THE BOOK OF AZRAEL

Amber V. Nicole is an author who works full time helping animals as a vet assistant. When she isn't working, she is dreaming of far-off places with dragons, magic, and swords. She loves a good villain and plans to tell many stories showcasing them in the spotlight.

Instagram: **@amber.v.nicole**
X: **@Amber_V_Nicole**
TikTok: **@amber.v.nicole**
Facebook Group: **Emotional Victims Of Amber V. Nicole**

By Amber V. Nicole

The Book of Azrael
The Throne of Broken Gods

THE BOOK OF AZRAEL

GODS & MONSTERS

BOOK ONE

AMBER V. NICOLE

HEADLINE
ETERNAL

The right of Amber V. Nicole to be identified as the Author of
the Work has been asserted by her in accordance with the
Copyright, Designs and Patents Act 1988.

First published in 2022 by Rose & Star Publishing

First published in Great Britain in this paperback edition in 2024
by HEADLINE ETERNAL
An imprint of HEADLINE PUBLISHING GROUP

15

Map design by Dewi Hargreaves.

Cataloguing in Publication Data is available from the British Library

ISBN 978 1 0354 1450 5

Offset in 8.65/12.97pt Crimson Text by Jouve (UK), Milton Keynes

Printed and bound in Great Britain by Clays Ltd, Elcograf S.p.A.

Headline's policy is to use papers that are natural, renewable and recyclable
products and made from wood grown in well-managed forests and other
controlled sources. The logging and manufacturing processes are expected
to conform to the environmental regulations of the country of origin.

HEADLINE PUBLISHING GROUP
An Hachette UK Company
Carmelite House
50 Victoria Embankment
London EC4Y 0DZ

The authorised representative in the EEA is Hachette Ireland, 8 Castlecourt
Centre, Dublin 15, D15 XTP3, Ireland (email: info@hbgi.ie)

www.headlineeternal.com
www.headline.co.uk
www.hachette.co.uk

AUTHOR'S NOTE

This book explores some potentially triggering themes. A list of content warnings can be found on the Rose & Star Website.

ONUNA

ECANUS

Pamyel

Silver City of
Hadremiel

Boel

ANDSUN
ISLES

Jaeoul

AARIN

Omael

Valoel

Adonael

Charoum

Conah

Tadheil

BAIRNISLE SEA

NAIMER SEA

NOCHARI

San Pavlao

Ecleon

THE DEAD OCEAN

NOVA'S ISLAND

Kashvenia

Hayyel

IPIUQIN

Naaririel

Arariel

Ruuman

N
A
I
M
E
R

Ophanium

Eoria

S
E
A

El Donuma

THE UNKNOWN DEEP

EL DONUMA

Morael

Chasin

ZARALL

Tirin

THE DEAD OCEAN

ONE

DIANNA

"Seriously? You're supposed to be these ancient warriors, feared by all, and you flinch? The worst part hasn't even happened yet."

I raised my fist once more, and it connected with his cheek this time. His head whipped to the side, the bones crunching beneath the force of my knuckles. Cobalt-blue blood splattered across the hardwood floor of the upstairs office in this oversized mansion. The bound celestial in the center of the room shook his head once more before correcting himself. He stared at me, his face bloody and his brow furrowed with pain.

"Your eyes," he said from between split and swollen lips, pausing to spit blood at my feet. "I know what you are." He had fought hard, his hair matted to his head with sweat and blood. His hands were bound behind his back, and his muscles bunched beneath the torn fabric of a once decent suit. He slumped in the chair at the center of the once prestigious room. "But it's impossible. You cannot exist. The Ig'Morruthens died in the Gods War."

I hadn't started my life as an Ig'Morruthen, but it is what I had become, and my eyes would always give me away. When I was mad, hungry, or anything but mortal, they burned like two fiery embers— one identifier among many that proved I was no longer mortal.

"Ah, yes, the Gods War." I tilted my head to the side as I regarded him. "How did that go again? Oh, right: thousands of years ago, your world crashed, burned, and fell into our world, disrupting lives and technology. Now you and your kind pretty much make the rules, right? Now the world knows about gods and monsters, and you are the great do-gooders who keep all the bad guys under lock and key."

I moved closer, grabbing the back of the chair as he tried to tilt his head away from me. "Do you know what your fall did to my world? While you all rebuilt, a plague swept through my home in the deserts of Eoria. Do you know how many died? Do you care?"

He didn't answer as I pushed off the chair. I raised my hand, my knuckles wet with his blood. "Yeah, I didn't think so. Well, you bleed blue, so I guess everything isn't what it seems after all."

I crouched in front of him, pieces of glass crunching beneath my heels. The only light came from the hallway, spilling through the door and illuminating the disaster of an office. Several pages from books and other debris littered the floor, along with the broken desk I'd thrown him through.

The celestial was the reason we'd come, and it was a long shot that the one artifact Kaden was looking for would be here, but I checked nonetheless. My bound and beaten celestial said nothing as he watched me search through the ruins of the room. The stoic face he put on was a shield, disguising what he was actually feeling.

Noise flooded the floors beneath us as the others living here screamed their last screams. Gunshots rang out, and a menacing laugh followed. His eyes flickered with rage as I walked back to him and placed my hands on his shoulders. In one fluid motion, I threw one leg over his lap and straddled him.

He whipped his head toward me, a look of pure disgust and confusion edging into his features. "Are you going to kill me?"

I shook my head. "No, not yet." He tried to recoil, but I grabbed his chin, forcing him to face me. "Don't worry. It's not going to hurt. I just need to make sure you are the one we're after. Bear with me. I need to concentrate for this to work."

Blood trickled from one of the several gashes littering his face. I gripped his chin and angled his head before leaning forward to slide my tongue over the cut. I was then tossed out of this office and thrown into his memories between one heartbeat and the next.

Blue light flashed across my subconscious as rooms I'd never been to appeared and disappeared. Laughter from a woman years older than him rang in my ears as she brought a tray of food into a small living room. She was his mother. Images converged, and I saw two gentlemen talking about sports and yelling in a crowded bar. Glasses clinked, and people laughed, trying to be heard over several large flat-screen televisions hanging on the walls. My head throbbed as I probed deeper. The scene changed, and I was in a darkened room. Waves of golden-brown hair danced around the edges of a woman's small frame. Her moans grew louder, and her back arched off the bed as she squeezed her breasts.

Good for you, but not what I need. I closed my eyes tighter, trying to focus. I needed more.

I was traveling the cobblestone streets of Arariel in a large vehicle with blacked-out windows. Sunlight darted behind the buildings, the shimmering yellows and golds enhancing the beauty of the scenery. People hurried along the sidewalks, and bicyclists wove through the traffic. Sunglasses shifted against the brim of my nose as I turned my head, looking at my companions. Three men sat with me in the back, the inside of the truck larger than I expected. Two others were in front, one driving and the other speaking on a phone in the passenger seat. They were young, clean-shaven, and wearing the same fitted black clothes as the celestial whose mind I was currently in.

"Have they heard anything else?" I asked, my voice no longer feminine, but his.

"No," the man across from me said. His hair was swept to the side and held there with so much gel that I could smell it even in the blooddream. He was lean compared to the guy next to him, but I knew he was just as powerful. "Vincent is very tight-lipped. I think they know the attacks are not just frequent. They have a target. We just don't know what it is."

"We have lost a lot of celestials—too many too soon. It is happening again, isn't it? What they taught us?" the man next to me said. His voice was quiet, but I could hear his apprehension. He was a large mountain of a man, but the way he twitched when he asked told me he was scared despite all that muscle. His fingers intertwined and unclasped several times over before he turned toward me. "If it is—if it does—he will come back."

Before I could answer, a short laugh caught me off guard. I turned to look at the man in front of me. He had his arms tightly folded as he stared out the window. "I think *him* coming back scares me more than facing them." This guy seemed young, too. Gods, how many celestials looked like college frat boys? This was what we were up against?

"Why?" I asked. "He is a legend, a myth at best. We already have three of The Hand of Rashearim here. Anything that could kill them either died in the war or has been sealed away for centuries. It's just another run-of-the-mill monster who thinks they have power." I paused, looking each one of them in the eyes. "We're fine."

The man in front opened his mouth to respond, but closed it as the car came to an abrupt halt. The sun glared down at us as we got out, closing the door behind us. Vehicles filled the curved driveway, and more continued to arrive. Celestials crowded the entry. Some gathered in small groups, others hurrying from place to place.

I adjusted my jacket and smoothed the edges down once, then twice, the nervousness seeping into my very core as I took the steps to the entrance. A large marble-and-limestone building greeted me, the golds, whites, and creams almost gaudy. Several large domed wings swept out on either side, with large arched windows lining every floor. I saw people walking across the stone bridges that connected the various buildings. They all wore similar business clothing and carried folders and briefcases. As I watched, several people exited the building, talking and laughing. They headed down the street as if a fortress did not sit in the middle of the city.

The city of Arariel.

My vision blurred as I pulled myself from the memory. The beautiful streets of Arariel faded, and I was back in the wrecked and dimly lit office. I had everything I needed now. A small smile curved my lips as I turned his face toward me.

"See, I told you it wouldn't hurt ... but this next part will."

His throat bobbed once as he swallowed, the smell of fear clouding the room.

"What did you see?" The voice, thick and heavy, came from behind me. A small thud sounded as he dropped something fleshy on the floor. He strode into the room, his presence almost as encompassing as my own.

"Everything we need," I murmured as I stood from the chair. I spun it around in one fluid motion so that Peter faced Alistair.

"He is a celestial? We have seen plenty of them, Dianna," Alistair said as he rubbed one hand across his face. Blood stained his skin and clothing from the destruction he'd wreaked downstairs. His normally perfectly combed silver hair had a few strands out of place and was streaked with crimson.

"I saw Arariel. He was there. They spoke of Vincent, which means *he*," I shook the chair with our bound friend slightly, "works with The Hand."

A grin, sharp and deadly, caressed his features. "You're lying."

"I'm not," I said, shaking my head and pushing the chair toward him. "I've tasted it. This is Peter McBridge, twenty-seven, second-tier celestial. His parents are retired, and he has no other connections to the mortal world. The fortress is in Arariel. His colleagues talked about us and what we've done so far. They spoke about The Hand of Rashearim and even mentioned Vincent."

The guy in the chair stuttered as he craned his head, looking from me to Alistair and back. "How did you see that? How can you know?"

We paused, looking at Peter as his eyes bounced between us. I crouched and leaned in closer. "Well, you see, Peter, every Ig'Morruthen has a little quirk. That was just one of mine."

I patted Peter's face as he continued to look at us in horror before I met Alistair's gaze again. He gave me a slow, mischievous smile and said, "If what you say is true, then Kaden is going to be very, very happy."

I nodded once more. "I found our way in. The rest is up to you."

I stepped back from the chair as Alistair stepped forward.

"Now, Peter, do you want to see what Alistair can do?"

The celestial struggled, trying to break his bonds, but he was too weak, too beaten to muster the strength. I scoffed. Some warriors these were! Taking this world for Kaden would be a piece of cake.

"What are you going to do to me?"

Alistair stepped forward, standing in front of Peter. He raised his hands, his palms hovering inches from either side of Peter's head. "Just relax. The more you struggle, the more it hurts," Alistair murmured.

Alistair's eyes glowed the same blood red as mine as a black mist formed between his hands, connecting his palms. It rippled and danced between his fingers, passing through the celestial's head. The screams were my least favorite part; they were always so loud. But I guess it was to be expected when someone was having their brain ripped apart and put back together again. Granted, Alistair had a few celestials under his control, but none with a rank as high as this, and none that had been this close to that damned city. Kaden would be happy for once.

The screams abruptly stopped, and I raised my head.

"You always look away," Alistair said, a smirk twisting his lips.

"I don't like it."

I didn't mean for that to slip. Kaden did not accept weakness, but I had been mortal before I had given up my life. I had been mortal, with mortal feelings, mortal views, and a mortal life. No matter how far I'd gone or what I'd done, my mortality sometimes snuck back in. Many would say it was a failing of my mortal heart. It was just another reason I had to be stronger, faster, meaner. There is a line you cross for survival—one I'd crossed centuries ago.

"After everything you've done, this," he pointed to the now silent celestial, "disturbs you?"

"It's annoying." My hands flew to my hips, and I let out an exasperated sigh. "Are we done?"

He shrugged. "Depends. Did you happen to see anything about the book?"

Ah, yes, the book. The reason we were running all over, searching Onuna.

I shook my head. "No, but if he can get close enough to The Hand, then that's something. A start."

His jaw clenched, and he shook his head. "Won't be good enough."

"I know." I raised my hand, cutting off whatever else he was about to say. "Just get on with it."

A smile, cold and deadly, lit up his face. Alistair reminded me of ice, from his hard, chiseled cheekbones to his empty stare. He had never been mortal, and serving Kaden was all he knew. He raised his hand in a silent demand, and the celestial stood. No words were needed. Alistair owned his mind and body.

"You will remember nothing that happened here today. You belong to me now. You will be my eyes and ears. What you see, I see. What you hear, I hear. What you speak, I speak."

Peter mimicked the words Alistair spoke verbatim. The only difference was the tone.

"Now, clean up this mess before you have company."

Peter said nothing as he stepped around Alistair and started to straighten up the office. Alistair came to my side as we watched him. We weren't even here to him anymore; he was a mindless puppet that Alistair controlled. I fought the urge to shift uncomfortably, knowing I was the same to Kaden. The only difference was that I knew it. Peter was long gone now that Alistair held his mind, and no power on Onuna could break that hold. As soon as he wasn't useful anymore, Alistair would discard him, just like the others before him. I had helped, just as I had for centuries. A part of me ached as I watched him go about the tasks he had no choice but to perform.

Damn mortal heart.

Alistair's clap shook me from my thoughts as he turned toward me. "Now help me clean up the bodies downstairs." He stepped past me, heading for the door as he shouted over his shoulder, "Peter, tell me where you keep those heavy-duty trash bags."

"Kitchen. In the third cabinet on the bottom shelf."

I turned on my heel, following Alistair out of the room and down the stairs. "What are we going to do with them?"

The smile he threw over his shoulder was purely wicked. "There are plenty of Ig'Morruthens at home who are probably starving."

Two
Dianna

Shadows separated in waves around Alistair and me as we portaled home to Novas. The warm salt air and an eerie quiet greeted us. Novas was an island off the coast of Kashuenia, but it wasn't just any island. It jutted out of the vast ocean like a ferocious beast threatening to claim the surrounding sea. I'd always assumed it was another fragment that fell to our world during the Gods War. Kaden had claimed it, shaped it, and made it his own. I suppose it was our home, although *home* was a latent term. Novas never felt like home to me. Home was with my sister, and oh, how I missed her.

I heaved several thick black trash bags across my shoulder and followed Alistair. The sand stuck to our blood-soaked shoes, making the trek even more cumbersome. Trees lined the vast landscape, the sun peeking through the many branches, creating a soft, peaceful glow. It was deceptive. Soft and peaceful were things not known here. The beach itself seemed welcoming. Salt scented the air as gentle waves lapped at the shore. The crystal-blue water was inviting ... if you didn't consider what lurked beneath the surface.

"It's quiet," I said as our feet hit the pebbled lava rock path. "It's never quiet."

"Securing Peter took longer than we thought, I guess," Alistair said, glancing around as if just now noticing.

I shook my head and sighed, knowing he was right. If we were late, Kaden would be pissed, regardless of the information we'd secured. Unfortunately, the unnatural silence of the island was not a good indicator of his mood.

We kept going, our pace slowing as the large structure came into view. Several wide steps led up to the twin double doors. Iron fences encompassed the front, adding a modern twist to the massive home Kaden had carved out of the active volcano that kept adding to Novas island. We pushed the doors open and entered, heat embracing us as we stepped into the entryway. It was warm and dry inside the house, but not overbearing. Kaden's home realm was long forgotten, sealed after the Gods War. Where he came from was much warmer than Onuna, and the volcanic island was the closest he could get to the feel of home.

I dropped the heavy bags on the floor and placed my hands on my hips, calling out, "Honey, I'm home!" My voice rang out through the vast open-ended entryway.

Alistair scoffed and rolled his eyes, dropping the large bags he carried next to mine.

"Childish." The word echoed from above us, and I looked up. Tobias watched us from the large balcony that lined the second floor. Sunlight streamed through the skylights, bronzing his rich ebony skin. He adjusted the cuff links on his dark blue button-up as he regarded us.

Alistair let out a low whistle. "All dressed up, are we? Has it started already?"

Tobias shot Alistair a quick smile that reached his eyes. It was one I never received from Kaden's third-in-command "You're late." His eyes cut to mine, quick as a viper's and just as venomous. "You both are."

I blew him a kiss. "Did you miss me?" I had grown used to Tobias's less-than-friendly demeanor. He had never said so, but I assumed his antipathy toward me was a result of me becoming Kaden's second-in-command when I was made. That had made Tobias third and Alistair fourth—not that Alistair cared. As long as Alistair had a home and food, he didn't care who Kaden preferred.

"Oh, but just wait until you hear why," Alistair said. "Also, we brought dinner for the beasts."

The beasts.

Tobias's lips turned up as he looked at the bags surrounding us and back. "They will be grateful, but you two need to get ready. Have someone else bring it to them. We don't have time."

As if on cue, the creatures started to sing, and my gaze dropped to the stone floor. A chill ran up my spine at the chorus of laughter. It always reminded me of hyenas, and it freaked me out. I knew how far down they were, and it always astounded me how the acoustics worked such that we could still hear them. Miles of tunnels snaked their way into the mountain, connecting rooms, chambers, and dungeons through numerous levels.

"Is he locking them up while we have guests?" I asked, raising a brow.

Alistair and Tobias shared a grin before Alistair shook his head at me and moved toward the back of the house. Tobias pushed off the banister, disappearing upstairs as I stood there. I wrapped my arms around myself, staring at the floor as if I could see through it.

"Guess that answered that question." I sighed.

It wasn't like I was scared of them. Kaden had made plenty of Ig'Morruthens since his time here, but they weren't like me, Alistair, or Tobias. They looked more like the horned gargoyles mortals plastered on their buildings. I often wondered if they had seen the Ig'Morruthen beasts and copied them in their art, trying to banish their instinctual fear of the monsters. The beasts were powerful and vicious, craving blood and flesh. They could communicate, but saying they could talk was giving them too much credit. They could mimic, but their speech was limited.

Footsteps came from the outer hall as a few of Kaden's lackeys approached and stopped near me. I kicked the bag closest to me. "Take these downstairs and make sure they eat. I have to get ready for a meeting with the who's who of the Otherworld."

THE CLICKING OF MY HEELS ECHOED AS I MADE MY WAY DOWN THE winding obsidian staircase to Kaden's main hall. I always referred to it as his "ego feeder." It screamed megalomaniac, from the tapestries to the extravagant furniture.

Voices filled the hallway as lights flickered against the stone walls. I picked up my pace, smoothing the edges of the sleek black dress I'd thrown on. I had known I was going to be late, but I'd had to take the time to wash the blood off of me. The voices grew louder as I got closer. Fuck, it sounded like a full house.

Two more of Kaden's lackeys stood outside the double doors of the meeting hall. They wore suits I knew they couldn't afford, but were a part of their uniform for tonight. Kaden had promised eternal life to those that pleased him and bent to his will, but I knew they would likely be reduced to mindless beasts rather than end up as Alistair, Tobias, or I. They bowed as I drew near, and I swallowed a breath to calm my nerves. Without breaking stride, I donned the face of the Bloodthirsty Queen. It was who they were expecting, who they feared —and rightly so. She had earned her reputation over the centuries.

Voices died as soon as I stepped over the threshold and entered the massive meeting hall. There were way more Otherworld creatures here than I had expected.

Double fuck.

The dark waves of my hair draped over my shoulders and back as I held my head high. I strode toward the long obsidian table that dominated the room. It was lined with chairs formed of the same sharp stone that made up this volcanic cavern. Tall cauldrons stood against the walls, each of them holding a small flame.

Eyes bore into every inch of me, but the ones that made me hesitate were the ones that burned crimson: Kaden. My maker, my lover, and the only reason my sister lived. She was why I did every single thing he asked.

Kaden stood at the helm of the table, his hands behind his back.

His eyes met mine for a split second. He was gorgeous, the tan-and-white suit contrasting beautifully with his ebony skin. But only the ignorant would not see the monster that lay in wait beneath his handsome demeanor.

I heard footsteps behind me. Good; I wasn't the last to arrive. I took my place at Kaden's right as the remainder of the attendees entered. Kaden did not speak or greet me, not that I had expected him to. No, his focus stayed on who was coming and who hadn't shown. Murmurs and whispers slowly died as everyone filed in. They stood, waiting for Kaden to sit before they would dare.

Tobias stood on Kaden's left, dressed in a dark blue button-up dress shirt and dark pants. He twirled the silver chain around his neck between his fingers as he surveyed the room. He was always keen and always watching. Alistair stood near him, no longer bloody, wearing a white button-up shirt and dress pants. They were both deadly and had earned their places as Kaden's generals.

I watched as Alistair leaned over and whispered to Tobias, "The vampires sent a second. Neither he nor his brother showed."

I looked at where the king of the vampires would normally sit and saw that Alistair was right. The area where Ethan and his people would have been was occupied by four lower members.

Triple fuck.

Tobias nodded, dropping his chain and looking toward Kaden. Kaden's nostrils flared, the only indicator of his anger.

To the right of the table stood the Habrick Coven. At least ten male and female witches were in attendance, all arranged perfectly around their leader, Santiago. His hair had so much gel in it that my nose burned. His Italian suit fit tighter than the black dress I wore—and that was saying something. He met my gaze and smiled slowly, as if he'd caught me admiring him. His eyes roamed over me like they always did, and it made my stomach lurch. With his good looks, he assumed that no woman could resist him. He was wrong, and he had learned that over the last few years in his many failed attempts to get into my pants.

I shook my head and turned back to face the room. Even with the number of Otherworld creatures that had showed, I felt it still wasn't enough for Kaden. He was their king—the king of all kings—and he wanted his due.

As if he'd read my mind, he turned toward me and adjusted his suit jacket before giving me a regal nod.

Showtime.

I raised my hands, summoning the power he'd given me. Fire erupted in my palms, circling and dancing playfully. I tossed the balls of energy toward each torch. Flames grew, illuminating the room and casting shadows in the far corners as a hush came over all those present.

Kaden sat, and I lowered the flames to a dull, pulsating dance. One by one, the clans, covens, and their leaders sat. Kaden's eyes swept the room as he drummed his fingers against the table in a steady beat. No one said anything—not a word.

"I will say I am happy with those who made it." Kaden's voice filled the room. To some, he would sound calm and collected. All I heard was rage.

"Santiago. Your coven is as lovely as ever." Kaden nodded toward him as the witches held his gaze, proud and powerful. I admired them, even if I hated their leader.

"The dream eaters." Kaden motioned toward the clan of Baku, sitting next to Santiago's coven. Their eyes seemed to showcase a smile they physically couldn't. Where a mouth should be, there was just a slit with skin stretching across it in diagonal lines. They were creepy bastards, and ones I tended to avoid. Through the centuries, I had heard stories that some clans were actually peaceful and were called upon to expel and eat nightmares. I had only encountered the ones that instilled terror in dreams for the right price.

Kaden's voice shook me back to reality as he went on. "The mind-yielding screamers." I noted the banshees on the left. They were an assortment of women, the clan consisting of only females. Apparently, the gene relied heavily on both X chromosomes. All that attended had very light or very dark hair and were dressed in blazers or fitted dresses that screamed money—no pun intended.

Their leader, Sasha, had her long, almost blue-tinged hair pulled back in a half-up, half-down style and wore a silk pants suit with an open-front blazer. She was nearly a hundred years old, but she looked as if she were in her prime. They definitely had style, but I had seen Sasha use those death screams on someone, causing their head to rupture into several pieces. It took weeks to get the brain matter off of my favorite shoes.

"I see the powerful." Kaden motioned toward the shades, who only nodded in response. Their bodies didn't seem solid, their forms wavering like smoke. They were a clan of assassins and tricky creatures by nature. One leader controlled them, and if you took Kash out, it would be bye-bye, good night assassins. The only problem was that you would have to get close enough to him. His family, like most, had risen to power over the centuries, cutting a bloody path for anyone who paid well. I did admire their loyalty to Kaden, though. I'm sure several factions had paid Kash and his family to at least attempt a hit on my scary boss, but the shades had never betrayed him.

"I see the ferocious beasts of legend." Kaden's still crimson eyes focused on the werewolves. This pack was led by Caleb and held in high regard throughout our world. He was quiet unless spoken to, but the power he displayed with just a look made goosebumps run across my arms. His dark hair was clipped short, his beard tidy and shadowing his jaw. Maybe he could teach Santiago how to do his hair, so it would not look like a slicked mess. I snickered, and Alistair cut his eyes to me as I tried to cover it with a cough. I liked Caleb.

These werewolves were not the typical horror movie type. Their wolf forms were more wolf, but their size alone would scare anyone, mortal or not. The males tended to be a little more stout than the females of their pack, but the females were more vicious. Caleb kept his family to themselves, but they came every time Kaden called. They were elusive and secretive, preferring to stay out of politics as much as possible, but they were all here.

"I mean, even the mortal council showed!" Kaden gave Elijah and his group a slight nod. Elijah was middle-aged, with a distinguished smattering of gray at his temples. He adjusted his suit as if he were important in a room full of monsters. Kaden had helped the politician rise through the ranks, gaining a great informant and an even better source of money laundering.

The crimson fire in Kaden's eyes flared as he focused on the three sitting vampires. "And yet, only a handful of the blood stealers show." His voice dripped with venom, and the energy in the room tightened. Everyone tensed, the quiet a thrum against my senses as Kaden's fingers stopped drumming against the table.

"Where is your king?" It was a loaded question, and one I knew had no correct answer.

One man stood, straightening his tie and suit jacket as he cleared his throat. "Mr. Vanderkai was unable to make it and sends his deepest apologies. Others have been testing his current rule, and he is dealing with that at the moment."

Kaden leaned back in his chair, folding his hands in front of him as he stared at the vampire. It was quiet for what felt like ages. The man shifted from one foot to the other, and if vampires could sweat, I knew he would be.

"He seems to have a lot of those problems lately," Kaden finally said, his tone light as he resumed his tapping on the table. "When was the last time he showed?" he asked, turning toward Tobias.

Tobias's eyes bore into the vampire, a smirk edging his features. "It's been a while, my liege. Months."

Kaden nodded, his lips turning upward. "Months."

"Yes." The gentleman cleared his throat. "But the prince has taken his place at the last few meetings."

"Yes, the brother. And where is he?"

"He couldn't make it. Both wanted to be here, I assure you, but they really needed a strong hand to deal with some of the issues we are currently experiencing." The words felt forced, as if he knew what would happen if he lied.

"I get that," Kaden said. I heard collective breaths being released, the tension subsiding from some of those around the table. But not for me, and not for anyone who really knew him. "It's hard keeping balance, especially among others during times like these. When compared to what we once were, what the world once was, our numbers are small in the grand scheme of things. Threats loom, and anxiety and fear get the better of us. That's why, above all else, we have to stick together." The tapping stopped as he leaned forward. "You know what I mean?"

The vampire nodded once. "Yes. I agree."

Lie.

Kaden smiled slowly, a pure white menacing gleam. He slammed his hand onto the table, and the room shook. The doors at the entrance slammed shut, trapping all of us. The table split in half, separating and pushing everyone to the sides as blistering thick steam billowed into the room. No one jumped or moved, staying in their seats. If they felt fear, they didn't show it. They knew what was coming, and the one thing Kaden hated more than anything was weakness. Kaden stood, a king before his pit, because that's exactly what it was: a hollow, echoing pit.

I swallowed the lump growing in my throat as I watched, keeping my hands folded in the center of my lap. I could see Tobias and Alistair with shit-eating grins lighting up their faces. The temperature increased, molten lava swirling in the hole at the center of the room. Smoke curled upward as hot volcanic bubbles popped on its surface.

"Go ahead. Get in." Kaden waved the vampires toward the pit.

"You're insane," the female vampire spat as another scanned the room, looking for another exit.

The other creatures made no move to help. They knew Kaden's wrath wasn't for them, and they didn't want it turned their way.

Kaden's laugh echoed through the smoke-filled room as he placed a hand on his chest. "Am I? Or do I just not like insubordination? Dianna." My eyes swung toward him. "If you would be so kind as to help our friends."

I slowly turned my head back toward the vampires, and keeping my gaze focused on them, I stood. My hands flexed at my sides as I walked toward them. The Otherworld creatures tensed as I passed, but their faces betrayed nothing. I was Kaden's weapon. I was powerful. They knew it, and I knew it. I was a blade made of fire and flesh.

Kaden's voice echoed as he continued. "Maybe I have trust issues. You see, this isn't the only time your king has had these *inconveniences*. Given our time frame and what we have to accomplish..." I stopped next to one of the female vampires, and she looked at me with fear in her eyes. "... I just cannot have weaknesses."

She screamed as I grabbed her by the arms and pulled her toward the pit. Her spiked heels caught my shin a few times as she fought against my hold, but the struggle was brief. I tossed her over the edge, her screams lasting mere seconds as she fell. Flames flared around her body as she hit the lava pool and was consumed.

Another vampire ran past me in a panicked effort to flee. I snapped my arm out with blurring speed. Talons burst from my fingertips as I made impact, puncturing his gut. He gasped, his body curling around my hand as he gripped my wrist and met my gaze. Fear and panic filled his eyes as I lifted him and tossed him into the fire below.

The third went much like the second. He tried to escape, tried to fight, but in the end, his screams for mercy echoed off the obsidian walls as I launched him into the lava. I wiped my clawed hand across my blood-splattered cheek and strode over to the last living vampire in the room. He had given up, knowing there was no way out and nowhere to run. He had curled into a ball on the stone floor. I grabbed him by the lapels of his suit jacket, lifting him and turning to hold him over the pit.

A soft shine of tears coated his yellow eyes. "Please," he begged, "I have a family."

Family. The word echoed in my mind, and I felt my canines retract. The bloodlust nipped at my heels, begging me to succumb, to let my beast off the chain. *Family.* The word was like a pulse, reminding me that this wasn't me. Each beat of my heart was for her, and remembering that she existed brought me back from the edge of madness. *Family.* This time the word was wrapped in the sound of my sister's laughter, and with it came the memory.

Gabby shook her head, laughing at me as I tried and failed to land a piece of popcorn in her mouth.

"You have terrible aim for a superbeing." She giggled as she threw a handful at me.

I kicked my foot out, hitting her softly on the leg. "Hey, I'm the trained killer here!"

She burst out laughing. "Please! You cried at the end of The Locket."

"That was a sad movie. It had a sad ending. You just pick terrible movies."

We laughed about that dumb movie for hours. We sat on the over-priced couch I'd bought her as a graduation gift and made a complete mess of the apartment she loved so much. Her graduation was months ago, and I hadn't seen her since.

The pain of that thought forced me from the memory. I blinked a few times at the vampire I held suspended over the void as the world came back into focus. *Family.* Beyond the hazy smoke, I met the twin red flames of Kaden's eyes. The message was unspoken, but still clear. Don't hesitate, don't think, just finish it—because if he sensed weakness in me, he would take her, too. Without breaking eye contact with Kaden, I retracted my claws from the vampire's neck and opened my hand, letting him fall into the pit.

Kaden smiled as the man disappeared. Then he willed the portal closed, and the table moved with the occupants still seated, sealing itself back in place. The creak of the door behind me flooded the now all-too-silent room as the remaining smoke seeped into the hall. A few people coughed and adjusted their chairs, the stone scraping against the floor.

I looked at the crimson stain that decorated my knuckles and nails before dropping my hands to my sides. I held my head high, my feet moving before my brain registered what I was doing as I walked back to Kaden's side. Alistair and Tobias were watching me, assessing me, but I was careful not to show my disgust at being covered in gore. I stood facing forward, my hands clasped in front of me.

No weakness. Ever.

"Now that you have taken care of that, why have you called us here?" Kash, the leader of the shades, asked. His accent was thick as the shades shuffled behind their puppet master.

"Simple. I have word of the Book of Azrael."

Several gasps and whispers filled the room as Kaden finally sat. Alistair, Tobias, and I remained standing. We were always on point, fearless and destructive.

"Impossible," the leader of the Baku hissed.

There was a moment of silence, and then everyone began talking at once, all agreeing with the Baku, arguing that the book was nothing more than a myth. The sound of so many raised voices was overwhelming in the stone hall. The werewolves were the only ones not speaking. They just sat, watching and listening.

It didn't surprise me that the mortal politician, Elijah, was heard over the rest. "Even if this text is found, it's been thousands of years since the Gods War. How would we read it?"

"Read it?" Santiago scoffed. "If it's even real, you know what it brings with it."

Silence fell as they all looked at Kaden.

"The World Ender," a soft feminine voice said from the left corner.

Everyone turned to look at Sasha and her sisters. The banshees had been quiet since this started—almost as quiet as the werewolves. Sasha's eyes glazed over as if she were lost in thought. It wasn't until someone tapped her on the shoulder that she realized she'd spoken aloud. Her long blue hair shook with her head as she straightened her white suit coat and cleared her throat.

"Ah, yes," Kaden said, rubbing his chin before placing his hands on the table. "The fabled World Ender. The legend. The Son of Unir. Wielder of the Blade of Oblivion. And where is he?"

No one spoke.

"Exactly. He hasn't been seen or heard from since their home world, Rashearim, blew up. Destruction that was caused by him, correct? Isn't that how the story goes? He is the boogeyman of the Otherworld. Tales to keep you all in line."

"They aren't stories. They are true. The Otherworld itself is outside of our reach because of him, because of them," Santiago interjected. The witches with him nodded, staying close. Their eyes were fixated on us, waiting for us to strike or make a move against them for Santiago speaking out of turn. "Celestials still walk this plane. The Hand still walks this plane, and if The Hand still exists, then it has a body, a head. The World Ender is that head."

"And heads can be severed." Kaden's words were venom.

Silence fell once more, the words sinking in. I smelled it before the rest did: fear. My life and time in Kaden's world had not been as long as most, but to see how they feared this World Ender more than Kaden spoke volumes.

"I get it. You all fear him. But he is not what you think he is, even if he lives. He has not been seen for centuries. Pay no attention to the fables others have built in his image. If he was as strong and skilled as they say, where is he? I have destroyed hundreds of his kind, yet he does not show. He is a coward, weak, damaged. This *World Ender* is not a god like the ones before him. He has no real power—but we do. They tell you their lies, trying to shove them down your throats. They want to bend you to their will. Once I have that book, we will rule, all of us. No longer bound to the shadows or repressed by those who deem us unworthy and less-than. Change happened the minute they spilled their own blood in their own world. And now?"

He stood and leaned forward, his hands splayed against the table. He met the gaze of each leader, and only a few of them shifted in their seats.

"Now it's time to take back what is ours, what was stolen from us. We had no choice before they sealed the realms. None. How many of your people are beyond those doors? Hmm?" He pointed towards Santiago, then the others. "Or yours, or yours? Do you wonder if they still live?"

Those words hit their target.

"And this book? You have it?" the leader of the shades asked.

Kaden clicked his tongue. "That's the next part. I do not have it yet, but soon. Elijah," he pointed toward the mortal and his council, "has been kind enough to provide intel on the celestials. We have infiltrated their ranks, which is the reason I called you all here. We need to be united. Once I start the process of opening the realms, we can't be seen as weak." He looked pointedly at the empty seats of the vampires. "Not even for a second. I need you all with me, and if you're not..." He glanced at the center of the table, letting the threat hang above them.

One by one, they all agreed by saying yes in their native tongue. The werewolves were the last to speak, and I knew I wasn't the only one who noticed.

THE WATER RAN BROWN IN THE OBSIDIAN SINK AS I WASHED THE GORE from first my face, then my hands. Ever since Kaden had turned me, I had scrubbed blood from my body every day. I had become a creature that could rip memories from blood, summon flame in an instant, and shift shape into any beast I wished. Every single time I had to feed, I felt less mortal. But it was the price I paid for her life. The sad part? Compared to the alternative, I didn't hate it. For the first time in a long time, I'd slipped up. I'd hesitated, and he'd seen it.

I turned the water off and grabbed a hand towel from the shelf, wiping away the specks of blood that still clung to the side of my face. My reflection showed me a shadow of the person I used to be. My face was harder now, the lines of my cheeks and jaw sculpted. The sharpness of my features was alluring to everyone, except me. I remembered my face as softer, kinder maybe. The edge of the cloth grazed my lips, the plump softness that shielded canines sharper than steel when the monster inside me clawed its way to the surface.

I was described as "beautiful" and "exotic." The words made me inwardly flinch, as if I'd been slapped in the face. I knew I was deadly, cruel, and lethal. For her, for us, I had allowed Kaden to leash me. I had carved her a place of peace with claws and broken bones, paying for her safety with rivers of blood.

"Please, I have a family."

The desperation in his voice echoed in my head. I closed my eyes tightly, drowning it out. I tossed the cloth to the side and grabbed the sides of the sink. My fingers dug into the granite until I felt pieces of it crumble. Were they not the same words I'd whispered that night years ago? I'd lain on the floor, holding her hand. As the cold feel of death had gripped her skin, I'd begged someone, anyone, to help her, save her. I'd been willing to offer my body, my life, my soul, anything to anyone who would answer.

"Everything okay?"

My eyes flew open, and soft brown irises looked back at me, no longer those iridescent embers. I stared at Kaden through the mirror as he leaned against the bathroom door, seeming to take up more than his fair share of space. He was taller than me, which was saying something, since I was well over average height for most women. I wasn't a cute, petite little thing like every movie or book craves. I was lacking in the breast department, but made up for it in my hips. They were the only curvy part of me. I was lean, with strong, supple muscles, a fighter in every sense of the word. After my turning, I'd trained every day with Alistair, Tobias, and even Kaden. I'd been beaten until I passed out more times than not. It had taken years before I'd learned to hold my own. Kaden wanted warriors, and I'd soon learned why.

He stood with his arms folded and a look of intrigue on his face. It wasn't the look of worry, like normal people would understand. I knew he didn't care about my well-being, only that I was still in line, still obedient.

"I'm fine, just a little tired," I responded, standing a little straighter.

His eyes narrowed slightly. "Hmm."

"I want to go see my sister."

He pushed off the doorframe as his lips turned down in a small frown. "Not now."

I'd known he would say that. It had been months since I had seen Gabby, and I missed her. He used her as bait. Do what he asked, and I would be rewarded with visits, even as they became fewer and further between.

"Remember that I love you."

She had said those words just before we'd hung up the last time I'd spoken to her on the phone. Damn, I couldn't even remember when that was. It seemed her voice flooded my head often these last few weeks, keeping me grounded, and more importantly, keeping me mortal.

Kaden's footsteps were light as he came up behind me. I watched his reflection move closer. He stopped a few inches away from me, his chin resting above my head. He gathered the strands of hair from around my face, gently pulling them back. His fingers slid through the silky mass as if he enjoyed the sensation, his gaze holding mine captive in the mirror.

"You hesitated."

He knew.

His right hand slid down my hair once more before reaching the ends and drifting over my bare back. "Something you want to tell me?"

"Not for the reasons you think." I kept my eyes on him through the mirror, refusing to look away. Just like with an animal in the wild, if you took your eyes off your prey for a second, it was over.

"Mm-hm," he murmured as he traced my spine, stopping at my lower back. His fingers dipped beneath the thin seam of my dress, and I shivered against him, still not breaking eye contact. A small smile softened the curve of his lips before he dipped his head toward my neck. "You're so beautiful." His words danced across my skin, his breath quickening the pulse thrumming beneath his mouth. His tongue flicked against my skin, sending another shudder through me as his hand moved higher to cup my breast. He teased his thumb across my nipple slowly, deliberately dragging a soft moan from me. I leaned back against him, rocking my hips, feeling the hard length of him pressed against my ass.

His lips trailed from my neck to my jaw, leaving a blistering trail. "You belong to me. You are mine in every way." He kissed and nibbled every place he touched. "Do you understand?"

I nodded and let my head fall back against his shoulder, allowing him better access. The thin line between pleasure and pain always elicited a response from me, and he knew it. He reached up with his free hand and fisted it in my hair, tilting my head to the side. Then he leaned into me, pushing me harder against the sink, leaving no room for me to escape. My eyes flew open as I felt the touch of talons against the curve of my breast. He opened his eyes and kissed the shell of my ear. His burning red gaze bored into me as he dragged those sharp claws to the center of my chest.

"But I can't have weakness, even from you. Not now, not when we are this close. Do you understand?"

I nodded as his nails pricked my skin. Ig'Morruthens were strong and almost impossible to kill—almost. We all had a weakness, one thing that would destroy us. The trick was trying to figure it out before we ripped you to pieces. I had been decapitated, lost limbs that grew back, and even had my neck snapped, but none of it had killed me. The only thing that had not been destroyed was my heart. So, through the process of elimination, we had deduced that I would die if my heart were removed from my body. My stupid mortal heart was my weakness.

"Yes," I said through gritted teeth, "I know that."

His fingers pressed harder, digging into my chest. I didn't scream. I wouldn't give him the satisfaction.

"Then why did you hesitate?" His voice was a breathy whisper in my ear.

Lie.

I couldn't tell him the real reason. If he thought for a second that I prioritized anyone above him or his cause, he would end me here and now.

"Because," I hissed, "he has a family. By killing him, you are only creating more enemies for yourself." I panted again, trying to breathe through the pain. "It is a complication with how close you are."

He held my gaze for what felt like eons before his eyes melted back to their hazel shade and he released his hold on my hair. I felt his fingers ease from my chest, and he slid his hand from beneath my dress. He gripped my hips and spun me to face him so quickly that I almost fell to the side.

His body pressed into mine as he leaned forward. "You care for me?"

"Yes." I reached up, rubbing a hand over my chest. The skin had healed, but the wet stain of blood coated my fingers.

It wasn't a complete lie. I had cared for Kaden in the beginning, until a few hundred years of excusing his behavior had grown old. He had never shared his secrets with me, but I knew there were parts of Kaden that were deeply damaged, and I felt for him. Kaden wasn't always as vile as he seemed. There were moments—fragments, at least —where I could see something deeper within him. Something in his past had turned him jaded, cold, and vicious. So, yes, I cared for him, but it was never love. It wasn't like those stupid movies Gabby insisted on making me watch. It wasn't the emotion the poets wrote sonnets about, or the way forms of literature describe it, but I cared. I would never be free of Kaden, and even in this limited way, caring made it easier to stay.

His lips brushed my cheek. "Good. Don't hesitate again."

I nodded, my hands still clutching the fabric of my dress. Kaden still had me pinned between the sink and his hard body.

"Let me go," I whispered. It was a request and a silent demand, one that meant more than where he had me now. One I often dreamed about when the fighting and violent nature of my life got to be too much. One I knew would never be granted. I ached for a life outside of this. A life with my sister. A life where I was loved and could be loved. Just a life. But I knew his answer before he spoke, and I knew without a shadow of a doubt that he meant it.

Kaden leaned back, his eyes dancing over my face before he lifted my chin, forcing me to meet his gaze.

"Never."

THREE

DIANNA

I flew through the crisp night air, high above the clouds, above civilization, above it all. Sleek black wings beat against the current, propelling me forward. One of my favorite things about being an Ig'Morruthen was the ability to shapeshift into whatever and whoever I wanted. Kaden had told me the ability came from the ancient ones, who could bend their bodies into any form they desired. Some could change into terrifying, magnificent creatures so massive that they blocked out the sun. They didn't have the prestigious royal blood, but they were gods in their own right. They were feared and respected. Well, they were until the Gods War had wiped them out.

Stars danced above me and in every direction. I beat my wings harder, rising toward them. Surrounded by such beauty, I wondered what would happen if I just kept going. I felt true freedom at that moment, and I reveled in it, never wanting it to end.

The shape I'd taken was one Kaden had shown me centuries ago, and one of my personal favorites. Mortals would recognize the beast as a wyvern. They were similar to the mythical dragon, but I was bipedal in this shape, unlike those four-legged, fire-breathing beasts. My hands and arms were stretched, forming the massive wings. Horns and scales swept over the crown of my head, ending in fine, sharp points. My skin was thicker in this form and covered by armored, scaled plates. A long razor-tipped tail swung behind me as I dove and danced between the clouds.

The stars were my only company, and I savored the solitude. I closed my eyes and spread my wings as far as possible, riding on the wind. The plus side to Kaden's mortal connections was they wouldn't shoot down a flying, fire-breathing beast. So, for the moment, I was at peace. I was not Dianna, the fire-wielding death queen, or Dianna, the loving and thoughtful sister. I just was.

"Bring me the head of the brother."

Reality intruded as Kaden's voice echoed through my subconscious, the memory of the night before playing like a movie behind my closed eyelids.

Kaden stood from the bed and grabbed his clothes, dressing quickly. He'd never stayed, never held me—not once.

He paused at the door, his hand on the handle, and turned to look at me. "And Dianna, make it messy. I want to send a message."

"As you wish," I replied as I sat up, pulling the sheets toward me. Kaden didn't speak or say anything else as he left the room. The slamming of the door echoed throughout the volcanic home. I covered my face with my hands and sat there for a few minutes longer.

He hadn't just asked me to bring him a prince's head. No, he was asking me to kill a friend. Drake was one of the very few beings I trusted completely. And I knew without a doubt that I had no choice.

My eyes snapped open, and I concentrated on propelling my streamlined body faster through the night sky. With each powerful beat of my wings, I shoved aside my feelings, locking them away once more.

I smelled the seawater from the Naimer Sea before I saw it. Music and the sounds of a vibrant city soon filled my ears, telling me I was close. Tirin was a beautiful city in the heart of Zarall and currently owned by the Vampire King. Actually, the entire continent of Zarall was owned by Ethan Vanderkai, Vampire King and the sixth son of the royal bloodline. Every vampire that spawned from the eastern to the western hemisphere was under his rule, but he wasn't the one I was looking for tonight. No, I was here for his brother, the Prince of Night, Drake Vanderkai.

Kaden had introduced me to many beings through the centuries, and there were very few I would call friends, but Drake was different. I did consider us friends. His family had worked closely with Kaden for years. They had their hands in almost everything, so they often knew how to obtain the artifacts and items Kaden sought. That was the main reason Kaden was so angry. He wanted that book, and he knew they would be a great source of help in finding it, but then they had stopped showing up to the meetings.

At first, Ethan had sent Drake in his place. I hadn't minded. It was nice to have someone to talk to, laugh with, and not be on guard with all the fucking time. But then Drake had stopped coming, and this last time was enough for Kaden. He wanted blood—and what Kaden wanted, I provided.

I knew it was another test of my resolve. When I had hesitated in front of Kaden, his paranoid brain assumed I was slipping. I had to show him I wasn't, regardless of my friendship with Drake. I couldn't risk my reputation and position. If either were called into question, I risked *her*. That was unacceptable, so I would prove my loyalty, starting with Drake.

I dove beneath the clouds, focusing on the valley below. Multicolored lights were scattered over the land, mirroring the stars above. People were out enjoying the night, and the sounds of voices, car horns honking, and music floated to me on the balmy air. Bright white beams of light were beacons, calling all who were willing to the inner city. There was a party tonight, like all nights, and I was headed into the heart of it.

The ocean danced off to my left, gentle waves lapping at the shore as I soared above the mountains. I glided around a neighboring cliff before pulling my wings back slowly, beating them against the air to slow my descent. The music drowned out any noise they made, and the mortals were too drunk and preoccupied to notice me.

Black smoke curled around me as I shifted shape in midair and dropped to the street. I landed in a crouch, several people jumping out of the way. They spilled their drinks and shouted at me to watch where I was going. I ignored them and adjusted my thick twin braids so they hung over my shoulders.

Lights varied from silver to red to gold as I reached the inner city of Tirin, known as Logoes. It was a popular neighborhood, renowned for its beauty and historical monuments, but most notorious for its nightlife. Everything you could want or need was available in Logoes, with numerous bars, pubs, and upscale lounges. Tourists and locals flocked to it, seeking to unwind and let loose, unaware of what awoke as the moon crested in the sky.

I moved through the crowd easily, looking like just another mortal out for the night in my black tank top, leather pants, and heels. It only took me a few minutes to reach my destination. The club was in the heart of Logoes, and a long line of people waited to pass through the massive entrance. The red neon sign above the door cast a crimson glow over everything. This was one of Drake's favorite places—something he owned that wasn't his brother's.

The mortals cursed and yelled as I pushed past them to reach the front of the club. Twin bouncers folded their arms and shifted to form a wall before me. They were the overly muscled, idealistic types made to intimidate people, usually the drunk and stupid, and keep them from trying to enter. One had a shaved head with tattoos decorating the back of his neck, and the other sported a long, dreadlocked ponytail. Their eyes glowed gold as they recognized me, but I didn't give them a chance to move.

"Sorry about this, but he should have shown."

I slammed my hands against their chests, forcing them back. Fire erupted where my palms had connected, their bodies ash before they hit the floor.

The doors burst open, splintering into a thousand tiny pieces as I entered. Behind me, the people in line screamed and ran for their lives. The crowd inside didn't even notice, continuing to dance and gyrate against each other.

The inside of the club was larger than what it seemed from the outside. Yellow, blue, pink, and red lights danced off the walls. The dance floor separated the DJ booth from the large circular bar that took up the middle of the room. People shouted at the bartenders, trying to be heard over the music.

I'd taken a step toward the soft red glow at the back of the club when a hard object smacked into the back of my head. I flinched, but my body didn't move. Another perk of being an Ig'Morruthen was that our bones were thicker, meaning we were harder to knock unconscious. I turned to see another vampire holding a gun with a look of complete shock on his face. I whipped my arm out, tearing a hole through him and incinerating the remains.

That got everyone's attention. A woman near me screamed, and the eyes of the vampires in the crowd fluoresced yellow, their fangs extending as they turned toward me.

It was going to be a long night.

My blood-soaked shoes squeaked as I walked up the stairs. I was covered in ash, blood, and probably more than one being's visceral organs. I stopped short at the top of the stairs, scanning the large lounge. There were multiple black sofas against the back wall, with matching chairs and small tables placed around the area. The room was dim, with red up-lights in the corners. There was a smaller bar up here, but it only served the type of drinks the Otherworld creatures craved. It was empty, except for the one person I was here for.

Vampire royalty always made my skin crawl. Their power dated so far back that my senses weren't sure what to make of it. Only four vampire families had enough power to inherit the throne, and one had turned to dust before I was created. The remaining three hated each other and had fought savagely for a chance to rule. The Vanderkais won and had been in power for a while now. Their victory had been due in large part to Kaden, but that didn't mean they were his lackeys. The older they got, the more powerful they became, and power was all I felt from the back area of the lounge.

I strode toward the source, stopping to lean against the end of the crescent bar as our gazes met. His golden eyes bored into mine, but neither of us spoke. I swiped my arm across my forehead, but only managed to smear more gore across my face. He took a deep pull on his cigar, the red ember at the tip flaring. He was lounging on one of the large sofas with one arm draped across the back. He looked as if he didn't have a care in the world and wasn't bothered by the carnage I'd inflicted downstairs.

Another pull on the cigar lit up the side of his face, the glow highlighting the dark curls clipped close to his scalp. Drake was a gorgeous predator, and the rich brown of his skin gleamed, enticing the unwary to touch him. It was another perk of vampirism. Everything about them was designed to attract their prey.

"You look rough." He took another tug from his cigar and crossed one of his legs over the other.

My fists clenched. "Why didn't you show? And don't give me some bullshit excuse about problems or enemies you have to deal with."

Drake didn't say anything, which only pissed me off more. I took one step forward, then another. He tapped the cigar out against the silver tray on the table next to him.

"Kaden is trying to open the realms, Drake. It means freedom for us, for our kind. No more worrying about the celestials or The Hand. Why are you and Ethan suddenly so against that?"

His eyes roamed mine for a second, searching for some sign that I was joking, but only pain edged my voice.

"He has a point. I would like to not be hunted—my family or me—but his beliefs are clouded." He stood, unbuttoning his jacket and carefully taking it off. "Ethan won't follow, nor will I. He's a tyrant, Dianna. No matter what pretty picture he paints."

I closed my eyes tightly, trying to hold back my tears. "You know you can't talk like that. You know what that means."

"I know." His voice was barely a whisper and suddenly closer now. I opened my eyes and was unsurprised to find him only inches away. He lifted his hand, brushing the loose hairs that had escaped my braids away from my face. "And will you, his pretty weapon, be the one to execute me? My brother? Our family, too?"

The part of me that was still good screamed at me to stop as I grabbed him by the throat, but I had no choice. He didn't struggle as I lifted him and tossed him through the back wall. Wires sparked in the large hole made by his body, and several pictures fell to the ground as the building shuddered from the impact. Dust and debris filled the air as the wall crumbled.

"You know what happens now. You knew when you repeatedly sent others to the meeting what Kaden would do and how he would react. He was never going to tolerate your disobedience, Drake!" I yelled.

Twin blades flew from the hole, heading straight for me. I slapped one out of the air, and the other whizzed by my head. But they weren't meant to kill, only to distract. The air flew out of me as he tackled me to the floor. We crashed into the bar, and it burst into shards of wood and glass.

"When he comes back, you need to make sure you're on the right side. You think this book Kaden wants isn't going to start another massive war?" he snapped as he pinned me to the floor. He held my arms crossed against my chest with one knee on my stomach.

"Oh, you can't be serious! You, too? He is nothing more than a legend, yet you condemned your whole family for it? They are stories, Drake—stories to keep us in line. They all died. The old gods are dead. The Gods War, remember? All that's left are the celestials and The Hand; that's it."

"Gods, he has you so fucking whipped!" He slammed his fist across my face, rocking my head to the side.

I faked a slight spell of unconsciousness, and as I felt him relax, I slammed my knee into his groin. He lurched forward, and I freed my arms, tossing him off of me. I rolled to my feet, but he had recovered by the time I was up. He was standing with his fists in the air and a shit-eating grin on his face.

My chest tightened. Drake was the one who had made me smile when I first turned and was dealing with the fact that I no longer had my freedom or mortality. He wasn't just my friend; he was Gabby's, too. He was always there when I needed him, and now I had to kill him because he and Ethan had decided to switch sides. I had no choice, and that only pissed me off more. I raised my hands to match his, clenching them into fists before dropping them.

"I don't want to do this." My voice cracked, but I didn't care. I didn't care if he saw it as a weakness.

He dropped his fists, his expression softening. "Then don't. You are one of my best friends, Dianna. I don't want to fight you. You're just as strong as him, if not more so. Stay with me, with us. We can help and protect each other."

I smiled softly, knowing he meant every word he said. Then I was in front of him. His eyes went wide as his mouth gaped open once, then twice. He looked down at my fist lodged in his chest. My hand curled around his heart, and I felt it beat. His life was in my palm.

"I said I didn't want to. Not that I wouldn't."

He smiled at me as his hands touched my wrist. "Better to die by what you think is right than to live under a lie."

I held his gaze as I willed the flames from my hand. His body lit up from the inside, but his smile didn't waver. It was the same smile that had comforted me when the nightmares got too bad. The same smile that curved his lips when he told me jokes, making me laugh, even when I felt like dying. I watched with contained horror as the same smile that could light up a room disappeared forever.

I stood there for I don't know how long, my hand still outstretched and full of what remained of my friend's heart. A loud, upbeat ringing filled the room, and I thought it was odd that they would still play music when the club was destroyed. Then I felt the vibration against my hip and shook myself from my daze. I wiped my hands on my jeans and pulled the phone from my pocket.

"You can go see your sister now."

I scanned the ruin of the room, my gaze catching on the camera mounted high on the wall. Kaden had seen everything. I nodded once toward it and hung up the phone before disappearing from the wreckage.

FOUR
DIANNA

I formed in the middle of Gabby's apartment. The black smoke that came with the teleport dissipated as I dropped my bags onto the floor with a loud thump. It was eight in the morning in this part of the world. I had checked before I left just to make sure she would be home.

"Gabby!" I yelled, throwing my hands up. "Your favorite and only sister is here!"

Usually, my random show-ups resulted in squealing and hugging, but this time, only silence greeted me. I looked around, noticing the new white sectional and the glass table cluttered with magazines. Several artistic pictures decorated the white walls. Gabby had revamped her style, but that wasn't unusual. She enjoyed decorating. The flowers on her kitchen island caught my attention, and my eyes narrowed as I strode toward the dozen assorted lilies. They were Gabby's favorite, and I didn't need to read the card to know who had given them to her.

A slow smile curved my lips as I turned and headed toward her room. I opened the door and flipped on the lights, taking in the clothes scattered across the floor. A pair of men's pants were thrown over the chair, and a pair of my heels lay on the fake fur rug against her bed.

"Well, well, well, this explains why you didn't answer my text messages!" I proclaimed loudly, placing my hands on my hips.

That got her attention.

Gabby jolted upright, grabbing the sheet to her chest as her lover turned to stare blearily at me over his shoulder. The toppled shaggy hair confirmed the identity of the man sharing my sister's bed.

A grin of delight curved my lips. "No way! You finally gave Big Dick Rick a chance?"

"Dianna!" Gabby grabbed a pillow and threw it at me. "Get out of here!"

I batted it away and laughed as I closed the door to her room.

PLAQUES. THERE WERE SO MANY PLAQUES. I STOOD IN THE LIVING ROOM staring at the degrees Gabby had earned from the University of Valoel. She had a life now, and I couldn't be happier. She had graduated with the highest degree she could get in healthcare. Gabby had always loved helping people, just like our mother. She was the light and hope in the family, where I was the darkness and destruction.

The door to Gabby's room opened, and she stepped out, followed closely by Rick. Seeing her happy made everything I'd suffered and endured worth it. She giggled at something that Rick whispered to her and sent him a flirtatious wink over her shoulder as they came down the hallway. Gabby wore a blue robe belted tightly around her small frame, her hair still a slightly tangled mess.

"Nice to see you again, Dianna," Rick said, a slight blush gracing his cheeks as he waved.

Rick Evergreen. The resident doctor had been after my sister since she moved to sunny Valoel a few years ago. I had met him a handful of times when I visited Gabby at work. My visits had become few and far between, and my heart ached at that fact. How much of her life had I missed this time?

"Rick. How long has it been? You look well." I let the last part linger, my gaze not leaving his. His scent changed, and I knew he feared me. His primitive mortal instincts were alerting him to danger, although he didn't know why.

"A few months, at least." He gave me a small smile, his throat bobbing as he swallowed hard.

Gabby shook her head at the exchange, familiar with my overbearing ways by now. She gently grabbed his arm and ushered him to the door. "You're going to be late for work."

I watched them smile at each other as if nothing else mattered. Rick leaned forward, kissing her softly one last time before she opened the door. Her expression was lit with love and joy as he stepped out. She waved and promised to call him later before closing the door.

A dull ache formed in my chest, and I looked away as my throat tightened. I longed to have even the simplest form of that, but I'd given up any chance of normalcy eons ago. I had given it up when I traded a life for a life.

Gabby's happy squeal pulled me from those dark memories. She ran to me and practically tackled me in a hug. "Oh my God, D! I missed you so much!" she whispered against my hair as I laughed.

"I missed you, too." I returned her hug tightly. It was nice being embraced and not worrying about my heart getting ripped out.

She pulled back, her eyes shining as she smiled. "How long can you stay this time?"

It was the unspoken truth of my visits. I stayed as long as Kaden allowed.

I shrugged. "I'm not sure, but let's make the best of it?"

"Sounds good. So, how about breakfast?"

I nodded and gave her a bright smile. Gabby turned and walked into the kitchen. I followed and jumped up on the nearest barstool at the long island. She reached into the fridge, pulling out an assortment of items before turning toward the coffee pot. I placed my hand under my chin as she stood on her tiptoes to take down two mugs.

"I like the white-and-brown theme you have for the place. The kitchen looks amazing."

"Thanks, it's actually new. Rick liked the marble finish, even though I told him I didn't need an upgrade."

My eyebrow ticked upward as I leaned across the counter, baiting her. "Oh, so now he buys you things for your apartment?"

Her eyes met mine over her shoulder as she added the coffee grounds to the pot and turned it on. "Well, he has been staying here lately."

"What?!" I gasped. "And you didn't tell me?"

"You're not the easiest person to reach."

A pang tightened my chest, stealing the excitement from me. I sank back into my chair and fumbled with my fingers. Gabby looked at me, catching the sudden shift in my mood.

"It hasn't been a long time, Rick and me." She walked back to the stove, reaching into a cabinet and pulling a pan out. "We had a few dates, and then he slowly just started staying over."

I forced a smile, meeting her gaze as she prepared breakfast. "I am happy for you. It's just the last time we talked, you guys were still playing the whole," I paused, making air quotes, "'We don't like each other' game."

She broke an egg over the pan and turned the heat up slightly. "D, it's been months since you've visited. Things change."

Those months that Kaden had me and the others searching for that book he was obsessed with. It had been months since I had been *allowed* to spend time with the only person in the world who loved me. Months. The word hung in the air a moment longer before I shook my head.

"Well, it's good to know that he's not just sending flowers to get in your pants." I smirked, but Gabby just gave me a small smile and shook her head. She knew me too well. She knew I used jokes and humor when my feelings got too real.

"You know, D, men sometimes do nice things just because they like you. It doesn't have to be about sex." She turned, holding the spatula to her chest, faking a gasp and holding the back of her free hand to her forehead as she mocked me. "Even flowers."

"I wouldn't know." The words left my lips before I realized what I was saying. I hated when Gabby worried about me, and I knew that comment alone would piss her off.

Her shoulders sagged as she scrambled the eggs in the pan before grabbing some bread and starting the toast. She didn't say anything, but I felt her anger from here.

"Gabby."

"I just… I hate him."

I stood and went to the fridge, pulling out the bacon. "I know, but you don't have to like him. Regardless, he is the reason I still have you."

She paused, placing her hands on the nearest countertop before turning toward me. "I'm here because you gave up your life for mine."

"Which I couldn't have done without him."

"I hate that he holds it over your head. That you have to do everything he says because of me."

I spun her to face me. My hands were firm on her shoulders as I held her gaze and smiled. "I don't regret it—never have, and never will. I knew the price when I asked, and I would rather answer his every call like a dog on a leash than lose you."

She smiled softly. "I know. I just worry about you. What have you even been doing this entire time? Where have you been?"

"Honestly?" I asked, stepping back. "Everywhere. Kaden thinks he's getting close to finding the Book of Azrael."

"What?" Her eyes practically bugged out of her head. "As in *the book*? The one he's been looking for forever?"

"Yup. But at this point, I don't think it's real. I mean, how could it be if he has not found it already? He is ancient, to say the least, and it's not like the war happened yesterday."

She stepped back, shaking her head slightly. "I always assumed a book such as that would be locked up tight."

"So, about that…"

She turned the oven on to preheat before turning to look at me. "Dianna."

I pulled out a pan and parchment paper. She watched as I started laying out the slices of bacon on the baking sheet. "So, remember how I told you the celestials have a sort of ranking system?"

"Dianna. What did you do?"

"It's not what I did, per se, but Alistair—"

She placed one hand on her hip as she brought her other hand up and rubbed her face. "Oh, gods."

"I think we might have found a way into Arariel, which means we can get close to The Hand, which means we will be closer to this book he thinks exists."

"What if it does? What does it do?"

I shrugged, moving past her once more to grab the cups she'd set out. I poured us each some coffee and said, "Honestly, I don't know. Kaden says it holds the key to opening realms. He wants normalcy for us. He wants us to live in a world where we are no longer burdened by the celestials or live in fear of The Hand."

"'Burdened'?" I turned and caught her stricken expression. "Would people be hurt?"

"Gabby, you know I would never let anything happen to you."

"I know that, but what about everyone else, D? If this book supposedly creates normalcy for him and his kind—"

"*Our* kind," I interjected, raising a brow. "I am just as much of Kaden as you are."

"No. I don't need blood, and I don't have to eat people for power."

The words hung between us. Gabby was right. She didn't need to feed like the rest of us, even if my diet of late was not mortal. Gabby was different; she was the closest thing to a mortal with an immortal life. I had asked Kaden after he changed us why Gabby wasn't like Tobias, Alistair, or me. He said she was so close to death that the parts that made us ended up weaker in her. She would live longer, but she couldn't change into anything she wanted and didn't have the urges we did.

Gabby was different, but so much better than any of us. The only power she seemed to have was a sort of empathy. That was the only way I could describe it. She could calm someone, heal them in a way. Her voice soothed, her touch brought comfort, and her presence alone seemed to make even the most irate patient quiet down. She wasn't a monster like us. No, she was an angel born out of the most brutal darkness.

"Gabby, there is nothing to worry about. The book doesn't exist.

It's been centuries since the Gods War and the fall of Rashearim. There is nothing left, no matter what Kaden believes."

She held my gaze for a moment, the look of concern never leaving her amber eyes. "I hope you're right, D. I do."

I smiled softly. "Hey, I'm the big sister, remember? I've always taken care of us, and I always will. Besides, I'm always right."

She snorted, rolled her eyes, and sipped her coffee.

"So, about Rick," I said, looking at her through the steam wafting from my cup as I took a sip.

"Oh, gods, here we go," she said.

"I'm all for happy naked fun, but you know it's temporary, right? I mean, I'm super happy you're finally getting laid, but I don't want this to be like that puppy you adopted years ago. He lived a long, happy life and died of old age, but you still cried for almost six years."

She turned away as the oven beeped, alerting us it was ready for whatever delicious dish Gabby was about to make for breakfast. She opened the refrigerator door and leaned over to grab a few items.

"First off, I loved that dog." She turned to glare at me over her shoulder. "And second, why does it have to be temporary?"

"Gabby, we talked about this. If you're going to date seriously, they have to be Otherworldly. Rick is mortal. He will grow old, while you stay pretty and annoying forever. What will he do when he sees you never get wrinkles or age spots, and your hair stays perfect for eternity?"

She opened the freezer, pulling out what looked like rolls of some sort before looking back at me. "Well, what if I asked Drake to change him?"

I nearly spit out my coffee at the mention of his name. I grabbed a paper towel and wiped my mouth. She moved around the kitchen, avoiding eye contact as she pulled a baking pan from the cupboard.

"Wait—what? You would want Rick to be an Otherworld creature? Gabby, that's permanent! You can't just decide to make the guy you're interested in into a vampire."

"Well…" She paused as she tucked a few strands of hair behind her ear. "I kind of want Rick to be a permanent fixture in my life. Maybe even marriage."

My shock must have shown on my face, because she started to chew on her lip, a clear sign she was nervous and unsure of my reaction. I didn't speak, because I didn't know what to say. I knew they'd been flirting for a while, but what Gabby was talking about meant she wanted him in her life forever. Since the Gods War, the rules and customs had changed. Shit, even the technology was different. Marriage wasn't a piece of paper you got that said you were bound to one another. It was beyond permanent and meant you were one in almost every sense of the word. When you married, you became true partners, the bond that of soul mates. "Gabby..." I started as she placed the rolls in the oven and turned back to me.

She raised her hand, cutting me off before I could go on. "Dianna, I know it's sudden from your perspective, but you've been gone for months. Rick and I have gotten very close, and something changed. Even before I saw him as anything more than a friend, he was there for me. He is there on the days when it's hard to get out of bed because work is exhausting. He is there on the days when I'm sad or stressed. I think I'm falling in love with him." She smiled at her own admission. "I know it probably sounds stupid to you—"

"It doesn't," I said, even though a part of me was sad I'd missed out on this part of her life. I felt like an intruder at times. I would swoop in, seeing bits and pieces, but was never truly here for her. Now my sister was in love, and I'd missed her telling me about it. There had been no phone calls where she gushed about him, because I hardly got to speak to her. There were no late-night movies or talks where she told me about the joys and struggles of the day, because I wasn't here. "If this is what you want, I am happy for you. I'm happy that someone can be here for you when I can't. I just want you to be happy. You know that."

She practically squealed as she engulfed me in a sideways hug, swaying with me. "I promise he is great and funny, and you will love him, too."

"Yeah, yeah." I pulled back to smile at her. "If he breaks your heart, I'll eat his."

She scrunched her nose, her arms still wrapped around me. "Okay, eww."

"I'm just saying."

She shook her head and rolled her eyes. "Okay, evisceration aside, do you think Drake would do it? Change him?"

The corners of my mouth turned up as I gave her an innocent smile. "So, funny story…"

My time with Gabby was the only time I felt mortal. On the first day, we stayed on the beach almost all day. Then that night, we went out for drinks before heading back to her apartment. The next day was nothing but lounging around and singing karaoke as we jumped from couch to couch. Our hair was up in lopsided ponytails, and our faces were covered in some weird face mask Gabby had spent way too much money on.

"Why do you only have mint ice cream?" I yelled from the kitchen as I held the freezer door open.

"Why do you hate things that are delicious?"

I snorted and grabbed the carton from the freezer before closing the door. "We need to go buy the twelve new flavors that came out, because this is just sad," I said as I scooped two spoons from the nearest kitchen drawer. I sat next to Gabby on the couch and handed her one.

"Less talking, more sharing." She snickered as she opened the large throw blanket and draped it over us. I scooped out a heaping spoonful of ice cream before passing her the carton and turning on the TV.

"What do you want to watch?" I asked, flipping through channels.

"Oh, check channel thirty-one. There was a cute movie I wanted to watch."

I turned to look at her as she shoved a spoonful of ice cream into her mouth. "Is this a romance again?"

She shrugged and gave me an angelic smile. "Maybe."

I shook my head and ate my ice cream as I scrolled through the channels toward the show she wanted. I stopped when the words dancing across the bottom of the screen caught my attention. A news anchor was discussing a recent quake near Ecanus.

"The strange thing about this was that it wasn't even a large quake for the area. The only real damage was to the three ancient temples." Images of the ancient ruins flashed up on the screen. They were similar to others that had appeared on Onuna at the end of the Gods War. My stomach sank, and I stood abruptly, nearly knocking over the coffee table. My phone—where was my phone?

"Dianna? Is everything okay?" I heard Gabby's voice from the living room as I ran toward her bedroom. Fuck, I had to find my phone! What if Kaden had called and I'd missed it? A quake in Ecanus? It was rare, to say the least, and the temples couldn't be a coincidence.

I pushed her bedroom door open and stopped just inside, looking around her room. Her bed was made, and the bathroom door to my left was cracked open. I spotted my phone on the dresser. I breathed out a sigh of relief and grabbed it.

My heart calmed in my chest when I saw I didn't have any new messages. Okay, I hadn't missed a call, but I knew the quake wasn't just a random act of nature. I felt it in my gut. I turned and left the room, taking my phone with me.

Gabby stood up and placed her ice cream on the table when I walked back in. "Everything okay?"

I nodded and sat back down. Gabby curled up beside me, waiting for me to answer, her eyes filled with confusion and concern.

"Yes, sorry, I thought I heard my phone."

Her eyes narrowed, telling me she didn't truly believe me, as she looked from the phone in my hand back to the TV. I didn't give her a chance to ask another question as I picked up the remote and changed the channel. "So, what was that movie you wanted to watch?"

GABBY DIDN'T INVITE RICK OVER ONCE WHILE I WAS THERE. SHE wanted time with me, which I appreciated. On the days she had to work, I mostly stayed inside, raiding her cabinets for food and just relaxing. It was nice not being on call for a change, but I kept checking my phone, afraid I'd missed a call or text. The random quake had me on high alert. I knew Kaden wasn't just sitting on his hands while I was away, but wondering what they were up to left me with a sense of unease. I was terrified Kaden would show up and take me back, but as the days bled into a week, I grew more comfortable, less on edge. That's what Gabby did for me: she grounded me. The beast inside me never truly went away, but her proximity kept it at bay.

On her next day off, we hopped in the car so Gabby could show me around. As she drove, I dangled my hand out of the open window, making waves on the wind as I watched the rippling hills pass by. The summer air held a hint of chill, telling me fall was on the horizon.

"I want to take you to a couple shops. You will love them, I promise," Gabby said as she turned the radio down.

I nodded as she slowed, the traffic getting heavier the closer we got to downtown. The cars were all sleek and sharp. Everything was similar to that style now. It was another reminder of the creatures that had fallen from the sky centuries ago. They had changed the very fabric of our world.

"What do you think the world will look like in ten years?"

"Huh?" She glanced at me. "What do you mean?"

I shifted in my seat, folding my arms as I looked at her. "The celestials. They have impacted Onuna so much. I wonder how much more they will change our world."

"You really hate them, don't you?"

I snorted. "Don't you? They're the reason Mom and Dad are gone, and why our home is practically nonexistent."

"D, they didn't kill Mom and Dad. The plague did."

"The plague was caused by whatever bacteria they brought down with them."

She sighed. "That was just a coincidence. There is no proof that was the cause. Besides, I work with a few celestials. They're nice."

"What?" I sat up so fast that the seatbelt practically choked me. I adjusted the sudden grip it had across my chest. "Gabby, you can't be friends with them. They will try to hurt you if they know what you are."

She glanced at me and shrugged. "I'm not, and they don't. I have just spoken to them a few times in passing. They seem normal."

"They're not normal, and they're not friends. Please tell me you will stay away. If they know what you are, or if Kaden finds out—"

"He'll what? Kill them?" She side-eyed me with a fake laugh.

I didn't respond.

"Oh, my gods. He would, wouldn't he?"

"You know he would." I rested my chin against my fist and stared out the open window. Neither of us said anything else.

We parked and wandered through the market areas she was obsessed with. After a few hours of buying things we didn't need, we had worked up an appetite and stopped at a small restaurant. The place was packed, but we didn't care. We asked for a table toward the back because I liked to keep an eye on every exit. Call it a habit of my lifestyle, but I never liked my back exposed in any room. We laughed as we ate, and we were fighting over the last bite of dessert when she said, "This has been nice. I've missed you."

I gave her a genuine smile. "It has. I missed you, too. Now, on the count of three, we open them?"

She grabbed for one of the crushable red-and-pink-style candies that held the year's fortune. I knew they weren't real fortunes, but Gabby loved the mystery of what if. "You know you're going to open before three. You have no impulse control."

"Pfft." I rolled my eyes, leaning back in my chair. "I have all the control."

She just shook her head as she waited for my countdown. I began, and on three, we ripped them open and broke them in half. I took the paper out of mine and read, *"A big change is coming your way."*

"Well, that's stupid." I sighed and popped the candy into my mouth. I looked up at Gabby. "What does yours say?"

She shrugged and handed it to me. "Well, it didn't tell me I won a large lump sum of money, so that's a bummer."

I giggled and took the small paper, reading out loud, *"A single act can change the world."*

I shrugged, handing it back to her. "Either I'm old, or these fortunes don't make sense anymore."

"Well, you do look like you're starting to get wrinkles." She lifted her hands, patting around her eyes. "Especially right here."

I crumpled my napkin and tossed it at her. "Shut up."

She laughed at me before taking another bite of her food.

NOT WANTING TO STAY IN THAT NIGHT, I CONVINCED GABBY TO GO out. I told her to invite Rick, but she said he was working late. Our game plan was to hit as many places as possible before the sun rose.

Gabby's ombre brown-and-blonde hair was curled, the waves dancing against the back of her white fitted dress. It stopped mid-thigh, and I practically had to beg her to wear it tonight. I told her that if Rick did stop by, he would love it. I even convinced her to take some sexy selfies and send them to him on the car ride to the club. My short, soft green dress had a halter top that tied around my neck, leaving my arms, shoulders, and back exposed. I had let Gabby curl my hair and pull it into a half-up, half-down style.

The club had three levels, and people were packed in on every floor, dancing, laughing, and flirting. The memory of the destruction I had inflicted on Drake and his club in Tirin threatened to overwhelm me with grief. I closed my eyes tightly, trying to shut it out.

"You good?" Gabby yelled.

My smile was forced as I opened my eyes and nodded. I wasn't there. I was with her, and I was okay. We shuffled further inside, and I pushed thoughts of Drake aside.

We danced for what felt like hours, pausing only to take a shot before going back to the dance floor. You couldn't move without bumping into someone. A large chandelier took up the ceiling from the front of the club to the back door. Colored lights danced over the crowd as everyone laughed and sang along with the music. It had been so long since I'd felt so free. I'd forgotten what it was like to just let go for a night. We danced with anyone who approached—men or women, it didn't matter. We just had fun.

After the next song, Gabby snagged me and pointed toward the back and the bathroom. A flashing neon sign signaled our target as we made our way through the crowd, bumping into people and apologizing mid-laugh like fools. But our amusement fled when we saw the line. We sighed, knowing we didn't have much choice in the matter. Gabby sagged against the wall, reaching down to massage her ankles while we waited.

"I haven't done this in so long, I forgot how much my feet usually hurt in the morning." She snickered as she straightened. "Well, except that you practically live in heels."

I smiled back as the music behind us thumped loudly. "Yeah, but that's also because I'm a masochist."

She swatted my arm and giggled. "Gross."

"I'm kidding, I'm kidding," I said, smiling back at her. "… Mostly."

She shook her head and grinned back at me. "I am having fun, though. We should definitely do this more often." She paused. "Well, when we can."

I nodded, knowing that once I had to leave, we probably wouldn't be together again for months.

The line shuffled forward, and we moved up a few paces. Gabby leaned against the wall as I rocked back and forth on my heels. Several women passed as they exited the bathroom, but only one stood out to me. I stopped rocking and stood straight, my every instinct going on alert. She was tall, and her skin was darker than mine, a deeper shade of brown. Her unbound jet-black hair cascaded in thick curls down her back. The purple sparkly dress she wore accentuated curves that would make any living creature take notice.

She reminded me of a goddess given mortal life. The women in line stared, their comments and whispers tinting the air with jealousy. She made eye contact with me, smiling as she waved. The silver rings decorating the fingers of both her hands caught the flashing lights and seemed to glow. She continued down the hall and back into the club. My gaze followed her as she disappeared into a wave of dancing people. I turned back to Gabby, a weird sensation flushing my body. The hairs on my arms bristled, and a chill caused me to shudder. Celestial? I pushed off the wall slightly, waiting to feel that static-like tingle they give off, but there was nothing.

"She's so pretty—unnaturally pretty," Gabby said, nodding toward where the woman had disappeared. "Do you want to go talk to her?"

I shook my head at her and smiled, but the pit in my stomach told me something was wrong. "No, I'm good. Besides, I really have to pee." We shuffled forward, the hairs on my arms still raised in alert and my heart pounding as if a threat lingered nearby.

Had Kaden called, and I did not answer? Was he here now? I held my hand out. "Gabby, I need my phone."

She reached into her small clutch and handed it to me. I checked and breathed out a silent sigh of relief. I had no missed calls or texts.

"Everything okay?" Gabby asked as I turned to stare at where the woman had disappeared into the writhing crowd of dancers.

I nodded as the line moved forward again. "Yeah, everything is fine."

After our bathroom break, we went back to the dance floor, laughing and twirling to the next few songs. I still had an uneasy feeling creeping up my spine that I couldn't explain. It was like my brain was trying to tell me something, but I didn't have the words for it.

We were mid-song when Gabby broke away and started squealing. I turned to see what had caused her excitement and saw Rick pushing through the crowd as best he could. She shifted around me and ran into his arms. Her delight in seeing him was obvious in her smile and the kisses she pressed to his face as he lifted her against him. I just smiled and gestured toward the bar, leaving them to dance while I went to get more shots.

I leaned over the bar to get the bartender's attention. He did a double-take and finished the drinks he was making before coming over.

"Two tequila shots," I practically shouted over the music. He nodded and tossed a small towel over his shoulder before turning to get the drinks. When he set them in front of me, I slammed the first one back, not even a burn tickling my throat. I sighed and turned back toward the dance floor. I could see Gabby's smile from here as she peered up at Rick. A warm bubble wrapped around my heart. I loved seeing her happy.

"Your friend looks happy."

The words caught me off guard. I was so distracted watching Gabby that I hadn't felt him approach. I turned to face the stranger, angling my body in a more defensible pose. His hair was cut close to the sides of his head in a fade, deep waves layering the top. He leaned against the bar next to me, his muscular build taking up more than his fair share of space. How long had he been there without me noticing? He was watching where Gabby and Rick had been swallowed up by the crowd, but glanced at me as he turned back toward the bar and took a sip of his drink.

"Not my friend," I replied coolly. "My sister."

He smiled, the shine of his perfect teeth sending goosebumps along my arms. "Sister? My apologies."

I smiled back, focusing intently on him, all of my instincts roused and on alert. He was handsome in that bad-boy kind of way. His beard was perfectly trimmed and neat. The tattoos that graced the back of his left hand and arm were etched with beautiful precision against his dark complexion. They disappeared beneath the rolled-up sleeve of his shirt and made him look even sexier and more dangerous. My eyes caught on the thick silver rings that decorated a few of his fingers. They had a strange assortment of twists and turns, the solid metal seeming to glow, radiating an unfamiliar power.

He wiggled his fingers. "Family heirlooms."

I met his eyes, realizing I must have been staring, and gave him a small smile. "Cool."

Something about him felt off. Wrong. The goosebumps still decorated my arms as I focused on filtering out the blaring music and smells of every mortal here. The sweat, lust, vomit, and alcohol faded. I heard the beat of his heart, the rhythm slow and steady. He smelled mortal, his scent one of cologne and a hint of citrus, but nothing Otherworldly.

The music came back, and his voice flooded my ears once more. "You all right?" His eyebrow ticked as he took another drink.

"Fine." I nodded back, smiling softly.

"So…" He lifted his glass, taking a sip. "Are you just here with your sister, or…?"

He let the words trail off, and I knew what he was implying. Normally, I would have been more than happy to indulge him. I would have been tempted had it been any other time, but I was here with Gabby, the sister I rarely got to see.

I took my last shot, slamming it back before placing the empty glass on the bar in front of me. I stepped forward, and he straightened to his full height as I invaded his space. It annoyed me to discover that he was indeed taller than I. Many men could not claim the same.

"Look, I get it. You have this whole bad-boy thing going for you, and I'm sure plenty of women here would love for you to bend them over this very bar, but it's not going to be me. Trust me. I am actually doing you a favor, because I mean it when I say…" I paused, a slow smile curving my lips. "I would eat you alive."

I patted him on the arm and walked away, leaving him at the bar. I shoved through the crowd, trying to make a path toward Gabby. Rick and she were still laughing as they danced around each other. As soon as she saw my face, she stopped, causing Rick to bump into her.

"What's wrong?" she yelled over the music.

"Nothing," I said, cupping my hand near my mouth. "I'm just a little tired. Give me my phone, and I'll meet you back at the apartment."

Gabby's eyes scanned mine, but she nodded and handed me my phone. I leaned forward, kissing her on her cheek and waving goodbye to Rick.

I shoved past the growing crowd of newcomers and out the door, where the cool night air greeted me. People milled about on the boardwalk, laughing and joking in the pools of light created by the streetlamps. I raised my phone to check for any missed calls or texts, but the screen remained clear. My unease didn't lessen as I lowered it to my side and willed my body into shadowy black mist.

FIVE

DIANNA

I t had been two weeks since I'd heard from Kaden or the others.
Two weeks to spend time with my sister. I loved it, but that
gnawing sense of unease kept forcing me to check my phone. I
couldn't place it, but I knew something must be wrong.

Gabby and I had just finished watching a movie at the local theater
and were walking down the sunny boardwalk toward an outdoor
restaurant. Birds chirped in the trees lining the path, and the people
we passed were laughing and happy. Everyone was out enjoying the
afternoon sun. Gabby wore a large brown hat and a pair of the largest
black sunglasses I had ever seen. I had been teasing her about them all
day. Her bronzed skin glistened, offset by her white tank and tattered
blue shorts. Her simple, understated beauty drew a few second
glances and compliments from passing pedestrians.

I'd opted for a black spaghetti-strap tank, the hem fluttering over a
white leather skirt. I was her opposite in every way, although we were
both wearing matching pairs of white sandals. She liked them because
they showed off the pedicure we'd gotten that morning.

"This is one of my favorite places," Gabby said, grabbing at her hat
as the wind picked up. She led the way to the open entrance, passing
beneath the sign that read THE MODERN GRILL. Tables and chairs

surrounded the bar, and TVs hung from the ceiling. The place was packed, and the noise blasted us as we drew closer.

"It looks busy. Maybe we should have made reservations."

She waved my concerns away. "No worries, I know the owner."

I smirked. "How many times have you been here?"

She grinned at me, but her tone was gentle as she said, "Not that many, but his wife had to have heart surgery a month back, and I was her nurse. They are super sweet, and he said I would always have a table here no matter what."

"Ah, my sister, the sweet caretaker," I said with a grin, following her further inside.

Gabby playfully swatted at me before turning to wave at an older gentleman. The owner was thrilled to see her, and Gabby made the introductions. I figured we would eat inside, but the waitress led us to a deck at the back of the restaurant. The tables sat a little further apart, and the view of the ocean was breathtaking.

The warm ocean breeze curled my hair around my chin, and I moved the errant strands out of my way. Gabby took her hat off, placing it on the edge of the table as our waitress took our orders. We watched as a few children teased the waves crashing against the shore, their laughter a song in the air.

"This is paradise. I don't think I could ever get tired of the ocean," Gabby said, pulling me from my thoughts.

"Yeah, it definitely beats the oceans of sand we grew up around," I said, looking at her as she watched the kids on the beach, a smile teasing her lips. The sun cast a shine over the ombre waves of her hair, making her look almost angelic.

"You remind me of Mom, you know." I folded my hands underneath my chin as I spoke. "You take after her, especially when it comes to helping others. I know she would be proud."

Gabby's eyes lit up with pleasure. "I hope so. And please, if I take after Mom, you definitely take after Dad. Headstrong, always trying to take care of everyone else but themselves, and that attitude." She whistled under her breath. "Definitely Dad."

I couldn't help but laugh. "I miss them. Sometimes I wonder what our life would have been like had they not gotten sick."

"Me, too." She sighed. "But I have to believe everything happens for a reason, even stuff like that. We can't live in the past, D. Nothing grows there."

"Oh, you and that pesky optimism."

She giggled. "Someone has to be. Do you remember that hiking trip we took in Ecanus? You thought we would get lost because you couldn't read a compass. That was one of my favorite vacations, even if I did get in trouble for feeding the wildlife." She laughed, covering her mouth with her hand at the memory. "I love the freedom you gave me."

Gabby dropped her hand and smiled at me, but I felt mine slowly slipping. We never really talked about my sacrifice—what I gave so that she could live. We didn't like to think about the price, and it resulted in a fight every time it came up. She didn't like Kaden, Tobias, or Alistair. She didn't understand Kaden's power over me, and I never wanted her to feel like it was her fault. I'd stayed for her, suffered for her, and I would do it again in a heartbeat.

"Yeah, and all you had to do was almost die," I joked as the waiter returned with our water and appetizers.

She mixed the greens of her salad, covering it with a thin dressing as she stirred. "I am being serious. I'm happy here with my job and my life. I want that for you, too."

My stomach sank. I knew where this was going. "Gabby…"

"What?" she asked innocently, her attention on spearing her salad. "I'm just saying—"

"I can't leave, and I don't want to fight with you about it," I cut her off, my voice stern. "You know this, and you know I hate talking about it."

She shook her head, placing her fork down. "Have you ever tried?"

"Gabby. Seriously. I can't. Have you even thought of what that would mean? He pretty much owns me. Remember what we just said about the life you have? That came with a price—a price neither of us likes talking about."

"I know that." Her voice was soft but held a hint of the same temper we both carried. She may not have had my powers, but my sister was feisty, especially when it came to those she considered hers.

The fire that burned beneath our skin was there in her. Mine was just literal. "But—"

I put my fork down and placed my head in my hands, frustration filling my voice. "There is no *but*, Gabs. He owns me. I don't know how much clearer I can make that."

"No one owns you."

I felt the Ig'Morruthen that lay beneath my skin wake, and I dropped my hands. My eyes flared, and I could see the embers reflected in the sunglasses atop her head. "He does, and in every way. We can pretend that these last two weeks are real and that we are the perfect sisters who braid each other's hair, go out for drinks, and paint our nails. But the absolute truth of it is that we are not. We both died centuries ago in that damned desert. Whether you want to admit it to yourself or not, we're different. *I'm* different."

My sister didn't flinch. She wasn't afraid of me and knew I would never hurt her. "You can't blame me for wanting you to be happy. I want something normal for you—something besides the bread crumbs he feeds you to keep you in line."

"Gabby. This isn't some movie you watch on TV, where everyone gets to live happily ever after. That's not my world. It never was. There are no flowers, no cute words, and no sweet promises. My world is violent and real, and permanent."

She shook her head, the waves of her hair dancing with the movement. "You think I don't know what's going on, even though you don't tell me? I saw the bruises when you arrived. You don't sleep, tossing and turning every night. You're on edge all the time. I see the way you watch doors and windows, how you act when we go out. I see the way you flinch when someone brushes up against you. Why don't you fight back? You have the skills and are strong. Why do you let him—"

"Stop!" I slammed my hands on the table, causing the entire thing to shake and groan. I knew it had split from the force, but the tablecloth hid the cracks. Several people stopped eating and stared at us. Those inside the building didn't notice the commotion, the noise drowning us out. I closed my eyes tightly, willing the flames to recede.

"Look…" I flicked my lashes up and looked at Gabby, placing my hand over hers. "I have everything I could want. Money, way too many clothes that you steal whenever you can, and I can literally go anywhere in the world. I mean, you like the vacations we've had. You said it yourself."

"That stuff is material, D. It doesn't make you whole."

"It makes me enough."

Gabby slipped her hand from beneath mine and wiped a tear from her cheek. "You gave up everything for me, and now you're forever bound to someone who will never love you, never care about you beyond what you can do for him."

"I know, but that's not realistic. Not for me." My heart ached. It was unspoken, but I knew Kaden didn't love me, nor did I love him. All Gabby wanted was the best for me, the same things I wanted for her, and it broke me. "Hey, look at me." When she did, I continued, "I don't regret it, you know? Not a second of it. I would give my life a thousand times over for you."

"You shouldn't have to." Her lip quivered, and I realized this had been bothering her since I'd arrived. She had kept her feelings behind the same kind of wall I'd constructed around my emotions. I hated seeing her sad, even for a second, so I did what I always did and tried to lighten the mood. "Hey, last I recalled, I am the older sister here, okay? I take care of you. It's kind of like my job, but with terrible benefits. The healthcare is shit, and I'm not even talking about the amount of money I spend on the collect calls when I'm out of town..."

Gabby's laugh was bitter as she carefully wiped beneath her eyes.

Our waiter returned with our food and refilled our glasses. Gabby smiled as she picked up her fork and twirled a few strands of pasta. She raised the bite toward her mouth, but stopped. Her eyes widened as she looked past me—and then I felt it. A cold chill ran up my spine, and I knew darkness loomed at my back. The birds had disappeared, and the children had stopped laughing. Even the sound of the waves was muted. It was as if life was attempting to hide from what had just arrived. I stood fast enough to flip my chair and spun, catching Tobias by the throat.

"You know what happens when people sneak up on me, especially when I'm with her," I hissed, my nails elongated and pressing into his throat.

He only smiled at my threat, his eyes a reflection of mine as he leaned into my grasp. He knew I couldn't hurt him or Alistair. I couldn't kill them, because it would be a death sentence for Gabby and me.

He bit his lip and wrapped his hand around my wrist. "Squeeze harder. I almost feel something."

I rolled my eyes and let him go with a slight push before righting my chair and sitting back down.

Alistair's laugh filled the outdoor patio. "Someone is tense. Miss us?" I didn't answer him, and Gabby sat frozen. Alistair turned to her. "Lovely day, isn't it?" I heard the scrape of a metal chair as he grabbed one from a nearby table. He flipped it around and straddled it with his long legs as he sat beside me.

My stomach knotted, and I picked up my phone, afraid I had missed Kaden's call. But when the screen lit up, I saw I had no messages. I clenched my jaw, annoyed I hadn't sensed them sooner. How long had they been nearby? Had they overheard Gabby and me?

Tobias lurked in my peripheral, and I focused on controlling my irritation. He knew I hated when he did that. "What are you doing here?" I asked, turning to face them both. "Kaden hasn't called."

Alistair reached over, stealing a meatball from Gabby's plate and popping it into his mouth. He glanced at Tobias and swallowed before saying with a grin, "He's busy."

They snickered at some private joke. I didn't care. They'd always had their secrets. It was something I had grown accustomed to over the years.

The wind shifted, and my mouth watered. I fought back the hunger and said, "You both reek of blood, with a hint of something foreign. What's happening? Why hasn't he called?"

Alistair smirked, shaking his head. "Aren't you always complaining that you never get to see your lovely sister here?" he said, looking pointedly at Gabby, a predatory sheen in his eyes. Gabby remained silent and still, not taking her eyes from them.

"Besides," Tobias cut in, "you weren't needed."

Alistair chuckled again. "Understatement of the century."

That got a laugh out of Tobias.

Gabby slammed her fork down on the table. "Don't talk to her like that!" she snapped. They both turned to her, quick as vipers in the flesh, their smiles and laughter gone.

"Oh, yeah? And how do you want me to talk to her, huh? Or perhaps talk to you?" Alistair's grin was cold as he leaned in close to her. "You know, it wouldn't take much to get into that pretty little head of yours. I could make you do whatever I wanted, any time, any place." His eyes roamed over her. "Anywhere."

"Alistair." It was a warning. They could talk to me however they wanted, threaten me, but no one disrespected Gabby.

He turned back, knowing damn well he'd pissed me off. Gabby didn't say anything as she leaned back in her chair, inching away from him.

"Don't worry, Dianna. We know the rules. No one touches your precious sister," he said. He was clearly annoyed, but lost interest as a pretty little waitress passed.

"Enough small talk." Tobias sighed, folding his arms. "Kaden is tied up at the moment, so we are here to collect you. Your visitation is over."

Gabby's eyes met mine, and my heart sank. Two weeks… At least I had gotten two weeks.

Alistair pushed to his feet, and I stood. I walked over to Gabby, and she rose to hug me tight. My eyes burned as I whispered close to her ear, "I'll be back as soon as possible. I promise." I pulled back, holding her gently by the arms. "Remember that I love you."

She nodded once before I let her go. I stepped around her, moving away from the table, Alistair and Tobias following me. I wanted them as far from Gabby as possible.

"Where are we needed now?"

Alistair rubbed his hands together slowly. "Oh, you'll love it. We're going back to El Donuma."

My stomach dropped.

"Ophanium, to be exact. Our little celestial friend Peter finally came through."

"El Donuma? But that's Camilla's territory. You know she hates me."

Alistair only shrugged. "She fears Kaden a lot more."

"Stop talking," Tobias snapped, and I turned to look at him. His eyes weren't on me, but on something or someone inside the restaurant. The red around his irises began to burn, and I followed his gaze. I didn't see any threats. No Otherworld beings were in the vicinity.

"Here?" Alistair asked, staring at Tobias and then glancing toward the restaurant.

Tobias shook his head, and Alistair cursed.

"What is it?"

"Nothing," Tobias said, giving Alistair a meaningful look. I scanned the area once more, trying to figure out what had caught their attention, but I still saw nothing of concern. With a shrug I knew would irritate them, I turned back to Gabby, offering her a small smile. "I'll be back as soon as I can."

Gabby nodded again, and I waved as we left my sister, the restaurant, and whatever had spooked two of the most terrifying creatures I knew.

SIX
DIANNA

My paws beat against the forest floor as I zipped between the large bushes and shrubs, outlining the lower part of the mountainside. The shape of the sleek feline beast I'd donned allowed me to slip easily through the dense forest. The animal's smooth black fur and dusky rosettes blended perfectly into the shadows beneath the trees.

We had made it to Ophanium hours ago. Kaden wasn't waiting for us, and when I asked about him, all Tobias and Alistair would tell me was that Kaden had sent us ahead to scout the area. A large tomb had been found in a remote area of the forest. It was interesting that it wasn't on any local maps, and the residents that lived closest to it seemed unaware of its existence. Alistair had pulled the information from Peter's mind. Peter had heard talk of moving relics closer to Arariel. They were planning to clear Ophanium in the next few days, so we made sure to arrive first.

A deep roar cut through the trees, causing birds to take flight. My ears tipped forward, and I cut to my left, running toward the sound. I raced up an incline, passing a small ravine as the trees thinned. I slowed as I caught Tobias's scent. He sat on his haunches with his ears forward and his tail twitching. He didn't turn as I stopped next to him.

His red eyes focused on the overgrown dirt road that wound toward the top of the hill. Twigs snapped behind us as Alistair approached.

"One last pass," Alistair said, his telepathic voice clear in my mind. Tobias lowered his head once in a nod.

"Why? It's abandoned. The road hasn't been used in ages. It's an old tomb. Let's just go," I thought at both of them.

"Why can't you just do what you're fucking told?" Tobias's voice echoed between us.

"Because I don't have to listen to you. Last I checked, I was second-in-command."

That pissed him off, and if he could have killed me on the spot, I swear he would have.

"Now, now, ladies, you're both pretty." I could feel Alistair's sarcasm and slight irritation, even through his mental voice. *"One last pass, and then we call Kaden. Those were his orders."* The last part was directed toward me.

"Fine."

Without another word, they turned and headed back into the thick overgrowth. Tobias went left and Alistair right. I heard the soft thud of their paws as they took off, venturing deeper into the forest. I started to follow, but stopped when I felt a tingle run down my spine, as if something large had flown overhead. My ears lay flat as I looked toward the sky, but I saw nothing. I glanced at the ruins and then back to where Alistair and Tobias had disappeared.

If I'd felt a celestial here, we needed to get to whatever they were coming for first. It wasn't like we couldn't take them, but we didn't need a member of The Hand showing up. I didn't want to wait to confront them. It would only give whoever it was more time. Decision made, I headed toward the ruins, trotting along the dirt road and over the hill.

The mountainside was desolate. Ruins of a once established village were all that remained, and nature was reclaiming the land. Several homes had caved in, and green vines draped every square inch. I hopped from the top of one ruined building to another, the bright crescent moon and stars my only light. I looked around but didn't see a temple or monument anywhere—just more of this broken, once vibrant town. Maybe Kaden was wrong? Maybe Alistair had finally made a mistake. But if that was the case, what was that energy I'd felt earlier? I swore it had to be one of them, yet I saw no one and felt nothing.

I jumped down from my high perch. Dust rose around my paws, but my landing was silent. I had taken a few steps back toward the road when the fur along my back stood on end as if someone were right behind me. I whipped around, baring teeth and claws, expecting a fight, but only crumbling buildings greeted me. My tail swished from side to side in agitation. Not seeing anything, I turned to continue on my way, when my hackles rose once more. *What the fuck?* There wasn't anything around me. I scented the air, checking and triple-checking, but there was nothing and no one around me. That was when I stopped. There wasn't anything around me—but what was beneath me?

I walked forward, once more heading for the road. The tingle along my spine eased, my hackles resting. I turned toward an abandoned building on my left, the feeling still fading. I probably would have looked insane to anyone watching me walk in circles around an abandoned city, but I knew I'd felt something.

I almost gave up, but it hit me again on my last pass by the same building. I spun toward the pull of the sensation, and the static along my fur seemed to increase. My eyes locked on the ground, animal instincts telling me my prey was near. I sped up, paws beating silently against the dirt. My head hit solid concrete as I collided with the wall of a crumbling structure. I hissed and sat back on my haunches, shaking my head.

Black smoke curled around my feet, engulfing my entire being. A breeze played over my skin, dispersing the dark mist as I changed back to my natural form. The black jeans and red crisscross tank I wore still looked as clean as when I'd put them on—a perk of Kaden's blood. The magic we used to change only altered our outer appearance. It meant we didn't have to deal with nudity when we changed back. I needed all my clothes, please and thank you. My hair was tied back into twin thick, long braids, making it easier to keep it out of my face during a fight, and a fight was what I was expecting.

My heels crunched against the rocky sand as I stepped inside the ruins of the stone building. It didn't look like anything special, but it was the source of the energy. Dust swirled in the air at my intrusion. The moonlight shone through the missing parts of the house, high-lighting the neglect. A half-broken table sat in the middle of the room. The remains of other pieces of furniture took up more space to the right, waiting for the forest to reclaim them.

The hum pulled at me as I walked further into the house, my skin prickling like static electricity danced across it. I checked what should have been a bedroom and a kitchen area, then returned to the main living room. There was nothing surprising. The space was destroyed and abandoned. What was I missing? I placed my hands on my hips with a sigh, tapping my foot against the floor. Then I froze when I heard the hollow echo, realizing the animal had been right: there was a sublevel.

I crouched, my hands roaming across the stone floor, pressing hard every few steps, looking for a weak spot. I'd practically crawled to the broken table in the middle of the room when a stone finally gave way. A sharp hiss filled the air, and I jumped to my feet as several carved stone bricks slid away. The table split, and the narrow space beneath opened. I peeked in to see a gaping black abyss staring back at me.

"Talk about creepy," I said to the empty room. Well, I had been through worse. This was nothing. I shrugged and jumped into the darkness.

I fell for a few seconds before my feet hit solid ground. I landed in another crouch, my knees taking the impact. Dust tickled my nose, telling me the floor beneath me was the same gritty sand as above. I flicked my hand out and summoned a small ball of fire into my palm. It danced there, the walls around me glowing and shadows licking at my skin. My own personal torch revealed a wall at my back, so forward it was.

There were no paintings or engravings on the walls to hint why these tunnels were here or where they might lead. I crept along, trying to move as quietly as possible. Nothing but darkness lay in front of me, and I was careful to watch for trapdoors or traps. I was considering turning back to find Tobias and Alistair when the hallway opened into what looked like an old and deserted library. Tapestries eaten away by time hung on the walls, the red and gold so worn that it looked as if they would disintegrate with one touch. I squinted as I made out what appeared to be a three-headed lion in the center of one, recognizing it as a mark of the celestials.

Broken candlesticks lay upon the massive, worn table in the center of the room, and an assortment of shelves hung precariously on the walls. Another tattered tapestry bearing the three-headed lion beast hung from the high ceiling. It danced and billowed as if a draft spun through the room, but the air felt still.

Statues, half-formed and decayed, lined the back wall. I moved closer, raising my hand and growing the small flame in my palm, increasing its light. The stone figures stood in different poses, holding what looked like broken swords, spears, and bows. Their faces were chipped, and half of their features were missing, but I knew who they were. They were the old gods.

Fuck. Alistair's sources were right. Peter hadn't been lying. This was one of their temples—and an old one at that.

"An ancient buried library. Good for you, Peter," I whispered to the empty room. No wonder Kaden wanted us here. If that book did exist, where else would you hide it? I felt my stomach roll. Could it actually be real?

I shook my head, turning away as I glanced around the room. "Bookshelves, yes. If I were an ancient book that could open realms, I would probably live there." I was talking to myself to calm my nerves. The sensation of being watched was overpowering. I walked between the decaying bookcases. Some still stood while others were broken in half, nothing but heaps of wood. I ran my finger through a layer of dust before wiping my hands on my pants. Other than the grime, the shelves were mostly empty.

The silence was a heavy weight as I stepped around the corner and spotted what looked like some old, weathered scrolls. The crunch of debris beneath my shoes was the only sound in the room as I drew closer. I reached forward, picking up a scroll. The rough texture was abrasive against my hands, the material made from something not of this world.

As I read through the ancient texts, I noticed that most of these dated back hundreds of years or further. They spoke of mortals and how they interacted, their languages, and the places of the world. I didn't see anything of importance, but I would take them, anyway. Kaden wanted anything that belonged to the celestials. I started gathering what I could, placing them on the heavy wooden table in the center of the room. I figured I would collect as much as I could and carry it out. Alistair and Tobias would be here soon, anyway. They would come looking for me once they figured out I hadn't followed.

The air in the room shifted, and I paused. Maybe they were here already. I spun toward the door, expecting to see them glaring at me, but the carved arched doorway was empty. I shook my head and turned back, searching the room again. There was nothing that should have my instincts screaming at me, but I couldn't shake the feeling of unease. I stayed on alert as I walked back to the shelves, searching for anything else that might interest Kaden. Some of the texts I found were so old and fragile that they crumbled to dust in my hands. The shelves of the last bookcase were bare. It was another dead end, which meant another useless mission.

I extinguished the flame from my hand and closed my eyes, pressing my forehead to the ancient wood of the bookcase with a sigh. I was so over this. So—

Goosebumps slid up my arms as a chill danced along my spine. I opened my eyes, raising my head slowly. Vibrant blue light filled the room, casting eerie shadows in the corners. The darkened silhouette of a man stared back at me, cobalt lines glowing beneath his eyes.

Not a man, was the only thought I had before a silver knife cut through the shelf in front of me, splitting it in half like it wasn't as thick as a tree. The wood sizzled and popped as if the blade were hot. I jumped back to avoid being split in two and landed on my ass. I scurried backward on my hands, moving away from the glowing blue creature.

He approached steadily, the blue tribal design that decorated the exposed skin of his hands, arms, and neck pulsing as he spun his silver blade.

"What are you?" he sneered. "No creature alive should have the power to wield flame."

So, I wasn't insane; he had been watching me the whole time. How? How had I not seen him?

"Oh, you liked that? Want to see something cooler?"

I didn't hesitate. I sat up, throwing my arms forward and releasing twin flames that tunneled toward whatever the fuck he was. His eyes widened for a split second before he ducked to the side. My fire set the shelves ablaze, the flames crawling up the walls, eating everything in their path. The tapestry that hung from the ceiling burned, the crest of the celestials turning to ash and raining down on us.

I jumped to my feet, watching the blue creature rise from the floor. His ivory skin nearly shone in the flicker of the flames. He looked mortal, and yet not. His body glowed with that peculiar light, and his beauty was captivating. Jet-black hair was tied back in a long ponytail that swayed behind him. The sides were cut in a few zigzag patterns, highlighting the silver earrings lining both ears. He was gorgeous, in a *wants-me-dead* kind of way. He stood a foot taller than me, but it wasn't his height that I found intimidating. It was that light and the blade he twirled in his hand. Those made my skin crawl.

We sized one another up, slowly circling, not once breaking eye contact. I copied any move he made, keeping myself a safe distance from him and that silver sword. He was a born fighter, his face holding no rage or anger, his emotions controlled. He assessed me, looking for weapons, not knowing *I* was the weapon.

My gaze caught on the silver rings decorating his right hand. Déjà vu struck me as I remembered the woman who had smiled and waved at Gabby and me in the club. She'd had the same silver rings, and I'd seen those same bands on the hot stranger at the bar. He'd said they were family heirlooms.

"What are you?" I practically hissed, repeating the same question he had asked me.

A smile crept along his lips, making the lights beneath his skin pulse for a second. "I am a Guardian of the Etherworld and the Netherworld. The Hand of Samkiel."

I froze. It was only for a second, but it was long enough for him to notice.

The Hand.

Fuck. I had hoped to never come face-to-face with one. Yet here he stood. *Double fuck.* Two of The Hand had been near me, near my sister, and I had been none the wiser. Their presence meant that this book was probably real, and Kaden was closer to finding it than he knew. So close, in fact, that we had kicked a hornet's nest and were now on The Hand's radar.

"Your eyes." He twisted that blade once more. "I know what you are now. Beasts of legend whose eyes drip as red as the blood they consume. Only one breed of creature could wield that much strength and harness that much dark power: the Ig'Morruthen."

He was standing a few feet away from me, and then I blinked. When my lashes lifted, he was in front of me, his blade crashing down. I threw myself to the floor, rolling beneath his strike. I hopped to my feet, but he was already there. Fuck, he was fast! I swung my fist out, but he sidestepped, swinging that blade at my head. I bent back and twisted away from him, the tip scraping across my side. The wound burned, and I hissed, instinctively covering the cut. Blood pooled in my hands as I looked down at the perfect slash in my top.

"This is one of my favorite shirts!"

He looked at me like I was crazy, and for a split second, he was distracted. I jumped, propelling both of my feet into his chest and sending him crashing into more shelves.

I landed on my back, but quickly placed my hands on either side of my head and flipped to my feet. He was sorely mistaken if he thought a little pain would slow me down. He recovered quickly, jumping from the rubble and launching himself at me. I heard him cut through the air, debris and papers flying in his wake. He barreled straight for me, and I shot my fist out, preparing for a counterattack. I expected it to hit, my fist to sting for a moment as it connected with bone, but all I got was air. Then he was behind me.

What the fuck?

I dove forward, rolling into a ball as I came to a stop. I felt the swing of the blade and knew if I had hesitated even a moment longer, he would have chopped my head off. He advanced on me again, faster this time, driving his blade down at me. I rolled to the side, the sword burying itself in stone rather than my body. Adrenaline coursed through me, and I took my chance. I jumped to my feet and brought my knee up to smash against his face. I felt and heard the crunch as he flipped backward, his blade still stuck in the floor. He straightened and wiped blood from his nose, the same color as the light that shone upon his skin.

"You're a fast creature," he said, shaking the blood from his fingers, "but I am faster."

"Yeah, I'm learning!" I shouted back, the fire from my first attack crackling around us.

"How do you exist?" His words were as swift as the blade he sliced toward me. "You and your species were extinguished when Rashearim fell."

I dodged two more of those powerful swipes. He didn't make contact, but the blade made my skin tingle just being near it. "I could ask you the same thing."

He lunged forward as I jumped over the large table in the center of the room. I landed on the floor and spun. I kicked the table, sending the massive structure flying toward him.

The lights on his flesh seemed to dance as he turned, slicing through the table with ease. The two halves clattered to the floor, a new cloud of dust rising into the air.

"How many more of you have survived all this time?"

If I focused, I could predict his moves. Every time he came at me, it was a fake-out. He wanted to play this game, pulling information from me until he had what he wanted. I wouldn't fall for it, and I needed to remain focused. I had already noted his tell: the tip of his foot would shift just before he moved in the opposite direction.

"You know, I heard stories about The Hand!" I shouted from behind one of the fallen shelves. He may have wanted information, but so did I. "Fabled warriors hand-selected by some douchebag god. All special in their own way, all powerful, and yet only a few survived the Gods War." I laughed loud enough for him to know it was an insult. "Some warriors."

The shelf behind me crumbled as two arms shot out, grabbing me around the waist and yanking me back with enough force to send me sailing across the room.

"You know nothing of us, creature. None of The Hand fell. We are still as many as the day Samkiel chose us. And once he learns of your existence, he will come back."

"Come back?" I pushed up on my arms as his words blasted through my subconscious. Did he mean the god Samkiel? "You're lying. All the old gods are dead."

"Is that what you believe?"

He lunged again at blurring speed, but this time I was prepared. I waited, counting the seconds it usually took for him to disappear and reappear before rolling away. I heard a thud as he drove his blade into the space where I had been. My foot lashed out, catching him in his gut and sending him flying. I wasted no time in hopping to my feet and grabbing the hilt of the silver sword. I yanked, pulling it from the floor in one fluid motion. The blade hummed beneath my hand, a sharp, searing pain eating at my palm. I ignored the sensation and spun it, testing its weight and balance. It held no runes or markings. It was basic, and yet not. The edge was razor-sharp, the blade slightly curved at the tip. I had never seen a metal like this. It looked silver, and yet a sheen danced across its surface as if it were crafted from stars.

Movement had me looking toward the fallen debris. I pointed the weapon at my newest friend. "You know, you're starting to get predictable."

He rose from the pile of broken wood, paper, and stones, wiping the dust off as if it were nothing. He stopped and looked at me with my hand on his weapon. If he was capable of shock, I would say that was the expression that flashed across his dangerous features.

"You know, you won't be able to hold that for long. It will turn you to ash."

"Hmm. Good to know." I shrugged, frowning slightly. "But I think I can hold it long enough to cut your head off."

He didn't charge me, only tilted his head slightly, a small smirk curving his lips. "In the face of absolute death, you make crass, sarcastic assumptions? Cameron would have liked you."

"I don't know who that is." I shrugged, spinning the blade as he had.

He flexed his right hand, and one of his silver rings lit up for a second. Then he held another sword—a near replica of the one I had.

"Oh, come on," I said, which only made him smile.

He advanced, steel on steel ringing out in the ancient library. I wasn't by any means an expert swordsman. I rarely used them, just trained with the basic wooden staff here or there. This? This was not my style, and he knew it. I ducked a swing of his blade and raised back up, driving mine upward. He blocked, and I aimed for his chest, head, anything I could hit, but he was too quick, too fast, too skilled. For every one I missed, he connected. I had cuts along my arms and legs and a fresh one across my cheek. My hand burned where I held the hilt of the sword, so I tossed it to the side. It was no use to me and was only causing me more pain.

His foot caught my midsection, sending me sailing across the room. I pushed to one knee, the other foot flat on the ground, preparing to rise.

"I give you credit. You've lasted longer than I thought you would. Especially unskilled with a weapon like that. It would be impressive if it weren't for what you are."

I wiped the blood that dripped from my cheek. "Are all of you massive dicks?"

He chuckled, the sound making him seem mortal, if not for his weird glowing tattoos. This needed to be over now. I stood and took a step forward, faking a slip as if I was getting too tired to even stand. My knees hit the floor hard, my breathing labored as I leaned forward on my hands.

"I can't fight anymore. I can't fight you. You're too strong."

He walked closer, tossing the blade from one hand to the other. He was all arrogance and ego.

Perfect.

He stopped in front of me, raising the blade, the tip of it touching my chin and forcing me to lift my head. He was ready to end me.

"You put up a good fight. It's been a while since I have had a worthy opponent."

"Please," I begged, looking up through my eyelashes. I forced fresh tears to my eyes and lowered my head. I needed him to get closer. "Just make it quick."

"I am not going to kill you. Samkiel and the Council of Hadramiel will place their final judgment."

The tips of his boots took up my vision. I raised my head slowly, a brief, wicked smile curving my lips. He'd fallen into my trap. Before he realized what was happening, my body dissipated and reformed behind him. He didn't have time to react as my foot connected with the backs of his knees, forcing him down. I grabbed him under his chin, my other hand at the back of his head.

I leaned next to his ear and hissed, "Simple men, even supernatural ones, are always falling for the damsel-in-distress act."

I forced his head forward and twisted quick and hard. The sounds of bones breaking echoed in the empty library.

His body sagged, his head turned at an ungodly angle as he dropped to the ground with a thud. I stepped over him and quickly gathered the books and scrolls that had scattered when I threw the table. I had to hurry. If there was one, there was bound to be another, and neither Alistair, Tobias, nor Kaden had shown up. I grabbed what I could and moved toward the door.

"That was a mistake," he said from behind me.

I stopped as I heard the bones in his neck snap back in place.

"What's it take to kill you?" I snapped, turning and dropping the piles of papers and scrolls.

"More than that." He launched himself at me, swinging his sword. I caught the blade with my free hand. I was done playing games. His eyes widened as he tried to yank it from my grip and failed. Talons grew, replacing my nails as I tightened my hold on the weapon. My skin burned beneath the strange metal, but I was done with our violent dance. "Okay, I'll try harder then."

He yanked on the sword, but I held tight. The blade cut into my hand, but I ignored the pain and squeezed it with everything I had. The blade snapped in half, shards falling to the floor as a thunderous boom rang throughout the room.

I smirked, and it was his turn to stumble back. "Oops. I broke your toy."

"Impossible," he whispered.

I flexed my hand, the cut on my palm healing slowly ... too slowly.

"Not really." My head tilted to the side. "Apply the right pressure, and anything can break. Even you."

It was my turn to take the offensive, and I sailed toward him. Shadows and steel danced between us for what felt like hours, but was actually mere minutes. We ended up where we'd started, circling each other. We were both panting and bleeding, but neither of us was letting our guard down. It didn't matter how much I hurt him; he still fought. He was a true warrior.

"Looking a little worn out there, champ. Stamina giving out?"

He sneered, rotating his new blade. "Don't be so cocky. I've fought creatures far bigger and far worse than you."

"Oh, yeah? Were you bleeding this bad then, too?" I grinned as I pointed toward his right leg. "What about the limp?"

He stopped and had the audacity to smirk. The glow beneath his skin grew brighter as he closed his eyes and took a deep breath. I watched as the bone in his leg popped back into place with a single snap. He opened his eyes, shaking his head at me. "You really don't know who you are dealing with, do—"

His words cut off as a clawed hand burst through the center of him. He screamed and reached for his chest, the blue tattoos on his skin flickering.

"I do," Kaden's voice, deep and animalistic, whispered from behind him.

SEVEN

DIANNA

Red eyes glared balefully as Kaden flung the celestial toward the middle of the room. His body skidded and stopped as Kaden's head whipped toward me.

"You were told to wait," he snapped at me, all fangs and anger.

"I thought it was abandoned."

His eyes bored into mine a moment longer before I heard footsteps behind me. I didn't need to turn around to know Alistair and Tobias had entered. Kaden said nothing else as he slowly returned to his mortal appearance, the spikes bending and withdrawing beneath his skin. He strode over to where the member of The Hand was struggling to pick himself up off the floor, the blue tattoos on his skin continuing to flicker. As Kaden approached, he clutched at his chest, holding his head high in defiance. Tobias, carrying two spiny daggers, kicked him back to the floor. Alistair stood at Kaden's side, a knife held in his hand.

The warrior looked up at Kaden, then at Tobias and Alistair before speaking in a language I had never heard. He spat that colorful blood on the floor near Kaden's foot as he struggled back into a sitting position.

"Ah, the ancient language of Rashearim." Kaden's smile was slow and filled with menace. "I admit it has been a while since I have heard those words." He took the spiny blade that Tobias offered him. He held it in front of the man on the floor. "Do you know what this is?"

The warrior recoiled, fear flashing in his eyes. "The forsaken blade." He breathed the words. "Made from the bones of ancient Ig'Morruthens."

Kaden chuckled and shot Alistair and Tobias a triumphant smile. "Good, good, and you know what it does to you and your kind, yes?"

It was obvious that he did, but the warrior didn't respond, and the reek of fear didn't permeate the room. I would return the compliment he had given me: faced with absolute death, he wasn't afraid.

"Don't worry. I am not going to use it on you. I have a better idea." Kaden held the blade by the hilt and said, "Alistair has this nasty habit of ripping into minds and pulling out any information I need, turning them into a shivering pile of useless goo in the process. Now..." Kaden clapped a hand on Alistair's shoulder. "I am going to have him make you my mindless slave, like several of your brothers before you."

The warrior grimaced at Kaden's words, continuing to hold his chest. He looked at Alistair, who gave him a sadistic grin.

"I'm not afraid of you. Any of you," he sneered.

Kaden flashed a crooked smile and said, "So cocky. So arrogant. Just like him to believe that you are the only powerful force in this realm or the next. Isn't that right, Zekiel?"

The warrior's brows furrowed, and for the first time, I saw a touch of fear in his gaze. "You know my name?"

My heart skipped once more. How much did Kaden know, and how much had he not told me? I felt my temper rise, but I calmed it as Kaden went on.

"The Hand of Rashearim. Samkiel's guard. Or is his name Liam now? Once I get what I need, I'm going to enjoy ripping you to pieces and sending the parts back to your brethren. I hope he sees what is left of you."

Zekiel's eyes widened at Kaden's words. His expression hinted at fear, but that wasn't the emotion I sensed coming off of him. It was something else. Resolve? He was preparing to fight. I knew from the way Kaden tilted his head and smiled that he smelled it, too.

"Speaking of hands..." Kaden flipped his sword and severed

Zekiel's hand. A blood-curdling scream echoed within the burning chamber as Zekiel grabbed the stump. Kaden wiped the blade against his pants before handing it back to Tobias. I was used to how quick and violent Kaden's temper could be, but it never made the scene any less gruesome.

Kaden kicked the severed hand to the side, and Zekiel hissed between clenched teeth, staring daggers at us. "I would hate for you to summon those pesky blades. Now," Kaden looked down at Zekiel, "where were we? Ah, yes. I want The Book of Azrael. Where would it be?"

"I'll tell you nothing!" Zekiel spat at Kaden as he cradled his arm. Blood oozed between his fingers, the same blue shade as the light that flickered beneath his skin.

The corner of Kaden's lips twitched. "That's what they all say."

Alistair's eyes blazed red as Kaden glanced at him. Alistair focused on Zekiel and stepped forward. He raised his hands, dark smoke flowing from his palms and into Zekiel's head. Zekiel's back bowed, and his eyes rolled. He let out another tortured scream as Alistair ripped into his mind. I winced, the sound piercing my ears. After all these years, I should have been used to this, but it was always horrifying. It was a few agonizing seconds that felt like years before Alistair stopped. Zekiel pressed his hand to the floor and panted as he lifted his head. Blood stained his teeth as he smiled, the sweat collecting on his forehead.

"Well?" Kaden said to Alistair, not taking his eyes off of Zekiel.

Alistair seemed stunned as he glanced between Kaden and Zekiel. "Nothing. I hit a barrier. His mind is strong, but not impenetrable. I'll need more time."

Kaden raised his brows and shrugged. "That's fine. We have all the time in the world."

Zekiel chuckled, staring at Kaden as if he could will his death. "No, you don't."

He kept his gaze focused on Kaden. I watched his mouth move as the ancient language poured from his lips. Kaden growled but only managed one step forward before Zekiel slammed his hand upon the ground. Circles of pure silver formed around each of us. I looked down as several glowing symbols appeared in the one encasing me. Alistair and Tobias screamed as a surge of electricity shot through me.

I fell to my knees, the pain blinding. My limbs felt weak and constricted, but I forced my head up. My teeth clenched as I tried to control the agony surging through my body. A blanket of light encased my prison like an opaque fog. I looked to my left, where Tobias had been standing. He was encased in his own silvery circle. His scream was that of a being in mortal pain, and he was shifting from one creature form to the next. Black smoke danced across his body as he scratched and punched, trying to free himself. I didn't need to see Alistair to know he was doing the same; I could hear him.

I gritted my teeth, my back bending as another surge of power ripped through me. What had he done? Sweat drenched me as I tried and failed to stand. Kaden roared, the sound one of pure rage and malice. My head snapped toward the center of the room, and I saw that Zekiel had managed to stand.

His eyes met mine for just a moment, and then he tore past us without a second glance, limping and cradling his arm against his midsection. I willed myself to turn, watching as he cleared the door. Fuck, we were going to lose him! A part of me snapped. He was the closest we had gotten to finding the book and getting some answers. We'd had a member of The Hand. I couldn't let him leave. I wouldn't.

My bones ached, but I pushed against the power holding me in place, the shapeless mass swirling around me bending. My knee wobbled as I slammed my foot to the ground. I strained, sweat dripping from my forehead. My teeth ached at how tightly I had clenched my jaw. I shoved upward, propelling myself into a standing position. I placed my hand on the barrier surrounding me, and hissed as my skin blistered. It was going to hurt, but I needed to get out.

I summoned every bit of resolve I had and closed my eyes, focusing as I blocked out the pain, the screams, and the shouts. My body shook as scales replaced skin, and wings, talons, and a tail formed as I became the beast of legends. I didn't hesitate to think about it, but shot out of the circular entrapment and through the roof. The beast screamed in pain and fury, my body feeling as if it had been scoured by fire and glass.

I BURST THROUGH THE CAVERN CEILING, DUST AND DIRT SPEWING INTO the air around me. My thick wings beat once, twice, and I was airborne. I shook to settle my new skin and remove the memory of the pain. I spotted Zekiel limping toward the entrance of the ruined city and slammed into the ground in front of him. Inky black smoke covered my body as I shifted back into my mortal form.

"No! You shouldn't be able to escape that. Not unless you are one of the—" Zekiel stopped, his eyes wide and fearful. "It can't be. Samkiel must know."

I took a step forward, and he took two back. "I can't let you leave."

"You really have no idea, do you? Your powers, your strengths?"

I stopped and shook my head. He was still bleeding from both his chest and his wrist, the wounds Kaden had inflicted doing their job. The only thing that could truly kill the celestials besides weapons made by the divine was us. We were mortal enemies in every sense of the word, and looking at him now, I could see why. The light that had shone so brightly in the library was now dim and fading. He looked mortal. He looked as if he were dying, but I couldn't let that happen. Not before we got the information we needed from him.

"Look, you're bleeding out, and once I drag you back downstairs, Alistair is going to shred you from the inside out for what you did. There is no escape, no running. Never." The last word slipped out on a whisper, revealing my own fear and reality.

He reached up, grabbed one of his earrings, and snatched it off. It glowed in his hand before turning into a silver knife.

I threw my hands into the air in frustration. "Oh, come on! How many of those things do you have?"

He didn't respond other than to twist the blade and press it directly over his heart. Instinct took over, and I grabbed the dagger before it pierced his chest. I held his hand between mine as he met my gaze, his expression shocked and sad. He knew there was no escaping, and this was his last choice. I couldn't help but feel for him. Gabby had the same look in her eyes when the desert had tried to claim us. It was the look you got when you had given up all hope, abandoned all reason, and accepted your fate.

"He can't get his hands on that book," Zekiel said, his voice barely a whisper. "You don't even know who Azrael was. If he made a book and hid it, then it's not meant for your kind to find."

I tried to pull the knife further away from his chest, but his grip was strong even with one hand. "And killing yourself is going to stop that? You know where it is?"

He shook his head. "No, but my death will have a purpose. It will bring Samkiel back."

My heart thudded loudly in my chest. "You mean *the* Samkiel?" He was real? Fuck. Zekiel didn't answer, so I shook him again. "Isn't he the World Ender?"

Zekiel's knee shot upward, connecting with my gut. I doubled over, and he twisted out of my grip. His fist connected with my cheek hard enough to send me flying. I landed on my ass and whipped my head back toward him.

"Athos, Dhihsin, Kryella, Nismera, Pharthar, Xeohr, Unir, Samkiel, grant me passage from here to the Asteraoth!" Zekiel cried.

Asteraoth? No! That was the heavenly dimension, far beyond time and space. Fuck!

He glanced at me one last time, and I saw tears form in his eyes. He tipped his head back to face the sky and plunged the dagger into his chest.

I was on my feet in a second, but it was too late. My fingertips barely touched the silver hilt before he twisted the blade. His body went stiff as the tattoos on his skin lit up. The light raced to the center of his chest and then exploded in the most vibrant, blinding blue beam, shooting straight into the sky. I raised my hand to shield my eyes and spun away.

I peeked back, expecting to still see the beam, but nothing other than darkness greeted me again. I looked down at my hand and the silver blade I still held, both coated in the blood of the man who was no longer here.

"What did you do?"

My head snapped up to see Kaden staring at me from the ruined building. One of his hands gripped the side of the house, his clothes disheveled from the assault within the silver circle death traps. What I saw in his eyes had me questioning everything and filled me with terror. For the first time in centuries, I saw fear in his eyes.

EIGHT

I t happened almost every night. Every night, my body willed itself to sleep regardless of my rebellion, and every night, the dreams assaulted my conscience. Upon waking, the room would be vibrating from the energy pouring from my body. The carved wooden furniture would bend until breaking, shards littering the already destroyed room. My control over my power was insufficient, and it had been for a while now. Night terrors of past battles, long fought and long over, plagued me. Tonight was different, though. What began as the same blood-filled battlefield became something else.

The battle armor covered me from head to toe. It was sturdy enough to withstand massive blows from the beasts we fought, but it was light enough to allow us to move with ease. The ground beneath my feet shook violently, making the massive beasts in front of me falter. It was only for a moment, but it was a moment too long for them.

I swung the double-edged sword high, slicing the head off of two advancing serpentine Ig'Morruthens. Viridescent blood leaked from their carcasses as they fell to the ground, and steam billowed from the wounds my blade had made. The traitorous gods had called upon our mortal enemies, the Ig'Morruthens, to aid in their rebellion, and it had cost us so many lives.

The flames rolled over the landscape, limiting my field of vision. The fire consumed any material it could find, and my heart bled at the sight of what remained of our ruined world. A loud boom punched my ears, accompanied by the vibration of something landing behind me. I spun, raising my sword in expectation of another enemy.

The Goddess Kryella blocked my strike with her broadsword. "Rest, Samkiel." She lowered her blade, wiping it on her beige armor. Her long auburn twists peeked out beneath the slightly dented helmet she wore. Kryella was one of Rashearim's fiercest goddesses.

I lowered my weapon, the battle raging around us. I saw the silver and blue specks of gods and celestials splattered across her brown skin, and the droplets of gore beneath her eyes were reminiscent of some primal war paint. She was covered in the blood of our own.

"How many?"

Kryella lifted her helmet, allowing parts of her face to show. Her gaze remained fixed on me, the silver of her eyes piercing. She shook her head. "Too many. Get to your father. If he falls, our world does, too."

She said no more as the silver light grew on the exposed parts of her armor, and she shot back into the heart of the battle.

I stumbled forward, catching myself as the realms shook. Gods were dying, their bodies erupting like miniature stars. Rashearim burned as far as the eye could see. Once plentiful mountains and valleys were now a desolate wasteland. The structures of gold, our homes, and our city were now concave, broken, and destroyed.

The sky screamed as the monstrous Ig'Morruthen responsible for the flames that consumed our world flew above. Fire erupted from its throat as it lit more of Rashearim aflame. It was winged death and large enough for target practice.

The silver lines on my skin glowed brighter as I picked up my spear and sent my power into it. The shaft shook as I held it above my head. Another large flap of its wings, and the beast dipped behind a rolling black cloud. I waited poised and precise for it to circle around. It was aiming for any infrastructure it could find in its quest to demolish our people. But unbeknownst to the Ig'Morruthens and the traitorous gods, my father and I had sent as many as we could to the nearest livable planet for refuge.

Another blast of flame erupted, sending embers sparking through the smoke, and I heard the telltale beat of wings. I followed the sound, and when I saw the tip of a wing and tail dance out of the thick, dark cloud, I threw my spear. I held my breath as the bright silver projectile tore through the air and disappeared. A loud, ear-shattering scream echoed as my weapon hit its mark, and the beast fell. Its body landed amongst several of its brethren, smashing a few beneath its bulk.

The uninjured monsters turned scalding red eyes on my men. Fury radiated off of them as they prepared to charge. Twin silver beams landed next to the enormous beast. The traitorous gods didn't hesitate to join in the slaughter of the celestials. Then they spotted me. I summoned a sword into each hand and ran toward them. The ground beneath my feet vibrated, and my surroundings shimmered. Everything blurred, and then I was in a different location.

There were no more burning ruins. The stars and galaxies that had covered my horizon were gone. Instead, I was in a large bronze room. Columns soared to the high circular ceiling as an orchestra filled the space with music. My mind had thrust me further into my past.

Before the Gods War.

My father stood before me, his attire a mix of the heavy, gold-encrusted armor and red-and-gold garbs that flowed around him like sheets. Jewels were entangled in the thick curls of his hair, with gold crests pressed on certain ones, some with emblems of battles, and one I knew by heart, gifted by my mother. A large black-and-silver crown with six points sat atop his head. There was a point for every major war fought and won under his rule, all of them long before my existence. The edges were long diamond shapes with a single silver jewel in the center. He only wore his crown when duty or propriety demanded. This day was a celebration, and one where I'd overindulged.

He turned to me, his dark hair longer than even mine. Silver veins glowed beneath the exposed parts of his deep brown skin. The twin lines that ran along his arms, throat, and face were the same silver as the eyes that bore into mine. He was angry, the weight of his ire a crushing force. The golden staff in his hand stabbed the floor, causing cracks to spread beneath his feet.

"I have spoken to you about this several times, yet you hear nothing. If you were not my child, I would assume you deaf!" he bellowed.

I swayed on my feet. The savaee liquid I'd consumed may have been too much. "Father. You're unnerved."

Another stab of his staff, and the floor vibrated as he moved closer. "Unnerved? I would be less unnerved if you did not parade yourself in such a manner. The realms have slowly been devolving into chaos. I need you more focused than ever. The Ig'Morruthens seek power over any realm they can claim, and if they grow in numbers, even we will not be prepared to stop them. I need you to be focused."

My breath left me in a sigh, knowing far too well what followed. "I am focused." I swayed on my feet before correcting myself. "Did I not cease Namur? I have earned the name World Ender from the realms we have taken back. I deserve a moment of peace, without blood and politics. Are we not supposed to indulge after victorious battles, be amongst our people?"

He sneered, shaking his head. "Our people can indulge. You cannot. You will be king. Do you not comprehend that? You have to show your face, not sway upon your feet or dip your cock in any celestial or goddess that shows you a sliver of attention." He paused, a single hand rubbing his brow. "You have so much potential, my son, yet you squander it."

I turned away and lashed out, throwing the chalice so hard against the nearby column that it became embedded in the stone. "I cannot rule them. They will not allow it. I'm not you, nor will I ever be. The title was supposed to pass to one of them. They know it, and I know it. I am nothing to them— nothing but a half-breed bastard. Aren't those the words they murmur when they think I do not listen? The stares... They insist I prove myself again and again, and still, I am not enough."

For a moment, his eyes closed as if he were in pain, but then he opened them and looked at me. His gaze pierced me as he rubbed one hand across his thick beard. He shook his head at me. "You are more than enough, Samkiel. You know my visions, what I have seen. I have seen far beyond this place and time. You are the best of us, even if you do not see it now."

I scoffed, mostly to myself, as I rubbed my hand across my forehead. "They will never accept me, no matter how many Ig'Morruthens I slay or worlds I end to save others. My blood is not pure like yours or theirs."

"You are perfect the way you are. Do not worry about them. They will have no choice. You are my heir. My son." He walked forward, stopping in front of me before placing his hand on my shoulder. My anger dissipated as he said, "My only."

"You force them, and they will retaliate." I knew they would, just as I

knew they would not accept me. I did not want to rule, but alas, my father, my blood, left me no choice. "Words like that bear the semblance of war, Father."

His shoulders lifted so carelessly, a small smirk forming on his lips as if the mere thought were a fever dream. "I have made enemies for less. Old and powerful enemies. I fear no wars."

My gaze met his for a moment, the effects of the savaee wearing off as my reality bored into my brain. "I will never be a leader like you."

"Excellent. Be greater."

His voice was all but a whisper, drowned out by a loud banging that serenaded my ears. I called out, but my father's face and form twisted like stardust.

My eyes popped open. Energy, bright and vibrant, shot through them, hitting the ceiling and causing a few large chunks of marble to fall around me. The hole above my bed had been there since my first night here, and it grew every time I slept. It was the physical manifestation of the emotions I could no longer contain. I sat up, wiping at the moisture that stained my cheeks. I despised seeing him, despised reliving anything that had to do with him or my past. The battles, the war, the good and the bad—I despised all of it. My hair clung to the sweat-drenched muscles of my shoulders and back. It was much too long now, but I didn't care.

Cups, tables, and chairs were levitating off the marble floor from the energy I'd expelled. Even after all the centuries, it was a power that still got the best of me. I raised my hands, massaging my temples and trying to regain my focus. As the pieces of my household dropped, the dull ache throbbing in my head subsided. The headaches were getting worse. They were a steady beating drum that plagued me more and more frequently. The guilt and regret I felt were becoming overwhelming.

I cradled my face between my hands, loose curls dropping forward like a thick curtain to block the light. The muscles in my body were still tense and aching. I had kept up the same training routine I'd learned before the days of war. It was the only thing that helped. The harder I worked or lifted or ran, the easier it was to chase away the thoughts that threatened to devour me.

On the days it got too bad, and I could not force myself to leave my palace, I stayed inside. That was when the hollow, aching feeling became the worst. It consumed me, a dark mist creeping from every corner of my consciousness, devouring my very will to exist. I did not want to move or eat on those days. It was then I would just lie there, watching the suns rise and fall, unaware of how much time had passed. I'd toss and turn, not having the strength or effort to even rise. Those were the worst days.

How many years had it been since I'd shut myself away? I had lost count.

The battered and worn sheets bunched around my hips as I placed my feet on the floor. Scars ran in zigzag patterns over my thighs and knees. My body was littered with them. The one I hated the most was the deep one on my shin. The memory of that one always brought back the night terrors. If I had only been a little faster... I closed my eyes again, drowning out the cries before I opened them.

I scanned the room, stopping at the long, gold-framed reflective glass on the far wall. Silver lines decorated my feet, legs, stomach, back, and neck, and under my eyes. I immediately regretted seeing my reflection. The thick, dark mass of hair reached to the middle of my back, and an overgrown, unkempt beard obscured most of my face.

The glow of my eyes reflected off the mirror, casting the room in a silver haze that reminded me who I was, where I was, and what a failure I was. They called me a protector. I scoffed and uncurled my fist, throwing a blast of blinding power at my reflection, reducing the glass to mere particles of sand. I stared at the new hole I'd added to this massive, run-down estate. Perfect—my house now resembled the complete disaster of the world I'd built.

I'd cobbled this planet together from the remains of Rashearim that had floated past the veil of the Netherworld before the realms had sealed. Once it had settled, the Council of Hadramiel returned, settling halfway across the world from me. I wanted to be alone, and they did not question their king. I had instituted the proper procedures so that they and the celestials could run things without me. What was the point? The realms were sealed for eternity, and anything that might have been a threat had died with Rashearim.

Light, clear and crisp, peeked from the open expanse above my head as the sun pressed against the horizon. I stood and shuffled to the hollowed-out portion of the room where I kept my clothes. The space was a disaster, with fabrics lining the floor in clusters and hanging off the shelves. It was a mess like the rest of me. I needed to leave, run—anything to make the growing tension in my head decrease.

I put on a pair of cream slacks and headed out of my quarters. I descended the carved steps and reached the main foyer. It opened into a large space with only a small dining area sitting to the right with a table and chair I had crafted. I didn't know why I'd made them. I did not allow or want company, and they just collected dust like every other piece of furniture in the house.

Nature was attempting to reclaim my home. Vines sought refuge, growing through the window on the far wall. I hadn't bothered with clearing them out or moving them. I did not bother with anything anymore.

An electric buzz filled the room, causing me to sigh and close my eyes. My hand immediately went to my forehead as I rubbed my brow, the ever-present throbbing increasing. I knew what that was, and I ignored it every time. I dropped my hand and turned toward the large mantel over the remnants of the hearth I had sculpted. A small, colorless device beeped, the tiny blue light on its side flashing. It was a way to keep in touch with others if they needed me. It was supposed to only be used in an extreme crisis. However, they had yet to follow that order.

Another beep sounded before a shimmering, imperfect silhouette formed in front of me.

"Message request from the Council of Hadramiel," the robotic monotone voice echoed.

I'd never get any peace. "Allow."

"Samkiel."

My fists clenched, pure energy dancing across my knuckles. I hated that name.

The once shapeless silhouette vibrated out of focus before returning as the embodiment of a tall, curvaceous woman. Her long blonde hair was loosely braided and ran down her side. Imogen. She resembled the Goddess Athos who had made her. The only difference was that Imogen was pure celestial and one of The Hand—my Hand.

A gold hood covered most of her hair, and her dress reached the floor, the hem puddling around her. She clasped her hands together as she looked at me—or more accurately, through me. The message could be sent, but they had no visual until I responded and granted permission.

"It has been a long period since the last message was sent, and alas, we received no response then, as well as all the other times. I worry about—" She paused and rephrased. "Our concern for you grows, my liege."

The drum in my head grew louder. I despised that word, too. It was a title thrown on me at birth, like all the others.

"Upon request from Vincent, Zekiel has ventured to Onuna. A situation seems to be developing there. The others seek your counsel and await your word."

Onuna—the world in between where the mortals and lesser creatures thrived. If there was a situation, Zekiel could handle it. They all could. They did not need me. No one did, and they were better off without me. Trained from the minute they were created, they'd served under the gods who'd made them until it was time for me to have my own celestials under me.

Unlike the other gods, I could not create celestials. My mother was a celestial and my blood impure. So instead, I selected the ones I knew were strong, intelligent, and, at the time, my friends. The Hand was everything legends had spoken of because I'd made them that way. They were trained killers, and everything I had learned, I'd taught them. Anything that could be a threat to them had died when our world did. Nothing could touch them.

My attention returned to Imogen as she paused, seeming to choose her next words carefully. She turned her head to the side and back. "I long to see you once more. Please come home."

Home. She meant the city beyond the high cliffs. Our actual home had turned to dust among the stars, and now we lived on the scraps of it. I had no home. None of us did, not truly.

The image in front of me faded, and the shapeless silhouette returned. "Shall I send a response, sir?"

My fists clenched once more, that dull ache in my head ceaseless. "Disregard."

It spoke no more as it returned to the irritating device. The room was once more empty and silent. I needed to get out. I spun, heading through the foyer and into the main hall. Silver flames burst to life as I passed, suffusing the empty beige halls with light. My energy roiled beneath my skin, begging to escape.

I pulled open the oval door and stopped, remaining in the shadows just out of reach of the sunlight. The view was almost overwhelming. Colorful fowl chirped as they flew by in flocks. The evergreens and shrubs swayed in the wind, their shades of green, yellow, and pink almost iridescent. It was a world filled with life—and yet I felt nothing. I felt so disconnected from everything. My throat tightened as my gaze dropped, my toes mere inches from the light outside. I moved to take a step forward and took two back instead.

I would try again tomorrow.

TOMORROW CAME, AND SO DID THE NIGHT TERRORS. THEY WERE WORSE than the last, and I woke when I erupted out of my bed, clutching my chest. I could not stop the increasing waves of pressure. I was on my feet, pacing the room before my body even registered what it was doing. My heart hammered in my chest so hard that I was sure it would fall out. I concentrated on breathing in and breathing out, but it was not helping. I couldn't control the tremors wracking my body, couldn't stop the onslaught of memories shaking me to my core.

"I am ashamed of you. I had such high hopes, and now I am left to clean up your mess. Again."

I covered my ears, squeezing my head as if I could drown out the noise.

"You're a fool if you think we would ever let you lead us."

My knees buckled, and I hit the floor, screams echoing throughout the room.

"What a waste," a female voice laced with venom hissed from above me. The Goddess Nismera. Her silver hair, sharp features, and armor were bloodied by the death of our friends, our family, and our home. She was a traitor in every sense. Her heel dug into my breastplate, keeping me still. The sounds of ripping flesh and metal on metal filled the air. She held the sharp edge of her sword at my throat. I grasped the blade, blood seeping through my fingers, my grip sliding. The metal pierced my throat, and I did not know how long I could stop it from going further. "You will get the fame you so desperately crave, Samkiel. That title you love so much. They will know you now as what you truly are: World Ender."

The wall in front of me exploded as power, hot and bright, seeped out of my eyes and obliterated everything in its path.

TWO SUNS I HAD BEEN RUNNING AND TRAINING. MY BODY ACHED FROM overexertion. I didn't stop until my right leg slipped out from under me, my muscles yielding when I would not. I tumbled over a small incline and through a few bushes. Twigs snapped and bit into my skin as I landed on my back in the foliage near a small ravine. Fowl erupted in bundles from the trees, startled by the noise. The forest grew silent after their squawks of departure. Light poured through the canopy as I lay there for a moment, panting for breath.

The sound of rushing water caught my attention, and I turned my head to see twin waterfalls cascading down the side of a jagged cliff. Different-sized rocks and boulders lined the edges of the small lake at its base.

I sat up on my elbow, staring into the rushing water of the creek. When was the last time I'd bathed? I did not know. When was the last time I ate? I did not know that either. My legs shook as I pushed myself off the rocky ground and stripped, tossing the sweat-drenched slacks off to the side. I stepped into the crisp, clear water and waited for the sting of the cold. It should be cold, it should be freezing, yet I felt nothing. I shook my head and waded toward the lake, not willing to think about what that lack of sensation meant for me.

After rinsing the ghastly odors from my body, I put my slacks back on. Regardless of them not being the cleanest, I had nothing else. I had forgotten a shirt and shoes when I'd run from the house after my most recent night terror, but I didn't want to go home. I did not belong there—but then, I didn't belong anywhere.

Not having anywhere else to go, I stayed close to the lake. Night fell, and a million or more stars lit up the sky, casting a similar reflection across the water. I sat with my knees raised and my arms resting upon them. I had gathered a few woodson berries from a nearby hanging branch. My appetite was limited as of late, but I forced myself to eat, and the nutrient-rich fruit eased the headache some. As the broken moon rose high, the forest creatures began their unique orchestra of howls and yips.

I ate another berry, spitting the toxic seeds out to the side. The remains of Rashearim floated across the sky, creating a ring around the planet. Another casualty of the Gods War, the moon looked like a giant had taken a bite from it. Beyond it, a galaxy spun, swirling together a variety of iridescent colors. Stars whipped past, leaving small dust trails in their wake. I used to find the view alluring—captivating, even—but no longer. After you floated among them, praying for a death you would never receive, you learned to despise them. Several meteors flashed as I lowered my head, eating another berry.

"I keep having the same night terrors. They have increased in frequency this last century. It's as if this overwhelming darkness is hanging over my head, just waiting to suffocate me." I paused, popping a few more berries into my mouth. "If only I had been faster that day. I wish I had been faster that day." I whispered the words into the night. Maybe if they weren't trapped in my head, they would give me some peace.

"I hope you know that I've stopped everything we argued about— the sex, the festivities, the drinking. I have no need or longing for the things that drove a wedge between us, and I know now how irresponsible I was. How much I truly did not care, not when it mattered—and when I tried to be better, it was already too late. They need a leader, and I am not you," I said, knowing I was speaking more to myself and not to my father. He was long gone from any realm I could ever reach, but relief filled me anyway, lifting a weight from my chest.

"You do not need to hide," I called out to the beast hiding nearby. "I hear you. You have nothing to fear from me." I plucked another berry from the branch. Fallen leaves crunched beneath the powerful hooves of the Lorveg Stag as he stepped into the clearing. I watched as his antlers broke through the bushes, six on each side. He was old. His pure white fur was spotted around the front, and he nearly glowed in the moonlight. He was lean, but massive at the same time. This was one of several creatures we'd managed to save. We'd placed them here, and then, like any creature, they'd evolved. The stag had four eyes, and his clear gaze never left mine as he continued to take one step after another. He stopped at the water's edge, and I waited for more to come. They usually stayed in groups.

"Where is your family?"

No response, not that I'd really expected one. He lowered his head to take a long drink, and I turned back to picking at the berries, the purple hue staining my thumb.

"Alone as well?" I looked at him and nodded. "I am assuming that is not by choice, and for that, I apologize." He paused as I spoke, lifting that massive head and staring at me. I picked a berry, chewing and discarding the seeds once more, but that had gotten a response, so I went on. "She keeps trying to reach out. I know she cares for me—they all do—but I told them to only contact me for the utmost of emergencies. But there are none, because they are The Hand, the best of the best. Instead, they send messages inquiring how I am and if I am well." I stopped, blowing out a breath before continuing. "The man she knew—they knew—isn't here anymore. He has been gone for quite some time now. I do not know who I am anymore."

The leaves crunched once more, and I looked up. The stag lowered his head as he stepped a little closer. He stopped near me and stretched his neck, extending his snout, sniffing toward the berries.

"The seeds are deadly for you." I placed the bundle of tangled branches on the ground and picked a single berry off. I put the fruit in the palm of my hand and focused. Silver light ran along my arm, making the markings glow and reflect off the white of his fur. He did not move or try to run. He only stared at my hand. The berry in my palm vibrated for a small second as I concentrated. The seeds disappeared one by one, leaving the translucent purple skin intact.

I held my hand out to him, the lights dying beneath my skin. "Here you go."

He looked from me to my outstretched hand and back before running his snout over my palm and taking the berry. I watched as he lifted his head and chewed, his eyes never leaving mine.

I shrugged. "It's simple. If I focus hard enough, I can erase the molecules that make up the integrity of the seeds." He tilted his head as if he'd understood me, which was insane. "But that is of no interest to you."

I forced a small smile and rested my arms on my knees again. "All this power, and still I could not save him." I snorted. "Them. The world. They were counting on me, yet they are gone, while their king sits in a dense, undiscovered forest, speaking to you as if my problems are of any concern."

He moved closer, nudging my arm with his snout. I collected a few more berries and removed the seeds again before offering them to him. He delicately plucked them from my palm and chewed thoughtfully.

"That's all of them. You should probably go. The darker it gets, the—"

My words were cut off as a whisper blasted through time and space. It was deafening, as if his voice were amplified.

"... Samkiel, grant me passage from here to Asteraoth."

The ancient words, the chant, meant only one thing. It meant death.

I surged to my feet. The sky lit up a bright, vibrant blue as a star that was not a star raced past and toward the Great Beyond.

No.

The remains of Rashearim shook beneath my feet, the ground threatening to split. Power radiated off me in waves, trees bending and breaking in half. The water on the lake's surface rippled, and the stag took off, escaping the force of my rage.

Imogen had said Etherworld, so that was where I went.

I BROKE THROUGH THEIR ATMOSPHERE, A CRESCENDO OF SOUND following my entry. Massive clouds circled me, thunder rolling across the sky in an ominous portent of my arrival. Lightning flashed all around me, as if the planet were defying my power. I ignored it, arrowing toward my destination.

The dark clouds lightened as the Guild came into view. It had been established here eons ago as a base of operations and a safe spot. There were locations like this on each major continent. They were places of education for celestials in training and provided links to our people, old and new. Within their walls, they housed archives of information and ancient weapons.

I dropped to the ground, lights, sirens, and screams overwhelming my senses. Several dozen celestials and mortals stood outside the large palace building. Some held small devices in both hands and were pointing them at me. Others were armed with the ablaze my family had created eons ago. They kept shouting, repeating words I did not know as lights, bright and blinding, shone from behind them.

I raised my hand, shielding my eyes from the glare. I peered from behind my hand at the numerous large metal boxes with circular appendages lining the area. Static filled my ears, entwined with the yells and chatter. It was too much, too loud. I gritted my teeth, the thrumming in my skull reaching the point of agony.

My skin lit up as I reached out and closed my hand into a fist. The lights burst, sparking and raining shards of glass. I raised my hands, drawing power from the boxes, and that damned noise ceased. The shouts and demands erupted with tension, and I raised my hand again, preparing to neutralize that threat as well. Then I heard a voice that was as familiar as my own.

"Liam."

I spun toward him, dropping my arms at once. My oldest and most trusted allies stood before me, their expressions a mixture of shock and sadness.

"Who?" I spoke in our language, my tone demanding and callous, reminding me more of my father than my own.

The strongest of The Hand, Logan lowered his head, his face distressed. "Zekiel."

That one word felt like a blow, and I knew this was not going to be a simple visit to Onuna. Logan was one of the oldest celestials and the only surviving remnant of the celestial guard formed by my father. I had grown up with him, and he was the closest thing to a brother I had. He was just as tall as I, and he had more than enough muscle to not fear anything breathing, so when his voice cracked, I knew it was time to pay attention.

"It's more than that, I am afraid." Vincent stepped around him. Even his normally stoic features seemed drawn.

"What has happened?"

And then there was the word, the one I never wished to hear again.

"War."

NINE
LIAM

The day since my arrival was spent with celestials and humans I didn't know trying to greet me and fawning over my arrival. I sighed as I shut the computer Logan had given me, closing my eyes while my brain tried to process the instructional videos he had pulled up. Languages, time zones, politics, and every major event that had transpired since I'd left Onuna centuries ago. My temples ached, and I rubbed them as I heard footsteps drawing near. Everyone was so eager and invasive, fawning over me in their eagerness to greet me. I braced myself for an onslaught of more people, and was relieved to see just Logan walk in.

"I have some clothes for you. They should fit well enough until we get you something in your size," Logan said. I recognized the language he used as the one native to the area. Over six thousand languages existed on this plane, and I had only learned half in the last twenty-four hours.

I gave an indecipherable grunt of agreement, still rubbing my eyes and forehead.

"I know it's a lot to take in at once, but I'm here to help, like always."

I nodded again.

"How are you? I mean, it's been centuries. I've missed you, brother."

My eyes opened as I dropped my hands. There was that word again. Imogen had said she missed me as well, just in a different language. It was genuine, yet I felt nothing. I hadn't felt anything in years, and I knew what it was, knew what was happening to me. The worst part was that a part of me didn't care.

I nodded again as I stood. The colors on Onuna were a duller version of those found on Rashearim. The golds and reds looked rustic, and the room was a weak attempt to recreate what we'd had back home. Logan said nothing as I walked to the oversized bed where he had draped clothes in shades of black, white, and gray.

I picked out an ensemble and started to change. A suit was what Logan had called it. Parts of it were too tight, the jacket digging into my biceps and the pants into my thighs. Logan was leaner than me by a few pounds—nothing drastic, but enough to make the clothes uncomfortable. I leaned over to tie the shoes, and my hair swung down into my face.

"Do you want to shave or get a haircut, maybe?" he asked, gesturing to his own head before scratching it.

"No."

"I'm just saying, you're about to meet a lot of people, and—"

"I do not care about my appearance, and I am not staying."

I did not mean the words to come out as harsh as they did. The look in his eyes reminded me of the many times my father had raised his voice. "I apologize. I just would like to take care of the threat that stole Zekiel's life and return to the remains of Rashearim. This was not meant to be an extended stay."

Worry knitted his brows for a brief moment before he corrected his expression. His eyes darted from mine as he lowered his head and nodded once. "Understood."

My fingers ran across the clothes Logan had given me. They were ill-fitting and made my skin itch, the material rough, unlike the soft fabrics from Rashearim.

"Sorry, my liege. I didn't know you were coming, or I would have gotten you something that actually fit," Vincent said before giving Logan a pointed look. As if Logan would have known of my return before him.

"Do not call me that," I said, a slight growl in my voice.

Logan chuckled softly from behind me. Vincent led us upstairs into a large chamber. Just inside, a mahogany bookshelf held an assortment of small statues. Paintings hung on the walls, and a desk with items scattered across its surface was off to the right.

"We can always get you something else. You'll need a place to stay—"

"That will not be necessary," I said, turning from the large oval casement. "I will not be staying long."

They glanced at each other, and I could feel their concern and disappointment. I knew I should have felt a tug of guilt. They cared and wanted me to stay, but I felt nothing. I just wanted to return to the fragment of home I had left. The noises and lights were becoming overwhelming. I felt confined, and it didn't help that everything here was noisy. The mortals talked continuously, and I could hear them through each room.

Logan and Vincent said nothing for a long moment, waiting for my next command or order. They did not understand how hard it was just being here around them after what had occurred. I despised it.

"What information have you gathered regarding Zekiel's death?"

I watched their demeanors shift and sadness return to their eyes, but the topic had to be discussed.

Vincent moved first. He hurried to the large desk, picking up a folder and opening it.

"Some of the ruins and temples created from the pieces of Rashearim that fell to Onuna have been hit. Whoever these creatures are, they seem to be searching for some old texts or items. We do not know what they are seeking, but they are determined to find it."

Vincent handed me a stack of photos, the images of half-destroyed places.

"I sent word to Imogen. Has she not been able to reach you?" Logan asked, his gaze questioning.

Is that what she'd meant about the "growing concern"?

I did not raise my gaze to look at him, but responded as Vincent handed me another photo. "She informed me of a growing concern, but I was unaware of the gravity of the situation."

It was kinder than the truth. I knew, and did not care. How terrible had I become?

Vincent flipped a few more images my way. A light knock echoed against the door, and all of us looked up as Neverra, fourth-in-command, entered and bowed.

"Sorry to interrupt, my liege."

Logan made a motion across his throat with one hand. "Babe, he doesn't like that."

Her eyes widened as she straightened. "Sorry." She cleared her throat before walking to Logan and giving him a quick hug. An image danced across my consciousness of when they had first met. It was long before I had formed The Hand, when Rashearim was a more joyful and cheerful place. Long before wars, long before death, long before the fall.

She folded her hands in front of her and said, "I just wanted to let you know that the mortal council has started to arrive."

I nodded once as Vincent checked the gold device on his wrist. Vincent had worked with the mortals, balancing politics and global problems in my absence. He'd been a part of the embassy for years. It "kept them in the loop" was how Logan had worded it. Trust had grown between mortals and celestials through the centuries, allowing them to form working relationships. Mortal liaisons were a predominantly significant benefit. They kept the peace, easing the melding of worlds and cultures. It was an easier transition once the Onunians learned just how small they were in the grand scheme of things.

I'd given Vincent the title because, out of all the members of The Hand, I'd known he wanted it. It gave him power and control, things he'd never experienced under Nismera. Vincent was a great leader. I'd known that since Rashearim. It was one of many reasons I'd selected him—another being that I did not want it. I'd shut myself off from the world, and that was how I intended it to stay.

Vincent cleared his throat, gaining attention once more. "I have set up a meeting of sorts, my l—" He paused. "… Liam. They wish to speak with you and be debriefed on what has been happening the last few months."

"I would like a brief history of that as well. You spoke about sending Zekiel to one of our bibletoceas. Why did he not return?" I asked, looking through the images of more buildings in ruins.

I looked at Logan. "Etherworld is one of the simplest realms to run. There are very few Otherworld creatures that roam here. The beasts they originated from are imprisoned in other realms, sealed by my blood and the blood of my father." I stopped, that gnawing pressure in my head and stomach returning. "So, I ask again, what can kill one of The Hand? Have you all not been training? Slacking while you indulge in the finer aspects of your duties?" I asked, indicating the room around us.

The lights flickered once, then twice as the pressure built in my head. "There should be nothing living that can best any of you, but I still hear the dying chants and see the life light bleed across the sky. Tell me why that is."

I knew it was cruel, but the words emptied from my mouth like poison. I sounded like *him*, and I knew it.

"I have an answer for that," Vincent said as he moved closer, opening the file he'd brought with him. "I have a few leads. There is one in particular, a female and two male companions. We got a few glimpses of her from the various security cameras. We ran them through facial recognition but came up mostly empty. That is, until Ruuman." He handed me another photo.

I studied the tall, slender woman with long, wavy black hair. She was exiting a building and wore some type of reflectors on her face.

"How is this of importance?"

"She showed up for the first time at an excavation site. I had several celestial guards in place, but they were no match for her. The site was destroyed, along with a few of the celestials. It looked as if a bomb had gone off."

I raised a hand and rubbed at my overlong beard as I processed Vincent's words.

"I did some more digging to see if I could pinpoint a name or location, but came up empty. Until this," Vincent said, handing me another photo. It was a clearer image of the same woman. The woman smiled brightly at another female, the same flowing, thick hair framing her heart-shaped face. I could not make out all the details, but I could see that they were carrying translucent bags filled with food items. She did not appear to be a threat. She seemed like a happy and content mortal out for a day of shopping.

"I do not understand," I said, looking between Vincent and Logan, my head throbbing.

Logan glanced at Vincent before saying, "We tracked her to Valoel. I had Logan and Neverra watch them for a few days before deciding to engage. She was spotted out one night at a club."

My brows furrowed. "A club?" My brain ran through the mountains of information I had gained over the last few hours. "The stylized playing card with the clover or the bat, used in various games the mortals like to participate in?"

Neverra silenced what sounded like a small chuckle as Logan cleared his throat. "No, here it is similar to the festivities like Gariishamere. Except with more clothing and fewer orgies." He paused and tipped his head in thought. "Sometimes."

Vincent rubbed his temples. "That last bit of information was unnecessary."

Logan scoffed. "Like you are any help?"

"Regardless," Vincent said, glaring at Logan, "we learned, thanks to Logan, that the woman with her is her sister, Gabriella Martinez."

Vincent handed me another photo. This one held a crystal-clear image of a woman smiling brightly. Her clothes were a dull shade of blue, and she had what looked like cards pinned to her shirt.

"Neverra found out she works in a hospital. She seems like your normal twenty-eight-year-old mortal woman. She graduated college and lives in an upper east side apartment."

"And the other one?"

"Nothing. No one can find a single thing about her. It's as if she doesn't exist."

I looked at Vincent. "How can that be?"

"I didn't know at first, but then we saw this," Vincent said.

He placed another photo in my hands. The same two women sat in what appeared to be an outdoor foyer. The space was bathed in sunlight, and an ocean sparkled in the background. Other mortals sat around them at different tables, some eating and others lost in conversation. But it was the two figures standing near the dark-haired woman that held my attention. My brows furrowed as I squinted and brought the photo closer.

I froze but did not speak as my grip tightened on the image, crinkling the edges. From the woman's posture, they appeared to have been mid-argument, and there was no mistaking the crimson glow of their eyes. My heart skipped for the first time in a millennium.

My chest tightened painfully, and a wave of nausea hit me as I broke out in a cold sweat. The sound of metal clanging against metal rang in my ears. The smell of blood and sweat from battles long since fought assaulted my nose. I heard the roar of the fabled beasts as they destroyed my friends, my family, and my home. The sound pierced my ears like blades, reminding me of the powerful wings beating against the sky. Flames poured down in torrents, the heat so strong that ashes were all that was left of anything. The world shook with their roars as hundreds of gods and celestials were incinerated around us. I whispered the one word I thought had died with Rashearim.

"Ig'Morruthens."

LOGAN, VINCENT, AND NEVERRA STAYED CLOSE TO ME AS WE HEADED to the main floor. I flipped compulsively through the images Vincent had shown me. Ig'Morruthens, alive and on Onuna. How? It shouldn't be possible. Those that had not died on Rashearim were locked behind the realms. Yet three of the beasts stared back at me with three sets of blood-red eyes. Three monsters from the Otherworld were on Onuna.

Voices filled the main foyer. Aids and support staff accompanied their leaders, mortals milling about within the cavernous room, but I barely noticed. I closed the file and handed it back to Vincent.

Fire sizzled down my spine and lit up my nervous system. I stopped so abruptly that Logan nearly ran into me. My head whipped to the side, and I scanned the room, looking for the source of my unease.

"Is everything all right?" Neverra asked, placing a gentle hand on my arm. The touch grounded me as the burning awareness eased. I saw nothing, but felt something. I searched the crowd but only found the faces and heartbeats of mortals.

"Yes," I said as I shifted away from Neverra's touch and closed my eyes. It was the only thing I could say. What else could I tell them? Their worry would only increase if they knew that the images alone had sent me straight back into the war. After one look at the glowing embers of their eyes, I could feel and see everyone dying around me, my hands slick with blood no matter how many times I washed them. "I am fine."

I opened my eyes and held out my hand. "Shall we continue?"

The three of them shared a concerned look before Vincent nodded and took the lead.

The chamber was a large circle with tiered bench seats surrounding an open space at the center. Every mortal leader from each country was here, and it was congested, to say the least.

The mortals greeted me as we descended the stairs, every person either shaking my hand or bowing. By the way Logan apologetically explained that I was new to their languages, I knew my facial features must have given away my internal feelings of disgust. They were looking at me as if I would save them, as if I were the answer to their prayers. I should have felt shame that I cared so little for their plight. The echoes of that thought sent my mind wandering back to a time far from this.

"Samkiel is king now, regardless of my place. Which you would have known had you and your ilk accepted the formal invitation to the royal ceremony," my father, Unir, said. The ancient words inscribed on the staff he held glowed slightly, a clear sign of his irritation. I stood beside him, covered head to toe in plated armor. The only thing visible were my eyes.

The Feildreen bowed. Their small, compact shape and pointed ears reminded me of green-skinned children, but they were much more mischievous. "My apologies, my king." His eyes darted to me before he straightened. "We sent a distress beacon a few days ago. Ig'Morruthens advanced, and we lost several—"

"I will evacuate you, your family, and as many as I can from this planet," Unir said, cutting him off. "You have a day to prepare."

A day was all he'd given them, and that time had passed. We stood at the edge of a cliff, overlooking a desolate wasteland. A camp of Ig'Morruthens occupied the once thriving valley. The sun still shone, but it was nearing the horizon. As soon as it set, the beasts would wake and continue to destroy this planet. They would conquer and twist it, claiming it for their armies.

I sighed, folding my arms as far as I could across my armor. "You must teach me that one day," I said, nodding toward the streak of clear light disappearing in the distance. My father had removed every Feildreen from this planet. He'd sent them out of the star system and to safety on a new world where they could live without having to worry about monsters slaughtering them.

My father glanced at me, his helmet resting at his feet as he sliced a round yellow fruit with his dagger. "I would hope you would never have to use it. I wish for no more wars, no more evacuations, no more suffering."

He peeled a thick piece from the fruit and offered it to me. I removed my helmet, tucking it beneath my arm before accepting it and taking a bite.

"Samkiel, do you remember what I taught you? About the Ig'Morruthens and who they follow since the Primordials fell."

I swallowed before speaking, watching him as he continued to cut the fruit. "Yes, the four Kings of Yejedin: Ittshare, Haldnunen, Gewyrnon, and Aphaeleon. The Primordials created them to rule this realm and the next."

He nodded once. "Yes, Haldnunen died by your grandfather's hand during the First War, although he made sure to take him with him. Aphaeleon fell at the battle of Namur, which leaves the remaining two."

"And now they seek revenge."

My father nodded as he ate the last few pieces of the fruit and tossed the toxic core to the ground. He picked up his helmet and placed it on his head. Wisps of curls escaped from the braids that stuck out of the bottom, the few gold-encrusted clamps shining in the waning sunlight. "Revenge, yes, but a part of me fears something much worse. If there is a breeding pair, we may end up outnumbered long before any war begins."

"Breeding? You always spoke of them being made, similar to the celestials, not born."

"Unlike most of the gods, they breed." He folded his arms, not looking at me as he went on, but I felt the shift in the conversation. "Speaking of breeding—"

"No."

"Samkiel, you are king now. You will need to choose a queen soon." He paused. "Or another king, whichever you desire."

I let out a deep groan. I hated speaking about this. "What I desire is not to be attached and leashed to someone for eternity. I choose neither."

"You can't live off the spoils of flesh forever."

"Oh, yes, I can."

The slowly retreating sunlight gave me a chance to change the subject. Praise the gods. "How many do you think are down there?" I asked, pointing with the tip of my blade.

"A few hundred." He made no motion to move, his voice quiet as he said, "If you focus, you can feel them. They are made from the same floating chaos as all things. Which means a part of us is a part of them. Everything is connected." He turned to look at me. "Go ahead. Try it."

I closed my eyes, drowning out the rustling of leaves from the southern winds and the movements of small creatures scurrying across the ground. I felt myself center and became aware of ... something. It was sharp and tingly and made my entire being quake. I felt dozens ... no, hundreds of beings. I took a step back, opening my eyes and turning to my father. He was in the same spot, his gaze focused on the field below.

"You felt it?"

"Yes, hundreds. Is that why you said not to call for the others? You knew."

He nodded. "With your power and strength, you should not require an army for hundreds."

He was right. I had taken back several worlds from the Ig'Morruthens over the years. A few hundred would not be a problem.

As if he could read my thoughts, he said, "Do not get above yourself. The Ig'Morruthens are an arrogant species, but they are not ignorant. They are smart and calculated, which makes them more than a normal threat. Even with what they lost, they will not bend willingly."

I heard the rumble before I felt the planet shake beneath our feet. The sun had made its descent, and night was making its presence known, as were the creatures below. I turned to watch the cavern and the barren land around their camp.

Flames slowly lit, one by one, as the Ig'Morruthens began to stir. They resembled thick-horned beasts, some walking upon two legs and others multiple. Weapons were draped across their backs, but my focus was on the beast chained in the cave. The massive creature was meant to burrow into the ground and erupt on command, demolishing cities. They used it to terraform planets, and I had witnessed its effectiveness several times. It was hard to kill, but not impossible.

I pushed my helmet back onto my head and summoned another ablaze weapon. "They either bend, or they break."

A small laugh escaped him as he placed a hand on my shoulder and shook his head. "You have gained your crown and been king no more than days, and yet you already speak as one."

His hand dropped, the humor draining from him as he eyed the field and the creatures swarming it. The feared King of the Gods replaced my father. I might bear that title now, but no matter what, he would always be revered and respected as such in my eyes.

"What shall you have me do, Father?"

"Simple. Use the title you have earned," Unir said. "End worlds, my son."

"And what do we do while these beasts destroy our cities and homes?"

I sat up straighter as the world rushed back. I shook my head, trying to banish another memory from my past. Logan's gaze fixated on me, worry etched on his brow. I waved him off, and after holding my gaze a moment longer, he returned his attention to the room.

Several voices spoke at once, exclaiming their support of the question and demanding an answer. It seemed that while I had been lost in the past, the reverence the mortals had felt for me had morphed into frustration and anger.

"We have kept our eyes on the creatures of the Otherworld. A civil war seems to have started among whoever they are. A Vampire Prince has been murdered. There have been multiple disappearances, not to mention the destruction of property."

An Ecanus ambassador was the next to speak. "We have reports of attacks and missing people throughout our world. Something is stirring between the Otherworld creatures. I have entire towns afraid to venture out at night for fear of being taken by red-eyed monsters."

Vincent waved to the room and said calmly, "Yes, and I have sent celestials to those areas. They have neither seen nor found anything close."

A woman stood, slamming her hands down on the table. The suit she wore was similar to that of her colleagues. "You mean like the destruction in Ophanium that you blamed on another quake?"

"If the God King were here sooner, maybe this wouldn't have gone so far," another mortal ambassador quipped, staring at Vincent before looking at me. That ache formed once more in my head as a muscle in my jaw ticked.

Logan cleared his throat before I had a chance to speak. "Your world lives because of what Liam sacrificed. Do not forget that. We are here, and we are doing everything in our power to help you and the mortals."

"It's not enough. Something is coming, and even if we don't have your powers, we can still feel it. How many things can we blame on natural disasters?"

The mortals spoke all at once again, arguing and agreeing with each other. I pressed my fingers against my brow, the pain in my head growing with each beat of my heart. It was worse now than before, an overwhelming pressure starting at the top of my neck and radiating through my skull. A thousand voices echoed through my mind, demanding answers and help from me.

"Silence!" I commanded, sweeping my gaze over them. Logan and Vincent sprang to their feet, preparing for a danger that was not there, and I realized I'd spoken louder than I intended. I lifted my hand to run it through my hair and saw that my skin was lit with silver.

I stood, my chair creaking as I relieved it of my weight. Aware that my eyes were glowing, I closed them and took a shaky breath, pulling the energy back. When I opened my eyes, my skin had returned to what they would consider normal. Their gazes were alert, filled with wariness as they waited to see what I would do next.

What was happening on Onuna was nothing compared to the horrors I had witnessed over the centuries, yet they needed reassurance as a child would. The mortals reeked of fear, and fear was a powerful motivator.

"You're frightened. I understand that. You're mortal. We are not. The monsters and beasts of legends died eons ago. The seals that hold the barriers to the realms are intact. Your world is safe, and will remain so as long as I breathe."

It was a half-truth, given the pictures I had seen, but I hoped it would reassure them. I'd locked myself away, thinking the threats had died with everything else. I'd made no effort to know this world or these people. Truth be told, I did not care much about their petty concerns, even if I understood them. I had not been here, and I had no right to claim to be their protector.

Vincent stood, raising a single hand as if to calm a growing, thrashing sea. "Yes. There is nothing here we cannot handle."

The female ambassador from Ipiuquin spoke up, her voice rising above the others. "I mean no disrespect to Your Majesty, but we are worried. Our ancestors passed down the stories of the fall of Rashearim. You cannot blame us for being unnerved. Is this the beginning of what our ancestors feared? Have you and the celestials brought the war here to Onuna?"

I met her unwavering gaze, her eyes filled with anger and accusation. Her attitude and the fact that she had even asked set my blood to boiling. "It is not. The ones who started the Gods War are long turned to ash."

She shook her head and gestured to the room. "You will have a civil war on your hands if the population of Onuna thinks those beasts of legend have returned. We will not lose our world as you lost yours."

Voices rose in unison as all those gathered added their agreement. The words stung, hitting a part of me I hated. I should lash out, correct them, but the words froze in my throat. I understood they wanted to keep their people safe. It was the very thing we had fought and died for on Rashearim. They were afraid of another cosmic event.

"One of your own died, yet you promise to keep us safe? Tell me, God King, why should we trust anything you say?" another mortal demanded.

Vincent's features tightened, and Logan lowered his gaze at the mention of Zekiel's demise. Yet again, the mortals raised their voices, speaking over each other in their attempts to be heard.

I searched my mind, needing the right words, but the languages and images I had absorbed in the last few hours were still being processed. I raised my hand once more, the crowd falling silent after a few moments.

"I understand, I do, and—"

"Boring."

A male voice cut me off, and all heads turned toward a young man lounging on one of the benches. He wore the same colors and style of clothing as his colleagues, but I could not place which region he represented. The only thing that set him apart was the nonchalant expression on his face. His legs were outstretched in front of him, and he held a cup in his hand. He shook it before slurping loudly from the small plastic tube attached to it.

"Excuse me?" Vincent asked, arching a brow. "Do you realize who you are speaking to?"

"Yeah." He took another drink and shrugged. "And like I said ... boring. When do we get to the part where you all slaughter millions?" He paused, taking another sip before pointing with a single finger. "Or, oh, I know: how exactly you became king? Or what about how the destruction of your planet destroyed ours? You all act as if you're a gift to Onuna, when in reality, you are a curse on this world."

Vincent looked at the people sitting around the bold man. The lead ambassador, whose face had turned a bright shade of red, said, "I apologize on behalf of Henry's behavior. He is still new and learning. His radical views—"

The ambassador's words stopped as Henry stood. People moved out of his way as he shoved past, still sipping from that cup.

"So, this is where you all meet to discuss world events? Hmm, I expected more," he said, shaking his head as he started down the stairs. "It does look like a fortress from the outside, but it is easily accessed. I honestly thought it would be harder to get in, but..." He trailed off with a small laugh and a shrug.

Henry shoved the cup into the hands of a woman he passed. He placed a single hand in his pocket before taking the steps, one at a time, slowly and deliberately. The prickling feeling at the back of my neck returned. Something was wrong with this mortal. Was he infected? Ill?

"So, you are him?"

Step.

"The feared king. What a title. Your hands must be soaked in blood."

Another step.

"The legend himself. The fastest, the strongest among his people, the most beautiful son of Unir." He paused, his eyes roaming over me from head to toe and back once more. "I don't see it. With the misshapen hair and overgrown beard, you reek of this unkempt vibe. You're taller than I thought you'd be, and I see the lean muscle fighting machine you have going for you, but I guess I expected more from the one they call World Ender."

"Who are you?" The voice that left me was not my own. It resonated deeper, and an emotion long buried filled my tone. That name—I hated that name.

Another step.

"Oh, silly me, I forgot I was still wearing this." He pulled at the suit, lowering his gaze before his eyes swept up to me. Black, smoky mist formed at the base of Henry's feet and crawled up his body. The shoes he wore slowly turned to midnight-black heels. The darkness climbed up the legs of the man, replacing them with slender feminine ones. It continued to twine and swirl around his form, revealing the ruse before disappearing.

Impossible.

Several people gasped as the mortals scurried toward the exits. I had not realized I had moved until Vincent and Logan appeared at my sides. Henry was gone, and in his place was the woman from the photos. They had not done her justice. The grainy images had not captured the extraordinariness of her.

She was captivating. What I had seen as dark hair was as black as the abyss itself. Her heart-shaped face seemed more angular here, and her dark brows arched over her eyes, framing their dangerous glow. Her lips were full and painted a shade darker than blood. She reminded me of the fanged riztoure beasts from home, striking and beautiful, but deadly. Very deadly. Her outfit was more revealing than the suits the others wore. She had on loose yellow fighting pants with the same color top, if that's what you would call it. The edges looked sharp, and it dipped too low in the front. A long matching jacket billowed on the waves of darkness she had summoned.

She placed her hands on her hips, staring past me. She nodded at Logan and said, "Hello, handsome. We meet again. I met your lovely wife a few minutes ago. Neverra, right?"

Logan moved forward, but my arm shot out, stopping him.

"What have you done with her?"

"Nothing she didn't deserve."

Another step.

"If you touched a single hair on her—"

I raised my arm, cutting Logan off. I needed to know more about this mystery woman, and if he jumped into a fight fueled by emotions, I might lose our newest lead.

"Good boy, keep your bitches in line." She gave us both a wicked smile. "So, Samkiel, this is your Hand? Not very intimidating, if you ask me. All you have to do is cut one of their hands off, and they're powerless."

I felt Vincent shift next to me, but he didn't step forward.

"*You* are the one who killed Zekiel?" My voice was as hard as granite.

"They say you're a god. Hard to kill and damn near invincible. Weapons have to be forged to snuff out that precious light." She took another step before stopping, her head tipping ever so slightly as she gauged my people and me. "Does that make you fireproof?"

A slow mischievous smile curved her lips as she turned both hands palms-up. Twin flames erupted from them, her eyes shining a fiery red. I reached out to stop her, but was a fraction of a second too late, and the room erupted into flames.

TEN

LIAM

Flames danced and spread in every direction as a loud beeping noise screamed in every room. Black clouds of smoke rolled along the ceiling. My ears rang as I looked around at the wreckage. The room was completely demolished. Large support beams had fallen from the ceiling, and sparks popped from broken wires. Many of the mortals had been crushed beneath the debris, and the smell of blood was overwhelming. I lifted the large piece of concrete off my body, easing the pressure on my abdomen and legs.

A cough to my right had me turning to see Logan pushing a large metal object off of Vincent. Logan helped Vincent up, both of them covered in a thin layer of dirt. They scanned the wreckage, looking for me. Logan's eyes were desperate when our gazes locked.

"Neverra," he said, the depth of worry in his tone nearly painful.

I waved him away. "Go."

He said nothing else as he pivoted and dashed from the room. Vincent stumbled toward me.

"Are you all right?"

"Fine. I need you to clear the building. Get as many to safety as you can."

He coughed. "What about you?"

I ripped the burned jacket off before rolling up my sleeves. My hand flexed, and one of the silver rings vibrated on my finger. I called forth the ablaze weapon, the silver broadsword sharper than any man-made steel.

"I'm going to find that woman."

SMOKE HUNG HEAVY IN THE AIR, CASTING A HAZY GLOW. SEVERAL people ran past me, coughing as they darted toward the exit. The building shook once more, telling me she was still here and on the warpath. I pushed a stranger out of the way as large chunks of stone fell. "Get to the exit."

Her eyes, large and glazed, stared at me.

"Go!" I commanded.

She didn't wait, mumbling her thanks as she sprinted down the hall. Another explosion shook the cavern, and I stumbled slightly. My mind reeled as memories of Rashearim tried to overcome me. But this was different. It wasn't war. There weren't thousands of them. There was only one—only her. It would be different.

The siren's loud, persistent beep slowly died. The once well-lit area was now a smoky, dark hall, the lights flickering as they struggled to stay on. Water fell from tiny metal devices in the ceiling, soaking the hallway and attempting to drown the blaze she'd left behind. I heard murmurs and shouts mixed with the sloshing of wet footsteps as more people hurried out. I closed my eyes and rolled my shoulders, slowing my breathing as I tried to pinpoint her location. My father's words replayed in my mind.

"If you focus, you can feel them. They are made from the same floating chaos as all things."

The screams of the mortals, scared and in pain, faded away. I cast my senses out like a net, and heard the clicking of heels. A shiver ran through my entire being, causing the pit of my stomach to roll. I hated the way they felt. It reminded me of the horrors of war and ruin. I shook off the memories as awareness of her filled me. My eyes flew open, and I snapped my head back to look at the ceiling.

Found you.

The silver glow of my eyes shone brightly in the dark, waterlogged space. I focused my gaze on the ceiling and crouched. With a powerful push of my legs, I shot upward at blinding speed. I smashed through several layers of stone and marble before coming to a stop several stories up. A hallway stretched before me, and large charred archways stood to my left and right. The staircase was broken, the steps leading into thin air. This woman was the definition of destruction.

My steps were light as I moved down the hall. I felt her before I heard her, my senses pulling me left. I crept closer, peering from behind the half-singed wall, and saw her tossing things out of the room. What was she doing? I tightened my grip on the ablaze sword as I stalked forward, my shoes making a small squeak with every step. There was no point in hiding. There was no other way out of that room.

Something heavy hit the wall, making the pictures shake. A thunderous roar washed over me as another piece of furniture flew through the open doorway and burst into a thousand pieces. I moved quickly, afraid she would leave the room and continue her reign of destruction. That was something I could not allow.

I stopped at the entrance, shards of wood and glass crunching beneath my feet. The door lay off to the side, ripped from its hinges and discarded. "You seem to be in distress."

Her head snapped toward me. She gripped the large table in the middle of the room, a deep scowl of frustration twisting her features. Books and other sacred items filled the enormous shelves lining the walls. Vincent had said that they were storing most of the relics they had collected from our other guilds. I placed one foot past the threshold, then the other. She straightened and squared her shoulders, but did not move to escape. I gave her credit. Most beings who knew of me ran the second they saw me with a blade.

The flashing lights behind me lit the room, but it was not on fire or covered in water. That meant whatever she was hunting, she thought it was in here.

"Looking for something?" I asked, pointing my blade toward the piles of discarded books, scrolls, and papers.

Her eyes never left mine, nor did she make a move.

Interesting.

Her gaze narrowed. "Damn, you are durable. I really thought dropping three stories on you would buy me a little more time."

I took another step forward, and she finally stepped back. "Time for what? What are you looking for?"

Her eyes flashed red as she shifted a bit, unhappy that she had given ground. "Loving the new outfit and hair. So, fire burns you but doesn't hurt you. Good to know."

That comment caught me off guard. My hair was singed, but that wasn't what caused me to pause. She was testing me as I was her.

The Ig'Morruthens are an arrogant species, but they are not ignorant. They are smart and calculated, which makes them more than a normal threat.

I wanted to continue this small game and find out exactly what she knew of me. Maybe she would give me a hint of who the two men in the photos were.

"It is true. Fire, while a nuisance, cannot kill me. Nothing can."

A small quirk of her lips was the only indicator that my words had any effect on her. She stepped away from the table. It was a small move, but I saw her place one foot behind the other. It was not much to the untrained eye, but I knew she was preparing for an attack.

"I've heard that. They say you can't be killed, but I don't think that's true. Everything has a weakness, even you. I mean, if that were the case, then where are the rest of the gods?"

Her smile returned—the one that made me clench my teeth. She was all poison and acid with her words, throwing them as weapons. It was a way to distract your enemy, and a smart tactic. If your opponent allowed their emotions to override their senses, it gave you a huge advantage.

I would be a liar if I said it did not sting. That topic was an open bleeding wound for me, one that refused to heal. The only problem was that it only fueled my anger and resolve. What she assumed would weaken me only made me stronger.

Her smile lingered, her arrogance showing its face as she raised a single painted nail and tapped her cheek before pointing it at me. "You see, I think you *can* be killed. I just think I need to try a little harder."

My grip tightened on the hilt of the blade. "Many thought the same. Many are dead."

Her smile remained in place as she charged at me. She was quicker than I expected, a dark dagger flashing toward me. I tilted my body to the side as she drove the blade toward my throat. She paused, her eyes going wide with frustrated anger as she realized I stood there no longer. Her irises pulsed with a crimson glow as she struck at me again. I raised my blade, the dagger connecting with my sword. I held her there, studying the knife.

"A forsaken blade," I hissed. "How do you have that?"

The blade had been made by the Primordials and handed down to the four kings eons ago. They were weapons made of bone and blood, made to destroy gods. Her smile turned lethal as she tried to force it closer to me, but to no avail. Was she really going to try to fight me? Kill me? After everything she knew? Here, of all places, when Vincent or Logan could come at any second?

"I cannot tell if it is ignorance or stupidity that has driven your decisions today."

She hopped backward, flipping the blade to her other hand and whipping it toward me. I sighed and blocked it. She threw a kick, but I knocked her foot away, sending her off balance for a mere second. She corrected herself, flipping her hair from her face as she held the blade in front of her.

"Oh, don't pretend to want to understand me. You and I are nothing alike," she snapped, launching at me once more. She did not stop, no matter how many times I blocked her or sent her flying off her feet. She was fierce, using any object around her to her advantage. I lost count of how many tables and chairs I had cut in half after she used them as both weapons and shields.

We went blade to blade again and again, but she gave no quarter. She was quick, and I realized I recognized her style of fighting. "You fight like one of The Hand."

She used a backflip to correct herself from her fallen position and raised the blade to attack once more. "You like that? I'm a quick learner, and Zekiel was so kind as to show me a few things before he turned to ash."

"I am not impressed. You're slow, ineffective. A dull comparison to what they are." The energy in the room charged, the papers and scattered debris hovering just off the floor. I felt my eyes change and knew silver burned in them. "And besides, I taught them everything they know."

She smirked and shrugged, but did not show an ounce of fear. "Didn't do Zekiel much good. Are you used to always failing?"

I moved without realizing it. Emotion drowned out logic, which was ignorant on my part and a win on hers.

My blade swiped at where she had stood—only she was not there anymore. I had only a moment to realize she'd baited me before I felt her blade ram itself into my back. If it was meant to be painful, I did not feel it.

Her painted nails grasped my upper arm as she stood on her tiptoes to whisper in my ear. "You know, I thought you didn't even exist. It wasn't until Zekiel exploded into ash and light that I knew he was right. His death would bring you back." I felt her twist the dagger in a tight jerk as she spoke. "Do you burst into light when you die, too?" She yanked back, ripping the blade free.

I turned my head and saw her eyes widen in confusion. Anger flashed across her face, and she actually growled.

"I cannot die," I said as the skin on my back healed.

Her throat bobbed once, and her grip on the blade tightened. "That's impossible."

"So is the power you possess." I turned fully, and she took a step back. She realized what she'd done and stopped short. "I hope you know you will not be leaving this building."

Her face scrunched. "We'll see about that." She charged again, her arrogance and anger outweighing the sane part of her brain. I needed to immobilize her, and she'd given me the perfect opportunity to damage her without killing her. She was the closest we'd gotten to any lead, and she was not leaving. I would not allow it.

I swiped my blade upward as she passed me. She took one step, then another, before stopping. I turned and flicked the blood from my blade as her arm fell to the floor with a thud. She hissed and grabbed where it had once been.

"That was a hundred-dollar jacket, you asshole!" she spat, looking at her ruined clothes, unconcerned with the missing limb.

"Excuse me?"

Her lip curled upward as she took the ruined jacket off and threw it to the side. Her crimson eyes seemed to glow a shade brighter as her lips formed a thin line. Veins protruded upon her neck from the strain, and a small crack echoed through the room. I watched in shock as her arm grew back, tissue and muscle forming from the stump of her missing limb.

"Regeneration," I whispered in disbelief, but my eyes did not lie. "No living creature should have that power."

She snarled again as she flexed her hand. "Funny, that's exactly what your boy said. Actually, it was—"

Her words died in her throat as a sharp whistle rang out. She glanced at me, and my stomach rolled. She was a distraction, and she was not alone.

"Sorry, lover, playtime is over."

The gleam of her teeth as she smiled was the last thing I saw before black smoke encompassed her. Her shape grew, and massive black wings emerged from the cloud. They were no fragile appendages, but thick and powerful, with tips as sharp and lethal as any blade. She slammed them against the floor, bracing them against the stone for support. I took a step back as a long, spiked tail whipped out, shattering the nearby table and sending paper and priceless artifacts in every direction. A large, taloned foot stepped out of the darkness, and then the smoke completely cleared, revealing the beast from my night terrors.

My heart stilled. I could not deny or question it. The pictures were true—Imogen's message, the reports, the urgency, everything Logan and Vincent had suspected. The Ig'Morruthens were alive, and they were in the Etherworld. They were on Onuna.

She looked at me, and if monsters could smile, I swear she did. She winked one massive glowing eye and went airborne. The ceiling exploded under her massive strength, rubble raining down from the hole she made. Her black wings beat once, the downdraft sending debris spinning around the ruined room as she rose toward the sky and away.

No. I would not lose. Not again.

I took a deep breath and tapped the power my father had passed down to me. I had locked it away, the feel of it too painful and reminding me too much of him. The books, broken tables and chairs, and discarded glass rose, every object near me levitating. I lifted my hand and grappled, trying to get a hold of the invisible force that allowed me to connect with any living or inanimate object. I hissed in victory, my teeth bared in a feral smile as my fingers found purchase. Then, using every bit of my will and raw strength, I braced my feet and pulled hard.

Her scream nearly shattered the sky as she stopped mid-flight. Her head whipped back, the look of shock on her reptilian features nearly comical as I forced her descent. I stepped to the side, continuing to pull at her massive form. She beat her wings and clawed at the air as I pulled her back, forcing her through several layers of the building.

I let up, everything near me dropping to the floor. The beast's outraged shrieks drowned out the crash as it all fell. I paused for a second, taking a breath as my headache reformed tenfold. A wave of dizziness washed over me before I steadied myself. I'd expended too much power way too fast, and I had not been training or eating properly. I took a shuddering breath and jumped into the massive hole, passing through several floors. Rubble made up of concrete, stone, and wires surrounded me as I landed, the impact reverberating through every nerve and exploding in my head.

She lay crumpled on the floor. Her body shuddered before returning to her mortal form. Her clothes were still present, but dirty. So, it was not a full transformation like with other beasts of legend. Interesting. I lowered into a half squat, preparing to pick her up. Her red eyes snapped open, and she glared at me. Smoke curled out of her nose as her lips pulled back, and a soft orange glow formed behind her teeth. She was going to spit fire at me.

I clamped my palm over her mouth, my fingers wrapping around her jaw, holding it closed. Her eyes bulged, and she grabbed my wrist, talons digging into my skin. Silver light ran down my arm, and I sent a blast of energy into her. Her body jolted, and her eyes rolled back before she went limp.

I leaned forward, studying her. The glossy, dark strands of her hair covered half of her face. In sleep, she looked normal and not the destructive creature that had showed up only an hour prior. But that power I'd witnessed, the strength she had, was not normal—not at all. There were only four Ig'Morruthens I knew of that could assume the form she'd taken. That made her an important factor in what had been happening in my absence. I slid my hands beneath her and stood, hoisting her into my arms. I cradled her against my chest and walked down the destroyed hall. Several celestials stood around the main entrance, forming a small circle. Some were covered in debris, and others had parts of their clothes burned off, while a few looked to have just arrived. Vincent saw me first and pushed through the group, Logan at his side.

"You got her," Vincent said, flicking his wrist and returning his blade to his ring.

I nodded. "Neverra?"

Logan swallowed. "She is a little dizzy, but fine. She got knocked out when *she*," he pointed to the woman in my arms, "first showed up."

"What about the mortals? Celestials? A lot of casualties?"

They both looked at me and shook their heads.

"I assumed."

Several of those metal boxes with wheels were parked nearby, lights flashing and sirens screaming. Celestials formed a line as they helped who they could and ran back into the building for any survivors.

"What are we going to do with her?" Logan asked, nodding at the sleeping creature in my arms.

"Get answers."

ELEVEN

LIAM

"She has been unconscious for at least a day. Maybe she is dead and hasn't disintegrated yet?"

Vincent sighed from where he was leaning against the large bathroom sink. "Don't the old ones disintegrate? It's been so long since we have seen any Ig'Morruthens that I've forgotten."

I said nothing as I wiped the remaining eraser sheddings off the notebook Logan had given me. I moved my hand to the side, continuing to sketch.

"Keep your head still," Logan said as he turned my head to the side once more. I narrowed my eyes at him. "Hey, I'm trying to salvage what I can, since half of it got burned off," he said, holding his hands up in surrender. I did not say anything else as he continued to fix what he could. He ran the loud mechanical clippers over the back of my neck, leaving it bare.

"She is not dead. She will regenerate any damage she may have suffered." I knew she was alive because I could still feel her power if I concentrated. It made me sick to my stomach, even from several floors above her, but I did not tell the others that. There was no need, and we had more pressing matters at hand.

"Regeneration. I can't believe it. And you said she could control darkness? The shapeshifting makes sense. I didn't even recognize that she looked like any other mortal until it was too late," Neverra said. She sat on the edge of the sink, close to Logan. He stopped clipping my hair for a second and eyed Neverra. She had healed from her snapped neck, but Logan had not let her out of his sight. It wasn't surprising. They had been inseparable since Rashearim.

"Yes," I said as Logan's grip on my chin forced my head in another direction, and he returned to what was starting to feel like a form of torture. "Her powers are peculiar, to say the least. The only legends I remember are those of the Four Kings of Yejedin. They were created by the Primordials and could take the form of beast or man. But they have long since been deceased. The only way they could still exist is if a breeding pair survived and escaped the fall. It is a mystery, and I want answers, so we will interrogate her and document the information for future use."

"I forgot you used to scribe for the bestiary." Vincent's voice cut through the thickening silence. I looked up, pain filling my head as a memory flashed across my subconscious. I closed my eyes, my fingers tightening on the edges of the pages. It was only for a moment, and when I opened them, I was no longer on Onuna. I had been transported to a time when my mother was still alive, and I was far too young to worry about battles or fanged beasts of legend.

I sat cross-legged on the stone floor as my mama hummed to herself, contentedly pruning the flowers. The garden made her happy, and I think that's why Father continued to add to her collection. I would glance up now and then to make sure she had not wandered too far, and when she did, I followed. The many rows and variety of plants she had here created a small labyrinth.

Several celestials greeted us as we moved further into the garden. Guards stood at the entrances and bowed whenever we passed. I did not think I would ever tire of that. After a brisk walk, she stopped and started picking once more. I sat on the edge of a nearby fountain and swung my legs back and forth.

"Mama, why do I need to know this again?"

I dropped the small stylus, the onyx ink covering the side of my hand. I lifted it, rubbing it against my garb, which earned me an eye roll from my mother.

She rose from her kneeling position and plucked a few more flowers, placing them inside the thick woven basket she held. "Because, Samkiel, I want you to have skills other than just fighting."

"Yes, but I like fighting. This," I held up the paper and showed her, "I am no good at."

Her smile grew as she stepped closer, the gold-and-white trim of her dress dragging across the ground. She never wore a crown like Father, only a thin gold band that held her hair back from her face. I had asked for one similar to hers or Father's, but they always told me it was not time yet.

"It only takes practice, little one."

I huffed, crossing my legs under me and continuing with my learning. I knew there was no use in arguing. We would sit and stay here as long as she wanted. I did not mind. It was not as if I had any friends on Rashearim. I was the only child born in recent memory, and the only child with a god and a celestial as parents. Everyone else had been created, made from the light that now ran through my blood. My mother said I'd been conceived in love, which made the other gods envious.

"Can I ask you a question, Mama?" I did not look up, continuing to sketch.

"I fear you would ask, anyway." She laughed. "But, yes, go ahead."

"Do you not go to battle anymore because of me? I heard Father talking the other day."

"Samkiel, what did I say about eavesdropping?"

"I was merely walking past and heard him." I glanced up as she eyed me, one eyebrow raised. "He said you were sick because of me, and that is why you do not fight anymore."

The wind picked up as she strode over, making the colorful shrubbery around us dance. She stopped and knelt next to me, curving her long dress around her knees. She reached out and rubbed her hand over my head once before lifting my chin to look me in the eyes.

"I fear sometimes your father speaks too much, but I will not lie to you. I do not feel like I used to, but in no way is that your fault. Your father cares and is just worried is all. Besides, I would give up fighting and battles to spend a thousand days with you."

She kissed my nose, and I smiled. "Now, tell me, what have you drawn today?"

I lifted the paper and turned it toward her. "Monsters. This one Father showed me the other day when he returned."

She took in the massive creature I'd drawn. I had mimicked the shades and patterns as best I could. Her brows rose once more, but she smiled before saying, "Ah—another conversation I will need to have with your father."

I turned it back toward me and squinted at my drawing. It was not the response I had hoped for. "Do you not like it, Mama?"

Her hand went under her chin as she eyed me. "Why do you call it a monster, little one?"

I opened my mouth, then stopped. Could she not see it? "Because that is what it is?" I turned it back to her and pointed at the shapes I had crafted. "See the teeth and claws?"

"I see it." She reached inside the woven basket, pulling out a single flower. It was yellow with black dots lining the petals. "And what do you think of this?"

I shrugged. "It is a flower."

"Yes, but do you think it's pretty?"

"Yes."

"Do you know that a single petal can be toxic? It can even make a god sick if enough of it is consumed. So, even this could be a monster. It does not need teeth, claws, or any other scary feature to be deadly."

I watched as she slowly spun the flower by the stem, the sun dancing off the colorful petals. It was pretty, but it looked harmless.

"So, it can hurt someone? Kill?"

She nodded before placing it back into her basket. "In the right hands, yes, but give it a good home, a little care, and it can heal, too." She wiped her hands on her dress and stood in one graceful motion, smiling down at me. "So, you see, looks can be deceiving."

The sound of approaching footsteps had us both turning. Guards flanked my father, the clang of their armor as they walked a discordant note in the peace of the garden.

"Adelphia, what are you teaching my son in a garden made for you?"

My mother's smile turned luminescent at the sound of my father's booming voice. "Your son? I presume I also had a hand in this?"

The guards stopped short as my father reached my mother and swept her up in his arms to spin her around.

"You reek of the battlefield-and sweat," my mother playfully complained. She laughed as he ignored her, placing kisses on her lips, cheeks, and forehead before setting her on her feet and turning toward me.

"There's my little warrior." He picked me up, slinging me onto his hip and pressing a kiss to my cheek. A small giggle escaped me before I wiped it off with the back of my hand.

"And what is this?" He set me down and picked up my drawing. "Samkiel, I am impressed! You draw beasts as a scribe would."

"Yes," my mother said as she reached into her basket, taking the same flower out once more. "We were talking about monsters and how looks can be deceiving."

"Ah, yes, but a monster is still a monster, no matter how pretty it is."

The look they exchanged made it seem as if they were having a conversation I could not hear. It lasted only a second before the smile returned to my father's face, and my mother's lips curved.

She reached out and gently placed her hand on my cheek. "Come, now. Let's go home. It's time for dinner." She turned, and Father fell into step beside her as I hurried to keep up.

LOGAN TURNED OFF THE CLIPPERS, SNAPPING ME BACK TO REALITY. He stepped back, allowing me to see my reflection. It took me a second to clear my thoughts. Memories of her always hurt, and I was glad they were few and far between.

"What do you think? I mean, it looks better than the charred remains that were there before."

"It's not terrible."

I caught Vincent's grimace in the mirror and watched as Logan turned to glare at him.

For once, my appearance did not bring me immense revulsion. I did not resemble either of my parents now. The mass of waves that resembled my mother's chestnut hair were gone, as was the thick beard that so often reminded me of my father. It was new, a change I dreadfully needed.

I touched my cheek, rubbing my hand over the soft stubble that shadowed my jaw. I ran my fingers through the hair atop my head. The contrast to my old self was alarming, but necessary. My neck and head felt lighter, and the cut was more in style with the mortals of this world.

"I know it's different and probably not as perfect as a professional job, but..." Logan reached out, brushing away the small pieces of hair that had fallen on my shirt.

"No, you look fantastic, Liam. I'd never pictured you with short hair, but it looks great," Neverra said. "We definitely would have had way more problems on Rashearim if you had done his hair back then, babe."

Neverra's comment made Logan laugh. Soon, Vincent joined in, and they were all making jokes about our past. Memories of days long past danced through my mind, before a title, before a crown, before the fall. I wanted that again, to go back to how we used to be. They had not changed much, but I had. I watched them and knew some part of me was long gone. It had been so long since I'd felt a twinge of humor or joy. I wanted to laugh and remember how much beauty life could hold. I just wanted to feel.

"It will do." My words were harsh and loud. Everyone fell silent again as I stood, nearly toppling my chair. The bathroom felt too small, and I just wanted to leave. I grabbed the cloth Logan had used as a drape and ripped it off. "We have an interrogation to perform. I need all the information we have on her and those she came with."

They nodded, and the energy in the room shifted again. It was familiar, but not comforting. It was how the room had felt every time my father entered.

"Are you positive there were others?" Logan asked, placing the clippers down and folding his arms.

"Yes. I heard it, and so did she. It was a whistle that was a summons. I should have paid more attention. Maybe I would have felt them sooner."

"It's not your fault," Neverra said. "We all—"

"Yes, it is. Everything is. It is my reign. Any death is on my hands, and any form of destruction is a sign of failure. I should be better prepared. I am not, but that is not your concern. What I need from you, I have already asked."

Neverra nodded once. Logan and Vincent both lowered their gazes, and all three stood up straight, their humor from earlier gone.

"Yes, my liege," they said in unison before filing out of the bathroom.

I grabbed the notepad and handed it to Neverra as she passed. "Add this to the bestiary. I added the details of the attack, what form she took, and the abilities I observed. I need it updated, and once we find out about her colleagues, I will have that, too."

Neverra's gaze dropped to the sketch. "She is pretty for a fire-wielding death bitch that tried to kill us all."

"Remember, Ig'Morruthens are smart, calculated, and above all, monsters. A monster is still a monster, no matter what pretty shell it wears."

She nodded and left. Those words rang in my head. Had I become my father so completely? I gazed at my reflection in the large bathroom mirror. I stared as the image of my father, armor and all, flickered before me. No matter the shell I wore, I would still be Samkiel.

I was the reason he was dead and Rashearim had fallen.

I was the World Ender.

TWELVE

DIANNA

My eyes fluttered open, and I squinted at walls so white that they were almost blinding. I was in a room. Wait—a room? I quickly sat up and immediately regretted it. My head throbbed, and every muscle in my body ached. I groaned. Being hit by a convoy going full speed would have hurt less. I gripped my head, trying to ease the agony there.

The memory of silver eyes flashed through my mind. Samkiel had grabbed me and pulled me back, but how? I hadn't even had time to process what was happening before hitting the ground. Then he was standing over me, the water from the sprinklers raining down on his massive frame, plastering the ill-fitting clothes to his body. I remembered calling forth the flames to get him away from me. My throat had tingled before he'd slammed his hand over my mouth. I'd watched his eyes glow a shade brighter before silver light traveled down his arm, igniting those strange tattoos. Then I tasted his power and knew I was dead.

I turned around, looking at the room. If I was in Iassulyn, it was a shitty version. It looked like an insane asylum. My pants suit and matching crop top were gone. In their place, I was wearing a loose-fitting tank and black sweats. After a steadying breath, I pushed to my feet, my knees shaking. Gods, what had he done to me?

I rolled the waistband of the pants so they would stay on my hips as I glanced around. The *cell* was a ten-by-ten white box with one wall made of bars. I walked to a corner and slid my fingers against the walls. They were smooth, cool to the touch, and hard as stone. There was no furniture, no toilet, nothing. So, this wasn't a prison. It was a holding cell, which meant they weren't planning to keep me here long. My anger rose. If they thought they could imprison me, they were sadly mistaken.

I inhaled a deep breath before I expelled a thunderous roar of lethal fire. The cell went up in bright orange and yellow flames, singeing everything they touched. I let it burn for several minutes.

When I allowed the fire to die out, I expected to see a smoldering open expanse. Instead, bright blue beams glowed where the bars had been. Molten metal pooled on the floor, but otherwise, the structure of the cell was intact. It was another reminder that I was not dealing with anything mortal. I cursed and kicked the wall. The only thing I had done was turn the white of my cell an ashy, dingy color. I narrowed my eyes and placed my hands on my hips, glaring at the opening where the beams glowed merrily, mocking me.

Fine. I'd just have to try a little harder.

IT HAD BEEN TWO DAYS—TWO DAYS OF LIGHTING THIS PLACE UP, AND nothing. I had tried changing shapes and slipping through the beams, but I'd been electrocuted, my body thrown against the back wall.

I sat cross-legged, my cheek resting on my fist. I stared at the beams for a long time before I got up. Maybe if I endured the pain long enough, I could get out. I had gone through worse. How bad could it be? I stopped in front of them, the electric buzz filling my ears as I got closer. I reached out, my hand hovering mere inches away.

"Athos, Dhihsin, Kryella, Nismera, Xeohr, Unir, Samkiel, grant me passage from here to the Asteraoth." I saw what looked like tears form in his eyes as he tilted his head back and plunged the dagger into his chest.

I jerked my hand back as that night played through my memories again. Everyone thought I had killed him, and I let them. It had earned me immunity from Kaden and his horde. They saw me as a threat, and now so did Samkiel and his people. Little did they know those memories haunted me.

The look on Zekiel's face as he plunged that knife into his chest was one I was all too familiar with. I had seen it on Gabby's face and my own as I fought to save her life. It was the look you got when you'd lost all hope. I would never forget the sound of the blade entering his body. The single tear that fell from his eye before the blue light burst from him and he exploded into the sky would haunt me forever.

"I would advise that you don't touch those."

His voice preceded the three forms that shimmered and solidified in front of me. Flames burst in my hands, and I didn't hesitate to throw a fireball straight at his head.

Samkiel sidestepped and lifted his hand, stopping the ball of roiling flame. It rotated for a second beneath his palm, those damned gray eyes boring into mine as he extinguished it with a single clench of his fist.

I couldn't hide my shock. My voice was barely a whisper as I took a step back. "How did you do that?"

Samkiel... No, *Liam*. Kaden said they called him Liam now. He looked at me as he lowered his hand to his side, keeping the other in his pocket. "I am more prepared now that I am aware of your powers." His accent was thick, another sign he was not from here.

I swallowed, taking in his appearance. He looked so different. Who had made him hot? Why was he hot now? His shorter hair looked more modern than I thought it could. It was cut close to his head and styled with gel that made it stick out in different directions. His beard was barely a whisper of what it used to be, more a five o'clock shadow that curved around his annoyingly perfect jawline.

It didn't matter, the perfect sculpture they'd tried to make. He was still the World Ender. He was still the hated and feared god who would gladly end me and those I cared about. They could dress him up all they wanted, but I could still see the truth of him. He may not have had fangs, but I sensed the predator beneath those sad gray eyes.

"And if you are referring to how we appeared before you as you were preparing to throw another tantrum…" He paused, looking toward the man I had seen at the bar. "What is the word for that, Logan?"

"The mortals call it teleporting, sir, or portaling," Logan said, his hands gripping the front of the tactical gear that all but Liam wore. Liam wore a casual white shirt with the sleeves rolled up, and black slacks. Just as with the suit, they seemed too tight. I could see his muscles tense with every move he made. He had a strong yet lean build, made for speed, power, and killing.

I could see why they called him the most beautiful son of Unir, and how he could have brought even goddesses to their knees. He was every bit as magnificent as the books had described. He knew he was powerful, and it showed in the way he held himself. The gray hue of his eyes sparked with intelligence, and the bronzed color of his skin glowed with health. But beneath his new and improved mask, self-loathing lay heavy on him. He had it wrapped around himself like a cloak. I'd seen it at the meeting in how he responded and talked. He'd zoned out a couple of times, as if he weren't even on this plane anymore. Maybe taking him down would be easier than I'd thought.

"Ah, yes, teleporting," he said. "Think of it as a refraction of light or a displacement. Molecules are broken down to their purest form and reformed in another space, so to speak."

"That's so cool." I kept my eyes trained on him, ignoring the others. After tasting his power, I had no desire to experience it again. If I even felt it stir, I was prepared to fight. "I don't care."

The man on his left scoffed, shaking his head. "Do you know who you speak to?" His voice was a snarl.

A slow, mischievous smile spread across my face, but I never turned away from Liam. The shadows danced lazily around me. "Of course I do. The Son of Unir, Guardian of the Realms, Leader of The Hand of Rashearim." My smile grew dark. "World Ender."

Liam's gaze did not waver from mine. "You know me, and yet you still attacked the embassy. Why fight?"

I shrugged. "Call it a personality flaw."

He shook his head as if he couldn't believe it. "That's an arrogant notion. You know what I can do, and that death would be imminent. Yet you risked it regardless."

My lip curled up in a half smile, my canines slowly descending. "Arrogant? I heard that's your thing, not mine." I stepped closer, the shadows beneath me bending. "But I am curious, World Ender. What do you fear?"

My shape changed as my voice deepened, going dark, thick, and rich. "Most men fear the forests at night and the creatures that hunt." My form changed to a massive canine beast as I paced, snapping my jaws at them. Shadows danced once more as I changed. "Or is it beasts of legend that drive the hairs erect on your body?" I took up the entire space as I shifted into my favorite shape, the black-winged wyvern. "Or..." This time, I took the form of a man. I stopped in front of him, the same height, same look, same posture. "... is it what you see in the mirror?"

He held my stare for only a moment before his eyes darted away, and I knew I'd hit my mark. My smile was cruel, but it didn't last long. The celestial on his left stepped forward. Earrings lined his ears as they had Zekiel's, and I had no doubt that each of them would produce a weapon. His eyes were the same blue as the ball of light that shot from his hand, sending me sailing across the room.

"Vincent." Liam held his hand up. "It is fine."

Okay, so that was Vincent. I stood, straightening my ugly sweats as I laughed. His power may have a kick to it, but it didn't burn like Liam's. Although his build was leaner, Vincent was nearly as tall as Liam. His straight hair was as black as mine, and he had it tied back, half up, half down. I glimpsed a tattoo along his collarbone, the bold, dark tribal lines a beautiful contrast to his lightly tanned skin. It reminded me of the one I had seen on Logan at the bar. I wondered if they all had one.

Vincent folded his arms and narrowed his dark eyes at me. The corner of his lips twitched, making me want to smash my fist against his perfect angular jaw. His stance screamed retribution if I dared to insult his precious leader once more.

The sound of a door opening and approaching footsteps had us all turning. I recognized the woman as the same one I'd seen at the club. I had knocked her unconscious when I snuck into their meeting. She stopped beside Liam, the celestials that had followed her in fanning out behind her. They wore the same tactical gear as everyone else and stared at me with narrowed eyes that glowed the same iridescent blue. Oh, they were angry.

The woman met my gaze with a look that promised death before turning her back on me to address Liam. Guess we weren't going to be best friends. "We are ready, sir."

Ready? Ready for what?

"Thank you, Neverra," Liam said.

I didn't have time to voice my questions before the floor of my cell lit up. A circle formed around me, and I recognized the pattern as the same one Zekiel had used in Ophanium. The symbols around the circumference glowed, forcing me to the ground. I fell to my hands and knees with a hiss. The power beneath me made my skin burn, and I gritted my teeth. It wasn't as all-encompassing as in Ophanium. No, he meant to immobilize me, not distract me with pain. I raised my head as the cell bars disappeared, and Liam, Logan, and Vincent entered.

"If you wanted me on my hands and knees, you should have just asked," I sneered through gritted teeth at Liam. Sweat formed on my forehead as I pushed, trying to stand. I managed to lift my hands the tiniest bit before the circle pulsed indigo, and the invisible bonds on me tightened. I grunted as my palms slammed against the floor again.

Logan paused, surprise and caution flaring in his eyes. Good. They were scared. They should be, because if I—

"Ow!" I snapped as a cool metal cuff was slapped onto my wrist. I turned my head, seeing Vincent place another on my ankle. Before I could try to make a move to kick him in the face, Logan had my other wrist shackled. As soon as the last cuff snapped close around my ankle, it felt as if the air were being sucked from my lungs. I fell to the floor with a hiss, trying to catch my breath.

"You will be weak while the Chains of Abareath are upon you," Liam said. "A safety precaution for your interrogation."

The circle beneath me disappeared, and Liam stared down at me, his arms behind his back. He nodded toward Logan and Vincent. A low grunt escaped me as they grabbed me under my arms and hoisted me up. Any fight I had in me was gone. I felt weak and sick. They dragged me out of my cell, my feet dragging on the floor. For the first time in centuries, I couldn't feel my fire—and that terrified me.

Neverra waved the celestials forward, and they led the way. I heard footsteps behind me as we turned down the large hallway. We passed several cells identical to mine before pushing through the double doors. As they dragged me through the corridors and up a small set of stairs, I tried to get my bearings. The inside of this building wasn't as regal as the one in Arariel, and I wondered if we were still in the city. Wooden benches and chairs took up a lot of the hallway, but I hadn't seen any other people.

The sound of voices grew louder the closer we got to a large, dark wooden door. The celestials in front stopped, opening it wide enough for us to enter. Neverra went in first, and then they dragged me inside. I saw what looked like a large brown four-poster chair. The heavy wood was engraved with alien symbols, and the seat looked like it had seen better days. When Logan and Vincent hoisted me onto the seat, the cuffs around my wrists and ankles locked into place, securing them against the arms and legs of the chair.

I tilted my head back, shaking the hair out of my face as I scanned the room. A woman in a pencil skirt and matching blouse sat at the end of a long metal table. She had a laptop in front of her, and several notebooks were piled beside her. She didn't even look at me, her attention on Liam. I craned my neck, seeing several blue-eyed celestials glaring at me, and I recognized a few mortals from Arariel. Rows of seats formed a circle around the chair, so all could see the prisoner at the center. Hmm, so this was how they did interrogations.

"I thought I had killed you." My voice came out weak as I looked at the mortal man wearing a sling. He had bruises and a few burn marks, but I remembered him as one of the ambassadors.

He glared past his swollen eyes, but took a step back.

"Do not fear the Ig'Morruthen. She is completely disabled," Liam said, standing in the center of the room. Logan, Neverra, and Vincent flanked him, stoic and ready to defend him. Not that he needed defending. I pulled at my bonds, testing them, but I was held tight.

I laughed—actually laughed. It started as a small chuckle before growing to a full-body experience, and it took me a moment to regain control of myself. I watched everyone look at me and then each other and couldn't stop another fit of giggles.

Liam cocked his head to the side and raised an eyebrow. "There is something in this situation that you find humorous?"

"Yes." I tried to sit up a little more. "You. Them." I nodded toward the crowd. "This. Seriously, what are you going to do? Torture me? I thought you were the special chosen one who believed in peace and all things good in the world. Or, wait—are you going to hit me? Slap me around a little? If you do it hard enough, I might like it." The smirk dropped from my face as I leaned forward with all the strength I could muster. A few people in the crowd gasped, but Liam didn't move a single muscle. "Don't you get it? Don't you see, there is nothing you can do to me that has not already been done? You can't break me, World Ender."

He regarded me, an expression I couldn't define flashing across his face. It was somber and stirred something inside of me I didn't understand. It was so fleeting that I would have missed it if I hadn't been looking right at him.

"We will start with a series of questions. The chair upon which you sit is imbued with…" He paused and looked at Logan. He spoke in what I assumed was their native language. Logan responded, and Liam nodded before saying, "… a certain power. It will emit a sound, signaling to me that you are not being truthful. The runes will alight, and the more you resist, the more you will burn. If you do not answer, you will burn. You try to escape—"

I rolled my eyes, already annoyed. "I get it. I will burn."

"Very well. Let us begin."

Liam walked to the long metal table. The woman opened her laptop, looked at me, and then continued to steal glances at Liam. I watched as he shuffled through some pages before turning to me.

"The power I felt when you first arrived was not just yours. Especially given the signal that sounded before you attempted to retreat. How many of you are there?"

"Ninety-nine."

A shrill beep sounded, symbols lighting up on the chair and floor as energy, white and hot, blasted through me. I grunted, my body jerking with agony as every nerve in my body caught fire. The woman who had started typing looked shocked and glanced up at Liam.

"Can you give me an accurate assessment?"

I shrugged my shoulders, catching my breath. "Um … four hundred."

Agony ripped through me, rocking my body back against the chair. I hissed through gritted teeth until it stopped. I leaned my head forward and blew out a breath, my heart beating wildly in my chest. "Damn. You weren't kidding."

Liam looked at Logan, who translated my words once more.

"No, I am afraid I was not…" He paused, struggling with the foreign words. "… 'kidding,' as you say. Now, let us try again. Was the attack on the embassy in Arariel premeditated?"

"What's an embassy?"

Another shock, and my fists clenched around the chair's arms.

"They say you are a god, but not wholly—part god, part celestial. I heard you're a weak coward of a man who hid away for centuries," I snapped. I was beyond angry. Two could play this torture game, and I knew exactly what buttons to push.

"The information you have is not new. Everyone is aware."

"So, they weren't wrong?" I asked, shock skittering through me.

Everything Kaden had told us was a lie, and on top of that, Zekiel had been right. An actual deity lived—and I had brought him back. I thought I had spoken to myself, but when he leaned forward, I knew he'd heard me.

"Who wasn't wrong?" he asked, trying to appear calm.

I cleared my throat and shifted away from him, ignoring his question. "So, why do they call you Liam if your name is Samkiel? Embarrassing family name, huh? Other kids make fun of you?"

His nostrils flared as if I'd touched on a sensitive topic. "This is not my interrogation. It is yours. While you were indisposed, I did find out your name. It is Dianna Martinez, correct?" he asked, turning back to the papers on the table and flipping through them, his face stoic.

My lip curled as I shrugged my shoulders nonchalantly. "So, you've heard of me? Good for you. You've found out my name. I've lived a long time. I have many."

He nodded and leaned back, raising one hand to rest upon his chin, a single finger curving over his lips. "Lived a long time? And how long would you say?"

Dammit, I was trying to remain cocky and giving him too much information. I needed to focus on getting out of these damned chains, out of this building, and far, far away. I moved out of reflex, and the sting in my arms caused me to hiss.

"Are you done?" Liam asked, watching as I tried to recover from the pain.

"Not even close," I bluffed. Those shocks hurt too damn much for me not to respect them.

He gauged my expression and leaned back, turning the contents of the folder toward me. He licked his thumb and flipped through the pages. I didn't have time to read any of it and completely lost interest, until he held up the pictures. Rage twisted my gut as I blinked at the images of Gabby, Tobias, Alistair, and me. My breath hitched as I recognized where these had been taken. It was during my lunch date with Gabby. *Fuck*. That was what Tobias and Alistair had sensed. One of them had been close to us, and I hadn't known. My heart raced in my chest.

"As you can see, you and your comrades have been on our radar for a while now." He settled those piercing eyes on me once more. "So, tell me, who do you work for?"

My eyes met his, and I hissed. "I'll tell you nothing." Any information would damn me, but more importantly, it would damn Gabby. He already knew what she looked like and her name. I would rather have burned a thousand times over in this chair than allow anything to happen to her.

His lips thinned into a hard line. "I had assumed you would not, but I did hope for a different outcome. A more pleasant one."

What was he talking about?

The thought had barely formed in my mind when my entire being was consumed with pain. My head snapped back, and my body lifted off the chair as much as the magic would allow. The sudden burst of electricity was much stronger this time. It felt like I was burning from the inside out. I let out a blood-curdling scream, unable to hold it in, the sound shaking the room. And then it stopped as quickly as it had begun. My head fell forward, my hair blocking my vision as I panted in the sudden silence.

The crowd gasped as I flung part of my sweat-drenched hair from my face, tendrils clinging to my cheeks. I knew my eyes were bleeding red as my anger rose. It was a small, smoldering flame that I could feel even with these damned chains on, and I took comfort in it. I gasped out through ragged breaths, "Is that your idea of torture? This is just a Saturday night for me, baby. You're going to have to do better than that."

He shook his head, his face unreadable. "I do not want to torture you, but I have questions that need answers. Many of my people are hurt because of you, dead because of you and your kind. I need to find out why."

"Oh, please, I did you a favor. Half the mortals didn't even like you or your people. That entire meeting was one big circle jerk over who is and isn't in power. And now?" I looked around the room. "They think you're some great hero who can save them."

"Is that what you consider a favor? Senseless killing?"

I laughed in his face. "Oh, you'd know all about that, wouldn't you? Senseless killing? How many have you buried, huh? How many have you slaughtered, thinking we are nothing but monsters? If we don't look like you, if we don't eat what you eat, behave how you behave, then we are nothing and beneath you, right? I'm so fucking sorry. Allow me to pretend to care. Your kind has hunted and prosecuted mine for eons."

"How curious. You think to understand me? You are nothing but a creature built and designed for killing. Do not presume to know anything about me," he said, not missing a beat. "You are right, though. You are beneath me. Lower than a measly worm that the fowl pick up for breakfast." Every word dripped with hate, and I knew he meant it. I could see it in his face and in the expressions of those around him.

I hissed, leaning forward, the cuffs biting into my wrists. "Such a dirty mouth for such a noble man. Does it work? Does it get women off when you talk like that?" I leaned forward again, uncaring of the painful bite on my wrists. "They may look at you as a savior, but I know the truth behind those lovely eyes. Your hands are just as bloody as mine, Samkiel. You are no savior. You are a coward who hid away. At least I fight for something. Paint me as the bad guy all you want, but I'm not the one they call World Ender."

I waited for him to explode. I expected him to yell, for the room to shake, and for him to use that blasted power I had seen before. Everyone in the room held their breath, but all he did was stare at me.

"I'm going to ask you again. Who do you work for?"

I blew another strand of hair from my face as I tried to sit up better. "Are you ignorant enough to think a woman couldn't lead all by herself? Did they not do that on Rashearim?"

"The women on Rashearim are very different from you. They are respectful, with tremendous strength and intelligence. I knew goddesses who led armies and fought with dignity, not cheap tricks. You don't compare at all and couldn't touch them. I have met women like you. Do you know where the vile, vicious, and vindictive women like you are now? They are dead."

"Oh, baby, I doubt you've met anyone like me before."

Liam nodded once and dropped his hand, returning his gaze to the pages in front of him. I thought I had earned a small reprieve since I didn't immediately feel like I was being set aflame. Unfortunately, my relief was short-lived as the power ran through me again. My body rocked back as my hands clenched, the cuffs biting into my flesh. I felt the beast in me try to break free, the dark power coiling beneath my skin. The pain ended after what felt like an eternity, and I sagged in my seat.

"I'll ask you again—"

I didn't have the strength to move. Sweat drenched every part of me, and my body trembled. "Ask me over and over, and I'll tell you nothing. Burn me all you want, Samkiel, but you won't get anything from me. So, come on. Do your worst. I fear no kings and no *gods*."

The last part left my lips on a sharp hiss as I glared at him through my lashes.

Liam didn't move, but annoyance flickered in his eyes. He was growing bored with this, and so was I. "Are you sure about that?" he asked, leaning forward.

The damn cuffs rebelled as I shifted my hands and flipped him off with both fingers. He stared at me for what felt like forever. I dropped my hands, my wrists slamming back down against the chair, pain vibrating through my arms. He shuffled the papers before holding some up in front of me.

"I believe, as you said earlier, that everyone has a weakness." His voice was soft, almost a whisper. "And I believe you have one, too. I do not recall Ig'Morruthens sitting down and having lunch with mere mortals, but she's not like you either."

I blinked a few times, trying to stay calm and not show the terror slithering through me.

He moved more photos out of the way. "So, do you want to tell me who you work for, or who this woman is to you? And please do not lie to me."

My gaze stayed fixed on him. "Go fuck yourself."

Confusion flickered in his expression. I rolled my eyes and snapped at Logan, "Translate that for him."

When he did, Liam's nostrils flared for a split second, as if no one had dared to speak to him that way before. "If you will not answer, I will have to ask her."

"You go near her, and I promise it will be the last thing you *ever* do," I snarled, straining against my restraints. I felt my canines grow and my vision grow red.

The air was sucked from the room as pressure built, immense and oppressive. A storm made flesh; that's what Liam reminded me of. "Are you threatening me?" he asked, his eyes going pure silver. It was a color I had come to hate in the last few hours, and I knew it would haunt my nightmares.

"You know, I'm usually a fan of a quick death. A quick snap of the neck or a roasting tends to be my preferred method," I hissed. "But you? I am going to take my time with you. I'm going to hurt you in ways you can't imagine and laugh as the silver dies in your eyes."

He held my gaze. No one talked, and no one moved. He turned back to the table and sat. It was a moment before the heaviness in the room evaporated. The silver in his eyes faded, returning to their normal shade of gray. I nearly laughed at the thought; this man was anything but normal.

"After the many failed attacks on our temples, it would appear you are looking for a relic of ours. Please elaborate."

I didn't.

I didn't speak when asked what we were looking for, and not when he asked where I was from or who I worked for again. He asked question after question, hour after hour, and I burned with each one. I can't remember which one finally knocked me out, just that at that moment, I felt peace.

How strange.

Thirteen

Dianna

I didn't know how many days had passed, or even if it was days at all. All I knew was pain. He asked the same questions. I didn't respond, and the burning started. It was like electricity in my veins, reaching every part of me as my eyes bored into his. Hatred, pure and simple, grew with every moment of agony.

Sometimes I didn't scream, able to distract myself by picturing myself breaking free and ripping his head from his body. I imagined his blood painting the room, creating a masterpiece more exquisite than any famed painter could imagine. I dreamed of running out of this damned place to her, my only family. She was the only thing that kept me mortal, even if she hated me right now. That was when I screamed, because I knew I couldn't reveal the one truth that he wanted to know. He wanted to know about her. He wanted a way to control me.

Kaden had done the same over the last century, and I would not trade one master for another. So, I let Liam torture me and listened to him repeat the same questions without giving him an answer. The room eventually faded to black, like it always did. My body was threatening to give out. I didn't know how much time I had before one of those blasts would kill me. It didn't matter as long as she was safe. That was always my last thought before that sickening heat seeped into every pore, and the darkness claimed me. There in that empty space, my mind drifted off to relive the days leading up to this.

I LANDED OUTSIDE HER APARTMENT, MY FEET LEAVING CRACKS IN THE concrete, but I didn't care. Several bystanders gasped, staring at me in shock before running away. It was barely seven in the morning, but this couldn't wait. I pushed past the doorman and looked toward the nearest elevator. Several mortals were shuffling out, probably on their way to work. I didn't have time to wait and ran toward the stairs, taking them two at a time. I could have portaled to her floor, but I needed to run and feel something in my lungs besides the dust and destruction I had endured. Not bothering to knock, I nearly yanked her door from its hinges. Gabby and Rick were in the kitchen. They were *busy,* and I would have to bleach my eyes later, but I didn't care. We didn't have time.

"Get dressed," I snapped as I grabbed the blanket from the back of the couch and threw it at her.

"Dianna! What are you doing here?" Gabby yelled, grabbing the blanket and wrapping it around her.

Rick took in my clothes and gasped. "What the fuck happened? Is that blood?"

I was covered in blood, mine mixed with Zekiel's. My eyes lit up as his widened. "Get out. Leave. Go to work and forget you were ever here. Forget what you saw."

Rick's eyes glazed over, and he nodded. He grabbed his clothes and left, not caring that he was naked.

"Dianna, what the hell is going on? Why are you breaking into my apartment this early? Why are you covered in—"

I didn't respond as I turned down the hall, going to her room. My feet barely touched the ground as I pushed past her open door. She followed me, still yelling, but I could only hear Kaden's voice ringing in my head.

I stormed after him, nearly running to keep up.

"You knew!" I yelled after him. I grabbed the nearest object, a small antique vase, and hurled it at his back. It missed, my aim completely off as my anger rose. It shattered near his feet, and he finally stopped. "You knew he was still alive."

He turned slowly, the beast beneath his skin slithering, reminding me how alien he truly was. His ember-filled eyes burned as he stormed toward me, a single finger raised. I took a step back before stopping and squaring my shoulders. I knew his temper, yet I'd played with fire, anyway. "You," he spat, "killed a member of The Hand. He will seek retribution. They all will. I had a plan, and you fucked it up again because you don't know how to listen." He stopped before me, forcing me to look up at him.

"You shut me out. You knew this whole time, and here I was, thinking he was a fairy tale. Does Alistair know? Tobias?" He didn't answer, just looked to the side, and I knew they did. I threw my hands up, screaming in frustration, "Gods, Kaden! You don't tell me anything. How long has The Hand known about us, huh? How long have they been following us? You know two of them found me while you were doing gods know what? You bark orders and demand I follow."

One moment he was glaring down at me, and the next, he was gripping my chin painfully tight. He moved so quickly that I barely saw it. He leaned in and hissed between clenched teeth, "And follow you will. Don't, for one second, think you have any power or say over me. I made you. You'd be a dried set of bones if it weren't for me."

I jerked my face free, knowing it would bruise. "Yes." My eyes stung. "And that is something you like to remind me of every chance you get. You put us at risk, Kaden—all of us, including my sister. What am I going to do about my sister?"

He scoffed at the mere mention. "I don't care about her. She is not important."

"She is to me!" I snapped back, pushing at his chest.

He didn't move, but something changed in his eyes. He tilted his head slightly and studied me for a moment before nodding.

"Yes, she is, and just how far are you willing to go to keep her safe now that one of theirs is dead? He will come seeking vengeance."

The thought made my blood boil. No one would touch Gabby. I would make sure of that. "As far as I need to."

"You would fight a god?"

"No," I said without hesitation, "I'd kill one."

I yanked open the closet doors. Gabby's clothes hung precisely, arranged by color. Shoes lined the walls, and a space on the far left held her suitcases. I reached in, grabbed one, and tossed it on the bed, along with two smaller ones. I pulled clothes from hangers that broke beneath the force, and threw them into the bags.

"Dianna!" She reached over and grabbed my hand, stopping me in mid-motion. "What happened?"

"I fucked up." I pulled away from her and spun, moving back to the closet. She just watched as I knelt, grabbing a handful of shoes and moving back toward the bed. "I fucked up bad, Gabs."

"Is this about that quake in Ophanium a few days ago, and the freak storm in Arariel?"

I stopped, laid my hands flat on the suitcase, and looked up at her. Her hand was over her mouth as she stared at me.

"That wasn't a storm. Something came back... *Someone* came back, and now I need you to go to the safe house like we planned."

I finished packing and zipped up the suitcases before looking up at her. She hadn't moved. "Gabby, get dressed."

She didn't say anything, just stared at me as she gripped the blanket closer. "Why the safe house? Who came back?"

I had never lied or kept secrets from Gabby. The bond we shared was too deep. Since our parents died, it had just been the two of us. We had been looking out for each other for a very long time. She was my sister, my best friend—and I was about to make her hate me.

"I killed someone very powerful. Well, I didn't technically kill him, but my hands are covered in his blood. Kaden and everyone else think I killed him, and that's enough. If what Kaden said is true, then the last living god is coming back for my head. Now get dressed."

Her hand dropped, her mouth slightly agape. "D...?"

"I know. Now please get dressed. You'll be safe where we talked about. It's the one place that Kaden knows nothing about. Remember what I said. You will need to change your hair, change your style, don't use your name, and no passports. I have several credit cards stashed there, too. You'll wait until I come back to get you. It's just like we practiced."

The only difference was that we'd practiced this for when I eventually left Kaden, not for when I was about to be hunted down by an ancient god. She said nothing, but I saw panic settle into her eyes. Finally, she moved toward the dresser, dropped the blanket, and got dressed.

I grabbed her suitcases, tucking the small ones under my arms. As I left the room, I called out, "Grab any pictures you have of us, just like we talked about. We have to—"

"Dianna, what about Rick?" she cut me off as she followed me, jogging pants rolled at the waist, pulling a shirt over her head. She sat on the couch and tugged on her shoes.

I'd known that was coming. I also knew from her expression that she was still processing everything I'd said.

"You knew that was short-term," I said, keeping my tone even.

"Why? Why does it have to be?"

"You know why!" I snapped. I didn't mean to, but I did.

"Don't yell at me!" she snapped back, throwing her arms in the air. "You are giving me no choice again."

I spun toward her, my hands on my hips. "Excuse me? I do this because I have to. All I am trying to do is give you choices while I have none."

She snapped, pointing a finger at me. "You could have choices if you really wanted."

"How, Gabby? Do you have any idea how strong he is? Do you know the power he has over the Otherworld, and me? I know we talked about me walking away, but it was merely a dream. How can I? I'm sorry we have to move, okay? I'm trying to give you somewhat of a normal life."

"I will never have a normal life because of what you did."

Her words were like a slap to the face. My voice rose as I pointed at my chest and then at her. "Because of what I did? You mean what I gave to save you? How dare you?"

She spun, placing her hand against her forehead. "You saved my life. I know that, and I am not unappreciative, but at what cost, D? I'm moving all the time. The secrets, the bloodstained clothes, the monsters, and what about your life? Your happiness?" She stopped, pointing toward the suitcases. "This isn't living, not for me and not for you."

I threw my arms up this time, my chest aching at her words. They'd sliced me open and left me raw. "What do you want me to do, Gabby? What do you want me to do, huh?"

"Leave! Whether or not you believe it, you are just as strong as him. He made you, and some of him is a part of you. You need to fight back, or at least fight for something."

"I can't!"

"Why?!"

"Because if I slip, if I mess up, he will come after you!" My voice cracked, emotions pouring out of me. My vision blurred, but it was the truth, the absolute truth. "And I can't lose you. I wouldn't survive it."

She shook her head as tears formed in her eyes. "I can't do this anymore. I know you love me, and I love you, too. But, Dianna, I can't be the reason you suffer. It hurts me to know that you have to stay with *him* because of me. All I ever wanted was for both of us to be happy. You can't protect me forever. There was no point in saving me if I can't even live." She paused and shook her head. "I'll go to the safe house, but after that, I am done. We have been doing this for centuries, and I'm tired. I can't do this anymore. If the price of my freedom is to watch my sister become a—"

She stopped, and I felt my heart break further.

My fists clenched like iron, just like my heart. "Say it. If you have to watch me what?"

She held my gaze. I could see the pain there, just as I knew she could see mine. Her lips formed into a thin line, but her voice was steady as she said, "If I have to watch you become a monster."

I nodded slowly and dropped my gaze. "Ask me again why I didn't tell you what I have done." I felt the sting as more tears pricked my eyes, the room becoming blurry.

A monster.

She was right, but if a monster was what I was, then so be it. I wiped away the few tears that had escaped from my cheeks and strode toward her. I pulled one of the forsaken blades from the sheath on my back and stopped in front of Gabby. She looked from the blade to me and back. I reached out, grabbed her hand, and placed the hilt in her palm.

"If worse comes to worst and I don't come back for you, use this. Remember what we practiced: groin, thigh, throat, or eyes. Take it, and when you use it, mean it." I looked at her once more, memorizing her face, remembering her being happy and healthy. What I was about to do would either set us free or end me, and I wanted that image. I pulled her to me and placed a kiss atop her head, whispering against her hair, "I'm sorry that I stuck you with this horrible life. Just remember that I love you."

I turned away from her without saying another word and left the apartment. I was barely out of the building before my phone rang.

"What?" I snapped, causing two passersby to jump.

"We found a way in. Get back to Novas." Tobias's voice was short and clipped.

I didn't bother to respond, and the line went dead. I turned back, taking one last look, as if I could see her through the walls. Black mist swirled around my feet and caressed my body before I disappeared.

After my fight with Zekiel, my fight with Kaden, and then my fight with Gabby, it had been a day. We were currently in a hotel suite in Arariel where the ambassadors we would take over were staying. They had the information we needed and were our way into the meeting.

Tobias stood in the bloodstained room. He had assumed the form of a celestial female and was stretching. Out of the corner of my eye, I saw Alistair mimicking him. I wiped the blood off my face with the back of my hand, the memories of the mortal I'd eaten flooding my subconscious. I hadn't killed in years, not truly consumed, and my body felt like it was running on hot. A part of me loved this feeling—the part of me that wasn't mortal.

Tobias looked at me and said, "Don't make that face. You'll need every bit of strength if you are to survive a second with him."

I nodded. "I know."

"Bloodthirsty Dianna is always my favorite."

I ignored Alistair as I finished off the mortal I would become. I played back every bit of information from his memories. After I was done, I abandoned my sleek feminine form and shifted into the average male named Henry.

I adjusted the suit, making sure it was clear of blood. "Meeting is in thirty minutes. There should be a car out front in about five. They have every mortal council member present, The Hand, and him."

Tobias's smile was lethal, even in his prettier form. "Good."

Alistair stepped over a few bodies, stopping in front of me. "Remember the plan. Distraction; that's it. Keep him busy while we search for the book."

I nodded, agreeing to *their* plan, absently rubbing the forsaken blade strapped to my thigh. I smiled in my new form. "Of course."

MY DREAMS FADED AS I WOKE UP IN MY BRIGHT CELL. I LIFTED MY HEAD from my half-slumped position on the cold floor, my body screaming. The tears I wiped from my face were not from the pain I was in, but from that memory. I hoped she was safe, even if she hated me. Sweat drenched my clothes, but I refused to change, setting any clean clothing they provided on fire. I hoped I smelled bad. I hoped I was revolting and a complete mess.

My arms wobbled as I pushed up on my hands. The torture and the chains had sucked my usual strength out of me. I scooted back, wincing as every part of me protested the movement. My back hit the cold stone wall behind me, and I gritted my teeth. Between the shackles and the repeated bolts of electricity he sent into my body, I was useless. It was okay, though. As long as I was here, and as long as I didn't break, she was safe.

Footsteps descended the stairs, and I lifted my eyes toward the entrance to my cell. It was all the strength I could muster. I heard clapping before Peter came into view. He was dressed in overly cumbersome tactical gear.

"Well, well, well, you really have taken a beating these last few weeks."

I flipped him off, even that slight movement causing me to wince, the muscles in my arms screaming. "Fuck you, Alistair."

Peter's head tilted, and I saw the shine that let me know Alistair was in full control. He clicked his tongue as he stood in front of me, hands in his pockets.

"You look terrible. Are they not feeding you?" He smiled, knowing they had sent food, and I'd refused it every single time. I would rather starve than receive anything from them.

"Did you find the book?" My voice cracked, my throat aching from the number of times I'd screamed.

He sighed, dropping to a squat. "Unfortunately, no. Your distraction worked, even if Kaden would have preferred less destruction. Regardless, you've done great. Kaden is very happy."

I forced a smile that hurt my torn, dry lips and tried to sit up a bit more. "So happy that he hasn't even tried to come and get me."

Peter's body shook slightly, his eyes reflecting and changing. His voice deepened, and I knew I was not speaking to Alistair anymore. "I'm missing two blades, Dianna. I told you nothing could kill him, and yet you fought. That's why you're here, not because of me."

My eyes narrowed. "You also said he wasn't alive. You lied to me. How can I trust anything you say?"

"We had a plan, and you didn't follow it. You were supposed to distract him long enough for Tobias and Alistair to search. Then you were to leave, not get caught. Why would I rescue you when you were captured due to your own failings?"

I guess it was the mortal part in me thinking I meant something to someone, but that stung, too. I had been here for weeks, and none of them made a move to help me. Like always, I was alone.

"I will admit, your efforts have put Elijah right in the prime spot of power. Now I have a mortal working alongside the World Ender. It's only a matter of time before we find the book."

"Lovely."

"I won't risk exposure coming for you. This is a fortress meant to hold, Dianna. Besides, we are too close now. The book is what is important, not you." I didn't look at him, facing the wall and keeping my head against my arms. "Maybe this will teach you to listen to me. You got yourself into this. Get yourself out."

FOURTEEN

DIANNA

I think a few more days passed, but I had lost count. With no windows, only the dimming of the lights told me when night had fallen. Peter—or should I say Alistair's puppet—did not come back, nor had I expected him to. Liam and The Hand didn't make an appearance either. Only the celestial guards stopped by, checking to make sure I hadn't died and to see if I had eaten any of the food they'd brought. I would rather have starved than accept anything from them, so I stayed in the corner and slept. I dreamed of simpler times before the fall, when I had a home, a family, and the world made sense.

The lights came on in my cell, startling me from my dream. I raised my hand to cover my eyes as a group of celestials stomped inside. All were dressed from head to toe in what looked like their normal tactical gear, but as they drew closer, I saw that the padded parts were fireproof. Smart.

I thought we were going for another round of interrogation, and I had no strength to even attempt to fight. They hoisted me up by my arms, and I realized all the ones in my cell were regular guards. Liam and the members of The Hand were not in attendance. Maybe my interrogation was officially over, and they were finally going to kill me. It would be a welcome respite.

There was no strength left in my body, and my feet dragged on the floor. They hauled me through the underground prison, and as they pulled me through the doors, I heard people talking and chattering. Maybe he had decided to make a show of it when he burned me for the final time. I tried to focus, blinking blearily, and was surprised when we turned down a small hall. A double set of sliding glass doors opened, and the noise intensified as they pulled me over the threshold.

Light hit my face, and I winced. I forced my eyes to remain open, and as they adjusted, I looked around, hungry for the sunlight. It spilled into the underground garage through the wide-open doors on my right. Large, heavy vehicles were parked on the concrete floor, their doors standing open. Were they transporting me? Where?

The celestials carried me to the back of a large armored truck. One of them reached forward, twisting some lock that lit up a light blue before opening. Damn, they were serious. They hoisted me up, and I groaned as they sat me on one of the long benches. The cold metal nipped at my exposed skin. Two loud clunks, and my arms and feet were secured with more chains imbued with magic.

I looked behind the guard as he bent to secure my feet. The vehicle reminded me of an iron cage on wheels. The two behind were similar, and I would bet that the two in front were the same. It was a common tactic. It disguised the location of whatever cargo you were transporting, making rescue more difficult. Smart man, Liam, but it was a wasted effort. I knew no one was coming.

"The book is what matters. Not you."

I would be lying if I said those words didn't sting. I felt the kiss of the now familiar power that preceded a member of The Hand and lowered my head. A chill ran up my spine as I peered through the tangled mass of hair veiling my face. The truck shifted beneath Logan's weight, and he spoke in that language I didn't know. The other celestials looked from me to him and back. They shook their heads before closing and sealing the door. It was another smart move not to let me overhear whatever they were planning.

"Taking me out on a date, lover boy?" My voice was a crackling mess.

Logan sat down across from me, his gear sleeker and less bulky than the others. I looked him over as he crossed his arms and rested one ankle on his opposite knee. He wore no weapons that I could see —not that he needed them. Logan was a member of The Hand. He was a weapon.

"You know, I have not killed an Ig'Morruthen in ages, so please make a mistake. Liam said that if you try to escape or do anything that could endanger the team or me, I have permission to make you a foot-note in history."

I forced a fake pout on my lips, the effort painful. "Aww, do you always do what Daddy says?"

I didn't have a moment to savor my smart quip before he punched me so hard that my head hit the metal wall, and I blacked out.

That burning pinched my wrists and ankles as my body bounced, once more pulling me from my dreams. It stopped, then happened once more. I squinted and bit back a groan as I pulled my head up. My neck hurt from being slumped over. I rested my head against the metal wall behind me, my nose throbbing. Someone was talking, and I slowly opened my eyes, expecting to see the white walls of my little cell. I focused on Logan, and memories washed over me. Another bump rattled my aching body, proving their veracity. Logan sat in front of me with a phone pressed to his ear as he spoke with that beast he called a wife.

"Look, it's simple. We're dropping her off and heading to Silver City of Hadramiel for the meeting. Just meet me there, babe," he said into the phone.

Her response was simple and sweet. "Please, just be careful. We believed them to be extinct, and now there are at least three. I'm just worried about another surprise."

I rolled my eyes. If I had to listen to this the whole ride, I would vomit.

Logan turned, realizing I was awake. His eyes narrowed in disdain, and he ended the call with a promise to return to her. Logan gave me a look of pure contempt. I knew he felt they had won and taken care of the problem. He was a fool, not only in love, but in that he didn't recognize the threat looming over him and his precious friends. He was so mistaken if he thought I was the worst he would face. Compared to Kaden, I was damned near angelic.

"What? It's probably strange for you to hear someone care." He smirked. "I doubt anyone loves you," he said, folding his arms.

Ouch.

Logan was right. Kaden didn't love me. I doubt he'd ever used the word. What would it be like to truly be loved? I wondered what it would be like to be wanted for me and not my powers of destruction. I gave Gabby a hard time about the silly movies she loved so much, but I think a part of me craved it deep down.

In the small amount of time I had been held captive, I had seen the members of the Guild show signs of caring for each other. I didn't know why, but a part of me hungered for that connection, and I was afraid Kaden knew it. My kin and I weren't big on feelings and emotions. I blamed it on our intense need for blood and sex. I felt less mortal the more I fed. The more I drank and killed, the happier Kaden was. Those were the only times I felt he truly cared for me.

"No sassy comeback? Come on, where is the brazen woman who blew up an entire building and then threatened the king of this realm and the next?"

I glared and slid forward as much as my bindings would allow. "Pop open an artery, and I'll introduce you again."

I mustered as much power as I could, given my circumstances, and knew my eyes flashed red. The energy in the van changed, the tension prickling at my nerves. Logan might seem sweet to those he loved, but he was part of The Hand for a reason. I half expected him to punch me again, or maybe he would kill me and claim it was an accident.

I didn't know why I always put myself in situations that could result in my death. Call me crazy, wild, impulsive, or all of the above, but one thing I could say for myself was that no matter what, I was a fighter.

I might have been weak and starving, but I wouldn't let him see it. I would keep my facade as long as I could. If he moved closer, I knew I could use what strength I had left to strangle him with the chains, but if he managed to draw a weapon, it was all over for me. He must have gauged my thought process or come to the same realization, because his only response was a small chuckle. I would be lying if I said I wasn't slightly relieved. I didn't feel like fighting right now. My entire being still hurt from the power Liam had slammed through me over these last few weeks, and my hunger strike was affecting my healing.

Time passed, and Logan answered more calls, but he switched to that beautiful language. When he wasn't on the phone, the ride was silent, neither of us interested in another exchange. Why would we be? Our species had been mortal enemies since the dawn of time, or so we were told. Yes, the good guys are always straight and true. They sacrifice themselves for the ones they love and save the day at the last minute. In contrast, my kin and I were always subjugated as the villains. History portrayed us as merciless, cruel, vile creatures who sometimes oozed slime. I didn't know anyone who did, but I had heard stories of Ig'Morruthens that had in the past.

Gabby was right. I was a monster.

"So," I probed, "where exactly are you taking me?"

He didn't answer.

I sighed. "What's the point of keeping me alive? You all know I won't talk."

"You're talking just fine right now."

I nodded, relaxing my head against the back of the vehicle. "Ah, so it's the big boss who decided, then. Because I get the feeling that you and the rest would gladly have me roasted and toasted."

He smiled. "Oh, absolutely. After what you did to Zekiel, you'll be lucky to be free ever again."

The sound of his name made me look away. It always brought the memories crashing down on me. The way he fought for that blade with all his strength. The look on his face. Damn that look! He'd known that everything was—

"Hopeless."

"What?" Logan's brow rose.

I hadn't realized I'd spoken aloud and quickly changed the subject. I shook my head, turning my attention back to him. "So, if the big guy wants me alive, I'm assuming it's not to ask me out on a date?"

"If by 'date,' you mean keep you alive by any means necessary, since you are the only lead we have, then yes, a date. At this point, I'm sure he is ready to force-feed you."

"I'm wet just thinking about it."

He shook his head, his lip curling. "I don't get the crass attitude and jokes. You know there is no way out of this for you. There is no happy ending, yet you refuse to speak. Who has that much of a hold over you?"

I had no intention of revealing that information, because if they knew what Kaden held over me, they would use it, too. Gabby was the one thing that kept me in line. My eyes dropped to the symbol on his finger, and I nodded toward it.

"I gave up on happy endings a long time ago. Speaking of which, how did you two murderous little lovebirds meet?"

He didn't answer.

"She is beautiful. I see what you see in her. I'm sure others do, too. She must mean a lot, especially if you guys performed the Ritual of Dhihsin."

The Ritual of Dhihsin originated with the Goddess Dhihsin. It consisted of a ceremony that bound soul mates irrevocably. They were left with a stylized runic symbol with beautiful flourishes on the third finger of the male's left hand and the right of the female's. When they pressed their palms together, the symbols met. The marks were unique to each couple, and once they were complete, there was no divorce and no leaving. The bond was forever, and one of the most precious forms of love you could give to another person. It was one of the things Gabby absolutely loved about celestial culture. It was what she'd wanted with Rick—and I'd taken it from her.

Logan's eyes glowed bright blue before he answered. "I have strict orders to make sure you make it to Silver City, but if you mention my wife again, I will make your death look like a bad accident."

A cold smirk formed on my lips. *Gotcha.* "Silver City, huh? Oh, I am special. That's in Ecanus. So, that's where we're going."

Silver City was exactly that, and it made the rest of the world look pathetic. I had heard it was one of the celestial's famed locations, not that I or anyone I knew had ever been there. Legend said those that entered never made it out.

He realized what I'd said, and his eyes widened slightly. "Say something else, and I'll knock you out again. I have no problem doing it for the rest of the ride." He folded his arms and sat back, his eyes narrowing into slits.

"Don't worry. I think I prefer to nap willingly."

There were no windows in the truck, but we both looked in opposite directions to avoid eye contact. I decided to tilt my head back to try to get some sleep. He did say this ride would be a few hours, and trying to talk with him wouldn't get me anywhere. The hard floor I had been sleeping on was not comfortable, and for some reason, this metal bench felt better. I shut my eyes and drifted off.

I WAS JARRED AWAKE AS THE TRUCK ROCKED VIOLENTLY. MY EYES snapped open, and my senses went on alert when I heard the stress in Logan's voice.

"Convoy Two, do you read me?!" Logan yelled. "Convoy One, repeat what you said. Come in, come in!"

Logan was shaking me, one hand on my shoulder, the other on a black handheld radio. "Dianna, this isn't time for fucking beauty sleep!"

"I'm awake, you idiot. Calm down!" I shrugged his hand off me, but he didn't even notice. His eyes were alight again as he lowered the radio and shook it. Static burst from the speaker, followed by screams and a loud whooshing sound. He looked at me, fear creasing his features.

"What's goi—" My sentence was abruptly cut off as the truck slammed to the right. We tumbled inside, bouncing off each other as we flipped several times. I tried to stabilize myself by holding on to anything I could reach, but the chains were too constricting. Suddenly, the truck stopped rolling, coming to a screeching halt. I pushed myself up and looked at Logan, both of us bruised and bloody.

The vehicle lurched forward again as if something had kicked us like a child would a ball. The truck rolled twice more before coming to an abrupt halt, hitting something with a loud crunch. Logan's body crashed onto me, his weight pinning me to the metal floor. The edges of my vision went dark, and I gasped for air, trying to blink myself out of the gray haze.

The back door was ripped off, the reinforced steel tearing like a sheet of paper. A dark figure stood silhouetted in the opening. I felt Logan's body tense, but I knew he was already too late. The monster reached in and dragged him out. The last thing I heard before I blacked out was his scream.

FIFTEEN
LIAM. A FEW HOURS PRIOR.

"The convoys are ready for transportation," Peter said. He was one of many celestials that had moved higher in rank after the explosion. Vincent had spoken highly of him. He, along with a couple of recent graduates, seemed to want to help as much as possible. They even offered advice when needed, which Vincent liked. Back during my father's rule, only the council or high-ranking officials had the ear of their superiors.

I turned, nodding toward him and moving from the large window. Peter and three other men stood at attention, their hands behind their backs and eyes forward. All seemed right, but something felt off about Peter and a few others I had come into contact with. I could not pinpoint the issue, so I just blamed it on not being around anyone for centuries. They all had the potential to be more, which was good if war was where we were headed.

"You are dismissed," I said, and one by one, they nodded and exited the room. I took one last look at the fog rolling off the mountains. Arariel was magnificent, but nothing compared to anything on Rashearim. These mountains, although beautiful, were small and their foliage dull in comparison. I just wanted to be done with this and go home. The longer I stayed, the worse the blasted headaches were becoming. It did not help that I had not slept and had no intention of doing so.

I did appreciate all the various ways the mortals and celestials had found to burn off excess energy. Logan had shown me the gym, and that was where I spent most of my time. As I worked my body, I tried to figure out what these creatures were after and what their next move would be. It kept me awake, but so did the fear. I did not fear the Ig'Morruthen in the lower levels, but I did fear what would happen if I slept. I needed this to be done so I could leave.

I had turned away from the view when Logan opened the door and stepped inside, Vincent and Neverra filing into the room after him. They bristled with weapons and wore the new armored suits I had ordered. I may have been fireproof to some degree, but they were not. If she could wield such power, who was to say the others couldn't as well? It was a necessary precaution to move her, but I would make sure they were as safe as I could make them.

"We are ready," Logan said.

I nodded and headed out of the room, the three of them falling in behind me. We'd made it halfway down the hallway before anyone spoke.

"You were too kind," Vincent said.

He flanked me on my left while Logan and Neverra took up my right. I knew this was a topic they had previously discussed from the way they tensed. Vincent and I had always held each other to a high standard. Our friendship had begun on Rashearim when I was just the son of Unir. He had no qualms about questioning me. I sometimes liked it, but there were those moments he annoyed me to no end. "Was I now? Was torturing the beast not enough?"

"The clothes and food sent down afterward? What for? After what she and her kind did, let her starve," he said, a muscle in his jaw twitching. His anger and hatred had matured over the centuries. "I knew it wouldn't work. There is no kindness inside of them. Unir taught us that. All the gods did. She is a monster."

Several celestials bowed as we passed, and I grimaced. I despised it. Logan, Vincent, and Neverra headed toward the elevator, but stopped when I shook my head. My control over my powers was erratic at times, but I did not care to share that information with them. Instead, I led the way to the stairs, and we took them down to the main foyer. It was an open-ended space that led to the front of the building. "Yes, that is correct, but I feel there is more. There is more to her than just evil and destruction. I merely tried to appeal to those pieces. Besides, I cannot question a dried-up husk, and that's what she will become if she does not eat."

"Yes, but we cannot forget that she murdered almost the entirety of the mortal council. The ones that managed to survive have burns covering half of their bodies. Then there is the fact that she is the reason Zekiel isn't here."

I stopped and turned to face Vincent. "How could I not? Was I not there? I witnessed her raise her hands, saw the flames dance, and reacted a fraction of a second too late."

"And what of Zekiel?"

"Vincent…"

"Zekiel is gone, and you act as if coming back here is a tedious task. He cared about you, just as we do, yet you don't seem to be mourning him at all!"

I closed my eyes, the throbbing in my head coming back tenfold. Several lower-ranking celestials cleared the area as power swirled around us. The lights flickered before flaring a shade brighter. "Mourn? When do I have time to mourn? I am glad you have that luxury. Yes, Zekiel died. Many have, and we are on the brink of war again. There are always casualties, or have *you* already forgotten?"

Vincent's eyes narrowed. "I have done what was needed here, remember? You left me in charge. I know Logan won't say it because he doesn't want to hurt your feelings."

"Hey, woah, woah," Logan interrupted, stepping closer and raising his hand.

"But you're different now, colder. Liam, you have been gone for centuries, and I get it. You lost a lot, but so did we. You spent all that time on the remains of Rashearim, locked far away from the council. Imogen told us she hasn't been able to reach you, no matter how many times she has tried. You are not the same man who freed me from that wretched goddess, Nismera. You are not the same man who laughed and joked and drank with us like we were brothers. You are not the same man who forged The Hand long before the war. What happened to the man who thought to create a world where celestials are treated as equals instead of the mindless fucking puppets the gods made?"

"You are overstepping." I stepped forward, invading his space. Several lights busted in the hallway, and I heard Neverra usher out the remaining celestials.

"Someone has to," he retorted. "Are we brothers? Are we family, or just dispensable casualties to you now? You were always so afraid you would become as emotionless as your father. Well, look at you now. I don't see Samkiel anymore. I only see Unir. You are no better than him."

"Am I?" The room shook, and I knew the emotions and anger I kept at bay were on the brink of breaking free. "I do not wish to be a judge and executioner as he was. Someone needs to make accurate and concise decisions, and that has to be me. I left you in charge. You're right. You wanted to rule. That has always been your goal, and what do I come back to find? Half of the world is in turmoil, the mortal council does not respect you, and creatures from legends are terrorizing Onuna. They are destroying our places, killing our people, and you have no leads or a plan to stop them."

Logan stepped between us, placing one hand on Vincent's chest and his other on mine, pushing us further apart.

Vincent's eyes darted away from mine—a submissive tactic, and one I had seen all too often with him. "I'm trying."

"Try harder." He was right. I was cold, callous, and empty of emotion. The problem was that I didn't know how to fix it.

I stepped away from Logan's hand and turned, heading toward the sliding doors. "Logan, you will escort the prisoner to Silver City. Neverra and Vincent, you are with me. None of this is up for discussion."

No one else spoke as we walked out the doors into the garage. Several celestials were packing ammunition and supplies into the armored cars. The precaution was not for her but the ones who would follow, whom she refused to mention. Someone had a strong enough hold over her that she had not broken no matter what I'd done. I would admire that kind of loyalty if it were not attached to such a creature.

"Sir," a young celestial said as he opened the door of the nearest vehicle. I despised that as well. In my youth, I might have enjoyed the attention and praise, but I had come to realize it came with blood and death.

My jaw clenched as I slid into the back of the luxury armored vehicle. It had two rows of seats, which seemed excessive, and I opted for the one closest to the window. I turned my head just as Logan and Neverra were saying their goodbyes. She watched him leave before climbing into the car with me. Logan had supplied me with more videos of the mortal world, so I at least knew what these mechanical boxes were called now.

I watched Vincent take the lead vehicle with several other celestials, who beamed in his presence. He was right. He had led them while I was away, and I respected that. I would gladly hand it back to him the minute this was over. He was still upset. I could sense it, and I didn't blame him. I had come back and taken the title he loved so much. He probably hated me, but he could not hate me more than I hated myself.

Six cars would go with me to Hayyel before taking the underwater convoy to Silver City. Four armored trucks would transport the Ig'Morruthen the same way. We had a meeting with the new ambassador of Ecanus. He would take over this region, his predecessor having perished in the fire. Elijah was his name and the reason for this transport. I was not comfortable with her staying here while I was not present, and I couldn't risk the others coming for her.

It had been two weeks since the attack, and I wanted to leave with my every breath. I had not slept, and I knew my body would take the choice from me at some point. When that time came, the night terrors would overwhelm me, and I did not want to be here when that happened. I did not want them to see the shell of a man I'd become.

Regardless of what I did and what decision I made, I just felt isolated and alone. I'd spent my entire life being told who I was, what I was, and how to lead. But who was I really? I did not know, not truly. In my youth, I'd avoided my lessons while my father insisted I pay attention. I'd drowned the demons that tried to claim me with men, women, liquor, and training, pushing myself to be faster and stronger.

I strove to be something he would be proud of and worthy of the love they all gave me. It worked for a while, but everything I tried just seemed to cause more problems. When I recruited for The Hand, I'd taken the generals from the other gods, creating my own network, because until then, I was alone. It was selfish, and I knew it. I had no siblings. My mother had passed away when I was young, and my father only cared about me becoming king. A king had to love, and love was not selfish or cruel. I wasn't sure I knew how to love, if I were truly honest with myself.

Duty and honor I knew. I knew how to fight and kill, but not love. As King of the Gods, my father had loved those he ruled, and I had witnessed his undying love for my mother. It had stood unwavering against all obstacles and even survived her death. Logan and Neverra had been together for centuries. They never tired of one another and never sought more outside of their relationship. They were the definition of soul mates if there ever was such a thing, and I envied what they had.

I'd never felt that way about anyone. I had bedded, but never loved. Not even Imogen, though she'd begged for it. Vincent was correct: I had turned cold, or perhaps I had always been cold. Zekiel had perished, and I did not mourn. I shed no tears, even though he was a part of The Hand, had been with me since the beginning, and was part of the select few I called friends.

Vincent called Dianna a monster, but I knew that title belonged to me as well.

Neverra cleared her throat as the vehicle took a turn, descending the mountains. I had not realized how quiet I had been. "Don't blame them. They have missed you. Even Vincent, when he isn't being a complete ass." She snickered before smiling at me. "I missed you, too."

I let out a long breath, stretching my legs and folding my arms. "That's what everyone keeps telling me."

"Well, it's nice to hear from your friends."

I did not respond, only nodded.

"Look, I don't know what happened when Rashearim fell, but I know you lost more than we did. And for that, I am sorry. You have done a lot for us, Liam. In forming The Hand, you gave us a life we can be proud of. You saved so many during the war and gave us what we needed to rebuild on Onuna before you left. We have never forgotten what you did and the sacrifices you made."

I watched out the window as the road turned, snow-capped mountains and trees surrounding us on all sides. "You always were kind, Neverra. No matter the battles, you never lost that."

"It's my gift. And how I tricked Logan into bonding with me."

I faced her, attempting some sort of emotion. "I thought I helped with that?"

She smiled playfully, kicking me as the ponytail she wore swayed. "Not even. Although, I guess, kind of. I do miss those days on Rashearim. The parties we would have, and the times we would all get together to talk shit about the gods. They were all always so uptight." Her eyes glazed over as she pulled at the sleeve of her tactical suit. "I miss Cameron, even though he is annoying at times, and I miss Xavier correcting him. I miss sparring with Imogen, and the crazy dancing, when she wasn't completely wrapped around you."

"You know you can visit."

She shrugged. "I know. Logan goes sometimes, but I can't. Everything changed after the Gods War. I'm afraid I'll see them again, and all the happy memories will be just memories. Everything is so different now."

"That it is."

Silence fell between us once more. The road slowly widened as we reached the end of the mountain range. Towns and shops came into view, mortals going about their day. As we turned onto the highway, I said, "She almost got away."

Neverra jumped as if she hadn't expected me to break the silence. "What?"

"If I'd been a second slower, I wouldn't have caught her. I'm not fit to be anyone's leader, Neverra."

Her eyes softened. "Liam…"

"We are in over our heads. Both darkness and fire bend to her will, which makes her extremely dangerous—lethal, even. The worst part is that I don't think she has tapped her full potential yet. The chains barely held. You witnessed that. She refused to tell me who was with her or who her creator is, even under torture. My gut is telling me we have not even touched the surface of what is happening."

She nodded, her tone thoughtful as she said, "We did background checks, but the name Dianna Martinez brings up nothing. There are no records, no documents, nothing. She doesn't exist as far as the system is concerned, which probably means someone with a lot of power is keeping her hidden."

"And the relic they are searching for?"

She reached up, scratching at a single eyebrow. "Files, a few scrolls, and some ancient books have been taken, but nothing of importance. It's all text describing the history of Rashearim, but nothing detrimental."

I leaned forward, my gaze unwavering. "I need you all to realize how serious this situation is. We are not dealing with regular Ig'Mor-ruthens, and we are not prepared. These are not the beasts from the legends. If they can shift at will like her, they have evolved, and we are in trouble. If they can kill a member of The Hand, attack with free will and conscious thought, we are headed for another war."

She swallowed, fear etching her features. "What will you do if she won't talk? Will you use Oblivion?"

Oblivion was another subject we rarely discussed. I absently touched the ring outlined in black on my third finger. It was a weapon I'd created during my ascension. Only The Hand and my father knew about it, and they had all kept it a secret from the other gods until they could no longer. It was an obsidian blade from the darkest depths of our legends.

I'd created it from hate, devastation, and grief, emotions a god should never nurture. The blade did what no other weapon or living being could: it delivered a permanent death with no afterlife. The ability to create and wield such a weapon was what made me so dangerous and made the other gods tremble. It had earned me my reputation, my name whispered in hushed and fearful tones throughout the realms. It was one of my biggest regrets, but I knew I would bear the weight of using it again if it came down to saving this world.

"If I must."

Sixteen

Dianna

The crackling of the fire was the first thing I heard as the world started to come back. Then searing heat spread through my entire being. Warm liquid coated the back of my throat. It was pure ecstasy, but it was too much too fast, and I struggled to sit up as I started to cough. I immediately regretted the jerky movement when agony burst to life along my side. My eyes shot open as Tobias moved the half-drained corpse away from me and carelessly dropped it to the ground.

"Tobias?" It came out as a question as I tried to remember where I was. I felt like I was losing my mind. He looked at me with pure contempt as he reached over and yanked a sharp piece of metal from my side. I screamed, crimson warmth pouring from the wound. Yeah, I was definitely awake.

"You waited too long to eat. You were nearly desiccated."

I looked down at the slash in my side, watching as it healed completely, leaving only a torn hole in the dirty tank top I wore. I leaned my head back, my voice filled with exhaustion. "Didn't know you cared."

"Oh, trust me, I don't, but Kaden would be upset if he lost his favorite pet."

I rested my hand against my forehead as memories that were not my own flashed through my mind. Not one or two celestials, but several. How many people had Tobias fed me? Was I that far gone? After a few minutes of concentration, the noises stopped. I'd spent years training myself to compartmentalize and lock away the unpleasant memories I'd collected over the centuries.

After several deep breaths, I lowered my hand and looked around. Tobias and I were still near the overturned truck. The back door was gone, and I had no idea what had happened to Logan. I sat up a bit more and saw the other two vehicles lying crumpled nearby, metal pieces sticking out in every direction as if a meteor had crashed into them. The trees surrounding the road were ablaze, branches cracking and breaking as they burned. Tobias stood, and I struggled to my feet, wincing as I swayed. Despite how much he'd fed me, the pain was still nearly debilitating.

"Your healing is still slow? What did he do to you?" I knew he wasn't asking because he cared, but because he feared it could be done to him or Alistair as well.

I waved his concern aside and looked around. "I would have already healed if not for these damned cuffs. They drain my strength and leave me with nothing."

He tilted his head, his red eyes matching the fire that danced around us. "Very well."

He grabbed me by my arm, dragging me with him as he strode through the wreckage. I hissed in pain, my abdomen throbbing. Given I still had the restraints around my ankles and wrists, I struggled to keep up. The road was cracked and burnt as if something or someone had fallen from the sky. In my mind's eye, I could see what had happened. Tobias wasn't by himself. Alistair had come, too.

I didn't think they would come for me. I would be lying if I said a part of me wasn't relieved to be free, but I would have preferred not to have been in the damn vehicle when it flipped. The ringing in my ears subsided enough that I could hear a gurgling scream and a crunch. I could make out a dark figure moving with a slow, predatory stride toward one of the crushed vehicles. Alistair.

He had a larger version of one of the forsaken blades and was twirling it in his hand as I heard him say, "You know, I am so glad my little trick worked. I whispered a little convincing among your troops, and it got back to the right ears that Dianna only needed one member of The Hand to escort her. I figured Tobias and I could take one of you. It still took a bit of effort, but better to separate the herd. You know what I mean?"

Alistair was looking down at someone I couldn't see, one of the destroyed vehicles blocking my line of sight. Even with my super hearing on the fritz, I heard a distinct *clink* as he drove the dagger down and hit metal. I heard a pained groan and knew it was Logan. He had fought back and was still alive. That's why the surrounding area was on fire and there was so much destruction. He'd held his own, but by the sound of his rattling gasps for air, I didn't think he had much time left.

Alistair pulled his arm back, punching the dagger into Logan several more times. His eyes were awash in red, and his grin grew with every grunt of pain from Logan.

"Don't kill him, you dumbass," Tobias said as we rounded the crushed vehicles.

Alistair had his arm raised, preparing to stab Logan again. The forsaken blade was long, and where one blade should be, this one was split in half. The entire sword was covered in Logan's blood, including the blackened carved bone hilt. Blood splattered Alistair's arms, hands, and face. He slung the gore from the blade and took a step back, his burning eyes glazed with battle lust.

Logan was lying propped up against one of the crumpled trucks. He was clutching at his side, trying to stem the blood pouring from between his fingers. Damn, Alistair had really done a number on him. He had a slash on his forehead and blood dripping down his face, and one eye was swollen almost shut. The protective vest he'd worn had been ripped away, revealing a bloody shirt. His body was riddled with stab wounds and deep gashes. His eyes and tattoos were alight with that blue shine I detested, but the glow dimmed and flickered with every labored breath he took. Five more minutes, and he would be dead, just like Zekiel.

"Having fun?" I asked, looking at Alistair.

"Dianna, you look terrible," Alistair said, not missing a beat.

"Oh, yeah? It probably has to do with the weeks of torture and the fact that you idiots flipped a vehicle with me in it!" I yelled the last part as I stared at him.

"Oh, please, as if that did any damage to you," he said before stopping and looking at me. "Why are you still limping and holding your side? Didn't you feed her?"

Tobias held up one of my wrists, and I winced at the stretch it caused on my wound. "These. We need them off of her, because I am not carrying her ass all the way back."

Alistair raised a brow and nodded. "Yeah, fuck that. I'm not carrying her either."

"Sweet, guys. Seriously, so caring. Now can we get these off, please? Check his pockets."

Alistair turned back, and Logan met his stare defiantly. Alistair hissed insults at Logan as he dug around in his pockets for the key, but Logan just grinned and snapped his teeth at him. A few seconds later, Alistair stood and strode toward Tobias and me. Several keys jangled on the ring he carried. I snatched my wrist away from Tobias and held my hands out, desperate to have the cuffs off.

"I thought you weren't coming?" I said. Alistair met my gaze as he tried several keys. He glanced toward Tobias and then focused again on the cuffs. "I didn't think Kaden would come for me."

"Well, Kaden wants his bitch back," Tobias said from behind me. "After Alistair heard they were transporting you with a member of The Hand, he formed a plan."

Logan coughed. "How did you hear that?"

Alistair grinned, still working on the cuffs. "Oh, we have spies everywhere in your little establishment. I guess you can know now. You will be dead soon, anyway."

"No," Tobias snapped, "he wants him back alive. He may know where the book is."

There was a soft *clink,* and I felt my power rush back tenfold as the cuffs on my wrists fell away. They hit the concrete, that damned blue light of the runes blinking out. I took the key from Alistair and unlocked the ones on my ankles.

I let out a loud sigh as if I'd slipped into a warm bath after a long day. The surge of energy was almost orgasmic. The wound on my abdomen healed instantly, and the broken bones I had ignored popped back into place. I stretched my body and neck like an athlete preparing for a match. The color returned to my skin, and my body filled out now that the cuffs weren't suppressing the absorption of the fresh blood. It felt so good to feel like myself again. I hadn't realized how draining the enchantments were. I felt my eyes light up as I narrowed my gaze at Tobias and Alistair.

"Now I feel better." My voice was my own again, no longer raspy or hoarse.

"You almost look pretty again, except for the massive tangled mess on your head," Alistair said.

I flipped him off as we turned toward Logan. He saw me healed and tried and failed to sit up.

"You won't win. No matter how many of us you kill." I could have sworn I saw tears forming in his eyes, the shine reflecting the flickering flames.

"The light is fading fast, and we need to move quick if we're going to get any answers," I said.

Alistair moved in to finish the kill, and I saw regret soften Logan's eyes. He knew what fate awaited him. Alistair crouched beside Logan. "Look, Dianna, he wears the mark of Dhihsin on his finger." Logan groaned in pain as Alistair lifted his hand to show me.

"Yes, I know. He's married to another member of The Hand," I said, raising my brow.

Alistair whistled under his breath. "That's a big step, my dying friend. I heard the mark seals your life to theirs. Your power becomes their power and vice versa. I always wondered, if one died, if the other would soon follow. What does she look like? Shall we pay her a visit next?" He grinned at Tobias and laughed as Logan tried to move, desperate to defend his precious wife. He screamed with the pain, but I couldn't tell if it was from the physical or emotional torment. "So, tell me, do you love her?"

It was a stupid question and nothing more than a taunt. He knew the answer just as I did, but Alistair was a pure sadist, and he had found a raw nerve in this topic. Logan's eyes burned with desperate rage as he spat, "Fuck you!"

Alistair's laugh was pure menace. "I hope for her sake that she does die with you, because what Kaden has planned is going to shake this entire realm."

Planned? What did he mean? Did he know something I didn't? Was Kaden keeping more secrets from me? My irritation grew as I felt Tobias look at me and smirk as if he could read my mind.

"You'll lose," Logan rasped. He grimaced, looking between us. "You all will."

Alistair lifted the forsaken blade again. "After all of my kin you have killed, I'm going to enjoy this." He pressed the sword to a leaking wound, allowing the blood to pool on the tip of it. Alistair stood and walked over to me, the blade dripping.

"Let's make sure he's even worth it before we bring him in." Alistair held the blade toward me. "Come now. Give it a taste."

I scowled at his double meaning before grabbing his wrist and bringing the sword closer. I ran my tongue over the flat of the blade, the sweet blood of the celestial filling my mouth.

Logan's blood was like drinking straight sugar. My cheeks tightened as my jaw clenched, and I shut my eyes hard enough to scrunch my nose. Several images flashed through my mind all at once. Logan was surrounded by Liam and The Hand. I recognized Vincent and Zekiel, but not the two other men. Their hair was long and in an assortment of braids and twists. They wore silver battle armor that clung to their muscular frames, and their helmets rested near their feet.

They stood around three massive golden statues in a large, well-manicured garden and laughed. I knew instantly that this was not Onuna. Their surroundings were foreign and breathtaking. Mountains higher than I had ever seen rose in the distance, clouds thick and opaque crowning the tops. Large double-winged birds in an array of colors flew overhead, chirping actual melodies that filled the air. It seemed as if they had all snuck away from something important and were hiding out.

Liam looked younger, healthier, and happier. He smiled, proving that the rumors of his beauty were true. They were joking and goading each other. Liam chuckled and slapped a blonde man on the arm for some remark he'd made. In that memory, he was not the cold, hard torturer I had known the last few weeks.

A flash, and another image invaded my mind. A battlefield appeared. Men fought, sword against sword, all around me. The ground shook as blue and silver beams of light shot into the sky. Horrifying screams rent the air, sounding like the pits of the Other-world were being ripped open. Someone yelled, and I turned as several armor-clad soldiers rushed forward, gold spears and blades in hand.

I ducked out of sheer habit, hitting the ground hard. Only this floor was not a rocky battlefield, but cold stone tile. I looked up to find I was in a white and black kitchen. I heard a feminine laugh and jumped to my feet. It was her, his wife, Neverra.

"We wouldn't have to order takeout if you learned how to use an oven," she called out toward an open living room area. I heard Logan's response on the wind of a laugh before the kitchen melted away.

Music blasted my ears as I was dropped into the middle of a large ceremony. I spun as couples around me laughed and danced. Twin chandeliers hung above my head, the lights on them seeming to flicker with a mind of their own. Logan's voice had me turning, and I watched as he lifted her and spun. It was their bonding day. The crowd cheered as Logan set her back on her feet, but the happy couple were completely oblivious to the world around them.

My head began to throb, his memories coming too fast. He was dying, and I needed to hurry this up. I closed my eyes and focused until a more intimate moment played inside the memory. I was back in their home, only this time I was in their room. Neverra ran in, giggling like a child as she jumped on the bed, Logan close behind her. They played and rolled as he whispered love words between kisses. Her laugh was joyful, her eyes filled with a love that defied words as she wrapped her arms and legs around him.

THE BOOK OF AZRAEL

Neverra. That was his last thought? He was facing certain death, and still, his mind drifted to her, his friends, and his family.

"Anything?" Alistair asked, snapping me back to a reality filled with blood. The fire still blazed, and a nearby tree snapped, sending sparks floating through the thick haze of smoke. Tobias raised a brow, waiting for my response.

I shook my head, coming out of my fugue state. "No book. Not even a mention."

Alistair shrugged and turned back to Logan. He knelt before him, waving the blade at his face. "Well, bad news, buddy. We are going to take you with us. Then I'm going to dive into that brain of yours and sift through every corner of your mind. I am going to examine each memory you have, including the ones of your friends and that wife you love so much. Then I am going to turn you into my mindless puppet. I've always wanted a member of The Hand as a pet."

"I won't help you destroy my family," Logan sneered. I saw the silver blade form in his hand. It was smaller than the others, a dagger, and I knew what he was about to do. "Forgive me, Neverra. I love you."

Something snapped in me. I had never experienced the kind of love he had with Neverra, but I knew if I were dying, my last thought would be of Gabby. She was the only constant in my life, and I'd give up everything for her.

Memories from the hot, burning desert flooded my mind. The empty hollow ache of starvation and the chill of an incurable illness made my stomach clench. I would never forget how I held on to her, feeling her slip further away with each labored breath. Her body had been giving out as I'd pleaded with her to stay, knowing there was nothing I could do to help her.

Then those words. They were so similar to what I had spoken. What was this feeling? Was I sad for him—sad for the love he would never again see? Or was it pain—pain for the woman he was leaving behind? Would she feel lost and abandoned, too, like I did at the mere thought of losing my sister?

Fight back! Fight for something! Gabby's voice echoed in my head.

I didn't have time to process whatever emotions I was feeling, and

I took no time to think. I grabbed the blade from Logan as he tried to drive it into his heart. His eyes widened with despair, realizing he would not get the death he wanted.

Alistair chuckled and said, "Good job—"

His words ended on a gasp as I yanked the blade from Logan's hand and spun, shoving it up through Alistair's chin. His eyes rolled back, the tip of the blade protruding from the top of his head. His limbs went limp, and his body stayed upright for a second longer before going up in flames, hot, bright, and burning. It took mere seconds, and he was ash, the fire inside of him turning on him like an abused pet let off its leash.

As the dust settled, I spun the blade and shifted my stance, putting myself between Tobias and Logan. The hilt of the dagger burned in my palm as I faced Tobias, preparing to fight him. Shock and rage distorted his features, and his eyes burned with hatred.

"You traitorous *bitch!*" His eyes raked over me as he stalked forward. I lifted the burning silver blade in front of me and shifted into a defensive stance.

A blue beam shot past me, hitting Tobias hard enough to send him into the burning foliage. His scream was not of death, but of hate and anger. I felt the compression of the air as he shifted, the trees rustling as he took off, wings beating against the inky night sky.

I looked back at Logan. He stared at me and dropped his hand, the light running up his arm slowly disappearing. My heart hammered in my chest as I dropped the silver blade. I didn't move and didn't speak, my ears ringing.

What had I done?

My gaze shot up, searching the night sky where Tobias had fled. He would tell Kaden. Kaden would come for me. *Fuck.* He would go after Gabby! I'd never be safe. She would never be safe.

I spun on my heel, needing to move fast. The dusty remains of Alistair rose around my feet as I hurried to Logan's side. He leaned his head against the destroyed vehicle behind him, the glow of his tattoos fading. His hand hung loosely at his side, his wounds still open.

"You're bleeding out, Logan," I said, crouching in front of him. I wiped what was left of Alistair from my hands. My voice was calm, in direct contrast to the panic screaming inside me. "I need to cauterize the wound before it's too late."

"What … what did you do?" he stammered in disbelief, looking at the ashes on himself and back at me. A part of me couldn't believe it either. Not only had I just slaughtered Alistair, but I was also about to save a member of The Hand.

I was so fucked.

"Do you want to see her again?" I asked, cocking my head to one side.

He tipped his head in a slight nod, grimacing with pain even with that small movement.

"Okay then, shut up and try not to scream too much." I lifted my hand and concentrated, needing it hot enough to cauterize. The veins in my palm and fingers lit up a golden orange, and I laid them over the worst of the damage, trying to stop the bleeding from the devastating wound. He howled in pain, gritting his teeth hard enough to break them.

"That should 'hold until we get you some help." I stood, wiping my hands on my sweats. My gaze was pulled back to that burnt spot on the road. One decision, and I'd sealed my fate.

Logan grunted as he tried to stand, and I reached out to help him. He jerked back for a second before realizing what he was doing and stopped. I didn't blame him for still being fearful of me. We did not trust each other, but maybe we could reach some common ground.

"Let me help you."

His mouth formed into a thin line, but he nodded. I grabbed his arm and wrapped it around the back of my neck. He grimaced and kept his right hand on his midsection. I put my arm around his waist, trying to give him the leverage he would need to stand. He pushed to his feet and swore. He hopped, trying to keep pressure off of his badly twisted right leg.

"So, Silver City, right?" I said, as if the last few minutes hadn't happened.

"Yeah, the Grand Estate in Boel," he said through gritted teeth. "It will be a full house, though."

"Grand Estate?" I sighed, mostly to myself. "Oh, fancy. I guess it's a good thing we brought our party clothes."

He made a noise that resembled a snort, and I could tell he immediately regretted even that minute movement. I pulled him tighter against me and focused. Power surged through me from the celestials Tobias had fed me and the brief taste of Logan. I felt the familiar heat right before I disappeared from the site of my betrayal.

SEVENTEEN

DIANNA

F lames danced around our feet, and black smoke clung to our
bodies as I portaled us to the front of the Grand Estate itself.
I knew I was in the right spot from the garbled description
Logan had given me. The building looked like an actual castle. Dark
stone formed the walls, and multiple towers with small window slits
rose at the corners of the massive beast. Lights lined the cobblestone
driveway and shone from the building. Gardens graced the grounds,
meandering pathways cutting through the beautiful array of plants.
There were so many vehicles parked out front that it made even me
nervous.

I shifted, supporting Logan as he leaned more heavily against me.
"Logan, where would they most likely be?"

"Third floor," he grunted. So, the third floor was where I went.

Multiple gasps and screams filled the room as our forms solidified.
The smoke dissipated, bits of the mahogany floorboards chipping
away beneath my feet. Somewhere in the room, glasses hit the floor
and shattered. The people near the long white tables filled with food
stopped and turned toward Logan and me. I recognized some of those
here from my little interrogation stint. They all cleaned up well,
wearing dresses and tuxedos instead of the tactical gear I was accustomed to seeing them in.

"Sorry, did I interrupt a party?"

There were mortals mixed into the crowd, but the energy in the room told me there were more celestials in attendance than I was comfortable with. Their eyes lit and turned toward me when I spoke. Guns were pulled, and the safeties clicked off as the barrels were pointed in my direction. Whispers and murmurs filled the room as they took in my bloody clothes and the even bloodier figure at my side. It took them a moment to realize he was one of their own.

Without those damn cuffs on me, my senses were back to a hundred percent, and I turned toward the one person I was looking for. I felt him coming long before I saw him, the energy vibrating off of him like a live wire. The Hand fell in behind him, and together there was so much power that it was sickening.

"I have lived for several millennia," his deep voice echoed from the back of the crowd, "and surprising me is hard to do. But you continue to surprise me."

"Hello, lover. I missed you, too," I purred. The crowd parted, and Liam appeared. I held Logan up by his torn collar. "I have something for you."

A look passed over Liam's face almost too fast for me to catch. Fear? Relief? Or curiosity?

A shrill voice burst through the crowd, drawing everyone's attention. "Logan!" Neverra cried out as she ran past the mortals. Liam's hand darted out, stopping her headlong rush, the silver dress she wore swinging around her ankles. I yanked Logan closer to me, causing him to grunt in pain.

I held him with one arm and shook my head. "Not so fast. Put the blades and guns away. I saved him, and I can end him just as fast."

"You wouldn't," the one I remembered as Vincent said, stepping forward with an ablaze weapon in hand. "You'd be swarmed in seconds."

I smiled, making sure my canines showed. "Wanna bet?" My grip tightened on Logan, and he grunted in pain again.

"Please, please don't." Neverra's voice came out on a quiet sob.

"What is it you want?" Everyone fell silent, his tone powerful and commanding.

I shrugged. "Simple. I want a truce."

Vincent laughed, but no one else did.

Liam's jaw clenched as if the thought disgusted him. "You have no power over me, and I do not have to make any deals with you. I could kill you right here and now and think nothing of it."

"You really are a cocky, arrogant son of a bitch, aren't you? That strong, and yet your world still fell?"

"Watch your tongue." His words came out as a threat, one I knew he could deliver on.

I shrugged and gripped Logan's arms, pulling him in front of me as a shield. "Fine, don't make a deal. Your boy is bleeding out, anyway. Why don't I make it quicker?" I yanked his head back by his hair, exposing his throat. I brushed my fangs against his neck and heard Neverra gasp.

"No! Stop!"

I watched them, my lips hovering over Logan's pulse. Liam took a small step forward, Neverra clutching his arm in a near death grip. She didn't look at him, as if she was afraid to take her eyes off Logan and me. "Samkiel. Liam, please! Please," she begged. Neverra took a deep breath, holding back tears as she whispered, "I cannot exist without him."

I watched as Liam's eyes filled with fury, and a muscle clenched in his jaw. I grinned and slid my tongue over Logan's neck before lifting my head. My fangs retracted, and I knew I had won this round. Their union was all-binding, and if he refused, he wouldn't just lose Logan. He would lose Neverra, too. She would never forgive him if she lost her soul mate.

Liam's face didn't change as he stared at me. "Let me guess. You would like protection?"

I nodded, and Vincent sighed audibly.

"But not for me," I said.

Liam regarded me intently as he folded those powerful arms across his chest. "For who?"

"My sister."

The crowd started murmuring again, every eye in the room on the tableau. Even Neverra looked at me for a moment, taking her eyes off Logan.

"Why would an Ig'Morruthen need protection?"

Vincent cut in before I could respond. He looked at Liam, pointing at me with his sword. "You can't be considering this—"

"She is not an Ig'Morruthen like me," I snapped, interrupting Vincent. Liam's head swung back toward me as I continued. "I will help you find what they are looking for, help you kill him. Then, after, you can do whatever you want to me. I'm yours. You can kill me or lock me up for eternity. I don't care. But for her, I ask for immunity. She is innocent in this. She always has been."

Liam didn't say anything, and he didn't move. For a second, I was terrified he would refuse after I'd revealed so much.

I grabbed Logan a little harder, causing him to hiss. "Do we have a deal?"

"If I agree, there will be no freedom for you. You will pay for the crimes you have committed. Do you understand that? Regardless of the help you provide."

I knew what that meant, but I didn't care. I'd die afterward anyway, but Gabby would be safe here, and maybe she'd finally have the life she'd always wanted. They could keep her safe, and if Kaden was dead, she would be free.

There was no point in saving me if I can't even live. Gabby's words played verbatim in my head.

I nodded in agreement. "I accept, but I'll need more than your word."

His gaze narrowed as if he couldn't believe someone would question him. "My word is law. No one would disagree."

"Sorry, Charlie. I have trust issues. I'll need something a little more permanent and from my world." My smile grew slowly. "Sign it in blood, my blood and yours, sealed and unbroken. Right now."

Vincent interrupted again. "Liam. No."

"Silence," Liam commanded without turning his gaze from me. Vincent stood down as if he'd suddenly remembered who was in charge.

I rolled my eyes at the male display of dominance before

reminding them who I had in my hands. "Your boy is fading fast. I only cauterized the wounds, not healed."

Neverra came to Liam's side, not releasing her grip on his arm. "Liam, please, I beg you."

"You can't!" Vincent said again, causing Neverra to shoot him a death glare that made me reassess her power.

"Ticktock!" I shouted, reminding them who was still bleeding. "I feel his heart slowing."

Liam took a deep breath before squaring his shoulders. "Very well."

He flexed his fist, his rings glowing as he summoned an iridescent silver blade. He gently pulled away from Neverra before slicing a cut across his palm. Vincent let out a disgruntled groan as the others in the crowd began to whisper. Neverra held her hands to her mouth, waiting for the opportunity to save Logan. Liam stepped closer, a small pool of silver-colored blood in his palm.

"So, he does bleed."

Liam didn't respond as he stopped in front of Logan and me. His features were like stone, but they softened as he looked at his friend. I didn't look away, but shifted Logan so he stood more upright. Mostly because he was slipping, but also as a shield should Liam change his mind and try to kill me. I willed my double canines down and raised my hand to my mouth, biting deep into my palm.

I stretched my hand out, blood dripping to the floor. "Repeat after me. Blood of my blood, my life is sealed with yours until the deal is made complete. I grant you my maker's life in exchange for my sister's life. She shall remain free, unharmed, and alive, or the deal is broken. My life is yours after, to do with what you must."

He took a deep breath, and I held mine. I was afraid he would pull back, but he reached out. His thick, callused hand encompassed mine. I felt the power surge through me in a shot of white-hot electricity. It didn't burn like before, but sent my entire nervous system into overdrive.

That was the moment I knew I'd made a huge, horrible mistake. Images, quick and deadly, flashed through my mind as I stared into Liam's eyes. He didn't know my power, didn't know what I saw, but oh, did I see.

He'd been covered from head to toe in that silver battle armor, only this time I could see it so much clearer. A three-headed lion crest took up the center of the breastplate. No matter the muscles that wrapped his massive frame, he moved with the stealth of a predator. From the blood and viscera covering his armor, he was every bit the feared warrior king of legends.

He has many names, and they all mean destruction. I knew Kaden had been right.

The battlefield was littered with the small, thick bodies of creatures I didn't recognize. It was a massacre, but there were no armies, no one but Liam and the corpse of a massive serrated-toothed beast. He stood upon its scaled body, the skin shredded and its powerful jaws slightly ajar. I watched as he walked atop the head before jumping off. He jerked the double ablaze swords toward the ground, slinging the thick ooze from them. He stopped, his head whipping toward me as if he saw me, and I flinched.

The real world came rushing back as the lights in the room flickered, struggling to stay on. The air felt condensed, but neither of us turned from the other. I heard Vincent yell from the corner, begging Liam to think about what he was doing. The crowd shuffled backward, some grabbing the sleeves of others as they retreated. Liam glanced at Logan, his jaw clenching as he looked back to stare daggers into me.

"Blood of my blood, my life is sealed with yours until the deal is made complete. I grant you your sister's life, free, unharmed, and alive, for your maker's life, or the deal is broken. In return, your life is mine…" He paused, his next words making me wish I had other options. "… to do with what I must."

My palm burned as if it had been branded, but Liam showed not an ounce of discomfort. As soon as the words left his lips, the lights turned back on, burning a little brighter than before. As Neverra rushed forward, I released Logan. She caught him before he touched the ground, gathering his torn and brutalized torso to her. His blood stained her silk dress, but he didn't make a sound as he somehow found the strength to wrap his arms around her and hold tight. Several celestials joined her to help support him.

"We need to get him to a healer," Neverra said, cradling him.

A celestial pushed through the crowd, this one not armed. He went to Neverra's side, kneeling next to her. "Follow me. We will get a room set up."

Neverra's eyes raked over me, as if she didn't know whether to thank me or slaughter me. It didn't matter either way. I said nothing and turned away, only to find Liam's gaze focused on me.

My palm continued to burn, even as I felt it heal, and I wondered if I'd traded one monster for another.

EIGHTEEN
LIAM

"So, you sent a message asking for help, and when they came, you killed one of your own. Is that correct?" I watched her movements and gestures, trying to gauge her responses. We were currently in a lower level of the Guild. Upstairs, the staff was busy repairing the damage Miss Martinez's entrance had caused.

Vincent had refused to leave my side and had brought several celestials from his unit. She sat at the end of the table, its length separating us, but the tension swirling in the air was a heavy weight. Anger was such a powerful emotion. It didn't ease the situation that she was still wearing her bloodstained clothes, ash and debris clinging to her skin and hair.

Every celestial in the building was brimming with energy, and a wellspring of power hid beneath her calm façade. I didn't think she was even aware of the boiling intensity of it.

Her shoulders sagged as she sighed, clasping her hands together and placing them on the table. "Yes, more or less. How many times do I have to explain this?"

"Your explanation makes no sense," I said as I twirled the pen between my fingers. "There is no way you could have communicated with anyone while in your cell. We watched your every movement."

She folded her arms and leaned back in her chair. "Well, it's good to know you've watched me piss. I guess we're best friends now. And, as I said, Alistair, the one I killed, knew I was here. He had numerous spies on your precious team, and Peter was his mindless puppet."

Several people shifted and murmured, the tension ratcheting up a bit more. I raised my hand, and the room quieted again. Maybe having them in here was not the best idea.

"Spies?" My headache was growing, throbbing behind my eyes. The effort to adapt to this new world had been more difficult than I'd expected. So much had changed, and I needed Logan here to translate. I rubbed my temples, knowing he would be out of commission for a while, and I would not risk him while he was healing.

Logan had fought by my side in battles, both small and large. I had seen him beaten and broken after going up against some of the Otherworld's strongest. So tonight, when I saw him so close to death, the light of his power flickering, I had hoped to feel something. But there was no sorrow or fear, and the complete lack of emotion for someone so close to me was terrifying. Maybe I wasn't *feeling* the love and friendship for Logan, but I remembered it and my promises to him.

"Those spies look like your guys, but work for us," Miss Martinez said. I stared at her, realizing that for the first time, she had offered information instead of making me work for it.

"That's impossible," Vincent said. "If any of your kind got close, we would have known."

She glanced at him and shook her head. "Nope, but you might now. Alistair is dead, and any mind puppet he had should be dead as well. Enrique in tech, Melissa in weapons, Richard in forensics, and you know Peter in tactical. You may have a few dead bodies on your hands now that the puppet master is ashes."

The room went silent as everyone digested the information.

"Vincent. Take the others and see if Miss Martinez's accounts are accurate."

"With all due respect, sir, I am not leaving you."

I turned to meet his gaze, my stare brooking no argument. "That's an order." I saw his jaw clench and knew he was biting back his words. "I will be fine."

He nodded once before glaring at the smiling woman who was

quickly becoming a thorn in my side. Vincent growled low in his throat before spinning on his heel and leaving the room. His men followed, leaving Miss Martinez and me alone.

She watched them leave before turning back to me. "I don't think your friends like me."

"You and your kin have murdered several of ours through the ages. If you add in the recent attacks and the massive loss of innocent mortals we were charged with protecting, why would they ever like you?"

"Ouch, you wound me, Samkiel."

I continued, disregarding her comments. "Why betray them?" I knew there was more she was not telling me, and I intended to find out.

"That's what evil, terrible monsters do, or whatever words you spoon-feed your soldiers."

Deflection was an interesting skill, and it was obvious she was well versed in it.

"You seek immunity for your sibling; that I understand. But you risked it without any assurance I would agree. That screams impulsive and erratic, and I already know that isn't your style. Which leads me to believe you need my help desperately, and whomever you just betrayed scares you more than you care to admit."

Her eyes narrowed. "Nothing scares me."

"If that were true, you would not be here," I insisted.

She didn't respond, and I assumed her pride was causing her to say no more. We sat there in silence, the only sound that of footsteps above and beneath us. She finally sighed. "You asked who I worked for. His name is Kaden."

The name meant nothing to me. It was not one I had ever encountered on Rashearim. Given who they had targeted, I had assumed it would be someone from my past.

"I do not know that name." I wrote it down and glanced back at her. "Can you give me a description? Height, body mass, powers? Things of that nature."

She nodded, leaning forward as she listed them off one by one. By the time she was finished, I had a small list of sorts, but still, nothing that stuck out to me.

"That last power—you said he can bend land? How so?"

She shrugged, resting her chin on her hand. "He has this flaming portal thing. I don't know where it goes, only that what goes in doesn't come out."

"And the other creatures you mentioned, why do they follow so blindly? Does he have power over them as he does with your sibling?"

Her back went straight, and her energy bristled. I noticed that anytime someone mentioned her sister, she always had a visceral reaction. She knew it too and averted her gaze, trying to conceal the crack in her armor. She cleared her throat and deliberately placed her hands palms-down on the table. "To them, he is King of the Otherworld."

I wrote that information down as I spoke and did not raise my gaze this time. "There is no King of the Otherworld, for there is no Otherworld. That realm and all the beasts inside it have been sealed for—"

"Yes, I know. A thousand or so years."

My eyes lifted as I folded my hands in front of myself. "Good. You know your history. So, is this the reason you work for him?"

She was choosing her words carefully, but she was still answering my questions. "Working for, yes … and more."

"More?"

She shrugged. "Well, I was fucking him."

The word did not register. "'Fucking'?"

She threw her head back and laughed, her tone mocking as she said, "Oh, gods, that explains so much about you. Anyway, I'm talking about sex. You know, intimacy—that thing two or more people do, usually without clothes, but sometimes with?"

She made a descriptive gesture with her hand, and I rubbed the bridge of my nose before lowering my hand with a sigh. I was losing my patience. I didn't understand how she could be this bloodthirsty beast and yet make light of the grave situation we were in. "Yes, I am aware of what that is, and it is irrelevant. I need something I can work with, not past interactions. I do not care what you have been through, only how you can be of use."

A small laugh escaped her as she folded her arms and leaned on the table. "Since we're being honest, I don't give a shit if he wins or kills you or this precious family you have. I'll help you, as I said, but only if Gabby gets what we agreed on. The second you try to back out or double-cross me, you're dead."

Her threats meant nothing to me. I had fought and killed creatures far worse than her. Besides, I could not die, no matter how many nights I wished for it. True immortality had been thrust on me for the salvation of every world. It was a lonely, detrimental burden.

"It is sealed in blood, so you have my word."

She shrugged, sitting back. "I've seen greater men betray for less."

"Who are the other two that were with you? Since you and Kaden are mates, are they your children?"

"What!" The word was nearly a shriek. The shrill tone hurt my ears, and I flinched. She shook her head with a look of pure disgust on her features. "Kaden and I are not *mates*, or whatever you people believe in, and I do not have children. You know people also have sex for fun, right?"

"I am very aware, but a breeding pair of Ig'Morruthens made creatures far deadlier than their parents in my world. It is rare, but possible. I only assumed—"

She held her hand up, her palm facing me. "Please, never assume again. They are my brethren, or so I call them. Kaden made me, but they followed him from the dimension he came from."

"Dimension?" My brows furrowed. "As in realm?"

She nodded.

Unfeasible.

She must have misunderstood, or the man claiming to be Kaden was a liar. My father and the old gods had fought, leading to the closure of those dimensions eons ago. Nothing escaped, especially not anything that powerful or ancient, but I could not deny what I had seen so far.

"How many are there that possess the power you do?" I asked.

Her expression softened for the first time since I'd met her. There was no false bravado, no illicit comments, just sadness etched in the depths of her eyes. "There is only me."

My chest ached with an echo of a memory I did my best to keep buried. For a split second, I felt something. It was short and fleeting, but the way she'd said it triggered an emotion, and for a moment, I reveled in the ability to feel anything. As fast as it came, it went, a flutter of hope extinguished by my reality.

"But…" I cleared my throat, sitting up and folding my hands. "The others, your brethren, they are Ig'Morruthen, too?"

"Yes, but only I was made from Kaden's power."

"He made you? How?"

She avoided my gaze, as if the memory were too painful and poisoned her mind. It was something I was intimately familiar with. "My sister was dying. I offered my life, and he took it. That's all you need to know."

I wrote down everything she said. "Very well. So then, you were mortal before. Where did you come from?"

"Eoria."

The word was clipped, her tone crisp and cold. I felt the energy in the room change and watched her warily. The name was familiar, and it took me a moment to recall why.

"Eoria is a lost civilization, dating back a thousand years."

Her eyes held mine, all power and mystery. "Not lost. Destroyed by the fall of yours."

That put her age far greater than I had imagined. I was surprised, given how she looked and the nature of her speech. I flipped a page before continuing. "So, in all this time, he has not made another?"

"He has tried, but failed. The ones who have taken his blood turned into these winged beasts, lacking any mortal emotions. They are loyal only to him, following his every command. They are called Irvikuva."

I wrote that down next. "I have not heard of these *Irvikuva* before. How many of these does he have?"

"Oh, an army," she said nonchalantly, as if it did not just make this entire situation extremely dire.

"So, you must be of higher rank to him? Yes? Am I wording that correctly?"

She nodded. "Yes, so to speak. We would be what The Hand is to you. Tobias, Alistair, and I are his generals, and he just lost two." Her hands fisted, her expression going flat. "Except you all seem a tad bit nicer to each other. Some say he was lonely, having no equal or whatever, but let's just say he doesn't treat me like his equal." Then she realized what she had revealed and looked around the room before running her hands through her hair. "Anyway. Alistair and Tobias came with him, from what I hear. I never really questioned it. My only concerns were my sister and surviving."

She had given me more than enough information to determine that they were more of a threat than I'd previously thought. I would not be returning to the remains of my home anytime soon, not if she was telling the truth and was correct.

"My last question for you this evening, Miss Martinez, is what is it you are all searching for?"

She looked at me as if I'd asked her the most basic question. Her thick, dark lashes fluttered once in disbelief. Her aura changed, reminding me of the first time I'd seen her. I saw again how deadly she actually was.

"I am shocked you don't know. Kaden wants the Book of Azrael."

Azrael.

The chamber doors opened. I strode through, my helmet tucked beneath my arm and long white and gold threads flowing behind me. Logan and Vincent were at my heels, their spears drawn, wearing the same silver battle armor. The world shook once more, knocking the ancient scrolls from their holding places along the walls of Azrael's study. The ceiling cracked, raining fine white dust on the large desk. Azrael hurried around, packing as many items as he could into his satchel.

"We are out of time."

His head snapped toward me, his long black hair braided on either side of his face. The cobalt lines on his skin glowed a shade brighter at our intrusion.

"No, your father wanted me to take as many as we could for the new world."

My voice was granite. "There will be no new world. We can only evacuate a selected few. War is here, and I need you out on the battlefield."

He picked the satchel up from the table, the muscles in his arms tightening as he clenched it to his chest. "I cannot," he said, anger infusing his tone.

"You can, and you will." I nodded toward Logan. He stepped forward, calling forth another spear. He paused, his arm outstretched, waiting for Azrael to take it.

"I cannot!" he shouted, slamming his palm onto the table. "Victoria is with child. I will not leave my babe fatherless."

The muscles in my jaw ticked. That explained Azrael's erratic behavior lately. "A baby?"

Vincent and Logan looked at me but did not speak.

"I am sorry, my king. I follow your lead and do what is best for our people, but I must think of my family. If you fall, if the world falls, I may be able to transcribe a weapon strong enough to help the survivors, but I cannot if I am dead."

Azrael was the one who had helped me forge the rings that The Hand wore, helping me shape metal and minerals. He was my friend, even though his loyalties lay with the God Xeohr.

"You know this is treason, regardless of the reason, correct? Abandoning your guard while we are at war?"

"I am aware, and prepared to fight if I must."

I nodded once, reaching behind my back. Azrael straightened, dropping his pack and calling forth a weapon made of silver light. Logan and Vincent stepped forward to flank me, holding until I gave the order to execute.

I ripped three long threads from my back and stepped forward, placing them in his hands. "For your child. If I cannot save this world, I hope you find another one."

His eyes held a fine sheen of moisture as the silver weapon he held disappeared. He fisted his hand around the threads and grabbed his satchel. He placed a hand on my shoulder and gave me a small smile. "You are not like him. I am so sorry the other gods cannot see it."

The memory faded as Miss Martinez's face came back into view.

"You and your brethren are mistaken, I am afraid. There is no Book of Azrael. He is dead. A mere legend."

She raised a single brow and tapped her nails on the table. "Isn't that the same thing they said about you?"

I sat back in my chair, exhaling a breath. "This is more than enough information to start with. I will need your sister's location if I am to collect her. You killed one of his and have turned on him. From what you have said, Kaden will likely make a move against her."

Her back snapped straight, and her eyes flashed. She jumped from her chair, nearly toppling it over. "Yes, of course. I need to change clothes. I'm disgusting."

"I can quite agree with that, but you will have plenty of time to do that while I am away."

Her brows furrowed. "But I am going with you."

I leaned forward, grabbed the notebook, and closed it as I stood. "No, I am afraid you are not."

"Oh, yes, I am."

With a wave of my hand, the double doors behind her opened, and several celestials walked in. Her head snapped toward them, and a look of pure rage settled over her features when she saw the silver chains covered in runes they were carrying.

"Cuffs? Again? Seriously? I helped you!"

"Barely." I placed my hands behind my back and waited for them to proceed. "But the fact remains that I do not trust you. I do not trust that you will not attempt to stab me in the back after I collect your sister. You have already proven that you are capable of such. So, now I will have you wait in a cell below until I return. Hopefully, your sister is more cooperative."

She snarled at the advancing celestial guard. Then she paused and turned to look at me. Her eyes blazed as she glared at me. "I won't go."

The lights flickered as I lost my patience and strode toward her, invading her space. I stopped inches from her, forcing her to crane her head back to look at me, but she held her ground. Her attitude and demeanor made her height seem more than it was, but looking at her from this angle, I realized the difference in our sizes. Invading one's space was a scare tactic taught on Rashearim. Usually, the weak backed down, but knowing Miss Martinez, I knew she would not. "You will, or I will carry you myself."

The corner of her lips raised as she glared up at me. "You wouldn't dare."

Her failed attempts to get me to drop her were just that: failed attempts. My first impression of her was correct. She was every bit a Riztoure beast if I'd ever encountered one. When cornered, they would lash out by whatever means necessary, and that was what she was currently doing. She clawed, hit, and bit at any part of my shoulders and upper back she could reach. It was annoying but had little effect, which seemed to just make her angrier.

"Let me go!" she snapped, slamming another fist against my side.

"I offered for you to go peacefully, but you refused. Just as you refused when one of my men placed the cuffs on you, and you broke his nose. So this, Miss Martinez, is your fault."

"What are you laughing at?" she snarled. I knew she was not asking me, but was addressing a member of the team following us. The celestials we passed said nothing and avoided us, not wanting to get close to her, I would presume.

I adjusted her over my shoulder as we reached the solid white door at the end of the hallway. I raised my free hand, and the small electronic box came alive, running a thin light over my palm. The edges of the door lit up, lights running in parallel lines across its surface before it hissed open. That only encouraged Miss Martinez to increase her efforts to flee.

"This is ridiculous." She clawed at me once more. "What are you made of? Steel?"

The hallway behind the door lit up at our entrance. There were fewer cells here than in Arariel, but I only needed one. I stopped in front of an open-ended expanse and placed her on her feet before taking a quick step back.

The moment her soles touched the floor, she charged me. She stopped short when several cerulean bars slammed down in front of me, the runes transcribed on them turning in counterclockwise circles. The cell behind her lit up, showcasing the metal bed attached to the wall and a small bathroom at the very back.

"Seriously?!" she snapped at me, folding her arms. "So, bringing back your boy meant nothing?"

I placed my hands behind my back as I tilted my head slightly. "Please, do not assume that because you responded to a few questions that there is any trust between us. You are, in mortal terms, a felon. I do not trust you, and I will not risk anyone else's life. You will be fine here until I return."

Her expression changed at my words, desperation crossing her face as she raised her hands and wrapped them around the bars. Her skin sizzled, and small puffs of smoke danced off her palms. She did not wince or show any sign of pain as she stared up at me.

"Please, let me go with you. Gabby doesn't know you, and if you show up without me, she will be scared."

I nodded once before turning away. "She will be fine."

"Samkiel!" she yelled, and I stopped, my shoulders tensing. I despised that name, and a part of me wondered if she'd used it just to get a reaction from me.

I took a calming breath and looked back at her. "Vincent will be down to monitor you while I am gone. You should have fresh clothing in your cell, and you might want to take a shower. If you value your modesty, I suggest you change before Vincent arrives, for he is not to leave your side until I return."

"Please, let me come with you," she begged. She looked at me with those big hazel eyes and thick lashes. I wondered how many men had fallen for this act.

"No."

"Samkiel!" she screamed as I turned my back on her. I could smell the sickening stench of burning skin as she unleashed her fury against the bars. The celestials followed me out, the thick door sealing behind us and cutting off the sound of her protests.

I turned toward the celestial closest to me as we paused in the main hall. "Do you have the address?"

He flipped through a small tablet, and several pictures popped onto the screen. I saw trees lining a white sand beach, an ocean stretching toward the horizon. There were small domed buildings and one large one with a lot of windows. Barely clothed mortals were everywhere. I took the tablet, bringing it closer as I looked through the images.

"This is where we think she is. It looks like a resort of some sort."

"Very well." I handed the tablet back and turned to leave, saying over my shoulder as they started to follow, "Stay with Vincent. I am afraid our guest will be less than cooperative until I return."

I heard an audible gulp and a few feet shuffling as I left them there.

NINETEEN

LIAM

My feet sank into the sand as I landed. From the images on the tablet, I knew I was in the correct place. Sandsun Isles was a peculiar place for a safe house, but given how far it was from other large landmasses, maybe not the worst. Several mortals walked past me, their eyes lingering as they whispered about my attire. I was way overdressed for the environment.

The waves crashed against the shore, the sound a constant bass thrum. Giddy screams and shrieks of laughter cracked the air, causing me to flinch.

I am not at war.

I am not at war.

I needed to get this over with promptly. I took a breath to steady my rising heartbeat. The rustic brick path beneath my feet meandered forward in loops and curves, breaking off in multiple directions. One led to the massive multi-windowed building in front. I could hear every person residing at the resort—their laughter, snores, and screams of pleasure. There were two thousand seven hundred and forty-four mortals by the heartbeats I counted.

It was not a hideout at all, but a smart tactic, nonetheless. If Miss Martinez wanted to hide something precious to her, it was a good idea to put it in a large group where it wouldn't stand out. I passed beneath several trees, the path skirting two large pools of water with multiple people either sitting around them or swimming. It seemed idiotic, considering the ocean was mere feet away, but I had not been around mortals nearly enough to know if that was normal behavior.

I shielded my eyes as I entered the building. The lights were almost brighter than the sun Onuna orbited. I came to a stop, uneasiness gripping me. Several people paused mid-motion, staring at me as they whispered amongst themselves. That did not unnerve me. I had been the center of conversation since the day I was born. No, there was something else, but I couldn't pinpoint it. I scanned the room, but only mortal heartbeats took up this main area and the floors above me. What was it? After several moments of searching and not finding anything, I shook off the feeling, assuming the noises were just getting to me.

People gathered around a massive statue spewing water at the center of the lobby. Large potted plants graced the corners of the room. One wall was nothing but clear glass, showcasing a breath-taking view overlooking the rest of the island. Several mortals stood near or around two long, large white desks, like the ones at the Guild. The staff there was helping and answering questions for the guests. Maybe that's where I needed to go? I strode forward, looking for a way to get upstairs. If I could not find it, I would ask.

"Excuse me, sir? You seem to be lost. May we help you?"

Two men stepped in front of me, forcing me to stop. They were a few inches shorter than me, with matching black attire and a blue-and-white rectangular symbol upon the breast. Their posture told me they assumed some position of importance here.

"Yes, how do I reach the twenty-sixth floor? Am I asking that correctly?"

"Listen, buddy. I think if you belonged up there, you would know how to get to the twenty-sixth floor." The guy on the left spoke, reaching up and patting me on my shoulder. I turned my head to look at his hand.

"Please, do not touch me."

He gasped and yanked his hand back, cradling it against his chest.

"Son of a bitch, that was like the strongest form of static electricity I've ever felt!"

"What the f—"

A ding sounded from behind me, and I turned to see an elevator open. Several mortals exited as I strode toward it, ignoring the shouts from behind me and the mortals that stepped aside to let me pass. I slid inside just as the doors closed.

Several symbols lit up on the panel, the writing foreign to me. Every single language from every single realm I had memorized since I was a child overwhelmed my brain. Logan should be here with me, helping me as he always had. The lights dimmed as I lifted my hands and rubbed them over my face.

I thought of Logan and the way he had slumped against Miss Martinez as she supported him, his body beaten and bloody. The worst part was that I saw him bleeding, near death, and I had not felt a single thing. There had been no pain in my chest like when my father died, no immense rush of power telling me to destroy the creature who dangled him like a trophy. I was truly broken.

It was true what they said about the old gods, how their emotions crystallized over time, making them harder than stone. My father had shown me their statues when I was a boy as a reminder not to let our feelings define us. If we truly loved and lost that love, if our hearts were broken, it would destroy us. I knew I was on the cusp of losing myself. I'd known it the second Zekiel had died. He was one of my oldest friends, and I'd felt nothing.

I just wanted to go home, to get away from the gazes that begged me to be the person they remembered. That was why I was here. I needed to find Miss Martinez's sister and figure out what all of this was about so I could avoid war and go home. I dropped my hands and opened my eyes. Okay, I needed to focus. I scanned the small buttons and thought back to the languages and images Logan had shown me when I first arrived. There had been letters, numbers, and signs. Wait, numbers—I needed twenty-six. The images blurred as my mind connected. I blinked, and suddenly I could read them.

I pressed the number twenty-six, and the button lit up.

THE ELEVATOR OPENED ON A LONG HALLWAY LINED WITH DOORS. I stepped out onto a shiny stone floor and paused, unsure how to proceed. With a small shrug, I started knocking. After several awkward conversations, I finally found the one I was looking for. It was subtle, barely there, but I could feel the hum of power. She was like a small flicker of flame where her sister was a raging wildfire. The scent she carried was similar to Miss Martinez's spicy cinnamon, but with a hint of something more, something pure. I knocked lightly on the door and waited.

"Who is it?" I heard a small voice respond. It was followed by a noise that sounded like a small slap and a whispered, "Shit."

I scratched my head, pondering how to word it correctly without frightening her. "Miss Martinez works for me, and she sent me to retrieve you."

I hoped that was adequate. Shoes met the floor, and I heard shuffling inside. Then there was a loud crash and more rustling. I stared at the door, wondering what she was doing in there, and heard her say, "One minute."

I placed my hands behind my back, waiting patiently. A small ding sounded, causing me to turn toward the end of the hall. The elevator opened and paused as if someone had stepped off, but no one was there. The hairs on the back of my neck rose, and I felt my nostrils flare as I inhaled deeply. A small breeze traveled down the corridor, yet there was no scent, no footsteps, nothing.

Peculiar.

A small click pulled my attention back to the door as it creaked open. I had time to register that she looked very similar to Miss Martinez, but there were some differences. Her hair was darker on the top, turning lighter toward the ends, and her aura was striking. It was iridescent and danced around her, calm and peaceful. I stared at it, studying the colors, watching as they morphed to dark intensity as her arm swung out.

A forsaken blade sank into my abdomen. She let go, leaving the blade protruding from my stomach, and covered her mouth with both hands. I put my hands on my hips, glanced down, and then back up at her. Her eyes widened, and she stepped back a few paces as I sighed. I grabbed the hilt of the dagger and pulled it from my gut. "It seems you are more like your sister than I previously thought."

Her eyes bulged, but her gaze was focused behind me, her body frozen with fear. I felt my nape prickle, and my instincts blared an alarm. I spun to face the three figures. Their outlines resembled men, but they were nothing but a black void with tendrils of smoke dancing off of them. Where eyes and features should have been, there was nothing but darkness.

I flipped the forsaken blade in my hand and slammed it into the formless skull of the one nearest me. Its scream was a pulse of air as it shook and burst into a million bits of darkened debris. The two next to it bent their heads as if looking at the remains of their kin.

They snapped their attention back to me, their hands twisting simultaneously, larger copies of the forsaken blade forming in their palms. As one, they swung, aiming for my head. I darted into the room and slammed the door shut before turning to look at the terrified woman.

I grabbed her hand and placed the hilt of the dagger into her palm, firmly closing her fingers around it. "Take this. That door will not hold, and you will need protection."

She looked at her hand, at me, and then back. A blade slammed through the door, splinters of wood falling to the carpet. I grabbed her shoulders and shook her, trying to jar her from the fugue-like state.

"Gabby, focus! Hide behind any large object you can find," I commanded.

She closed her mouth and scurried away to duck behind one of the large sofas. The door burst off its hinges, sailing across the room toward me. I batted it away and faced the two shadow figures, brushing the dust and wood splinters from my shoulders.

"That was quite rude," I said. When the lights in the room flickered, I knew my eyes had changed to that pure silver glow. I rolled up the sleeves of my white button-up shirt.

"I am assuming Kaden has sent you for retrieval?" I asked, watching as they steadily made their way toward me. They did not speak nor respond to my question. As they stepped into the sunlight streaming in through the window, I could see they were not pure shadow. They had form and wore ancient battle garb.

Very well then.

A single ring on my right hand vibrated as I summoned the ablaze weapon. Their formless faces tilted toward it, and I felt another slight breeze as four more forms walked through the walls.

"Interesting."

I twisted my blade and stepped forward just as the one closest to me advanced. Metal met metal as I blocked his attack and sent my sword through his darkened skull. The other spectral creature came at me from the side. I twisted, meeting his blade next.

With our blades locked, I backed away as they advanced. Out of the corner of my eye, I saw one dart past me.

I dropped one hand from the hilt of my sword and summoned a second blade. In one smooth motion, I spun and threw the dagger at the creature, impaling it against the wall as it reached for the woman. I completed the turn, using my momentum to sweep the legs out from under the one I'd been fighting. He fell to the floor, and I dropped to one knee, plunging my blade into his chest. He shrieked and reached for the blade before bursting into ash. A third ran from the wall. I caught my sword before it hit the ground and pivoted as he came at me. I sliced the air, the tip sliding through his stomach. Shadows burst from the cut as he disintegrated.

Two more came from the wall, and I sighed. How many of them were there? One rushed me; the other went for Gabby. I slid under its outstretched arm as he thrust his blade at me, and I cut out the back of his knees in one fluid motion. He fell hard, and I stood up, slicing off his head. It rolled to the end of the couch before disappearing in the same smoke they'd come in on.

I heard a feminine scream, and the center of my palm burned, sending searing pain up my arm. My head snapped in that direction, and I saw one of the creatures dragging Gabby by her hair. He had a blade sticking out of his leg, but continued to walk toward the door. She fought, fists flying, but her blows just went through his body. I looked down at my palm and the glowing, pale orange symbol beneath my skin.

Blood of my blood, my life is sealed with yours until the deal is made complete. I grant you my maker's life in exchange for my sister's life. She shall remain free, unharmed, and alive, or the deal is broken. My life is yours after, to do with what you must.

The blood deal. She was harmed, and it was threatening to break.

I strode toward the spectral creature, and he stopped. Gabby's struggles increased, terror and adrenaline aiding her efforts. He dropped her and turned toward me, yanking his blade up to block my swing. His head hit the floor and exploded into ash. She coughed as she looked up at me, the front of her completely covered in his remains. I sent the ablaze weapon back into my ring and held out my hand.

"Come now. We are leaving."

She grabbed my hand, and I hoisted her to her feet. Her entire body was trembling, but she still stopped to pick up one of the forsaken blades. Hmm, maybe she was a fighter, just like her sister.

She clutched it to her chest as she looked up at me. "You killed them? You're so fast—and your eyes! Are you the one that came from the storm? Are you the good guy? Where is my sister? Is she okay?" Her questions came in quick succession.

"If you come with me, I will take you to her."

She nodded eagerly, and I ushered her toward the door. I stopped short when black smoke shimmered in the room. It bent and twisted, and I knew the creatures were reforming. Without asking, I pulled her to me, and she squeaked as I lifted her off her feet before heading for the door.

"I apologize for my roughness, but we must leave this instant, and I am much faster on my feet than you."

She nodded and clutched at me with her free hand, still clinging to the forsaken blade. I tucked her close to me and rushed down the hallway. I turned briefly, shielding her as best I could, and shot a ball of pure energy at the shadow figures that followed. The two my power touched disintegrated. The third jumped aside and continued toward me.

I had clenched my hand to call forth my blade when a pat on my back made me stop. I spun around, putting Gabby back on her feet and pressing her behind me in one smooth movement. She gripped the back of my shirt and moved with me as I backed her against the wall. A man—or something that resembled one—stood before us.

"So, you are him. The World Ender in the flesh. I am honored."

He was entirely encased in inky black armor, his head covered with a dark hood. One opaque eye stared back at me, the other hidden or missing. He held his hands in front of him, passing a small black orb between them. The shadow creatures emerged from the room and went to the man's side.

"You are their conjuror?" I asked, slowly shifting to make sure the woman was still shielded. Her grip tightened on my shirt, and I could feel her peering around my arm.

"Conjuror? You are from a different time." He smiled, and it was far wider than it should have been. "Hand over the whore's sister. That is all we came for."

"Such a derogatory term. And unfortunately, I cannot do that."

His head tilted to the side as he spun the orb on his palm. Shadows curled around his feet, and one by one, creatures formed until they surrounded him.

"Do you really want to risk more lives for someone that means absolutely nothing to you?"

"She is innocent. Therefore, she means everything."

The creatures next to him drew their weapons and stepped forward in unison.

"Then you are truly a fool. You can't save everyone, and soon this world will belong to him."

My wrist flicked, the silver ablaze weapon forming in my hand. The probability of ending them all while keeping her alive was slim, but not completely zero. I just had to be fast enough to cut a path to him.

The floor shook, causing all of us to pause and catch our footing to stay upright. The conjuror looked as surprised as I felt.

"Does the ground frequently shake here?" I quietly asked Gabby behind me.

She shook her head. "That's not a quake. That's my sister."

The words had barely left her lips when flames burst through the floor. The fire consumed the conjuror and his creatures as if it had intelligence. It burned hotter than the cursed Otherworld, destroying everything in its path.

A black figure shot through the hole in the floor and out through the ceiling. The hallway went dark, and a loud, piercing alarm went off as water rained down from the sprinklers. I shielded Gabby with my body so she was not blinded or scorched. The creature flew back through the massive hole in the roof and landed. The fire died quickly, as if sucked back into the beast. It glared balefully up and down the hallway before settling back on its haunches and folding its wings against its sides. It tossed its head as a shimmer ran over its body, and damp, raven-colored hair was thrown over its shoulder.

My jaw ticked. "How did you get out?"

TWENTY

DIANNA

"You son of a bitch!"

I stomped forward, my hands clenched into fists. The smoke alarm continued to blare, and water from the sprinklers soaked us.

"I told you to take me with you. I swear to any gods that are left, I will decapitate you if she is so much as—"

I stopped as Gabby's head poked out from behind Liam's massive frame. My heart stuttered with relief. The last time I had seen her played over in my mind, and my gut ached. I knew she hated me and was probably beyond pissed, but I didn't care. As soon as I'd felt that sting on my palm, I knew she was hurt or worse, and I'd lost it.

Gabby pushed past Liam and ran at me as her face crumpled. Her body collided with mine, almost knocking me off my feet. I stood there in shock as she squeezed me tighter, her head nestled in the crook of my shoulder.

"I'm so sorry for what I said." Her voice was a mix of whisper and sob. "I haven't heard from you in weeks, and then he shows up and not you, and I was so worried that the last thing you would hear me say were those words, and I'm so sorry." She pulled back. "I didn't mean it. I'm just so scared and—"

"Gabby." I reached up, cupping her face. The sprinklers above us died, and I gently wiped the water and tears from her cheeks. My eyes burned, her words meaning more than she knew, but I hadn't forgotten we were not alone or safe. "I know. It's okay. I love you. I'm just glad you're okay. We will talk about it later," I said, glancing at Liam.

Gabby nodded, remembering where we were. She tightened her hold on me, and I hugged her back before stepping away. Her body continued to tremble as she wiped her nose on her soaked sleeve and took a deep, jerky breath.

Liam was staring at us with the strangest expression on his face. I stepped in front of Gabby as she tried to compose herself, and I glared at him. He ran his hand through his hair, slicking back the dark, wet strands. His biceps bulged with the movement, and his drenched shirt clung to him, revealing muscles I didn't know he had. Gods, he was beautiful, but he was a complete and utter dick, and I was over beautiful but cruel men. So, I did what I did best and poked at the beast.

"You look like a drowned rat. Oh, and Vincent is downstairs and pissed. He is a terrible bodyguard, by the way."

Anger replaced whatever emotion had caused that look on his face. He took a few steps forward, stopping a few inches from me. Gabby shifted so that she stood next to me, her gaze wary. "How did you escape?"

"Escape?" Gabby asked, but neither of us responded.

I shrugged. "Oh, I broke my wrists to get those damned cuffs off. Vincent became concerned, so he rushed in to stop me, and well, here we are."

"It seems I will have to try something else, then."

I lashed out, pushing at that thick chest. Liam barely moved. "No, you're not locking me up again!"

He looked from his chest to my hand, the corner of his lips tilting. "Did you just strike me?"

"Lock her up?" Gabby questioned, holding up her hands and looking at us.

Liam ignored her, glaring at me. "I cannot trust you."

"Well, you need to learn, and quick. I didn't make a blood bond with you to have you keep me in a damned cell while you try to do everything yourself. Especially when it puts my sister at risk."

He finally glanced at Gabby and then back at me. "She was fine."

"Oh, yeah? Then you guys didn't just get attacked by shades?" He didn't respond. "Exactly. So, I say you needed me, and you will need me even more if we are to look for this book. You don't know my world."

His lips formed into a thin line as his hands went to his hips. The white, wet shirt strained over his chest and shoulders, momentarily distracting me. I watched a single muscle tick in his jaw before he sighed. "We cannot work together if you do not listen to orders."

"I am not yours to order around," I scoffed.

"Isn't that what you said with that deal we made? For your sister's life, you are mine."

"The fuck I am!" The way he said it made me want to light him on fire. I opened my mouth to set him straight, but stopped when Gabby slapped my arm.

"Seriously, D? Again? Another deal?"

I turned toward her, rubbing my arm. "Ouch! It's different this time. It's nothing like Kaden's deal."

Liam didn't say anything else as he stepped past us. Gabby glared at me, shaking her head as we both turned to follow him. Liam stopped, standing over the hole I'd made in the floor. It was one more reason he would hunt me. I watched as he held his hand out, his power dancing along his fingertips. The hallway shook as pieces of wood, brick, and metal came forward, sealing the massive hole as if nothing had happened.

Gabby sucked in a deep breath, slapping my arm. "He can do that?"

"Apparently." I rolled my eyes, shaking my head as I extended my hand in a wave. "Gabby, this is Liam—or as the old world knew him, Samkiel, ruler of Rashearim. You know, when it was still around."

He whipped around, his silver gaze so intense that I thought he would incinerate me on the spot. But he only glowered as he lowered his hands and headed for the elevator. "We are leaving," he said, his voice a deep growl.

Gabby walked ahead of me, our soaked shoes squeaking with

every step. She stopped near Liam and pressed the button to call the elevator.

"I am so sorry for stabbing you."

That got my attention. "You stabbed him? Gabby, I am so proud!"

They both shot me a glare as I held my hand up for a high five. I shrugged and lowered it as Gabby shook her head.

"Thank you for saving me. Dianna told me to protect myself if she didn't come for me herself. As you can tell, she has a lot of bad people after her, and they often try to use me to get to her. So, I am sorry." She smiled up at him as I rolled my eyes again.

He looked down at her with no contempt or ill will. "You're welcome. You should be trained to defend yourself properly, especially given your situation. And although it is unnecessary, I do appreciate your apology. Maybe you can teach your sister some manners." He looked back at me, his scowl returning tenfold.

I pushed past Liam as the elevator opened, stepping in first. "Excuse me. I have manners."

Gabby and Liam looked at me as if I had lost my mind before joining me in the elevator. I pressed the button for the lobby and leaned against the wall, watching as my sister continued to smile up at Liam.

"So, you're the one they all fear? You're a god?"

He started to respond, but I cut him off. "Oh, he is, and you should see the way they all cater to him. Pretentious is an understatement."

He gave me his death glare again, and I grinned at him, accustomed to the look.

Gabby's mouth fell open. "Dianna! Be respectful."

"Gabby, no."

"He saved me."

"Oh, did he? That's nice. He tortured me."

"What?" Her head snapped toward him as she shifted closer to me.

"And why did I do that, Miss Martinez?" he asked, tilting his head toward me and raising a single brow. "Do you think it had anything to do with you killing a member of The Hand? Or maybe it was your assassination of mortal ambassadors and celestials? Or could it have been that you attempted to fight and kill me, all while burning down one of my Guilds in Arariel?"

Gabby gasped. "Dianna. Tell me you didn't."

"Oh, you just had to say something, didn't you?" I pushed off the wall, my temper getting the better of me.

"I apologize, but I do not see the point of hiding behind lies."

"You are an arrogant asshole." I took a step closer. "You know, I know a man like that—and I betrayed him, too."

He pushed up from his leaning position. "Is that what you would like? You want to betray me? Go back on the blood deal you and I made?"

"Oh, now you care about the deal? I begged you to take me with you to get her. But no, you want to act like some big tough, macho leader who can do everything by himself. Well, guess what? You can't. If that were the case, your world would still be whole and not shards shoved into ours."

Liam was in my space before the words had fully left my lips. His face was inches from mine, his eyes molten silver. "If you mention Rashearim with such disrespect one more time—"

Gabby's small frame pushed between us. "Hey, let's all calm down. Please." She turned toward me, and I took a deep breath before spinning and heading back to the other side of the elevator. "Okay, tensions are just running high right now. All of us are filled with adrenaline and so forth. Let's just take a breath and try not to break the elevator."

I looked around, not having realized it had stopped. The lights flickered as Liam seemed to notice, too. He moved as far away from me as possible. His eyes slowly returned to normal, but Gabby stayed between us.

"Dianna."

I looked at her, my arms folded.

"Apologize."

"Over my dead body."

"Dianna. That was harsh, especially if you did everything he said you did. Plus, he saved me. Twice. You are not this vile, mean person."

"Last I checked, you said I was a monster." I didn't mean for the words to come out as quick as they did, or around Liam, but I couldn't help it.

"You know that I was just upset. You have never been a monster. Not to me."

Her words eased some of my tension, and my shoulders relaxed as I glanced at Liam. Maybe I was a little high-strung because I was so worried about her. I had felt my hand burn and thought the absolute worst.

Liam's expression seemed to soften at Gabby's words. Well, it was soft for him. He always seemed annoyed or pissed.

The quiet beep let us know we had made it to the lobby. The doors opened, but I made no move to leave. "Listen, I get that you're some leader of the universe, but that means nothing to me. Nothing. Her..." I stopped and pointed at Gabby, who gulped. "She is it. I don't care about Kaden's plan to end the world, or yours to save it. It's all just one giant cock-measuring contest, anyway."

The doors opened and closed as I continued to talk, neither of us breaking eye contact.

"But if you can promise that whatever you do, she can at least have a happy, normal life after this, then I..." I stopped and sighed loudly as I rolled my eyes. "I am yours. We have to work together and find some common ground, or regardless of who is stronger or meaner, we will lose. So, can you at least agree to listen to me, let me help, and not just order me around?"

He stared at me for a long moment as the doors opened again. The air felt thick, charged, and I knew we had gathered a bit of an audience.

He released a breath. "I accept your terms."

"Fine," I snapped.

"Fine," he said, pushing away from the wall and exiting the elevator.

Gabby and I stepped into the lobby and were stopped short by several celestials. I heard Vincent directing people to the spots that had sustained the most damage and sending others to check on the mortals.

Liam had closed the hole in the floors and ceiling, but from the flashing lights, it looked like emergency services had been called. A crowd had gathered beyond a barricade the rescue teams had erected outside the main entrance. I watched as several celestials urged the growing crowd away from the scene.

"Vincent, what part of my order to keep Miss Martinez at the Guild did you not understand?" Liam snapped as he strode toward Vincent. Well, at least he had a new target for his anger.

Vincent's voice was distressed as he pointed to where Gabby and I stood. "I can't control her. She brought us here with a thought. I had no time to stop her."

I laughed, covering it up with my hand as I caught Gabby staring at me, her gaze holding a hint of sadness.

"What?" I said. "I did what you said. I fought back, and now I have a way for this to all be over. You will finally have a semi-normal life."

She reached out, lightly squeezing my arms. "Oh, D, trading one powerful man for another isn't a way out."

"So, this is where I'll be staying?" Gabby asked, spinning around in the huge living room. The setting sun peeked through the large windows overlooking the busy city of Boel. The cream and white furniture in the living room surrounded a glass table littered with several magazines. A chandelier hung from the ceiling, dripping with small clear jewels. A kitchen took up the right corner of the apartment, and there were two bedrooms on the opposite side.

"Do you like it?" Neverra asked.

"Hey, at least it's not a cell," I said, trailing the two of them as she showed Gabby around. Gabby's smile faded, and Neverra glared at me. Oh, look, they were all like their boss. Goody. I was still wary of her, of all of them, despite the deal I had made.

Neverra smiled at Gabby and redirected her attention. "The fridge is already stocked, and if you need anything else, all you have to do is ask."

"Thank you," Gabby said before she turned and looked at me. She gave me a once-over and caught my gaze. Without looking away, she said to Neverra, "May I speak to my sister alone, please?"

Neverra's smile dropped as she looked at me. "Absolutely. I will be just outside the door." I heard her shoes click against the floor as she exited.

As soon as the door closed, Gabby whispered, "I'm in the freaking Silver City! It's too fancy. This is too much. And she is so nice."

"I find her a right bitch, but then again, I did bring her husband back to her half dead."

"Umm … what?"

I waved my hand. "Another story, for another time."

I stepped forward and flipped one of the magazines over before walking to the window. "Anyway, this is only temporary," I said with a shrug.

She flopped on the couch with a huff. "How long is temporary?"

"Until I find this damned book, or kill Kaden. Both would be preferable."

I sat next to her and rested my elbow on the back of the couch, propping my head on my palm.

She leaned her head back, staring at the ceiling. "I can't believe you're actually going to do it now."

"Well, you told me I needed to stand up, and I guess I finally listened."

She turned to me, folding her legs beneath her body. "But at what cost? What happens to you once this is over?"

That I didn't know. In my head, I had assumed jail or some weird godly prison. But in my heart, I felt that once this was over, I would be executed after everything I had done. I was well aware that Liam and his celestial entourage didn't like me, but none of it mattered as long as Gabby was safe.

"Honestly, I don't know."

"Did you even ask before you entered into another wager?"

"No."

She rolled her eyes, the act so familiar that it was soothing. "I hate that you do that self-sacrificing bullshit. You're not Mom or Dad, Dianna. You don't have to take care of us like that anymore."

I twirled a piece of my hair, avoiding her gaze. "We've been doing this for how long now?" I dropped my hand. "Fighting, protecting, hiding? I just want it to end." I placed my hands in my lap and looked down before confessing, "I killed Alistair."

Gabby sat up so suddenly that she almost fell off the couch. "What?!"

"They were transporting me to a different location. Tobias and Alistair showed up and almost killed Logan, one of Liam's men and Neverra's mate. Anyway, I saw his dying thoughts through his blood, and they were all of her." I stopped, pointing toward the door Neverra had left through. "That was it—no malice or cruelty. Everything he felt was just love and happiness, and I couldn't do it. So, when Alistair moved in to finish Logan, I killed Alistair."

My vision became blurry, and I tipped my head back, trying to stop my emotions from overwhelming me. I took a deep breath, but when I met her gaze again, I knew my attempts had been futile, and tears filled my eyes.

"You were right. I haven't been happy for a long time. I am not happy with Kaden, and I have been faking it for so long. These last few weeks have been terrible." I sobbed, and I couldn't seem to stop.

Gabby gathered me into a hug, and I wrapped my arms around her. She ran her hands through my hair as I quietly cried. I could always confide in Gabby. Sure, we fought over everything. What sisters didn't? But we always had each other's back. She was the part of me that kept me mortal and sane.

She patted my back. "D. You are my sister, and I love you. What he had you doing was wrong. You didn't have a choice, but now you do. If you can save a few people or make it right with the littlest of things, try, okay?"

I leaned up, looking at her as I patted my face dry. "I'll try."

She smiled and nodded. "And be nicer to Liam."

I scoffed, reeling back. "Now you're asking too much."

"He saved my life, and it was so cool! You should have seen how fast he moved when he was cutting those shadow guys in half."

"He is not 'cool' or anything pleasant, Gabby."

"I didn't mean it like that." She looked back down at the pillow she was holding.

"You always try to see the good in people. It's a terrible flaw." I grinned at her and hopped off the couch, running away before she could retaliate.

I'd made it across the room when I heard Gabby yell, "Hey!" The pillow hit my back just as I opened the door. Neverra raised an eyebrow as it bounced off of me and out into the hallway.

"Don't worry about it, just some sisterly bonding," I said, waving my hand. Her expression was familiar, but I was used to being judged.

A shimmer appeared on my left, and I spun toward it to see Vincent there. I growled, adrenaline pounding through me. "I will never get used to that."

"Hopefully, you won't be here long enough that it will matter," he said, giving me a once-over.

Okay, I deserved that. Neverra nodded at him. "What's wrong?"

"Liam has summoned her."

The word "her" dripped with acid, and a chill ran up my spine. My fists clenched at my sides, and I closed my eyes, feeling for the unrelenting static-like power. As soon as I tapped into it, I opened my eyes and grinned at Vincent. "Tell my sister I will be back later." He reached out to grab me just as I disappeared from the hallway.

"Summon me? I am not yours to be summoned!" I snapped after forming before Liam.

"Are you sure?" Liam tilted his head to the side, watching me as he relaxed at the end of a long table in what appeared to be a meeting room. He folded his hands atop the papers he had been reading as he met my gaze. "I recall you telling me twice now that you are."

My eyes narrowed, and I took a step forward. I felt the flame in my hand before I realized I'd summoned it. He watched me as if daring me to try it. The door behind me burst open, Vincent and Neverra rushing in. I quickly extinguished my fire.

"Vincent said you summoned me. Kaden did that, and I hate it."

Liam glanced at Vincent, then back toward the stack of papers in front of him. He waved a hand as if he did not care in the slightest. "I merely asked for your presence. If that is not the correct terminology, I apologize."

"Are you saying you're sorry?" I was genuinely shocked.

"Yes, Miss Martinez. Not all of us are beasts," he said, turning a page.

"Did you just call me a beast?!" I roared, the flame tickling my palms again.

He ignored my outburst as he looked back up. "Now that we are all here, there are some things we need to discuss. Miss Martinez has made it very clear she refuses to be left out, so that is why she is here … if she would kindly extinguish the ball of fire in her palm." He looked toward my hand, and I rolled my eyes before calling back the power. "Perfect. Now, any questions?" he asked.

"No, sir," Vincent and Neverra responded.

"Excellent. Let's begin." He waved his hand toward the seats. I took the chair at the other end of the table while Vincent and Neverra sat on either side of Liam. As if I didn't feel alone enough already. Just to be obnoxious, I got up and sat right next to Vincent. He glared at me, but said nothing. Liam ignored the byplay.

"As you said, several of the celestials Alistair had control over have died. He had completely destroyed their minds. I have funerals to prepare and staff unavailable as they mourn. Thanks to your efforts, Logan is going to live, but he will remain in the med wing until the end of the week."

I felt Neverra's eyes boring into my skull, and I swallowed a growing lump in my throat.

"Vincent, the leads you had have run cold. Movement has increased, but not by much. They are no longer actively coming after us, and I assume it is because Kaden has lost most of his muscle."

"Aww, you think I'm muscle."

They all glared at me, and I mouthed "sorry" before sitting back in my seat.

"When retrieving Miss Martinez's sister, I was attacked by a creature that looked like this." He slid a paper forward. He had drawn several of the shades, and the likeness was impressive.

"You can draw?"

They all just stared at me.

"Okay, not the point. Tough crowd."

His eyebrow quirked. "I can find no records of these beings in this world, and I don't recall them from Rashearim. As I was saying, I don't know what they are called, but they seem to follow and respond to a conjuror of sorts. If you—"

"They're called shades." Everyone looked at me. "They are a large clan led by Hillmun, and they are not morally good or evil. The ones we fought work for Kaden—or, well, they did. You won't have to worry about seeing them anymore, at least not that clan. Just add that to the growing list of reasons Kaden will want me dead."

They all seemed taken aback and stared at me in shock.

I smiled like it was no big deal. "Sorry for interrupting."

"No, that information is relevant," Liam said and started writing everything down. When he finished, he turned toward Vincent, sliding him the pages. "Add that to the bestiary, please." He looked back at me and folded his hands. "Do you have any idea where or when his next move may occur?"

I bit my bottom lip, thinking. "I don't, but…" I paused, knowing the next words out of my mouth would probably result in either his death or mine. "I know people who might."

"There are others that would betray your maker?"

I nodded. "Not everyone was keen on Kaden's latest obsession, and he has been brutal in his search. As a result, he has made enemies that have chosen to bide their time."

Liam steepled his fingers, studying me across the table. "And who are these people?"

"Let's just say I have connections."

"I would assume your connections are the same as his. So, tell me how you perceive them helping us if you, his consort, killed one of his generals in cold blood."

I didn't bother to correct him. "Simple. Kaden's ego is almost as big as yours, if not more so. He won't tell anyone about me killing Alistair because it would make him seem weak. He will not advertise that he couldn't control the woman he created. I would bet he is already weaving a story about how the great World Ender overpowered Alistair and took his favorite toy."

I hated referring to myself as such, but I did so, nonetheless. None of them moved as I leaned back in my chair, folding my arms. "So, you figure out what you are willing to do, while I go pack and say goodbye to my sister. Again."

I pushed away from the table and stood. Vincent's and Neverra's chairs went tumbling as they jumped to their feet, blades appearing in their hands. I smirked and pushed my chair in.

Liam held up his hand, and they moved to his side in unison.

"Forgive them. You remain a threat, no matter how much you help. You have one hour to prepare and say your goodbyes. Then we are leaving."

I looked at him sitting at the head of the desk with Vincent and Neverra flanking him. Their eyes were glowing blue, and their weapons were drawn, ready to kill me at his word. I knew it wasn't the same, but I had the sense that Gabby had been right. I had traded one powerful master for another.

TWENTY-ONE

DIANNA

"D, what are you doing?" Gabby called from the living room.

"Looking for wires, cameras, or listening devices," I said, reaching further under the table. I stood and placed my hands on my hips and sighed. "I know they have to have one somewhere."

"Why would they have cameras? Don't they have super hearing?" she asked as I scanned the room, narrowing my gaze on the shelf against the far wall. My heels echoed as I stomped across the pretentious shiny stone floor.

I snorted. "Please. Kaden has cameras all over the place, and not just for sexy fun times."

"Gross!" she yelled.

I snickered as I turned a chair over, checking underneath it. I found nothing and placed it back down before going to the nicely decorated shelves.

"Well, maybe they don't," Gabby said with a shrug, watching me carefully.

I turned, curling my lip at her. "Are you serious? You just met these people. You are too trusting, Gabs. It will be the death of you."

She frowned, taking one of the many pillows off the couch and wrapping her arms around it. "Maybe they are different. Not everyone is like Kaden and his people. Besides, you said these are the good guys, right?"

I ran my hand over every corner and crack, but found nothing. My frustration rising, I picked up a plant and inspected every leaf. "I never said they were the good guys, just that they are against Kaden."

After coming up empty-handed, I placed the plant down and moved into the kitchen. By the time I was through searching, every cabinet and door was open, and I had examined every pot, pan, and kitchen utensil.

"Nothing?" Gabby asked, her hand resting under her chin as she watched me.

I leaned against the kitchen counter, blowing a strand of hair from my face. "Nothing. Dammit."

"See, maybe we can trust them. Besides, you made another deal, and I am sure Liam can't break that."

I scoffed and rolled my eyes. "I guess so."

"So, what's the plan?"

"Go find all the flunkies who don't like Kaden. Maybe I'll beat them until they give me the information I need. I am going to search for that fucking ancient book with an ancient god who is as rude as he is powerful."

Gabby lightly tapped the back of the couch and sighed. "I feel like something bad is going to happen."

"I mean, probably." I shrugged. "But we do what we always do. We take care of each other."

"So, you don't trust him?"

"Not at all. You and I have lived long enough to know just how cruel and vindictive powerful men can be. He may preach that he wants this book to protect the world, but he has the same drive as Kaden. They are both after power, and that never ends well."

"So, what do you want me to do?"

"Be friends with them. See what you can find out and what they're really after. Get as much information as you can. Maybe find a way we can stay under the radar once this is done. I'm thinking of drinks on that beach you love so much. What is its name?"

"Liguniza Beach off the coast of the Naimer Sea." Her sigh was wistful as she thought of it. "Ugh, the water is so clear, and there's a cliff that overlooks the entire ocean. The sunset from there is everything."

"Okay, yes, we will go there, have drinks, laugh, and forget all about monsters and gods."

Our smiles turned into laughter that had my cheeks hurting after a few seconds. After everything that had happened over the last few days, it was nice to see her happy again.

I basked in Gabby's joy, knowing that everything I'd said was a lie. There would be no beaches for me after this. My fate was sealed, but maybe she could go. She and Rick could create the life she wanted. And if she befriended the celestials here, they would protect her. Then maybe she wouldn't be as alone once I was gone. That would be enough for me.

My smile died as a chill ran down my back. The hairs on my arms rose as that all-encompassing power drew closer. Our fun time was over. It was time to get back to business.

I pushed away from the counter, my throat tight as I said, "I promise to call as much as I can."

She nodded and stood, following me as I strode to the door. I pulled it open right as Liam raised his hand to knock. He stopped, lowering his hand as Neverra stepped up to his side.

"Miss Martinez," Liam said, looking over my head at Gabby. "Neverra will be one of two of your companions while we are gone. Logan shall join you in a few days. They will be staying here with you. With the recent attack, we don't want to take any chances. I fear you may be a target until this book is obtained."

"Sounds lovely," Gabby said. I knew she wasn't exactly thrilled. But true to form, she was taking it in her stride.

I gathered Gabby close in a tight hug. "Okay, I'm going to go save the world from impending doom. You just stay out of trouble."

She laughed wetly. "Out of the two of us, I am not the trouble-maker."

"That's fair." I squeezed her once more before pulling away. I held her gaze a moment longer before turning and quickly walking out the door.

Neverra stepped inside, and I heard her say, "What happened here?"

I reached behind me and closed the door as their voices picked up.

TWENTY-TWO
DIANNA

L iam sat in one of the lounge chairs, absorbed in his studies. An array of computers and readers surrounded him, and he had been hunched over them since we boarded.

I was leaning against a high glass table, picking treats off a silver tray. Plush chairs were arranged in comfortable groupings, and a liquor cabinet was tucked against the wall. I thought I'd heard Vincent say this convoy had twelve rooms. It seemed like a lot, but when they could go anywhere in the world, it made sense they would have space. The convoys had replaced trains once celestial magic and technology became one.

"You know, I'd always wondered if the celestials' convoys were nicer than the public ones used in the cities," I said as I popped another small piece of chocolate into my mouth. "I can definitively say that they are."

Liam glowered at me, which had been his response each time I said something. It had lost its effectiveness over the last hour, and I had started to poke at him just to see how long he would keep it up.

"We're going to have to communicate if we're going to work together, you know." I popped another piece of candy in my mouth and grinned at him.

His face held no humor, as usual. "I am busy."

I rolled my eyes as I pushed off the edge of the table and walked to the large window. We were passing through the mountain range, the various shades of green and brown broken by the foamy white of cascading waterfalls. I had never been to this side of Ecanus, and I never dreamed I would be seeing it from a luxury convoy.

I stepped away from the window and sighed, flopping onto the lounge opposite Liam's. That earned me another glare over the multitude of screens. "How much longer until we get to Omael?"

"Too long."

I had a feeling he enjoyed being stuck with me as much as I did with him.

"I just want to make sure we get there on time. Nym is a high-end fashion designer who rarely stays in one place for long."

He waved his hand toward me, the lights from the computer screens casting a blue glow over his features. "I do not see how a designer of fashion will be of any help to us."

"I told you, she is at the end of Kaden's..." I paused, thinking of how to word it. "...*friends* list. She may have information on a certain excommunicated witch that could help us."

Liam raised a single brow. "Excommunicated?"

"Let's just say she wanted a position, and someone disagreed."

"And this woman in Omael can help?"

I nodded. "Yes. She can also help with passports, IDs, credit cards, you name it."

"We do not require any of that. I can go anywhere and do anything in the world I wish. No one will stop me. I do not fear your Kaden, and I do not want to prolong this *journey* any longer than necessary."

The way he waved toward me when he said "journey" let me know what I'd suspected was right. He didn't want to be around me, and I most certainly didn't want to be around him.

I stared at him, sure he was joking. When I saw he wasn't, I scoffed. "Seriously? You can't use anything that is personally yours. He can track all of that. I killed a crown prince in Zarall, and Kaden watched the entire thing from the other side of the world. He has access to the type of technology you can't imagine, and he has solid connections. I want to stay off the radar as much as possible. Kaden has already sent his shadow assassins after my sister, and that was just a warm-up. I will not risk her because my presence annoys you. I know you don't know him, but he will go to extreme lengths to get..." I paused, the thought alone making me hesitant. "... to get what he wants."

I waited for him to continue arguing, since that seemed like the only time he wanted to speak to me, but he didn't. Instead, his eyes bored into mine, a single muscle ticking in his jaw. He lowered his gaze and resumed flipping through the screens in front of him.

THE NEXT FEW HOURS WERE MOSTLY SILENT. MY NERVES WERE SLOWLY getting the better of me as my new reality sat in. I'd had no choice. I refused to let Gabby suffer anymore for my actions and decisions.

The lounge chair was comfortable, and I tried to nap, but nightmares plagued my sleep. I woke as I sat straight up, clutching at my sides. Liam's eyes flicked to mine and held. He didn't ask what was wrong, and I didn't offer any explanation. There was no way I would tell Liam that I'd dreamed of Kaden's laughing face as his damned beasts dragged me back to him.

I rubbed a hand over my face and swung my feet off to the side. Then I stood and wandered to the window, watching the changing scenery. The snowcapped mountains were further away, and the trees on the hills were filled with color, announcing the onset of fall.

"We are almost there," Liam said.

I felt his wary gaze on me, as if he were afraid I'd set something on fire. I nodded, still lost in the nightmare. He studied me for a moment longer before returning to those damn screens. How long had he been watching them? Vincent had set up the workstation and supplied Liam with more videos before we left. Liam was using the travel time to continue to familiarize himself with Onuna. His vocabulary already seemed more normal and less formal. I wondered how smart he actually was. Learning history and languages as quickly as he did was no easy task.

"How's your head?" I asked as I folded my arms around myself and looked at him.

He didn't look up. "Fine. Why do you ask?"

I shrugged. "I figured you would have a headache with all the videos Logan and Vincent feed you. Learning the languages, history, and culture as quickly as you have is quite the task. Plus, you haven't slept since I've been here, and that's been almost a month," I said.

That got his attention, his dark brows furrowing deeply. "And how would you know that?" He folded his arms, the shirt straining over his chest and biceps.

"You radiate power. I can feel the energy you give off through the walls. Even in that fortress of a building, I could feel you pacing back and forth these last few weeks."

Fear flashed in his eyes. It was so quick I would have missed it if I hadn't been holding his gaze. "My sleep schedule is none of your business."

He wanted to play? Fine.

I tilted my head. "Actually, it is. If we are going to kill Kaden and find this mythical book you think doesn't exist, then I need you to be in top-tier-god fighting condition."

"I assure you I am fine." He shifted in his seat as if the mere conversation were uncomfortable. "Besides, I was more than capable of taking care of you and the shades your maker sent."

I shook my head and rolled my eyes. "It's honestly surprising how I can even sit in this convoy without being suffocated by your massive ego."

"It is not ego. It is merely a fact. I have lived far longer than you. I have fought and slain beasts far greater and more powerful than you or the shadow-benders Kaden sent."

"They are not 'shadow-benders,' and you don't have to worry about them anymore, since I killed their leader. That was the last clan known. The rest died eons ago—which is another reason Kaden will be pissed."

Puzzlement filled his expression. "Kaden would be angrier that he lost his allies than by the fact that he's lost his consort?"

The corner of my lips twitched. "'Consort'? What does that even mean?"

"You both derive pleasure from each other. That is what you said. Yet Kaden does not care enough about you to make you his..." Liam paused, his brow furrowing as if he were searching for the word. "The mortal word for it is *wife*, I believe."

I shook my head, memories of the last few years making me uncomfortable. If Kaden ever mated, I had no idea who it would be with. He never spoke of love or showed he had any experience with the emotion. It seemed beneath him. As long as I had known him, the only thing he truly desired was power. "That was not our relationship. Kaden and I are not connected like that."

"My point entirely. He cares about the allegiances he has more than his own consort. Which would not be peculiar, except for how close he keeps you."

"If you call me a consort one more time, I will incinerate this convoy with you in it."

"It is perfectly fine to have consorts. I've had many. Almost all the gods did—male and female—but they do not mean anything. *You* do not mean anything."

My chest tightened. I knew that, and it was one reason among many why I was here. "Gods, you're a fucking joy to be around."

"I do not know what that means."

I held up my hand. "You don't have to tell me what I do or do not mean to Kaden, okay? I already know."

He merely shrugged as he leaned back, all power and arrogance. Most women would want to climb him like a tree in that position, but I was imagining stabbing him again. "It was not my intent to offend you, Miss Martinez. If we are to work together, we need to at least be honest. Communicate, as you put it."

"Oh, so you *do* listen to me."

"It would be nearly impossible not to, with the high pitch of your voice every time you speak."

I shook my head, pursing my lips. Gods, he was a dick, but I ignored the jab. "That's another thing. Call me Dianna. You can't go where we're going and call me Miss Martinez. Everyone will know exactly who you are by the formalities alone."

"Because your kind are not polite?"

I snorted. "My kind? You really are every bit of the self-righteous, pretentious asshole they said you would be. I get it. You're a spoiled brat who grew up in a magical world where everyone literally worshiped your ass."

"Volatile." He cocked his head to the side. "That is what you are. One statement you do not agree with, and you lash out. Not to mention, you are very crass and rude."

"Like you aren't?" I snapped. I was already annoyed, and we were just beginning this journey.

"I have been polite. I have given your sister shelter while you are working for me, even though you blackmailed me into the bond by threatening the life of someone I care about. So please, *Miss Martinez*." He emphasized the words on purpose, which only set my blood to boil. He leaned forward, folding his hands in front of him. "Tell me how I have been rude."

"Everything that comes out of your mouth is an insult."

"Have you not insulted me? Or brought up things just to throw them in my face? Things you can't begin to understand."

I started to respond, but he held up a single finger, stopping me.

"I am not done. Before you dare bring up your captivity or the means by which I attempted to extract vital information, may I remind you, *you* attacked me and mine first. You tried to kill me. I also explained the consequences if you did not tell the truth, and you proceeded regardless."

I leaned forward in my seat, snapping, "Oh, don't play the martyr! Your precious Hand isn't around, and you don't have to save face here. You would have killed me the second I gave you what you wanted."

I watched the muscle tick in his jaw once more before he gave a curt nod. "You are correct. If you had given me the information I needed, I would have had no further use for you. Do not forget, Miss Martinez. You made yourself a threat, and one very similar to those I have executed in the past."

I leaned back in my chair. "Is that what you plan to do to me after this is over? Execute me?"

The corners of his mouth turned up. "I think it's too late for you to worry about what I will do to you afterward. Wouldn't you agree?"

I swallowed hard at the realization because it was true. It wasn't a surprise. I had considered the possibility, and we hadn't discussed the fine print when I made the deal. My focus had been on ensuring Gabby remained safe and alive. Maybe a godly prison was not in my future. Maybe he really would end me. I looked away from his penetrating gaze, watching as the mountains and trees zipped by.

"I changed my mind. Maybe we shouldn't talk."

Ding.

"Let me do the talking."

Ding.

"That should not be a problem, since that is all you do," Liam said.

I turned to glare at him, but he just stared straight ahead, his hands clasped in front of him as the elevator rose.

Ding.

"I'm serious. If she even suspects who you are, I doubt she will help."

Ding

"And why is that?"

"I don't know why, but some people are afraid of you." I tapped my foot, watching the numbers crawl higher.

"Good. That proves some of you are intelligent," Liam said, glancing at me meaningfully.

"Did you just call me stupid?" I snapped as the elevator doors opened. I shook my head and turned toward the open layout of her apartment. It was a large, bright suite with hardwood floors. Windows made up the back wall, showcasing the city. Various paintings of people in different poses hung studio-style and spotlighted.

I stepped forward and called out, "Nym!" I walked a little further inside. "It's Dianna. I hope you're decent."

"Oh, Dianna, decent is for old crones." I heard the patter of her bare feet as she rounded the corner and stopped. Her short blonde bob swayed at the abrupt pause. Her eyes met mine, and then she glanced at Liam as he came to stand beside me. "And you've brought company." She wrapped the sheer white robe around herself, failing to cover the overpriced lingerie beneath.

"Am I interrupting something?" I asked with a grin.

She waved a hand, still looking at Liam. "Oh, no. It's early. I was just making coffee. Come in." She turned, heading toward the hallway on the right, leading us further inside.

"This is Kaden's informant?" Liam asked, sounding skeptical.

I shrugged. "Kaden likes pretty little things that do whatever he says."

He turned to face me, his familiar scowl in place. "You don't say?"

I arched an eyebrow at him as if daring him to continue, but he just turned and followed Nym.

I shook my head and took a deep breath, trying to calm my nerves. As I started after them, I whispered to myself, "*This will work.*"

The living room was filled with artistically designed furniture that looked horrifically uncomfortable, but seemed to be Nym's style. A small kitchen sat off to the far right, and a bedroom with its door slightly ajar was behind me. Nym was in the kitchen, pouring coffee into cups that probably cost as much as a nice car.

"So, Kaden got you a new sidekick?" she asked as she placed one cup on the center island and turned back to the coffee.

I felt the charge in the room as Liam bristled. He opened his mouth to say something, and I kicked him with the side of my foot. He glared down at my foot, then up at me. I mouthed for him to shut up and slid my hand across my throat twice. His nostrils flared, and I assumed I'd offended him with my disrespect. We argued silently until Nym turned back around with the other two cups of coffee. We faced her as if in sync, both of us oozing innocence and calm as if we weren't about to rip each other's heads off.

"Yes." He forced a smile that looked more like an aggressive baring of his teeth. "I am to help Dianna."

Even if it was said with a growl, the sound of my name coming from him made my breath catch. Slightly shocked at my reaction, I explained it away as just relief that he was playing along. Nym nodded, pink dusting her cheeks as she pushed the cups closer to us. I took a seat at the island, and Liam followed suit, the stool creaking beneath his weight. I picked up my cup and sipped while Liam made a face at his and nudged it away.

"So, what's with the surprise visit?" she asked, taking a sip of her coffee and eyeing us both.

"Kaden has me," I paused, "well, us, on another *round-the-world* mission. But we need to stay low profile."

She nodded as she placed her cup on the table. "Sounds about right. So, what do you need? Cards? Passports? Clothes…?"

"All of it, really."

"I can do that." She leaned forward, her robe slipping down her shoulder as she placed her hand underneath her chin. I knew the flirtatious display wasn't for me. "So, what's the mission this time? Word on the street is that he's had all of you searching for some ancient artifact."

"Yes. We are still working on that, but Kaden has me going a little further underground."

She nodded, lifting a brow. "Makes sense. The Otherworld has been buzzing lately. I heard rumors about that freak storm in Arariel. Some are saying it brought something ancient back."

A chill ran up my spine as I glanced at Liam from the corner of my eye. He didn't move or shuffle, just sat listening.

"I think it was just a weird weather anomaly."

"Beats me. All I know is everyone is suddenly looking for a way to get on Kaden's good side, and they will do just about anything to make it happen. Well, except for me. I would rather stay out of whatever that man is up to if I can. I will do my part and then go about my business."

"Speaking of that, I know you helped hide an ex-member of Santiago's coven. I need Sophie's location."

She smiled, lifting her mug slightly. "Whatever you want. I would hate to face Kaden's wrath for refusing you."

"Thanks ever so much." I smiled, but my stomach sank at her words. I knew I was definitely on Kaden's bad side. The only thing I'd gleaned from this conversation was that word of Alistair's death had not spread.

"I need to make a few phone calls, but the passports shouldn't take more than an hour."

I felt Liam bristle next to me, but he stayed silent. I knew he didn't want to extend this little trip with me longer than necessary, but we needed these new IDs if we wanted it to work.

Nym pushed away from the island and walked toward the bedroom. Liam glared at me, annoyed about having to wait even an hour.

"So, how's Kaden, anyway?" Nym called over her shoulder as she entered her bedroom. "You know, I have not seen him in months. Tobias stopped by for the Omael Metropolitan Fashion Show two weeks ago, but only to pay me for my last little involvement. He seemed really uptight. Well, more so than usual."

I turned sideways on the barstool to respond to her. "Yeah, sounds like him. And Kaden is Kaden."

Nym returned, holding a shimmering black bag and her phone. "Well, at least you have decent muscle to look at on this long trip," she said, smiling at Liam as she stopped in front of me.

I fought to control my facial expressions. I didn't want her to see me cringe at her comment. She winked at Liam before handing me the bag.

"There are a handful of credit cards in there that are untraceable, and a few burner phones, because I know how easy it is for you to lose things. The passports will take at least an hour if I'm going to fake them right. I have at least a week's worth of clothing for you, but him…" She stopped and looked him up and down again like she wanted to lick him up. "Lucky for you, we are in Omael. I can get anything I want here, but your height puts me back at least an hour. I just have to make a quick call to one of my guys, and then I will get started."

As she walked away, typing on her phone, the lights flickered. I glared at Liam and pointed toward the lights. "Stop it!" I hissed under my breath.

Liam's nostrils flared, the muscles in his jaw flexing. "Another hour?" he growled, too low for Nym to hear as she walked out of sight.

I lifted my hands and pantomimed choking him. He snorted derisively, his eyes daring me to put my hands on him. We glared at each other, another battle of wills taking place between us. A light burst, raining shards of glass onto the floor as Nym returned with a dress tossed over her shoulder. Liam and I sat side by side, smiling as if I hadn't just threatened to choke him.

Nym jumped and laughed, looking at her light fixture before shrugging. "I swear, I pay so much for this place, and if it's not a random leak, it's the godsforsaken lights."

I didn't correct her, letting her believe it was a random electrical occurrence and not the ill-tempered god sitting next to me.

"Okay, I have someone on the way for passports."

"Sounds lovely. Thanks again, Nym," I said. I was smiling more than the news warranted, but I wanted to give the illusion that everything was fine and dandy.

"Not a problem." Nym sat her phone on the counter and turned her attention back to Liam. "So, your accent. I've never heard it before, and I've been from here to Naaririel. Where are you from, handsome?"

I watched his jaw clench briefly, and then his features softened. He relaxed as he looked at her, and my worry that he would blow our ruse eased. He smiled, and my breath caught at the devastating beauty of it.

"Far away," he said in the understatement of the fucking year.

WE HAD LEFT NYM'S WELL OVER SIX HOURS AGO, AFTER SHE SUPPLIED US with enough to get us through our little adventure. I was especially happy with the darkened sedan she had loaned us for the trip.

I yawned and rubbed my eyes. Why was I so tired? It was probably due to the stress I had been under over the last few weeks.

"That is the fifth time you have yawned in the last hour."

I sat up straighter at Liam's words and glanced at him. His eyes, like always, were drilling holes into me. I focused on the road. "You're counting now? Do my yawns annoy you, my king?"

"Do not call me that," he snapped.

"Why not? Don't you own the universe or something?" I mocked.

"Because you do not say it out of respect." I saw Liam's hand clench against his knee. "You only say it to pester me."

"Oh, look," I faked a smile his way, "he's learning."

Liam didn't respond, but his energy roiled in the small confines of the car. I stubbornly refused to admit to him that I was tired. After drinking the coffee at Nym's, you would think I'd have been more alert.

I drove deeper into the forest, the beams from the headlights jumping as we hit another small bump. Thick trees lined the gravel road, their beautiful colors dulled by the darkness. Adonael was a small city nestled against a forest that continually threatened to reclaim it. When the shards of Rashearim fell and sank deep into the planet, they carried minerals that set nature into overdrive. It was one of the few good things to come out of that experience.

The small wooden cabin was secluded, but Nym knew where Sophie lived, because she was the one who helped her stay off the radar. Sophie had been kicked out of Santiago's coven years ago for a little stint that had put him on the celestial's radar. Since her excommunication, she had been doing readings and spells for unsuspecting mortals. I think she wanted the cabin so far out for aesthetic purposes. She was eccentric, to say the least.

I pulled into the slightly curved driveway and placed the car in park. The light next to the door showcased a small wraparound porch. Several potted plants hung from the rafters, and a small bench covered in throw pillows was a welcoming touch.

I saw her silhouette through the window as she stood and walked from the living room and out of sight. Good, at least she was home. I opened my door and stepped out, my boots crunching against the small rocks. Yips and howls lit up the night, another reminder that the cabin was located in the depths of the Adonael forest.

"This is your friend's home?"

I shrugged as Liam came around the front of the car. He studied the house as if he were memorizing every door, window, and square inch.

"'Friend' is a stretch," I said and walked toward the porch, Liam at my back. "Let me do the talking, okay? I doubt she knows anything about me breaking away from Kaden, so we're going to play it off that I am still working for him, and you are just my overgrown, annoying muscle, as Nym said."

He sighed, and the porch light flickered as I knocked lightly on the door.

"Stop that! Play it cool. Just don't, you know, talk or speak or move much."

The door opened, and Sophie froze, her brunette hair swaying behind her. Her mouth went slack, and her eyes widened as she took in first me and then Liam.

"Hey, Sophie, long time no see."

Her eyes were like saucers and focused on Liam. She froze in place, and I snapped my fingers in front of her face.

"Sophie!" I dropped my hands and smiled. "Honey, you're drooling."

She shook her head as if coming out of a daze, but I knew it was something other than attraction, even as she plastered a small smile on her face. It was fear, plain and simple. I could smell it.

"Dianna. It's been a while. What brings you into town?" Sophie stepped back, opening the door wider, and we entered. She was apprehensive, but that wasn't unusual. If she still thought I worked for Kaden, she would assume I was here to collect on the debt. Add in the man looming at my side, and I am sure she thought it was a debt to be paid in blood.

We walked further inside, and Sophie closed the door behind us.

THE BOOK OF AZRAEL

The cabin had modern conveniences, but it looked as you would expect a cabin out in the middle of nowhere, owned by a witch, to look. It was an open concept, and from the entry, we could see the small dining area in the kitchen and the stairs that led to the second level. The fireplace in the living room was dark, but the thick fur rugs added warmth. The brown-and-beige color scheme gave the cabin a homey feeling, if you discounted all the mounted animal heads on the walls and the clear jars full of who knew what.

She walked toward the fireplace and raised her hand. A tiny spark of green energy flew from her palm, and the logs burst into flames. Sophie was pretty, especially considering she was pushing four hundred years old. Liam's eyes followed her movements, but I couldn't tell if he was looking at her ass in the tight spandex pants she wore, or if there was something about her little magic trick that had caught his attention.

"Look, I don't have a lot of time. I need your help."

That got her attention, and she turned to face me. "Oh, do you? I thought you'd all forgotten about me after my little mishap."

I snorted. "'Mishap'? You tried to double-cross Santiago, and he found out. You're lucky Kaden didn't throw you in the pit."

She shivered at the mention and tugged at the sleeves of her white top. "So, you're not here to collect my head or something?"

"Nope. I need you to keep it, and help me find an ancient artifact."

"The one Kaden has been looking for?" Her shoulders seemed to tense.

I cocked my head to the side slightly. "And how would you know about that, being excommunicated and all?"

"The creatures of the Otherworld talk, Dianna. You of all people should know that."

"How much have they talked recently?" Apprehension rippled through me, and I struggled to hide my unease. I wandered around the room, running my fingers over the jars lined up on a shelf. They shared space with various ferns, dust collecting on the jars she rarely used. A few held feathers, and one a weird foot from gods knew what. There was a jar of eyeballs that more than likely had once belonged to mortals, and another filled with insects. I picked up the jar with the bugs and shook it slightly.

"Why? Do you have something you want to hide?" She looked at Liam, her gaze raking over his form. Thank the gods that he remained silent. "New boyfriend, maybe?"

"No," I snapped in disgust. "He is here if you decide you don't want to play nice. Then we would tear you into tiny pieces."

She glanced at Liam and back to me, clearly thinking about how he could dismember her. "I'll pass on that. So, how am I supposed to find this artifact if Kaden's right-hand woman can't?"

Good. If Sophie thought I still worked for Kaden, that meant she didn't know about Alistair. "Don't you have a spell or something you can do? I mean, it's ancient and probably cursed, so you know, right up your alley."

She nodded once and sighed. "I might have a spell or two I stole from Santiago's grimoire."

I winked, placing the bug-filled jar back on the shelf behind me. "Knew I could count on you, Soph."

"Okay, let me run upstairs and get some supplies. I'll be right back." She looked at me and then at the jars behind me. "And please don't touch anything."

I smirked at her. "I promise."

She glanced at Liam once more before heading upstairs. As she disappeared around the corner, I stepped closer to Liam and whispered, "Good job. I'm actually impressed. You didn't say one word." He didn't turn or glance my way, showing no irritation at my comment, which was strange. His gaze remained fixed on the stairway as if he could see through the walls. "What is with the staring thing you two keep doing?"

He didn't answer, and his stare never wavered.

"You want some alone time with her? If she finds the book, I can run and grab it. You two should be done by the time I get back, and it might actually help to remove that large stick up your—"

"Your friend is lying to you," he said with such surety that I was taken aback.

"What?"

He turned toward me with a look of confusion on his face. "How can you not see it? The fidgeting, pacing, and lack of eye contact. Even if that were not the case, her scent alone spiked the second we entered."

"Yeah, that's because she's sweating over you, Mister Tall, Dark, and Annoying. Sophie isn't smart enough to double-cross anyone, and even if she did, who would she turn to? Kaden owns the largest coven, and Santiago hates her. She has no one."

He held my gaze and cocked his head to the side. "Neither did you, and now look where we are."

My smile faltered as unease twisted my gut. "I'll go check on her, make sure she's actually grabbing the stuff for the spell."

He went to lead the way, and I raised my hand, pressing it against his chest. I couldn't stop myself from flexing my fingers against all that hot solid muscle. "Wait here, just in case."

He looked at my hand, then back at me. "I am growing tired of you instructing me on what I shall or shall not do. I am the king of this realm and every realm in between. You do not *command* me. Remove your hand."

I did, letting it drop to my hip. "Yes, a king in another world, but not this one. Just wait. Please."

His eyes scanned mine, his nostrils flaring once. "Five minutes."

"What?"

"Four."

Realization clicked.

"Oh, it hasn't even been a minute yet," I said before heading up the stairs as quietly as possible.

The hallway was dimly lit and small. Pictures hung on the walls, but they were not of Sophie or her friends. They were impersonal paintings of flowers and landscapes, the kind you would see in a hotel. That was weird. I knew Sophie well enough to know she loved to look at herself.

I lifted a frame and noticed a receipt taped to the back. What the fuck? She'd purchased it today? I lowered the picture and continued down the hall. I passed a small end table with an assortment of knick-knacks on top. There were three doors off this hallway, two of which were closed. The third, at the very end, was ajar, and shadows danced within the dimly lit room.

"I told you she would come." Sophie's voice was a whisper, but it stopped me in my tracks. I pressed against the wall and crept closer.

"If she brought the World Ender with her, he won't come," a deep male voice responded.

I peeked inside and saw Sophie standing next to a large armoire, her hands clasped before her as she pleaded with someone in the mirror. The mirror held no reflection, only a dark, murky shimmer. I couldn't see or make out who she was speaking to, but I could feel his energy filling the room. It had to be one of Kaden's men.

"Listen, I can still bring her in."

"Let's hope," he said, and the mirror flashed before returning to normal.

"Well, once a traitor, always a traitor," I said as I pushed the door open and stepped into her bedroom.

Sophie jumped and spun. She met my gaze as she pressed against the dressers behind her. I saw her arms move and shook my head. "You have nothing here that will kill me. You know that, right?"

She swallowed hard. "You don't understand."

"What don't I understand? The creepy creature you were talking to in the mirror, or that you're not as excommunicated as I thought? Or maybe Kaden has been lying to me about a lot of things." The last part made me seethe. "How much did he offer you for my head?"

"Why does it matter? You would do the same."

She lifted her hand, and the door behind me slammed shut. I looked over my shoulder, knowing the sound would alert Liam. When I turned back, Sophie stood with a small crossbow cradled in her hands.

"The plan was perfect. Nym texted me everything. I will take you back to Kaden. Once he is done with you, I'll be back in the coven, and Nym will get a seat next to Kaden."

Before I had time to react, she pulled the trigger. Instead of one single arrow flying at me, several small needle-like projectiles raced through the air. They hit me square in the chest, knocking me onto my back.

I propped myself up on my elbows as my canines descended. I was going to rip her to shreds. She stood at my feet, a smile nearly splitting her face.

"This won't kill me, you dumbass," I snarled, looking up at her.

She placed a hand on her hip, lowering the crossbow. "No fucking duh. But that coffee you drank at Nym's had a little extra something in it. I'm sure you've been feeling the effects. The arrows carry the same poison. I think I'm going to like being rich, and I can't wait to be back in the coven. I will rule alongside Kaden as Onuna burns."

The strength seeped from my arms, and I collapsed back on the floor. Poison? They had poisoned me! Nym had double-crossed me. I looked down at the needles sticking out of my chest and tried to reach for them. But my arm was too heavy, and my hand dropped to my side before I could touch them. I coughed, my throat starting to ache as darkness played at the edges of my vision.

"Trust me," my voice was cracked and weak, "that's not a seat you want."

"Says the one who has all the power. You wouldn't understand. You've always been Kaden's favorite." She pressed her foot against the needles, forcing them deeper into my body. I gritted my teeth, fighting against the pain. "Now, I am going to hide you in the closet and go downstairs to distract the World Ender until my backup arrives."

A wave of nauseating dizziness washed over me, and I knew I wouldn't be conscious much longer. Sophie leaned down, looking at me with a smug smile as she waved. "Night night, bitch."

Then the door exploded with a loud boom, the ground shaking as shards of wood erupted into the room. Sophie's eyes went wide, and she lifted the crossbow, aiming it above me. She had no time to pull the trigger before an invisible force sent her flying. Liam stepped over me as the room flickered in and out of focus. A whoosh sliced through the air, followed by a solid thud.

The world went black, but a tug and a sharp, piercing pain in my chest pulled me back to reality. I wavered in and out of consciousness, Liam's irritation a familiar comfort in a sea of agony.

Tug.

"—infuriating—"

Tug.

"—disobedient—"

Tug.

"—aggravating woman—"

As the last needle left my chest, I felt like I was floating. I was cradled against a hard, warm surface, my arms and legs hanging limply. My eyesight grew blurry, the effects of the poison taking over. The last thing I saw was Sophie's head near the foot of her bed, her dead eyes unmoving and staring.

TWENTY-THREE

DIANNA

"Bounty on your head."

"Let me go."

"Never."

"Kaden wants his bitch back."

"A seat next to Kaden."

My eyes refused to open even as I lurched into a sitting position. A wave of nausea flooded me, and I expelled the contents of my stomach. I felt someone holding me, hands gripping the back of my neck. As my body tried to slump, strong arms propped me up. Something warm washed over my lips and the side of my face before I was gently laid back down. Everything hurt, and even with my eyes closed, the world was spinning.

A thick, sweet liquid filled my throat, and a pleasant coolness took away the pain as I drifted off once more. There was no more stomachache, no more dizziness, just darkness seeping in and encompassing me once more.

MY EYES POPPED OPEN, AND I FROZE. "I'M DEAD. I FUCKING KNOW IT."

A huge golden door flanked by massive twin torches stood before me. The flames flickered and danced much higher than any I had ever seen. Ancient carvings were etched into the surface of the door, depicting a battle I was not familiar with. Through that door must be the final judgment before I was sent to Iassulyn.

I looked down and saw I still wore the white tank, dark jeans, and heels. I pulled at my shirt and peeked at my chest, but saw no trace of Sophie's attack. Weird. Well, if I was dead, at least I would be comfortable and fashionable while I haunted people.

Wait—what about Gabby? I turned, trying to find a way out. I needed to get back to Gabby. She would be alone and definitely angry if I died. What if Liam didn't uphold his part of the bargain because we hadn't found the book?

I stopped, distracted by the carvings on the walls. They matched the door, and there were so many scenes. Some were depictions of battles, while others were of people doing everyday tasks. Torches lined the hall as far as I could see, long crimson silk curtains blowing in the wind. The area was dark except for the dim flicker of the flames.

"Hello?" I yelled, turning in a circle. "Anyone home? Do I request a final judgment, or are we all just aware I shouldn't be here? The joke is on me. I get it now. Come out!"

To my surprise, no one answered. You would think a big place like this would be crawling with people.

Frustrated, I was about to yell obscenities to see if that got a reaction when I heard footsteps approaching from down the hall. It sounded like just one person, and they were coming in fast.

Okay, well, great job, Dianna. You probably pissed off an ancient beast. I retreated, looking for a place to hide. Whoever or whatever was coming was in a hurry.

I kept moving backward, afraid to turn my back, my hands searching for the wall behind me. I took one last step and blinked. When I opened my eyes, a wall with deep carvings took up my vision.

Did I just walk through a wall? What is happening?

I spun, and my breath caught as I took in the expansive room. I took one step and then another, my shoes not echoing on the shiny stone floor. The absence of sound was deafening. I stopped in the middle of the room to take it all in, my gaze catching first on the golden columns standing tall in the corners. Sheer fabric hung from the massive carved windows and danced as if blown by a soft current of air. I tipped my head back and spun in a small circle, gaping at the night sky.

Oh, shit.

I definitely was not on the mortal plane anymore. The galaxy I saw through the half-missing roof was made of stars and planets that did not belong to my world. They lit up the cold sky, the colors ranging from reds to purples and a mix of blues. Meteors streaked through the empty spaces as the nebulae spun. It was the most beautiful thing I had ever seen. No painting or image could compare.

Grunts and moans pulled me from my admiration of the extraordinary view, and I realized I was not in some fancy mausoleum, but in someone's bedroom. What prick would have a room with an open ceiling showcasing the freaking galaxy?

There was more rustling, and I crept toward the sound. A four-poster bed emerged from the darkness, fabric draped around the spiraling spires at each corner. My eyes locked on the couple, and I stopped, afraid to make my presence known. I watched as soft feminine legs were thrown over thick masculine shoulders, her ankles linking behind his head. He thrust into her, eliciting a chorus of screams and groans in both feminine and masculine tones.

Nails raked down a muscled back, leaving small pink scratches in their wake. He hissed and gathered her hands, holding them at the wrist above her head. Desire flared and coiled in me as I watched that powerful body slam into hers. She screamed a name, and the heat pooling at my core was extinguished as if someone had dumped a bucket of cold water on me.

I should have noticed sooner, given the glowing silver tattoos marking his entire body, but I had never seen him naked. I knew this scene would forever be burned into my memories. The realization came with a pang of disappointment.

Fucking Liam.

"Please don't stop," the woman groaned.

A gruff response followed, making me want to throw up.

I have died, and this is my punishment. This is worse than Iassulyn. I threw my hands up and looked away from the erotic thrust of his hips. I didn't know how I had ended up in Liam's memories. It was impossible, unless—

I paused as the realization of what was happening hit me. I was in a fucking blooddream! My hands went to my face, covering my eyes as I shook my head. "No, no, no, no..."

I dropped my hands, looking at my palm where I had cut it. A small, thin scar ran parallel to the lines, and I knew Liam had one to match after that stupid blood deal. But if that were the cause, I would have dreamed sooner, especially since I'd napped on the convoy. Unless he'd fed me? My chest tightened. Had I been so close to death that he'd been afraid I would die? Had he fed me to keep me alive?

"You idiot!" I kicked the bed where he and whoever this mystery woman was were currently switching positions. "Why would you do that?" I said, choking out the words.

It was a drawback of being what I was. If I drank too much or *ate* somebody, fragments of their memories would bleed into mine. I couldn't control the blooddreams, and I hated the images and emotions that came with them. That, among other reasons, was why I tried not to consume blood. Fortunately, the dreams rarely lasted long, and with the sounds coming from the bed, I was pretty sure they would finish soon.

I looked around, wondering why the memory was important to him. I got that he was a guy, but typically the memories I saw in blooddreams had affected the being profoundly. Usually, what I saw were acts or feelings of such emotional impact that they had become a part of what made the individual who they were. Maybe it was because of this mystery woman? Was she a long-lost love, a fling, or maybe an ex-wife? Liam didn't carry the mark of the Ritual of Dhihsin on his hands, just those silver rings, so I knew he wasn't mated.

I felt my chest tighten at the thought of Liam being bound, but before I could process the emotion, the large doors behind me burst open, and a tall man strode into the room. I knew this man. His long, braided hair was decorated with bright jewels. I had become accustomed to the blue lines that ran along his arms and neck to pool like indigo flames in his eyes. Every member of The Hand had that same shine. Logan wore what reminded me of a mix between a tunic and battle armor, one side of his chest exposed.

"Samkiel! My apologies, but your father fast approaches," Logan said, closing the door and striding straight through me as if I were a ghost. He tossed the sheer curtains around the bed aside as the woman gasped, surprised by the intrusion.

I tore my gaze away from Liam as Logan's words sank in. Liam's father was headed this way. I knew I was in a blooddream, but the thought of seeing him filled me with unease. Kaden had told us stories about how powerful and cruel the gods were. One touch could turn a being into dust, and their anger could make the very stars tremble. Their weapons carried more power than the sun, and they were more than happy to turn them on us.

"You were supposed to distract him, Nephry," Liam said, his voice husky. So, Nephry was Logan's real name.

Liam climbed off the bed, wrapping a sheet around his hips, but not before Logan and I got a good look at all his assets. Why was I not surprised that he wasn't lacking in that department either? Why couldn't it be small and not practically a third leg?

I studied him openly, deciding that I would take the opportunity to look my fill. He was gorgeous, after all. The Liam of the blooddream was different. He wasn't the Liam I knew. He seemed happier and less irritable, but still with that cocky attitude. The Liam of Rashearim was younger and unbroken, with an aura that reeked of arrogance.

Unlike when I'd first met him, only a dark stubble shadowed the perfect line of Liam's jaw, with no sign of that ghastly beard he had arrived with. His dark hair lay in heavy waves on his massive shoulders. Health, youth, and vitality emanated from him. His eyes burned molten mercury, and every time he moved, the silvery glow seemed to gild his skin. It was as if his power were looking for a way out. I understood now why I could sense him any time he was in my vicinity. He wasn't just powerful. He was power.

Liam took a step toward Logan, but his gaze was focused on the door. "How long before he arrives?"

Maybe it was because I hadn't had sex in a month, but Liam naked was a work of fucking art. I would never tell him, but seeing him even half naked made my mouth water, my nipples tighten, and my core clench. I couldn't deny my physical responses to him, but it changed nothing. He was still a prick.

"I did as much as I could. I even got the nymphs to play a little song," Logan said, waving toward the closed door behind him.

Liam patted his friend on the shoulder as he strode past him to the table. He poured something into a golden cup. "I missed another coronation, so it is without question he will be ill-tempered."

"Another coronation, Samkiel?" the woman said, her voice still husky with pleasure. She swung her legs off the side of the bed and stood. The soft light gilded her pale skin, and she nearly glowed with feminine beauty. Her gorgeous long blonde hair swayed over her shoulders as she moved, the curls that fell forward barely concealing the soft swell of her breasts. I had witnessed their wild play, but not one shiny strand was out of place.

I threw my hands up and said out loud, "You've got to be kidding me. Is everyone here perfect?"

It only got worse when she turned and walked with elegant grace to a chair, picking up a long embroidered dress. Her every move was poetry in motion, the soft light streaming through the broken ceiling caressing her lean feminine curves. The glowing lines of color that traced her delicate form matched Logan's. I was surprised that she was a celestial, because she was everything a goddess should be, stunning from head to toe.

"Hello, Imogen. Looking ravishing as always," Logan said, winking at her.

"No more ravishing for me, thanks. Samkiel has taken care of that aplenty." She smiled, clasping the dress together at the back.

"I'm sure he has." Logan smirked, looking at his friend.

Liam shrugged mid-sip, his eyes filled with smug male satisfaction. He finished his drink before giving Imogen a devastating smile. "Do you blame me?"

Oh, gods. I was going to be sick if I had to watch Liam flirt.

Before I had a chance to find a way out or force myself to wake up, the air in the room shifted. Logan and Imogen straightened, and Liam's expression turned sullen. I felt the power coming our way even in the blooddream and fought the urge to flee. I heard what sounded like a small army approaching as Logan went to stand by Imogen.

The door opened, and several guards entered. They spread out, standing against the walls in pockets of shadows. A man, much taller than Liam but built almost identically, strolled in. His hair was nearly the same length as Liam's, but instead of falling in waves, it was coiled in a mass of long thick curls that draped down his back. A few strands were twisted with golden bands that shone against the starlight spilling in. The shine of the encrusted jewels was a beautiful contrast to his rich brown skin. A dark beard lined his jaw, adding to its strength instead of concealing it. I now knew where Liam received his devastating good looks.

He gripped a long gold spear in his right hand, the shaft glowing and a golden light pulsing near the bladed tip. The staff was engraved with what I recognized as the language of the gods, the same runic letters etched deep into his battle armor. They circled the three-headed lion on his breastplate and pulsed gold on every metal piece he wore, including the skirt that met the tops of his leather boots.

The power he emanated reminded me of Liam's, except his seemed to take up the entire room. Even in the dream, with my senses dulled, I could feel it. It was as if I had opened the door to be greeted by the sun.

I backed away, feeling the hairs on my arms rise. The Ig'Mor-ruthen in me whipped and coiled, sensing danger and clawing to escape. My every instinct knew he was a threat, and I knew who he was.

The God Unir.

Imogen and Logan knelt, their heads bowing as he entered.

"Father," Liam said simply, meeting Unir's gaze.

"Where were you?" Unir asked, the words making the room vibrate.

"If you are here, you need not ask," Liam sniped coldly.

He took one look around the room, motioning for Logan and Imogen to stand. "Leave us."

Imogen looked once more at Liam before a vibrant blue light encased the two of them. My gaze followed them as they shot through the open ceiling and into the sky. My heart twisted as I remembered how Zekiel had done the same in his death. I took a deep breath and returned my gaze to the stare-off that was happening between father and son.

"That means all of you!" Unir bellowed, driving the butt of the staff against the stone floor.

The room shook, the power inside of him roiling. I backed up, my instincts screaming at me to run as the entire room threatened to explode. Liam didn't even flinch, unfazed by his father's display of anger.

The guards quickly dispersed, closing the door behind them. Unir sighed and shook his head before taking a seat and leaning the staff against the wall. He stretched his legs out in front of him and propped his elbow on the arm of the chair. He rubbed the bridge of his nose, and I smiled, having seen Liam do the same many times. It was obvious where he had picked up the habit.

"Would you like some, Father?" Liam asked, pouring another cup of the golden liquid.

"No," Unir retorted sharply. Now I knew where Liam had gotten that from, too. Unir's eyes were still closed, as if the god had a headache. "You drive me mad, my son. A simple task is what I ask of you, and you still cannot complete that."

"I hardly see how it is of major importance, Father. It was a coronation service for celestials who survived a battle a mere child could have won."

"It is of great importance that their *king* shows his face. Instead, you hide it between a woman's thighs."

Liam pointed to his father with a single finger. "To be fair, I'd accomplished that task well before the coronation began."

"Samkiel."

"We keep training our warriors for a threat that may never come," Liam said, taking another sip.

"It is better to be prepared for war than for war to come and you are not," Unir said, meeting Liam's gaze.

"I am prepared, just like the rest of the celestials. I formed The Hand, and they train day in and day out. Besides, we have you and the other gods. No one would dare invade Rashearim." Liam smirked and set his glass down.

"Do you hear yourself? When you speak, your words drip with pride, self-righteousness, and arrogance." Unir's eyes flashed with irritation, and I had to agree with his dad on that one.

"Perhaps. Or perhaps I just do not see the importance." Liam shrugged—and before I registered what was happening, Unir was across the room, knocking the glasses and wine off the table.

"You do not see! How could you? All you see are your own selfish desires. The many lovers, the liquor, the gatherings you attend with your friends. They are not your friends! We did not make them for that purpose. Their purpose is to serve, obey, and fight when we war!" Unir bellowed.

Normal people backed down when someone that massive and full of power advanced or raised their voice, but not Liam. He didn't move as he watched his father. "You speak to me as if I am not your son. I know the ancient laws. You've made me eat them, forcing them down my throat on a daily basis since I was an infant, and I know of my *friends.* They are sentient beings, and they feel just as I do. If they are given a purpose they believe in, they will follow. Why do you think they left the other gods? It is because I do not see them as objects to control."

Unir ran his hand over his face and nodded. "The other gods see this. They see it and fear a rebellion within our ranks."

"A rebellion? From who?"

"You."

"How?"

"The weapon of Oblivion you carry. You have ended worlds, and now you gather their soldiers to fight for you. Thoughts of an uprising tease their minds."

Weapon of Oblivion? What did that mean?

"I would never. I do not even wish to lead. That is your dream, not mine. I was born into this and had no choice."

Unir tilted his head back as if he was truly exhausted. "There must always be one ruler. You know this. Otherwise, the realms would tear themselves apart. There has to be one constant, one king who puts their own selfish desires aside for the greater good. A god must not be selfish. That is the utmost law."

Liam sat on the steps that led to the dais where his massive bed rested. He ran his thumb along the rim of the golden chalice he still held. "But why does it have to be me? Give it to Nismera. She is next in line."

"She was, until your birth. Now the crown falls to you. You are my only child." Unir met Liam's gaze. Emotion, nearly violent in its intensity, flashed across his face. "I will bear no more."

"Why?"

"You know why."

"Because of what happened to Mama? You are afraid of what could happen to another?"

"No." Unir took a deep breath and rubbed the back of his neck, the action almost mortal. He looked away as a hint of sadness danced across his features. "I loved your mother, and I will never love another. You know our relationship was secret at first. Eventually, the truth came out, and I had to defend that which I held dear."

"Like you do with me?"

Unir smiled and said, "Similar, yes. The gods do not like sharing their gifts, even if the ones before us and the ones before them handed them down. So, yes, I understand why you care for your friends. You see them for what they are, not what they were made for, the same way I did with her. It is truly a gift, Samkiel. I do not wish you to lose that, but they will never accept it. Wars have been fought over simpler things than a title. My visions have gotten worse recently. I see worlds burning, realms ripped apart, and battles in which far too many die. So, yes, I fear war."

Liam nodded as he glanced up. "Very well. What shall you have me do now, Father?"

"First?" His eyes roamed around the room. "Clean up this mess, get dressed, and let us try to salvage some part of this day. Meet me in the main hall."

Unir picked up the golden staff and strode toward the door.

"Why did you not bring her back?" Liam called to his father's back. Unir froze and bowed his head, but did not turn around. "You could. It is one of your gifts."

"When she passed, I would have pulled the entire universe apart to bring her back, but I knew it was wrong. Resurrection, no matter the circumstances, is forbidden. You do not gain something so precious as a life without paying a hefty price. There are some things that even we cannot afford," he said before opening the doors. The guards waiting outside stood at attention. Without looking back, he quietly closed the doors behind him.

I watched as Liam stared after his father. He had lost his mother. I could relate to that pain more than I liked to admit. He hung his head, letting the cup he held fall from his hands. It rolled down the steps and spun in a slow circle on the floor. A part of me felt sorry for him, while another remembered the predator beneath that pleasantly taut skin. He was the World Ender in every sense of the word. It was like I was seeing the real him, not the short-tempered, rude asshole I had come to know. What else had happened to him to cause such a drastic change?

I stepped toward him, not sure what I was going to do. Before I could find out, the room swayed and started to dissolve.

TWENTY-FOUR

DIANNA

Cool, soft sheets wrapped around my torso as I turned over, nestling further into the warm bed.

Wait—why was I in bed? My eyes popped open, but I slammed them closed just as quickly. I draped my arm over my face, the light in the room blinding.

I lifted my lashes carefully, squinting as I took in the room. There was a large window to my right. The thick cream-colored curtains hung to the floor but were pulled back, allowing sunlight to spill into the room in golden beams. I stretched my arm out, my fingertips barely reaching the edge of the massive bed. The overfilled comforter slipped down as I propped myself up on my elbows. This place wasn't nearly as elegant or vibrant as the Rashearim I had seen in the dream, so where was I?

"You are awake. About time."

I jumped and rolled. An undignified squeal of alarm left my lips as I fell off the bed, my body hitting the floor with a loud thud. I grasped the comforter, pulling it around myself and glaring at the large man lounging in the chair on the other side of the room. My anger turned to confusion when I saw the books, papers, and laptop on the small table in front of him. He wore beige jeans and a white sweater with the sleeves pushed up to his elbows. His biceps flexed as he crossed his arms and glared at me. He was angry. Well, at least that was normal.

"Where are we?"

"How are you feeling?"

"Are you ignoring my question by asking me another question?" I narrowed my eyes and struggled to my feet. My legs threatened to give out, and I gripped the edge of the bed, holding tight to the comforter. I swayed and felt Liam's hands grip my shoulders, steadying me. I hadn't even seen him move, but there he was in front of me, holding me at arm's length.

"Your question is irrelevant, since we will be leaving soon," he said. His gaze roamed over me, assessing my every move as if he were looking for some sign that I was about to drop dead. "Now, answer my question. How do you feel?"

I glanced up at him and turned to sit on the bed, leaning on his strength more than I would ever admit. "Fine, I guess. A little tired, but fine. What—" I started to say something else, but lost my words when my memories came rushing back.

I looked down, pulling the tank top I was wearing away from my chest. The puncture wounds, and the spiderweb of black veins around them, were gone. I was clean and dressed in a dark tank and matching lounge pants with no sign of the blood I knew had poured out of me.

"Did you undress me?"

His mouth set into a hard line, his hands flexing on the curve of my shoulders. "I apologize. Does your chest usually hemorrhage something that looks like tar? Or do you normally seize when shot? You were disgusting, possibly dying, and you are worried if I undressed you?"

"I don't want you to touch me." I remembered what those hands did, how painful his touch could be, and I wanted them nowhere near me.

He recoiled, drawing back as if I had burned him. "Please, do not insult me, Miss Martinez. The desire to touch you is, and will always be, the farthest thing from my mind or intentions." He placed his hands on his hips, shaking his head as he regarded me. "One of the female celestials cleaned you up after assessing your wounds. You were covered in bile and absolutely reeked. Even I am not cruel enough to let you fester in that."

I glanced at the chair and the mess around it. "How long have I been out?"

His eyes followed mine, and he said, "Two days, six hours, and thirty minutes."

"You counted?"

"Yes? Why is that surprising? Your absence has only extended what I assumed would be a short adventure."

"Oh, I'm sorry. I didn't plan to get shot by an angry witch," I snapped, shaking my head.

I rubbed at my chest and glanced at the trash can sitting close to the edge of my bed. Through the haze of being awake and lost to the world, I remembered someone holding me as my body tried to rid itself of the toxin. Liam said that there had been celestials helping, but I remembered his voice, his scent, and the feel of his arms. Maybe that was just a fever dream.

"She poisoned me. No, *they* did. Sophie and Nym poisoned me."

The bed next to me sank, and I looked at Liam as he sat. "That I deduced." He rubbed his hands together, his silver rings connecting every few passes. "I do not understand why the man you shared your bed with, your maker, would make you violently ill just to force you to return to him?"

I snorted. "Let's just say 'shared' is a loose term, and I honestly don't know why Kaden is so set on getting me back. Sophie said she didn't know how much poison she would need to take me down, so maybe they just meant to incapacitate me and overdid it."

He made a noise, which I accepted as a grunt of agreement.

"Where is Sophie?"

He met my gaze, his face flat, but his eyes burning with remembered rage. "Which part?"

A memory flashed through my mind. I remembered the door busting open behind me as I lay on the floor. Liam had stepped over me, and I saw Sophie's decapitated head roll toward me, her hollow eyes staring. Liam had done that. I gulped and ran my hand over my throat. His eyes followed the path of my hand, but he didn't say anything.

"And Nym?"

"Detained, but breathing."

I nodded once. "One last thing, since we will be stuck with each other for a while." I reached behind me, picked up a pillow, and whipped it at him. "You can't feed me your blood, you idiot!" I picked up another pillow, aiming for his head. He swiped it away and glared at me. "I don't just consume the blood. I ingest memories with it."

He cocked his head to the side and tossed my fluffy weapon to the floor. "Memories? That's not possible."

"Oh, it's very possible." I held up the last pillow on the bed, ready to attack. "And I just got a backstage pass to images and sounds I wish to cut out of my brain."

"If that is the case, you should have had these dreams prior. Since the blood deal, my blood is in your system, as yours is in mine."

I slowly lowered my feather-filled weapon as I thought about it. "Well, I guess it wasn't a large enough quantity. I don't know. I didn't make myself like this, and I haven't really slept since we made the pact. Just that nap on the convoy."

His eyes narrowed. "Yet, here you are, critiquing *my* sleep schedule."

"Not the point," I said with a glare.

"Correct, that's not the point. What did you see with this power of yours?"

My chest clenched as I recalled Liam's and Unir's private conversation, and I felt the color drain from my face as the images of him and Imogen played back through my mind. I cleared my throat, pushing my discomfort aside. I didn't know why the memory of their screams and moans made my stomach flutter. It couldn't be embarrassment. I had done so much worse… or better, depending on how you looked at it. The logical part of my brain tried to convince me it was because I didn't see him that way. Liam was a legend, our version of the boogeyman, and he'd tortured me. Granted, I had tried to kill him and played a part in the death of one of his own. He was the

World Ender, and that name and title rang true, from what his father had said. But to me, he was Liam, uptight, arrogant, and opinionated.

"Who is Imogen?" I blurted out before I realized what I was going to say.

Liam looked surprised for the first time since I'd met him. "How do you know that name?" His voice came out a gruff whisper.

I blamed the beast that resided in me for taking over and forcing the words out like vomit. "Is she an ex-girlfriend? Is she dead? Is that why you're so miserable and mean?"

"Do you ever try to temper your vocabulary when you speak to me? You are so crass at times," he said, his tone filled with anger.

"Not really. But you didn't answer the question. Did you love her?"

If she had died, that could explain why he acted so cold. Losing your family and the one you loved the most could mess up even the strongest of us.

His jaw clenched before he raised his hand to his temple, rubbing it for a second. I had seen him do that several times, but had said nothing. That was a question for another time.

"Not that it is any of your business, but Imogen is not dead. I did not love her, nor is she my…" He paused, waving his hand as if trying to digest the words. "… anything you previously stated."

"Oh, Liam, I didn't know you were a player, but it makes complete sense. Given your title, I'm sure you could have anyone you wanted, goddess or not. Good for you."

He let out a long, exasperated sigh as he pinched the bridge of his nose. Okay, I'd irritated him. "Miss Martinez, please focus."

"Right, anyway…" I looked up as I tried to recount the events. "So, I saw you and your girlfriend-not-girlfriend naked. I was also in another world. The building I was in wasn't like anything I have ever seen, and that was before I was in your room. The ceiling was missing, and I could see so many planets and stars. It was—"

"Rashearim," he whispered. He said the word as one would say a dead relative's name. I watched the color drain from his face, his massive body seeming to crumple in on itself. He seemed so sad.

It was at that moment that I figured it out—why Liam was the way he was, and why he didn't care about his looks. I knew why he was so abrasive and so closed off to everyone, even those he claimed were his friends. He was consumed with grief and overwhelmed with pain. Liam was mourning.

He cleared his throat and asked, "Do you always get such vibrant renditions of one's past?"

I looked down, messing with a piece of the comforter. "If they're strong enough." I looked back up, dropping my hand. "I had assumed all of yours would be boring. No offense."

His scowl returned, replacing the haunted sadness in his gaze. I would take it. I much preferred the angry, disappointed-in-me Liam over the hurt one. Thanks to my stupid mortal heart, Liam hurting made me feel things I would rather avoid.

He turned his head as if lost in thought before clearing his throat and saying, "It is fascinating. Could this give us insight into where Kaden is hiding? I assume the two of you shared the same blood, correct?"

"Actually, no." I scrunched my nose. "He never let me. He always talked about how his memories would damage my mortal brain."

Liam looked skeptical. "Or he was hiding things from you."

I nodded, knowing it was probably the latter—especially given how Kaden had lied to me. "Or that."

"Is this power transmittable?"

I scoffed, grabbing the pillow and raising it once more. "Excuse me? Like a disease?"

He stared at my non-deadly weapon and placed his hand on the pillow, forcing me to lower it. "In essence, yes. You and I have shared blood, and I need to know if this is something I might experience."

My ears burned hot as I flushed, thinking of the things Liam might witness if he saw my past. "I actually don't know. I hope not, but I've never shared my blood with anyone."

"So, it's possible." He paused. "How long does this power last—the dreams?"

I shrugged. "Not long, usually. A day or so with mortals, but you're different. So, that I don't know either."

"From my studies, Ig'Morruthen powers and skills range based on species and type. Since you and your brethren seem to be a type not classified within any text Vincent has, is there anything else I should know about your gifts?"

I studied him for a moment, weighing my options and deciding if I should tell him the truth or leave him wondering. With a sigh, I shrugged and said, "I'm sure if you dream, you'll see all my gifts. But, no, you've seen all I can do. You have seen me shift, and you've seen the fire I wield. And now you know about my blooddreams."

"'Blooddreams'? Hmm." He nodded as he seemed to mull over my powers. "Please let me know if you have any more of these visions, yes?"

I gave him a mock salute. "Sure thing, boss. I'll be sure to let you know if I have any more vivid sex dreams about you and Imogen before Logan interrupts."

His eyes narrowed on me, as if he knew exactly which day I had seen. I would be lying if I said it wasn't intimidating, especially after seeing how he had stood up to his father without flinching. "That was not the only incident that occurred that day. What else did you see or hear, Miss Martinez?"

I heard the catch in his voice and knew he was concerned I'd seen too much. That got my attention. "I saw your father, Unir. He is a lot taller than you, which is saying something. I could feel the power in that memory of yours, but I couldn't understand the language. Then I woke up."

It was a lie, but I felt their conversation was too personal to repeat, regardless of me seeing and hearing it. Even if it was an unfamiliar language, I was in his head, so I understood what was said.

I smirked, knowing it would annoy him. "Why? Is there something you don't want me to see?"

He stood in one fluid motion, his speed reminding me that even though he felt some mortal emotions like sadness and grief, he was far from mortal. "I think it's time for us to leave."

So, he did have secrets. Color me surprised. "Where are we? And don't ignore that question again."

"A hotel on the outskirts of Adonael."

Everything clicked, and overwhelming dread filled me as I scooted off the bed in a hurry. "What? I told you nothing fancy, Liam. Under the radar," I snapped as I looked around the room. It was a decent size, even for a hotel. I needed to find my shoes, and we needed to get out of here fast. "Why is it so hard for you to listen?"

"Excuse me? I did not do this out of leisure. You were unconscious, and I had no idea how their spells worked or what to do. I wasn't sure if feeding you was the right thing. I needed information, and I couldn't get it from these off-the-radar places you recommend."

I dropped to the floor, looking underneath the bed for the heels I had been wearing. Not finding them, I stood and glared at him. "Yeah, but how did we get here? You can't drive, so that means you called someone, which means it could be traced. If Kaden or his lackeys went to Sophie's house looking for me, they probably know where we are."

"You know nothing of me or what I can and cannot do. Your lack of trust in my abilities is insulting. I am a king, remember? I can do and get anything I wish."

"Oh, trust me, I haven't forgotten, you spoiled brat," I said under my breath.

He made a sound of disapproval, letting me know he'd heard what I said, but he didn't comment further. "I phoned Vincent after what transpired. This is one of many celestial-owned establishments. I will always be provided for if I ask."

Just like that, the empathy I felt for him evaporated. He was such a spoiled asshole. I wanted to comment on how I had seen firsthand how well he was taken care of, but I managed to restrain myself.

"I had Sophie's house secured and brought you here. This was the closest place where you could rest, and I could stay by your side to ensure you didn't die."

Liam had just confirmed what I had already deduced from the papers and mess around that chair: he had stayed with me.

"Besides, I cannot lose you."

"Aw, that's so sweet," I half joked. I knew he didn't mean it in a sweet way, but irritating Liam was my new favorite pastime.

"Your death would be a great inconvenience, given the mission we must complete. So, with that said, you will not be out of my sight again. That means you do not command me or tell me what to do."

I rolled my eyes as I continued to search the room for my shoes. "There he is. I thought I'd lost the terrifying man-god for a second there."

He glared at me before pinching the bridge of his nose. "If you die, I have no Otherworld leads on this ridiculous notion that Azrael left behind a book. You are my best chance of predicting and stopping the attacks."

I nodded as I gave up my attempt to find my shoes. I would just have to go barefoot until I could get another pair. "Such a gentleman. I see why women fall at your feet."

His nostrils flared, his jaw set in a hard line. "Must you make quips every second you breathe?"

I smiled, knowing I'd finally gotten under his skin. "Why do they bother you?"

"You are absolutely tormenting. You realize that, correct?"

"I love it when you flirt with me." I winked, causing a vein to pop forward on his forehead, which only made me laugh. If he could have killed me on the spot, I knew he would have. "Fine, fine, that's fair."

"So, we agree then? You will not abandon me while you go and talk to any of your so-called friends or informants?"

I strode toward him, and he subtly shifted his weight, preparing for an attack. I stopped a few inches from him and held out my pinkie. His gaze dropped to my hand, looking at it as if I'd offered him a dead animal. "I pinkie-promise that I will never abandon you, Your Highness."

His gaze flicked to mine, some emotion I didn't recognize flaring behind his gray eyes. I grabbed his hand, forcing him to pinkie swear as he looked from our joined hands and back at me. "I do not understand this."

"It's something fun Gabby and I did when we were younger. It stuck through the years. Back after our parents died, I had to steal for a while to survive. This was one of many things we came up with to make sure I came back. You can't break a pinkie promise. It's like the law, but not your boring laws."

"You stole?" Of course that got his attention.

"Not everyone is born with a silver spoon in their mouth, Your Majesty."

He let my comment slide before he nodded slowly. "Very well. Pinkie promise."

It was so strange to hear the words leave his lips that I actually smiled. That seemed to unnerve him more than my annoying quips, his eyes widening just a fraction. I dropped my smile and my hand.

"I should have known Sophie wouldn't be reliable," I said, purposely changing the subject.

He put his hands in his pockets. "Do all your friends shoot you in the chest?"

I wrinkled my nose slightly and shrugged, thinking about it. "I know this may surprise you, but I don't have a lot of people that care about me. My sister, sure, but friends? All my *friends* are through Kaden, and that means there are very few whose loyalty lies with me." I forced a bitter laugh and curled a strand of hair behind my ear. I waited for him to agree, to say something rude or mean, but for once, he didn't.

A somber look crossed his face. Did he feel pity for me? Whatever it was, the emotion was gone as quickly as it came.

"With that in mind, we will need a new plan," he said. "Your friends are unreliable and dangerous. Unless you have some other informants that could be of assistance and won't attempt to return you to Kaden, I think we need to return to the Guild in Boel."

I bit my lower lip, my chest aching with uncertainty. There was someone, but I wasn't sure I wanted to bring him into this. I had made him a promise, but we were in an end-of-the-world type of dire situation. I had given him and his family a way out, a chance to escape. If I went to him, I would be dragging them right back into my mess with Kaden. I would be putting a target on his back.

"I may have another plan, but you'll have to make another promise."

"Will I now?" he asked, raising a single brow.

I nodded. "This man is supposed to be dead, and his location has to remain a secret," I said, all humor gone from my voice.

Confusion filled his eyes. "I do not understand."

I wanted my ruse to last longer. I didn't want him to get even a glimpse of the real me, and I didn't want to bring down anyone else with me. "Promise me that if I take you there, if I show you my world, you won't act as the almighty law enforcer."

"Miss Martinez. I don't know if I can make that—"

I grabbed his hands and clasped them in mine. I didn't realize how much bigger his hands were compared to mine until I held them. Rough calluses marked his wide palms, and I knew he had earned them through battles long fought. I looked up, trying to will as much pleading in my gaze as I could. I rarely begged for anything, but I would do whatever it took to keep my friend safe. "Please. This isn't me commanding you, I swear. This is me begging. These are my actual friends, and they hate Kaden just as much as you."

"If innocents are hurt—"

"They won't be, trust me. And if they are, then by all means, enforce the law all the way."

He was silent for so long that I was afraid he wouldn't agree.

"Very well. Then I promise." He looked down at where I still held his hands. "Does this require another pinkie?"

I shook my head as I laughed, a small snort escaping me. "No, it doesn't." I dropped his hands and turned, heading to the bathroom to take a shower.

"Wait. Where are we going?" Liam called right before I closed the door.

"Zarall. There is a Vampire Prince I was supposed to kill that I didn't."

TWENTY-FIVE

DIANNA

"Another stop?" Liam groaned and shifted in the passenger seat. Granted, I saw his point. We'd had to get gas several times, and I was hungry again. Since I was trying my best not to eat people, snacks it was.

"Yes, another stop. Don't you want to get out and stretch your legs? We have been trapped in this car for hours now."

"No, what I would like is for us not to drive everywhere when faster forms of transportation are available."

"And I have told you at least seventeen times why we can't."

He waved his hand toward me, clearly agitated. "Yes, yes, you and this obsessive radar."

I rolled my eyes. "Besides, I have to pee, and I'm hungry."

He gave me an exasperated look. "But you just ate a few hours ago."

"You know, normal people eat more than once a day."

"You are not a normal person—or a *person,* for that matter."

I bit my lip as I threw the car into park. "Gods, it's a surprise you have any friends at all."

"Says the one whose friends repeatedly try to kill her."

My gaze narrowed. "Someone is cranky. When was the last time *you* actually ate?"

He avoided eye contact and stared toward the small convenience store. "Just hurry up," he snapped.

I turned fully in my seat, placing my arm on the steering wheel. "Liam. When was the last time you ate?"

I knew he hadn't eaten yesterday or the day before, since I had gotten food and ended up eating it all. It just now occurred to me that I hadn't seen him eat or sleep. Although, what I had been doing could barely be considered sleep. Images of Rashearim and Liam's past still plagued my dreams. Luckily, they consisted more of battles and less of the orgies.

The air in the vehicle felt condensed, as if his agitation had physical weight. The locks on the door popped up, and my door opened. I jumped slightly and looked behind me. Had he done that? Of course he had. My mind flashed to the attack on Arariel when I'd tried to escape. I'd felt an invisible force, like a large hand had wrapped around my tail and yanked me back.

"Five minutes," he said gruffly as he leaned against the passenger door, arms folded. He was such an arrogant ass.

"I cannot pee in five minutes. I would have to run through the store," I said, throwing my hands up.

He didn't say anything, only raised a brow as if challenging me.

I sighed heavily, tilting my head back briefly before looking at him again. "Ugh. Give me ten minutes."

"Eight."

"Liam."

He looked at me as if I had asked him the most idiotic question, when all I'd done was say his name.

"Did you assume I was... What's the word?" He paused, looking away for a second as he searched for the word he wanted. "Joking? When I said I did not want you out of my sight?"

"Fine." I groaned, throwing up my arms again.

"You have seven minutes now, since you want to argue."

I narrowed my eyes at him. If I could have choked the life out of him, I would have.

I didn't bother arguing. There was no point. Liam would only count down more, and I didn't want to risk him following me inside. I shook my head and glared at him a moment longer before jumping out of the car. I closed the door a little too hard, but he was a complete ass, and his high-and-mighty routine was wearing on my nerves. It was a power trip, and I was so sick of dealing with men and their egos.

A bell dinged overhead as I pushed the glass door open. The attendants glanced my way, the one at the register smiling as she handed cash back to the person she was helping. Several shelves filled with snacks and supplies of every variety formed aisles in the small space. A child picked out a bag of candy, and her brother opted for chips, while their parents smiled indulgently.

I swept my gaze across the store, making sure I knew where everyone was and noting my exits. The frozen drink machine called to me, and I went straight to it, gleefully mixing three different colors until it formed a purple concoction. There was enough sugar in that sweet brew to keep me awake for at least a few more days.

I took a sip and kept an eye on the cashiers as I wandered through the small store. The bell above the door rang several times as people came and went. I grabbed a few bags of chips and some sandwiches before heading to the register. One of the cashiers started sweeping, watching me from the corner of his eye as I placed my purchases on the counter. The bell dinged again as the only other customer in the store left.

"Why are you here?"

A beep sounded as she scanned my chips.

"That's rude, Reissa. No 'hello' or 'how have you been'?"

She narrowed her eyes at me and said, "Everyone from the Otherworld knows how you've been. Kaden put a large sum on that pretty head of yours."

Another boy came from the back, glancing at me sideways as he passed to the other register. He looked to be in his late teens, but it was hard to tell.

"That's what I hear. So, are you planning to chop it off, then?" I said, leaning forward to take a long sip from my drink.

Reissa scanned the last sandwich and bagged it before placing both of her hands on the counter. She met my eyes, holding my gaze. "I just want to live in peace with my children, Dianna," she said, nodding toward the two boys. "Besides, any violence would only alert that large man in your car. Although he's not a man at all, is he?"

I glanced behind me, taking another sip of my drink and making sure the car and Liam were right where I had left them. I had parked so that he did not have a line of sight into the store. "Anatomically, yes. Everything else, I would go with no."

She shook her head and slowly pushed off the counter, tying the bags closed. "Why would I help you, Dianna? If Kaden finds out, he will not only have my head, he will go after my children as well. The risk is too great."

"That's fair." I reached forward with my free hand and grabbed the back of her head. My fingers coiled in her hair, and I slammed her face onto the counter, holding it there.

"You know, I tried to be nice the first time I asked for help. It got me shot in the chest and poisoned, so I don't think I want to be nice anymore."

I picked up her head and slammed it down hard against the counter again.

I heard the broom drop as her sons rushed forward to protect their mother. I glanced at them, my lips curved in a wicked grin.

"Oh, yes, please do. I haven't burned anyone alive in at least a month."

"Stop." She grunted beneath my hand. "It's okay."

The boys skidded to a stop and glanced at her before glaring at me.

"Let's play a game. You tell me what I want, and I don't barbecue you and this place."

"You wouldn't."

Reissa yelped as I slammed her head against the counter once more. "I hope my reputation hasn't taken that much of a hit."

She made a noise under her breath, but didn't comment further.

"Come on. Don't be like this." I leaned closer, my hand pressing harder against her skull. She grunted from the pressure. "Would you like to see your sons on their knees, begging for death while I liquify their organs from the inside out?"

I couldn't really do that. I had tried once, but they'd ended up combusting long before the actual pleading started. But it was still a good threat, and I knew it had worked when I smelled her fear.

"Okay, okay, okay," she pleaded, and I eased up, lifting my hand. She pushed off the counter and smoothed her hair with a couple of small movements before straightening the front of her slightly wrinkled shirt.

"Besides," I said, turning the straw in my drink to break up the ice that had clumped up at the bottom, "the less noise we make, the better. We don't want tall, dark, and annoying getting out of the car."

"So, it is true. You have the World Ender in your palm. Well, if anyone could corrupt a god, it would be you."

My lip curled up in disgust at her innuendo. "What? Is that what everyone thinks? That I fucked my way out?"

"You are everything he hates. Why else would he not have incinerated you at first sight?"

Smoke curled from my nostrils, and I knew my eyes had flashed red. The cup in my hand sizzled and then melted, the blue-and-purple liquid falling to the floor with a splat. "I may not be under Kaden's rule any longer, but that does not make me any less of a threat. Disrespect me again, and you will be the last of your eight-legged race."

She stared at the sticky mess on the floor, then reluctantly met my eyes. Her throat bobbed once as she swallowed hard. "Sorry, it's just—"

"The Otherworld talks, I know, I know." I shook my hand, slinging off the remains of my drink.

Her sons hadn't moved, but their bodies were tense, and their hands fisted. I saw their shirts ripple around their shoulders, the legs that they kept hidden beneath their skin moving in an intimidation tactic. Cute. It wasn't until I took a breath, calming the current of anger roiling through me, that I heard movement from behind the metal door. She had more than just the two boys with her.

She waved toward one of the boys, silently ordering him to clean up the mess. She watched him leave to grab the mop before turning back to me. "What do you need?"

"A safe way to get past El Donuma. Camilla will have my head if I set foot in that area." I had about four minutes of my allotted time left. I needed to hurry this up.

"Ah, yes, the Witch Queen. Maybe if you had given her what she wanted, she wouldn't hate you and Kaden so."

"Kaden made Santiago his main witch bestie, not me. I know her power rivals his, but Santiago has a dick, which automatically gets him a leg up." I turned toward her sons. "No offense."

"If I help you, what do I get in return?"

I shrugged. "I don't know. What do spiders want?"

Reissa's fist slammed down on the counter, causing the machine to glitch. Several eyes popped open along her forehead, her mortal disguise slipping as needle-like spines poked through her bad wig. "We are not spiders! You know I hate that comparison."

I smirked, amused that I'd pissed her off. "Are you sure about that? Between the legs and eyes, and oh, let's not forget the weblike creations I know you have in the back, it all seems to add up to spider. What's on the meal plan today?" I leaned closer, sniffing the air. "I smell deer and ... ohhh, hitchhikers."

Her lip curled back in anticipation of her fangs descending. "Is your diet any better?"

"I gave up mortal a long time ago. I'm practically an Ig'Morruthen vegetarian now."

She shook her head and took a deep breath, her many appendages and eyes disappearing as she resumed her mortal shape. She ran a hand over her wig and said, "I have a way you can sneak past El Donuma, but you'll have to ask him yourself. Lines have been drawn, Dianna. Kaden has lost two generals, and his faction is shaken. No one trusts anyone anymore."

I looked at my hands, imagining the blood that marked them even now. All I saw was red. After what I had done, Kaden would never stop hunting me, and his entire infrastructure had to be on the verge of a civil war. If they thought he couldn't keep even his closest in line, he would have to do something drastic to regain control. I clamped down on those thoughts and met her gaze, my fingers tapping on the counter.

"Where is he, this man who can help me?"

She reached under the counter, taking out a small gray lockbox. She dug a key out of her apron and unlocked it. After rummaging through a few phones, she chose a small black one. She opened it with a flip and turned it on.

I glanced at the large clock on the wall. Fuck, I was running out of time. I glanced out the glass doors, hoping Liam wasn't on his way in. She typed a number into the phone before handing it to me.

"A festival has popped up in Tadheil. He will be there. I'll tell him to expect a call from this number. Be there when he tells you to be, because he will not wait."

I sighed and shook my head, knowing Liam would throw another fit once he found out. "I don't have time for a festival."

"Make time, because whether you like it or not, there is no one who will want to help you now."

I didn't say anything else as I took the phone from her and put it in my back pocket. I grabbed my bags and headed toward the door. The bell chimed once more as I exited—and slammed into what felt like a brick wall.

"Son of a—" I looked up, rubbing my head. "Liam."

"You lied." Liam's gaze narrowed on me, his arms folded.

My pulse quickened. Had he heard me talking to Reissa? Had he seen everything? If he knew what they were and what was kept in the back, he would destroy them and the store. I may have threatened them, but I had no intention of following through. They were a small family, and I would not be responsible for them losing each other.

"You said you had to use the bathroom, but what is that?" He pointed at the bags in my hand.

I released my breath, the tension in my shoulders subsiding. "Oh, this? Yes, I got us snacks." I smiled and walked around him, hoping he would follow. I breathed a sigh of relief when I felt that harrowing power behind me a moment later. Thank the gods. I headed to the car, opening the driver's side as he walked around the front. He didn't give the store a second glance.

"You took too long," Liam scolded as he slid into his seat and closed the door.

I shrugged. "I told you, I got snacks. You need to eat something."

Liam massaged his temples as if the very thought was too much for him. "Can you please drop that subject?"

"What's with the headaches? Growing restless? You know what will help? Food and sleep."

"No." His tone told me to drop it.

"Seriously, you can nap in the car. I promise not to drive us off a cliff."

"Just go."

"You know, keeping everything repressed isn't a solution either."

Liam dropped his hands. "If I want your counsel, I'll ask. Now, may we please continue? You've already wasted enough of my time."

I slammed the bag of snacks against his chest. "That's the last time I say or do anything nice for you. You have one more ego trip before I lose my shit, Liam. You know you're not a king or savior to me, right? The outside of you may look great, but on the inside, you're just a bitter, mean, ugly asshole."

I couldn't help it. I was tired of him talking to me as if I were his servant, and I was more than ready to fight if he didn't change his tone. His expression was incredulous, as if he had never been spoken to like that before. Which, from what I had seen of his past in my dreams, I knew he hadn't. Everyone worshiped him, hanging on his every word.

Liam didn't respond or make one of those grunts he did when he was displeased with something. He just took the bag I'd practically assaulted him with and turned away from me. Without another word, I put the car in reverse and drove away from the gas station.

WE WERE ON THE OTHER SIDE OF CHAROUM BEFORE LIAM FINALLY passed out, and I thanked the dead gods above. I had stopped a few more times to actually use the bathroom, and each time, I had to listen to him complain about how much time we were wasting. He hadn't touched the snacks and had yelled at me when I reached back to grab a bag of chips while driving. I told him it wasn't like we would actually die if we got into a car accident, but he didn't find that as funny as I did. But as the sun set once more, he finally nodded off. His arms were folded, and his head rested against the window as his eyes danced behind his eyelids. He even slept angry.

While he was asleep, I dug out the small phone Reissa had given me. I maneuvered it so that my hands were on the wheel as I dialed Gabby's number. Another bump had the car jumping, and I looked over to make sure Liam was still asleep.

"Hello?" a sleepy voice answered after a few rings.

"Gabby, shame on you for answering numbers you don't know."

"Dianna!" Gabby practically yelled my name, all sleepiness disappearing from her voice.

"Did I wake you?"

She yawned, and I heard her groan as she stretched. "No. I'm usually awake at one in the morning."

I giggled. "Ass."

"What are you doing? Are you okay? How's the trip?"

I put the car on autopilot and pulled one leg up to rest my arm on my knee. The road was empty, the stars the only light on the back road I had taken.

"I'm driving, and yes, I guess. And let's just say it's complicated."

"Is Liam still a pain in the butt?" I heard a small slap as she covered her mouth. "Oh, wait, am I on speaker? Can he hear me? You do know they have super hearing?"

I laughed quietly. "Yes, and don't worry, he is actually asleep."

"He sleeps?"

"That's what I said." I looked over, watching as his chest rose and fell steadily. It was strange to see him asleep, since it had been days of him just glaring at me. I had to admit, I liked the peace and quiet his sleep brought.

"Apparently, he's a deep sleeper, because I've hit like three small holes in the road, and nothing."

"You're also a terrible driver."

"Hey, you're the one who taught me."

It was her turn to laugh, and the sound was a balm. I'd been betrayed, gotten shot, been poisoned, and had to deal with Liam's constant attitude. This trip had worn on my nerves more than I let on. I wished I could just go back and eat terrible junk food as Gabby cried over another sappy movie. My chest tightened because I knew that would never happen again.

I cleared my throat and sat up a little straighter. "How is it there? Are they nice to you?"

"They are. Neverra and Logan actually spend a lot of time with me. I know most of it is to monitor me, but it's still nice. They have a medical wing, and given my background, they've put me to work."

"Oh, so Logan is all healed and friendly. Good. And let's be honest, you would still want to work even when you didn't need to."

"I like helping people. Even people that heal at an alarming rate." She snickered, and I heard her shuffling around. "But yes, they are nice. Neverra likes all the sappy movies you make fun of me for, and I made her and Logan do a face mask with me."

"Replacing me already! I am offended."

I joined in her laughter this time. It was nice to forget, even for a few moments, that I was in the middle of some gods-versus-monsters war.

"No, no, you know I could never replace you. Who would steal my shoes and clothes? And no one can complain and nag like you. Or annoy me. Or—"

"Okay, okay, I got it."

She was quiet for a moment. "So, do you really think you will find the book before Kaden?"

I shifted slightly in my seat, sitting up a bit more. I placed my leg back down, gripping the steering wheel and turning off the autopilot. "Honestly, I don't know. Liam thinks it's not real, and I feel he would know. But at the same time, the Otherworld is terrified. Kaden is up to something, and the people I can trust are slim to none."

"Well," she sighed, "I am relieved that Liam is with you. At least nothing will hurt you while he's around."

I went quiet, not wanting to mention that I'd been poisoned. It was done, and it would just cause her to worry, but she must have read into my silence. Damn sister bond.

"D? What is it? Please tell me you're not hurt?"

"What? No, I'm fine. I just wish I were on a trip with anyone but him. He's such a dick at times, Gabby. I know he's a protector of realms or whatever, but how do people actually like him?"

I heard her sigh and suspected I was about to get a lecture. "Well, from what I gathered from Logan and Neverra, he wasn't always like he is now. I mean, think about it. He's an ancient warrior king from another world. I'm sure he's suffering from their version of PTSD, depression, or worse."

I glanced at the ancient warrior in question. He leaned heavily against the window, his breathing steady and his ridiculously long lashes shadows against his cheeks.

"Depression, huh? Look at my sister, psychoanalyzing gods."

"I'm serious. It would explain the erratic behavior, mood swings, and uneven temper. Trauma affects the brain dramatically, and given he has lived a long, long time, who knows what the side effects are? I'm just saying, be careful."

"Yes, Mom."

She snorted. "Okay, I'll let that slide. And who knows? Maybe he's just lonely. Logan and Neverra said he's been isolated for centuries. They haven't seen him since Rashearim fell."

"Oh, please. That man has not been alone since he reached puberty. You should see the blooddreams I've had. Gods, goddesses, celestials, you name it, they all bend over for him. If it's not some battle or party, he's busy getting his cock wet."

"Wait—what?" Her voice was loud and shrill before she quieted to ask, "Dianna, what?"

"I know, right? I mean, I thought *I* was experienced."

"Wait, he fed you, and you've seen him naked?" She practically screamed the question in my ear.

"Yeah, it would be fantastic if it were attached to anyone else."

"Dianna, stop deflecting. I don't care about that. He fed you, which means you were hurt enough for him to be worried. What happened?"

Well, shit. I could fake a bad connection and hang up, but I hadn't spoken to her in a while, and I didn't want to end the call just because I got caught.

"Okay, well, it's a long story. The short version is that Sophie and

Nym may have poisoned me, and Liam fed me because he thought I was dying."

The phone went silent for a moment before she asked, "But you're okay now?"

Guilt churned in me, and my hands tightened on the wheel as I heard the fear in her voice. "Yeah, I'm fine. Pinkie swear."

She sighed, and it sounded like she'd flopped back on the bed. I could picture her jumping up to pace once she had heard about the blooddreams. My sister was always worried. "Well, I for one can't wait until this is over and we can go back to a semi-normal life. There will be no Kaden, so you'll actually have a life this time." She paused for a second. "What do you think about going back to Sandsun Isles? They have a secluded, unmarked part of the beach I found while I was in hiding. They have cliffs we can dive off of, and it's so beautiful. We haven't been to a beach together like that in at least thirty years. I won't even invite Rick. It will just be a nice, relaxing, fun sister trip. Let's make it our first vacation. Please, please, please!"

"Okay, okay, okay, sounds like a plan. Stop begging." My lips curved in a small, sad smile as my vision grew blurry. I hadn't told her the terms of my deal with Liam, and I wasn't sure if I would be going to prison or if he had something worse planned. Liam never told me what he was going to do with me, and I'd rather not know.

She was quiet for a moment longer, silence hanging between us. I'm sure she was sensing my emotions, even from this far away.

Gabby took a breath. "Listen, I know it's hard right now. I know, whether or not you want to admit it, that you're frustrated and probably mad. But I believe in you. You've been through so much, D. So much. You're the strongest person I know. If this stupid book exists, you will find it. You're stubborn, but resilient. You can survive anything."

I wiped at my face, covering my sniffle with a small laugh. "Thanks for the pep talk."

"You're welcome. Now pull over somewhere and get some sleep. You shouldn't be driving this late. I don't care what Liam says."

I looked over at the sleeping god and yawned. "That actually sounds like a plan. I think I see one of those shady motels up ahead."

"Perfect for you, I guess," she said with a laugh. "Call me tomorrow if you can."

"Yes, ma'am."

She snorted into the phone. "Remember that I love you."

I smiled and echoed the words back to her before hanging up.

A large, half-lit sign pierced the darkness ahead. Gabby was right. I was exhausted and tired of being trapped in the car.

The sign flickered on and off, and I could almost hear the buzz of the lights. I turned in, noticing only one truck parked toward the back of the building. I pulled up to the office and saw a small woman sitting at a counter, watching TV. She had a cigarette between her fingers, and smoke floated in the air behind the glass.

I put the car in park, but left it running. Not wanting to wake Liam, I carefully opened the door. I would love not to have to listen to him complain. When he didn't so much as shift, I hopped out and gently closed the door.

A small bell dinged as I entered, and the woman, who looked to be in her late fifties, turned toward me. She put out the cigarette and lowered the volume on the TV.

"Hello, dear. Looking for a room tonight?"

"Yes, please," I said before leaning back and making sure Liam hadn't woken up.

"He's cute," she said as she plucked a key from the large brown board behind her. "You picked the perfect hotel if you and your boyfriend want to get loud. We don't get much in the way of customers this far out."

I held up my hand, the look of disgust on my face making her pause. "He is not my boyfriend."

"Really? That's a shame." She smiled as she came to the counter and handed me the key. "It will be forty dollars, miss."

"Forty bucks for a single night?"

She shrugged. "As I said, we don't get a lot of people this far out. Mostly truckers or..." Her voice trailed off as she looked me up and down, then flicked her gaze toward Liam. "... you know, *working women*."

The way she said the last part had me glaring at her. "I am not a prostitute."

"Like I said, not judging." She held up her hands in defense.

I didn't say anything as I dug out the cash I had stolen. People really should learn to lock their cars, especially at rest stops. We couldn't use any of the cards Nym had given us because I knew they were being traced. I unfolded the bills and slammed the forty dollars down before snatching the key from the counter and turning to leave. Her laugh followed behind me as the volume on the TV increased and she went back to her show.

TWENTY-SIX

SAMKIEL

"Samkiel, hold your hands out." My father demonstrated as we stood in the pavilion above the dining hall on the outer banks of Rashearim. Clouds ringed the mountaintops, and a light breeze brought the mouthwatering scent of food from the feast. I wanted more than anything to be there.

"I cannot do it," I said, growing frustrated. I could hear my friends gathering down below and wanted to join them.

"You must learn to control your powers, or they will devour you. Do you wish for that fate—to combust and be reduced to nothing but ash in the wind?"

The columns of gold surrounding us vibrated with the power of his tone. The symbols carved into the stone of the pavilion flared brightly as my father grew frustrated as well.

With an exasperated sigh, I shook my head and said, "No."

The enormous silver city below was awake and buzzing with activity. We had been up here since sunrise. I was tired of training, but he persisted.

"Now, concentrate. Every thought you have and every emotion you feel comes from your center. Your anger," he pointed to my stomach, "comes from your gut." He pointed at my chest next. "Your desires come from your heart, and your idiocy..." He reached out and ruffled the hair atop my head, making the strands dance across my shoulders. "… comes from here."

I swatted his hand away before holding my palm up once more. "All right, all right."

"Now, focus."

His eyes lit with a pure silver glow that matched mine. I watched as energy formed above his palm. At first, it was just a spark, but then it began to swirl in a small circular pattern. Whips of energy spun off it in the same color as the power that ran through our veins.

"Once you get the energy outside of yourself, it is easy to manipulate. It can be shaped," he danced the ball of light between his fingers until it formed a small blade, "or just used as is." It reformed into the original sphere. "Power has its limits, though. What you give, it takes. If you feed it too much, it will drain you. That is something you always have to remember, especially in battle."

I nodded along, his words replaying in my mind as I concentrated. *Core, heart, brain. Center, focus, release.*

I took a deep breath and turned my palm toward the ceiling, repeating the six words like a litany.

Core, heart, brain.

Center, focus, release.

The energy sparked within my palm, sending a wave of power through my entire being. The twin lights on either side of my body pulsed beneath my skin, the power racing toward my hand. I looked up and saw the wide smile on my father's face. He was proud. Of *me*.

I focused harder, willing it to shape itself. The small orb formed, but did not hold for long. Sweat drenched my brow as I concentrated. I could do this. I knew it.

"Breathe, Samkiel."

Did he not see that I was breathing?

My fingers curled at the tips as I tried to hold it together. I wanted a blade like he'd made. I just needed to push a little harder, and—

The ball grew larger than my entire fist. The light inside of it became blinding. It writhed and turned, twisting in on itself. My power was not whole or tame like his, but a broken ball of energy threatening to devour everything in its vicinity. It shot toward the sky, punching a large hole in the ceiling. The force of the explosion washed over us, and pieces of stone rained down, the debris covering us in a layer of white dust.

Unir brushed a long black strand of hair from his face. His brow creased as he placed his hands on his hips, his look of pride replaced by a scowl.

The aching pit in my gut formed again as I dropped my gaze. I would never be as powerful as him or have his control. A lump formed in my throat as I took a slight step back. I looked at the hole in the ceiling, and a thousand voices filled my head, reminding me that I would never be good enough.

My temper snapped, the rubble around us vibrating against the floor. "I do not know why you push me so hard all the time! I am not like you!"

"Samkiel."

"I am not normal, and I am fine with that. You are the one with something to prove, not me." I spun away, my fists clenching at my sides. The lights along my body pulsed, and chairs and tables slammed into the walls in my wake.

I'd barely reached the steps when I felt an invisible force tighten around my midsection, pulling me back. My feet barely touched the floor as he used his power to turn me around, forcing me to face him again.

He placed me back on my feet and said, "Look." His face held no anger as he pointed up.

"I do not need to see my failures to know..."

The words died on my lips as the rubble around us floated toward the ceiling. Piece by piece, the hole slowly filled in, mending itself. My father's outstretched hand glowed dully with power.

"... How?"

He smiled once more. "The same power that runs through my veins flows through yours. Yes, given the technique or strength of the wielder, it can damage, but it can also rebuild and heal. Even the strongest among us have learned how to use it to heal. You are not a failure, nor will you be." He clapped his hands together and dusted off his clothing. "Now, let us try again. Hold your hand out."

You are not a failure. The words rang true for me. I studied every day in anticipation of becoming king. Not every deity was happy about my accession, and they were sure to let me know. But the only opinions I cared about were those belonging to my friends and father. If I did not fail them, maybe I would not fail at ruling. I nodded once before I smiled and raised my gaze to his.

My eyes widened as a shimmer settled over my father's image, distorting it. I took a step back, then another. No, this hadn't happened—not here. Silver liquid ran from his eyes, then from his nose and mouth. The room darkened and shook. We stood rooted in place as the building blew away. Screams and roars ripped through the air. Orange lightning danced between billowing yellow clouds.

The stench of blood and death hung above the remains of Rashearim. My head spun as I saw legions of celestials fighting one another. Metal sang as their weapons clanged, light vibrating off of them. The world shook as many fell, their bodies exploding in light and shooting into the sky.

My father stared at me, his clothes bloody, his face scarred, and those eyes—those dead, empty eyes.

"Are you happy, Samkiel? This is what you wanted, yes?" It was my father's voice, but the words were cruel.

My body felt heavy, and I looked down, seeing the bloodstained armor wrapping my frame. I held a silver spear covered in blood in one hand and a broken shield in the other. "I never wanted this," I said, shaking my head so hard that my vision blurred.

"You are a World Ender. Another one of my mistakes. We would have been better off without you. *I* would have been better off without you." He advanced, one broken leg dragging behind him.

"Stop." I dropped the spear, yanking the helmet from my head and tossing it to the side.

"What a waste."

"No."

I took another step back.

"I was a fool to think you could lead us. You've only led us to destruction."

"You do not mean that." I stopped as he approached, my body

shaking. He was in front of me, his hands reaching out and grabbing my shoulders, his nails digging deep.

"You should never have been born. Your mother would still be here. Rashearim would still be here."

"I said stop!" My power burst from me, the illusion around me shaking, but not dissipating. I grabbed him by the throat and lifted him off his feet. "Why do you haunt me?! What do you want from me?! I do not understand!"

I shook him as he clawed at my wrists, black talons dragging across my flesh, the pain biting.

"Liam," he choked out, his hands grabbing at my arms. "Liam, you are dreaming. Wake up."

His voice cracked and changed, becoming more feminine.

"I did what you asked of me, Father. I did what you begged of me! You wanted a king, so I became a king. So, why? Why will you not let me rest?"

"I," the voice choked, those nails digging in harder, "am not your fucking father."

Bright amber swept over his irises, obliterating the silver. Fire, hot, fierce, and burning, shot from his eyes, sending me flying backward. My back hit a hard surface, and I slid to the floor. I pushed myself onto my elbows, coughing as I lifted my hand to shade my eyes. My head throbbed so hard that it felt as if it would rupture. The world around me shook and scattered as I blinked a few times.

The images of Rashearim disappeared, replaced by a darkened room. I heard the crunch of footsteps approaching and turned toward the massive hole in the wall. A set of eyes, burning red, shone through the dust, and I sat up as a tall, slender figure stepped through the wreckage. Her thick hair danced around her bare shoulders as if it had a life of its own. She was wearing a tight tank top with thin straps and matching loose black pants. She was stunning. A dark goddess brought to life. She was—

"Liam!" The voice was mangled. "What the fuck?"

She was Dianna.

I shook my head, coming back to reality, the aching throb easing. I was on my feet in the next second.

"Miss Martinez."

"Stop. Calling. Me. That." She bit off the words. I would be lying if I said I did not flinch just a little. Her eyes burned with Ig'Morruthen rage, and her voice was a broken croak. Her voice... No!

I was in front of her in the next second, gently cupping her jaw. She winced and slapped at my hands as I tipped her head back.

"That hurts."

I did not think as I leaned down to gather her up into my arms. I cradled her against my chest and walked through the hole she had made when she'd tossed me through the wall.

"Put me down," she said, her voice a deep, strangled mess.

I obliged, setting her on the half-broken bed. The room was in shambles, and the roof was completely gone. It was just another display of my destructive nature. I lowered my head, my hands rubbing against my temples as I closed my eyes and concentrated.

I opened my eyes, the shine from them illuminating the small, dark room. Everything began to vibrate, and I heard the rumble from overhead as the roof repaired itself. The appliances and furniture became whole again, the chairs no longer in pieces. The bed Dianna was sitting on jolted as the broken frame was fixed. Once the massive hole in the wall filled itself in, I looked at her. She looked around the restored room, her eyes huge. She had her hands pressed to her throat, and I could see the purple-and-black bruises forming on her delicate skin.

I crouched before her, and I knew I had moved too fast when she jumped and scooted back, startled at my sudden movement. She watched me warily, as if expecting another attack.

"Let me see," I said, slowly reaching out but not touching, waiting for her permission. "Please."

She studied me, her gaze flicking to my hand. I knew she was remembering the pain my touch could bring.

"I promise I will not hurt you."

"You already did," she said, her voice growing raspier as her throat swelled.

"Please. Just let me fix this."

She held my gaze, and whatever she saw convinced her to drop her hands. I nudged her knees apart and maneuvered myself closer. She swallowed at my proximity, causing her to wince in pain again, but she didn't pull away.

I placed a hand on either side of her slender throat and closed my eyes, remembering the words my father had taught me so long ago. I felt the surge of energy crawl from my center. It traveled down my arms and filled my hands before passing into her. I heard her soft gasp and opened my eyes. Threads of silver light circled her throat like a necklace, casting her in an ethereal glow.

A bone snapped back into place with a sickening pop, and I watched as the bruises disappeared, leaving her beautiful bronze skin smooth once more. I shifted away and stood before sitting next to her on the bed. We were quiet for a long moment, the silence deafening.

"You broke my larynx, you dick," she rasped, continuing to rub her throat.

"I am sorry." To say I was ashamed would have been an under-statement.

She nodded and looked out the window as if lost in thought.

"Where are we?" My voice did not sound like my own.

"A hotel. Not as fancy as yours, though." She attempted to joke, but the words were cold. Her usual humor and spark were missing, and I hated that I was the cause. I lowered my head and sighed, rubbing at the bridge of my nose.

"I am sorry."

"You apologize a lot for royalty."

"I truly did not mean to hurt you. I did not know it was you." It sounded so inadequate to say that I hadn't known where I was or who she was at the time. It was inexcusable that the king of Rashearim didn't have control of his powers.

"Do you have outbursts like that every time you sleep? Is that why you don't want to?"

I felt the bed shift, but I stayed where I was. I nodded, my shame keeping my tongue glued to the roof of my mouth.

I rubbed my hands over my face, working at finding my voice. "I should not have slept, but I am just so *tired*." My hands fell to my lap as I turned to look at her. "I told you I did not want to wait! I told you I did not wish to prolong this more than I had to! Now you see why. I am volatile, Miss—" I stopped. "Dianna. I cannot be here for long periods of time. My body requires sleep, no matter how much I wish it did not."

I did not mean to snap or scold her, but the emotions I kept buried so deeply seemed to explode around her. Between the erratic, impulsive behavior she regularly displayed and her crass, rude, sarcastic comments, she brought out a side of me that had lain dormant for centuries.

I saw how she had responded and lit up around her sister, which told me more about her than I was sure she would want. Gabby's aura seemed to encompass Dianna at times, her light reaching out to tame the wild beast that lay beneath Dianna's skin. She may not have been mortal anymore, but a part of her still felt and loved. It was that part that made it difficult to dislike her. She roused emotions in me that made me forget what she was and what she was capable of.

"I am sorry. I did not mean to yell. It is just, I do not wish to sleep. Ever."

"Because of the nightmares?"

I slid my hand over the back of my neck. "Is that what they are called here? I refer to them as night terrors. Memories long past that result in…" I waved to the now clean room. "This."

Dianna was quiet for a few moments, seeming to process what I had said before asking, "Does anybody else know?"

"Nobody knows. Just you," I said, glancing at her. She had angled her body toward me with her legs crossed and her hands in her lap. "How did you stop me? I have always been afraid to be around anyone when those happen. I am afraid of the damage I cause and having anyone in the vicinity who could be hurt."

Dianna shrugged. "Well, I heard you whispering in your sleep, and then every piece of furniture in here started levitating. The whole building actually shifted. I tried to wake you up, and…" She paused and reached for her throat before dropping her hand. "I thought you were going to pop my head off, so I reacted."

Guilt bit at me again. It was another reminder that being around her made me feel when nothing and no one else had been able to reach me. "You are a lot stronger than you think. Especially if you can disarm me."

She let out a short laugh that was mostly a snort. "Thanks."

Silence fell once more, and an uncomfortable air of tension filled the room. I did not know what else to say, other than to apologize once more.

"You know, I used to have nightmares, too. Actually, I still do sometimes." She looked at her hands as she played with one finger, then the next. "Gabby helped me a lot when I first turned, but I still dreamed of the blood and fighting. The screams I heard in the night were a constant reminder of what I had done for Kaden. What he made me do."

My chest tightened. I understood what she was saying and was deeply familiar with the guilt and pain. "Did they ever stop?"

She held my gaze, her eyes shadowed. "They came less often. On the really bad nights, I would sneak off to call Gabby. If I had them when I was visiting her, she would hold me." She broke eye contact and lowered her head, tucking a strand of hair back from her face. "It's nice to have someone there for you, someone who understands. Otherwise, you keep it all bottled up, and you explode. Kind of like you did tonight."

"Yeah."

"Liam, you are far too powerful to let that happen. If I hadn't managed to wake you, you could have flattened this whole area. You could have killed—"

I stood abruptly and started to pace. "I am aware."

"I'm not being mean, and I'm not trying to fight, but what about your friends? Can you talk to them?"

"No." I spun to glare at her, the one word coming out aggressive and rough. I saw her flinch and turned away to resume my pacing. "No, I cannot."

The silence was almost deafening until she said, "Gabby taught me not to live in the past. Well, she's trying to, at least. She said it's pointless, because nothing grows there. You've seen a thousand plus worlds and have lived a thousand plus lives. I can only imagine what you've done and what you've seen. I'm sure that even the blooddreams couldn't show me all that you've experienced." She caught my gaze, her eyes boring into me, seeing things I didn't want her to know. But her expression was soft and filled with understanding. "It's okay to not be okay, Liam."

My chest tightened, and I was quiet for a moment. I'd never had anyone there for me. Not like this. Not when I'd bared pieces of my soul and revealed my weaknesses. She was my enemy, yet my enemy was the only one who seemed to understand me and the demons I fought. Even so, her words were the farthest thing from the truth.

"It's okay to not be okay."

I shook my head. "Not for me."

"Then how about we make a new deal?"

That caught my attention, and I stopped to focus on her, my head still pounding. "A new deal? Have we not made enough?"

"This one doesn't involve the book, or even the monsters we may or may not fight."

I was silent for a moment, but curiosity got the best of me. "Does this require another small finger?"

A small smile—a real one—graced her lips, and my chest tightened once more. "Yes. We are stuck together for this crazy mission. If you're wrong about the book, the world will probably end, so why not call a truce? We should stop fighting and try to be friends." She held her hand up, cutting me off as I went to speak. "It's just while we have to work together. The two of us bumping heads all the time is getting us nowhere."

"That I can agree upon."

"Good, that's a start. And while we're together, you can share your burdens with me. I promise not to judge or ridicule or make you feel less than because of them. Your burdens become my burdens."

"Your burdens become my burdens?" My brow quirked.

"Yes," she said. It was as if a pebble had dropped into the middle of a quiet lake. In the grand scheme of things, it meant nothing. Yet it started a small, seemingly insignificant ripple, and something shifted.

"Okay."

"So, in light of our newly formed alliance, I'll help you with your nightmares. Sometimes it's easier to talk to a stranger than the people you care about, and I promise not to share anything you tell me, okay?"

I shook my head. "This is not something that words can simply cure."

"What did we just say about arguing?" she said, the smirk she usually wore returning.

Frustrating woman.

I pursed my lips and sighed. "Very well. How do you intend to help me?"

She scooted backward on the bed until there was enough room for me and patted the space next to her. My curiosity turned to concern.

"Come here, and I'll show you."

I had heard similar words before, spoken by celestials and goddesses alike. Usually, it was an invitation, and they were soon upon their knees, worshiping me with their hands, mouth, and tongue. My pulse quickened, the blood in my ears thrumming as it threatened to travel elsewhere. I tried to speak, but my mouth had gone dry. I cleared my throat and tried again, managing to say, "There is only one bed."

"Great, you're observant. I'm so proud. Now come here."

My toes flexed against the carpet. I must be misreading her intentions. She did not mean that she wanted to have sex with me. Sweat broke out across my back. "But—"

"I promise to be on my best behavior, Your Majesty. Your virtue is safe with me," she said and pressed her hand over her heart. "I promise."

"That's not what I meant." I shook my head. Why would a thought like that even cross my mind? What was the matter with me? I did not and would never see Dianna in such a way. "Fine."

I swallowed hard, putting one foot in front of the other until I reached the bed. I sat on the very edge, and she rolled her eyes, scooting further back.

"Liam, lie down."

I eyed her once more before lying back, my body tense. She lay down next to me, but stayed on her side, propping her head up on her hand.

"What is this supposed to do?"

She laughed, the pure white of her teeth flashing in the darkened room. "You look so uncomfortable. Just relax. You've had women and men in your bed before. Sometimes all at once. I've seen it."

"That's not—" Why was my brain not working? "That's different."

"Why? Because they weren't Ig'Morruthen?" she asked, an edge to her tone.

"Well, no, because... Why are we talking about this?" Why was I fumbling over my words? "This is not helping me."

She rolled her eyes and said, "Just relax."

I took a deep breath and shifted, lying on my side to face her.

"So, from what I hear, Logan is your best friend, but also works for you? You call them The Hand, but they're celestials, right? What's that mean?"

I did not understand how this was to help me, but I answered her question. "My father made Logan, but he was not conceived. All the celestials were created by one god or another. The celestials are not born, and they have a shadow of our powers."

She nodded, and I could tell she was focused intently on me. "You mentioned your father in your nightmare. Do you want to talk about him?"

"No." It came out harsh, but those were memories I would not share with anyone.

She swallowed before changing the subject back. "Why make something so similar? Weren't they afraid they would rebel?"

"The celestials don't have the power to rebel successfully. I always thought they made them because they were bored and wanted something to rule over, since they could not control each other."

She smirked, the corners of her mouth turning up and her eyes sparkling. "How do you not know?"

"I know it is difficult to believe, but growing up there, I mostly did not care. I got what I wanted, who I wanted, and barely had to lift a finger. That was the benefit of being king. So, I did not care about politics, which was a mistake on my part. As you said, I was spoiled and self-righteous."

She absently scratched at the nape of her neck. "I didn't mean that."

"Yes, you did. Do not apologize. I appreciate the honesty."

Dianna smirked, and her words dripped with sarcasm. "Oh, yeah?"

I narrowed my eyes, adjusting my arm beneath my head to get more comfortable. "Sometimes. It is not something I am accustomed to. Everyone has always been so cautious around me, bowing all the time, which I loathe. They call me 'liege' or 'sir,' as if my name has no meaning anymore. As if my title is all I am or will ever be to them. Half the time, they are afraid to say the wrong thing. It makes me feel as though I am no longer a person to them."

"Well, as you told me, you're not a person—not really."

It was my turn to be shocked. I raised up on my elbow. "Oh, so you *do* listen to me?"

Her eyes softened as a smile lit up her face. I froze, and for a moment, I forgot how to breathe. I had never seen her truly smile—not a real one. It brightened her face, making her seem almost godlike. "I only listen every time you talk. How could I not? You're usually complaining—loudly."

I dropped back down, placing my arm under my head once more. "You said no more fighting."

She shrugged. "That wasn't fighting, more so picking at you, joking."

"I don't understand the difference."

"Don't worry. I'll teach you. So, back to The Hand and the celestials. They weren't born? How do they feel like they do? Neverra and Logan are married. The joy and laughter I saw in Logan's memories were true love."

"The celestials are sentient beings created by my father and the other gods. Their primary purpose is to serve. As you saw, they can love true. Their high metabolism requires that they eat a lot. They are highly sexual and have the same passion for fighting. They are brave, quick to adapt, and very good at war, making them the perfect killing machines. It made them invaluable during battle."

She nodded along, and I could feel myself relaxing. My nerves settled a little more as we continued to speak.

"So, the ones who follow you, the ones left, they listen to you?"

"They do. I handpicked them, recruiting them away from the other gods on Rashearim. I needed my own legion, so to speak."

"And so, you formed The Hand."

"Yes."

She snorted. "So, why does Vincent make that face every time you tell him something?"

I felt my lips tip in a small smile. Dianna's eyes flicked toward them, a brief look of shock appearing in their depths. I cleared my throat. "Vincent has never liked anyone having power over him. I blame Nismera for it."

She did not mention my sudden change in posture or tone, just continued. "Who is that?"

My blood ran cold at the memory, the scars upon my throat and calf burning. "An ancient, cruel goddess. She perished during the war. She made Vincent and a few others. Vincent is the only remaining member of her line."

She nodded again before scooting closer. She must have seen my sudden wariness, because she smiled. "Close your eyes."

"Why?"

"I promise I won't hurt you. I don't even have a forsaken blade on me this time."

My gaze narrowed at her attempt at humor. "I am not worried about you hurting me."

She cocked her head to the side, the beautiful dark waves of her hair spilling over her shoulder. "Then what are you worried about?"

She waited patiently. I held her gaze, and it took a few moments, but I did what she asked and closed my eyes. Her breath was a whisper, the rich, spicy scent of her washing over me. I could feel the heat of her body inviting me to move closer. I was not nervous, but another emotion was crawling through me. It was like tiny needles were dancing across my skin. I was feeling an odd combination of anxiety and anticipation.

"Can I touch you?"

My eyes threatened to fly open, but I remained still. I was thousands of years old and had done things Dianna could not even dream of, yet her question set my blood to boil. I did not move, and my breath hitched as I said, "Yes."

Maybe I did need a different sort of release. It was something I had deprived myself of for centuries. Then again, I had not had the desire until now. Dianna was forbidden, but no one needed to know. It was something to consider.

Wait—no. What was wrong with me? Why was I thinking such things? It was Dianna, not some consort begging to fulfill my desires. I thought about moving away, telling her this wasn't working, but discarded the idea when I felt her fingers comb through my hair. My eyes flew open, and she gave me a small, gentle smile.

"My sister would do this on the nights that were bad for me. It wasn't much, but it helped. I always loved my hair played with while I drifted off to sleep. It was just a comforting touch, reminding me I wasn't alone. As I said, it's not a lot, but it's enough."

Not alone.

Her words struck a chord in me, dampening the spark of lust and replacing it with another emotion. It was more than overwhelming, and this other emotion was one I wasn't familiar with. It was something warm and happy, but also sharp and painful. I had lived alone with a harrowing emptiness for so long that I wasn't sure what to do with warmth and peace. The words could not encompass the feelings, and we shared more than she knew.

"Sorry I burned half of your hair off, but this looks better, anyway. You don't look all mangy anymore."

"No fighting," I mumbled, which only got me a small giggle from her.

She slid her fingers through my hair, her nails a light whisper upon my scalp. She did not have to tell me to close my eyes again; I did it all on my own.

"So, how did you get Vincent to work for you?" Her voice sounded like a hum now, a soft lullaby urging me toward sleep.

"Logan and I slowly convinced him to spend time with us on Rashearim. He is a lot bolder now than he was back then, but he had a good reason for it. Nismera abused him in ways he still has not told us about."

"Poor Vincent. Legends made The Hand out to be monstrous and deadly, but they seem so mortal."

"Mm-hmm, you have not met them all. I have a few like that. They worked with my father, and by law, worked with me. So, we spent a lot of time together. They are more 'mortal,' as you say, than others. I did not want their entire existence to be about fighting and following every command. I wanted more for them."

Her fingers were a repeated dance against my scalp that I soon memorized. "Where are the others?"

I yawned before responding, "On the remains of my old world. I reformed the parts that did not disintegrate. It is small, not as large as this planet, but as you said, it is enough. They still work for the Council of Hadramiel in the city. It looks similar to Silver City, only much larger."

Her hand stopped, and I opened my eyes. The look on her face was almost comical. "You put a *planet* back together?"

"Yes." I was confused. "Oh … I forgot that is not a normal occurrence for your people here." I propped myself up on my elbow as she continued to stare at me as if I had grown a second head. "It is not as difficult as it may seem. My father and his father before him and his before him created several. My great-great-grandfather created Rashearim." She didn't move or speak and just kept staring at me. "Are you all right?"

Dianna shook her head and tucked a stray strand of hair behind her ear. "Yes, sorry, I just didn't know you could do that. I mean, I know you're a god, but I just didn't expect you to be that powerful."

"We can talk about something else, if you wish."

Her gaze flicked to mine, then down to her hands. "There actually is something I wish to tell you. Especially if we're going to start on a clean slate and at least try to be cordial, if not friends, while we look for this book."

I tensed, wondering what else she had been hiding from me. "All right."

She took a deep breath before looking at me again. "I didn't kill Zekiel in Ophanium. He was badly wounded because of Kaden and tried to escape. I stopped him and had every intention of dragging him back. He summoned a silver blade and spoke of you, and how you would return and…" She stopped, as if the memory were painful. "It all just happened so fast. I tried to stop him, but I couldn't, so…" Her words trailed off once more, and I studied her as I waited for her to continue.

My nostrils flared as I inhaled deeply, expecting to pick up a scent change that would tell me she might be lying. I searched her eyes, looking for the beast who had destroyed the Guild in Arariel and caused so many casualties. But she remained somber, and I saw nothing that would indicate she was not being truthful.

Learning the truth of how Zekiel had died hurt me more than I thought it could. I was happy that I felt something, even pain, but it seemed that I was having trouble controlling my newfound emotions.

"Why did you not tell me sooner?"

I saw the pain flash through her eyes, quickly followed by what I thought was anger, but soon realized was resolve. "Would it have mattered? I'm not good, Liam. I had every intention of dragging him back to Kaden, who would have done much worse. No matter what Gabby sees or thinks, I *am* a monster. I do what I have to do to protect her. I always have, and I always will, even if it means fighting a god." She forced a smile.

I had seen her fall back on humor or a crass comment when a topic became too real for her, so seeing her fake that smile, I decided to give her a way out. "You fought terribly, by the way," I said.

"Excuse me?" Her mood seemed to shift, the haunted look leaving her eyes as she smirked. "I stabbed you, in case you forgot."

"You caught me off guard. Do not think it will happen again."

She rolled her eyes. "Sure thing, Your Majesty. Now lie down and close your eyes."

"So forceful," I said, but eased back down and closed my eyes.

I felt her settle before she spoke again. "Can you make a celestial?"

That was odd, but not considering the other questions she had asked. "Unfortunately, that power is only available to the gods created from Chaos. Why do you ask?"

Dianna sighed softly, and I felt the bed dip a little as she moved closer to me. Her fingers slid through my hair again as she said,

"Gabby. I spoke to her earlier, and it seems she really likes Logan and Neverra. It's the first time in a long time I've heard her so happy. She kept going on and on about them. I don't know. I think she would have loved to be a celestial, and if she were, she wouldn't be tied to Kaden or me any longer. She could have a semi-real, normal, happy life."

"If she truly desires it, she could stay and work for me. There are more than enough jobs, and besides, we have a deal. She will get her normal life however she sees fit."

I felt her stiffen against me, the lazy scratches against my scalp stopping. I was about to open my eyes, afraid I had said the wrong thing.

"Thank you, Liam." Her fingers threaded through my hair once more.

"You are welcome. I have not talked to anyone in… Well, I cannot remember the last time."

"Well, you can talk to me, when you're not being a dick."

"I assume that is a euphemism for my actions and not the physical body part."

"Yes." Her small laugh shook the bed. "Now go to sleep."

I do not remember how long it took me or if we continued to talk, but sleep came, and the nightmares did not.

TWENTY-SEVEN

DIANNA

"Rise and shine, Your Royal Highness," I said, shaking Liam's shoulder. He was facing away from the door, still in the same position he had fallen asleep in. Honestly, if I hadn't been able to see his chest rising and falling, I would have thought he was dead.

I leaned closer to him and whispered, "Liam. If you die, does that mean I won't go to a godly prison or whatever?"

He groaned as he slowly turned over. I stood and placed my hand on my hip. "Hey, sleeping beauty."

He stretched, his shirt riding up to reveal a strip of bronzed skin over the defined muscles of his abdomen. His hands hit the ugly headboard, and his feet hung off the other end, the bed way too small for his massive frame.

"What time is it?" Sleep edged his voice, making it an octave deeper. He rubbed his eyes as he sat up on his elbow, part of his hair sticking to the side of his head. He was the most beautiful and annoying thing I had ever seen. I shook the thought from my head.

"Almost eight."

That woke him up. He sat up and swung his legs off of the bed, placing his feet on the floor. He rubbed his face once more before looking at me. "We need to leave. Why did you let me sleep that long?"

"Because you don't sleep, and you need it." I picked up the bag from where I had set it on the old, worn chair when I'd come back to the room. "I burned the rest of the stuff Nym gave us, so I went out and got you some clothes. She might have poisoned the clothes she sent, and you need to blend in. I want to make a pit stop before we get on the road, so hurry and get dressed."

"'Pit stop'?"

"Yes. Paige, the sweet old lady who runs this place, told me about a small breakfast area a few miles outside town. I'm hungry, and you need to eat, too."

I could tell by the look on his face that he was about to refuse.

"Look, if we're going to try this whole 'let's be friends' thing, you have to eat."

I watched him open his mouth to say something, but I cut him off.

"Ah, nope, I don't want to hear it. You may fool your friends, but you can't fool me. I haven't seen you touch one piece of food since we started our little journey, and it's been almost a week. That's probably why you keep having those headaches, too. I honestly don't know how you keep all of that," I waved a hand toward his physique, "in shape while not eating."

"Do not tell the others," he said, the corner of his mouth lifting. "Please."

"Your secret is safe with me, Your Highness."

His eyes narrowed at me. "Also, stop calling me that."

"I will if you eat."

He held my gaze a moment longer before looking at the bag. "I do not need the clothes. I am assuming they are the wrong size, just like everything else Logan has given me."

I scoffed. "Well, I'm sorry. I didn't…"

My snarky words died as he stood, the air around him shivering as thread and cloth spun out of nothing. His worn, faded jeans shifted into a clean dark pair that molded to his powerful thighs and ass. His new shirt was off-gray and clung to his broad chest and wide shoulders. My mouth went dry as a black jacket formed on his body, tapering a few inches past his waist. He held his arms out. "What do you think?"

"You're fine. It's fine." I stumbled over my words, gripping the bag against my chest. The man was ridiculously beautiful. "How did you do that?"

Liam shrugged, dropping his arms to his sides. "It is all material. I can mimic the fabric of the garments you wear. It is far easier to manipulate on this plane. The air on Onuna is filled with useful particles."

"Oh, okay," I said, as if any of that made sense to me. I was too busy fighting the urge to peel him out of those clothes that fit so well. I shook my head. "How did you come up with this?"

"I have paid attention to what the mortals wear. Your garments are far sturdier than the sheer fabrics of Rashearim. I suppose that is because mortals have such thin skin, and the seasons change rapidly here. You said I needed to blend in. Am I not doing it right?"

"No, no, it's great, honestly. I'm just surprised you can do that, I guess."

He studied me for a moment. "You are scared?"

"Not scared, just apprehensive. You're a lot more powerful than I expected."

His face seemed to drop, the hard and expressionless man from yesterday threatening to return. I didn't want that. I preferred this Liam. He had talked to me through the night, and he cared what I thought of his outfit. I stepped a bit closer and narrowed my eyes, smirking as I poked his chest playfully. "What *can't* you do?"

Liam looked down at my finger, his face softening as he put his hands in his pockets. His lips formed a thin line as he thought. He tipped his head back and squinted at the ceiling. I snorted and rolled my eyes at his theatrics. He looked down at me with a playful glint in his eyes. He shrugged and said, "I cannot bring back the dead."

"What? Have you tried?"

"My father could, and I tried on a dead fowl when I was younger. It did not work. Some gifts only he had, I suppose."

"Well, I guess you can't have everything. You'll just have to settle for creating planets and clothes out of nothing." I lightly tapped his arm, hoping to keep this version of him with me a bit longer. "Okay, let's go eat now. I'm starving."

Liam made a low sound of amusement in the back of his throat as he followed me out the door. "So forceful."

The diner was a lot cuter than I had imagined. It was small and reminded me of those movies Gabby loved so much. The interior was rich and rustic, filled with wooden tables surrounded by mismatched benches and chairs. We could see the cooks flipping and frying an array of food through the pass-through window as the wait staff hurried to serve the hungry patrons.

There was a family in a booth at the back, the older child coloring on a small tablet while the woman spooned food into a baby's mouth. A group of teenagers sat at the opposite end of the restaurant, lost in conversation. A few people sat at the counter, watching TV while they ate. It was a nice, quaint little place.

"How's your head?" I asked Liam from behind my mug as I took a sip of my coffee. He barely fit in the booth, but he didn't complain. I'd told him I liked to be by the window, and he had nodded and let me lead the way. Gabby said I people-watched, but really I just wanted to make sure no one could sneak up on me. Several mortals walked along the sidewalk, completely oblivious to the god stabbing at the eggs on his plate.

"Better," he said before taking another bite. I was happy he was eating and hadn't fought me on the large meal I'd ordered for him. I didn't know what he liked, so I'd gotten almost every breakfast item on the menu. The waitress hadn't even blinked, but I think she was distracted by Liam. That seemed to be an issue everywhere he went.

"Strange, it's almost as if I know what I'm talking about."

He swallowed the food in his mouth and said, "Now who is the cocky one?"

"Oh, trust me, big guy, I have nothing on you."

He smirked at me before cutting a piece of sausage. He'd eaten more than I'd thought he would, but I think it was mostly because I kept pestering him. I took another sip of my coffee as a chill ran up my spine. I shivered, causing my shoulders to shake.

"What's wrong?" he asked, mouth half full.

I looked out the window, hoping to see whatever had set my senses off. The hairs on my arms were raised with little goosebumps littering my flesh, but I saw nothing remotely Otherworldly or celestial out there. The street was busy with just your normal run-of-the-mill mortals going about their day.

"Dianna."

I realized I had been sitting and staring in silence for several minutes. "Sorry, nothing. I thought I felt something, but I could just be cold."

He nodded and methodically ate the rest of his food, but now he was alert, his gaze flicking between me and the window.

"You know…" I placed my coffee cup down and folded my hands on the table. "I did have a question I didn't get to ask last night."

"You asked many questions. What more could you want to learn?" Liam asked, taking a sip of his coffee.

"The realms. You said they're sealed. Which I know means our world is locked out from the others. My question is how?"

His face paled, and I heard static interrupt the music. The lights in the cafe flickered a few times, causing a few people to murmur in confusion and stare at the ceiling. I knew it was nothing electrical, but the man in front of me. My question had triggered a flashback, and I could tell he didn't want to speak of it.

"Is that too personal? I'm sorry. I mean, I have seen flashes of your memories, but nothing about that. Besides, the blooddreams wear off after a while."

Liam didn't say anything as he looked at me. He slowly lowered his cup and carefully placed it on the table. He reached up and ran his thumb along the bridge of his nose, the cafe returning to normal as he regarded me.

"It's fine. You said last night that speaking of things may help me."

"Yeah, but if you don't want to—"

"I do." He cut me off as he slipped his hands underneath the table. I could see his biceps flex and knew he was clenching his fists.

"It was the day after my coronation. My father was off handling council business. I remember that the halls were decorated for the festival. It was to be a massive celebration, and I was looking forward to all the fun." He placed his hands back on the table, folding his fingers together and leaning toward me as if he were afraid the mortals in the cafe would overhear. "One of Goddess Kryella's celestials found me at the gathering and told me Kryella wished to see me. I was already slightly inebriated and assumed she just wanted to spend time with me. I was wrong."

Kryella. Why did that name ring a bell? And then it hit me. I had traipsed through many of Liam's memories over the last few days, and I remembered him moaning that name. The moonlight had gleamed on her brown skin and reddish locks as they writhed against each other in the pool at the center of the temple. I had lost it and kicked at one of the massive golden columns, frustrated further when my foot passed through it. Then, when I'd discovered how long that girl could hold her breath underwater, I had prayed for the stupid dream to end.

"The celestial led me out of the great hall and to a temple across the city. It was the one Kryella used for her rituals. I believe Logan spoke of witches there. Well, Kryella was the first of her kind to wield what you all consider magic. Her power frightened even my father—not that she would have ever betrayed him. She, along with a few others, were the only true allies my father had."

Our waitress stopped by then, pulling Liam from his thoughts and the next part of the story. Liam continued after she had refilled our drinks and cleared our plates.

Liam's fingers tapped absently against the side of his mug, but his expression remained flat. "My father and Kryella were there, standing around a massive cauldron set over green flames. They looked to be in deep debate until they saw me. They wore their council garb, and their expressions told me the meeting had not gone well. I asked, but they refused to speak of it. Instead, they explained they needed me to seal the realms."

"Did they say why? I mean, this was before the Gods War, right?"

"Long before."

"So, why?"

"After my mother's death, my father grew paranoid. His temper had increased, while his patience had not. Kryella told me of the spell she wished to perform, and my father reassured me it was for the greater good." Liam paused for a moment and looked up, watching as the teenagers walked past us without a care in the world. As soon as they passed, he continued. "The realms must always have a guardian. My father feared war and had decided on a contingency plan. I was that plan."

Liam looked down at his hands, lost in thought. I was wondering if he would continue when he said, "It required blood—more than I had known I could give. She spoke a few words of enchantment, and the binding was done. I remember being so tired, I could barely stand, and then all went black. My father said I was unconscious for days. He blamed my absence on my untamed ways, so no one would worry, but the three of us knew the truth."

"And the truth was what?"

"The truth was that if my father were to fall, I would become truly immortal. My life would be bound to the realms, and I would never die. When I ascended, the realms would close, and we would no longer be able to travel between them."

I couldn't imagine that kind of pressure. It was literally the weight of the worlds on Liam's shoulders.

"But why? Why close all the realms just because he died? What about the other beings in those realms?"

"My father feared a great cosmic war. He had visions, images and dreams that came to him and then would come true. He saw the universe in chaos, and closing the realms was the only way he could see to garner peace. My father wanted to protect as much life as possible should the gods fall."

Anger burned in me on Liam's behalf, and I lowered my lashes so that he wouldn't see it. His father had not given him a choice before laying the burden of protection on his shoulders. Regardless of the need for a guardian or whatever other bullshit they had fed him, it had isolated him. They had laid the fates of worlds at his feet and given him no support, except what he had created. "I'm sorry."

His gaze flicked to mine for a moment, the corner of his lips twitching. "You have no need for sorrow. It was almost a millennium ago. But I appreciate it."

"Well, as a distraction, I have something that will probably make you mad." I clasped my hands together.

He tilted his head slightly and leaned back, folding his arms across his chest. "Why would I be upset?"

"You know the convenience store we went to yesterday? Well, let's just say a friend of mine who works there gave me a lead on how we can get into Zarall."

He closed his eyes, taking a breath as he swallowed. "You swore with a small finger that you would not leave me behind when you dealt with these 'friends' of yours."

"Technically," I held my hands up in mock surrender, "I didn't leave you. You were just a few feet away, sitting in the car."

"Miss Mar—" He stopped, his jaw clenching. "Dianna. How can I trust you if you keep things from me, but ask me to bare my soul?"

"And that's why I'm telling you. It's the last thing, I promise."

His face told me he didn't believe me.

"I promise, okay? Liam, no offense, but you are terrifying to a lot of people. You aren't supposed to exist, remember? You are our version of the boogeyman. Besides, they're flighty. I didn't want to risk the only chance we have of getting into Zarall."

He didn't say anything for a minute as he held my gaze. The intensity in the depths of his gray eyes awakened something feminine and needy in me. "I was not terrifying to you?"

A pang fluttered in my chest. This powerful and indomitable male was worried about what I thought of him. I had no idea how that was possible.

"Well, no, but I'm crazy."

"That we can agree on."

"Hey!"

For the second time, he smiled. It was just a brief flash of his stupid perfect teeth, but it undid me. It was the simplest thing, and I hated it. He smiled, and gravity shifted, pulling me toward him as if he were my anchor. I pushed the romantic nonsense from my mind. He had been so emotionless and cold until last night. The beauty and warmth of his smile had just come as a shock. That's all it was, no other reason.

"And what did your informant say?"

I crossed my legs underneath the table. "Well, we have to meet a guy at a little pop-up festival on the outskirts of Tadheil. If we leave soon, we should be right on time."

Liam nodded, closing his eyes as he rubbed the bridge of his nose. He was obviously mad, but trying to control his temper.

"I promise I won't keep anything else from you."

He opened his eyes, searching my gaze.

"Fine."

I smiled and reached into my back pocket, digging out my remaining cash. I scooted out of the booth, and Liam followed. He stopped, staring at the cash in my hand.

"Where did you get that?"

I looked down at my hand as we walked to the register. I gave him a small smile and said, "Okay, I promise not to keep anything *else* from you. Starting now. At this very moment."

He sighed, and I swore I heard a growl rumble in his chest.

Twenty-Eight

Dianna

We sat in the car in the unpaved parking lot. The festival was a lot larger than I'd thought it would be. Music filtered in through the windows, and purple, gold, and red lights strobed through the darkness. Rides moved and shifted, and we could hear the screams of those that had dared the roller coaster and the more exciting attractions.

People walked past the car, couples holding hands, families leaving with exhausted children asleep in their parent's arms. We watched as a group of teenagers ran past, whooping and laughing as they pointed at the rides.

"Are you okay?" I asked Liam for the third time.

He hadn't moved to open the door. Instead, he just sat and stared at the chaos of the festival. "Are they always screaming?"

"Does it bother you?"

"No." He glanced at me, then back as another set of screams filled the air. "... Yes."

I knew it bothered him, and I knew why. I had seen some of the battles he had fought and was aware of the scars he carried.

"These are happy screams, not calls to war or death cries."

He took a deep breath, his body vibrating with tension. I had made him perform his little trick again and change his clothes, wanting him to fit into the crowd better. The denim jacket strained over his biceps as he folded his arms. His anxiety was another presence in the car, and I had learned enough about him to know it wasn't out of fear for himself, but of what he could do if he lost control.

"I can go in alone."

"No," he snapped, and then cringed at the pitch of his own voice. "No. You promised you would not leave me. It's just…"

I shifted in my seat so I could face him. "Talk to me."

Liam hesitated and held my gaze as if trying to peer into my soul. It was not suggestive, but calculating. I could tell he was feeling vulnerable and exposed. I held my breath, almost desperate for him to trust me. Until last night, I would have said that was so I could gather information and use what I learned against him. The monster in me urged me to do just that, but the part of me that had reveled in the intimacy knew I would take his secrets to my grave. That was the part of me that existed only because Gabby existed, and it terrified me.

His fists tightened as he seemed to come to a decision, and he took another deep breath before saying, "The screams just remind me of before. It's as if my dreams become reality, and I'm back on Rashearim. I know it's not the same, but every time I hear the screams, I can smell the blood and feel the ground shake. I can see the monstrous beasts rip through the sky, and I'm right back there. It feels like my chest will surely burst."

I reached forward, placing my hand atop his and squeezing once. He glanced down at my hand before meeting my gaze again. He was so wrapped in sadness that I couldn't believe I hadn't seen it before. When I'd first met him, the shell of what I thought a god would be, I'd only seen arrogance, hatred, and contempt in his gaze. But there was so much more than that. I'd thought maybe it was a result of containing too much power, or maybe he had just grown tired of living. But when I looked at him through the lens of last night, I saw grief, sadness, anxiety, and pain. He was in so much pure, raw pain.

"Hey, I am the only beast you have to worry about, and I promise not to rip apart the sky."

The corner of his mouth twisted as he glanced at me. "You are not a beast."

"I mean, I have my moments." I shrugged, squeezing his hand once more. "We can leave? I can try to find another way to get us to Zarall."

"No, if this is our best chance, we have to take it." His jaw clenched as he pulled away from my touch. I could see him slamming up those shields he had so expertly built over the centuries. His face went blank again as he opened the door and stepped out. The cool night air greeted me as I jumped out of the car. I hurried to his side as he slid his hands into his pockets. Maybe I had overstepped in trying to comfort him, but I couldn't stop the compulsion. Damn mortal heart! It was all Gabby's fault.

"Look, we'll go in together, and I won't leave your side, okay?"

He nodded once before adjusting his jacket. I'd forced him to change his outfit almost six times. Everything he made caused him to stand out too much, but then again, that might be just because it was Liam. He could have worn a trash bag, and people would have still broken their necks to look at him. Not that I blamed them, but I needed us to blend in. He still stuck out, but I hoped it would be enough. He took another deep breath and looked past me. I saw his jaw tick again as he held tight to his composure.

"Just don't destroy this place, or electrocute anyone, or disintegrate the rides, or—"

"Dianna."

"Sorry." I held up my hands.

I tilted my head toward the entrance, beckoning him to follow me. He nodded and started walking. His footsteps were light next to mine, and I kept glancing up at him, watching the multitude of lights cast colorful shadows across his face. The muscles in his shoulders flexed every few seconds, coinciding with the laughter, yelling, and roars of the roller coaster as it sped through another loop. "I think I know why your nightmares are so bad. You haven't processed anything that's happened. You buried it, buried yourself, and now that you have been thrown back into everything, it's too much."

Liam didn't look at me as we got into line to buy tickets, his gaze scanning the crowd. "Is that so?"

"Yes, although I was not the mastermind behind that deduction. It was actually Gabby. I blame the psychology classes she took in school. It seems some of it stuck with her."

He finally looked down at me, confusion edging his features. "You spoke to your sister about this? About me?"

"Well, no, not really. I was just complaining because you've been a complete ass. Then Gabby said it's probably because of all you have been through. She thought maybe you just needed someone to talk to." I shrugged, happy that he was focused on me and not the anxiety of being in this place, but unsure of how he would react to my revelation.

He didn't respond, just stared at me, which unnerved me more. Then he made that small grunting noise he often did before nodding and turning his attention back to our surroundings.

"You need a friend, and lucky for you, I'm here." I playfully shoved him with my shoulder, lightening the mood and keeping him distracted.

He looked at me. "Lucky me, huh?"

That strange sensation of being anchored in him overtook me as I stared up at him. Something had changed last night. It didn't make sense, but I knew once this was over, I wouldn't leave. I wouldn't try to flee or avoid my inevitable punishment.

I wanted to believe it was because of Gabby. It would be the height of selfishness to run and drag Gabby with me, hiding from yet another powerful man. Especially since I knew she would be protected and truly happy with The Hand as she worked alongside the celestials. Maybe it was how Liam spoke about his friends or what he had sacrificed to give them the life they now led, but I believed him when he promised her a normal life. So, I wouldn't run, and I wouldn't fight anymore. I would deal with my sentence, whatever it might be, and I almost believed that Gabby was the only reason.

"Besides, maybe this will earn me a lesser sentence once we're done here," I said with a shrug, curling my fingers against my palm and the scar that ran across it.

The line moved forward, and so did we.

"Perhaps."

That gave me a spark of hope and the courage to ask, "And maybe

Gabby can visit me sometimes? I mean, even mortal convicts get visitation rights."

The young mother in front of me glanced back and pulled her children in front of her. I smiled at her, but Liam didn't seem to notice, continuing to stare at me. He narrowed his eyes and said again, "Perhaps."

My grin nearly reached my ears, and I placed my hands behind my back, swaying slightly. "Well, you didn't say no."

We had been at the park for at least two hours, and the only message I'd received from our contact was that he was running late. I stopped at one of the booths to buy a large, fluffy purple cloud of cotton candy and was stuffing my face when Liam complained again.

"What is taking so long? All of your friends are terrible and unreliable."

I sighed as I picked another small piece of sugary deliciousness and placed it in my mouth. I spun, walking backward as I eyed Liam. A group of young girls giggled as they passed, and a buzzer went off to the accompaniment of cheers when someone won a prize at one of the games.

"What? Are you not having fun? I thought you liked the cool shooting game and the bumper cars."

His lip curled in disgust as we continued to walk. "The small cars are violent, and they let small children drive. Do they not care for the small ones? It's ridiculous. Mortal lifetimes are fleeting, yet they build contraptions that could end them in moments."

I tipped my head back and laughed, the sound unfettered and full. When I finally got control of myself again, I wiped the tears from my eyes with my free hand and grinned at him. He was watching me with the oddest expression on his face.

"I have never heard you laugh like that," he said, a smile tugging at his lips.

My shoulders shook as I ran my finger under my eye, still giggling.

I fell in step with him, walking at his side. "You're funny." I bumped his shoulder with mine. "Sometimes."

"Sometimes?" His brow lifted as I stuffed my face with more purple spun sugar.

"Yeah, you know, when you're not being an ass."

He grunted, the sound filled with more humor than irritation. We walked side by side, silence falling between us. It wasn't the awkward kind. It was never awkward with him, just a comfortable quiet. Well, as quiet as it could be with the laughs, squeals, and giggles that floated in every direction here.

"What was with the small box with flashing lights?"

I took another bite of my cotton candy as I thought about his question. "The photo booth?"

"Yes."

I shrugged. "I just wanted proof that the all-powerful World Ender had fun for once."

He stopped, causing me to nearly trip over my own feet. "I do not like that name."

"Sorry," I said, grimacing. I reached out and touched his hand. "I won't say it again."

He nodded. "I would appreciate it."

"How did you get that title? I have heard it so many times in your memories."

He was quiet once again, all traces of humor long gone. "It's not something I wish to speak about if we do not have to."

"Got it, boss." I shoved another bite of candy into my mouth.

"Don't call me that either."

"What, you don't like that?"

"No."

His favorite word.

"Okay, what about Your Majesty? Your Highness? Oh, I got it." I turned slightly toward him, pointing. "My lord?"

He frowned, looking down at me. "Never any of those. Please."

I giggled, but stopped as a trio of women walked past us. They stared at Liam, interest apparent in their eyes. It was the same wherever we went. Not only was Liam devastatingly handsome, but the air of power he exuded made him nearly irresistible to both men and women alike. I didn't think he even noticed.

Liam watched the crowd carefully, but I could tell he didn't actually see the people. His head swung toward the sound of a crack followed by a bell ringing, and I noticed a vein throbbing in his neck. He rubbed his temples, but dropped his hand when he noticed me watching him. It had been like this all evening. He was trying so hard to keep whatever demons nipped at his heels at bay, but his jaw was clenched so tight that I worried he would break his teeth. I wished there was some way to hurry this up, but it was out of my control. So, for the time being, I would distract him with games, overly surgery treats, and photo booths—anything to keep him from self-destructing.

"How is your throat? I assume I did not hurt you too much?"

I choked on the piece of cotton candy I had just stuffed into my mouth. My hand went to my chest as I coughed, trying to clear my airway. His comment and my little fit got us a few looks and whispers from the crowd of nearby teens.

Liam stopped abruptly, reaching out to make sure I wasn't dying. He placed his hands on my shoulder and back, supporting me as I cleared my throat and caught my breath. "Did I say something wrong?"

I waved him off, indicating that I was fine, and he stood straight, dropping his hands. I ignored the fact that I immediately felt bereft at the loss of his touch. "No. Well, yes, but no. We really have to work on your phrasing."

I spotted an empty table between some of the less popular and quieter rides. I led Liam to it and hopped up on the table, resting my feet on the bench. Liam straddled the bench and rested his elbow on the table, watching the frenetic activity of the festival.

I lowered my cotton candy close to Liam. "Want some?"

He turned up his nose, about to refuse, when he looked at me again.

"Trust me. This is amazing."

He eyed me cautiously and took it from me as if he were handling a dead animal. I watched as he tore off a piece and reluctantly placed it in his mouth. His face scrunched at the sweet taste, his eyes closing for a moment before he opened them. He shook his head as a chuckle escaped me.

"It's, umm…"

"Sweet?"

He nodded but took another bite. He seemed more prepared for the second taste, and the tension in his features eased. "Yes, but it is enjoyable."

I leaned back on the table, using my hands as support. "Good."

Liam said something else, but I didn't hear it. A shiver caressed my spine, and goosebumps littered my arms. The hairs on the back of my neck stood on end as I sat up and turned to look behind me. The Ig'Morruthen in me had gone on high alert, ready to attack or defend. It was the same thing I had felt in the cafe and Ophanium. Was another celestial here? I peered into the deep shadows, but nothing stood out.

"Dianna, your eyes."

Liam was standing in front of me, blocking me from sight. I shook my head and closed my eyes, willing them to return to normal before blinking them open.

"What's wrong?"

"Nothing." I looked behind me again. As quick as the feeling had come, it was gone.

"You said the same thing at the cafe." He looked behind me as if he could find what I couldn't. "What is it?"

"I don't know. I thought I felt something."

Liam stared into the darkness for a few moments before returning his gaze to me. "I do not see nor sense anything."

I wrapped my arms around myself tightly. "Maybe I'm just cold."

"Ig'Morruthens do not get cold unless they are in harsh climates, like the planet Fvorin. You should not be cold." He reached out, stroking his fingers along my forehead. "Is this a side effect of the poison your friends so kindly gave you?"

I swatted his hand away. "It's not the poison. At least, I don't think so. I feel fine. I just thought I felt someone or something."

I knew it couldn't be Kaden. He wouldn't show up anywhere near Liam. I had seen the fear on his face when Zekiel died. He feared

Liam, whether he wanted to admit it or not. If it had been a celestial, they would have approached to fawn over Liam as they all did. I looked behind me once more. Maybe Tobias? No, he was more Kaden's bitch than I was.

My thoughts derailed as Liam placed his jacket over my shoulders and pulled it closed over my chest. It draped me like a denim blanket, and I looked up at him in surprise.

"I saw someone do this before you forced me into those tiny, aggressive cars."

I grinned. Liam had been quietly watching everyone around us the entire time. I thought he had been monitoring for potential threats or fighting the demons scratching at his subconscious. Instead, he had been observing and learning mortal behavior. Although he didn't realize how intimate the gesture was, it was nice.

"Thank you," I replied, the corner of my lips turning up as I wrapped his jacket around me. I dipped my chin, burying my face against the collar. I surreptitiously inhaled deeply, taking in his clean, masculine scent. His white T-shirt hugged his torso and was a nice contrast to his tanned skin and muscled arms. The sight of him drew attention, and he turned as he heard the whispered comments from a group of women. He didn't say anything as he sat beside me, but I could tell his mood had soured.

"Don't like the attention?"

Liam rubbed his hands together and lowered his head. "I am not comfortable being out in public. I detest large crowds and would much rather be by myself. There was a time when I used to enjoy gatherings, which I am sure you are aware of, having seen so much of my past. Now I hate it when they stare at me." He rested his chin on his hand, watching as people passed. They would glance at him, then avert their gaze, some not as sneaky as they thought.

"Want me to set them on fire?" I nudged him once more, this time with my knee.

"Absolutely not," he mumbled, not lifting his head. "I just hate it. 'Hate' is the right word, yes?" he asked, tipping his head to look at me without taking his chin off of his hand.

I nodded. "Why? What's the real reason?"

Liam sighed and faced forward again. "It's not important."

"If it bothers you, it is. Besides, we have time to kill. Enlighten me."

An upbeat melody filled the air as the ride closest to us started up again. Liam was silent for a moment, and I wondered if he had heard me through all the noise.

"I do not know. I suppose I feel as if they can see everything I have done. Every mistake, every wrong decision—and they blame me for it."

My brow furrowed. "You know that's not true."

"I told you, it's not important," he said, his harsh tone returning.

"Hey." I pushed at his shoulder, not hard enough to hurt, but enough to get his attention. He sat up and looked at me. "It is, but not for the reason you think. It's important because that's something else you'll have to work on. You're projecting what you feel. They don't know you, just like we don't know them." I wrapped his jacket around me tighter and leaned closer to whisper, "And I'll let you in on a little secret. They're not staring because they know you as an ancient warrior king, or for the battles you've fought or the ones you've lost. That's all in your head. They're staring because they think you're gorgeous."

He pulled back and blinked at me in surprise. "Gorgeous?" He said the word as if it were the most disturbing thing he could imagine.

"That's the part you heard out of everything I said?" I rolled my eyes and placed another piece of cotton candy in my mouth. "Is this the part where we pretend you're not?"

He shook his head, his gaze snagging on my lips as I swept my tongue across them.

I sighed, giving in. "Yeah, you know. Attractive, good-looking, desirable." That seemed to click in his godly brain, because the corner of his mouth twitched. "Especially when you smile."

He shook his head and chuckled, the sound a velvet caress along my skin. Liam was lethal in more ways than one. "You call me one thing, then another. Your opinion changes like the wind."

"Oh, trust me, my opinion has not changed. I mean, you did look terrible for a while there. Plus, I still think you're a complete ass at times, and you have an ego the size of the moon, but I'm not blind."

His smile drooped, which only broadened mine. "Hey, at least I am honest."

"That you are."

I continued to smile, taking the last bits of cotton candy and popping them into my mouth. "Since I have pried your deep, dark secrets out of you, I guess I could let you in on one of mine."

That got his attention, curiosity edging his features. "It seems fair, yes."

"Okay," I said, pointing my cotton candy stick at him. "Don't laugh, but as lame as it sounds, I do want what Gabby worships in her silly cheesy movies. Well, I did. I tried to get serious with Kaden once. He pulled away from me then. He's been different ever since. Definitely more of an open relationship type of guy. Or a monster, I guess."

His eyes bored into mine a fraction of a second too long. "Pity. I wouldn't share."

Heat filled my cheeks, his comment catching me off guard. I rolled my eyes, swatting him with the empty cotton candy stick. "Liar. I've seen you share plenty of times."

Liam grinned as he dodged my failed attempts at assault.

"Is that a normal godly thing? All the giant parties and raging orgies."

Liam's laugh made my knees go weak. "No," he said, glancing at me before scanning the crowd again. "It's a way to pass the time, I suppose. And not all gods are like that. Not when they find their *amata*."

"What's that?"

He shrugged, shaking his head ever so slightly. "In your mortal tongue, it means 'beloved one.' It is what Logan and Neverra have."

"Oh." I nodded slowly. "The mark of Dhihsin?"

He turned to me, his forehead creasing as he tried to find the right words. "Yes, but more. It's the reflection of your soul. I don't know if that's a proper translation. The mark of Dhihsin just shows the world the bond you two have already established."

"So basically, your other half."

"In simple terms, I suppose, but it is much more than that. It's deeper. It is a connection that words cannot fully convey."

"Does everyone have one? Do you have one?" I didn't know why I suddenly cared so much, but I did. The images I had gotten from Liam's subconscious told me he didn't. But what if he'd had a mate and lost them? I could see him being in so much pain that he shut the memories out.

"No. Despite your stories and legends, the universe is not that kind." Sadness crept into his storm-colored eyes.

Maybe Gabby was right. Maybe the powerful, terrifying World Ender was lonely.

I leaned into him, jarring him from whatever cruel thoughts plagued his head. "If you did have one, what would they be? If you had to choose."

He pursed his lips, thinking for a moment. It was a distraction, sure, but it was also fun to actually talk to him.

"If I had the choice, and I had to choose, I would want an equal. A partner in every aspect of my life, like what my father and mother shared."

I meant for the conversation to make him venture further from the ghosts that haunted him, but it seemed he couldn't escape, no matter how he tried. So, me being me, I did what I did best: I counteracted with humor.

"I don't know." I sighed loudly to draw his gaze back to me. "Seems nearly impossible. You would need someone who could handle your massive ego on a regular basis and respond to your every beck and call. Not to mention—"

"Quiet, you." He snorted, this time nudging me with his shoulder.

My back pocket buzzed, interrupting our verbal sparring. I pulled out my phone, reading the text that flashed across the screen.

Ferris wheel. Now.

I showed Liam and nodded toward the large spinning wheel. He stood and helped me from the table, our moods sobering as we headed to the back of the carnival.

TWENTY-NINE

LIAM

The smells here were atrocious, yet the horde of mortals didn't seem to notice. I had seen a pack of D'jeern cause less destruction, and that was saying something, given they were large, clumsy beasts with several horns where their eyes should be, and rotten, jagged teeth, and they ate the remains of dead creatures.

Although the festival was an assault on my every sense, there had been moments when I'd enjoyed myself. I would never admit it to her, but the presumptuous dark-haired woman strolling in front of me may have had something to do with that.

I might not want to admit it to myself, but I enjoyed her companionship. That was something else I would not share with her. To think I could be cordial, even happy, around an Ig'Morruthen was preposterous. The old gods would have thought I'd gone insane, but it was true. I wasn't as trapped in the past when she was near.

Dianna would still have to pay for her crimes against my people and the mortal world. My chest felt heavy at the mere thought of punishing her, but it was the law, and I was the enforcer. But even if this bond of ours was only temporary and fraudulent, I was thankful for the respite she had provided me.

"You're doing it again." Her euphonious voice filtered through my consciousness, snapping me back to the present. The jacket I had given her rolled off her shoulders, revealing more of that golden bronzed skin. She claimed everyone was staring at me, but I had noticed every eye that lingered upon her since we entered this obnoxious place. At last count, it was forty-five—no, wait, there was another, make it forty-six. I told myself I was only keeping track for safety reasons, nothing more. She had enemies, and I was still unsure of this alleged contact of hers. I did not need her poisoned or unconscious again.

"Doing what, exactly?" I asked as we rounded a corner. A line of mortals waited patiently to board baskets attached to a monstrous lit-up circle. They laughed and squealed while I cringed, hearing every piece of metal that struggled to stay together. Their lives were so short, yet they risked death needlessly.

She led me past the rides and deeper into the shadows. No lights or music danced here, and no mortals either.

"The quiet sulking thing," she said as she ducked beneath a few metal bars supporting a flapping piece of plastic. I followed after her, which seemed to be a common occurrence lately.

"Must you pay so much attention to me?"

Her hair was a mass of waves and curls that danced over her shoulders as she turned, a mischievous grin curving her lush lips. I knew her next words would be snarky or crass, but before she could say anything, we heard footsteps against the gravel path. Her mood sobered, her bright smile fading.

An ill-kept man emerged from the darkness, his clothing worn and dirty. His shirt was half tucked into jeans that hung loosely on his hips. The odor that surrounded him in a nearly visible cloud was almost worse than the smells hanging over the festival. I stepped in front of Dianna, shielding her body. She may know this man, but I did not, and the last informant had shot needles into her.

"You are late."

The small, skinny male's eyes widened. "Oh, man, you're huge! Not in a bad way, though. You're just tall and, you know, big. You're really him, aren't you? The one everyone in the Otherworld is whispering about?"

Dianna came to my side, answering before I could. "Yes, it's him.

Now, what took so long? We've been here for hours."

He held his hands up, looking at Dianna, who stood with her arms folded and hip cocked to the side. He swallowed hard, his eyes moving over her form with obvious male interest. Forty-seven.

"Look, you're lucky I even showed. You're blacklisted, sweet cheeks, which means no one from here to the Otherworld wants to help you."

I felt her posture change, a bit of that cocky edge she wore so well dropping away. That bothered me. The air around us became charged as clouds billowed in the distance, my temper festering. I wouldn't allow anything to dim her spirit.

The thin, smelly man went on. "I know your connections are limited, but the Otherworld is stirring. They say he found the book."

I heard her sharp intake of breath and folded my arms. I looked at him as if he were insane. "Your sources are lying to you. It is impossible. The book does not exist."

He shifted from one foot to the other, looking around before he said, "Look, dude, I'm just telling you what I know, okay? You came back, and everyone is on edge. It's chaos out there—and it got worse when you stole his pretty little girlfriend."

I heard Dianna scoff next to me. He met her gaze, placing one hand in his pocket. "Word on the street is that Kaden is beyond pissed, and he's looking for revenge in a big way."

"If he's so angry, why have I not seen him?"

He shrugged, still shifting from foot to foot. I could smell the anxiety seeping from his pores, and my distrust of him grew. "He's smart. I don't think he will strike unless he knows he can take you out."

He stepped a foot closer and leaned toward Dianna. He craned his head forward and whispered, "I heard he doesn't care how he gets you back. Alive or dead, he has a price on your head. I heard he would drag you back in pieces if he had to."

Dianna did not move or say anything, but I felt the panic ripple through her. I looked at her and saw her struggling to maintain the cool demeanor she always projected.

Before I realized what I was doing, I had stepped in front of her again. I grabbed the front of his dingy shirt, lifting him off his feet. "He will *try*," I said, my voice a menacing growl even to my own ears.

His eyes widened as his feet kicked at the air, his hands scrabbling at my wrists.

"You are wasting our time and supplying empty threats. Tell us how we can get to Zarall, or this meeting is over."

"Hey, hey, I don't want trouble, okay? I got the call, and I'm here to help. You need a flight to Zarall, and I got you one. You'll meet a friend of mine. Don't ask his name; he doesn't want to be any more involved than he already is. He is flying a shipment in, and you guys will hitch a ride with the cargo. It's a small plane, but it will get you in undetected."

"What airport?" Dianna cut in.

"International Airport. It's a few miles from here. He will be at one of the back hangars." His beady eyes glanced away from me and toward her. "Time is of the essence, sweet cheeks, so don't make him wait."

I heard the sound of her shoes scraping against the rocks as she turned and walked away. I dropped the pitiful excuse for a man, and he fell to his knees. Dianna did not bother to look back. I knew something was wrong with her, and it bothered me more than I liked to admit.

"It is strange to see," the man said as he picked himself up off the ground, wiping his hands on the knees of his jeans. "The son of Unir and an Ig'Morruthen working together. The stories said you two were destined to spill each other's blood until the stars died, yet you seem more than cozy together."

I did not respond to his comment or care for his opinion. I turned away from him and followed Dianna.

FOR THE FIRST TIME SINCE WE HAD STARTED OUR LONG TREK, DIANNA did not speak. I looked over a few times during our drive to the airport to make sure she was still in the car with me. Her face remained guarded as she drove with one hand on the steering wheel. She leaned her elbow against the window, her free hand against her lips as she chewed on her thumbnail.

"This is the first time you have been silent since we started this trip."

No response.

"Usually, you have a million things to say, in rapid succession."

She didn't even offer me a flick of her gaze as she maneuvered the car smoothly through another turn. Her silence was all-encompassing. I didn't know how to help her as she had helped me the last few days, but I knew I had to try. I was lost in thought, trying to figure out how to make her talk to me, and was surprised when she stopped the car.

The lights from the vehicle lit up an abandoned road. I could see large brown metal buildings off in the distance, and chain-link fences ran along both sides of the road. Overgrown grass threatened to reclaim the pavement, and small insects danced in the beams cast by the headlights. The only other light I could see from here was the blinking red one atop a tall tower. I watched as an airplane accelerated with a deep roar of sound, speeding down the runway before taking flight.

Dianna pulled out her small black phone before getting out of the car. She did not even bother to close the door before she lifted the phone high and walked away. I sighed and stepped out of the car to follow her.

"Dianna."

She said nothing as she circled the area before climbing atop the vehicle, still holding the phone above her head. She was such a peculiar woman.

"I have terrible service out here," she said as she sat and folded her legs in front of her. With one hand, I grabbed the side of the vehicle and hoisted myself up. The car shook and leaned to the side before righting itself.

I sat close to her and watched over her shoulder as she quickly typed out a message, letting our contact know we were here and waiting. Then she pressed the small send button and stared at the screen, as if willing a response to appear.

I glanced at her, half of her face illuminated by the glow of the phone. "Are you planning to remain silent for the remainder of this trip?"

Her phone made a small beeping noise. She quickly read the message and closed the phone before I had a chance to see what it said. She nodded, and I waited for her to answer my question, desperate for her to speak to me. I longed for her to do any of the annoying things she had pestered me with over these last few weeks. Instead, she took a breath and pulled her knees up against her chest, wrapping her arms tightly around them.

"He'll be here at dawn. So, we have a while."

"Dianna." I lowered my head toward her, trying to get her to look at me. "Will you please tell me what is troubling you?"

She did not speak as she tipped her head back, looking up and avoiding my eyes. I followed her line of sight, seeing what she saw. Stars dimly lit the night sky, and a crescent moon hugged the horizon. It was not as beautiful as it was on Rashearim, but it held her gaze. I leaned back and studied her profile, the cool night breeze teasing at the loose pieces of hair around her face.

"So, all of those are other realms?"

Her question caught me off guard, but I didn't hesitate to answer. "Some, yes. Some are ancient dead worlds that were alive long before even my father was born."

She still wore my jacket, and she wrapped it tighter around herself. "So, there were gods before you?"

I knew she was avoiding whatever was really weighing on her, but I refused to press. I was content that she was speaking to me. "Oh, yes. Many. Honestly, I was ignorant as a child. I should have paid more attention, but from what I recall, there are great beings that reach past even the universe. They are formless, giant things. My father said that's where you go when you pass. Another realm that even we cannot reach, beyond the stars, beyond time—everlasting peace."

She nodded as her eyes scanned the glittering darkness. "I envy you."

My brow furrowed as I stared at her. "What?"

She shrugged, her eyes reflecting the moonlight. "I'll never get to see those other worlds. This realm is all I will ever know. But I wish I could see more."

"Maybe one day."

She turned to me then, a small smile tugging at her lips. There were no tears in her eyes, but sadness etched her beautiful features. "We both know once this is over, if I'm not dead, it's whatever godly prison you have for me. We don't have to pretend."

I said nothing. I had been thinking about what would become of her once all of this was done, and my options weighed heavily on my conscience.

"I need another promise." She swallowed hard, as if the words were difficult to form.

"But I have already made you so many." I tried to lighten the mood. I wanted to soothe the pain I could feel radiating from her.

"If Kaden gets his hands on me, take care of Gabby, okay?"

Her words caught me off guard. "Is this sudden shift in your emotions due to what that man at the festival said about Kaden?"

"You don't know him like I do. I've been with him for centuries. Everything he says, he means, and he will follow through. He does not make idle threats, Liam. If he says he will drag me back, even in pieces, he will."

The way she looked at me, the way she spoke—it was as if her fate were already sealed. She was certain he would take her.

"I will not let him have you."

Her smile was small and did not reach her eyes. "I know what I signed up for, and I knew the risks. I knew when I killed Alistair and returned to you the price I would pay. The moment I decided to help you, my fate was sealed. Freedom and servitude went hand in hand with Kaden, and I gladly accepted his terms. I paid for Gabby's life and freedom with blood. You and I both know that I'm covered in it."

Dianna shook her head and stared at her hands as if she could see the blood on them. My playful hellion was long gone as the reality of our situation hit some deep part of her.

"I know I am not a good person." She paused and let out a short, humorless laugh. "Gods, I'm not a person at all anymore. I know my fate, and it's one I deserve, but Gabby is innocent. She always has been. I may have been the strong one who stole so we could eat, the one who fought so we could live, but she held me together. Her only fault is that she loves me. Even when I was at my worst and lowest, she never stopped loving me. She deserves to be happy. I've chained her to this life for too long. So, promise me. If something goes wrong and I don't make it, promise me you will keep her safe. Please. Just promise me."

Her eyes held no humor as she turned and stared at me, her vibrant light snuffed out. She was silently pleading, desperately begging me to keep her sister safe. I decided then and there that this woman should never beg. I understood she cared for her sister, but who cared for her? At that moment, she seemed so innocent. She was not the vicious, fire-wielding beast I had first met. She was just a girl who had been born into chaos. Kaden had backed her into a corner, her choices taken until she had reformed herself into a weapon. She had become what she needed to be to protect the only person who still saw good in her.

Not able to bear the sight of her so alone in the dark, I reached out and took her hand the same way she had done mine during my night terrors. It had comforted me, and I wanted to do the same for her. "I promise to make sure Gabby is safe. I also promise that he will never lay a hand on you again. If he even tries to take you away, I promise I'll make him regret ever being born."

"There's that ego again." She sniffled, shaking her head slightly.

I gave her a lopsided grin. "Ego? No, you have seen within my memories that I have made monsters and men beg for their lives."

"Oh, I've seen my fair share of begging…"

Her words caused the strangest feeling in me. It started in my diaphragm and poured outward. I threw my head back and laughed— truly laughed. It overcame me so quickly that the sound of it was a little shocking. I looked back at her, and the surprise on her face was satisfying. "You know way too much of me. I am afraid even The Hand would be envious."

That earned me a real smile. Dianna looked down at our joined hands. "I promise not to tell." Her thumb traced over the back of mine. "You're sweet when you're homicidal."

"I don't know what that means."

She glanced at me and gave me a small smile before tugging her hand from mine.

Half of that was a lie. I knew what she meant, but I found pleasure in watching her try to explain words and phrases to me. She shifted and lay back on the vehicle. I eased down beside her as she adjusted the jacket over herself. I saw her dip her chin and inhale deeply of the sturdy material before she pulled a strip of paper from the pocket.

"You kept them?" Her laugh was small and quick, but it calmed my nerves. "I thought you left them behind at the photo booth." Her eyes lit up with joy as she looked at the pictures.

"Yes, you suggested I should."

"I don't know if you listen to me half the time."

"I always listen."

She rolled her eyes before pointing at one of the images. "This one is my favorite." It was the one where she had been pointing at the flashing camera with one hand while trying to move my face toward it with the other. My look of pure confusion was captured forever. "The mighty king is friends with his archnemesis, the Ig'Morruthen."

I scoffed, causing her to turn toward me. "Not my nemesis. You would actually have to best me in a fight."

She playfully slapped my arm. Her tiny hits barely affected me, but it seemed to be some weird form of affection for her. "Okay, fine, not your nemesis. But what about a friend?"

"Yes." I nodded. "My friend."

That answer seemed to please her. She looked back at the pictures, caressing the image. "I like this one because it reminds me of how much I try to force you to listen," she said with a laugh.

I decided that was my favorite, too.

I didn't remember how long we talked, but somewhere amidst her laughter and smiles, I decided I would rip the world apart for her. When she had turned into me and wrapped her arms around my chest, the world had slipped away. It was a brief reprieve as I held her body curled against mine. It was a moment of peace—until the dreams that threatened to shred my soul shattered it.

Thirty
Liam

The silken sheets tangled around my legs as we giggled, laughed, and tumbled beneath them. I braced my forearms on either side of her head, holding myself up so as not to crush her. Her hair clung to her flushed face as she laughed up at me. I caressed the curve of her cheek, brushing back the caramel strands, unable to remember her name.

She leaned forward, kissing me once more before laying back against the bed. Clothes and pillows were strewn around my chamber, proof of the pleasure we'd enjoyed the previous night. Morning light spilled into the room, and songbirds sang as they flew by the open window.

"What if Imogen finds out?"

"I am not betrothed to Imogen."

She bit her bottom lip, tracing a finger along my jaw. "She speaks of you as if you are hers."

My words held no kindness, only truth. They were the same words I'd uttered to Imogen and several others who thought space in my bed meant my heart or my crown. "I do not love her, not as she loves me. Nor can I love you. You will not gain a crown by bedding me. If that's what you seek, I cannot give it to you. Do you understand?"

"Yes," she whispered, wrapping her arms around my neck. "I shall have you in any way I can." Her leg inched higher up my side as she ground her hips into mine.

"Is that so?" My smile widened as I leaned forward, slanting my mouth over hers. A soft moan parted her lips as I claimed them. I cradled the side of her face and jaw, gently tipping her head back to allow me better access as my tongue danced with hers.

I pulled back and licked my lips before slowly opening my eyes. My heart stuttered and then became a sudden hammering mess in my chest. A slender, golden-skinned beauty with thick, dark hair that curled around her face and shoulders had replaced the lush, pale curves of the woman beneath me. I pushed up and scooted away, staring at her in shock.

"Dianna." I breathed her name. "I do not wish to dream of you this way."

"Are you sure?" She sat up, drawing closer to me. The dark waves of her hair spilled down her back, revealing the sweet, lithe curves of her body and the soft swell of her breasts.

Something inside me snapped. My mouth went dry, and my body burned with need.

Dianna ran a single hand up my arm as that sultry voice whispered like a siren's song, "Stay with me."

I swallowed the lump forming in my throat as I raised my hand, brushing back a wild strand of hair that had fallen across her forehead. I lightly caressed her brow with a single finger—the same brows that she raised so often in my direction. I trailed my touch along the curve of her cheek—the same cheeks that brightened when she smiled. I cupped the side of her face, my hand curling around her jaw as I rubbed my thumb over the shape of her full lips. Oh, how I wanted to taste that beautiful, defiant mouth.

I wondered what it would take to make her lips part, make her scream. I longed to find out if she would bite and claw at me as I buried myself so deep inside her that she would never even think of allowing another to touch her.

"You already consume my every waking thought. Must you consume my dreams as well?"

She tipped her head back as I ran my fingers along her jaw,

watching as her pulse jumped when I caressed the delicate line of her throat. I moved slowly, memorizing every line and curve of her face. A soft moan escaped her as my hand slipped lower, tracing her collarbones before dipping into the valley between her breasts.

I knew then that I wanted to touch her like this for real, regardless of if it was wrong, a part of my brain whispering that it was forbidden. *We* were forbidden.

Her body coiled beneath mine, drawing me closer as if she were a wave upon the sea, and I was prepared to drown. My eyes met her hazel gaze, and I knew the moment would be branded in my memory long after I had turned to stardust. I leaned forward to—

I felt wet heat replace the warmth of her silky skin and forced my gaze from her eyes to look at my hand, shocked to see blood pooling beneath my palm.

No.

She coughed and raised her head, tears staining her eyes as a trickle of blood dripped from the corner of her mouth.

"You promised," she said, her words garbled.

No!

I pulled her to me, cradling her head as she coughed. I pressed my hand against the hole in her chest, trying to stop the bleeding, but it was no use. Her body cracked and bent before turning to ash.

I slammed my eyes shut as the power inside of me threatened to combust. The dark ring on my finger began to vibrate, Oblivion reacting to my rage and grief, eager to be summoned. An ache, pure and blinding, consumed me, the sharp agony making me want to destroy everything that had ever hurt her. The dark blade was all too eager to comply, and with it, I could reduce any living thing to mere atoms.

My eyes snapped open, and I paused when I realized I was no longer in my room. I looked up, scanning my surroundings. The scenery was completely different, as was I. I opened my arms and looked down at myself. Silver armor covered my body. My hands were clean, all traces of Dianna gone, and my chest ached with the loss. I spun slowly, my hands still outstretched as I looked around.

I was in the massive hallway of the Chamber of Raeul, the meeting and commerce building of Rashearim. Laughter and raised voices filled the cavernous space, carried in on the breeze that fluttered the cream-colored banners attached to the towering columns. I strode down the main corridor, passing statues of the gods in various battle poses, following the sounds of revelry.

I stopped at the large carved-out entrance of the meeting room. Several men and women sat at a long, thick table. They wore the same armor I did, but theirs was dirty, covered in various forms of dirt and debris.

I knew them all. It was us—The Hand and me. Logan, Vincent, Neverra, Cameron, Zekiel, Xavier, and Imogen. I could not place what battle we all reminisced about, just that I remembered this time. It was a happier time.

"Samkiel, you become any faster in battle, and you will not require us anymore!" Logan yelled as he leaned back, his helmet on his lap.

"That's incorrect. He may have the strength and skill, but not the brains!" Cameron shouted, holding up a cup as the others laughed.

"Continue that, and I will make sure everyone sees the brains you do not have," my own voice said from the far end of the table. The tone was relaxed and poised, but still dripping with overconfidence. I hated this version of myself. I did not remember who I was back then, and I certainly did not feel like him anymore. All these memories ever brought me were grief. I tried to focus, willing myself to wake up, but the scene continued to play out before me.

"How many Ig'Morruthens was that today? Ten? Twelve?" Xavier asked, stealing a bit of food from Cameron.

"Not enough," I heard my dream self respond. "Their numbers swell, yet the gods barely bat an eye."

Vincent took a large gulp of his drink and cleared his throat. "The less of them in this realm, the safer we will all be."

Memory Samkiel nodded and rubbed his chin. "I agree. They are mindless, destructive beasts. They have no real purpose except to be weapons for war. The quicker we free the realms of them, the better."

The others held their glasses high, cheering in unison before continuing to speak and laugh about some other nonsense.

"Wow. Harsh."

I did not move as Dianna appeared in my peripheral. We stood side by side, watching the scene play out before us.

"It was a different time. I was different. Arrogant." I sighed deeply. "I believed that killing was the only way to protect my home."

She tipped her head toward me, her arms behind her back. "Hey, you don't have to explain yourself to me."

"Is this a part of our deal? The blooddreams you mentioned? Is that why I dream of you now?"

A slow, seductive smile spread across her face as she bit her bottom lip. "Would you like that to be why? Would it excuse all the nasty things you think of me, hmm?"

I felt my jaw clench as I looked away from her.

"I mean, how could you ever be with a monster?"

"You are not a monster," I snapped and met her gaze, which only caused her to laugh.

"Don't worry, your secret's safe with me. Besides, I'm not really here, anyway. I'm just your higher self trying to tell you something."

I narrowed my eyes at her and demanded, "Tell me what?"

Dianna strode forward, closing the distance between us, and I held my breath. She reached up and caressed my cheek lightly. I refused to move as her gentle touch turned painful, her nails digging into my cheeks and dragging my face closer to hers. Those once enchanting hazel eyes burned crimson as she leaned in close enough that I felt her hot breath upon my lips.

"That this is how the world ends." Her voice was a sibilant hiss.

My hand shot up, clasping her wrist as she gripped my jaw tighter. She was so strong, turning my head and forcing me away from the room. I stumbled, and when I corrected myself, the scenery had changed once more.

I slid my hand along my jaw where her claws had sunk into me. There was no blood, and no scratches marred my face. I swallowed and looked around, trying to figure out where I was. I stood near a balcony, but it was one I didn't recognize. Through the open doors, I saw pyramids looming in the distance. Several smaller buildings made from the same stone were scattered in the space around them. The moon hung high, casting everything in silver and reflecting off the armor I still wore. It was gorgeous, but not my home.

The sound of many footsteps marching in unison made me turn. Torches hung on the walls, the small flames barely glowing. I stared into the shadows past the light, and silver-clad soldiers appeared as if summoned from the darkness. They carried thick oval shields at their sides and held ablaze weapons. I didn't take my eyes off them as they stepped forward as one, their boots slamming against the stone floor. These were my soldiers.

The wind whipped at me as my back hit the railing of the balcony. The soldiers stopped and shifted their shields in front of them. Then, as one, they pointed to something beyond me.

I peered over my shoulder and saw an orange glow lighting the sky. I slowly turned, gazing in horror as the once vibrant, beautiful landscape was reduced to ash and rubble. Crimson lightning struck in rapid succession, and thunder shook the ground. As the light flashed across the sky, a monstrous silhouette appeared in the clouds. Its roar echoed through air thick with ash and smoke, the sound so terrifying that it made the primal part of me want to flee. Wings, thick and powerful, beat at the sky, the rest of the Ig'Morruthen's body hidden within the billowing clouds. The beast roared again and sent thunderous flames across the already devastated land.

I knew this scene—only it was not happening on Rashearim. No, I was on Onuna. Was that what my higher self was trying to tell me? Was it trying to warn me of the complete and utter destruction of another world? I stumbled back and let loose a roar of denial and grief.

I bumped into someone and whirled around to see Dianna. Her eyes were solid white, but it was the thick bruise around her throat that made my stomach churn. It looked as if someone had broken her neck, pulling so violently that they had nearly ripped her spine from her body.

"Dianna!"

A sob escaped me as I reached for her, but I stopped when the shadows behind her moved. I glanced over her head and noticed the throne in the far distance. The figure that sat upon it had no face; only his shape told me he was male. He leaned one elbow on the arm of the chair, his fist supporting his chin. The armor he wore was pure obsidian. Spikes jutted from the knees and shoulders, mimicking the crown he wore.

Kaden.

A rumbling growl echoed behind him as what I thought was part of his throne moved. The tip of a thick, spiked tail whipped through the air and out of view. A large, bulky body emerged from the darkness, red eyes narrowing into slits as the creature glared balefully at me. It was the same winged beast Dianna had turned into, only larger.

"Look what you've done," Dianna said. I turned my attention back to her, her voice garbled by the devastating condition of her neck. "Look. You have brought destruction here."

"No! No, I did not." I shook my head rapidly from side to side.

Her voice was but a raspy whisper as she pointed behind me. "That is all you are. Destruction."

"No."

"You see now, Samkiel. This is how the world ends."

More people shuffled forward from behind his throne. There were so many, several hundred filling the temple. All of them were covered in dirt and bleeding. Some were missing limbs, some were without heads, and others were mere skeletons. They raised any limb they could, pointing to the chaos behind me.

They began to chant, and I raised my hands to my ears, trying to block it out, trying to stop it. The sound was deafening, and it didn't help that the words seemed to echo within my head, growing louder with each step they took.

"No, I can stop this. Tell me how!" I shouted over the growing voices.

They kept coming, moving inexorably forward, pushing me toward the edge, repeating the same thing over and over again.

"This is how the world ends."

"This is how the world ends."

"This is how the world ends."

THIRTY-ONE
DIANNA

"Liam." I tugged on his arm once more, trying to wake him up. He kept mumbling as if he were talking to someone, and his face was contorted in pain. He had tossed and turned the entire night, which meant no sleep for me. "Liam!" I shouted, turning him toward me. I lightly tapped the side of his face a few times, trying to get him out of whatever loop he was stuck in. His head tossed, sweat slicking his skin as tears leaked down his cheeks. I couldn't stand to see him in such distress.

"Liam, for the love of gods, wake up, you idiot!" I yelled and shook him a little harder this time.

His eyes popped open, the silver of the irises blazing. I was thinking of a way to knock him unconscious again, so he wouldn't destroy me and the car, when the sound of his voice startled me.

"How the world ends." The words were barely a whisper.

Liam's eyes returned to normal as they focused on me, and recognition flashed in their depths. "Dianna?" He pushed away from me harder than I think he intended, causing me to land on my ass on the floorboard. "What are you doing?"

I sat up in the cramped space as much as I could. "First of all, ow, you jerk! Second, I was trying to wake you up. You were having a nightmare again."

He turned as much as he could and tried to stretch, groaning when he hit his head. "How did we get in here?" he asked, rubbing the top of his head and scanning the inside, his features still drawn from his nightmare.

"Well, I'm okay. Thanks for asking," I said, tossing a glare his way. "You fell asleep first, and I didn't want either of us to roll off the top of the car, so I moved us. The backseat has enough room for us to sleep comfortably. Except I didn't, since you kicked and turned the entire night."

He looked out the window, staring at the horizon and the rising sun.

"Where is your next informant?"

Something felt off. "What's wrong with you?"

"Nothing." He didn't even look at me.

"Um, he should be here soon. We can go wait," I said, waving a hand toward one of the deserted hangars.

Liam didn't say anything as he popped open the back door without touching it and slid out. I scooted to the edge, following him into the dawn. "Liam, you had another nightmare. Is that what's bothering you? Do you want to talk about it?"

He didn't look at me and didn't turn around. "No."

Okay, so we were back to that.

A FEW HOURS LATER, THE JET WE HAD TAKEN TOUCHED DOWN IN Zarall. Liam hadn't spoken to me the entire flight, and I didn't know why. I felt like I had made him mad, only I hadn't done anything. Maybe I'd revealed too much last night. Hearing how desperate Kaden was to get me back and knowing he meant to by any means necessary had more than rattled my nerves. I knew what he was capable of, and Kaden never said anything he didn't mean. Maybe I had pushed too hard, asked too much, and Liam had decided I wasn't worth it.

I was very confused. We'd had fun and talked, and Liam had actually laughed. I thought we were friends, and his sudden coldness hurt.

I wondered if I had done something wrong, and then I felt stupid for caring so much.

Stupid fucking mortal heart.

"This is where I let you two off," the pilot called back to us.

Liam finally turned away from the window and looked at me. I unbuckled my seatbelt and stood, utterly pissed at his rapid mood change.

The pilot stopped me at the door. "Remember, we have a deal." His shirt was coffee-stained, and his hair was messy. His unkempt and rumpled appearance matched the plane, making me feel lucky we had made it here in one piece.

I opened the hatch with a hard yank on the metal lever. "Yes, yes, I will make sure you're paid well."

He mumbled under his breath as I jogged down the rusty steps and hit solid ground. I heard Liam's footsteps on the tarmac behind me. The sun shone brightly against the rustic white-and-blue backdrop of the abandoned airport. I realized the pilot had dropped us off as far from the terminal as possible. There were no cars or anyone else in sight. It looked like we would have to figure out how to get to Drake's compound ourselves.

I glanced at Liam, who was looking everywhere but at me.

"Remember, these are my friends, and they are the good kind, so please, don't get sword-happy."

A muscle in his jaw tightened. "I have already promised."

I smiled and held my hands out. "That you did. Okay, now let's hold hands."

He looked at them, then back at me, his brows knitting together. I already knew he was about to object. "I don—"

I grabbed his hands before he could finish his protest. Black mist danced around my feet, and between one breath and the next, we disappeared from the airport.

LIAM HELD ANOTHER LARGE BRANCH AS I DUCKED UNDERNEATH IT. "Don't say anything."

"My only suggestion is if you wish to teleport, that we have a more accurate location."

I spun, my foot catching on a root. "I just said don't say it."

Okay, he had a point. I probably should have paid more attention when Drake had given me the details of where they would be once our ruse was complete. But it had been nearly three months, and it was all a little fuzzy.

"So, enlighten me. What about these so-called friends of yours is so special that we are trekking through this jungle to meet them?"

"Oh, look, *now* you want to talk. Sure you don't want to keep sulking the rest of the trip?"

He stopped short. "I do not sulk."

I rolled my eyes and leaned over, ripping at a vine that had wrapped around my ankle. "Sure. What do you want to call the last few hours?"

He looked away from me. "I was … thinking."

I rolled my eyes again and continued walking, lifting my feet a little higher this time. "Whatever. Look, I can try to get us closer."

"No. You have already tried, and it just pushed us further back. We will continue on foot."

I sighed loudly, wanting him to know how much he annoyed me. He held his ablaze blade close, using it to cut through some of the thicker foliage as we pressed on. The silence was getting on my nerves, so I did what I did best: I talked.

"Drake is the one I'm closest to." Liam stopped mid-swipe as if my voice had startled him. He nodded and continued hacking at the thick foliage as I went on. "He is technically the Vampire Prince, but he rarely acts like one. Ethan is his brother, and king. Long story short, their family came into power, and now they rule over every vampire on Onuna. Which may seem like a lot, but their numbers are actually pretty low, considering the population."

He cut a path in front of us, several branches falling to the ground. "And how does one come into such power?"

"Family. Kaden had recruited them long before I came around.

Ethan wasn't king then, but with Kaden's help, he rose to power. A few other vampire families wish he were not king, but I guess that's a given when it comes to someone in control. I'm sure you would understand that." I placed my hand on a rather large log and maneuvered myself over. Liam just picked it up and tossed it aside like a bothersome stick. *Show off.*

He shrugged, and I thought he would resume his silent cutting and go back to ignoring me, so I was surprised when he said, "To an extent, yes." I looked at his broad back as he spoke. "No one was thrilled about me becoming king, including me. It's more than just a title to be given. The responsibilities that come with it can be a heavy burden. The people who rely on your every word and watch your every movement…" He stopped, as if taken back to some part of his memory I couldn't reach. "It's overwhelming, and something I would not wish on anyone."

That piqued my interest. "So, if you had a chance, just say hypothetically, would you give it up?"

His eyes met mine, something flashing in the stormy depths. "To not be king?"

I nodded.

"In a heartbeat. Yes. If it meant I could be whoever I wanted, do whatever I wanted, I would give it up." Guilt flashed over his features as he shook his head. He started walking once more. He spoke his next words so quietly they were nearly lost. "But I cannot."

I followed, letting him lead once more.

"I never told anyone that before." He glanced back at me. "Please, do not repeat it."

I held my hand up. "Pinkie promise."

He didn't even attempt a smile. The look that flashed across his face reminded me of the Liam who had first started this trip with me, not the one who talked to me until we fell asleep. "No more of those."

"Okay," I said and dropped my hand to my side.

Liam turned and stalked away from me. It was silent again, and it hurt. Being around him annoyed me more often than not, but at other times, I just had fun. Fun was something I hadn't had in a long, long time, and it was something I hadn't known I needed. His withdrawal made me feel lost.

"Are you sure we are even in the correct place?"

I shook my head, clearing my thoughts. "Yes, I promise. He told me exactly where it would be. I just don't remember the jungle part." Sweat dripped into my eyes as I turned, checking behind us. "I can sense their essence, but every time I feel like we're getting closer, it's just more jungle. It's almost like—"

My sentence ended on a surprised yelp as I was tackled from the side. I was tossed in the air and then caught, the air rushing out of my lungs. I was spun in a full circle before muscled arms gripped me tight around the waist. Drake finally sat me down on my feet and smothered my face in kisses.

"Oh, how I have missed you!"

I smiled brightly up at my friend. I felt the tears sting my eyes and hugged him back. The last image I had of him was his face melting into ash as he'd said, *"Better to die by what you think is right than to live under a lie."*

My eyes widened in shock when the warmth of his body was ripped away. Liam held Drake by his throat. Drake's feet dangled as Liam held his blade close to his eye.

"Liam!" I shouted, running over and grabbing on to his arm. "Put him down!"

A look I had never seen outside the blooddreams graced Liam's face, and my heart stopped. He looked every bit the World Ender the stories foretold. Was that the same look he gave all who had fallen before his blade?

"He attacked you."

I tugged on Liam's arm. Drake didn't struggle. He just gripped Liam's wrist and eyed the blade. I slipped under Liam's arm, putting my body between him and Drake. "No, he didn't. He is just excited to see me. Please put him down."

Liam's piercing gaze focused on me, and I was mesmerized by the silver rimming his irises. I gently touched his chest, and for a split second, his face softened. He dropped Drake, his gaze never leaving mine as he clenched his hand and his blade disappeared. Liam took a careful step back, putting distance between us. I licked my lips and looked away, shocked to see that the forest had disappeared.

Drake rubbed his throat and shook his head at the guards circling us, silently ordering them to stand down. The dogs at their sides snarled and bit at the air, their handlers struggling to control them. They obviously did not like the smell of either Liam or me.

Drake whistled and ordered them back to their posts. The men nodded and backed off. I turned, taking in more of our surroundings. I hadn't been here before, and for good reason. We all wanted to make sure that even if Kaden tore my mind apart, he couldn't find their safe houses.

The paved driveway split and flowed around a large fountain. It was beautiful, but what held my attention was the massive castle. Yes, it was a castle, because why would any vampire family have a normal house? I placed my hands on my hips and leaned back to take in the full view.

Large, dark gray stone walls shaped the imposing building. Several towers rose from the massive structure, with long oval windows lining the front of the palace. I could hear water off in the distance, and from the smell of roses and jasmine, I knew there was a garden somewhere off to the left.

"It's an old family heirloom," Drake whispered in my ear.

I turned, slapping him playfully on the chest. "I hate when you do that."

"Mmm, I thought you liked it when I whispered sweet words in your ear?" he asked with a predatory grin. His voice was a throaty growl, but his gaze was focused behind me. I could feel Liam at my back and knew Drake was trying to agitate him. My only question was, why? And why did he think flirting with me would work?

I glared and flipped him off. He smiled widely before nodding toward the wide stone steps to our right. "We felt your power the minute you landed. I had assumed you would have found me sooner, given the directions I gave you, but regardless, I am glad you are here. Now, if you will follow me, my brother is waiting."

"Waiting?" I asked.

"Yes. It's time for dinner, and we have a lot to discuss."

Drake flashed me a dazzling flirtatious grin before starting up the stone steps. I sighed and followed him as Liam fell into step beside me.

"This is your friend?" Liam asked.

"Yes, an actual friend who doesn't get pissy and shut me out when something is clearly bothering him." I knew my words dripped with anger, but I was still annoyed.

The stoic glare I had seen so often on Liam's face returned, but he didn't say anything.

We reached the top of the steps just as Drake pulled open the large wooden double doors. The smell of food hit me as soon as I crossed the threshold, and my stomach growled.

"Hungry, Dianna?" Drake asked, glancing at me.

"Yes, very."

He laughed, but I barely heard him as I gaped at the interior of the castle, which was more impressive than the outside. A few guards stood by the door with weapons at their sides. They didn't look at or even acknowledge us as we entered the foyer. I heard heartbeats throughout the castle, probably mortal staff and guests. The presence of a few dozen vampires sent an icy chill crawling through me, raising goosebumps along my arms.

"This place is massive," I whispered as I spun, trying to take it all in. A large chandelier, the size of a car, hung from a ceiling that soared to a staggering height. Two large hallways branched off on either side of the entryway, the walls decorated with paintings old and new. A large staircase faced us, a red rug covering the smooth stone steps.

"Not necessarily," Liam said. "The halls of Rashearim would make this seem like a small hut."

Drake looked toward Liam, not missing a beat. "Size isn't everything."

I shot a look at Drake, willing him not to antagonize Liam further. Liam was already in a sour mood, and I didn't want to deal with it anymore tonight. Drake just shrugged as Liam continued to pass glances between us.

"Ethan has rooms ready for you both." He glanced at Liam before giving me a devastating smile. "I can show you to your room if you would like to freshen up. You both look and smell terrible."

"Thanks, I would love that."

"Ladies first." He smiled and held out his arm. I took it, slipping mine under his. Drake looked at Liam. "I'll have someone show you to yours."

I could have sworn I heard Liam growl behind us as we headed upstairs, but I chalked it up to exhaustion.

DRAKE HAD MADE SURE I HAD EVERYTHING I NEEDED. I GRATEFULLY used the shaving products. The hair on my legs and vagina had gotten a little out of control. There was an assortment of every type of soap, scrub, and exfoliating cream. I hadn't realized how much I'd missed actual soap. Was I being spoiled? Probably. Would I complain? No, never.

I filled the massive tub with way too many bubbles, and after a long soak and several scrubs later, I finally felt like myself. I got out and wrapped myself in a lush towel before wiping the steam off the mirror. My hair was a tangled mess, even after washing. I spent some time working the knots from the thick, wet strands and wondered if Liam's room was as nice as this one.

I stopped myself short. He was back to being rude and dismissive, so they could have put him in the dungeon for all I cared.

I closed my eyes for a second, willing the flame inside me to the surface, drying my hair a little faster. I stopped after just a few moments when I started to feel a little dizzy. A downside to eating mortal food and not mortals was that while the food sustained me, I didn't attain the level of power that came with consuming people. The plus side was that I didn't feel like a monster for crawling around inside someone else's mind.

My bare feet were silent against the cool tile as I left the bathroom, the lights going out behind me. The room they'd given me was huge, even for a castle this size. My toes curled against the plush carpet. It was so soft, and definitely better than in the cheap hotels where we'd been staying. The walls were a dark gray, and several matching pillows decorated a large sectional facing the flat-screen TV. Magazines were scattered across a glass-topped coffee table, flowers in a round orange vase adding a pop of color. They smelled fresh, as if they'd been cut from the garden below. I walked past them, my fingertips lightly brushing over the edges of the blooms.

A bed so big it could sleep five adults sat at the back of the room. Exhaustion hit me, the soft white bedding calling to me. I was tempted to fall into it and sleep for days. I shook my head, trying to clear the fog created by not enough food as I walked toward my favorite part of the room. The walk-in closet had taken my breath away when I first saw it. Every shoe that I could dream of lined the walls, and the range of colors was beyond amazing. Rows and rows of dresses, shirts, and pants hung on the racks.

My pleasure in my surroundings was dimmed as I remembered this wasn't just a normal visit, and I couldn't just stay here. I had work to do, information to gather, a book to find, and then I would probably be tossed into some godly prison realm.

A knock made me jump. The wet strands of my hair slapped my back when I jerked my head toward the door. My fingers tightened on the towel, pulling it tighter around me. I took a deep breath, trying to calm my nerves before calling, "Come in."

Drake's head popped in a second later, and a stab of disappointment pierced me. He caught my expression, and his grin widened. "Expecting someone else?"

I shook my head. "No."

He came in, closing the door behind him. "Dianna, you're absolutely glistening. Did you like the soaps? Half of those items in there are from Naaririel."

"Yes, thank you. You always take care of me." I smiled at him, relieved that I didn't have to be on guard here with him. He had been a constant in my life, his friendship steadfast and true. I knew he always had my back.

Drake was more dressed up than I thought he'd be just for dinner, looking amazing in a well-cut suit that enhanced his masculine beauty. He was a gorgeous man, but he did nothing for me—not like a certain annoying and rude god.

"Wearing just a towel tonight?" Drake asked with a grin.

I rolled my eyes and tugged the towel tighter around me. "No, and given what you're wearing, I guess I need to dress up."

He strode past me and into the closet. "If you wanted to just wear a towel, I wouldn't mind, nor would your new boyfriend," he said with a smirk as he rummaged through the array of clothing.

My heart froze. "Liam is not my boyfriend."

He cut a look at me. "You sure? He's awfully protective for someone who—"

I held up my hand. "Please, stop. Liam is not, nor will he ever be my boyfriend. I'm helping him, that's all. Remember what you said: it is better to die for something than live under a lie."

He shook his head. "Don't tell me you teamed up with the World Ender on my advice. I want you free from Kaden, not shackled to another powerful man who doesn't care about you, Dianna."

I huffed, blowing a damp curl from my eyes. "You sound like Gabby. And I'm not shackled to anyone. Trust me. He wants to be as far away from me as possible." He had proven that over the last few hours. "Besides, we have a deal."

"Oh, a deal, huh? What kind of deal?"

I shrugged, holding tighter to my towel. "A blood deal."

Drake nearly ripped a dress off the hanger as he spun toward me, worry a shadow in his eyes. "A blood deal, Dianna? With *him*?"

I stomped into the closet and slapped my hand over his mouth, not wanting him to alert every vampire in the mansion. "Shh, it's not that serious. I mean, we had one over chips that time."

He rolled his eyes and lightly gripped my wrist, pulling my hand away from his mouth. "That lasted for a few hours, because you gave in first. What are the conditions of this deal? No god would willingly share or spill their own blood."

I swallowed, not wanting to tell him that Liam had done just that for me more than once. "It's not important. We're here," I snapped back.

He shifted his hold, cradling my hand in his. "I worry about you, Dianna, especially if you guys are already fucking."

"It's not like that," I snapped, pulling my hand from his, my cheeks burning at even the suggestion. "Liam is not like Kaden. We are not sleeping together, or even remotely close." That last part sent bile to my throat, because in my heart, I felt like we *were* close. I had a more intimate connection with him than I'd had with any man I'd slept with.

"Is that so?" Drake asked as he held out a dress. "Then why do you reek of him, and he you? Your scents are so entwined, there is no differentiating between the two."

I walked over and snatched the dress from his hand. "If you don't believe me, that's fine. All any of you have done is encourage me to grow a backbone and leave Kaden. Then the second I do, the second I find a way, I get shit about it."

He placed his hands on his hips. "I have only been around you two for mere minutes, but I see the way you look at each other. You may lie to yourself and him, but don't make the same mistake, Dianna. I want more for you. He may not be like Kaden, but he is just as powerful. I don't want to see you hurt anymore. I want you to have the freedom to make your own choices and shape your own life."

"I have none. We both know that the second I gave my life to Kaden, my freedom and right to choose were gone. All I can do is try to give my sister a better life, try to give you all a better one. No more rulers. No more tyrants. Isn't that what you said Kaden was? Liam can kill him. I'm just trying to do the best I can, okay?"

That last part was filled with emotions I was careful to keep buried, and I suddenly felt overwhelmed. My vision blurred as tears filled my eyes.

Drake was in front of me before the first one fell, his hand cupping my chin and his thumb brushing my cheek. "I know, and I promise I'm not being mean. I just—"

His words hissed to a stop, and I knew exactly why. As the roiling heat of Liam's power appeared in the closet with us, my sorrow, fear, and regret no longer felt overwhelming. The ache in my chest eased, allowing me to breathe easier.

"Am I interrupting something?"

I jerked from Drake's touch and cringed, knowing Liam would see it as a sign of guilt and believe there was something between Drake and me.

"Do you knock?" Drake asked, dropping his hand.

"Not when she sounds distressed." Liam's voice thundered behind me, the lights in my room flickering ominously.

I stepped away from Drake and turned toward Liam, intending to calm him down before he blew a literal fuse here.

My breath stopped. He had showered and changed clothes. I'd been right: white was not his color. He wore a suit that actually fit, and fit well. It was all black, the shirt darker than the jacket and pants. My stomach fluttered at the sight of him. What was wrong with me?

"You have clothes. I mean, you changed clothes." My words came out a jumbled mess.

He stopped trying to glare holes into Drake and looked at me. "Yes. They were provided. Where are yours?"

I looked down, remembering I still clutched my towel.

"Oh, that—"

"Leave," he said to Drake, who bristled next to me.

"This isn't your domain, World Ender. You don't order me around in my own house."

Liam took a step forward, and I quickly moved between them. Towel or not, I would not let them fight. Liam stopped inches from me, the heat of his body a caress against my bare skin.

Liam glanced down at me, then back to Drake. "It's not your house. It's your brother's. You are but a prince, not a king. Now leave. I wish to speak to Dianna, and I do not trust or know you enough for you to be here."

I held up my hand before things got bloody. "Liam, you can't talk to people like that!" I snapped at him before turning to Drake and mouthing, *I'm sorry*, before saying, "Can you please excuse us? We'll be downstairs in a moment."

Drake's eyes flashed gold, and his jaw clenched before he leaned over to press a kiss to my cheek. He did it to piss off Liam, and it worked. Liam's power pulsed, and I knew he was imagining what it would be like to run Drake through. I waited for the door to close behind Drake before popping Liam on the chest and saying, "What was that about?"

He'd tracked Drake's movements like a predator hunting prey. His eyes focused on the door, until he felt my hand graze him. He looked down at his chest before meeting my gaze. "I dislike him."

I sighed, grabbed a few of the dresses Drake had pulled out, and strode past Liam toward the bathroom. "You don't even know him."

"He touches you without your permission. He's crass and overall excitable."

"How do you know he doesn't have my permission?"

The lights flickered once more as Liam followed me. "Does he?"

I actually laughed as I closed the bathroom door behind me. I shouted so he could hear me as I dropped the towel and picked up a dress. "He doesn't touch me like you make it sound, and that's how friends are when they care about each other. It's a sign of affection, Liam. Good grief."

"You do not do that to me."

My breath caught at his words. Liam didn't mean it like that. He didn't understand mortal interactions. He was still learning, right? I threw on the dress as my thoughts spun. It was a long-sleeved, short-cut black ensemble with an open back that wasn't too revealing.

I pushed my hair behind my shoulders, the thick waves tickling the middle of my back. I didn't bother with hairpins or clips, knowing I would be unable to tame it in this humidity.

After a quick red lip, I looked one last time in the mirror before stepping out of the bathroom. "Do I not hold you every night to keep your nightmares at bay?"

He was pacing, his hand on his hip and lost in his thoughts. He stopped mid-step, his gaze traveling slowly up and down my body. His voice was both husky and outraged when he finally said, "That's what you are wearing?"

I held my arms out and looked down. "What's wrong with my dress?"

He looked genuinely confused for a moment. "Dress? That is not a dress. You look as though you plan to bed him immediately after dinner."

My mouth dropped open. "Excuse me? I am not bedding anyone, you ancient jerk!" I gestured toward the dress I wore, the hem riding high on my thighs. "You can't even see anything."

"You see enough. It's practically an insult."

I placed my hands on my hips. "Where do you get off—"

He raised his hand, and the material I wore began to vibrate against my skin. I looked down and froze as the fabric of my black dress morphed into a vibrant deep red that matched my lips. It grew, spilling past my feet. The bodice fit me to perfection, the thin straps wrapping around my shoulders and crisscrossing over my back. Liam lowered his hand, and I spun toward the mirror. I gasped at my reflection. The dress was breathtaking—and he'd made it for me.

I felt regal and seductive with how the silky crimson fabric lovingly hugged the curves I had. The material was sheer, but not transparent like the garments the goddesses of Rashearim wore.

Liam appeared behind me, and my pulse quickened at the image we made. I felt like a goddess, especially with him in his sharp suit and freshly styled hair standing at my back. We looked like we were headed to a ball, not downstairs to a meeting that would probably end badly.

"There. That is better," Liam said, satisfaction and male hunger flaring in his eyes.

"He is going to be so mad." I smiled and glanced at him in the reflection. I ran a hand down the front of my dress and half turned side to side, looking at every glittering detail.

"Let him be." Liam's voice was a soft growl, making me pause. He was watching me as I spun. He always watched me, especially when he thought I wasn't looking. "I do not care. During large engagements, all goddesses and celestials wore similar garments on my world. Some flowed well past their feet, others barely touched the ground, but they all shimmered and shined like starlight upon the darkened sky. They were truly beautiful … and so are you. You are a queen and should be draped in the finest fabrics, not the cheap faux material he chose."

My throat tightened at Liam's words. That was how he saw me? I turned toward him, his face mere inches from mine and his scent surrounding me. I felt the heat rush to my cheeks and cleared my throat. "Thank you. For the dress. It's beautiful."

He smiled, realized what he had done, and stepped back. "You're welcome."

"Now, what did you have to tell me?"

"Tell you?" he asked, looking confused.

I stepped out of the bathroom, picking up the sides of my dress so I could walk. "In the closet, you said you had something you wanted to talk about."

"Oh, yes. No, I only said that so he would leave."

"Liam." My eyes widened as I snickered. "That's so rude."

"I apologize. There are just too many people here, and I can hear all of them. It's overwhelming." He sat on the edge of the couch and blew out a long breath. "And this palace of theirs seems too dense and tight. It's as if the walls themselves are trying to close in around me. You seem to be the only one I can stand to be around."

I moved around the couch and sat next to him. "That's actually sweet. I'm still waiting for you to say something mean as a follow-up."

"I am not mean to you."

"You certainly have been today."

He looked down at his hands, his thumb sliding over one particular silver ring. This one wasn't pure silver like the others, but had a ring of obsidian around it.

"I apologize, then. I did not sleep well last night."

"I know. I was there."

"If I upset you, I did not mean to. I promise it was not my intention," Liam said, the sincerity in his voice clear.

"It's fine. I'm used to you not being the most charming at times. I just thought we were friends and had moved past the whole mean part."

"We are." He shifted to face me fully, as if I'd said something that upset him. "I just... The nightmare last night was too much."

My brows furrowed in concern. "Do you want to talk about it?"

"No."

I nodded before sitting up straighter and sighing. Liam grew quiet once more, and I wished he would let me help him.

"I do want to talk about how much I do not want to go to this dinner."

I snickered under my breath. "I'm sure it won't take long. Plus, they have connections even Kaden doesn't know about. So, they could point us in the right direction to the book you say doesn't exist, and we can leave."

He held his hand out, his pinkie extended. "Promise?"

My chest tightened. "I thought you didn't want to promise anymore?"

"I am allowed to change my mind," he said, nodding toward my hand.

I smiled and held out my pinkie, and he grasped it with his. The act was so pure, yet it sent a small bolt of electricity to my very core.

"Yes, I promise."

THIRTY-TWO

DIANNA

The silence in the dining room was heavy and filled with tension. I stabbed at my food, the fork piercing the tender meat and hitting the plate. We sat at a long table, the light from the chandeliers reflected in the polished tabletop. Ethan sat at the head, and I sat next to Liam at the other end.

I knew the moment I'd entered the room that I'd made a mistake in wearing the beautiful gown. Ethan and Drake had looked at me, then glanced at each other. It hadn't helped that Liam held my chair out for me and even pushed it in. I knew what they were thinking, but Liam was just trying to be nice.

"Lovely dress, Dianna," Drake said, raising his glass to his lips. "Definitely not one of mine."

Yup, bad idea.

"Nope, not one of yours," I said.

"Where did you get it?" he asked before taking a sip of his drink, hiding his grin.

I took a breath, knowing he was trying to bait me. He wanted information, but he should have known not to play games with me.

"Liam made it, because all the ones you left me showed my ass."

He laughed and nodded in defeat. "It's a nice ass."

"So I've been told."

Liam's eyes flicked between Drake and me as we bantered. For a moment, the air became charged, and the room fell silent as the light dimmed. Ethan glared at Liam, and I felt my body tense as the aggressive male power in the room increased. I sighed. The dinner and our information gathering were going nowhere fast.

Ethan, the Vampire King, was every bit as beautiful as Drake. His gorgeous dark curls were thick on the top of his head, but shaved in a close fade at the sides. He wore a black coat with red lapels over a black shirt and matching dress pants. His shoes were probably more expensive than mine. Ethan was about the same height as Liam, with a similar strong, muscular build. Both men radiated power and were currently staring daggers at each other.

"How is Gabby?" Drake's voice broke the silence.

I swallowed a bite of meat before saying, "Great. I spoke to her earlier. She was recently promoted at the hospital. Well, before I..." My voice trailed off as I thought about how I'd uprooted her once more. We had made up from our fight, but her words still stung. It was okay, though. She would have the life she wanted, no matter what I had to do.

He cleared his throat, and I knew he sensed it was a touchy subject and was going to push. Before he could say anything, I turned to Ethan and asked, "Where is your wife? I haven't seen Naomi in ages."

Drake stopped mid-chew and stared at his brother.

"She is away. She wished she could make it, but she has more important things to attend to," Ethan said, breaking the standoff with Liam to look at me as I had intended.

I nodded, curious about what could be more important than Kaden trying to end the world and Liam returning, but I left the subject alone. Liam and Ethan sat in brooding silence while Drake and I went back to eating.

"Vampires eat?"

Liam's voice caught me off guard, and my eyes widened as I looked at him, shocked by his bluntness. He didn't meet my gaze, though, his eyes trained on Ethan.

"Yes. Shouldn't you know that, given your reputation?" Ethan quipped.

Oh, gods, this was going to be terrible.

"Incorrect. The vampires who ruled long before you were quadrupedal, vicious creatures."

Ethan's gaze didn't waver as he tapped his fork against his plate. "I'm sure they are all gone now?"

"Yes. The vampiric bloodline originated from the Ig'Morruthens, but evolution turned them into ... well, you."

"Evolution? Interesting. And what happened to our predecessors?"

"War. Something I plan to not let happen again."

"Is that so?" Ethan said, raising his glass to his lips and taking a sip. "Is that not the goal here? Why you betrayed the one they call Kaden? There is no victory in war, only death. Even the winning side loses."

I swallowed a lump in my throat as I sat slightly back. Ethan smiled softly, but there was no humor in it. Drake rested his elbow on the table and watched the back-and-forth of the conversation.

"I want to believe you, but your reputation makes me less inclined," Ethan said. "You have slaughtered countless creatures like us, and like Dianna. Even if you two parade around as friends, she is Ig'Morruthen, your sworn enemy for eons. It was not by choice, but she is a beast. We may drink blood to sustain life, but so does she. She has to consume mortal flesh."

"Technically, I haven't in a while," I said, raising my hand in the air. Drake snickered, but Liam and Ethan didn't look away from each other.

I had tried to make light of it, but my heart sank at the comparisons. I knew Ethan didn't mean it negatively, but I didn't need to be reminded of the darker sides of my nature.

Ethan was right, though; Liam was everything we were taught to fear. Yet I looked at him, and I saw the man who trembled at night over the world, family, and friends he had lost. I saw the man who asked questions over the most basic things and thought he was saving me when we first started this trip. Liam was my friend.

Liam was quiet for a moment as he stared at Ethan, and my nerves skyrocketed. "Dianna is different. I have seen evil. I've seen it born, what it craves, and how it acts. She may be stubborn and erratic. At times, she is rude or crass, even violent or dangerous, but not evil—not even a little bit."

I blinked a few times, completely shocked at his words, especially after everything I had done since we met. I took a few shaky breaths and curled a piece of hair behind my ear. Liam didn't look at me, but he didn't have to. I knew he meant everything he'd said, even the less than nice parts. He didn't think of me as a monster. I hadn't known I needed to hear those words from him. It was such a relief, I almost felt lightheaded.

"Are you in love with her?"

My mouth dropped open. "Ethan!" I snapped, glaring at him as Drake spit his wine halfway across the table.

"No," Liam said, completely ignoring Drake and me. "She is my friend, nothing more, nothing less."

Ethan arched one aristocratic brow. "Perfect, because we do not need another powerful man obsessed with her. However, Kaden is still obsessed, and he plans to rip everyone to pieces to get back what is his. You understand that, right?"

"Kaden is not in love with me," I snapped at Ethan, and caught Drake quickly looking down at his plate to hide his expression. "What?"

"Kaden has tracked you as far as the eastern border. Every contact that has helped you has met an untimely demise. He slaughtered even the ones closest to him that have failed to return you to him. His legion has crumbled since you killed Alistair and left."

My mind reeled at the information, but it made sense. It was why the shades had come after Gabby. He wanted to lure me back by using her as bait. I had fooled myself into thinking he would eventually give up, but I knew he was hunting me. It was why I'd been careful not to overuse my powers or teleport on our journey: I didn't want to alert him to where we were.

I gripped my knees underneath the table, my heart pounding. I'd just spoken to Gabby before dinner. Neverra and Logan were with her, and she was surrounded by celestials. She was fine. She was safe.

"That's not love," I said, lifting my head and looking at Ethan. "I am a possession to him. I always have been."

"A weapon, a possession, a lover. You are all of that and more to him. You were the only one that survived being turned by him, and please believe he has tried again since you left."

My blood pounded in my ears. If he had, that meant he had even more of those beasts. There I was, joking around and helping Liam, while Kaden was creating an army.

"You coming here risks everything you set out to do for us, yet we agreed to help you. Do you wish to know why?"

I held Ethan's gaze, and when I didn't respond, he said, "Because he is afraid of *him*." He pointed at Liam. "He won't attack or risk coming for you directly as long as he is on this plane. We heard of the attempt on your sister, and now that he knows she is out of his reach, he needs to find that book. He believes there is a code or answer in it on how to stop him."

Liam sat still, taking in every bit of information Ethan threw out. His hands were underneath his chin as he continued to stare at Ethan. I couldn't read his expression and couldn't gauge the thoughts formulating behind his gray eyes.

"We wished for you here. Once we learned what Kaden was really searching for and that the legends were not just legends, we planned to secede from his legion. I began to research you on my own, pulling from sources long buried by my people. Drake took my place at meetings, gathering any information he could get. Then something changed, and Kaden became obsessed with this book, committing dark acts in his desire to obtain it. He is holding meetings, slaughtering and torturing celestials, all to find this book."

"I am aware," Liam said finally. "The only issue is that the Book of Azrael is not real."

"He is killing because he believes it is."

Liam sat up straight and waved away Ethan's words. "He is wrong. Azrael is dead. He never made it off Rashearim."

Ethan's brows furrowed. "You must be mistaken."

"I am not. I saw Azrael's body in tatters after he helped his wife escape. The Ig'Morruthens had overpowered us, and he was ripped to shreds. He was turned to ash before Rashearim fell. How could I ever be mistaken?"

I felt the room charge. The plates on the table and the pictures on the walls slowly vibrated. The guards looked at each other, then at Ethan.

"Would you like to see the stardust of my homeworld?"

The lights flickered, a sign of his growing agitation as the heavy chandeliers above us began to sway. Drake watched the two men, his body tense. I moved my knee underneath the table, lightly bumping Liam's. The brief contact shook him from the grasp of his rising anger and grief. He looked at me, and his eyes softened as he held my gaze. He released a breath, and the room stilled.

"My apologies," Ethan said. "If that is true, someone has made a replica or copy. Camilla has found something in El Donuma and is offering it to the highest bidder. Kaden wants it."

I almost choked again. "Camilla?"

Drake nodded. "Yup, she found something a few days ago. Won't give any information, only that she found the book, knows where it is, and is offering a huge lump sum for the one who wants it most."

"Why hasn't Kaden stormed her coven, destroyed it, and taken it?" I asked.

"If she dies, the information dies with her—and you killed the one person who could rip it from her mind. So, my guess is he is waiting to see who gets it first, and then he'll take it."

Liam leaned forward, locking his fingers together. "How do we meet this Camilla?"

"I can try to get a meeting arranged. Camilla will probably agree to meet you if she knows you are here and interested, but she will not let Dianna step foot in El Donuma," Ethan said, avoiding my gaze.

Liam looked at me. "Why?"

"Let's just say she hates me."

"We really need to work on your relationship skills, so you have better friends in your life."

"Hey, I'm sitting right here!" Drake said, his tone offended.

Liam turned to him and said in all seriousness, "My point exactly."

I snickered as Drake burst out laughing. It was a nice release after the tension of the dinner and finding out that our search for the book had just become even more complicated.

For the next hour, we discussed battle plans and what we would do if Camilla accepted our request to enter El Donuma. Liam was finally eating his food, but I had long since abandoned mine. My stomach rolled each time I thought of what Ethan had said. Kaden may have failed at creating another me, but that just meant he had more soldiers for his army.

Liam was downing his food, not really paying attention to what he was eating as Ethan continued to talk about the obstacles we might face. Drake added a detail from time to time, but mostly just listened. I couldn't sit still any longer and pushed my chair back, the men at the table turning toward me.

"Dinner was great, but I'm tired. I'll see you all tomorrow," I said.

Not waiting for a response, I swept from the room. The guards flinched and reached for their weapons as I moved a little too quickly, but I couldn't bring myself to care. My blood felt like ice water in my veins as my brain ran in a million different directions. Liam was right. We needed to hurry things along.

My hope that no one would follow me was quickly dashed when I felt Liam's power rolling toward me. It felt like I was being followed by a thunderstorm. His large, callused hand grabbed my arm and spun me around. "Dianna. I have been speaking to you."

"What?" I stared up at Liam and realized I had moved a lot faster than I thought. We were halfway down a flight of winding stone steps.

"Where are you going? This is not the way to your room."

"Oh? You have that memorized now?"

His gaze narrowed, his hand still lightly shackling my arm. "I know that face. What are you planning?"

Damn annoying god. "Nothing."

"You cannot go to her. We have a plan, and you flying off to demand answers by firebombing a city is not part of it."

I let out an exasperated sigh and shook my arm out of his grasp. "That's not what I was going to do."

He placed his hands on his hips, his suit jacket flaring around them. "Oh? Then where exactly are you going?"

I had planned on finding a couple of mortals to feed on, so I would have enough power to fly to El Donuma. Once there, I would find

Camilla's estate and force her to give me the book. But I would not tell him that and prove him right.

Frustrated, I groaned and picked up the sides of my dress. I pushed past Liam and stomped up the stone steps. He didn't say a word as he followed me back to the main foyer.

We were silent, the words spoken at the table hovering between us. Kaden was building an army. He was desperate for me to come back. He was obsessed with finding a book Liam claimed didn't exist. And then there was what Liam had said. I was touched by his words, but at the same time, they left me feeling empty. Ethan had made it even more awkward by asking him if he loved me. We were friends—just friends.

I stopped before the front door and stared at it for a moment before looking back at him. "Do you want to get out of here? Just for a little bit?"

He tipped his head and gave me a questioning look, but agreed.

We walked along one of the cobblestone paths at the back of the castle. The forest was alive with the sound of insects and the occasional yip of some hunting four-legged predator.

He had given me his suit jacket to drape over my bare shoulders, even when I insisted I didn't need it. My body temperature ran a few degrees higher than most people's, and I was completely comfortable. Nonetheless, it was sweet and a break from the extreme coldness of his attitude earlier in the day.

I wondered if his sudden change in demeanor was a sort of apology for being a dick after the nightmare he refused to tell me about. But another part of me whispered that it was something deeper. Or maybe I was just feeling unnerved by what Ethan had said about the lengths Kaden was taking to get me back. I knew he wasn't acting out of love; love didn't exist in our world. Kaden had made that painfully clear through the centuries. I was nothing more than a possession to him, and he wanted his toy back.

"Dianna. Have you heard anything I've said?"

I shook my head, not even pretending. "Sorry. Dinner has my nerves rattled."

"Understandable," he said as we continued walking.

My feet whispered over the stone path, my gown swishing around my ankles with each step. "You seem happier."

He gave a low snort, the sound forced with a hint of agitation. "At dinner? How so?"

I glanced at him and nearly stumbled, the male beauty of him taking my breath away. The moonlight cast his features in silver and set his eyes aglow. His power was nearly visible, wavering in the air around us and encompassing me. I felt it as an almost physical caress, and in that moment, I felt safe. It was such a foreign sensation that it took me a moment to find my voice again. "No, sorry, not then. I was just thinking in general. You smile more. You weren't like that when I first met you. Although I was also trying to kill you."

"Yes, well, that is accurate."

"You also don't look as frumpy and untamed as you used to. The haircut and clothes that actually fit have greatly improved your appearance."

His gaze swung to me, his brows furrowing. "Is that supposed to be a compliment? If so, it is absolutely terrible."

"No, I'm just saying you're coming out of your shell, so to speak."

"Ah," he said, and we continued our stroll. "I suppose it's easier to be that way around you. You give me no choice."

I bumped my shoulder against his. The light tap didn't even move him. "Is that supposed to be a compliment?"

"I suppose." He paused, and I knew he was thinking. I had become used to the mannerism when he was trying to formulate the words for what he thought or felt. "There is a saying in my language, on my world. It doesn't truly translate, but it means 'to calcify.' Gods are at risk of reaching a certain point in their lives where emotions dissipate. It often happens after what you would consider a traumatic event. They lose a part of themselves and cease to care about anyone or anything. It is as if the very light inside of us goes out, and we turn to stone."

I stopped, and he turned toward me. "Stone? Like actual stone?"

He nodded, and the muscles in his jaw clenched. "It is impossible to tell when it will happen. I always assumed it was from a great loss— loss of something they valued more than anything in the universe. I feared my father would go cold after my mother's passing. The signs were there, but he didn't. A part of me fears that's what's happening to me." He looked down at his feet, and I could see the pain in the lines of his body. Which was a good sign, but I had been with him for almost three months now. I knew there were parts of him he had closed off.

I had seen how sexual he used to be, but he seemed to have no interest in physical pleasure since I'd met him. We had often shared the same bed, but it was never intimate. Liam's hands never wandered, nor did he rub up against me in the middle of the night, seeking release. If he did press against me, he kept his hands to himself.

I knew it helped him to sleep beside me. Sometimes he would move and shiver as if lost in some dream. He would wake up in a sweat, look at me, and go back to sleep. I never pushed him about the nightmares, assuming if he wanted to tell me about them, he would. I would never admit it, but sleeping beside him helped me, too. It was nice to have someone there. I didn't feel so alone.

I reached out and placed my hand on his shoulder, keeping my touch light so as not to overwhelm him. "I promise not to let you turn to stone," I said, smiling reassuringly.

His gaze danced across my face. "I doubt I could be around you long-term. You are far too invasive and intrusive."

I hit his shoulder this time with enough force to make him jump slightly, but not enough to hurt. A smile formed on his lips, and I knew he'd said it mostly to irritate me. "And much too forceful."

I swatted at him once more, but he took a step back. He was playing with me. I liked this Liam. He was different when he was with me, away from the others who demanded a king. He was almost normal.

"Well, you're not terrible." I shrugged, glancing at him once more. "At times."

"I'll take that."

We fell back in step once more, matching smiles on our faces as we walked. I glanced up and realized we had reached the garden. I'd forgotten how much Drake loved this garden. He had spoken of it often through the years. Although the story was less than happy. A woman he had loved as much as anyone could love another had designed it. She had chosen another, and it had broken him. But even though she'd built it, he had kept and maintained it. With his care, it had flourished into a monument of what could have been.

"What is this?" Liam asked as we stopped between the twin statues of two women holding large bowls that flanked the entrance. I tucked my hands inside Liam's jacket as I looked up.

"A garden. Did you not have those on Rashearim?" I asked, looking back at him. His face had grown cold. Was he mad—over a garden?

"This is a garden? It's terrible," he said, his face scrunched with disgust.

"Liam, you haven't even been inside yet," I said with a sigh. I walked into the garden, knowing he would be close behind. He always was.

The path opened up, splitting off to the left and right, thick, gorgeous flowers lining the walkways. Small lights were strung above, casting a lush glow over the plants and creating deep pockets of shadows. It was absolutely beautiful, even if Liam's lip curled at everything we passed. I headed toward the center, drawn by the sound and smell of fresh running water. Knowing Drake, he would have a fountain here, and I wanted to see it.

"Even their plants are atrocious," he said, reaching out to touch an assortment of purple flowers.

"Why do you find offense with everything associated with them? It's like you want to pick a fight."

He dropped his hand and rubbed it against his pants before looking at me. "I dislike them. Even the energy surrounding them feels disturbed. Something just feels off."

"They're probably just on edge because you're here. Remember, you're kind of a big deal, Liam. Drake is one of my oldest friends, and his family is currently helping us."

He put his hands in his pockets. "Yes, they are helping us. Which seems peculiar, given their fear of Kaden and what would happen if he finds out they betrayed him. What makes these powerful friends want to take that risk? I do not trust them, nor do I want you alone with them for too long."

I almost tripped over my feet as I caught the hem of my gown, coming to an abrupt stop. I picked up my skirt and faced him. "Excuse me? You can't tell me who I can and can't be around. That's not how this works, nor do you have any say over me. I am not your possession, just like I am not Kaden's."

"It is not about possession." His brows furrowed as he looked down at me. "I worry about you."

His words caught me off guard, and the snarky comment I had prepared died on my lips. I didn't know what to say, which was a first for me.

Liam's eyes softened as he looked at me. They were no longer hard or mottled by anger and irritation. His gaze moved from my face to my chest, a pained expression flashing across his features before he turned away. Confused at the change in his demeanor, I checked the fancy silk gown he had made me, thinking I had spilled something on the bodice, but there was nothing there.

"You don't have to worry about me. I've been alive this long."

"Barely," he grumbled, still avoiding my gaze.

I snorted and spun around, heading deeper into the garden. "And no, you don't have to worry about them. They have slowly been trying to secede from Kaden for a while now."

"And Kaden doesn't suspect?"

I shrugged. "He watched me kill Drake in Zarall. Well, the image of Drake, at least. He thinks he's dead."

Liam's gaze flicked to mine. "And the brother? The one who calls himself king? Kaden would not fear retribution for a family member lost?"

"I assume he thinks he's in hiding. No one would blatantly go against Kaden. They're not stupid. It would be a death wish. Despite your ego and what you think, Kaden is strong, powerful, and psychotic."

Liam made that grumble-grunt sound again that I had grown accustomed to. "I do not fear him."

It was my turn to grunt in annoyance. "You should."

I sighed as we fell into step with each other again, the creatures of the night filling the darkness with their song.

"There has to be at least one thing you like here?"

"No."

I snorted. "Okay, just say *one* nice thing about them. The mansion," I said, gesturing toward the beautiful structure.

"Pretentious."

Was he joking—joking with me? The laugh that escaped me prompted a genuine smile from him. He seemed to enjoy this, even if he was still surly.

"Okay, what about their outfits?"

"Too confining."

"Oh, come on, there has to be something you like?"

Liam tipped his face up, nodding as he considered. The corner of his mouth pulled up as if he were trying very hard to find a single thing. I was about to ask him another question when he said, "I like the language here. It's the closest thing to my mother's."

His mom? My heart lurched. He hadn't spoken of her, and now that I thought about it, I hadn't seen her in any of his memories either. The only thing I recalled was the mention of her death. I remembered his father's words and how sad Liam had been in that blooddream, but I had seen no memories of them together as a family. Could it be so terrible that he'd blocked it? I was afraid to ask, a part of me not wanting him to hide that rare playful side again. But he'd opened up to me, and I wouldn't waste it.

"What was she like?"

His throat bobbed before a muscle in his jaw clenched.

"If you don't want to talk about it, you don't have to. We can discuss the fun dinner."

A part of him seemed to relax as he huffed. "No. You have already seen and know so much about me. There is no reason not to tell you this as well. And as you have said, perhaps talking about this will help." He inhaled deeply, gathering his words. "She was kind and sweet, from what I remember. She got sick after I was born. I was too young to see it at first, but I noticed the changes as I grew. She was a warrior, a celestial under the rule of an old god, but her light dimmed when she was pregnant with me. Once she grew too weak to lift a blade, she transferred to the council. That's the problem with gods being born: the fetus takes too much. It requires too much energy and power from the mother as it develops. The risk is too great. That's why I am the only one."

"Liam." I didn't want to apologize again, because he didn't need it. He needed something else. "What happened to her is not your fault."

His eyes met mine, and I saw the burden of sadness that he carried ease. "Isn't it?"

"No. If it was known, then she knew the risks and still became pregnant. And you know what I think? I think she loved your father and you so much that she didn't care. I would bet all the money in the world that she didn't regret it. A family's love is stronger than anything, trust me."

He was quiet for a moment, and I realized we had stopped walking. He stared at me as if searching for the truth of my words. I think a part of him had been desperate to hear that it wasn't his fault.

"You surprise me, Dianna."

"So you have said."

He nodded and led the way as we continued our nighttime stroll. "What happened to your parents? Since I just bared my soul, I would like to know about yours."

"Well, since it's only fair," I half-heartedly joked. "Long story short, my mom and dad were healers. They loved helping others with what at that time was considered medicine. When the shards of Rashearim fell, it triggered a plague. They continued to help others until the illness consumed them as well. It has been just Gabby and me since then. We've always looked out for each other."

"Did you have any other family? People who could help you?"

I shook my head and looked down for a second. "No, we didn't. I kept us fed and gathered supplies." Liam's face didn't change as he waited patiently for me to go on. "I was a thief. It's not something I am proud of, but I did what I needed to for my family. I always have and always will."

"That seems logical. People tend to do what they feel is necessary in times of crisis."

I had expected Liam to scold me and was more than a little surprised when he didn't. He saw my expression and smiled. "I am not justifying it or saying it was right, but you do not know who you truly are until you have no options left. That is all." He shrugged, looking down at me. "Besides, I am not surprised. After all, you attempted— and failed—to steal from me."

"So cocky," I said, bumping my hip against him as he grinned.

I had subconsciously been following the sound of the water, and we stopped as the path gave way at the heart of the dreamlike garden. Stone statues rose at the fountain's center, several people holding various containers, water pouring from them into the pool below. It nearly glowed, the small lights adding a soft golden glow to the silver of the moonbeams. It was breathtaking.

"My mother had a garden on Rashearim." Liam's words startled me, and I turned to look at him, eager to hear more about his past. "My father crafted this elaborate maze of the most beautiful artwork and foliage for her. It was magical, and much better than this one. We never used it after she passed. My father left it to rot. I think it hurt him too much to visit it or see it again."

"I'm sorry."

He shrugged as if it didn't pain him. "There is no reason for you to be sorry."

He stepped forward, bending slightly to duck beneath the curved, tangled-vine archway. My footsteps were light as I followed behind him. I sat on the edge of the moonlit fountain, giving my feet a break. Otherworldly or not, heels still hurt after a while.

Liam didn't sit. Instead, he walked over to a large flowering bush and ran his fingers over the delicate petals of a bloom. He plucked a gorgeous yellow lily, slowly twirling it by the stem. I stared at him, transfixed by the sight of the powerful World Ender holding such a small and fragile bloom.

"Do you know how I got my name?"

I sat up a little straighter, adjusting the jacket around me and savoring the scent of him that lingered on it. "What? Samkiel?"

He didn't look at me, his gaze focused on the flower. "No, that name was given to me at birth. Although, it does carry more blood and death with it than I would like. I have done so many things over the centuries that I regret. There are so many things I've lost." He finally turned, his eyes locking with mine as he said, "People I've lost."

The somber expression I had come to hate flashed across his features. It was always a prelude to the grief that hid behind those lovely eyes. So, I did what I did best and annoyed him.

"You mean Liam? Yeah, I did wonder how you picked such a plain name."

"Funny." A breath escaped through his nostrils, his shoulders raising for a moment, and I assumed that was the closest I would get to a laugh tonight. "On Rashearim, we had a flower that put the beauty of this one to shame. It had rings of yellow and blue that moved in waves across the petals when you touched it. It was called *orneliamus*, or *liam* for short. They were my mother's favorite, and a symbol of strength and protection. They could adapt to any climate and were so sturdy, they were nearly impossible to kill. It took the death of the planet to eradicate them."

His eyes flickered to mine before he strode over and sat beside me. He angled the stem of the flower toward me, offering it to me. I felt my heart skip as I reached out to accept it. He gave me a small smile before he rested his elbows on his knees and clasped his hands together in front of him. "I wanted to be that."

Liam had given me a flower. A simple fucking flower, and my world tilted. It was the first time any man had given me flowers. It was the stupidest thing for me to obsess over, but this tiny yellow plant suddenly meant the world to me. I hated the way my stomach flipped as I glanced at it in my hand. Gabby got flowers, not me —never me.

"The great and powerful King of All, named after a flower. How ironic."

He grinned at me, and my breath caught. With the glow of the small lights and the moon shining down, casting a shadow across his features, he was absolutely and painfully gorgeous.

"I reveal so much, yet you do nothing but make a smart quip? You wound me."

I scrunched my nose and playfully swatted him with my flower, not hard enough to damage it, but enough to annoy him. "I'm sure I do, Mister Invincible."

"So many names for me, and I have very few for you. I shall fix that."

"Come up with as many as you like, as long as you don't call me a worm again."

His expression softened, a corner of his lip twisting. "You truly do remember all I say, don't you?"

"Only the truly terrible things."

"I'll fix that as well."

I felt a flush creep up my face before I turned away, tucking a strand of hair behind my ear. He didn't mean the things he said, didn't understand how they sounded to me. But his words, and the way he spoke them, made me ache in all the wrong places. "So, on a scale of one to five, how likely is it that we will all die?"

"Zero. The book itself doesn't exist. No matter what anyone claims."

"Okay, but say it does. If it does, on a scale."

He shrugged, a small frown tightening his lips. "Maybe a one. If the book is somehow a real relic that my people never got hold of, then there may be cause for some fear, but the likelihood is extremely low. Azrael never made it off of Rashearim, and anything he made died with him when the planet was destroyed."

An upbeat melody flooded the air, interrupting our conversation. Liam and I both turned toward the castle. It wasn't uncomfortably loud, but we could hear it clearly.

"What is that?" Liam asked, his lip curling upward in disgust.

"Music."

His head swiveled toward me. "I am aware, but why?"

His guess was as good as mine. I shrugged before craning to look past him toward the mansion. "I don't know. It's Drake. They're probably just playing something for the house guests who have woken up."

"Are you worried?"

I focused on Liam to find him staring at me intently. I raised a brow. "About music?"

"About dying."

His question struck me as odd. Not just that he'd asked, but the way he looked at me when he said it. I shook my head, the waves of my hair tickling my cheeks. "No. About my sister dying? Yes."

That cold expression returned to his face, as if I had said something wrong. "You worry so much for others, but not for yourself. Why?"

I smiled, but he didn't. "Am I not supposed to? I mean, I always assumed I would go out fighting, you know? That's how I see it. Now, Gabby? She is the one with the life and career and boyfriend. I don't have any of that. So, I'm not worried about myself. I can survive almost anything. Gabby, not so much."

He continued to stare at me as if I'd insulted him.

"What?" I asked. "Why are you looking at me like that?"

He shook his head slowly. "You are just not what I expected."

"What's that mean? Ig'Morruthens don't have feelings?"

"Not the ones I have encountered."

"Oh, yeah? What were they like?"

"Powerful, dangerous, ferocious, and not nearly as annoying as you." That earned him a shove that barely moved him, and yet he acted as if it did by grabbing his arm and rubbing it as he glared at me, a smile spreading across that ridiculously perfect face. "But equally violent."

We continued to talk, moving comfortably from topic to topic, some heavy and some light-hearted, but we didn't talk anymore about Kaden or the book. Time passed, yet it had no meaning when I was with him—and that terrified me.

THIRTY-THREE

LIAM

She had her hand under her face, the pressure of it pushing her cheek slightly upward, and her heartbeat slowed as sleep claimed her. A few dark, wavy tendrils of her hair covered half of her face as she lay facing me. How was it that she looked exquisite even as she slept? As I moved, carefully adjusting my arm beneath the pillow, I noticed the yellow flower in the small glass of water she had set on her bedside table. A smile tugged at my lips. It was such a small gesture, yet she'd held it as if it meant something. An unknown feeling pulled at my gut, and I thought about where I had gotten it from, knowing I could find her a thousand more that were even better.

"This is how the world ends."

The words echoed through my subconscious, and I closed my eyes. I had pretended to sleep so Dianna would not worry and actually drift off. I was restless and frustrated, too raw to risk reliving the blood, fire, and chanting. There were no words to describe exactly how I was feeling, but I knew I could not sleep.

"This is how the world ends."

Over and over, the damned dream haunted my waking hours. The horror of it had become entangled with the very confusing feelings I had for Dianna, adding to my emotional turmoil. I sighed, turning on my back and staring at the ghastly decorated ceiling. My fingers danced, tapping atop my chest. No, I couldn't see her like that. I wouldn't allow myself. I'd told myself after the dream that I would distance myself and keep it professional.

I turned my head toward her, watching as she slept peacefully. I knew I had been foolish to think I could stay away from her. My chest had tightened when Drake grabbed her into a hug. Then, when I was getting dressed, I'd felt the shift in her. It was slight, like a small pinch of pain and sadness. When I'd seen her distress and his hand on her, I'd known I would make his death slow and painful.

I had almost ripped him to pieces then and there, yet she had calmed me. Dianna had been doing that a lot with just her presence. She was nothing like the creatures from home, not even a little bit. She claimed to not be as caring as her sister, but she was. I lay there, watching her sleep until that voice floated into my head once more. I eased from the bed and watched as she shifted, reaching and curling into the pillow I had placed where I had been lying. Once I was sure she was settled and not going to wake, I slipped quietly out of the room.

"You're good at that," Drake said from where he was leaning in a doorway about halfway down the hall. "Lots of practice sneaking out of women's rooms, I assume?"

My eyes narrowed as I carefully closed the door behind me.

"How was the nightcap after your little date? You like the garden? You know, there are spots so far off that not even we would hear it if you decide to fuck her out there."

He straightened as I strode toward him, but I still towered over him. I glared down at him. The silver rings vibrated on my fingers, itching for me to summon one of the weapons. I could end him in mere seconds, turning his remains to nothing but ash. The only thing that stayed my hand was that I knew the woman sleeping a few feet away would never forgive me.

"I have killed men for less. So, make no mistake, if she did not care for you, I would have turned your body into embers for how you speak to me."

Drake smiled. It was slow and lazy, letting me know he found my threat humorous and was not intimidated.

"What are you doing here, Drake? What do you want?"

He nodded toward the ceiling. "Ethan wants to see you in the study. Come on."

I said nothing as I followed him into a large foyer. A few heavy and overly ornate benches and small tables sat in groupings, surrounded by thick foliage. A vampire couple sat deep in conversation, but fell silent as we passed. They sat up straighter, their eyes going wide. They didn't say anything until we were across the room, but I heard the whispers regardless.

The World Ender.

I shook my head as we started up the marble steps, clearing the images that always followed when I heard the title. We emerged at the top of the stairs, and I looked around. This area didn't seem to fit with the rest of the mansion. My eyes narrowed as I studied the paintings hanging on the walls. It looked like these were portraits of ancestors dating back decades. I heard stirring below us as the other house-guests began to awaken. I counted twenty-five heartbeats here, but could feel the essence of forty-one Otherworld vampires in the castle.

"You have a tremendous number of guests here."

"Yes, the ones under my brother's rule who are terrified of Kaden's retribution feel safer here, so Ethan opened the doors to our small and modest mansion."

I found Dianna's pithy comments did not bother me, but I had images of ripping his tongue out almost every time he spoke.

Drake stopped before a set of large onyx doors. What appeared to be a reptilian head was carved into the polished stone, the lines of the creature curling toward the handles that Drake gripped and twisted. He invited me into the spacious room with a sweep of his arm and a mocking bow.

Several comfortable-looking couches and chairs were arranged in small groupings. Every wall was lined with bookshelves that soared to the second floor. There was a spiral staircase at the back, the railing trimmed in gold.

An ember glowed from the chair in the middle of the room as Ethan looked toward me. "You smoke?"

I shook my head. "No."

"Not even for fun, I presume?"

Centuries ago, Logan, Vincent, Cameron, and I would sneak away from training to indulge in illicit remedies for what we considered fun. They were mild remedies that made the pressure put on me and others seem less.

"Not anymore."

Drake snickered. "I knew there was a bad boy underneath that cold facade. Why else would Dianna be drawn to you?"

"She is not drawn to me. She is helping me," I corrected him, cutting a seething glance his way. His grin only grew as he passed by me, putting himself between Ethan and me. He was protective of his brother, staying by him like a shadow. He was highly protective of Dianna, as well, although I assumed his motives where she was concerned were very different. His scent changed when he was near her, making me feel some emotion I could not explain.

Drake reached for a brown cylindrical object on the table near his brother and flicked a small silver box. A flame burst to life, and he lit the tip of the brown cylinder, puffing on the other end, smoke wreathing his face.

"Cigars. That is what they are called," Ethan said, watching me closely.

"Mind reading is a lucrative practice. It takes time to develop, if one has the gift and skill," I said, narrowing my eyes on him.

Drake chuckled, a small puff of smoke escaping his lips. Ethan only shrugged. "Ah, yes. It can be. Lucky for you, only a slim few in my world possess it. It is one of many skills my father passed down to us, but our ability is not nearly as strong as what Alistair wielded. I may catch phrases and flashes of what you think, but nothing as powerful as his abilities. Alistair was the last true mind-bender, and Dianna turned him to ash."

"Is that why you summoned me here? For idle chitchat regarding matters I am already aware of?"

He chuckled under his breath. "Yes, although I expected you sooner. Drake informed me that you and Dianna were enjoying the gardens."

Drake's grin spread. It seemed he was more of a shadow than I'd thought. He obviously kept tabs on everything that happened here, and he did it well enough that I had not sensed him when Dianna and I departed earlier this evening.

I felt the heat in my hands as my temper rose. "You, like your brother, forget who you speak to. I apologize for you being under the assumption that what I do or where I go is your concern."

Ethan stood in a fluid motion. As he strode toward the dark wooden desk, his predatory gait was proof that the modern vampire had evolved directly from the four-legged beasts I remembered. They were a mix of feline and reptilian, quiet and sneaky. They were a perfect predator, and one my ancestors despised.

"Your hate for us is not displaced, you know. On the other hand, we are not that fond of you being here, either," Ethan said, obviously reading my mind again.

"That is intrusive and beyond rude, no matter who you are."

Ethan smirked. "My apologies, Your Highness. It is just that time is of the essence, and it is more expedient." He placed his cigar on a small glass dish on the desktop and waved me over. I moved silently, stopping next to him as he flipped on a small light, illuminating several pages and a large map with dots on it.

"Drake was able to snag a few items out of Kaden's lair before he caught on to us."

I nodded once, my eyes scanning the map in front of me. "So, this was another reason you stopped showing up to the meetings Dianna told me about?"

"Yes, one of them. The other was that the danger in his lust for power far surpasses our fear of you."

"I do have a question. Obviously, Drake is not dead. How is it that Kaden saw his death? What part did Dianna play in the illusion?"

Ethan nodded once and said, "Yes. It was a ruse they formed once she found out we did not show up for the last meeting. Kaden wanted my brother's head in retaliation for me not showing yet again. Dianna could not kill him, so they devised a plan. My brother is *popular* with a few witches, who happily developed a cloaking spell. His death looked and appeared real, but it was not. It is the same type of spell protecting this home."

"Interesting."

"I meant what I asked you earlier at dinner. I want a deal."

Ah, yes—the question he had proposed while Drake and Dianna spoke freely, completely unaware of the separate telepathic conversation at hand.

My lip curled in disgust. "I will not share blood with you."

"I told you they made a blood deal," Drake said from behind me.

My shoulders tensed, but I kept my focus on Ethan. Had Dianna told him that? If so, why did it make me uneasy? What else had she shared with him? I shook the thought from my head, trying to ignore the emotions it aroused.

"If I do this, it would be for Dianna's sake, not yours. My allegiance is to the innocents, and you feed upon the innocents. What you do is forbidden, but Dianna believes you are her friends. Prove her right, and I'll grant you your pardon."

Ethan shook his head, a look of disappointment flashing across his face. "Very well. Is there some godly bond or oath that must be spoken or signed?"

"No."

Ethan's brows drew together. "If not that, how will I know you will keep your word?"

I tipped my head back, staring at the ceiling, frustrated that I needed to explain myself to someone once more. My patience gone, I met his gaze and laid it out for him in terms I hoped he would understand. "I could have this mansion you love so much raided and seized with one phone call. As a result, you and every being here would be arrested, and I could take the items you wish to give me. But because I made a promise to Dianna, I won't do any of that. So, that's your assurance, and the only *deal* I am willing to make."

A slow smile spread across Ethan's face. "Very well, a deal is set then." He glanced at Drake before saying, "She is something rare, that is for sure. No matter what Kaden did to turn her fully into a creature of hate and fear, she did not break. It's that heart of hers. It may be a mortal heart, but it is stronger than anything he has encountered. She may feed, fuck, and breathe like us, but she is not one of us. I think you know that deep down. She is different."

I knew it. Dianna had proven it repeatedly, but I would not discuss her with these two vampires.

"Before we continue, I have a question," Ethan said when I did not respond.

Irritation edged my tone as I regarded him. "What?"

"You have no intention of staying, correct?"

I was confused, but saw no issue with answering. It wasn't as if it were a secret. "No, I shall return to the remains of my home once this is finished."

"Told you," Drake said, his previously teasing expression now hard and cold. The ember from the cigar matched the orange glow burning in his eyes, revealing the truth of his nature.

Ethan's voice had lost all humor, his tone more serious than I had heard it, even when we were discussing the possibility of death and destruction. "A word of advice then, World Ender. Do not fill her head with pretty words. Do not make her beautiful gowns. Do not take her on midnight strolls through a garden or give her handpicked flowers. Kaden has fed her scraps for years to keep her in line. She is a woman who craves love, no matter what she says. If you have no intention of staying or being with her, don't court her and make her care. Don't be the one to make her fall if you have no intention of catching her."

I had no idea how I hadn't spotted Drake in the garden. I hadn't even sensed him. My temper rose, and the lamp on the table flickered. My gaze narrowed, and my voice filled with irritation. "Are you sure you are not in love with her?"

Drake's laugh echoed in the room, just annoying me more. Ethan's expression didn't waver as he held up his left hand. The intricate design of the Ritual of Dhihsin graced his finger. "In case you have forgotten, I am happily married." He lowered his hand as he went on. "Let's just say we owe her and want the best for her. We do not want to see her suffer any more than she already has."

"Very well," I said.

I held my hand out toward the middle of the room. My skin glowed with silver, the thick double lines forming along my legs, chest, and arms, and beneath my eyes. The silver rings spun on my fingers as I spoke the ancient words of summons. A circle formed, and the library shook, the force of my power pushing the furniture toward the walls. A silver beam shot straight up, and Logan and Vincent stepped out. As soon as they passed into the room, I lowered my hand, my skin returning to the smooth golden brown.

"So, that's what you truly look like?" Drake asked. His face was impassive, but I could see the instinctual fear of what I was in the depths of his eyes.

I did not say anything as Logan and Vincent walked toward me. They looked every bit the formidable warriors they were. Celestials took to warfare as if they were born for it, but I had trained the lethal strength into them. A subtle change came over Ethan and Drake, their postures becoming defensive. They watched Vincent and Logan, unsure whether they were a threat.

Logan and Vincent scanned the room, their eyes glowing a vibrant blue. They were on edge, and had every reason to be. They were trained to detect even the smallest threat, and this place had set their celestial blood aflame.

Seeing them relieved some of the tension I didn't know I had been feeling here in this foreign place, surrounded by enemies. Logan was whole and well beyond healed. And even if our last encounter had been less than pleasant, Vincent seemed cheerful and happy to see me. I was surprised to realize that I had missed them as well. After being empty and cold for so long, it was such a strange feeling.

I greeted them with a lift of my chin. "Here is what they have on Kaden at the moment. I want a member of The Hand with Gabriella at all times. I have learned that Kaden is very motivated to reacquire Dianna, and I fear he will try to snatch Gabby again. That also means tighter security."

Vincent glanced at the vampires before saying, "I have already added a few things to our guilds while you have been away."

I looked at Ethan and pointed at the map. "Tell me about this."

Fiery sparks swept across his eyes, and I saw the edge of his fangs as he said, "The map pinpoints spots where he might attack. They are places he has frequented in the past. There are several caves that we think are of significance. He seems to like being underground. Every place he has owned has had a dug-out area somewhere."

I nodded and said to Logan and Vincent, "Keep track of those. They have a dossier on Kaden. Read it and report to me anything I need to know or if you find anything further."

Logan nodded and gathered the folders and papers. He handed them to Vincent before rolling up the map. "We haven't seen an increase in attacks or missing persons. It seems to have gone quiet," he said.

"What about the Book of Azrael? Should we be worried?" Vincent asked, cradling the files and pages Logan had given him.

Logan and I shook our heads. "We saw him. He was dead, Vin. There is no way he made it off world, much less wrote a book."

Vincent's eyes darted between us. "Why is Kaden so sure of its existence, then?"

"That's what I am going to find out," I said as Ethan's words played through my mind. "I believe he is hunting her, and if that's the case, you should be safe, but I do not want to risk it." I clasped Vincent's shoulder. "Just be diligent and keep them all safe."

He gave me a smile and a quick nod. "Yes, my liege."

For once, that title did not haunt me, and I did not correct him. What was happening to me?

Logan groaned and rolled his eyes. "Please do not tell him he is in charge! He has been a bossy pain in the ass since you've been gone."

I smirked, not realizing how much I'd missed them until now.

Logan stared at me, his eyes going wide before he caught himself and cleared his throat. "We will be on our way. I'll call if anything changes."

I nodded and dropped my hand from Vincent's shoulder. I opened the portal once more and watched them leave. After they had stepped through and vanished, I turned back to Ethan. The papers and books settled as the force of the power from opening and closing the portal abated. "You have my word that you and yours will be safe despite your involvement in helping us."

I turned on my heel, heading for the door.

"Is it true you wield the Oblivion blade?" Ethan called out.

I stopped dead in my tracks and turned to glare at him. "How do you know about that?"

Drake's eyes danced between Ethan and me. "So, it's true."

"Who told you about that?" I repeated, my voice a mere whisper.

"Kaden. He said it was a weapon forged for pure destruction and true death, endless darkness for all eternity—no afterlife, no anything. The energy embedded in the blade could end worlds. Thus your name: the World Ender."

My jaw clenched. That weapon represented another part of my history I wished to forget. "And how would Kaden know of such a thing?" It was an impossibility, for no one who had seen it lived. No one but me.

"He is old, Liam, old and powerful. He has been digging for information on you for centuries."

My power spilled out, the doors behind me slamming open and vibrating against the walls. "Then he is well aware of what I am capable of," I said. I turned away, leaving the study and them.

The last thing I heard was Drake saying, "So, that's Samkiel. We're in such deep shit."

My feet barely touched the cheap rug covering the stone steps as the memories battered me, demanding I listen. My chest hammered at even the mention of that weapon and what I had done with it over the centuries. The sound of metal ringing against metal, blood drenching the ground, the way the roars and thunder split the air ran on a constant loop through my subconscious. How could he know?

I took a breath, nearly knocking a gentleman over as my shoulder connected with him. He yelped, rubbing at it as if he were shocked. The pounding in my head was too much for me to stop. I needed air. I needed Dianna.

Before I realized where I was headed, I found myself outside her room. I stopped, my hand clutching the doorknob. My vision cleared, and the pounding in my head subsided. My breathing calmed, and the tightness in my chest eased as I was able to sense her just beyond the door. I ached to go in, desperate to feel her body against mine. She had become a balm to my soul, but Ethan's words rang in my head.

"Don't be the one to make her fall if you have no intention of catching her."

I leaned my forehead against that perfectly ordinary door and knew the woman beyond it was more precious to me than I wanted to admit to anyone, let alone myself. What was I doing? War threatened this world, and I was spending time in gardens. I was distracted again, distracted by her and what I felt. I couldn't do it, not again, not here, and not to Onuna. So, I lowered my hand, and I left.

THIRTY-FOUR

LIAM

I t had been a few days since my meeting with Ethan and Drake. I had stopped sharing a bed with Dianna—and I hadn't known a single night of peace since. I tried to sleep alone and ripped a hole through the wall as I woke. The damage was facing the forest, and I repaired it before anyone was aware. They assumed a quake had shaken the castle, never suspecting the god upstairs. No one questioned it, no one but her.

"This is how the world ends."

"This is how the world ends."

"This is how the world ends."

I missed the nights when Dianna would comfort me, her hands rubbing down my sweat-soaked back as I'd rocked. I'd kept my eyes tightly closed, hoping the energy behind them would not rupture outward. Unafraid of the power I held barely in check, she'd remained close, whispering to me that it was just a dream. She would repeat the words like a mantra, trying to soothe me.

I hadn't told her I was no longer dreaming of Rashearim falling. The dead whispered to me, over and over, always ending with her corpse and its burning eyes. If it wasn't that, I was dreaming of her beneath me, with my cock buried so deep inside her that I could almost feel again. That frightened me more than anything, and I did not know how to tell her that all my dreams were about her. So, I stopped sleeping again and escaped to my room the second she was distracted, refusing to answer my door when she knocked. I knew she wanted to help and was frustrated and confused by my behavior. I didn't want to hurt her, but she couldn't help me. No one could.

At first, she seemed angered by my avoidance, but she allowed Drake to distract her. Their laughter seemed to grate on my nerves, so I retreated to the study. Ethan did not bother me there. No one did. That was where I stayed, reading, researching, and checking in with the Guild, waiting for word of where we needed to go next.

The days dragged on, and I grew restless. I decided I needed to exert some energy that did not involve more busted lightbulbs or electrical malfunctions. There was a gym in the very lowest parts of the castle, and when I was not reading or strategizing, that was where I ended up. When that stopped working, I would run the perimeter of the shielding spell for hours to keep the voices at bay. It helped some, but not enough. It was never enough.

Never enough.

THE SCREEN ON MY PHONE FLASHED BEFORE LOGAN'S FACE CAME INTO view.

"Anything?" I asked as a greeting.

He shook his head and held up a book. "Same texts as we had on Rashearim. The only ones that could even remotely be seen as dangerous are the ones that describe how our weapons are made and work. They are nothing of dire importance. There is no point in knowing how our weapons are made if there isn't a god to make them."

The birds chirped in the overly dense foliage as I sighed in frustration, rubbing a hand over my sweat-drenched face. I'd run until my legs wanted to give out before stopping and picking an isolated place to call Logan.

"I know you're annoyed, but what about the witch?"

I shook my head and turned toward the small mammal that peeked at me from a low-hanging branch. "We have heard nothing, and so we wait."

"Which you hate."

I nodded. "Yes, very much. What about the map?"

He closed the book, the world spinning on the screen as he moved around the study. "I sent a few recruits to the locations pinpointed on the map. They're just old abandoned mines and empty caverns. There is nothing there."

I spoke an ancient curse that had Logan smirking into the phone. "I haven't heard that one in a while."

"I wish for this to be over. If he is as old and powerful as everyone says, what is taking so long? If the Book of Azrael is real, why has it been so difficult to find, even for us?"

"Knowing Azrael," he paused, "maybe he didn't want it to be found. If the God Xeohr made him craft this book, maybe he had strict orders not to speak of it."

"You think Xeohr ordered him to make it?"

"Possibly. Azrael did not make items with any real power unless he was coerced. You know the whole 'too much power in the wrong hands' type deal. Maybe what's inside is that dangerous."

I rubbed my temples. "You give him too much credit. Azrael was waist-deep in the same perversions we were. He was one of us, even if I could not get him away from Xeohr. He just pretended to care about the words and lessons the gods preached."

"That's true." Logan's laugh echoed through the forest and forced a slight smile to my lips. "Why don't you ask the dark-headed beauty you're stuck with? Maybe she knows something?"

"No."

My smile fell, and he noticed.

Logan moved once more, and I waited for him to settle behind one of the desks. "You know, I overheard her sister on the phone with her, and she was complaining about you not sleeping with her anymore."

I groaned and lowered my head, rubbing my forehead. "That does not mean what you think it means."

He laughed. "Oh, come on. This is the same old story we've heard for eons. The great love-them-and-leave-them Samkiel."

"Do not compare Dianna to any of my past conquests." I snapped my head up, the phone flickering to black before returning to normal. I let out a breath, trying to contain the damaging power rippling beneath my skin. "It is not like that between us, and I will not speak of it again."

"Fine. Enlighten me, then: what is it like? Because the last time we spoke, we were all on the same side. Ig'Morruthens were bad, we were good, and now we are what? Working with them? Like the traitorous gods before us?"

My gaze flicked away from the phone as I remembered just how fast Rashearim had fallen because of that betrayal.

"Listen, I'm not questioning your rule, and I'm not being a dick. Neverra and I like Gabriella, but Dianna? Don't choose her. You could have any woman in the universe to scratch your centuries-long itch. Don't let it be her. Hell, call Imogen. We all know she's more than happy and waiting."

"I do not need anything scratched, and Dianna is not like the Ig'Morruthens from our time. She is different. You've seen it."

"Yeah, I saw her bend her shape with mere shadows, blow up an embassy, and kill how many mortals? Oh, and I also saw her shove a blade through the skull of one of her own."

I was growing frustrated, and he knew it. "We cannot think that way anymore. Do you know another reason Rashearim fell? The gods that turned used the Ig'Morruthens. They worked with them to slaughter almost all of us. So, yes, she has helped me, and has continued to help me, but that is it. No matter what you or the others think."

"Hey, I didn't say the others thought—"

My gaze narrowed, knowing well how frequently they all spoke. "I know you. I know you all."

"Okay, fair. We just worry about you. You've been gone so long, Liam." He paused, running a hand over his face as he sat back. "But you're right. They definitely had the upper hand. So, whatever you say, we will follow, you know that."

In the logical thinking part of my consciousness, I knew it came from a place of caring, but there was so much he did not know. Logan assumed I was the man he knew before the war, but Samkiel had died on Rashearim the second it was reduced to dust and rocks.

Logan was not completely unjust. My feelings toward Dianna had been the same as his, but that had changed. I cared for her, and the more I learned about her, the more I realized we had a lot in common. Being around her was easy, and there were times when I was with her that I did not feel like the feared king I was rumored to be. I was just Liam to Dianna.

"She was helping me with my nightmares."

He sat up slowly, swiveling his head from side to side, making sure no one else was in the room. "Nightmares? Of Rashearim?"

I nodded. "That, and what happened after I sent you all away."

"You mean, after you forced all of us from our homeworld while you stayed and fought."

I lifted a single shoulder, as if it were nothing. "The planet was erupting. None of you would have survived."

"Well, you didn't give us a choice on that."

"No, no, I did not. Your life and that of the others are not expendable. Zekiel's death is another thing that will haunt me for the rest of my very long life."

Logan ran his hand over his face. I knew the loss of Zekiel had cut him deep.

"There is another thing," I said, deciding to confide in this man who had stood by me for centuries, even when I repudiated his loyalty.

Logan focused on me again. "Oh?"

"I feel I'm developing the same sight my father and grandfather had."

"Seriously?" Logan's eyes widened in shock.

"Yes. I remember them telling me of their dreams and visions, warning me of what I may one day face. They were of the future to come, but not whole, and not always clear."

"Yeah, they were so utterly terrifying that your grandfather was almost driven insane by them." He leaned forward. "What did you see?"

I could not tell him I dreamed of her; I didn't even want to admit it to myself. So, I told him about the other part of my recent night terrors.

"The world was ending, just as Rashearim did. It was different, but the sky trembled with the same massive beasts. I saw a king, his throne and armor made of horns. I saw the living dead... But I don't know what any of it means, or how to stop it."

Logan's eyes darkened with fear and despair as he shook his head, placing a single hand over his mouth. "Damn."

"Damn is right."

THAT ALL-TOO FAMILIAR ACHE RETURNED TO POUNDING IN MY TEMPLES. I sighed as the light flickered on the desk, and I stretched, looking at the stacks of books surrounding me. I'd hidden away, burying myself in research as we waited for word from Camilla. Ethan's library held items dating back to the beginning of civilization. I had not found anything that mentioned the fall of Rashearim, or the celestials that had taken refuge here while I rebuilt the remains of our world.

If the information Ethan had given me was accurate, and Kaden was indeed as old as he said, then the beginning of civilization could give me clues. The mortals had ancient stories of mythical beasts. Maybe Kaden was an Ig'Morruthen that had escaped the Gods War and landed here, planning to rebuild his ranks. But the ones here had to be a subspecies. I had read and reread about firebirds that danced across the sky, skinwalkers who lured their victims to their deaths, and even dragons. All of them fit, and yet none of them fit completely.

Footsteps approached, and the door to the study slowly opened. I did not need to look up to know who my visitor was. She set a plate on top of the open book I was reading.

"Look, I made you something. See the face? It's grumpy, like you."

I kept my gaze down, my forehead resting on my hand. The plate held a thin brown cake-like disc with red, round half-sphere items forming its eyes. The mouth was made out of some white, foamy cream and was turned down in a frown. I watched Dianna put her plate down and shift a stack of books off the desk. She pulled over a large chair and sat down.

"Very funny." I shook my head and pushed the plate aside before returning to my book.

"Yup, exactly like that."

"I am not grumpy. I am busy."

Her fork dinged against her plate as she cut a piece of her food and took a bite. "You're not sleeping either."

I closed the book, knowing I could not focus with her around. "And how would you know that? I thought you and your friend would be too busy catching up to notice?"

They'd been catching up, indeed. There were several times I'd stumbled in on them in the middle of a joke. As soon as I entered, their laughter would die, and tension would fill the air.

She lowered her fork and leaned back in her chair, crossing her legs. "Oh, I don't know. Maybe it was that random 'quake,' or that they've had to hunt down issues with the electricity three times in the last few days. Or maybe a clue is that you have been avoiding me and haven't asked me to stay with you in two weeks."

Two weeks? Had the sun set that many times? Her leads were taking longer than promised, and we still needed that invitation before we could continue our search. In the meantime, I had been trying to piece together the mystery that was her maker.

"Your observations are bothersome."

She made a face, a breath leaving her nostrils in a snort. "Why? Because they're right?"

Yes, I said to myself, reaching for another book.

"You can't ignore me forever. Now eat."

She moved the book that I was using as my distraction and pushed my plate in front of me again. It was my turn to scowl, but I pushed the books aside and brought the plate closer to me. I picked up the fork, cut a piece, and took a bite. I glared at her as I chewed and swallowed before asking, "Happy?"

She smiled before starting to eat again. "Tell me why you aren't sleeping. More nightmares?"

Yes. Nightmares about your end.

I swallowed another bite of the sugary breakfast she'd brought me before saying, "I am not tired. I just do not wish to sleep. If what they say is true, we have limited time to find this book before Kaden does."

She stabbed at her food. "Yeah, and waiting on Camilla to accept the invitation is taking longer than I had hoped."

I nodded, hoping to change the subject. "So, why does this Camilla hate you so? Another friend who is not a friend?"

"Try an ex-lover."

I felt that tinge of heat again, the same as when Drake placed a hand on her. I'd never felt it before and did not know what it meant, only that I did not like it. Even her speaking of being with another caused something wild and vicious to awaken within me. I did not recognize these emotions.

She had said before that her relationship with Kaden was not monogamous, but after hearing about his extreme obsession with getting her back, I was surprised he'd allowed someone to get that close to her. "Kaden permitted that?"

A small laugh escaped her. "He didn't care about my relationship with Camilla. He was actually going to give her a seat at his table, but she came to care deeply about me, and *that* he did not like. So, he exiled her because I begged him not to kill her. Santiago got her seat instead. I never told her what I'd done, but she assumed I'd betrayed her and was responsible for her loss of power, and I guess in a way I was. I haven't spoken to her in ages. Kaden wouldn't allow it. She hates me because she thinks I didn't fight for her and chose to stay with Kaden. I mean, what we had was great and fun, but I didn't love her, not like she loved me. My decision could never be anything else, anyway. I wouldn't risk Gabby."

Her words echoed parts of my life, leaving me awestruck that we could be so different and yet have so much in common. I knew all too well about past lovers who felt more for you than you did for them. I knew how horrible that could make one feel.

"You are risking her now, being with me, are you not?"

"It's different with you." She paused as if catching herself and finished chewing a small bite before saying, "You are the only thing Kaden fears."

"You never told me the story of how you ended up in Kaden's grip. Just that you gave up your life for your sister's."

Her expression went blank, and I saw the shadows in her eyes before she looked at her plate and shrugged. "It's a long story. Maybe another time."

I nodded, knowing better than to push her. She would tell me in her own time.

"Do you like the crepes?"

I nodded as I took another bite. "Is that what they are called? They are divine. I think 'sweets,' as you call them, are my weakness."

She chuckled. "So, you do have a weakness. Your secret is safe with me." She winked before taking another bite. "Be thankful that Gabby taught me how to cook, because otherwise, this would be disgusting."

"You cooked breakfast for the entire estate?" Although my question was more in reference to the vampire that followed her every move like a Vennir hound in heat.

Dianna shook her head, snorting slightly and covering her mouth. "No, just us. You give me way too much credit. I'm not that nice."

She continued to eat, completely unaware of the impact of her simple statement. A small smile played on my lips, and I found myself relaxing for the first time in weeks. It was so easy to speak with Dianna, and I had missed being able to do so. The weight of the worlds seemed to lift from my shoulders when I was near her.

As good as that felt, it was a problem if I intended to leave once this book, real or not, was retrieved. Ethan's words bounced around in my head once more, and I bit back the things I wanted to say to her.

"Gabby is a good person, and I mean that," I said. "Mortals and creatures alike give off a certain energy—a true form, I suppose. Some call it the soul, whereas others refer to it as an aura."

"You can see that?" she interrupted, her eyes going wide. "You can see people's souls?"

I did not know if I'd upset her or misspoken, because she sat very still, staring at me.

"Yes. It depends on the person or creature, and I sometimes have to concentrate, but I can see most."

She placed her fork down and propped her elbow on the desk, resting her chin on her hand. She leaned in, fully engaged. "What does Gabby's look like?"

"Yellows and pinks, vibrant and warm, kind of like her." I placed my fork down, grabbing the thin white paper cloth she'd brought and wiping my mouth.

She beamed. "Yeah, that sounds like her. What about mine? What do I look like?"

"Very similar." I did not want to tell her what danced around her. I did not want her to feel less than what she was. Hers was vibrant, yes, but it was a mix of reds and blacks with a hint of yellow. It was pure swirling chaos, like the edge of the universe itself.

"Cool." She smiled and popped a piece of fruit into her mouth.

I cleared my throat. "I heard you speaking to your sister earlier. How is she?"

Her eyes seemed to sparkle at my question, as if no one had ever asked her that before. I did not mention what Logan had told me. Her phrasing of what we shared, or did not share, was no one's business.

"She's great, actually. She was able to work in the medical department at the Guild with some of the celestials there. So, she is more than happy. Thank you."

Dianna reached out, placing her hand atop mine. A frisson of awareness wound through me at her touch, calling to something I had thought long dead. The sensation caused the hairs on my arm to rise, and I wasn't sure if it was from a sense of alarm or a desire for more.

I slipped my hand from beneath hers and reached for my fork. Dianna's body tensed, and she slowly withdrew her hand.

The room fell silent again. It was not Dianna's fault, nor did I want to hurt her. I just was not used to how I felt around her. Dianna's touch set fire to a place inside me, and I found myself wanting to burn.

"Why do you and your sister always repeat that same mantra?" I asked in a rush, not wanting our conversation to end.

She tipped her head and looked at me with confusion. "What do you mean?"

"At the end of your calls, you always say, 'Remember I love you.' Are you afraid she will forget?"

She snickered softly and folded her arms on the table. "Oh, no. It's like a goodbye, I guess. My parents used to say it every day before they left. Gabby and I picked it up and have said it since we were young. I guess it stuck. It feels especially important given what I do now. It's just in case I never came back, which I know sounds kind of morbid."

"It's not. It's nice, and something for you two to share."

"Thanks." Her smile returned slowly.

I was about to ask another question when I heard footsteps approaching. The door slammed open, and both of us spun toward it.

"There you are! I've been looking everywhere for you," Drake snapped as he stalked into the room.

I had grown to hate his devilish grin, because it was always directed at the vicious vixen sitting in front of me. He wore a pair of loose black pants but no shirt, flaunting his muscled chest and the expanse of taut brown skin. As he knelt next to Dianna, I noticed his hands were taped up. She sat back and angled her body toward him, her smile bright. My chest ached, and I found I did not enjoy sharing her attention.

I scowled at him and said, "You need to come with a warning."

He glanced at me and smiled, completely unoffended. "Thank you."

"That was not a compliment."

Dianna laughed, and I felt like I had been punched in the gut. I hated the way they smiled at one another. I wondered if she thought of his perfectly flawless skin and dreamed of touching it. Would he let her if she asked? It was not like mine, marred and scarred from the battles fought throughout my lifetime. Sure, I might have been taller, and my muscle definition was more pronounced than his, but I would never be the flawless creature he was.

Dianna's eyes seemed to dance when he entered the room. The stories and legends from my past might hail me as some magnificent being, but with Dianna, I felt a slight nudge of self-consciousness.

What if she preferred men like Drake? Even though I knew I should not care, nor should it bother me, it did on some base level.

I hated the playful slaps of her small hand against his chest and shoulders. I felt those were reserved for only me, yet she did the same to him. She truly laughed when he spoke or made some crass comment. I'd only heard her laugh one time like that with me. Their laughter died whenever I entered the room, and I did not know why it bothered me so much, but it did.

"Ready to get hot and sweaty, cutie? I'll stretch you out before." He grinned suggestively at her, and my blood boiled.

I could not tell if they were past lovers, and I refused to ask. It was not my place, and I shouldn't care, but a part of me hoped he had never laid a hand on her naked flesh. It was a ridiculous notion. Dianna was not mine, and we were only associates … friends. But if that was the truth, why did my heart ache? The muscles bunched beneath my shoulder blades as my hands clenched into fists and then released. I was being ridiculous.

Dianna stood and gathered our plates as Drake rose. "Sure, let me change clothes, and I'll meet you downstairs."

"Where are you going?"

I could tell by how they both turned and stared at me that the question came out rough and a little aggressive. I hadn't meant to ask, but I had to know. She had just gotten here, and now he showed up, and she was off once more.

"Drake has been helping me keep up with my training over the last few weeks. Which you would know if you had bothered to leave this study and look for me."

Drake's eyebrows went up, but he did not interject. At least he wasn't a complete idiot.

"I told you we needed to gather all the information we can find on Kaden while we wait for Camilla to either accept or deny the invitation. That is why we are here."

"What is that supposed to mean? Have I not been helping?"

"As of late? No."

Her nostrils flared, and I knew I had hit a nerve. We had been getting along well, but her coming here seemed to stir up something.

"Well, if you had bothered talking to me, instead of shutting me out, you would know that you won't find anything written about Kaden in a book. But no, you would rather ignore me."

"I am not ignoring you."

She scoffed, her grip on the plates tightening. "Are you sure about that? When is the last time we had an actual conversation, besides me bothering you until you responded with a grunt or the word 'no'? Or how about when I go to your room, and you won't even open the door?"

I closed my eyes and rubbed at my forehead, that damn pounding starting once more. My voice was anything but kind when I said, "I will not share a bed with you any longer, when to do so gets me lectured by creatures far beneath me thinking I have ill intentions toward you."

The room shook before going eerily still, and I thought my power had broken the leash again. But when I opened my eyes and looked at Dianna, I realized it was not my wrath affecting our surroundings. It was hers. I glanced up and saw anger etched into her sharp features. White, wispy smoke coiled beneath her nostrils as she glared at me. The last time I'd seen her like this was just before the room exploded in Arariel.

"You have been avoiding me because they think we're sleeping together?" Her words were short and clipped.

My eyes went to the overly affectionate man at her side. "Have your precious friends not told you what they have said to me regarding you?"

Drake's eyes went wide as Dianna's head spun toward him. He held up his hands in mock surrender. "Hey, Ethan and I were just looking out for you."

The plates in her hands shattered, scraps of food and shards of delicate glass falling to the floor. "You two are like overbearing brothers!"

I smelled the fire even though she hadn't yet summoned the flames. Drake did too and took a step back, his eyes darting toward her now clenched fist. "Who I fuck, or don't fuck, is none of your or

Ethan's business. You put everyone here at risk because you're so concerned with protecting me."

"Dianna!" I said, my voice sharp.

"What does that mean?" Drake's brows furrowed, obviously unaware of my violent nightmares.

"And you," she said, turning on me. Her eyes locked with mine. I watched the anger fade, only to be replaced by sadness, and that was so much worse. "You couldn't even tell me? After everything, you suddenly couldn't confide in me? I am so sorry you find me so repulsive that the mere mention of *fucking* me makes you avoid me for weeks."

I surged to my feet, planting my hands on the desktop. Several pages of text floated to the ground as I growled, "Do not place words on my tongue. I did not say that!"

She took a step forward, coming up against the other side of the desk. "It's how you act!" A ring of red started at the edge of her irises and then flooded them, suffocating the rich brown. "Apparently, their opinions mean more to you than my feelings. So, I am done. I am done trying to be your friend. I am done trying to help ease your pain, and I am *so* done with caring. We have to work together, but I am not doing this weird back-and-forth shit with you anymore. We're not friends, Liam—and I see now that we never were."

She turned, and without a second glance toward me and the massive hole she just punched through my chest, she left.

Drake turned back to me and placed his hands on his hips as he sighed. "She's fine. She just needs to cool off, you know?"

My jaw clenched as my lips formed into a thin line. "Out."

His eyes lit up as a mocking smile curved his lips. He lifted his hand in a small salute and followed Dianna from the room.

As soon as the door closed, every object and piece of furniture around me exploded into a thousand shards.

I DID NOT SEE HER THE NEXT DAY, AND I WAS SURE SHE'D KEPT TO herself. The sound of her laughter was absent in the castle, but her words rang in my head. They were more upsetting than I cared to admit.

"We're not friends, Liam. We never were."

My eyes darted toward the door every time I heard footsteps. The hope that it would be her coming to throw another crass comment at me refused to waver. Maybe she'd forgotten to tell me something and needed to remind me how much of an asshole I was. I thought my eyes would burn holes through the door that day, but she never came.

I had not taken her feelings into account, only mine. I had agreed to a friendship, yet I'd shown Drake and Ethan more respect. She had helped me more than she knew, and I'd mistreated her. She was right, and I needed to make amends.

The clothes lent to me here were of higher quality than the ones I'd first received upon my arrival. I changed into a pair of long black jogging-style pants. The long-sleeved shirt was meant to fit snugly, but it was tighter than I liked. My ability to summon fabrics was out of my reach, since I had not slept. It was taking me more power to control the visions that plagued me and to stay awake. So, I had no other choice but to wear what was provided.

I sighed and left my room, taking the steps two at a time. The few houseguests I passed either ran from me or ducked and whispered to those closest to them. I continued on my way, using the connection I refused to acknowledge to track the fiery female. A loud thud followed by a grunt from a man in pain had me heading down a large corridor. There she was.

"Why are you taking your anger out on me? I apologized," Drake moaned from the floor as I entered. It was the same gym I had used before, but some things had changed. Black burn marks decorated the concrete walls like sooty dots. From the scent of fresh flame, I knew that at least half of them had been created recently, and the other half were maybe a day old. Smoke still spilled from the fresh singe marks on the large red pad covering the middle of the floor, and two dummies sat against the far wall with half their faces and parts of their bodies melted off. Ropes hung from the wall closest to me, the ends black and frayed. The only thing that seemed untouched were the large mirrors covering the wall, an assortment of metal bells and circular plates lined up before them.

My eyes stopped roaming when I focused on Dianna. Her clothes were not any I had seen her wear previously. They clung to her sleek figure, hugging the lean muscle and small curves too well. Her shoulders, arms, and midsection were exposed. She had tied her hair back, the tip dancing between her shoulder blades. She was breathtaking— and still beyond angry.

"Finally, someone else you can beat up." Drake slowly picked himself up off the floor, holding his side. His clothes were riddled with burn holes, proving she had not held back. Good girl.

"Go away."

That stung.

"No."

"I don't have any new information, and I'm busy, so go away."

She was trying to throw my words back at me, only with more venom. Drake hobbled toward a row of benches, sitting far out of the way.

"No."

Flames tickled the tips of her fingers as she stared at me. "You step onto this mat, and I'm fighting you, too."

Very well. I looked down and deliberately placed one foot on the mat. I looked up, holding her gaze in an unspoken challenge. She saw it and accepted.

Dianna's fist swung for my face. I pivoted to the right, letting it drift by. She spun, swinging her elbow for my chin. I leaned back, and it failed to connect. She threw a combination of punches and jabs, all of them missing their targets, which only frustrated her more.

"If you intend to hit me, you are doing poorly," I said, deflecting another punch.

"You are so annoying!" she said, throwing her leg in an upward kick.

"I came to apologize."

"Fuck off."

Dianna circled the ring, her fists raised and held close to her body.

There was no laughter in her today, no quips, and no jokes. She was all barely contained, untempered rage. She moved like a large feline predator, calculating, dangerous, and exceptionally impressive.

"I don't want to hurt you," she breathed.

"Says the one who can't even touch me."

Dianna moved again, this time with a punch-and-knee combo. I blocked with my hand, but the force behind her moves caused them to sting. She was a hard hitter, but still not accurate enough. She was trained, but not like The Hand or me. If she used her legs more, she would be quite effective. She had the length to reach her opponent, just not the correct skill. Not yet.

She moved closer, throwing a jab that I ducked. It flew by my head as her other fist shot upward, aiming for my jaw. I caught her by the wrist and spun her into me. Her breath came in harsh pants as I held her with her back to my chest. I locked her wrists against her body as she tried to break free.

"Your punches are strong, but uncoordinated."

"Burn in Iassulyn."

Drake's laugh echoed in the background.

She tipped her head toward the sound, sweat beading on her forehead. "Why are you laughing? I don't see you trying to fight a god."

Drake did not respond, but he did quiet down.

"Ignore him. I wanted to apologize, Dianna, not fight you."

"There is nothing to apologize for." Her breathing stopped, and I felt her twist her wrists in my hand. "We're not friends."

"Stop saying that!"

I felt her try to rotate her wrists, so I squeezed them tighter. "I am sorry for how I acted and have been acting. There is too much happening at the moment with me, and I am letting things bother me. I allowed people who mean nothing to get to me. You have helped me tremendously since we first started. I truly do appreciate it, and you. I am sorry."

She went quiet, some of the tension leaving her body as she stopped trying to free her wrists.

"You're mean." Her voice was barely above a whisper.

"I know."

"And rude."

A small snort escaped me, my breath moving a few loose strands of hair atop her head. "I know."

"Let me go."

My grip upon her wrists loosened, but not enough to set her free. Not yet. "I will once you say you are no longer mad at me."

She sighed. "Fine, I'm not mad at you."

I cautiously relaxed my grip on her wrists, releasing her hands. She took a step forward and spun, her fist shooting out too fast for me to deflect. I heard the crack both inside my head and echoing in the room as blistering pain shot through my nose and across my face. I reached up, cupping it with a single hand.

"What was that for?" I asked, squinting at her blurry image.

"For being a dick these last two weeks." She shrugged. "I feel better now."

I pinched the bridge of my nose, the small fracture healing and the bone popping back into place. I would give her credit; Dianna never surrendered. She reached up and tightened the band that held her hair back before rolling her wrists and taking up a defensive stance.

"You still wish to fight? I apologized."

"Tired already?" A slow smile formed on her lips, and I felt the energy in the room change. Her eyes shone with that familiar red ember glow. "I told you I was training. If you're done, Drake can replace you."

I do not know why that comment made my blood turn to ice, but it did.

"No, please stay. I would prefer to heal a little more before she breaks another rib," Drake said from where he was slumped on the bench. "Just please do not destroy this house. Ethan will kill me."

His comment caught me off guard and gave her a window. I did not see her move or her shape fade, but I felt the displaced air wash over me as she reformed, her fist aiming for my head. I moved, her knuckles barely grazing the top of my shoulder. Before I was able to recover enough to react, she spun one lean leg, her foot sailing toward my head. I bent back as she corrected herself, but I was not quick enough to avoid her second kick. The center of her shin connected with my shoulder hard enough to sting.

Drake let out a congratulatory cheer, but we both ignored him. Dianna held her fists up, one leg in front of her, her expression defiant and daring.

I rubbed my shoulder as the slight ache faded. "Your arms are less defined than your legs. There is more power there, given your hip-to-leg ratio."

She looked down as Drake said snidely, "I think that's his way of saying you have a nice ass. Which I agree with."

We both glared at him. He flung himself to the side as a fireball whipped toward him, colliding with the wall where he'd been sitting. Flames sizzled on the dark and singed stone.

"Hey! What did I say about destroying the house, Dianna?"

He caught my glare and decided to shut up. "Ignore him," I said again and turned back toward her. She was shaking her fists, extinguishing the lingering flames.

"With your powers alone, you're stronger than most of my celestials, but still not strong enough for The Hand or me."

She scoffed and shook her head, her eyes threatening to incinerate me. "I don't know. I held my own pretty well with Zekiel and you."

"I am not saying that it is a bad thing," I added, refusing to take the bait, not trying to argue with her. "I have trained for centuries; so have they. You have the right motions, just not the execution. You were also trained by someone who probably did not want you strong enough to overpower him. Dianna, you are already dangerous. Now let's make you lethal."

She squared her shoulders, the crimson glow of her irises easing as she nodded.

DAYS PASSED WITH STILL NO WORD. LOGAN REPORTED THAT THERE HAD been no suspicious movement or deaths. Despite that, or maybe because of it, I was on edge. Something felt off, but I was struggling to pinpoint what.

Dianna and I had trained every day, but that was the only time we spent together. We didn't speak of it again, but there was a distance between us that threatened not only our partnership, but our friendship.

She did not ask me to join her at night, and I did not go to her. A few times I'd stopped outside her door, my hand raised to knock, but I'd stopped myself each time. I kept telling myself it was better that way, since my stay was not permanent. Even if I yearned for it, I could not get attached to her warmth and the comfort she brought me.

Instead, I went to my room each night and lay on the bed, staring out the window. I watched the moon fall and the sun rise, same as I had on the remains of Rashearim. That deep, dark hollow feeling in my chest she'd chased away started to crawl its way back in.

I CIRCLED HER AS SHE STOOD WITH HER EYES CLOSED AND STANDING ON one leg, the other folded at the knee, the sole of her foot against her thigh. She held her hands, palms together, at chest level.

Dianna opened one eye, maintaining her stance as she said, "If you let me use my powers, I could show you just how quickly I could take you down."

"No." I stopped in front of her, my hands clasped behind my back. "You desired training, so we will train properly. Not whatever failed attempt you tried with Mr. Vanderkai."

She sighed before closing both of her eyes.

"Think of it this way. Your powers are phenomenal, but you are defenseless if you overexert yourself and no longer have access to them. You must know how to defend yourself and be aware of the boundaries of your capabilities."

Dianna peeked one eye open. "I've never had any issues before."

"That does not mean it can't happen. Trust me." I circled once more, stopping behind her this time. "I will teach you a technique my father once taught me."

She turned her head, looking at me over her shoulder. She didn't say anything, just nodded once and waited for me to continue.

"Extend your arms out for me."

She looked forward and complied. I moved an inch closer, the rich, spicy fragrance of cinnamon filling my nose. It was complex and Dianna's unique scent. I had missed it dearly over the last few days. I shook my head slightly, pushing those thoughts away and focusing.

"I will not physically touch you, but you will see what happens once I start."

She tipped her head back, her face inches from mine. "What does that mean?"

I raised my hands, my palms beginning to glow as they hovered over her wrists. Violet and silver light danced from me to her, tiny sparks of electricity connecting us. Her eyes widened, but she made no move to pull away or stop me. I followed the lines of her arms, allowing my power to lick at her skin.

She shuddered, swallowing hard before saying, "It doesn't hurt. Not like before."

"That's because I can control the intensity. If I wanted it to hurt, I could make it hurt."

She glanced at me as if she was about to make some smart-assed quip, but her expression closed down as she stopped herself. My heart clenched with disappointment as she looked back at her arm. "The movement under my skin. What's that?"

"That's your power. See the shadows that bend when I pass? It is preparing itself to act to defend you against what it senses as a threat. It's patient, just waiting for you to call it forward."

"Cool. Gross, but cool."

My gaze narrowed. "It is not gross. Just as the light inside me is a part of me, the shadows are a part of you. It is you, and it is not."

Her eyes met mine before she nodded again. I moved around in front of her, my right hand hovering inches above her skin, her power following like a shadow beneath her skin.

"My father taught me this mantra. It is very different from the one you have with your sister, but it helped me gain control and maintain focus. He labeled it as the main power source. The logic portion of your power comes from your brain." Tiny tendrils of her power followed as I moved my hand toward her head. Her eyes momentarily crossed as she tried to track the movement.

"The emotion and irrationality from your heart." I trailed my hand lower. I didn't touch her, but my palm hovered over her breast. Her breath hitched as her shadows seemed to dance and tease the sparks of my power. Something had changed. Her chest rose and fell beneath the sweat-drenched fabric of her top, my mind flashing to the dreams where I begged to touch.

I licked my lips and took a steadying breath. Dianna's gaze snagged on the movement, and I nearly groaned, forcing myself to focus once more. I moved to her side, tracing the line of her torso to hover over her belly. "And lastly, your anger, that fire you wield, comes from your gut." The shadows beneath her skin mingled with a vibrant red.

I pulled my power back into me, and the light died as I moved my hand to my side. I heard Dianna release a ragged breath, as if she had been holding it for too long.

"Core, heart, brain," I said. "That is the main trigger of your powers. One cannot exist or function without the other. Decisions made with one and not the other two can be deadly. True masters of the skill can control and manipulate all three."

"Let me guess: you're a true master?" Her eyebrow rose as she placed her hands on her hips.

"I have to be. My decisions cannot be based on what my heart tells me, no matter the cost. I cannot break or bend the rules because I wish it. The universe would be unbalanced if I used my power for selfish reasons."

Her eyes softened for just a moment before she lowered her gaze. "How do I control it?"

"Center, focus, release." I paused as the appropriate word entered my mind. "Or 'meditation,' as this world calls it."

Her hands dropped to her sides as she nodded. "Okay, teach me more."

"Very well."

We spent the rest of the evening on meditation. The practice helped to calm my erratic nerves, and I vowed to utilize it more.

Every day we worked on something new, but on the fifth day, we returned to sparring. We had decided that every time Drake commented, he had to be the target. It shut him up, and eventually, he stopped coming.

On the sixth day, I showed her how to hold and wield a blade. She was absolutely terrible at it. She hated it and preferred brute force, and while she agreed it was a good skill to have, she complained every single second.

"Show me how you fought Zekiel and lived," I asked, a wooden *bo* staff in my hand as I circled her.

Dianna held a matching staff and copied my movements, her body drenched in sweat and her breathing labored.

"It wasn't easy. He is fast, just like you."

"It's a skill—"

"I know, I know. It takes time to master."

She charged. Wood met wood with a loud crack that echoed through the room. I pushed her back, and she spun, correcting herself. She whipped it once more, aiming for my left arm. I moved, blocking the hit. No matter how many times she missed, she learned, corrected, and aimed a counterattack. She was determined, skilled in her own way, and resilient. She was a perfect weapon through and through, and she refused to quit or yield, no matter how many times she was bruised or hissed in pain when my weapon would connect as it did now.

Dianna's head whipped to the side, and a small trickle of blood formed on her lip. I lowered my weapon and rushed to her side.

"Dianna."

"I'm fine," she said, holding up her hand to stop my advance. I had noticed that she did not want me close to her. If she was hurt during our training, she did not want my comfort or for me to attend to her. It wounded me just as much as it did for me to see her in pain.

I stayed in my place, watching helplessly as she wiped the blood from her healing lip. "See. All better."

"Let me look," I practically begged.

She held up her staff, pointing it at my chest, keeping me at a distance. "I said I'm fine. Raise your weapon. Would you check on your enemy when you hurt them? No."

"You are not my enemy," I said flatly.

Pain flashed in her eyes, but all she said was, "Raise your weapon."

Before I could respond, she came at me. I slapped her staff away, but it did not stop her, and she charged again. Had she learned nothing? I shifted, preparing to block another hit. The staffs connected once above our heads, then on my left, her right, and then again as she spun, aiming for my throat. With a hard upward swing, I knocked her staff from her hand. I had a second to thrust mine forward, but she was gone, only a thin layer of mist remaining in her place.

I felt a heavy push on the back of my knees, and I fell forward. There was no time for me to process what had happened before her leg connected with the side of my face, causing me to spin hard enough to land on my back. I watched as she caught the wooden staff out of the air with one hand, thrusting the tip against the center of my chest.

"That's how I fought Zekiel." She panted, no humor in her gaze, only that same hard look she had given me since our fight in the study.

Dianna had combined what I had been teaching her with her own moves, creating a unique and unpredictable style of fighting that had caught me unawares. She had performed a perfect roundhouse kick that knocked me on my ass, and now she held a weapon to my chest. She never stopped thinking and was always calculating, figuring out how to turn a fight to her advantage. I was more than impressed with this beautiful, dangerous, magnificent woman.

She tossed the wooden staff to the side before stalking over to the small towel and water bottle she'd brought with her. She came back and lowered herself to the mat, but she hadn't brought mine or offered to share anything with me. The slight burned me more than any flame she could wield.

I rose to a sitting position and brought my knees close to me. I rested my arms upon them and just looked at her, transfixed by the light playing off the sheen of her skin.

"It's impressive what you have absorbed in this short amount of time. You are a quick learner, even if you hate the way I train, or me." I did not mean for that last part to slip out, but it was increasingly difficult to ignore how much this rift hurt. It was worse than any physical pain I had endured.

Her eyes met mine before darting away quicker than I could gauge her expression. "You are definitely bossy when you train, but it makes sense." She stretched her leg out, bumping her foot against mine. The contact was the first she had initiated outside of the ring. She realized what she had done, and her face dropped. She pulled her leg back and scooted a few inches away from me, and I had to will myself not to reach out and drag her back. I missed her playful swats and bumps. I just missed her.

"I apologize for my actions lately. I am growing frustrated with waiting, and it just has me on edge, I suppose."

She shrugged as she folded her legs in front of herself. Her eyes darted down as she picked at her shoelace. "You don't have to keep apologizing, Liam. Seriously, it's fine."

My brows furrowed as I turned to her completely. "Dianna. You keep saying that, but I really do not think it is fine. You—"

The doors behind us swung open, and Ethan strolled in, Drake at his heels. As per their norm, they were both dressed in all black, with Drake adding a hint of red. He reeked of illicit activities layered with a hint of lavender. I didn't care for either scent, but at least he didn't smell of cinnamon.

"Good news: the invite has been accepted."

Dianna hopped to her feet, wiping her hands on the leggings that hugged her ass and legs. "Great. When do we leave?"

"Anxious to leave me already?" Drake joked, but Dianna did not respond as she usually did. Maybe I was not the only one facing her wrath. Drake noticed, and his grin slid off his face.

Ethan's eyes cut to his brother, then back to us. "Her condition is that she only wants me and a few members of my line. I feel she wishes to make peace, since the world believes Drake to be dead."

Dianna nodded once, folding her arms. "I don't trust Camilla, but I can look like anyone. So, I can take Drake with me and—"

"Absolutely not." That had every head turning toward me, but I did not care. "You will not leave me here while you walk into a trap, or worse."

"You can't go with me. Not only would they recognize you, but you feel like a living supernova. Your power alone would alert them the second you stepped foot in the area."

Despite our audience, I squared off with her. "How would she not sense you? Even if you change forms, Otherworld creatures may recognize your power. You are not like them. You are a step above, if not more."

"As insulting as that is, the World Ender has a point." Ethan sighed, shooting a look my way. "Which is why we have these."

Drake stepped forward, holding a large engraved box. He opened it, revealing two silver chain-like bracelets.

I studied them, able to sense the power radiating off of them. "What enchanted item is this?"

"The Bracelets of Ophelia," Dianna whispered as she looked up at Drake, her smile returning. My jaw clenched as I realized this was another thing they shared that I knew nothing about.

"Please explain."

Dianna's smile dropped as she turned toward me. "They're a treasure and extremely enchanted. They are strong enough to make any Otherworld creature seem like a normal mortal. In short, they can cloak someone's power."

"A mutual friend let me borrow them," Drake added, looking pointedly at Dianna. "So please, be careful and return them. I would like to not piss her off." He closed the box and handed it to Dianna.

She met his gaze, a small smile dancing across her face as she took it from him.

I couldn't watch her smile at him anymore and turned to Ethan. "So, what is the plan?"

THIRTY-FIVE

LIAM

"This plan is horrific," I said to Drake, who sat on one of the nearby couches. We were upstairs in one of Ethan's old offices. There was a large painting of an elegantly dressed couple over a massive fireplace. Chairs and couches offered plenty of seating options, and bookcases lined the walls. His large desk was cluttered with papers and scrolls that we had studied the last few days, looking for something, anything, that could help us defeat Kaden.

The room was dimly lit. The only light we had turned on was the small one on the desk. I leaned against the fireplace, calling silvery flames to my hand before smothering them in my fist. The light flickered as I borrowed the energy from it to create the fire. I used to do similar tasks when I was young to calm my nerves.

"It will work. Trust me."

I made a noise low in my throat.

Drake's shadow took up the space near me. "You really don't like me, do you?"

"Should I?"

"What's your problem? Besides the fact that you hate all Otherworld creatures."

"I do not hate all Otherworld creatures. That is yet another story fabricated in the minds of those who do not know me."

He scoffed, folding his arms. "My apologies, my king, but how many have you slaughtered? How many died before the realms were sealed?"

I could see in the reflection of his eyes that mine had started to glow silver. I was so sick of my history getting thrown back in my face by those who knew nothing of what had happened or what I'd had to become. "You know nothing about me."

"Oh, so it's because of Dianna, then. Are you threatened by me?"

"I dislike the way you speak to her at times, but threatened? Never. I have known many men like you." I paused and lifted one shoulder in a careless shrug. "Gods, I used to be one. A simple flick of your finger, and you can have any woman you want—dozens at a time if you ask it."

Drake's brows rose. "Wait—when you say dozens at a time, do you mean—"

I raised my hand, cutting him off. "That's not the point. The point is that Dianna does not deserve to be spoken to like that or treated as just a conquest. She is not an object for you and Kaden to haggle over. So, no, I do not like you, nor will I pretend to be your friend. The only reason I have not killed you yet is that I promised Dianna I would be on my best behavior. Even if she hates me at the moment, I will not go back on my word."

He smiled a slow, cocky grin. "And you say you're not in love with her."

"I am not, but she still deserves someone in her life that cares about her beyond the physical acts you keep suggesting. Someone that respects her and treats her as an equal, not some pawn. She has no one but her sister."

His grin slipped as he folded his arms over his chest. "I agree. Gabby is her only family, and although we are friends, no one could get close to her. Kaden wouldn't allow it. He kept her on a tight leash —sometimes literally, from what I hear. I also think that Dianna was afraid to get close to anyone because he would use them as weapons against her, just as he did Gabby."

My teeth ached with how hard I was clenching my jaw. I hated thinking of her living that life for centuries, alone and afraid to form any relationships. She had been surrounded by beings that actively sought to hurt her.

When I didn't say anything and just stared at him, he went on. "I wasn't trying to piss you off by asking if you love her, but maybe to make you realize the feelings you keep denying. I also wanted to make sure you weren't like Kaden. We both can agree she is strong and beautiful, and that attracts powerful men."

"So, you are saying you are not in love with her?" I asked, the doubt clear in my tone.

He leaned against the mantle and shrugged. "I love her, but I am not in love with her. I have loved one woman in my entire existence, and she left a long time ago. I'm through with the whole love thing." Loss and regret flashed across his features. It was a look I recognized for different reasons. "What about you? Have you ever been in love?"

I paused as I stared into the fireplace, focusing on the glow of a single ember in the dying wood. "No. I never have. I've lusted, cared for others, but never loved. My father told me once that he would rip the known universe apart for my mother. I have never felt that way about anyone. Logan and Neverra have been together for as long as I can remember. They are inseparable and have put their lives on the line to protect each other. Sure, I care for my friends, my lovers at the time, but never like that. Maybe it's the godly part of me, but I do not think I am made that way."

"Made what way?"

I did not turn to see Drake's face, knowing I had revealed too much of myself. "I am a destroyer. The World Ender in every aspect, I am everything you should fear. I mean that with every ounce of my being, and not in the egotistical way Dianna assumes. I have burned worlds to their core and slain beasts large enough to devour this castle. The books were not wrong about any of that. I have always been a weapon for my throne, my kingdom, and my family. The Gods War started because of me. My world is gone because of me. How is there any room left in me to love?"

It was quiet for a moment, and I wondered if he finally understood me enough to not make jokes or wise quips. I glanced at him to see he was staring at the same ember in the fireplace. His throat bobbed once before he spoke, but I smelled no fear in the air. His voice was softer, and there was no hint of the trickster that had been with us the last few weeks.

"Don't you know? Love is the purest form of destruction there is." The corner of his lip lifted. "And you don't have to worry about Dianna and me. We have been friends for centuries. Just friends. We have never, and will never, sleep together. I love her, but not the way you think. Ethan had an allegiance with Kaden way before he became king. I was the one who found her begging and crying in that blistering desert. A plague had swept through Eoria, and many died. Kaden and his horde took advantage of it. He was looking for the book even then. We had been there a few days. Many of the mortals had fled, seeking refuge from the sickness, so blood was scarce. I was out hunting and passed a worn-down home. The female voice from inside was sobbing and praying to anyone who might listen. I ripped the fabric covering the makeshift entrance aside and found her sitting with Gabby."

Drake went quiet, obviously lost in the past. I waited, hungry for any information about Dianna. Finally, he took a deep breath and seemed to remember I was there.

"I thought of killing them both. They were mortal, and the illness had ravaged Gabby. She was dying. I could hear her heart stuttering, but Dianna didn't care. She begged and pleaded, offering anything if I would save her sister—even herself. I don't know if it was her eyes, the way she spoke, or the complete and utter pain in her voice that reminded me so much of my lost love, but I couldn't let her die. So, I took her to Kaden. I didn't know at the time that there was a possibility his blood would turn her into a beast."

Drake paused and shook his head. He cleared his throat before continuing. "Kaden took a piece of her out and replaced it with a piece of himself. I always assumed he had put darkness in her. It was painful and terrible. She fought for days as she tried to stay mortal and alive. And against all odds, she did. She doesn't come from some mythic family background. She's just a girl who survived out of sheer force of will, and that makes her stronger than us. It made her deadly.

He knew it, and the way he looked at her after that, I knew I had made a mistake."

My heart sank. It explained so much. Why Dianna was the way she was. Why she would never give up on those she held close to her. She'd been a fighter from the very beginning. Incredible. She was incredible. "You saved her and her sister that day."

His eyes held pain as he faced me. "Did I? Or did I just create more chaos? Ethan hated me for years for it. He eventually got over it, but he hated me. He believes in the whole balance thing, like you. Dianna and her sister were supposed to die that day, and he said I changed fate. He believes everything has a price."

I nodded slowly. "It usually does, yes."

"So, what's the price for her living?" His eyes begged for answers I did not have.

"That I do not know. I will say, regardless of her hostility and crude comments, Dianna's existence is not the worst thing in the world."

He forced a smile and wiped the side of his face with the back of his sleeve. "I'm nice to Dianna and give her what I can because I know how Kaden is, and I know part of it is my fault. She says we are overprotective, but someone has to be. So, no, you shouldn't feel threatened by me —but you should also stop trying so hard not to feel something for her. She may be the very creature you have been raised to destroy, but she is so much more than that. So much more. Take it from someone who lost their love. Don't take what you feel for granted. It is worth everything."

I shuffled my feet, adjusting my posture. "It's not like that with us."

"Sure. That's why the two of you are practically inseparable, why you can't keep your eyes off of her, why she was so pissed after what she learned about what Ethan and I said, and why you refuse to share her bed with her."

I ran my hand over the back of my neck. "I will admit it has become increasingly difficult to share the same bed with her. But she deserves better than me and this life she has been forced into. I wish for her the same things she craves so desperately for Gabby: a life outside of monsters, blood, and fighting."

"So that's what it is. Such a martyr. I hope you realize for both of your sakes what you're risking before he comes for her. And make no mistake: he will come for her. He's barely let her out of his sight for centuries."

"I won't let him have her."

"I hope not, because if you do, you won't see her again."

The approach of heavy footsteps interrupted our conversation. The doors were pushed open to reveal Ethan. He paused in the doorway, adjusting the lapels and sleeves of his jacket.

"Are we ready?" he asked.

I took one look and sighed. "That is a terrible disguise."

Ethan's voice dropped to the feminine one I had grown so accustomed to as he placed one hand on his hip. "Oh, come on! I thought it was perfect. I even have the bracelets. How did you know?"

Because I have every part of you memorized.

I shrugged. "The posture, the way you carry yourself. Ethan does not walk or recline like that."

A thick masculine voice flooded into the room from behind Dianna. "Touching, World Ender. I didn't know you cared."

The real Ethan walked up behind Dianna, the two of them similar but not.

"What are you two losers talking about, anyway?" she asked, clearly annoyed at her failed attempt at a disguise.

Drake cleared his throat as he strode toward them, his cool and annoying demeanor returning. "Oh, just politics."

Her nose scrunched, and she swatted at him, which was amusing given the form she wore. "Boring."

Drake raised the lapel of the thick black coat she wore, sniffing at it. She pushed him away, and he said with a chuckle, "It's a nice look, but you may need more cologne. I can still smell that lustful scent of yours."

The real Ethan rolled his eyes and shook his head. I met Drake's eyes, and for once, I did not have the urge to rip his head off. I knew that the comments and joking were a way for him to make her smile. It was a form of penance.

Dianna walked toward me—a peculiar sight, knowing what lay

beneath the fake exterior. She pulled out the silver chain bracelet, motioning for me to hold out my arm. I extended it, and she clasped the chain around my wrist. A small rush of air seemed to encompass me before disappearing.

Drake shivered. "Damn. Those are strong. All jokes aside, I think it will work. I can't feel the thick, electrifying power in the house right now."

Ethan—the real Ethan—nodded and said, "It will work."

THIRTY-SIX

DIANNA

I t didn't work. We had made a mistake.

I tapped my foot lightly on the marble floor of the large villa. Several Otherworldly creatures entered, flocking to the large pool area and the several juice bars. The inside of the villa was lit with hanging lights of gold, and soft, rhythmic music filled the air.

"Stop it," Liam said, his voice flooding my ears and breaking me from my daze.

I glanced at Liam, our height almost equal now, which was another thing to adjust to. "Stop what?"

He raised the glass he held and took a sip before saying, "Fidgeting. Ethan does not do that. Hold your head high and act like a king."

I nodded at a woman who smiled at me as she passed before whispering from between clenched teeth, "Oh, I'm sorry, and how do kings act?"

He looked at me like I was kidding. "Like you. Cocky and arrogant because they know how powerful they are."

I reached up to scratch my brow. "I feel like there was a compliment in there somewhere."

Liam shrugged. "Maybe. Maybe not. I will never admit to either."

I wanted to smile and maybe sneak in another sarcastic comment, but I couldn't. I was still mad … hurt? I didn't know. All I knew was that I cared way too much about what he thought of me. I cared too much in general. As always, Gabby had been right. All I'd done was trade one powerful man for another, except this one found me repulsive.

Liam avoided me like the plague, and I couldn't forget that fight in the study. His words had sent a sharp, piercing pain straight into my heart, and I still didn't understand why he had pushed me away. I'd thought he was my friend, and even though it hurt to admit it, I had wanted it to be something more. I spent my days locked in my room, even ignoring calls from my sister, because she would know. She would figure out how much of a fool I was.

I'd tossed that damn flower in the trash the second I could, and its wilted, dried-up leaves mocked me from across the room. I was dreaming of men who gave me pretty dresses and prettier words, as if my world weren't fire and hatred and pain. Gods, was I so desperate for even a crumb of kindness?

What a stupid, stupid girl.

"What are you thinking about?" Liam's eyes narrowed on me.

"Nothing." I shook my head. "Why?"

"Your scent and aura changed for a moment." Whatever expression passed across my face, he'd noticed. "Also, Ethan does not slouch."

"And how do you know so much?" I mumbled, pretending to look around as guests in black-tie attire continued to arrive. I could feel Liam's eyes still boring into me.

"I spent time with him while you were preoccupied."

I sighed, not caring if that was kingly. I was getting annoyed with the weird jealousy he had toward Drake. Liam had made it clear he found me repulsive, so I didn't understand why he cared. He had no idea what Drake and I had been through together. Drake had helped me survive.

I ignored his comment, the silence growing between us once again. That's how it had been since the study. He moved closer to me, his head lowering as if to whisper to me. My body tensed, and I wanted to lean into him. "How many do you think she summoned here?"

"Enough," I whispered back, taking a small step away. Liam noticed, and I could have sworn I heard him sigh. Camilla was known for her lavish parties, another reason she and Drake got along so well. The estate was one of many and located on a small unknown island close to San Paulao in El Donuma. It wasn't on any map, and she paid the government to keep it that way. I didn't know what that cost her, but it was enough that they also turned a blind eye to the strange disappearances that plagued the area. I didn't mention any of that to Liam. The less he knew right now, the better.

The mansion was open and grand, meant to impress and awe. A large circular fountain sat in the middle of the open expanse. Several paths branched off from that central point, like the spokes of a wheel. Lush shrubs and small trees lined each walkway. Columns, far smaller than the ones I had seen in Liam's memories, decorated the first and second floors. Lights shone on both levels, the building itself curving toward the main entrance and the large stone pavilion in the front. The river ran nearby, and boats docked, disgorging guests in a steady stream. Of course, we had to arrive in a helicopter, which seemed excessive to me, but appearances and all.

My guards suddenly stood straighter. Liam's back went taut, his shoulders squaring as a tall gentleman dressed in a white button-up and dark slacks stopped before us. Liam was acting the bodyguard he was supposed to be.

The man gave a slight bow and said, "My liege. She will see you now."

It took me a second to realize they were addressing me. I had grown so accustomed to people bowing and fawning over Liam that I thought he was speaking to him. I recovered quickly and nodded once before straightening fully. If I was going to portray a king, I needed to act like one. There was no more time for games. I kept my head held high as we followed our escort through a small gathering of people. They made eye contact before dipping their heads.

We entered a foyer, the lights dimmer here and the sounds of the gathering muted. A chill went up my spine, and the hairs on my arms rose. I stopped, the guards and Liam coming to a halt with me as I looked behind us. My nostrils flared as if I could smell whatever the fuck had me on edge. I felt the same presence that had been at the festival in Tadheil. I was sure of it.

"Kaden has been following her."

Ethan's voice rang through my mind, but this wasn't Kaden. I was intimately familiar with his power, and this wasn't it.

"My liege?" our guide asked, his gaze following mine. I turned back, adjusting my jacket and shaking my head once. "My apologies. I thought I saw someone I know."

He studied me for a moment before a brief smile curved his lips. He turned, extending his arm for us to continue toward the back of the house. "Just this way."

"What is it? This is the second time you've done that." Liam's voice was a whisper next to me as we followed the corridor.

"I don't know. Just be alert."

He watched me out of the corner of his eye before glancing behind us once more. I hoped I was wrong. There was no way Kaden would know what we had planned, let alone who we were visiting. It was impossible. I had made sure Drake stayed dead to everyone but me, and we had taken the safest route possible. But that chill, that feeling, told me we were being hunted. I just hoped I was wrong.

WE ENTERED A ROOM LARGE ENOUGH TO BE A SEPARATE HOME. An oblong table greeted us first, several oval-backed chairs surrounding it. Beyond that were two crescent-shaped couches, white and gold pillows lining the thick cushions. A large window sat to our left, the jungle pressing against the glass. A chandelier dripping with crystals illuminated the space, and flowering vines wrapped around the banister of the curving staircase.

"Welcome, Vampire King." Camilla's rich, sultry voice floated through the air, and her power filled the room. It pressed against my skin like the smoothest satin as she appeared on the balcony.

Camilla's lips were painted a deep burgundy, enhancing their fullness and making her emerald eyes gleam. The beauty of her face was a lure that many men and women had fallen for. Most of them had not lived to regret it.

Dark brunette waves cascaded over her shoulders as she started gracefully down the stairs. A toned, tanned leg slipped from the deep slit in her skin-tight black dress, one glossy heeled foot after the other taking the steps. My breath hitched at her feminine perfection, and I wondered if Liam's did, too. Despite her beauty, the click of her heels on the stairs was like nails on a chalkboard for me. I knew she was more than powerful enough to turn this night deadly.

"Welcome to my other home." She smiled coolly as she reached the last step, her hand resting on the railing. Her nails were the same shade as her dress and just as sharp as her tongue.

"Thank you for accepting the invitation. Although your hesitance was concerning at first," I returned.

Act like a king, Dianna, act like a king.

"Well, it's very hard to arrange a gathering this size. It was quite challenging, trying to get everyone here on time with all the conflicting schedules. You understand, right?" Her smile took on a seductive edge as she tipped her head toward me.

"Of course," I murmured, watching her carefully.

Camilla's smile didn't slip as she strode towards the middle of the room. She stopped at the edge of the table, tapping those long nails against the top. "I must admit, I was quite surprised you were interested in my offer. I had assumed you and your kin were done with anything involving Kaden. Especially after he sent his bitch to kill your brother."

I swallowed, giving her no indication I'd felt that little jab. "Yes, well, if I can get a leg up on him, then so be it. Payback and all. You understand?"

"That I do. Why do you think I'm doing this? I now have something over him. Over many people, actually."

I nodded once, as I had seen Ethan do, and held her gaze. He never broke eye contact. "Yes, from what I hear, you've found the Book of Azrael."

She clicked her tongue, waving a single finger in the air. "Oh, I found that—and something even better."

Several witches from the balcony slowly made their way down the stairs. Two men headed toward the kitchen, a woman and another man coming to her side. The male held a chair out for her, and she sat down. The two attendants joined her once she was settled.

Liam and I sat as the other two witches emerged from the kitchen with trays and several glasses filled with a bright red liquid. My nostrils flared—as did the guards'. Blood. Fuck. Liam was not a vampire or a creature born to consume blood.

"Drink?" she asked, folding her hands underneath her chin as she smiled at us. The other two men stopped short, offering the glasses to the guards and me. "I made sure it was fresh for you and yours. A merchant who thought he could steal from me. Typical men, you know, afraid of women in power."

"Very kind of you, but I am afraid we ate before heading here." I offered a polite smile, keeping my hands folded in front of me.

Her head tilted to the side, a puzzled look on her face. "Are you sure? You seem famished."

Was she testing me? Did she know? I absently ran a thumb across the bracelets around my wrists. No, I could still feel the magic against my skin. I was just paranoid.

I held her gaze as I reached for a glass. The crimson liquid stained the crystal glass, and my heart jumped slightly. The beast inside of me rose to the surface. Thirsty, I was so thirsty. I had to drink it for appearance's sake.

I smiled softly, careful not to show my teeth as I took the wineglass by the stem. The glass pressed against my lips, and the warm liquid touched the tip of my tongue. Fire exploded in my mouth and then my throat as I swallowed. I couldn't hold back a soft moan as I drained the contents faster than I'd intended.

That old familiar craving came roaring back tenfold. I wanted, no, *needed* more. I felt my skin prickle, the Ig'Morruthen within me slithering, begging to be allowed off the leash. Memories, brief and quick, slipped into my mind. A small man with scruffy hair, taking what looked like a stone of some sort. Pain accompanied a blast of magic. I saw Camilla's eyes watching from a dark corner as she told her men to execute, and then there was nothing.

I handed the glass back as my guards did the same. I didn't look at Liam, not wanting to see his disgust at what I had just done. He already saw me as revolting, and watching me feed, even from a wine glass, probably solidified his opinion of me.

From the corner of my eye, I saw him place an empty glass back on the tray. I kept my face impassive but wondered how he'd gotten rid of the blood.

Camilla's eyes gleamed as she continued to smile at me. "Theo, would you please take Mr. Vanderkai's guards out to enjoy the party? Oh, and the rest of the coven, too."

I held up my hand. "That won't be necessary."

"Oh, yes, it will."

I watched as the woman beside her stood, motioning for the other witches to follow. They headed for the door, waving at my guards to follow. A man stopped in front of Liam.

"Leave that one, please."

The man nodded and followed the others out. Once the doors were closed, Camilla said, "I want five million and protection for me and mine."

My brows lifted as I was momentarily taken aback. "Protection? Regardless of our familiar standing, I doubted your witches would want to be around—"

Her eyes cut past me. "I'm not talking to you."

I felt my heart skip a beat when I realized who she was asking. She knew. Fuck.

"Everyone wants a deal," Liam said with a sigh, briefly rubbing his eyes with his index finger and thumb.

She placed her hands on the table and stood in one fluid motion. Her movements were filled with graceful pride as she circled the table. Her eyes raked over Liam as if she were memorizing every line and muscle hidden beneath the thin layer of the suit he wore. His hair was freshly clipped, the sides in a small fade. The dark strands atop his head were tamed by the gel Drake had forced on him.

Liam was aware of his physical appearance and how others reacted to it, but he seemed to use it as he did any other weapon in his arsenal. Regardless of his intent, he drew attention wherever we went. Some of the members in Ethan's castle laughed and giggled every time he walked through the halls. Others stalked him just to catch a glimpse of him. He was gorgeous in a sickening way, and I knew it had not escaped Camilla's notice.

"Let's just say we know real power when we see it." She stopped short of us, her hand flat on the table and another on her hip.

"How long have you known?" I asked.

She glared at me, that fake politeness long gone. "First, the plane you took to get to Zarall crossed my border. You were in my territory for just a second, but it was half a second too long. I felt that sickening power of yours then. Second, Ethan sends lackeys for an invite when he hasn't reached out to anyone since you murdered Drake. Third, I would know the bracelets of that bitch Ophelia anywhere, and fourth," her eyes danced over Liam once more, "he is nothing if not godly. No mortal looks like that. Those bracelets might hold back a fraction of his true power, but his body is humming with it."

"Please, don't feed his ego. It's already big enough."

"I can imagine," she all but purred as she reached for him.

Before I realized what I was doing, I was on my feet, and I had ahold of her wrist. A growl, low and menacing, slipped past my lips as the beast inside me coiled. They both turned to look at me.

"Don't touch him. I am well aware of what you can do with your hands." My voice was guttural, nearly a snarl.

"Ah, there is the real you." Camilla sneered at me, her wrist still in my grasp.

Liam regarded me, and I was unable to read his expression. "Dianna. It is okay. Let her go."

I didn't move.

"Please," he said softly, and the Ig'Morruthen beneath my skin answered.

My jaw clenched, but I let her go. She cradled her hand against her chest for a second before cautiously rotating her wrist. It must have been the blood she'd given me that was making me so erratic. My emotions were heightened. That was all.

I stepped away, putting distance between us as Liam got to his feet. Camilla was staring at me with a smug grin. I wanted nothing more than to wipe that look off her face. My talons crawled from my fingertips, and I curled my hands into fists to hide them, the razor-sharp claws biting into my flesh.

"Interesting. I had assumed, given your reputation, that you could seduce even a god."

"I have not seduced anything."

"But you have seen it, yes? It must be massive and overwhelming, almost too much for one person to contain, much less handle."

My head reeled back, and my body suddenly ran hot. "What? No!" I snapped, avoiding Liam's gaze completely. "Well, I mean, once, but it was a weird dream thing." I closed my eyes, waving my hands in the air slightly. "Wait—why are we talking about his penis?"

Camilla cocked her head, one brow raised. "*I'm* talking about his power."

"Oh." I dropped my hands to my sides, my face feeling as if it were on fire. The massive room suddenly felt too small. "Yeah, I've seen that too."

She shook her head, ignoring me as she fixated on Liam. "I have heard stories—we all have—about the great World Ender. It is rumored that your father could shape worlds, yet you end them. You have a power like no other."

With a single flick of her hand, the lights in the room grew brighter. Flames crackled in the fireplace behind her as a slow wind fluttered through the room. The curtains lining the large windows opened, the stars in the night sky casting a pale glow over the floor. I watched as her magic swirled in green tendrils, forming a small ball that she danced between her fingers.

"I've shown you mine. Now, show me yours."

I rolled my eyes at the obvious attempt at flirting. Good luck with that. Liam showed so little interest in physical pleasure that I would have sworn he was made of stone if I had not borne witness to his past.

The lights dimmed, and a bright silver orb spun into existence on Liam's palm. I squinted my eyes, unable to look directly at the small sphere. It was so bright that it was like looking at a miniature sun.

Liam stared at Camilla, his expression of interest one I had not seen him give anyone before. My insides twisted.

Her eyes reflected the silver shine from his energy as she leaned in closer. "It's so beautiful." Her voice was a breathy whisper as she met his eyes. "And powerful. I can feel it."

The way she said that had me gritting my teeth hard enough to crack my jaw.

"Thank you. Yours is very impressive as well. The feel of your magic reminds me of a goddess from my time."

"The Goddess Kryella?" Her voice hitched. "You knew her?"

"Oh, trust me, he did," I piped in, but they ignored me, lost in some weird magic-wielding stare-off.

"Yes, I did. Kryella was the first to wield and bend magic. How did you learn? How did you know? Are you a descendant? She bore no children."

Camilla's lush lips curved in a bright smile as she tossed the green ball from one hand to the other. "No, not a descendant, but her teachings have been passed down for generations."

Liam seemed awestruck, and it made me sick. "Impressive. Truly. Mastering a skill like yours can take years, yet your appearance is the quite opposite of aged." He watched the green mass of her power, mesmerized.

Her smile nearly outshone the brightness of his power. She looked at him, taking the compliment, whether he meant it that way or not, to heart. Bile rose in my throat, the creature inside me snapping its jaws. "It's all energy. It belongs to no one. We just use and protect it. We practice, we focus…" She paused, turning toward me. "But we don't overuse."

Great, they had similar mantras concerning the use of their power.

I snorted and rolled my eyes again. It was not surprising that Camilla would take a jab at the blatant power Kaden forced us to wield. Especially since it highlighted another difference between Liam and me. But it was the only way I knew, and it got the job done.

"Truly, your control of your gift is astonishing," Liam said, not even looking at me.

"Thank you." She smiled before closing her hand, the green energy dissipating. The silver energy ball in Liam's palm broke off as he twisted his wrist. Shards of it darted toward every light fixture, and one by one, they turned back on.

"Now, time for business." She stepped a few inches closer to him, and I bristled again. I knew he was strong enough to take care of himself, but how she looked at him made my stomach churn. "I'll tell you where the book is, for a price."

I groaned loudly and waved a hand toward her. "You already named your price, Camilla."

"That I did, but I want it sealed."

"Sealed?" I folded my arms tightly as Liam finally looked at me. "You are out of your fucking mind if you think you're going to bind yourself to him in any way."

Camilla's brows shot upward, but I didn't care how I sounded or if I was overstepping. I knew some magic, especially dark, required blood to make a deal fully binding. I was no witch, and I couldn't cast or bind anything, but just the power of our combined blood had tethered our deal. There was no way I was going to allow Camilla to follow suit.

"Protective of the World Ender, Dianna?" Her lips curved in that vicious smile again. "How cute. Do you speak for him, too?"

"No," Liam cut in before I could respond, cutting a look toward me, "she does not."

I shook my head and turned away. He didn't know what Camilla would ask. She may look sweet and tempting, but a cold, conniving bitch lived beneath her skin. I didn't know what I'd expected. When had he ever listened to me?

"Good." She clasped her hands together and took another step toward him. She glanced between Liam and me before saying, "I want it sealed with a kiss."

"What?" I snapped. "I'm not kissing him!"

Liam turned away from me, but I caught his expression of what looked like pain. But that couldn't be right. It was probably just disgust. I knew he would never agree to kiss me, not even to find the book. Liam kissed goddesses, not monsters.

I couldn't kiss him, but for a completely different reason. I knew it would end me, and I would be lost. There was a part of me so hungry and desperate for his touch that I didn't dare acknowledge it. Instead, I'd buried it under jokes and sarcasm. I had used Drake to distract myself from my growing feelings for Liam. I kept my desire hidden, but I could not hide from myself. If I kissed him, I knew he would figure it out, and I didn't know if I could bear his rejection again.

She turned toward me, all pride and arrogance, a slow smile curving her lips. "Not from you. From me."

My blood boiled.

"No."

I thought the word had come from Liam, and was a little shocked to realize I had said it. The dark part of me was strong and making its presence known. It was because I had fed. At least, that was what I was telling myself.

She smiled once more, cold and cruel, because she knew she had power over me in that moment. "I don't think it's up to you. After all, you don't make decisions for him, as he said." She leaned in, pressing against Liam as she raised that perfectly manicured hand and placed it on his cheek. "So, World Ender, what will it be? I'll give you the book's location, and all you have to do is kiss me."

I watched as his eyes dipped to her lips. I gritted my teeth, a cold flash of anger ripping through my body.

"Seriously?" I asked, not caring how I sounded. "You're considering this?"

His eyes cut to mine. His gaze was sharp and held no hint of humor, or any trace of the Liam I had spent time with these last few months. "It is but a kiss, Dianna. Why does it matter?"

Why does it matter?

My chest tightened. He said it as if it didn't mean anything, and maybe it didn't matter to him. Maybe I had read too much into the stolen glances and intimate secrets we had shared. Obviously, what I felt was all one-sided. Oh, what a fool I was. I had fallen for someone who had no intention of catching me.

"You're right." I squared my shoulders, trying to ease the pain of what he had broken in me. "It doesn't matter."

"Okay." That was all he said, and all Camilla needed to hear. Her hand gently cupped his jaw as he lowered his head toward hers.

Stupid, stupid girl.

I gripped the arms of the suit jacket so tightly that I almost ripped the fabric. I had hoped it would be quick. Liam didn't seem like the type to lust after anyone. After what I had seen in the blooddreams, I knew he had been highly sexual at one point. But during the weeks I had slept with him, he had not tried to touch me intimately, and he'd had no physical reaction—not even in the mornings. I had assumed those bodily functions had died with the trauma of his past.

I was wrong.

What started out as a simple kiss soon deepened. Liam tilted her head to the side, devouring her mouth. She let out a soft but heady moan that made me nauseous. I refused to turn away, even when he let out a noise I had only heard from him in one of those damned dreams. He was enjoying it.

Tears threatened to blind me, but I would watch this, and I would let it kill what I felt for him. I had been so wrong. Liam did have those feelings; he just didn't have them for me. I guess you had to be a goddess or a magic-wielding, beautiful witch to get his attention. Maybe Camilla was less of a monster.

After what felt like an eternity, they separated. Camilla released a heavy sigh and said, "You really are everything they said."

One more comment, and I swore I would lose my grip on my more homicidal tendencies. I finally allowed myself to look away, not giving a fuck what that revealed of my emotions. I was pissed, but had no right to be. It was well known that Liam hated my kind. I was so angry with myself, and I felt so foolish. The one person I wanted, I couldn't have. Liam was not mine, and I was not his. We weren't even friends. I was a weapon. It was my own stupid fault for thinking I could be anything other than a tool to him or Kaden.

"Everything all right, Dianna?" Camilla asked in a husky whisper.

I met her gaze, knowing my face showed every bit of the anger and hurt I was feeling.

"Vaski lom dernmoé," I hissed in Eorian, a low growl vibrating deep within my throat.

Camilla's laugh was sharp and precise, slicing another wound into my soul. "Ah, so it's true. Ig'Morruthens are territorial."

I didn't say anything. The beast in me was snarling and clawing, begging for freedom, begging to rip her to shreds.

Camilla smiled brightly. Her red-stained mouth was swollen, smudged, and matching Liam's. She had won. She hated me because she felt I had taken a spot away from her. Now she had taken something from me: a kiss I hadn't known I even wanted. To her, we were even.

I couldn't look at Liam. I could feel the heavy weight of his gaze, and I knew he wanted me to meet his eyes, but I didn't care.

Camilla continued to smirk at me as she said, "Now that we've settled that, let the party begin." She raised her hands and clapped. The door to my right opened. I didn't turn or move, but my stomach dropped when I smelled the overpriced cologne.

"Hello, Dianna."

We had been set up.

"Santiago." His name left my lips in a hiss.

THIRTY-SEVEN

DIANNA

"Sorry to interrupt. It looks like your new boyfriend was having fun." Santiago smiled at Liam and the red lipstick on his lips.

"Santiago. Kaden's witch bitch. You look nice. Don't tell me you dressed up just for me?" I sneered. "How many times do I have to tell you? No means no."

Several of his coven stood on either side of him, all dressed in overpriced suits with those fucking leather shoes. I hated leather shoes.

He smiled and leered at me. "I missed that mouth. So has Kaden."

"Oh, yeah?"

I swallowed enough air to incinerate him and this entire building, but I didn't get a chance to use it. Camilla called forth that green, wispy magic and threw it at me. I heard Liam's shout as my body flew back. I landed in one of the chairs, and it rocked precariously, but corrected itself before it toppled over.

Green, glowing loops bound my wrists and ankles. I tried to break the fragile-looking vines, but it felt like an anchor was sitting on any part of my body they touched. I glanced up, seeing she had Liam strapped to the farthest wall with the same green bands biting into his wrists and legs. She had used several more on him, a stronger bond to hold a stronger being. I gritted my teeth as I struggled. My chair slid back toward the table, the legs scraping across the floor before coming to an abrupt halt, making my head jerk forward.

"You bitch." My veil dropped the second the words left my mouth. My form rippled and bent. The shape and masculinity I had imposed upon my body dissolved, and I was no longer the Vampire King, but myself. His clothes melted away with the facade, revealing the white lace top and pantsuit I wore.

Camilla's eyes roamed over my outfit. "Well, don't you look lovely? All dressed up like a boss, when we know you're more of a groveling bitch."

My head whipped toward her. I was furious. With everything that had been building between Liam and me, waiting for this stupid meeting, and being set up again, I was ready to rain fire. "Groveling? Last I remember, you were on your knees more than I ever was, Camilla."

"Ladies, ladies," Santiago said as he moved to stand at the edge of the table, smiling from ear to ear. "Fight later. We're in a time crunch."

His smile was overly cocky as he looked toward the far wall. Liam's eyes bled silver as he struggled against Camilla's power. She stood in between us, one hand raised toward me, the other toward Liam. She gritted her teeth as she pushed more power toward him. I could see the beads of sweat forming on her forehead. He was fighting to get free, and from the looks of it, he was about to.

"So, you're him? The World Ender?" Santiago asked.

Liam's gaze snapped to Santiago, and he gave him a once-over before saying, "And you are a dead man if you lay a hand on her."

Santiago laughed, placing a hand on his stomach. "Aww, Dianna, I think he is sweet on you. How cute."

I ignored his comment, looking from him to Camilla and back. "So, you two are friends now, huh? Guess I shouldn't be surprised."

Santiago laughed again. "Us? Who betrayed who first, Dianna?" His brow lifted as he ran his gaze over me. "Where is Alistair?"

I leaned forward as far as I could. "Unbind me, and I'll show you."

He shrugged, seemingly unbothered as he clicked his tongue. "Kaden wants you back, and he put an exquisite price on your head.

You should have been smart, like Camilla. She is promised a seat after helping to bring in you, him, and that damned book."

My gut sank, knowing what awaited me once I was back. I would probably never see the light of day again. He would keep Gabby from me. I knew I would never see her again.

"You'll have to drag me back." My voice shook, and I didn't care who heard or saw. "And I will fight you every step of the way."

Santiago's eyes flamed green with the force of his power as he leaned forward, his hands pressed flat against the table. "We have a long trip ahead, and you'll be begging to go back by the time I am done with you. I will make sure of it—and I will enjoy it."

"You'll die if you try," Liam said, cutting through my blinding hate as I glared at Santiago.

"Shut him up, Camilla," Santiago snapped, his eyes never leaving mine.

Another coil of magic wrapped around my throat, pushing my head back. It pulled tight, forcing my jaw closed. I bit my tongue hard enough that I tasted blood. I grunted, my head spinning and my vision going black from lack of oxygen. As quickly as it began, it subsided.

"Speak again, and I'll pop her precious little head right off." Camilla's voice filtered through my pained gasps for air.

She released a tiny bit of her power, and I lowered my head, wincing as I tried to swallow.

"Stop … the … idle … threats," I said, panting as I looked at each of them, tossing the loose tendrils of hair from my face. "He is only here for the book, just like the rest of you idiots. So, stop with the empty threats, shall we?"

I gave Liam a pointed look. He seemed to understand that I wanted to keep them talking. The tension in his jaw eased, and I saw his muscles relax a bit. He was still testing and pushing at his bonds, but he turned his attention back to Santiago.

"Is this your plan?" Santiago asked me. "Work with the World Ender and kill Kaden? Kaden can't die. You know that. Does he?" His voice was filled with such smug arrogance that I nearly rolled my eyes again.

Liam's eyes narrowed at that new little tidbit of information.

Everyone thought Kaden couldn't die, but that was because no one ever attempted it.

I shrugged, ignoring him. "Then where is he? If he is immortal and so all-powerful, why doesn't he just come get me himself? All I see is him ordering his fucking flunkies to drag me back. That's what you are. You know that, right? He doesn't give a shit about you or anyone. Only himself."

Santiago and Camilla laughed. Santiago adjusted his suit and stepped between my open knees. He leaned in close and brushed the back of his knuckles against the curve of my cheek, tucking the disheveled strands of my hair back from the side of my face. My whole body revolted. I leaned as far away from him as I could. The magic shackles and collar cut into my skin, but I didn't care. "Well, I guess it's a good thing I'm not desperate for his love."

He whispered that last bit in my ear before straightening once more. That part stung, and I ground my teeth as I tried to think of a way to disarm Camilla's spell so I could kill everyone in this room.

Santiago sighed, clearly bored. "It really was a valiant attempt, but we both know there is no way you can outsmart him, let alone beat him. You should have kept your perfect ass where it was. Oh, well." He reached behind him, pulled out a gun, and pointed it at me. He flicked the safety off before cocking it and placing it next to my temple. The cold bite of metal made me sneer as he pushed it against the side of my head.

"You're so weak. You had to bind me to beat me. Some man." His lips curled, and I knew I'd hit a nerve. Good. "What are you going to do, Santiago? Shoot me? It won't kill me."

He shrugged, the corner of his lip turning upwards. "It won't, but it will make it easier for us to drag you back."

I paused as what he'd said sunk in. I tried to look at him. "'Us'?"

He pointed toward the large window on the other side of the room. I felt my pulse quicken as several pairs of glowing crimson eyes looked at me from the jungle. Four large figures stood close to the glass, their horned wings extended. They grinned like primates, exposing sharp black teeth.

One pressed its clawed hand against the window, its thick talons waiting to shred me to pieces. Another ran a thick black tongue up and down the glass, leaving a trail of slime in its wake. I could see several more sets of red eyes behind them. Fuck. *That's* what I had felt. Santiago had brought the Irvikuva. He had brought a lot. We were so fucked.

Thunder rolled off in the distance as lightning flashed across the sky—a storm I didn't know was coming.

"Irvikuva? Seriously?" My voice was steady, but they would be a problem. They could seriously hurt me with their talons and teeth, hurt me enough to slow me down, and if he had brought as many as I thought, we were in deep shit.

He pressed the gun harder against my temple. "I'll give you credit, Dianna. Your little mutiny set his nerves on edge. But no matter what form you take, or the friends you surround yourself with, you will always belong to him. Kaden's pathetic whore."

I turned toward him and spat in his face. He reeled back, using his sleeve to wipe away the spittle.

"I love how men like you throw those words around like it's supposed to hurt, to mean something. Yet you're the same man who cried when he couldn't get his dick sucked."

The humor drained from his face along with the color.

"The powerful coven leader, who could have anyone he wanted, cried like a baby because he was told no. Who's pathetic now?"

He raised the gun, resting the barrel against my forehead. "You're a bitch."

"I know."

He pulled the trigger. I saw the flash, but I was gone before I heard the echo of the gunshot.

THIRTY-EIGHT

LIAM

The force of the gunshot caused the chair to fall over. Panic gripped me as I saw Dianna's body topple to the side. The wall that held me cracked and groaned as power, pure and blinding, shook the entire foundation. Debris rained down before us as thick bands of silver lit up beneath my skin, and I knew my eyes matched. My muscles clenched, straining the green magic tendrils holding me to the wall. I ached to rip this house from its foundation and destroy everyone inside. But I could not do so after what Camilla had shown me.

Visions had ripped through my subconscious as she'd kissed me. Images of Azrael's daughter, the book she possessed, and the town where she'd stayed filled my mind. Camilla had been working against Kaden for some time. In that exchange, she warned me to play along, or I would be putting Dianna in even more danger. I would have done anything to keep Dianna safe, but the pain I'd witnessed on the facade of Ethan's face had twisted my insides. I knew I may have done irreparable damage to the brand-new connection between us.

"You will meet Oblivion for that," I snarled at Santiago as he held the gun towards her limp form.

"Oh, yeah?" Santiago fired twice more, a cruel and sickening smile upon his face. I could see Dianna's body jerk with each crack of sound. I pulled at my bindings as the wind began to howl. The pulse of the approaching storm matched my beating heart. Camilla's eyes flicked to mine in warning.

"Do you have to do that?" she asked, turning toward Santiago.

"Call me a sadist." He shrugged, and I marked him for death. "Now, we have a flight to catch." He set the gun on the table before adjusting his sleeves.

I let out a nearly inaudible growl, knowing that I could not let him take her. My muscles clenched as I prepared to rip myself from the wall, but I stopped as the lights flickered. Everyone froze as darkness grew from every corner.

Camilla hissed at me, "What are you doing?"

"It is not me."

Black smoke curled around the edges of the table as a deep, vicious growl came from beneath. The room stilled as a wave of power rose from the floor. It wavered in the air like heat waves. My heart skipped as the power brushed against mine and I got a taste of it. It damn near rivaled my own in intensity. The table flew through the air with such force that it crashed against the ceiling, raining debris on the room.

Dianna.

It was the only thought I had as a large, sleek black beast launched itself at Camilla. It landed on her, teeth and claws flashing. She screamed, her blood splattering the wall near me. The green bands dropped from my body, and I slid down the wall, landing on my feet.

Santiago met my gaze, his eyes widening. Pure blind rage consumed me as I looked at him. I had never felt the desire to shred a being with my bare hands. He would die screaming for what he'd done to her. His throat bobbed once as he read the expression on my face. He shuffled backward, raised his hands, and clapped once, disappearing from the room in a flash of green light. Fucking coward.

An ear-shattering scream rang out, followed by a loud crunch. I turned and grabbed at the thick fur of the beast Dianna wore as she mauled and clawed Camilla. I yanked her off. One of her massive paws swiped at me, branding my chest.

"Not her! We need her!" I yelled as I tossed Dianna back, separating them. Her claws dug into the floor, tearing deep furrows in the stone until she came to a stop. Her red eyes bored into mine, and she hissed. A thick black tuft of hair raised along her back as she bared her teeth at me in defiance. Then her gaze locked on to something behind me, and her snarl grew to a roar. More flashing green orbs flew into the room, aiming for her. Santiago may have left, but his coven stayed and still planned to take her. Blood dripped from her jowls as she snarled and raced past me. Her speed was blinding. I turned in time to see her jump on a witch, her momentum sending them tumbling through the open door and out of sight.

I had a split second to formulate a plan before the thick glass windows behind us shattered. A hollow screech filled the room as the Irvikuva flew into the room. I shifted my body to protect Camilla.

Chaos ensued as the witches that came with Santiago opened fire. Bullets bit into my side, legs, and arms, which only pissed me off more. Mortal weapons were a mere annoyance for me. But the witch queen might be a different story. A single ring vibrated on my hand as I called forth my shield. The length covered my body with my father's three-headed beast sigil in the middle. I crouched with it in my hand, the bullets ricocheting off of it.

I called on a fraction of my power to throw tables, chairs, and glass in all directions. Witches and a few of the Irvikuva fell, bleeding from where they had been struck by the shrapnel. I dragged Camilla up by her arm, her blood-soaked feet slipping as we ran. We made it outside, the sound of a loud boom following us as the top floor detonated. I smelled the flames, and smoke soon followed as the whole building shook. The lights flickered as water poured from the ceiling.

Dianna.

I needed to get to her, but first, I had to deal with Camilla. I called my shield back into my ring and crouched over her bloody form. My hands lit with silver, the glow dancing over her body, healing the cuts and gashes that Dianna had caused. Camilla hissed in pain as her wounds knitted themselves closed.

"You helped me with the book, so I'll honor our deal. You take the ones closest to you and leave this island. I have to go find Dianna."

Roars sounded behind me, and I spun to my feet. I lifted my hand, silver lines bursting to life along my forearm. I shot a ball of energy toward the beasts charging us from the open door. They disintegrated, their bodies crumbling to ash and blowing away between one breath and the next.

I felt a tug on my sleeve and glanced back at Camilla. She was using me for a bit of leverage as she struggled to stand. When she finally managed to get to her feet, her legs were wobbly, and she pressed one hand against the nearest tree.

"She cares about you. You will need to remember that to make it through what Kaden has planned."

I didn't really understand what she was trying to tell me, but I nodded. "I think you might have ruined that."

"No." She shook her head with a small, blood-filled smile. "I only made her see."

A scream echoed through the villa, the sound piercing the noise of battle. I looked up to see a man thrown from the balcony. When I turned back, Camilla was gone.

I stepped back into the mansion just as a large explosion shook it. Monsters and mortals screeched in terror and pain. Flames licked at the ceiling as a large, billowing cloud of smoke pushed downstairs.

Dianna.

I turned, shielding my eyes from the thick orange glow. The foliage outside smoldered, and several people—friend or foe, I could not tell—ran around in flames. The large villa shook once more, the explosion followed by a pained screech and a curse. She was hurt.

I didn't hesitate or think as I launched myself through several tons of stone and brick to land on the top floor. I had a split second to ponder calling forth the Oblivion blade, but I couldn't risk it. My fingers clenched as I called the silver ablaze weapon, gripping it tighter as I squinted through the hazy smoke.

"Dianna!" I shouted. "Where are you?"

Movement came from my left, the heartbeat of the creature unnatural as I swung my blade. A foul odor followed as the beast's head thudded to the floor. Several more appeared out of the smoke, obviously searching for her. They had lost her, but they spotted me and charged. I dove and slid across the ash-covered floor, cutting their legs off at the knee. They screeched as they fell. I stood and stabbed all three in the skull. Their bodies matched the soot on the floor a moment later.

I felt the pull of her and was running toward the sound of a scuffle before I had consciously registered it. I skidded to a stop in the doorway of what used to be a study. The room was dark and a mess of ruined furniture. Curtains billowed in the wind as the Irvikuva fought a creature much more skilled and faster than them. They were already dead; they just didn't know it yet. Shadows appeared and disappeared, hitting them with punches and kicks.

Dianna.

She methodically dismembered them. Wings, arms, and legs flew around the room. Heads rolled, their black teeth gnashing and their crimson eyes wide. Blood sprayed the floor, ceiling, and walls. I was impressed, but I was always impressed with her. My mouth turned down in a frown as I realized she didn't need my help after all.

The building shook once more, and I grabbed on to the doorframe to steady myself. I could hear the infrastructure bend and tear. I knew the house was on the verge of collapse.

Hot breath tickled the hairs on the back of my neck. I spun, angling my blade upward and cutting the head off another beast. Its body crumpled to the ground as I completed my spin, coming full circle.

Dianna stepped from the shadows. The cream lace pantsuit she wore was covered in blood and filth. She raised her clawed hand, wiping blood from her mouth with the back of it. Her eyes were pits of crimson rage as she focused on me. For a moment, I, slayer of beasts, destroyer of worlds, feared her.

"Dianna." I said her name as a whisper, a plea.

"What?" The single word was sharp and full of anger.

I held my hand out to her. "The building is about to fall. We're leaving."

She looked at my outstretched hand as if I were offering her sour milk. She turned away, her lip curling in disgust. I did not have time to respond to her repulsed response as I heard the cry of several more Irvikuva coming for us.

"World Ender." The hiss raked over my nerves, and I turned. The hall was engulfed in flames, the demonic forms silhouetted in the thick smoke. They smiled and snapped their teeth as they strode through the fire unharmed. Of course. They were born from Kaden, and Dianna's powers came from him as well.

Dianna stepped forward, aiming for the hall, her claws extended and ready to fight. I grabbed her around the waist and pulled her against me before launching us through the ceiling. I used my hand to cradle her head close to me, protecting her from the brunt of the impact, but she still made an *"oof"* sound as we broke past the support beams in the roof.

The night sky greeted us for a split second as I headed for the cover of the jungle. My vision cleared as we got further away from the burning building. I dropped us to the forest floor with a loud thud. The moment our feet touched the ground, she shoved me away. I stumbled but quickly righted myself. I grabbed her arm, pulling her back to me a little too forcefully.

Dianna slammed against my chest and sputtered, "What are you—"

I covered her mouth with my hand and looked behind me. The beasts screamed as they burst from the burning mansion, taking to the sky in search of us. I slowly removed my hand from her mouth before pressing my index finger to my lips, shushing her. Her eyes remained crimson fire as she glared at me, but she did not speak.

I raised one arm, energy falling off of me in small waves. The temperature dropped, and the wind slowly picked up, fog creeping in from every direction. It was thick enough to confuse them and hide us, blanketing the surrounding forest in a misty haze. Thunder echoed nearby, the storm I had summoned in my rage at seeing her hurt, drowning out any sound of conversation. They would not be able to find us now. I looked down at Dianna, dropping my arm. "Okay, now we can—"

She pushed off of me hard enough to rock my shoulder back. "Don't touch me." She spun and stomped away. "Don't *ever* touch me." Her shoes sunk into the soft, dense ground as she practically ran from me.

"Dianna. Where are you going?" I called as lightning danced across the sky.

She threw her hands in the air, the thunder around us covering her yells. "Oh, I don't know! Maybe I'll find a way out of this damned fog you made, and then I'll walk out of this jungle, since I can't very well fly with those damned creatures around!"

I almost tripped over a thick vine as I followed after her. "Will you just wait up? I do not know my way around here."

"Great. Maybe you'll get lost."

I scoffed. "That was rude."

"I seriously do not care, Liam."

I stopped short at the undisguised venom in her voice. "I understand your hostility. Consuming blood heightens Ig'Morruthen emotions, and I would assume since you haven't partaken in a while, your body is in sensory overdrive."

She spun, the sudden movement causing her to nearly slip on the slick ground. Her arms windmilled as she struggled to regain her footing. Once she was stable, she glared at me and hissed, "Yes, Liam, give me a fucking history lesson while we're stuck here. Tell me more about myself. You know what else your stupid, prestigious teachings obviously didn't tell you? We fucking have feelings! I will not be a pawn for you, for Kaden, for anyone. Do you understand? You're so lucky I can't fly away right now without risking exposure, because so help me, gods, I would leave you so fast. I would take Gabby, and you'd never see me again."

Her words stung, and my heart hammered in my chest. Leave me? I did not like the way that sounded, or that she'd clearly considered it.

I snorted to mask the pain that suddenly made my stomach drop and my chest tighten. "I'd find you."

Her head reared back, that same disgusted look on her face as before. "How about you worry about that stupid book you all have a hard-on for?"

I shrugged, crossing my arms as she continued to storm away. "We made a deal, Dianna. You cannot leave me nor break it, regardless of your bad mood."

I watched her fist clench as her gaze grew deadly. "'Bad mood'? You are so lucky that I can't throw a fireball at your head right now."

"Listen, I know the fresh blood in your veins has you—"

"This has nothing to do with that!" she practically screamed.

"Then what is it? Is this because of your friend Camilla?"

Her crimson eyes narrowed into slits, and at that moment, I was afraid she would incinerate me on the spot.

"Friend? Ha!" Dianna barked a mocking laugh. "She's more *your* friend, now that you practically deep-throated her with your tongue!" she snapped before she turned and headed deeper into the forest. She almost slipped again, grabbing on to a nearby branch to steady herself.

The mix of her words confused me for a brief second before realization clicked into place, and relief flooded through me. I had feared I had destroyed what was between us, but Camilla had been right. If Dianna were truly done with me, she would have left regardless of the danger. Instead, she was spitting at me. Oh, she was angry—but she wasn't done. I shook my head, but was not stupid enough to show her my amusement or relief. She did not want to leave me. She was just upset that I'd kissed Camilla. I did not move an inch as I called out to her, folding my arms.

"You look absolutely ridiculous in your attempt to stomp away."

"Well, you look ridiculous always!"

I called back to her, "Your rebuttal is that of a child."

She stopped, spun around, and stomped back toward me. Flames burst into life around her hands as she curled them into fists. Without pausing, she threw a fireball at my head. I ducked, the flames singeing my hair as it whizzed by. I continued to dodge as she tossed not one, but two more. They sizzled and died as they met the wet forest floor. "Did you just call me a child?"

I smirked at her, knowing she would take it for the challenge it was. "It is how you are acting."

Her eyes narrowed. The flames still wrapped around her hand echoed in her crimson irises as she raised her hand and pointed at her forehead. "I'm sorry. Who just got shot in the head while you were busy sticking your tongue down Camilla's throat?"

My chest ached at the memory of the noise, her body falling, and Santiago's smile. He had grinned, as if shooting a bound woman was something to be proud of. He would pay greatly for that the second I got my hands on him, but I had to address her jealousy and pain before I could get to that.

"Santiago will perish for what he did to you, and there was no…" I paused, not wishing to lie to her. "There was very little tongue. And for your information, she showed me where our next target is."

She folded her arms over her chest, extinguishing the flames on her hands. She looked away as pain twisted her gorgeous features once more. "Oh, that's lovely. I'm glad your make-out session helped us solve a riddle. Congratulations. Do you want a prize?"

"Why are you so upset?"

Her head snapped toward me, and she advanced on me once more. "Upset? Why am I *upset*? You chose her over me—you know, your actual partner. I know your strength. You could have busted out of her control. But no, I had to get shot several times. Then the second I try to kill her, you toss me off like I'm…" She stopped, seeming to choke on the words. She was only a few feet from me now. "Like I mean nothing, when I'm the one risking my life, my friends, and my only blood to help you. I should have left Logan on that fucking burning street and killed Kaden myself."

She turned away once more, stomping off, and I didn't follow her this time. Instead, I appeared in front of her, grabbing her arms and making her stop. "Hey, I did not choose anyone over you."

Her eyes blazed once more. "Let me go."

I did, but she didn't move away, so I went on. "Dianna, she showed me visions when she kissed me. Showed me what our next move is. She has been working undercover like you this entire time. That is all, and the only reason she kissed me."

She looked up at me from under her lashes, pain still shadowing the depths of her eyes. "Is that why she brought Santiago in?"

"I cannot speak for that. What I do know is that I promise to dismember Santiago when we next cross paths, and you know I keep my word."

She was silent, and I was half tempted to step back, afraid she would set me aflame. I knew her temper was still present. I could feel it.

"No," she said, folding her arms and looking away.

"No?"

"*I* want to dismember him." She said it so calmly that I smiled. She still did not look at me, just kept her gaze locked in the distance. I carefully reached out, removing one of the several leaves littering her hair.

"We will talk about it."

Dianna looked at my hand before lightly slapping it away. "Don't touch me, and don't try to be nice to me right now. You have Camilla breath."

My smile grew as she seemed to lose some of that intense fire. "I don't see the big deal. It's no worse than you and Drake's constant flirting, or the laughter you two share over jokes I do not understand. At least I have gathered information."

She tipped her head, her eyes roaming mine. "Is that what that was? Payback? Were you trying to make me jealous?"

The way she asked made nerve endings I had not used in centuries come alive. It was softer than the tone she usually used with me, and the part of me I had silenced in order to survive screamed awake.

When she had reacted with disgust at the idea of kissing me, it had stung. I had never been rejected, and maybe it was just ego, but I had a feeling it was more than that. She didn't know how badly I had wanted it to be *her* lips beneath mine. I could still taste the red stain of Camilla's lipstick on my mouth, and I wanted to erase every trace of it with the taste of Dianna. It was an intense burning desire that tore at my very being.

"*Are* you jealous?" I asked, and a part of me prayed to the old gods that the answer was yes.

Dianna took a step closer without seeming to realize it. Her body was a few inches from mine, her scent imprinting itself on my mind with each breath. We were too close, and not just physically, but mentally as well. She consumed my thoughts, making me feel and question everything.

Her voice was a breathy whisper, and one she had never used with me. "Do you want me to be?"

Dianna's breathing hitched, and her gaze dropped to my lips. Her tongue darted out, leaving the plump curve of her bottom lip glistening. I ached to accept her invitation, savoring the feel and taste of her until only her scent lingered on my skin. I wanted to claim her as mine.

I knew nothing of love, but I knew I wanted her, needed her, and dreamed of her. It was the most inappropriate and irresponsible thing I could ever want for myself. I just wanted to feel, and a single touch from her set my body alight. I wanted her hands on every part of me, and I wanted it more than I had ever wanted anything. It was the most selfish desire in the world, but I wanted her more than a crown, more than a throne, more than air. I had confirmation that the Book of Azrael existed and the threat of war loomed, but all my thoughts centered on Dianna. Camilla was correct. She had seduced me. More than that, she owned me—and she didn't even know it.

I moved a fraction of an inch closer and lifted my hands to cup her face. My fingers brushed behind her ear, my thumb tracing her cheek as I leaned in.

Dianna's lips parted in invitation—but then her body jerked, and her features contorted in pain before I could accept. Her brow furrowed as blood filled her mouth. She looked down, and I followed the path of her gaze, seeing the long, curved talons piercing her midsection. My head snapped up, and I stared into the blood-red eyes of one of the Irvikuva. He smiled triumphantly at me over her head, displaying a mouth full of pointed black teeth.

"Liam?" she gurgled.

I was too slow. Dianna's fingertips brushed mine as she was yanked into the thick brush and out of sight.

THIRTY-NINE
LIAM

*F*uck. The word Dianna frequently used passed through my mind. I'd been so distracted that I hadn't sensed the creature until it was too late. My head throbbed as images from my nightmares assaulted my mind. There was blood, so much blood on her chest, her ashes... No, she couldn't die, wouldn't die. I would rip the very fabric of this world to atoms.

"Liam!"

Dianna screamed my name, the sound echoing through the forest, prompting me to run faster. Pain laced her voice, and it broke something inside of me.

"He plans to rip everyone to pieces to get back what is his. You understand that?"

Ethan's words rang in my skull as I sped through the forest.

"Dianna! Where are you?" I shouted, scaring birds from the trees in clusters.

Trees, shrubs, nothing stood in my way as power shot through me. I plowed through the jungle at an alarming rate, leaving nothing but flattened vegetation in my wake.

"Liam!" I heard her voice again from my right. I skidded to a halt, the ground beneath my feet bending.

"Liam!" No, wait, she was in front of me.

Again, my name rang out. This time from behind me.

"Liam!" That time it came from my left.

I won't let him have her.

I hope not, because you won't see her again if he does.

I cupped my hands around my mouth and shouted, "Dianna!"

I heard nothing but animals clearing the forest. I closed my eyes, concentrating and trying to remember everything I'd learned on how to focus. Failure was not an option. For Dianna, I could do anything. I slowed my breathing, controlling each breath, in and out. The forest fell quiet again, the snap of a branch above me sounding like a gunshot in the silence.

"Liam!" The scream was followed by sickening laughter.

My eyes shot open, meeting the red eyes glowing from the treetop. Talons dug into the bark of the trunk as the creature crept down the tree headfirst like some warped lizard. Its wings, thick and heavy, spread and closed as it continued to grin, its teeth covered in blood. Dianna's blood.

"Liam!"

I spun, another creature stalking out of the bushes behind me, its wings curving back as if it had just landed.

They could mimic.

"Where is she?" I asked, my voice not my own. My power pulsed with each beat of my heart, making the trees and foliage vibrate in time. The birds screamed, fleeing into the night sky.

The first creature jumped, the ground shaking with the impact of his feet hitting the forest floor. I angled my body to keep them both in sight.

The Irvikuva towered over me, its grin too large and exposing the jagged black teeth that dripped tissue. "Too late, World Ender. You failed again. She returns to the master now." Its tremendous head came closer, the stench of its breath overwhelming. "In pieces."

They laughed, a sickening heckling sound. The words coursed through me, awakening something dark I had kept hidden for eons.

I heard he will take her back in pieces if he has to.

Its smile froze in stunned shock, and its gaze dropped, looking at its midsection in confusion. Without making a sound, its body convulsed. It took a step back before turning into thick, black dust.

I had not known I could call the Oblivion blade forward that quick, but I did not have the time to overthink it. The silver lines etched my body in patterns that twisted and zigzagged toward my face. The second creature looked at me, then at the blade I held. Thick black-and-purple smoke oozed from the weapon. The sword was not silver or gold, like the spear my father and the gods kept. Mine was the absence of all color, absorbing all light. It was a true death blade.

The Oblivion blade was the one I'd made during my ascension. The legend of it had been passed down through time. A story told of how I ended worlds and the weapon that made it possible. Even the old gods feared it, and I had promised myself I would never summon it again. I had thought there was nothing that could force me to break my vow, but the way these creatures had mocked Dianna, her pain, and her fate had proven me wrong. Dianna was worth it, and I would risk it all for her.

I smiled and unleashed. A flick of my ring, and silver armor erupted over my body, covering me from head to toe. I would go to war for her.

The creature fled into the sky.

"Oh, don't run now. We're just getting started." I followed, shooting into the air behind it. It screeched like a wounded animal, fear and panic echoing through the night. I projected myself further and faster. As I slid past it, I turned my blade sideways, cutting it in half. Its screams died as it turned to ash.

I hovered, spinning in the sky, looking for my next target. In the distance, a plume of thick orange flame burst into existence. *Dianna.* I didn't hesitate to will my body forward, flying toward her with all the speed I could muster. My only goal was to save her, help her.

The ground shook from my landing, startling four more of those ghastly beasts. The half-burnt body parts of their brethren littered the area. Dianna had fought and fought well, but it wasn't enough. She was wounded and outnumbered, but I was here now.

The remaining four creatures were dragging a kicking and clawing

Dianna toward a massive hole in the ground. It was burning, sending thick black smoke into the sky. They were taking her back to *him*.

No.

They took one look at me and sped up. Their powerful wings opened, and they jumped, trying to make it to that hole with her. I threw my blade, aiming it like a spear. It caught the one holding her the tightest, and the Irvikuva disintegrated upon impact. As Dianna fell, I jumped, calling the blade back to my ring. I landed hard next to the burning pit. Dianna clung to the edge, the remaining three beasts pulling at her, determined to drag her in. I heard a pop and a tear as Dianna screamed in defiance. That was my girl.

I grabbed her wrists as the beasts below scratched and pulled at her legs. She maneuvered, using one of the kicks I had taught her, and hit one hard enough to send it falling. It disappeared into the fire below.

I pulled as hard as I could, dragging her out and clasping her close. I knew I was holding her too tight, but I wasn't sure I could let her go.

Two monstrous heads popped up. The Irvikuva grasped with their clawed hands, reaching for her, intent on finishing their mission. I cradled her against me as I summoned the Oblivion blade once more.

"Close your eyes."

She nodded and buried her face against the armored plates on my shoulder, clinging to me. I tossed the blade, flipping it and grabbing the hilt. I kneeled, stabbing it into the ground with enough force to shake the terrain. Spiderweb-like veins of purple and black raced toward the pit, killing everything in their path. The devastating energy blazed forward, reaching for the creatures. Their shrieks of terror were abruptly silenced when Oblivion's power touched them, and the ferocious wind caught the dust that remained. The fiery hole shook, smoke billowing as the flames crystallized and the portal went dormant. I yanked the Oblivion blade free before it could do any more damage and summoned it back to its ether.

Still kneeling, I cradled Dianna in one arm, easing her back to assess her and her wounds. I used my free hand to carefully brush the strands of hair from her bloody and torn face.

Her eyes raked over me. "Kn-ight in shin-ing armo-r."

"What?" Her words were broken by the slashes across her throat, but then they registered. Armor. I was still wearing it. With a flick of my thumb, the armor disappeared back into my ring.

"Where are you hurt? Are you okay?"

She shook her head as she gritted her teeth, her mouth coated in blood. I looked down and winced at the deep claw marks and puncture wounds over every part of her body. They had nearly ripped her arm off at the shoulder. I ran my hands over every part of her, finding the bones of one leg horribly twisted.

She hissed, and I stopped, looking back at her face. "Why are you not healing?"

"Irvi-kuva."

Of course. Made of the same blood, they could wound her terribly.

I started to draw the ablaze weapon to offer her my blood, but she gave a barely perceptible shake of her head and gestured to her half-ripped throat. A shudder of pain ran through her as I shifted. I looked down, noticing how twisted her hip was. I tasted fear when I saw the deep wounds torn into her flesh. There were just so many of them. I had assumed her injuries from our earlier altercation would heal quickly with her enhanced regeneration, but I'd been wrong. She was so badly hurt and bleeding heavily.

"Hold on, okay? I'll get us somewhere safe. Just stay with me."

She tried and failed to nod as I leapt back into the sky, desperate to get away from that place.

FORTY

LIAM

I landed in a dimly lit subdivision in a town called Chasin. I wanted to fly us further, but the snow at the higher altitude had slowed me down, and I could feel Dianna slipping away. I'd reached out, searching for any sign of celestial power as we soared.

The little town sat in the shadow of snowcapped mountains. It was quiet, with cars parked along the cobblestone streets and small houses lining either side. Trees spiraled toward the sky, and snow dusted everything.

Dianna groaned and shivered in my arms as my feet touched the ground. Her blood soaked the front of me, and fear gripped me as I felt her heartbeat slow. A part of me knew she would not die, but there was that little niggling doubt. What if she was wrong and did not know the true limits of her power?

I focused my sight on each home, seeing if I could pick up the celestials I'd sensed. My vision changed, allowing me to see the shapes of mortals, their hearts beating steadily. I stopped before the third house, the couple inside gleaming with the cobalt signature of a celestial.

Ah, there they were. Perfect.

I was on the porch in mere seconds, not bothering to walk. I used my foot to kick lightly on the door, afraid to let go of Dianna for even a second.

Several locks clicked before the door opened, revealing a small woman. To mortals, she would look to be in her mid-eighties, but I knew all too well she was pushing a few thousand years.

"Samkiel." Her voice hitched. I heard the other being in the house rush forward. They stared at me, their eyes flashing blue.

"May we use your home, please? My..." I paused. Dianna groaned in my arms, clutching me tighter. Words tumbled through my head, rushing forward to explain what she was to me, but I could not use any of them. Instead, I used the one that, while true, was so much less. "My friend is badly injured."

They nodded, taking in the bloody figure in my arms and stepping aside. The warmth of their home caught us in its embrace, the fireplace in the back licking at smoldering logs. I passed by the small living room, the gentleman ushering me toward the kitchen. He moved items off the table as the woman came in with several towels, placing them on the tabletop. I laid Dianna down on it, hearing her hiss as her back made contact with the surface.

"I'm sorry." I looked around the small kitchen for anything that might help.

"Do you have any herbs from our world? Anything saved?" I asked, looking between them. The woman scurried to a shelf and pushed against the gleaming wood. The wall gave way, exposing a hidden alcove filled with domestic treasures from Rashearim. She opened a small fridge, revealing several glass jars, their contents running low. She picked one and hurried back to hand it to me.

Secctree leaves. They were greenish-yellow and smelled terrible, but helped ease pain. I twisted the lid off the jar and plucked out a single leaf. I slid my arm beneath Dianna and carefully lifted her, bringing the leaf to her lips. "Open your mouth, Dianna. I need you to eat this. It's dissolvable, like that colored candy cloud creation you gave me. It will help with the pain."

She tried but failed, the muscles along her jaw straining. She was cut too deep. I shifted my hand, angling her head back and lifting her chin. She struggled weakly. I knew I was hurting her, but I had no other option.

"I know it hurts, and I am sorry. But with wounds this severe, it will feel like I am ripping you open again when I heal you. I have to do this."

Dianna's bloodshot eyes met mine, and I could see the acceptance in them. Her body relaxed, and I cradled her head a little higher so she would not choke. I slipped the leaf into her mouth, making sure it hit the back of her tongue. She closed her eyes and swallowed, her body trembling with renewed pain at the movement of her throat. I gently brushed a hand over her hair and laid her back.

I rolled up my sleeves and glanced up at the homeowners. The woman's gaze lingered on the crimson, shredded mess of Dianna's white pantsuit, her eyes filled with compassion and worry. "I have clothes she can wear once she is healed," she said before gently grabbing her husband's arm. "We will get your rooms ready."

"Thank you," I said.

They left the kitchen, their footsteps echoing down the hall.

"This will hurt, and for that, I apologize."

She nodded slightly, her eyes tracking my every movement. I clenched my fist, and when I opened it, silver light arced off my palm. It danced, the small whips of energy reaching for her eagerly. I started at her bruised and dirty feet, the shoes she had worn long gone. I directed the energy where it was needed, and her toes wiggled slightly as the skin beneath my hand healed.

The lights in the kitchen flickered several times as I drew more energy from the nearest power sources. The TV and radios cut on and off, static filling the room. I followed the lines of her legs, and she hissed when several large gashes on her thighs knitted themselves back together. A loud crack echoed in the room, and she twisted in pain as her hip popped back into place.

"I'm sorry, I'm sorry," I murmured, wiping the blood-soaked hair from her face.

Dianna eased, lying flat on the table again. She forced another short nod, and I straightened, summoning more energy to keep going.

My hand continued its journey as the power went out completely. I heard the couple murmur from down the hall.

The lights outside flickered, and soon the whole street was blanketed in darkness as I drew more energy. I hovered my palm over her lower abdomen and midsection. Her hand whipped out, gripping my wrist, and I stopped.

Dianna's eyes remained closed, but I could see the pain she tried to hide. She breathed in and out slowly, riding the wave of agony. I waited patiently, stroking her hair lightly with my free hand until she let me go with a shuddering breath. I concentrated once more, my hand tracing her ribcage, breasts, collarbone, and throat before moving up to ensure every scratch and bruise on that gorgeous face was gone.

The power kicked back on as soon as I called my energy back. Noise filled the kitchen as the TV played and the radio continued its joyous song. I took a step back as she sat up. Dianna gazed at me, her eyes softening before she looked down at herself. She raised her arms slowly, flipping them over to examine them before inspecting her legs. She swallowed and looked back up at me.

"How do you feel?" I knew I was hovering, but I couldn't make myself take another step away.

She rubbed her hands up and down her arms. "Cold, but whole."

"Good, good." I had so many things to say, but did not know how or where to start. She started to say something, but stopped at the light sound of footsteps in the hall.

"I have the guest rooms ready." The woman smiled shyly as she wrung her hands together. "There is a bathroom in both, not quite as large as what you're used to, my liege, but enough. Both rooms are at the end of the hall, and I tried to find some clothes that would be sufficient."

Dianna took a deep breath, her expression unreadable as she hopped off the counter.

"Thank you, Miss...?"

"Call me Coretta."

"Thank you, Coretta."

Coretta smiled again, clasping her hands in front of herself.

Dianna nodded as she straightened her torn clothes. She looked at me once more before heading down the hall and out of sight.

As I stepped out of the shower, I looked at the borrowed clothes the celestial couple had laid out. The plaid shirt and gray lounge pants fit well enough. I leaned against the small sink and stared into the steam-clouded mirror. I took a deep breath, centering myself before I drew a circle, slashing the ancient symbols on the mirror. It shimmered and rippled as if a small drop had fallen into a placid pool. When it settled, Logan's face appeared.

"Liam. I have been calling you for hours. Where is your phone?"

I stopped, realizing I had not seen or had one for a while now. "I do not know. What has happened?"

He scoffed. "You tell me. A part of El Donuma is in flames. A freak storm appeared, and there was a quake felt all the way to Valoel."

I looked down. I had not left the Oblivian blade in the ground for long, but apparently, it was enough for its effects to be felt that far.

"Fuck," I said with a weary sigh.

Logan looked taken aback, his brow raising. "Where did you learn that word?"

I ran my hand through the short, wet curls of my hair. "Not important. Kaden launched an attack. He has beasts that are smaller versions of the creatures from legends, including teeth, claws, and wings, everything. He sent them for Dianna. I acted."

He did not ask me to elaborate, only nodded. "So, that's the power we felt. I assume Dianna is safe."

"Yes."

"Good. Gabby may be small, but I fear she would try to skin all of us alive if something happened to Dianna."

"I'm sure Dianna will call her soon." I rubbed the side of my head.

Logan sighed. "Oh, thank the old ones. I would like to have my wife back. She keeps stealing her every night for these ridiculous movies. I hear them in the living room crying and assume the worst. But they tell me it's normal, and they enjoy it? It's confusing. Why do women like to cry so much?"

I smiled as Logan ranted, and he stopped when he saw it.

"You're smiling again. I noticed it at that vampire's castle, too. It's good. You even look decent once more. You've put on weight, which means you're eating."

My brows furrowed. "You noticed my lack of appetite?"

"I notice everything, brother. I just refuse to get scolded for calling you out for it, unlike Vincent and the dark-haired beauty you're currently stuck with." He smiled, the image flickering, and I knew it would not hold much longer. "That light seems to be glowing in you again. It's nice."

"Yeah."

My smile dropped, and Logan cleared his throat, obviously aware of the change in my mood. "Regardless of what has happened in El Donuma, we haven't experienced anything even remotely Other-worldly here. No attacks and no activity. It seems Kaden may be saving all his power and efforts for you two."

I felt the muscle tick in my jaw. "It would appear so. I need you and the others to research two witches: Santiago and Camilla. The moment you find anything on them, let me know. Santiago ran a coven out of Ruuman. Vincent probably knows something about him. Camilla operated one in El Donuma."

"Done and done, sir."

I shook my head, pushing up off the sink. "Don't call me that."

"Look at that. Even your language is changing." Logan smirked. "What about the book? Any leads?"

"Yes, actually. Azrael's daughter lives."

Logan stepped back, his eyes widening. "No fucking way."

I grinned at him. "Now, your language."

"Hey, I've been on this plane longer than you. Their words are contagious." He moved closer to the mirror. "Where is she? I mean, Victoria survived, even if Azrael didn't. I just figured we would have known."

"That's what I am going to find out."

He wiped a hand across his face. "This changes everything."

My stomach sank, knowing it had changed more than he could imagine. "Yes, it does."

"Do you really think he can end the world?"

I lowered my head and stepped back, gripping the sides of the sink. "I don't know. If my visions are accurate, then that's what will happen."

"Liam, your father said those are what *could* happen, not always what *will* happen. Even he had visions that never came to be."

"But why so strongly? Why is the same version repeated? It has to be a sign." I felt the words leave my lips even as I turned toward the bathroom door.

I could hear her heartbeat from here, and it drowned out the rest of the world. She had become a priority for me, and I hadn't been able to keep myself from monitoring the sounds of her survival. I had dreamed of her death, and saw it as that beast ripped a hole through her. It had happened, which meant the world ending part would, too.

I turned back to the mirror, the rest of the world rushing back. The TV and murmurs from downstairs flooded my ears. A car door opened down the street, and the sounds of slumber from the houses near us were loud in my ears.

Logan sighed. "What will you need from me?"

"Transportation in the morning. A convoy that can be undetected for where we have to go. And another phone."

"Done and done."

We spoke a few minutes longer before I dropped the connection with a promise to be in touch. Logan would inform the others, and I would fill in the Council of Hadramiel as soon as I had a chance.

FORTY-ONE

LIAM

My hand stayed raised as if to knock. It was the same thing I had done back in the Vanderkai mansion when I couldn't sleep but refused to stay with her. I was hesitating for the same reasons. The lights flickered downstairs as the celestial couple made what smelled like tea and settled in for the night. I allowed my knuckles to fall, knocking lightly on the door.

"Dianna."

"I'm fine." I heard the rustle of sheets and a sniffle.

I opened the door, concern a tight ache in my gut. I saw a brief glimpse of her eyes before she nestled back into the thick comforter. She had another thick faux fur blanket on top of that. Her dark hair stuck out the top as she curled into herself.

Her response was muffled, but I heard her say, "I said I'm fine."

"What's wrong? Are you crying?"

"No."

I walked further into the room, shutting the door behind me. This room, like mine, was small. A bed took up the right side of the room. Through the doorway, I could see a tiny bathroom, and there was a closet on the left. A window took up the farthest wall, the sheer curtains not blocking out the sight of the falling snow. I felt a draft run through the room and wondered if she was cold.

"Dianna."

"I said I'm fine. Go to bed. Don't we have to be up early or something? Isn't that what you and Logan said?"

I took another step closer. "Eavesdropping?"

"The house is small."

I glanced around the room. "That it is, and it is drafty. I was unaware it snowed this time of the year. It is cold outside." I knew I was rambling like a madman, but I would say and do anything to stay with her, no matter how idiotic I sounded.

"Liam, I'm tired. Go to bed. We can talk in the morning," she said, nestling further into her blanket cocoon.

She wanted me to leave. Was she avoiding me after everything that had happened? Well, too bad. There was no way I was going to let her put distance between us. I moved to the other side of the bed, and lifting the covers she'd wound so tightly around herself, I scooted inside.

She turned to look at me, exhaustion dulling her eyes. "What are you doing?"

"You told me to go to bed, so that's what I am doing."

"Not here. You have your own."

"I don't want my own." And I didn't. I needed to be close to her. I'd almost lost her. Couldn't she see that?

A pained expression crossed her face as she regarded me. "Aren't you afraid of what your precious celestials will think?"

So that's what this was about?

"No. And besides, I'm cold."

She scoffed and lay down hard enough to make the small bed shake and creak. "Gods don't get cold."

I copied her position, lying facing her, close, but not touching. "Oh, yeah? So, you know a lot of us?"

I saw her shoulder lift in a shrug. "Only one super annoying one."

My lips curved in a small smile. I would take any quip or jab Dianna threw at me as long as she was okay.

"Did you call your sister?"

She looked away. "No."

"Why?" That concerned me.

"I don't want her to worry, and I'm too tired to act like I'm okay tonight."

It was quiet again for a long moment. I hated the silence between us more than anything. I wanted to fix what was so broken, yet even with all my strength and power, I did not know how.

Images flashed before my eyes of us back in the forest before the attack. How Dianna spoke to me, looked at me, and how her lips parted before she was taken. Words I wanted to say bubbled up in my throat, yet they remained trapped there. I tried to force it, but when I spoke, what I said had nothing to do with how I felt.

"We should probably get some sleep. We need to leave at first light. Logan is arranging space for us on a convoy tomorrow morning. We are close to where Azrael's daughter lives, but we both need some rest after everything that has happened."

Dianna studied me, her eyes scanning my face as if she expected me to say something else. I didn't, and she nodded before rolling away from me.

I silently cursed myself. What was wrong with me? Dianna was not like anyone I knew. I had slain creatures the size of stars, yet this fiery, headstrong woman made me nervous. She was tying me up in knots. I needed to tell her how I felt, but I first had to figure out what I was feeling. I grimaced, already able to hear Cameron's mocking laughter if he ever found out. Gods, all of them laughing.

I absently rubbed my hand across my face as I stared at her back. She'd wrapped herself in as many covers as she could, leaving me with practically none. I lifted the blankets closest to me and fit my body to her back.

"What are you doing?" she asked, her body tensing.

"I'm getting close to you for warmth. I told you I was cold."

She snorted, then let out a yip when my feet touched the bare skin of her ankles. "Gods, you *are* cold! You weren't lying."

I smiled. I wouldn't mention that I could control my body temperature. It was necessary that I be close to her, and if that meant a small lie of omission, I could live with that. When she'd vanished, I had been terrified I would never see her again.

"No, I wasn't."

With a big sigh, she nestled back against me. She grabbed my wrist and pulled it over her, pressing my hand against her abdomen. We had slept like this before, when my night terrors were particularly violent. I held her close, my face buried in the crook of her neck, and counted her every heartbeat, every breath. I relaxed for the first time in weeks, the tension leaving my shoulders. The old ones spoke of absolute peace beyond worlds, beyond realms, and when I held Dianna, I felt it. It was a feeling I had spent centuries searching for. I took a breath, inhaling her scent as she shivered beside me.

I was allowing myself to get too close to her again, but I did not care this time. I savored the feel of her with me, whole and far away from Kaden. They had almost succeeded, almost dragged her back to him. I had almost lost her. Fear still quivered through me as I propped my head up, needing to make sure she was okay.

The curve of her shoulder was exposed by the overly large clothing, and I brushed my hand over it, shifting her hair to the side. She shivered, and I stopped, afraid I had hurt her. Was she still sore? Tender? I did not know if I had healed her completely.

"What's wrong?" Worry edged my tone. "Are you still in pain? Wounded?"

"No." Her voice sounded like a breathless whisper. "Your rings are cold."

Relief flooded through me. "My apologies."

My lips curved in a small, satisfied smile. Smooth skin met my fingertip as I teased my touch down her neck, tracing the exposed flesh I could see. My mind flashed back to her tears and blood. My chest and gut ached, but she was fine now. She was safe. Her skin was unmarred. No more gashes lined her shoulders or throat.

"I am sorry if I hurt you when I healed you."

I could see the edge of her grin over her shoulder. It was short, but it was enough. "You know, you apologize a lot for royalty."

My smile was genuine. "So you keep telling me."

It was quiet once more as I caressed the few loose hairs from her cheek. I scanned the edge of her face. There were no marks, no bruises, no bullet holes. My traitorous mind willingly supplied the memory of the sound of the gun, her falling, and Santiago's grin. Death would be a kindness once I was finished with him.

The bed shifted as she rolled to her side, facing me. I cupped her shoulder, caressing the silky warmth of her skin.

"You came for me," she said, looking up at me through her thick lashes. I swear, I melted. "You saved me even when you didn't have to. You had the information you needed and could have left me to go find the book, but you came for me."

I was shocked by her statement. It was such a ridiculous notion, and it had never been an option. Who would ever abandon her? Although, given the company she had kept, I saw why she would question it.

"I'd never abandon you."

A soft smile graced her face as she raised her hand and ran her fingers through my hair. She had done the same many times since that first night when I'd almost demolished the motel. I lifted my head, seeking more of her touch, and she cupped my face in both hands. I lowered my forehead to hers, and my eyes closed as I savored the feeling. Dianna's cinnamon scent engulfed me, seeping into my every pore. Her breath mingled with my own as my nose grazed hers. I was suddenly aware of how perfectly her body fit against mine, and how it would be the death of me. We were silent, the trauma of the last few hours weighing heavy between us.

"I tried to fight, but there were too many," she said.

"You were perfect."

She shook her head, her forehead rocking against mine and our noses rubbing. "No, no, I wasn't. I'm not that strong."

I opened my eyes and pulled back to cradle her face, brushing my thumbs against her cheekbones until she met my gaze. "Dianna. They outnumbered you. I have seen seasoned and blooded warriors fall when attacked by too many." I searched her hazel eyes, happy to see they were healed and no longer bloodshot. They were whole, pure, and perfect, just like her.

She snorted. "I am no warrior."

"Yes, you are. Along with being brave, stubborn, crass, and volatile, you are one of the strongest people I know. You fight me on everything. Which is saying a lot, considering everyone trembles when I enter the room." She chuckled and closed her eyes. "Hey, look at me. You would have to be an ignorant fool not to think you are anything but extraordinary, Dianna."

Something shifted in her hazel eyes when they met mine. It was small, but world-shattering.' Her lips slanted over mine, and for the first time in my entire existence, I froze. Her kiss was light, tantalizing —and everything I never knew I had been missing.

She pulled back and looked up at me, her fingers tracing the line of my jaw. A slow, mischievous smile curved her lips. "You still have witch breath."

Something snapped in me, and I was afraid it was my self-control. Desire coiled and burned in me, and I let it.

"Then fix it," I dared, throwing down the challenge.

I shifted, tucking her beneath me. Our mouths came together with enough force to rattle the heavens above. I could not have explained it even if the gods themselves gave me a century to do so. There were no words to describe how Dianna's lips felt against mine, but with that first kiss, my gravity shifted. I may not have the words to do justice to her or what I was feeling, but I knew if she would let me, I would happily spend a millennium trying.

My hands ran through the silken tresses I had dreamed of each time I'd allowed myself to dream. My body ached, an eternal need I'd never known flaring to life, begging to be sated. Every nerve ending I had was suddenly awake and screaming, demanding to be touched, demanding to touch.

I tipped my head to the side, deepening the kiss. She moaned softly as my tongue dipped past her lips and danced across hers. I tangled my hands in her hair, hoping she wouldn't pull away, hoping she wouldn't change her mind. I had kissed and been kissed thousands of times in my lifetime, but nothing compared to this moment. With the right person, a kiss was so much more than a kiss. It was pure, unfiltered ecstasy. A part of my soul had been waiting for this woman, and one kiss from her had undone me. A voice I couldn't ignore quietly insisted that she was what I had been missing.

It's her.

It's her.

It's her.

For the first time in centuries, I felt that old familiar feeling rushing through my veins. Arousal, sharp, intense, and burning, slammed into me, my body reacting so strongly that my head spun. I groaned as she wrapped her legs around me and lifted her hips in sweet feminine demand. My hands dropped to her ass, pushing her against me and holding her there as I ground against her. She moaned against my mouth, her tongue dancing against mine, and I knew I would move planets to hear that sound over and over again.

Dianna's nails scraped lightly over my nape as she pulled me closer. She sucked on my bottom lip before nipping at it, as if marking every place Camilla had touched as her own. The slight twinge of pain made my cock jerk and my blood boil, leaving any critical thinking part of me far behind. I wanted, no, I *needed* more.

I reverently cupped her breast through the thin fabric of her shirt, my thumb rubbing across her nipple. She moaned, circling her hips, pressing her soft heat hard enough against my throbbing erection that I almost came right then and there.

The sound of footsteps shuffling and a TV turning on had us breaking apart. We looked toward the door, then back at each other. Dianna playfully pushed at my shoulder.

"You're too loud," she whispered.

I scoffed, keeping my voice low as I raised up on one arm. "I'm too loud? *You're* too loud."

The smile she gave me was the first real one I had seen in weeks.

She glanced at the door, then back to me, biting her kiss-swollen lower lip. My gaze snagged on her mouth, and I was drawn back in. I lowered my head, but her hand pressing against my chest stopped me. She giggled and said, "We probably shouldn't have loud make-out sessions in a house with super-beings."

I nodded once, even though every fiber in my being rebelled. "You're right."

"I mean, they did offer us their home and help us. It feels rude to keep them awake because you're too loud."

Dianna's eyes gleamed with mischief as she played with me. I couldn't have kept the smile from my face even if I'd wanted to. I never could with her.

"Me?"

She nodded as she slipped out from under me, the feel of her body sliding against mine making me bite back another groan. She grinned knowingly before turning to face the bedroom door.

I cleared my throat and said, "It is quite rude."

I settled behind her, wrapping my arms around her waist and pulling her back against me. Dianna wiggled as she got settled. A jolt of pleasure ran through my body as the curve of her ass rubbed against my cock. She had me aching, and she'd barely even touched me. The woman was pure evil. My eyes closed as my head fell into the crook of her neck, a slight groan escaping me at the intense pleasure that shot through me.

"Dianna."

"Hmm?" she asked as she rubbed against me another time. My hand flew to her hip, putting a stop to her current torture.

"Bad girl."

"What are you talking about? I'm just getting comfortable."

I popped her ass lightly enough not to sting, but hard enough to get a small squeal from her. "You know what you're doing," I whispered in her ear as my grip tightened on her hip.

"I don't know what you're talking about," she said, her voice breathless.

Very well. Two could play that game, and I loved a challenge.

My hand splayed on her hip, the tips of my fingers brushing against the oversized shirt she wore. "Earlier, you wished for me not to touch you. Is that still your wish?"

Her head turned toward mine, her breath tickling my lips. I heard her swallow as she regarded me. She reached back and caressed the side of my face. "No."

"Very well." I slipped my hand beneath the thin fabric of her shirt. My fingers spread wide as I ran them over her ribs and higher. "But you'll have to be quiet. It's a small house."

Her smile slowly died, that perfect mouth opening slightly as my hand ran over the curve of first one breast, then the other, cupping them and squeezing firmly. Her eyes fluttered closed, and her moan was more of an exhale as I ran my fingers over her nipples, teasing them to small, tight points.

I changed my mind. Dianna's laugh was my *second* favorite sound.

She pressed her head back against me as I tugged and pinched one nipple, then the next. She ground against me, moaning again. It was a soft whisper of what I knew I could make her feel. Pure, exquisite pleasure burst inside of me every time she moved, her ass brushing against my already aching cock. I reveled in it, but it was not my pleasure that I was interested in tonight. I just wanted to give her some joy amidst all the pain she had endured at the hands of Kaden, me, anyone.

Dianna turned her head and teased her mouth along the line of my jaw, my neck, and any part she could reach, setting my body on fire. Her fingers gripped at my hair as she curved her body further into mine.

"You know, I was not truthful earlier," I whispered, my hand slipping from beneath her shirt.

"Hmm?"

"You have the most phenomenal ass." I snaked my hand under the waistband of her pajama pants and cupped one cheek, eliciting another softer moan from her. "I am almost ashamed to admit how many times I have looked at it, fantasized about it."

She pushed into my hand, her breathing quickening. My smile grew brighter. So, that's what my Dianna liked. She liked to hear the words. Very well.

"Do you wish to know why I avoided you? Why I couldn't bear to spend another night beside you?"

Her lips fell from the side of my neck, her nose scraping against the stubble on my jaw as she looked up at me. The burning embers in the depths of her hazel eyes lit up the room and my entire world. She nodded once, her hand still lightly resting against my face.

"Because I could not lie there, close to you, and not wish to be inside you."

I inserted my knee between her thighs and lifted, opening her to my touch. My hand dipped between her legs, and she gasped as my fingers found her more than wet.

"Is this all for me, Dianna?" I asked as she grew even slicker beneath my touch.

She nodded desperately, her eyes squeezing shut as my fingers teased from her entrance to her clit and back. Her hips moved in tandem with me, and she bit her lower lip to hold back her cries of pleasure. Slowly and deliberately, I teased her before dipping a single finger inside. Her pussy clenched around the single digit right as a heady moan escaped her lips, much louder this time.

"Shh." I reached up with my free hand, cupping her mouth and whispering in her ear, "Do you wish to wake the entire neighborhood?"

I didn't give her a chance to respond as I drove my finger deeper. Dianna was already more than wet, but I moved slowly, not wanting to hurt her. There would be no pain. I would make sure of it. She had endured enough.

Dianna ground against my hand, stopping briefly as I slipped the single finger out to the tip before adding another inside of her. Her head fell back, exposing the vulnerable line of her throat as she moaned against my palm. I couldn't resist the temptation of her neck, sliding my mouth over her pulse, feeling it pound against my lips as I sucked and kissed. She reached up, holding on to my arm and bearing down on my hand, begging for more.

My lips brushed the shell of her ear. "Feels good, doesn't it?"

Her response was muffled as she moaned against my hand, but the clenching I felt around my fingers at my question was more than enough of an answer.

"Would you like to see what else I can do, Dianna?"

A sharp nod was her response, and I felt my power radiate through my veins, pulsating with heat.

"I told you before that I could make it hurt if I wanted it to … but I can also make it feel like this."

She froze for a moment as she felt that invisible power, like second hands, slide over her breasts. I felt the small puff of air against my palm as she gasped and clenched hard around my fingers. Her eyes widened before rolling back as I sent that invisible force to her clit.

I wanted to see if Dianna had the same sensitive spot as my lovers before. I curved my fingers inside her, her hand tightening around my arm as I pumped harder. A deep moan vibrated against my hand as her movements became feverish.

"Yes..." I nipped at the skin of her neck. She whimpered at the sound of my voice. "Ride my fingers like you'll ride my cock when I take you beneath the stars."

She did, pressing her ass back against me as I lifted my knee higher, opening her more. Her body trembled as she bore down, my fingers meeting her every thrust, pushing deeper inside of her. My magic teased at her clit, licking and sucking. Her breath was coming in small, harsh pants against my palm, her grip painfully tight on my arm. She arched into me, and her body tensed as she reached her peak and was released.

Dianna shook and bent against me. The walls of her pussy clenched tightly around my fingers as I continued to draw every last bit of orgasm out of her. Her head fell into the crook of my shoulder, the whites of her eyes showing as her eyelids fluttered. Transfixed, I watched as wave after wave of pleasure washed over her. Hungry for more, I moved the power against her clit again, causing her to moan as another tremor ripped through her. I swore she screamed my name into my palm.

It was addicting to watch her pleasure and know it was only for me.

I waited for a few moments before easing my fingers from inside her. I brushed kisses along her shoulder and neck as I removed my hand from her mouth. She sagged against me before turning her head to look at me.

"I'll never admit to how amazing that was," she panted. "Your ego is already large enough."

I smiled and slipped my hand from beneath her pajama pants before pulling them up.

"That was only my hands. How deprived are you, my Dianna?"

Something flashed behind her eyes, her smile fading slightly as her eyes searched mine.

"What?" I asked, hoping I hadn't just offended her. I was merely joking.

She shook her head. "Nothing."

I watched as she rolled over to face me, that all-too-familiar mischievous gleam lighting her eyes. I grabbed her wrist as I felt her fingers reach for the waistband of my pants.

"Not tonight. We have to leave early, remember?"

She looked confused. "Are you sure? It would only take me five minutes."

I couldn't help but laugh. "Dianna, if you touch me, I promise that neither of us will sleep tonight. I am barely hanging on to my control, and the first time I take you, I do not want either of us to have to worry about being quiet." I pressed a kiss to her forehead. "Go to sleep."

She smiled, truly smiled again as she nestled her hands beneath the pillow under her head. "Yes, Your Highness." She closed her eyes, and I watched her for a moment before grabbing the large blanket and covering us both with it. I laid down facing her, watching her sleep and listening to the rhythmic beat of her heart as she slumbered.

Dianna was safe and whole. My dreams had come to fruition, but I hadn't lost her, and she hadn't died. A part of my heart sang, knowing she was okay, while another part stirred with emotions I barely recognized. I watched her sleep as long as I could before my eyes forced themselves closed.

No matter how much peace I'd found tonight, the nightmares still came.

FORTY-TWO

DIANNA

I found out I loved waking up with Liam—especially when I woke first and could wake him by taking him into my mouth. His cock touched the back of my throat, and the sound that rumbled from his chest made my core melt. He gripped the back of my hair tighter and bit his bottom lip to muffle his groans.

Were we still at the home of the sweet celestials that had taken us in? Yes. Was I in the least bit concerned that they would hear us? No. Did Liam think he could give me multiple orgasms, and I wouldn't return the favor? Apparently.

I looked up at him as I slid my tongue from the base of his shaft to the crown of his cock in one long, slow lick. His free hand was above his head, gripping the headboard tightly. His gaze was focused on me, the silver of his eyes shimmering hotly from beneath hooded lids.

I wished I had more time to explore him. I wanted to find every spot that made him moan and discover what would happen if he lost himself in desire. But I could hear the homeowners stirring in the kitchen and knew our time was running short.

I wrapped my hand around the base of his cock, his girth enough that my fingers did not meet. I tightened my grip and stroked, marveling at the size of him. Slowly, I twisted my hand, going from the base to the crown and back again as I watched him.

Liam was absolutely beautiful, and I couldn't help but explore the parts of him I could touch, sliding my free hand across the planes of his abs and the sensitive skin of his inner thighs. His hips lifted, pushing his cock against my palm. I felt so powerful, making this god writhe.

"I'm going to make you cum really quick," I whispered and licked my lips. Liam groaned as quietly as he could, his head falling back deeper into the pillow as he nodded. "I promise, next time I'll make it last longer. Just try to be quiet." I loved that we were developing our own private jokes, deepening the intimacy between us.

I flashed him a devilish grin before swirling my tongue over the tip of his cock. His silver eyes found me once again as I teased the sensitive underside of his shaft with small, short licks.

"Dianna." His voice was a low growl of impatience.

I laughed softly and closed my mouth over him. With one hand, I stroked his massive length, and with the other, gently massaged his balls. I heard him slam the pillow against his face as he tried, and failed, to cover his moan. That sound, and knowing I was the one who'd caused it, drove me wild. I increased my pace, his hips thrusting as he matched my rhythm. He no longer gently held my hair, but gripped it tightly in his fist.

I groaned around his cock, sending vibrations through the hard length filling my mouth. He responded by thrusting harder. I felt the tip of him hit the back of my throat, but I didn't stop him. I wanted more.

Liam groaned again, and I had the fuzzy thought that he didn't care anymore who heard. "That feels so *fucking* good, my Dianna."

My Dianna.

There was that word again. I didn't know if it was the possessiveness in it or the way he said it, but it made my body run hot, and I felt myself grow slick. If he didn't finish soon, I wouldn't care who was in this damned house. I wanted to feel him inside me, and I would take him hard and fast.

"Look at me."

I barely recognized his voice, but I knew I could never ignore the need in it. My gaze flicked up. The pillow he'd had over his head was gone, and he watched me with molten silver eyes. "That's it, baby. You're so fucking beautiful. I love the way you look when you suck my cock."

Liam knew what those words did to me. He had figured it out and would use it. With one last loving caress over his balls, I gripped his shaft with both hands. I tightened my fingers around him, trying to mimic how it would feel if I straddled him and took him deep. I wanted to show him how I would squeeze him for every filthy word he whispered to me.

His hips thrust up, and I felt him twitch. His shaft swelled, stretching my lips tight, and I knew he was close.

"Suck me harder. Please, baby, please."

So I did, sucking hard and sliding my tongue along the underside of his shaft as my hands worked in tandem, worshiping his body. I savored the taste of him and the pleasure he was experiencing, wanting to give him more.

"I'm so close," he said in a breathy groan, his hand gripping my hair tighter. "I'm so close. Come here."

I moaned against him, keeping my pace. He was a fool to think I didn't want him to release in my mouth, down my throat. I wanted to taste him. He must have read the intent in my expression, because his body shook, and the intricate silver lines of his tattoos raced across his skin. They were there for just a fraction of a second, as if he had lost all control of his form. His hips thrust hard, both hands gripping my hair. He tossed his head back, and I could feel his entire body tense as he spilled into my mouth.

My name left his lips in a perfect cry that I knew even a TV couldn't drown out, but I cherished it. I stayed still and purred contently, letting every last drop escape him and pour into me before I swallowed. His breathing was ragged and his body trembling with aftershocks of pleasure as he relaxed back against the bed. I licked up the side of his shaft, cleaning up any drops that had escaped. He grabbed my shoulders and pulled me up and away, tucking me against his side as he tried to catch his breath.

I laughed. "Even gods are sensitive?"

"Very." He sounded so spent, so relaxed. I liked this Liam. Actually, that was a lie; I liked all versions of him, even the grumpy ones, even if I wasn't supposed to.

I ran the back of my hand over my lips, but he caught my wrist, stopping me.

"Don't wipe me away."

My heart clenched, but I snorted and said, "There's the bossy and arrogant god-man, and I'm not, but I have drool on my face."

"I don't care. Don't do it again." He pulled me across his chest and gave me a hard, quick kiss.

I smiled against his lips. "Does this make us mortal enemies with benefits?"

His brows furrowed.

"Or I guess friends with benefits."

He looked at me like I had slapped him across the face. I pushed back, my hands braced on his chest so that I could read his eyes better.

"'Friends'? Like you and Drake?"

"Oh, eww, no. I have never done anything like that with Drake."

"Well then, don't associate me with him."

I rested my head back against his chest. "I didn't. I was saying—"

Whatever I was about to say died as a shrill ring filled the room. We looked at the door as the sound came again. I realized it had been ringing off and on all morning, but we had been a little too preoccupied to notice.

Reality rolled over us, and I pushed off Liam, allowing him space to move. He climbed out of bed and adjusted his clothes before opening the door and grabbing the phone.

"It's Logan. The convoy—we missed it."

"… Oops."

I SAT AT THE DINING ROOM TABLE WITH OUR LOVELY HOUSEMATES, shoving another piece of toast into my mouth. Coretta made the best toast ever, and I hadn't realized how hungry I was until I made it downstairs and smelled breakfast. Her husband sat across from me, reading on a tablet about the chaos that I may or may not have been a part of last night.

The memory of talons dragging across my skin was still fresh, and I shivered. But I was okay. I was alive and whole and not taken. I was okay.

"How did you sleep last night?" Coretta asked, making me bite my tongue.

I hissed, raising my hand to my lips. Had they heard us? Liam had covered my mouth, but a few licks to a certain part of him, and he'd practically crawled out of his skin. The noises he made were my new favorite addiction, and something I wanted to hear again as soon as possible, but I didn't want to discuss our early morning activities with this sweet couple.

"Fine," I finally got out. Her husband's brows lifted, and a grin tugged at the corner of his mouth, but he didn't look at me. "What about you?"

She turned from the stove, bringing a plate of eggs and sausage. "Very well, dear." She smiled at me as she sat beside her husband and picked up her cup of coffee. "I was worried about you. Those cuts were deep, and I can't imagine the type of creature that could do that. I'd assumed they'd died with Rashearim."

Phantom aches echoed through my body at the mention of those claws digging into my flesh. The fear I had felt at being dragged back to Kaden would haunt me for a long time.

Before I could respond, the stairs creaked, and footsteps approached. As usual, I felt him before I saw him. My senses went on alert—not in fear, but in my primal need to have him, *truly* have him. He came to my side, blocking my peripheral view as he sat.

Both celestials smiled up at him in welcome as I continued to stare like an idiot while eating. Was he always this attractive? A hunger stirred in me once more, and it had nothing to do with the breakfast in front of me.

His hand slid down my back as he sat, and I shivered, leaning into his touch. After last night, I realized Liam's way of showing affection was definitely physical touch, and he had confirmed it once again this morning.

"Thank you for letting me use your home. I do apologize for the sudden emergency."

"Please, it's the least we could do." Coretta smiled at him. "Did you find the phone? A courier brought it early this morning."

He sat mere inches from me, his thigh brushing mine under the table as he gave me a small smile, noticing the plate I had made for him. Another brush of his leg spoke a silent *thank you* before he picked up the fork without a second thought. It was nice to see him eating and feeling better.

A foreign sense of contentment filled me—and it terrified me more than anything I had faced. Liam could destroy me.

"I did. Thank you for making sure I got it. We have to leave soon to catch the next convoy." Liam glanced at me, taking a sip of the freshly squeezed juice. An unspoken *"since you made us late"* hung in the air as I nodded, not one bit ashamed about this morning.

"Sounds great."

"Oh, my liege, I wanted to thank you and that sweet Vincent once more for all the lovely gifts and sweet messages you have sent."

Liam and I looked at her as she smiled brightly at us, her husband following suit. "Yes," he replied, reaching out and grasping her hand tightly. "Our son passed, but we heard how heroic he was during the attack in Arariel."

I forced myself to swallow the now dry piece of toast. Their words hit home, as I knew I'd been the attacker.

Liam felt my unease and cleared his throat, gracing them with one of those bright, beautiful smiles. "Yes, well, we only wish to help in any way we can. Just know that he is at peace in the Asteraoth now."

Asteraoth was the realm beyond time and space where the dead went, and where we could never reach.

She smiled and wiped a stray tear from her eye. "That's all we want for our dear, sweet Peter."

My knee jerked, hitting the table hard enough to rattle the plates. Liam shot a glance of concern my way as the couple looked at me.

"Sorry." I forced a smile, even as acid turned in my gut. "Leftover muscle pain from the attack last night. Weird spasms."

"It's okay, dear. Why don't I make you some herbal tea before you go? It works wonders on pain." She rose, none the wiser, as she headed toward the pot.

Liam's knee brushed mine, the same as I had done for him during the dinner at Drake's. It was a small yet comforting touch that seemed to ground me. I watched as the mother of the man I'd not only beaten within an inch of his life, but then turned over to Alistair, made me tea to help my aches and pains, when I'd caused her the greatest grief of her life.

MY SMALL, FEATHERED WINGS BEAT ACROSS THE SKY. I WAS HIGH enough to see but not be seen, and the local bird shape I had taken made it easy. One last circle, and I landed in a clearing out of sight of the temple entrance. It was shrouded by miles of woods, but I had no trouble spotting the World Ender where he leaned against a tree. I shifted back to my base form as I approached.

"I see now why the old gods nearly won." His eyes raked over me with what looked like an expression of admiration. "Your powers are more than convenient."

Liam fell into step with me as we started toward the temple where we were supposed to meet Azrael's daughter. "Oh, yeah? You want to use me?"

I meant it as more of a suggestive joke, but I think the humor was lost on Liam. "Never," he said, his voice pained. "I would never even suggest such a thing. I appreciate you. Truly."

My heart seemed to skip a beat at his words. Call me a stupid fool, but no one had ever spoken to me like that—no one. I either did what was expected of me, or messed up and then heard about it nonstop. No one ever *appreciated* me.

"Anything?" he asked as the temple came into sight. It was overgrown with moss, and tourists buzzed around it, laughing and talking.

I shook my head. "Nope."

A half smile graced his beautiful face. "I told you. You are just paranoid."

I playfully slapped his shoulder as we came to a stop at the edge of the temple grounds, staying in the shadows. A heated look crossed his devilish features. At this point, I was convinced he just liked the fact that I touched him. "Not paranoid, but I don't trust Camilla not to set another trap."

"Nothing will happen to you." His smile dropped as the icy rage snuck back into his eyes. "Not again."

A brief smile crossed my face as those phantom pains suggested otherwise. Even now, they ached, but I didn't tell him. Images flashed of him slamming to the ground, covered in the same armor I had seen him wear in the blooddreams. Samkiel, the feared king, had come for me, a literal knight in shining armor. I couldn't wait to call Gabby and tell her about it. She would love it. It was everything her romantic movies and books swore was real.

I gave him a small smile and nearly jumped when a group of tourists walked past us, chattering and taking pictures. We stood outside the large temple in Ecleon on the Nochari continent. The structure was made of carved green stones and was deep in the middle of yet another jungle, vines and vegetation threatening to take it back. The sign at the entrance said it was built in remembrance of the founding of this area.

I slapped my arm, and another tiny insect fell to the forest floor. I had fallen silent, but so had Liam, which was nothing terribly abnormal. We had traveled for a few hours in a cramped, tight space surrounded by tons of people. It had put both of us on edge. The constant shuffle and bumping into others had been uncomfortable, but it was the only convoy we could get on short notice.

I sighed and folded my arms, blurting out, "Why didn't Vincent or you tell them the truth?"

"I knew that has been bothering you."

I turned toward him. "Why lie?"

It wasn't guilt that made me ask. I knew what I was, even if Gabby and Liam saw me differently. I did what I had to do, and I would always do whatever it took to keep her safe. But a part of me cared what he thought of me, which scared me more than I wanted to admit. He didn't act like it, but I couldn't help but wonder if he felt guilty about last night.

"Sometimes, a simple lie is better than a harsh truth. In truth, he did die in battle. But that was Vincent's decision not to tell them the whole truth, not mine. I was unaware of the connection when we stopped last night, or I would have taken you somewhere else."

"Why?"

He faced me, and I held his gaze, sensing that what he wanted to say was important. "Because you have been lost in your own head since you found out who they are. I may not have known you very long, Dianna, but you have a tell. Your tell is that somber silence that takes you away from me. The one that shuts me out."

"I don't regret it, Liam. You know that, right?" And I didn't. "I would do anything to keep Gabby safe. I will fight to destroy any threat to her. She is all I have left."

"I am very aware," he said, but worry still grew in my gut. I hated that I suddenly cared so much about what he thought of me.

"And how does that make you feel … now?"

I saw the moment he realized what I was asking. Heat flared in his eyes, the hunger and naked need in their depths shocking. He leaned forward, pressing his hand to my lower back and pulling me into the curve of his body. His breath tickled my ear as he whispered, "If we weren't so preoccupied with finding this book, I would show you in seven different ways how much it does not affect how I feel about you."

My heart thudded in my chest, a small, mischievous smile spreading across my face as I brushed my lips along the curve of his jaw, savoring the rasp of his stubble against their softness. "Only seven?"

"Let's see how much you can handle first." I felt him smile as his hand cupped my ass, low enough that he was able to graze his fingers across my center. I yelped, and his laughter sent another ripple of heat through me. He stood and turned back toward the temple, pulling my back to his front. "So, that's what has been bothering you?"

"No." I sighed. "Yes."

"Do you wish for me to feel a certain way about you? It's not as if I didn't already know what you are capable of."

"I killed him, or at least helped. And I've killed a few of yours."

"And I helped wipe out all of yours." His arms tightened around me in a small hug. "We were both blinded by willful ignorance. There are things I have done that make me wish I could claw the memories from my mind. But we grow, we learn, and we do better. I am not making excuses for you or myself, but I know how far you will go to protect your sister. I know what Kaden has forced you to do. You seem to think I am this pure, good being, when the old gods taught me how to end worlds."

"You are to me."

I felt his chuckle against my back and could hear the smile in his voice. "Dianna being nice. Have you grown ill?"

"Shut up. I am always a delight," I said, elbowing him playfully in the ribs. "You know, you have a tell, too."

His breath tickled the top of my head. "Oh? Enlighten me."

"You're a kicker."

"What do you mean?" he asked.

"I noticed the first few times you shared a bed with me. On the nights when your nightmares are the worst, you twitch, sometimes kick. Not hard enough to hurt, but it's as if you're trying to run away from something. You did it last night, too."

He was silent for a moment too long, and I was afraid I had said the wrong thing.

"I thought my dreams would subside, but I feel they have only gotten worse."

"The nightmares?"

He nodded, but I felt him raising those walls again.

I turned in his arms and looked up at him. "Liam. Talk to me."

His throat bobbed once, and he looked past me, staring at the temple instead of me. "My father, his father, and those before him had visions, images that foretold of what would come to pass. A story grew that my great-grandfather went insane from them, and now I am afraid maybe I am, too."

"Insane?"

He nodded. "My father told me how his grandfather got lost in not being able to change the horrors that may come to pass, and now I'm afraid I may be headed down the same path, because I can't get them to stop. You have helped tremendously, but this new dream seems to be one even your presence cannot penetrate." He forced a smile that made my insides twist with worry.

"Are these the same ones you were having back in Morael?"

His response was a simple nod.

"You mentioned a dream last night. Is it the same one? What else happens?"

Pain and horror flashed through his gray eyes as if a storm brewed there. "It's not important."

"It is if it's bothering you."

"What's bothering me is that we are still waiting, even though we were the ones who were late." A muscle ticked in his jaw, and I knew he didn't want to talk about the dreams anymore. At least he had opened up some, but I was worried about what he wasn't telling me. I wouldn't push, wouldn't ask for more than he wanted to give.

"So, what time did this girl say again?" I asked, allowing him to change the subject.

"She is not 'this girl.' Her name is Ava."

I rolled my eyes. "I'm sorry. *Ava.*"

A snort escaped him. "She is Azrael's daughter. Which means she is a higher-ranking celestial by blood. I am going to play it off as you being my second, for appearance's sake. Please be respectful and nonthreatening," he said, narrowing his eyes at me.

I held my hands up innocently. "Hey, I can do a little role-play, if that's what you want."

He shook his head, but I saw the grin even as he tried to hide it. "She said she would be here at four-thirty. Right as they close."

Right. I had used Liam's phone on the convoy to call Gabby. I let her know I was alive and okay before Liam took it and called the woman we were supposed to meet. She refused to tell him where she actually lived, which seemed weird to me, but I figured if anyone had a right to be paranoid, she did.

I watched the sun grow closer to the horizon. "Maybe she isn't coming. Probably chickened out or something."

He tilted his head back, clearly frustrated with the situation. "Can you try to be positive?"

"Yes. I am positive that I hate the jungle."

Liam started to say something, but stopped when a petite, dark-haired woman came strutting along the trail. She pushed past tourists as they headed toward the exit. We straightened, and I took a step, putting a little distance between Liam and me. She waved as she walked toward us. Her outfit was similar to mine, just a white tank and light-colored pants. Her boots were thick, and she carried a back-pack over one shoulder.

"Sorry to keep you waiting," she said as she stopped before us, her short pigtails swaying perkily. A man followed her, his back hunched from the weight of the pack he carried and his eyes darting between us.

"Ava, correct?" Liam asked, stepping forward.

"Do I know you?" I asked at the same time. My senses had gone on alert, an odd but familiar feeling twisting my gut.

"Gosh, no. I think I would remember someone like you," Ava said with a laugh, waving me off before turning to Liam. Her smile grew as she leaned forward to hug him. He froze, his arms trapped at his sides. The force of her embrace shook him. I moved quickly, prying her off of him and forcing her to take a step back.

She realized what she had done, correcting herself as I stood between her and Liam.

"I'm so sorry." She laughed, covering her mouth with her hand. "It's just that my mom spoke so much about you. Now you're here, and it's so unreal."

I arched my brow. "So, you usually touch people you've never met before?"

Liam shifted next to me.

"Well ... no," she stammered, her gaze bouncing between Liam and me. "I'm sorry."

"It is fine. Dianna is just..." He paused. "Protective."

When I looked up at him and he met my gaze, his eyes softened as if he appreciated it.

Ava cleared her throat, and Liam seemed to remember where we were. He turned back to her, but took a step closer to me. "Your mother? Victoria? Where is she? I had hoped to see her today as well."

Her eyes gleamed as she reached behind her, fishing in her bag. I tensed and felt Liam go still. After being attacked almost everywhere we'd gone, we were more than a little on edge. But instead of a weapon, she pulled out glistening white-and-blue fabric. The material shimmered in a way that was not of this world. Liam stepped forward and touched it, his expression unreadable.

"She kept this with me. I guess my dad gave it to her for me, kind of like a baby blanket. She said you gave it to him before Rashearim fell." Her eyes filled with tears. "She passed a long time ago."

"I am truly sorry," Liam whispered, handing the dazzling blanket back to her. "Keep it. Maybe you can use it for your children one day."

She nodded before stuffing it back into her pack. She gestured toward the man behind her. "I'm sorry for my rudeness. This is Geraldo. He is my celestial guard. He has been with me for a really long time."

Geraldo gave a shallow bow, his eyes flashing a vibrant blue, his gaze never leaving me.

"Sorry, Geraldo doesn't speak much. Especially with her here."

"Excuse me?"

"Ig'Morruthen, right? I can feel your power. My mother told me they had eradicated your kind in the Gods War, but there is no denying your power. You practically vibrate with it. Plus, Camilla filled us in."

I felt Liam stiffen next to me. Well, there went our plan.

She tried to smile at me, but it looked more like she was scared. "I'm sorry. I wasn't trying to insult you."

"You have nothing to fear from Dianna, I promise you. She is my —" Liam paused, and I waited. I guess I hadn't thought about what we were now. Were we even a thing?

"Friend," I said, since Liam seemed to be tongue-tied at the moment. "I'm his friend."

Geraldo was still watching me, and I was sure he saw the hunger in my expression even though I tried to hide it. Uncomfortable, I looked up at Liam to see he was staring daggers into my soul.

Geraldo leaned forward, his accent thick. "But she is with Kaden, yes?"

"No." Liam's voice was a threatening growl.

"I am not *with* Kaden, nor do I belong to him." They looked at me with disbelief so profound that it bordered on amusement. "It's a long story."

"I'm sorry. That's just not what we'd heard," Ava said, glancing back at Geraldo.

"Well, it's the truth. Now, can we hurry this up? I'm getting eaten alive by insects," I said, slapping at one of the annoying beasts.

Liam gestured toward the jungle and said, "Very well."

We said nothing else as we headed toward the temple, Geraldo and Ava taking the lead. We stayed within the trees, surrounded by vines and bushes as the last of the tourists left. Liam grasped my arm and slowed his pace, letting Ava and Geraldo move a few paces ahead. He leaned over, his voice a hot whisper against my ear and low enough that no mortal could hear.

"'Friend'?" he hissed through gritted teeth.

"… What?" I asked, confused. I glanced at him, then toward Ava and Geraldo, who kept walking. Then it clicked: he was pissed about me calling him my friend earlier.

"That's *eight* ways now, because when we leave here, I'm going to fuck the word *friend* out of your vocabulary."

He let me go and strode ahead without giving me a chance to respond. I forgot how to breathe and just stood there watching him walk away, my core having gone molten with need. When my brain started functioning again, I had to nearly run to catch up to them.

Streamers of tape and warning signs in various colors cautioned people to keep out. They had blocked off a portion of the back part of the temple where rocks and rubble had fallen. There were no guards in sight. They probably had to clear out the guests before making a sweep this way.

"So, how did you and Liam become friends?" I felt Liam's glare at

Ava's question. I didn't look his way as we ducked under the tape and made our way to a doorway cut into the heavy stone. Gods, he hated that word. "I heard your kind is a 'kill first, ask questions later' type."

Ava and Geraldo pulled flashlights out of their packs, offering Liam and me our own. Liam took one, but I ignored it. I concentrated, and a bright flame burst to life, dancing on my palm.

The ruins in this section of the temple smelled of mold and stagnant water. Joy. With a sigh, I turned and headed down the stairs overgrown with moss and vines, one broken step at a time. "Oh, trust me, I can still kill."

Why did I find her so annoying? Was it because she'd hugged Liam? Was I that possessive? Maybe I was just hungry.

"She will not kill. Dianna, please try to be polite."

I made a face behind Liam's back, and Ava, who was walking next to me, snickered.

"My apologies, Ava. It's just that we know nothing about you. Actually, we didn't even know you existed until Liam stuck his tongue down a witch's throat."

We reached a carved stone wall, and Liam spun, shaking his head at me. "Dianna."

"What? It's true." I ignored him and patted his chest as I slipped by him.

"Umm, well," Ava said, her eyes wide.

"Oh, come on. Use your big girl words." Yup, she annoyed me, but something was off. I felt it. I knew it. My instincts were on high alert, telling me I had to protect Liam, but I didn't know why.

"It's a long story," Liam said, throwing another glare my way.

"If they have been in touch with Camilla, shouldn't they already know it?" I asked suspiciously. Geraldo's eyes flared with cobalt fire, earning him a smile from me. I knew he carried one of those ablaze weapons. They all did. My talons grew from the hand I held at my side. He noticed, and my smile grew. "Oh, please, tell me that's a threat."

Geraldo stepped forward, his silver rings vibrating on his fingers. Liam grabbed my arm, hauling me back.

"What is wrong with you?" His face held no humor. "I apologize. She is usually a little better-mannered." He glared at me. "Sometimes."

"Seriously? They show up, offer a little bit of information, and you believe them? You're not the least bit curious about how they have managed to hide this book? Why hasn't Kaden found it yet? Camilla hid them for how long? They're celestials, but never came to you or The Hand? Do you just trust them because they're celestials?"

I lifted a brow, the talons in my hand receding as I willed him not to dismiss me. Liam studied me for a moment before saying, "Regardless of Dianna's rash behavior, she does have a point. Where have you been, and why haven't either of you contacted the Guild?"

Ava looked at Geraldo. When he nodded, she took a deep breath and said, "The truth is, we have been in hiding. My mother insisted that we remain isolated. A friend of a friend met one of Camilla's associates a few months ago. That was how we learned of the uprising Camilla was a part of. Long story short, she doesn't want the book in Kaden's hands any more than we do. This isn't just any book." She looked at Liam, her gaze intense. "You knew my father, and you are familiar with the weapons and machines he designed. Azrael created a manual, so to speak. Inside this book, there are a thousand plus secrets from Rashearim. It was a contingency plan, made for the celestials should you ever turn. It holds the secrets to a lot of things—but most importantly, how to kill you."

"What?!" I stepped forward. "Liam can't die. He is immortal. Truly immortal."

"No, he's not." Ava looked at me, her eyes soft and kind. "He can. That's why Kaden wants it. It's a book to open realms and end worlds. And it all starts with his death." She nodded toward Liam.

Death?

I had never considered his death. He was larger than life, indomitable, and irreplaceable. He was their king, yet his people had made something to kill him.

"I would love to see anyone try." I turned, staring at Geraldo. "Now, *that's* a threat." And one I meant with every part of me. I didn't know why I was suddenly so protective and possessive of Liam, and I wasn't keen on examining my emotions too closely.

Liam squeezed my arm, drawing me back to him. I hadn't realized I had taken a step closer to them.

"I won't let that happen." My eyes met his, my words a vow.

He had said those words to me several times, and he'd always kept his promise. It was Liam—annoying, beautiful, rude Liam. He'd told me of his nightmares, his past. He'd made me stupid dresses and given me flowers. He'd saved my life and kept me from being dragged back to Kaden. He saw me—the real me—and didn't turn away. He had healed me. I didn't know when it had happened, but he was mine, and I would tear anyone who so much as touched him to pieces. I owed him that, at least.

A shadow of a smile crossed his lips. "I know."

"I'm sorry. I really am, but—"

"Save it. Your father made a book to kill someone he was supposed to protect. There's no excuse. Let's get this over with."

Ava nodded and shifted uncomfortably before we continued, heading deeper into the temple. I had finally realized what had been nipping at my heels.

Death.

The word hung in the air, and as the sun set, I felt it join us in the temple.

THE HOLLOW ETCHINGS OF THE SKULL'S EYES STARED BACK AT ME. MY flame illuminated it, making the shadows dance against the walls. The flashlights had died, and I had lit several wooden torches for Geraldo and Ava. Liam used his silver light to push back the darkness.

"Creepy-ass temple."

"This isn't even the main one." Ava's voice echoed behind me. I turned, the fire dancing in my palm. She leaned over her backpack, taking out what looked like a map. The paper was thick and bluish-gray in the torchlight. She unfolded it and spread it out on a large rock.

"See this? This is where we are. My mother had catacombs built throughout the lower parts of the temple, connecting them with several other nearby structures."

"Nearby?"

The light from the torch she had set between two crooked stones cast a glow over half her face, the rest of her lost in the darkened background. Geraldo hovered over her shoulder as Liam watched, arms folded.

"Yes. There are thousands of temples and structures in this jungle that have yet to be found by mortals. Most are too scared to venture too deep. It's easy to get lost and die from a venomous creature or succumb to starvation."

"So, where do we need to go?" Liam asked, jarring all of us. He had been quiet most of the trip, only speaking when Ava slipped on a smooth, wet stone, or when Geraldo almost got impaled by some ancient booby trap.

"Give me just a second." Her finger traced the path of several lines before stopping at a small square box.

"Why this temple, this place, though?"

Ava looked around the darkened room. "My mom loved this place, the country, and the people. She loved history and culture. When she landed here after the fall of Rashearim, she decided to stay. The language was easier for her to learn, since it was closer to that on Rashearim."

"That is true." Liam nodded.

She smiled before a touch of sadness crossed her features. "She just liked it here and thought my father would, too."

"But why the temple, though?"

"Victoria was highly skilled in architecture and combat. I would assume she helped build many structures here and wanted to stay close to the people she loved," Liam said.

Ava nodded in agreement. "You're correct. As I said, she loved it here. She fought in several rebellions, and when she died, she wanted to be buried next to the ones closest to her. I think she knew the book was too dangerous to leave unprotected, and she built many of these with that in mind. These catacombs are a maze of tunnels engulfed by a wild and primitive jungle. They're the perfect hiding place."

"If Dianna is finished with her questions, may I ask which way now?" Liam was on edge, and I suspected it had something to do with the part of the dream he wouldn't tell me about.

Ava stood, the map in her hand. She picked up the torch and pointed toward one dark tunnel. "That way."

None of us spoke as we headed down the corridor, this one damper than the previous one as part of the jungle tried to sneak its way in. Ava took one turn and then the next. We followed, walking for what felt like hours. We ducked beneath a thick canopy of spiderwebs and came around a corner to find our way blocked by a large stone mass.

"Great. We're lost," I said with an exasperated sigh.

Everyone turned toward me, their expressions less than amused. I shrugged and mouthed, *"What?"*

Liam shook his head before peering over Ava's shoulder. Her brows were drawn together in concentration. "No, this is the right way. I know it." Geraldo came closer to further illuminate the map she held. "See? The line runs right past this corridor."

I edged nearer, taking a closer look. She wasn't wrong; a thin line went right through that huge rock. Hmm. I brushed past Ava, studying the solid stone.

"What are you doing?"

I shushed Liam as I pressed my ear against the stone. I raised my knuckles, tapping against the solid barrier. Thick noises vibrated back as I moved along the wall, continuing to knock as I went. After a few feet, a hollow response echoed back. I jumped when the sound changed. I grinned and cried, "Found it!"

They all looked at me as if I had grown horns. I quickly ran my hands over my head, ensuring I hadn't before I asked, "Have you guys not watched any adventure movies? Hello! A mysterious wall that isn't a wall?"

Liam just looked at me like he thought I had gone crazy. I sighed. "It's a false door. A trick wall. It's literally in every adventure movie."

Realization dawned in their eyes as they caught on.

"I assume it was locked by celestial magic. So, come on, big guy. It's your turn," I said, waving Liam over.

He strode toward me, and I couldn't help my sigh of pleasure at watching him move. He stopped short of the door, giving me a once-over. I smirked, all cocky and arrogant. "You'd be lost without me. You can say it. You're welcome."

Liam's gaze flicked up in his version of rolling his eyes, but he said nothing as he turned and raised his hand. His lashes lowered, and when he raised them again, his eyes gleamed that ethereal silver. He pressed his palm to the wall, murmuring in a language I couldn't identify. Beautiful silver and blue symbols burst to life, etched deep into the stone. They formed a glowing hexagon, marks zigzagging inside and out. The wall shifted and slid back before moving to the side. The lack of sound was surprising. With the weight and age of it, my mind expected noise. Ava and Geraldo were behind us in a second, almost giddy at what we had found.

Liam glanced at me before ducking his head and stepping through the newly revealed doorway. I followed him, with Geraldo and Ava right behind me.

The sound of grinding stone was loud in the darkness as steps formed beneath Liam's feet. Flames lit the torches mounted on the walls in a single whoosh. The webs and vines draped from the ceiling waved in a mystic wind. I reached out and gripped the back of Liam's sleeve, making sure I wouldn't trip over my own feet. He looked back at me with an expression I couldn't read. Was he still mad about my whole "friend" comment?

"Look, you are the one making stairs appear out of thin air, okay? I just don't want to fall," I said. It was half true, but the wind rushing through here had also sent a chill up my spine. It was the same sensation I had felt at the festival, and the same chill I'd felt at Camilla's right before we'd been attacked.

We reached the end of the steps, only to find another dark tunnel. Twin torches shaped like metal claws lit the mouth of the tunnel, but the inside was midnight black. Several carved stone monsters lined the walls, their faces frozen mid-scream. I held my hand higher, casting the light in a larger sphere, illuminating more figures. They were creatures of battle, wearing the same armor I had seen in Liam's dreams. I swallowed. We were getting closer.

The sound of trickling water caught my attention, and I realized the ground had grown slick. The smell of stagnant water and mold assaulted my senses. I could see liquid seeping through sections of the stone wall. Great, my feet were going to smell like death. At least with my immune system, I wouldn't get sick.

"I always wondered just how deep this temple went. My mother would never let me venture this far down. She said it was forbidden. She used to set guards to watch over this place. You know, to keep mortals far away, but they're long gone now," Ava said, looking at her map and squinting.

I moved closer, making sure the flame in my hand stayed away from the old parchment.

"Thanks." She smiled before tracing the line on the map. "It should be up this way," she said, stepping into the black maw of the tunnel.

We had only been walking a few minutes when she skidded to a stop, the path ending in a hanging cliff. Pebbles skittered as they fell, the silence heavy until we heard them hit the water far below. I gulped, raising my hand over the edge, trying to see how far down it went.

"What do you think? A good eight to ten feet?" I asked, leaning a little further over. Liam grabbed me, not roughly, but just enough to steady me so I didn't fall over. I looked back at his hand, then his face.

"At least thirty feet," he said.

I peered back into the gaping hole. "Well, good thing we're all immortal."

"The way the rocks hit tells me it's deep enough. Maybe an underwater cavern, but we will not know until we go."

We both turned toward Ava and Geraldo. They nodded, and Ava tucked her map away.

"Shall we?" Liam gestured toward the open expanse.

"Ladies first." I grinned, and he rolled his eyes.

FORTY-THREE

DIANNA

The jump hadn't been the worst part. The worst part had been the blistering cold water at the bottom. After we crawled out of the pool, we dumped the water out of our boots and tried to dry off as much as we could before continuing. Ava's map was a wrinkled mess, the images blurry but still readable.

We slogged through about a mile of disgusting water, our feet submerged in gods knew what. I was getting frustrated with my clumsiness, and Liam didn't seem pleased either. My boots caught on roots, rocks, and cracks, but I managed not to break my neck.

None of us knew how long the tunnel was, and we were all growing irritable and tired. Hours had passed, if not a day; I couldn't tell. My heel caught on a rock, and my body lurched forward. I caught myself against the nearest wall, cursing and muttering as I pulled a stringy green mass from my boot and tossed it aside.

"I hate..." I slipped, catching myself as I pushed off the wall. "... the jungle."

Liam paused, waiting for me. "From what Ava showed us, it's only a little further."

I huffed and stood upright. "Pretty sure you said that an hour ago." I didn't tell him how much it had hurt, landing in that damned icy pool. I refused to acknowledge the phantom aches from the night before. The aches and pains and the sluggish healing were due to not eating like I was supposed to.

Ava and Geraldo stopped and looked back. Liam sighed and said, "Your healing is close to that of a god's. How are you not able to keep up?"

I threw my hands in the air. "Oh, I'm sorry! Were you almost ripped to pieces, dragged through the jungle by beasts, and then magically glued back together last night? No, I don't think so. I'm just still a little sore, okay? Give me a break." Plus, it hurt to keep up when every path we took was uneven or involved some obstacle.

I tried to stand up straighter, and my abs twinged in protest. I bit back a gasp and held my side for a second before dropping my hand.

His features darkened as he raked his gaze over me. "You didn't tell me that."

"Well, we were…" I paused, realizing Ava and Geraldo were staring at us. *"Busy."* I created another flame and forced my feet to move.

Super healing didn't matter when the ones ripping into me shared my blood. Sure, I had healed thanks to Liam, but I still felt tender and sore on the inside. I hadn't wanted to tell him last night; I hadn't wanted him to stop touching me.

Liam studied me, taking in my posture and expression. He allowed the sphere of energy in his hand to fizzle as he strode toward me, his boots echoing with each step.

I watched him come, his power preceding him and wrapping me in warmth. Before I realized what he intended, he lifted me. One arm cradled my back, and the other supported my legs.

The air whooshed out of me at his sudden hoist. "Liam, what are you doing?" I grunted.

"We have a bit further to go. You can't walk if you're not healing properly." Ava and Geraldo shared a look, but said nothing as Liam cradled me against his chest. I wrapped an arm around his broad shoulders, the ache in my legs and feet subsiding.

"Well, if I knew you'd carry me, I would have said something a lot sooner."

He snorted and brushed his lips against my forehead before turning with me in his arms. "How much further?"

Ava and Geraldo stared at us with identical expressions of aston-ishment. At Liam's question, Ava shook her head and said, "Oh, umm, just a little further."

Liam nodded before spinning around and heading down the path.

No one said anything as we trudged along. I kept my hands linked loosely at the back of his neck, my body singing in relief. Liam carried me for what felt like another hour. He never complained, seemed uncomfortable, or acted as if I were a burden. It was nice for a change.

The silence within our little group was deafening, but I didn't have the energy to come up with anything clever or sarcastic. Ava never spoke, only pointing out our next direction.

There was nothing to indicate that the next turn was any different from the thousands before. But as Ava led us up a small incline and around a corner, beams of sunlight spotlighted several fallen stone monuments. Everyone stopped and blinked, our eyes adjusting to the sudden light.

Liam gently set me on my feet and took my hand. I followed him, passing beneath a large pillar that had fallen against the oppo-site wall. We stopped when we saw the four stone coffins in the room beyond. They sat diagonal to each other and were elaborately engraved. The ceiling was high and came to a sharp point at the center of the crypt. Like every other place in the gods' forsaken temple, moss and vines covered the walls. I could see smaller rooms through open arched doorways, more coffins resting at their centers.

"Why would Victoria want to be buried so far from civilization?" I asked, slowly turning to take in the mausoleum. "And in such a damp, dingy place?"

"She didn't want to put the city she loved at risk. It was safer to hide the book and her remains far from the place she called home," Liam answered, stepping forward. "Which is Victoria's tomb, Ava?"

Ava shook her head. "I don't know. She didn't want to put me in danger by telling me. The only thing she left me was the map, and it ends here."

"Very well. Spread out and see what each of you can find." Liam inspected the first two coffins, and I checked the remaining ones.

They all looked like normal ancient coffins. The figures carved into the lids looked like soldiers, swords clenched in their stone hands.

Ava and Geraldo had split up, each taking a smaller room. I could see their torchlight forming shadows on the stone walls as they moved around. I cast my flame again and took the room furthest from the entrance.

A hiss greeted me as I entered the dark room. A snake, coiled and prepared to strike, danced at my feet. I lowered to my knees, carefully reaching out and grabbing it. It hissed and spat before settling, its long body wrapping around my arm.

"Hey, little guy, do you want to show me where the magical ancient book is?"

A beam of sunlight shone through a small hole in the ceiling, spot-lighting a coffin at the back. I moved closer and saw that, unlike the others, this one had a woman on the front. The snake in my hand seemed to recoil. Perfect. Animals always knew. I sat it down, watching it slither away before turning back to the coffin.

The woman's hands were crossed over her chest, the marble stunning and untouched. She had long, flowing hair, and her face was in perfect peaceful repose. Rings decorated her fingers, and the mark of Dhihsin was clear. Despite what the artist had carved into the stone, I could feel the sadness that lingered. My heart twisted, understanding a bit better now what it would mean to lose a mate. This was Azrael's wife. I leaned closer to get a better look, bracing my hand on the lid.

Pain seared through me, and I hissed, jerking back. The skin on my palm blistered and bubbled before healing over.

"Fuck!" I snapped.

I felt the rush of air behind me. "Dianna, what is wrong?" Liam caught sight of my healing hand and grabbed my wrist, pulling me closer. "You're hurt? How…" His words died as he noticed the coffin.

"I think I found her," I said. Liam looked at my already healed hand and pressed a kiss to my palm before releasing my wrist. My breath caught, and I curled my fingers into a fist as he circled the coffin.

Liam ran his hand over the lid, barely making contact. His eyes shimmered, the silver rings on his fingers glowing. I watched as tiny tongues of electricity sprang from his palm, flicking out to taste the stone. The coffin creaked and hissed, the carvings glowing with that cobalt blue that had become so familiar to me. He withdrew his hand, sweeping out his arm to push me behind him. The lid slid to one side, the sound of stone on stone nearly obscene in the silence.

I stood on my tiptoes, trying to see over Liam's shoulder. A clothed figure lay inside, its mummified hands crossed over its chest.

"It's not Victoria," I whispered.

Liam shook his head. "No, it's not. When celestials or gods die, the energy that makes us returns to where it came from. There is no body to bury. This must be one of her trusted subjects."

I stepped a little to his left as he peered further inside. In the tomb lay the remains of what could possibly be a man. The wear and tear of time had left a grayish hulk covered in a white shawl. Beads and jewels lined the neck, and it held a worn and tattered book in its hands. It was thick, at least a thousand pages, but was not made of any type of paper I had ever seen. Various symbols were engraved deeply into the brown leather cover, and silver latches held it closed.

The Book of Azrael.

We'd finally found it. Not only had we found it, but we'd found it before Kaden and Tobias.

Liam reached inside the crypt, carefully detangling the man's fingers from the book, whispering an apology as he lifted it from the tomb. Liam's eyes shone, and that beautiful smile flashed against the dark stubble that shadowed his jaw. I stared at him, stunned anew at his beauty, and knew I would do just about anything to see him truly happy. I didn't know how he had made it past my guard so quickly, but there was no doubt he had roused emotions in me that I thought I would never feel.

"We did it," he said, slamming his lips against mine. The kiss was short but blistering. He pulled back, and I grinned, nipping lightly at his chin. He tightened his arm around me, fitting my body to his.

"More like *you* did," I corrected. "I was mostly the hired muscle."

"No, we did it, Dianna. You're right. You have always been right. I could not have done this without you," he said, his eyes searching mine.

My chest suddenly felt tight. "I'm sure that thick skull of yours would have figured it out eventually."

"Always with the sassy quips." He grinned before kissing me quickly once more.

"Of course. Who else will keep you humble?"

I looked down at the book pressed between us. The energy coming off of it was nipping uncomfortably at my skin. I gently pushed myself out of his embrace. Liam, who seemed to notice everything about me, immediately transferred the book to his other arm. I finally understood what Kaden had meant when he said Alistair and I would know once we found it. I couldn't describe the feel of it, but we would have known.

"Damn, that thing packs a punch. I can feel the power coming off of it in waves." I shuddered.

He took a reluctant step back, trying to move it even further from me as if he were afraid it would hurt me. "Sorry. Look, let's get this back to the Guild. I'll need to call the others and inform them," he said, stepping in front of me to lead the way. "Besides, you need a shower. You smell absolutely terrible."

"Hey!" I yelled. "I'm sure you smell just as bad." I picked up my pace, following close behind as he left the room.

"At this point, I do not care. Although, I have smelled worse. Long battles with creatures whose secretions alone took days to wash off," Liam said, flashing me a wild grin.

"Okay, you have to quit smiling. You're starting to freak me out now," I said, side-eyeing him.

"What can I say? I am happy. We got the Book of Azrael. Anything that comes now, we can deal with. What's the worst that can happen?"

Liam flinched as I popped him on the shoulder with the back of my hand.

"Ow, what was that for?" he asked, rubbing his shoulder.

"Are you insane? You can't say that!" I hissed.

Liam shook his head, still grinning as he rubbed his arm with his free hand. "So forceful."

I smiled back, about to make a sassy comeback, when we heard footsteps coming our way. Our heads snapped up as Ava and Geraldo joined us in the main antechamber.

"You found it. That's it, isn't it?" Ava asked, stepping forward.

Liam lifted it in the air slightly. "Yes, and it seems your mother had a seal on the tomb, so only I could open it."

Geraldo nodded. Ava sighed, placing her hands on her hips as she smiled. "Well, that explains why we couldn't get it open the last few times we tried. I mean, we burned through a lot of celestials."

My eyes widened as her words clicked. "What did you say?"

Ava didn't move or respond. Her body was frozen in place, that sweet face of hers stuck in a permanent half smile. Geraldo's gaze stayed fixated on the book Liam held. We stood there like that for about half a second before I realized we were fucked. So fucked.

Liam must have felt the change in the air right before I did, because he went rigid. Ava's body jerked to one side, her arm bending at an ungodly angle as her neck rotated to the side, the bone beneath protruding. We were looking at how she had died.

Geraldo's body dropped, his spine misshapen and parts of his skin sluicing off, exposing the tissue beneath. Bite marks and gashes appeared, as if a wild animal had mauled him. He jerked up, both his and Ava's eyes wide open and a dull white. At that moment, I knew that what I had smelled earlier wasn't just disgusting stagnant water, but them. They had been dead and rotting this whole time.

I stepped back, grabbing Liam's arm as he stared in shock.

"We need to go. Now!" I snapped.

"What is this?"

"Death. And only one person has power over it."

Ava's and Geraldo's heads snapped back, their broken jaws opening obscenely wide. Only one creature had enough control over the dead to keep a celestial bound to their flesh, and I knew it was too late. A hollow howl echoed out of their throats, filling the mausoleum and calling their master forward.

The ghastly wail was piercing, and I covered my ears. Liam winced, and I saw the brief flash of silver as he slashed his blade through Geraldo's neck. His head bounced and rolled on the ground, but his body stayed upright.

I pulled on Liam's arm. "That won't work. They're already dead, and what's controlling them is only using them as a beacon."

My point was proven as that damned wail continued to pour from the stump of Geraldo's throat. For the first time since I'd met him, Liam seemed to be in shock. He called his blade back into one of the many rings that decorated his hand.

Ignoring what was left of Ava and Geraldo, I spun, looking for another way out. I knew what was coming, and it wasn't something we were ready to fight. I wasn't even fully healed.

The cracks that had allowed light through filled with several pounds of mud and rock as I dug at them. Talons replaced my nails as I searched, hoping for another secret door. We had to get out of here, and fast.

"Dianna, stop!" Liam snapped, pulling me from my search. "There isn't another way in or out. I told you that."

"We have to try!" I cried, yanking my arms back.

I could see the worry fill his eyes as he recognized the near terror in me. "What is coming, Dianna? Who is coming?"

The room suddenly went silent as Geraldo and Ava stopped wailing. I heard footsteps and a whistled soft melody coming down the hall. I spun toward the doorway as the sound of heavy boots hitting the ground drew closer. Liam stepped up beside me, and I swallowed, my gaze fastened on the doorway. The energy in the room changed, and the whistling stopped.

Tobias entered the mausoleum, his hands in his pockets as if he were out for an evening stroll. He wore a slim, dark jacket that wrapped at his waist, and matching pants. As he moved into the light, I realized that the dark color of his clothing was due to the blood soaking the fabric. He stopped and pulled his hands from his pockets. His eyes glowed as he began to pick the gore from his dark talons. He had killed and eaten every guard surrounding the entrance of the temple. I could smell it.

"Well, well, well, the bitch can do something right."

"Tobias," I sneered, stepping in front of Liam.

If I stood at just the right angle, he wouldn't see the book in Liam's left hand. We needed to get out of here before Kaden showed up. I could probably take Tobias on my own, but we would be seriously screwed if Kaden made a guest appearance.

"Samkiel. World Ender. Destroyer," Tobias taunted, staring at Liam. "A creature of so many names."

I could feel Liam's energy coming off him in waves, and I didn't need to look behind me to know his eyes were glowing. The last part of Tobias's words must have hit a nerve. What did Tobias know about him that I didn't?

"And what do they call you?" Liam asked, his voice edged with anger.

"Oh, I'm sorry, did Dianna not tell you who I am?" Tobias asked, putting his hand to his chest, acting offended. "I figured she would have, since... What did you say again?"

He lifted his hand, and Ava's corpse lurched upright, her voice repeating my words back. "I'm his friend." The words left Ava's cold lips in my voice, except the octave was gurgled and mangled. Tobias dropped his hand, and Ava's body fell, rotting on the floor.

"She was a good puppet," Tobias said as he watched Ava decay. "They both were—although they weren't going to last much longer, since you decided to take your sweet-ass time and jump into that blasted water. Dead flesh doesn't last long when wet," Tobias said, stepping close to one of the coffins. He swiped his fingers through the dust on the lid and rubbed it between his fingers.

"You have control over the dead," Liam said, a touch of surprise coloring his tone. "Necromancy has been forbidden for centuries."

"I'm not the only ancient being who has committed atrocities, God King," he said. "Does she know everything about you? Did you tell her about the Oblivion blade? Did you tell her how many of ours you've slaughtered with it? Did you tell her the truth—or did you guys just skip to the part where she opens her pretty legs?"

"Go fuck yourself, Tobias," I snarled, my talons digging into my palms.

"She is a monster, Samkiel, and one of the worst," he snapped back, an evil grin lifting his lips. "Don't let those bashful eyes and sweet smiles fool you. She has killed and relished in it. She didn't become Kaden's second just because she's good on her knees."

I felt Liam stiffen behind me, and for a moment, I was concerned about what he would think of me after hearing that comment. He knew what I would do for Gabby, but he didn't know just how blood-thirsty I could be. But my concern should be the Ig'Morruthen standing in front of our only exit, and the idea that he might get the book. It shouldn't matter that Liam and I hadn't shared everything about our pasts. I shouldn't care, but a part of me did.

"Oh, are you quiet now? Don't want your new boy toy to know how absolutely terrible you are? She is sweet, I know, but she is just like us, World Ender. No matter what those pretty lips murmur near your cock," Tobias said, walking over to another coffin. "You know I can smell you on each other? It's sickening. I can only imagine what Kaden will do once he learns of her betrayal. I wonder if he will make Gabby scream for you as he tears her limb from limb."

Something in me snapped, and I launched toward him at full speed. I barely heard Liam yell, "No!" I slammed Tobias against the wall hard enough that pieces of stone rained down on us.

I realized too late that he had been baiting me, and I had fallen for it. He grabbed my arms, twisting and flipping, changing our positions and driving me against the wall. Tobias's eyes glowed a bright red in the darkened room as he grabbed my throat, lifting me. His claws pierced my skin, my back scraping along the rock.

Where was Liam?! I couldn't see him past Tobias's shoulders, the room beyond in deep shadows. I wasn't usually the damsel-in-distress type, but I could have used a little help here while Tobias was distracted.

"You're weak, Dianna. Have you not been eating right? Less protein in your diet?" he asked. He smiled, and I saw his teeth grow to points. He cocked his head to the side and inhaled. "Oh, you haven't, have you? That's why you're not healing. Are you pretending to be mortal again? How well did that work for you the last time?"

Liam was behind Tobias in the next instant, his eyes a burning silver as he grabbed him by the shoulder. I felt Tobias's hand tighten around my throat, and then he was being tossed through the air. He flew through one of the internal walls and landed with a loud crash, the stone piling down on top of him.

"What did I teach you about emotions? Control, Dianna," Liam said, helping me up from my crouched position. I cradled my throat, my fingers sticky with blood.

"Yeah, I didn't really think that one through," I said, my voice raspy. I stood, leaning on Liam's arm. "Liam, he's stronger than me. He was out there feeding off the guards. We have to leave."

The low rumble from where Tobias had landed had us whipping our heads in that direction. He emerged from the murky darkness, wiping dust and pieces of stone off his clothes as if he hadn't just been slammed through a wall. He glared at us, straightening his jacket and regaining his composure. There was not a single scratch on him.

"Now, that was just rude." Tobias cracked his neck before stepping out of the rubble. "You asked me who I am, Samkiel." The timbre of Tobias's voice changed, making the walls vibrate, and I knew what was about to happen. "Allow me to show you."

Tobias's body cracked and bent as bony protrusions, thick and piercing, grew from his shoulders and elbows. His skin turned inky black with a red sheen, and his flawless features became more angular and sharper. Four horns sat atop his head, pointing toward the ceiling. His talons lengthened and curved, and sharp serrated teeth gleamed as he smiled at us.

The air grew heavy, Liam's power filling the room and pressing down on me. I glanced at him and saw unfiltered shock on his face. I wrapped my hand around his wrist, but he paid me no mind.

"Haldnunen," Liam whispered.

Tobias's smile was icy. "I have not heard my real name in eons, Samkiel."

"It's not possible." Liam's breath hitched. "You perished alongside my grandfather. I saw the texts, read them. I know them."

"Is that what your father told you?" Tobias clicked his tongue. "Your family is full of liars, Samkiel. Too bad you won't be around to figure that out."

Liam squared his shoulders as he glared at Tobias. "It does not matter who or what you are. It will take an army to detain me."

Tobias's laugh was cold and downright deadly. He stretched his arms out to the sides, squeezing his hands into fists. His talons dug into his palms, drawing fresh blood. He spoke in the ancient tongue of Ig'Morruthens. Blood welled between his fingers and dripped onto the floor. It sizzled, dark smoke swirling as it made contact with the stones. "Well, it's a good thing, Samkiel," he said, his voice deep and menacing, "that I have bodies to spare."

The mausoleum shook as the stone absorbed his blood. Liam and I watched in horror as the lids slowly slid off the coffins. Hollow wails and moans filled the crypt, the ground busting open beneath us as the dead rose.

FORTY-FOUR
DIANNA

P op!
My hand hit Liam's shoulder once more as we ran. "'It will take an army to contain me,'" I mocked. "You just had to use your giant ego, didn't you?"

Another *pop*.

"You did not tell me Tobias was a King of Yejedin," Liam snapped as we ran through a crumbling tunnel. The undead creatures wailed and charged after us.

"A what?" I panted as I reached behind us, throwing another fireball. Liam yanked me around a corner and pushed me against the wall, pressing his body over mine.

"The crown embedded in his skull," he said quietly after the dead passed us.

We were covered in dirt, debris, and gore after fighting our way out of the crypt.

"Well, I didn't know," I whispered. "I thought they were horns."

He looked at me like *I* had grown horns. "They are not horns. They are a crown. He is one of the Four Kings."

I gaped at him, my eyes going wide. "Four?"

Liam stared at me, his expression dazed as realization dawned. "It explains so much. Their power. Who Kaden is. Why they can hide from me. Dianna, they are older than even me! Centuries older." He reached up with one dirty hand, rubbing it frantically over his head before his eyes bored into mine. "That makes you a queen—a Queen of Yejedin! If he is one of the four, that's why he is so vicious, so territorial. Why he will do anything to get you back."

My stomach roiled at Liam's words, and I felt bile fill my throat. No, he couldn't be right. And yet my heart hammered in my chest.

"No. I am not Kaden's. I am not his queen."

Liam's breathing came in short pants as he looked at me. "We need to get back to the main room. I put the book back into the tomb when we first started fighting, and I do not wish to leave it there."

I swatted at his chest. Even covered in gods knew what, I could still see his scowl. "You mean the same room Tobias is still in?"

"Yes," he hissed, the sound barely a whisper. "I will kill Tobias while you get to it. The tomb is cracked enough that you will not hurt yourself."

He didn't give me an opportunity to argue, and I contemplated hitting him again as he crept closer to the opening of our hiding spot. Liam kept a hand against my stomach, holding me in place as he peeked around the corner. He nodded and took my hand, leading me back toward the coffin room at a run. I kept looking back, making sure the dead hadn't turned around. So far, we were in the clear.

As we got closer, I could hear stones clashing and Tobias yelling in frustration while he searched for the book.

We stopped at the edge of the massive door. Liam's eyes raked over me. "Remember what I taught you."

I nodded and called the flames, igniting my hands. I peeked into the room and saw the undead stumbling around.

"Queen or not, please be careful."

I met Liam's gaze, but could not decipher the emotion in his eyes. His thumb flicked over his ring as he called forth his armor. An ablaze weapon formed in his hand, this one much longer than the ones he had summoned before. He pressed his lips to mine in a hard, fast kiss before charging into the room, flying toward Tobias. I heard them grunt as they collided, and the mausoleum shook.

Fuck.

Okay, Dianna, he's distracted. Get the book!

I ran into the room, the falling debris cascading all around me. My body hit the wall as the undead rushed me, biting and scratching. I slammed my knee against the head of the closest one, crushing his skull into powder before incinerating several others. I used my foot to kick off the wall, propelling myself forward with enough force to decapitate a few more.

I landed in front of the room I needed. The sounds of feet rushing toward me and groans behind me told me the ones I hadn't hit were closing in. Dammit. I needed to find that book so we could get out of here. I ran inside and scanned the room, squinting as I elbowed one undead out of the way. He dropped his rusty ancient sword, and I grabbed it before he could recover.

The sound of stones falling made me look up. Tobias and Liam were having an aerial fistfight above us, the temple quaking every time one threw the other against the walls or ceiling. *Concentrate, Dianna.* He was still immortal—fully immortal. He would be fine. I spun, cutting down every dead creature that got too close as I searched the room.

The area was a complete mess. How the hell was I going to find Victoria's tomb now? I tossed a few scattered remains to the right side as another undead reached out to grab me. I thrust my blade through that one and then felt something jump on my back. Its skeletal arm reached around my throat, and I grabbed it, jumping up and slamming back onto the ground, crushing it beneath me. Before I had time to get to my feet, another undead reached for me. Its decaying nails grabbed the front of my shirt and lifted me. I maneuvered my arms beneath it, lifting them high and dropping my elbows, severing its bony arms. I grabbed the blade and stabbed the one crawling at me in the skull.

I looked down, noticing the arms dangling from my shirt. I ripped them off, a shudder of revulsion going through me. "Eww." I dropped them on the ground and stomped them into pieces.

Tobias screamed, and the room shook again, knocking me off my feet. I dropped my weapon as I fell and watched in dismay as it slipped through a crack and disappeared.

Tobias's power must have flickered, because the undead all stopped and grabbed at themselves, patting as if to make sure they were still in one piece.

I lifted up on my elbows and saw the familiar marble finish. I jumped up and ran toward it. Something slammed into me from behind, forcing me to the ground. My breath rushed out of me as I hit the cold floor face-first, the undead ripping and tearing at my back. Every time I tried to push myself up, more piled on top. I heard slashes against the concrete as the undead with weapons stabbed through their own, trying to gut me. I screamed as a sword tore into a still-healing wound.

The mausoleum shook hard this time, a narrow crevasse forming in the floor. It felt as if a huge piece of the temple had fallen, but what I heard next told me it was probably Tobias throwing Liam.

"You lost your blade, World Ender. You're distracted. Are you worried about her?" Tobias laughed coldly. "Did she get under your skin? Would you like me to cut her out?"

The floor cracked once more, shaking as if a convoy were speeding through. The air lit up with Liam's power, the strike disintegrating a few of the undead. Liam leaped back into the air, the force of him leaving the ground knocking several more of the creatures off me.

I dislodged the sword from my abdomen, my lip curling in a snarl as I stood back up. Three undead charged me. I gripped the sword by the hilt and spun the way Liam had shown me, using my upper body momentum to swing the weapon over my head and down, decapitating them with one smooth stroke. More came, and I cut them down, too. It was a dance I didn't know I knew. By my tenth kill, the ancient sword fractured, breaking off in the skull of one of the undead.

I had bought myself a slight reprieve, but it wouldn't last. I spun, looking for the marble coffin, but it was gone. Double fuck. Liam and Tobias's fighting wasn't helping; the temple shuddered and rained debris every time they hit a wall.

Liam flung Tobias through another part of the mausoleum, and I made my move. I raced toward Liam as he stalked after Tobias and grabbed his arm. His eyes were molten silver, hot with battle rage as he turned and glared at me through the small slit in his helmet. His gaze, combined with the debris and blood covering his armor, turned him terrifying. I nearly took a step back, but his features relaxed as soon as he saw my face. I pulled him to the farthest end of the crypt just as Tobias dug himself out.

Liam and I were pressed against a crumbling bit of stone wall. We had fought, but it made no difference. No matter how many I burned and kicked or how many he cut through, they kept coming. The cavern shook again as I heard them above us, beating their way inside. More of the undead were forcing their way through the entrance. I feared Tobias had summoned every buried mortal for miles. Dust fell as those not trying to tear us apart searched for the book.

"Where did you go, World Ender? I was just starting to have fun!" Tobias roared.

He ripped coffins from the ground, tossing them against the walls, causing more debris to shift and fall. If we didn't get ripped to pieces, we would soon be buried alive. At least thirty of the undead surrounded us. All were skeletal, draped in tattered clothes, decaying skin clinging to what was left of them. Others looked battle-worn, with limbs missing and helmets rusted from time. They carried weapons I could only assume had been buried with them, ranging from swords to rusty battle axes. I couldn't risk getting decapitated while they destroyed this building. We needed a new plan.

"How many dead are buried here?" I whispered to Liam as I peeked around the corner. Some of them tossed about debris in their search for us. I moved, pressing against the wall as I flexed my hand. Every muscle I had was screaming. I was weak, and I knew it.

"Too many. Far too many," Liam said as he turned from side to side, calculating our odds before looking at me, assessing my physical condition. He touched his ring, and his helmet disappeared, his sweat-drenched hair clinging to his head. "How much fight do you have left?"

I shook my head. "Not enough. Every time I think I have the upper hand, more show up. He's too strong. Alistair was the same. There was a reason Kaden kept us three close to him. The only difference was that they embraced their nature, whereas I didn't. I'm not that strong, Liam!"

His gaze did not waver. "Yes, you are."

Another loud crash had us both ducking. I moved quickly, crawling behind a half-destroyed column. I knew we were fucked, especially if Tobias was this king Liam thought he was. Tobias would have been enough of a challenge, but he had raised every corpse in the general vicinity, and we were outnumbered. I didn't know how we were going to keep him from getting the book. I knew Liam could use the ablaze weapon and finish Tobias off, but the dead army could easily overpower him if he were distracted by me. Liam wouldn't be able to help it, because he was nice and good and everything I wanted to be. I could only think of one option, and it wouldn't end well for me. A part of me hated it, but I knew what I had to do.

"Liam," I said, not caring if the dead or Tobias heard me, "you have to leave. You get to the book, you take it, and go. We are not both going to make it out of this temple alive."

"Yes we will."

"We're outnumbered and battered. I'm still not at a hundred percent after the jungle, and this cavern will fall eventually. We need that book." I paused, swallowing a growing lump in my throat. "You need the book. That's all that matters."

It was true, even if it hurt me. It was true.

His battle-weary eyes scanned mine. "No."

"There is no other way."

He gripped the silver blade tighter and leaned forward on his knees. "I'm working on it."

"Why not use the dark sword one, like before? It killed in seconds!"

His eyes narrowed. "I told you to close your eyes."

"You know I don't listen." I smiled softly, even as tears stung my eyes. I knew if this plan worked, Tobias would drag me back to Kaden, and I would never see him or my sister again.

He shook his head, turning back to the horde of dead crawling around. "I cannot use it here. The space is too small. It would not only eradicate everything here, but you as well. I will not risk it."

My point was proven. I sighed, knowing what was next. "I can distract him long enough for you to get the book and leave."

"No."

"Your favorite word—what a surprise. Listen, this was the plan all along. Above all else, you get the book. It's why we have a deal. Just take care of my sister. Please." I grabbed the collar of his breastplate and tugged him closer to me. His forehead touched mine as I closed my eyes, breathing in his scent once more. I wanted it engraved in my mind long after my body turned to ash. I wanted to remember every day I had spent with him, even back when we hated each other. My chest tightened, tears threatening to spill because I knew this was goodbye. "You promised."

He shook his head again. "No." He stated that one word, cutting off any reply I may have had. "I'm not leaving you."

I ran my hand over the sweat-drenched side of his face before I kissed him hard and quick. "Maybe in another life," I whispered against his lips.

I wasn't going to give him a choice. I jumped to my feet and tore off to the right. My hands scrabbled in the debris as I picked up an array of discarded bones and wrapped them in a discarded piece of cloth. I hoped Tobias was so driven by his need to have the book that he would be stupid enough to believe I had it.

I stopped at the entrance of the cavern. My eyes met Tobias's long enough to force a look of desperation as I gripped my ruse tighter in my arms. His nostrils flared, and I ran. Tobias roared as I fled. If he didn't bring the book or me back, things might not end well for him.

I held my slowly healing midsection as every head turned toward me. I heard Liam's curse, but he didn't follow. The undead let out a hollow scream and charged after me. I ran down the darkened tunnel, putting some distance between us before I stopped to throw a wall of fire behind me, lighting up the tunnel. The undead at the front ran through the flames and fell to pieces, but it wasn't enough. Those behind them just stomped over the corpses to take their place. I crouched and jumped, slamming through slabs of stone and landing on an upper level.

"Bad move," I hissed, the top of my head throbbing as a single trickle of blood ran down my forehead. My skull would heal, but it would do so slowly. I got to my feet and pushed forward. The space grew smaller, and I went to my hands and knees. I could hear the tapping of water up ahead, and I knew I had made it to an antechamber above where we'd started. I couldn't hear Tobias or Liam.

The sound of scratching had me looking back to see the undead scrambling after me, their decaying jaws opening and closing as they crawled. Fuck—they must have piled themselves on top of each other to reach me. I was moving to shoot another string of fire when the stone beneath me exploded. A clawed hand grabbed me by the midsection, yanking me through the hole.

"Where do you think you're going?"

He tossed me down, my body hitting the floor hard enough to knock the wind out of me. He was on me before I could react, ripping the cloth from my hands. Bones scattered, and my ruse broke.

"Tricked you," I whispered as his knee dug into my ribs. "You lose."

Hatred, pure and blinding, filled his crimson eyes as he grabbed me by the scraps of my shirt. "We'll see about that." Jagged teeth ripped into my throat, and I screamed as he sucked any remaining energy I had right out of me.

BLOOD POOLED IN MY MOUTH AS TOBIAS DRAGGED ME BACK INTO THE room by my hair. I clawed at his arms, but it was useless. He had drained me, and I knew what he was about to do.

"Oh, World Ender!" he called out in a sing-song voice, taunting and teasing. "I have something of yours."

The undead parted, their feet shuffling as they moved to the side. I couldn't see Liam, but the fighting had stopped as soon as Tobias walked in.

He dropped me for a split second, but before I could scramble away, he yanked me up by my mangled throat.

Tobias turned me to face Liam. Liam's armor disappeared, as if seeing me like this made him vulnerable in more ways than one. Tobias chuckled as his claws forced their way into my chest to squeeze my heart. I lurched forward at the intense pressure. The pain was overwhelming, but I couldn't scream. My lungs burned, as if the mere effort of taking in air was too much. I felt my power wane, and I grew dizzy. One squeeze, one movement, and I was dead.

"Tsk, tsk, not so fast, World Ender. Another step, and I rip her pretty little heart out," Tobias snarled. "And we both know even you won't be fast enough to save her."

I could see Liam in front of me. His expression was disastrous. He just needed to get the book and leave. Tobias wouldn't let me go, especially after what I had done to Alistair. If he didn't kill me here, he would take me to Kaden, who would do much worse.

"Just … go…" I managed to gargle out after grabbing Tobias's hand and getting his grip to loosen enough for me to speak.

I could see the calculation behind Liam's eyes as he looked between Tobias and me. He was formulating some plan; I just didn't know what. Idiot. There was no hope for me. There never had been. I just needed him to leave.

Tobias used his free hand to grab my jaw. "You hesitate over her?" He shook my head, and I winced. "Fucking pathetic. You have bathed in our blood for centuries, just like your father, and his father before him. Yet one pretty face, and suddenly you have a heart? I don't believe it."

"Let her go." The words weren't harsh or cruel. They were soft, spoken as if he knew Tobias would make him suffer if he said the wrong thing.

Oh, Liam, you fool. Why can't you just leave me?

Tobias chuckled, sensing it, too. "You know what? I have an idea. You could run that damned blade through us both. Come on, World Ender. It will save you so much time. Think about it: two Ig'Morruthens, one sword, and you get the book. You can make it look like an accident. No one will miss her anyway," Tobias teased, using his hand to shake my head at his last statement for effect.

A pained moan escaped me, causing Liam to flinch and take a step forward. Tobias had a point. If he killed us both, that would leave

AMBER V. NICOLE

Kaden alone with no book. Kaden would lose his muscle. His ranks were already divided and in shambles. Liam and his friends would be safe for a while. Yes, Liam would lose me, but the world would be safe. That had been the plan all along. Pain wracked me again, but this time it wasn't from Tobias's less-than-gentle ministrations.

"You can't do it, huh?" Tobias taunted. "Is that weakness I sense? After all these centuries, does the mighty, powerful destroyer finally have a weakness?"

"If I give you the book, will you let her go?" Liam asked, his voice barely audible.

I felt Tobias stiffen, a devilish grin pulling at his lips as his face came close to mine. "Yes."

"I have your word?" Liam asked.

"Yes, give me the book, and I will return sweet little Dianna back to you," Tobias said, annoyance edging into his voice.

No, he wouldn't. *Liam, do not be that dumb!* I tried to speak, but it just came out as a gargled gasp.

Liam's face twisted. "Very well. It's in the sealed coffin closest to you," Liam said, gesturing with his sword.

"I'm no fool. I know it's sealed so only you can open it," Tobias snapped. "You open it."

"I will," Liam said, holding a single hand up in defeat. "I just need to get over there."

Tobias looked from the coffin to Liam and back. He nodded, moving us both further to the side so Liam would have enough room to get the book without being close enough to strike. Liam's eyes never left mine as he slowly walked to the coffin. His hand brushed the side, and in one solid motion, he flung the lid across the room. He must have been gentle before, but with the way he sent it rocketing across the room, I knew he wasn't in the mood for games.

He reached inside, his gaze still focused on me, and grabbed the book. He waved it in the air and said, "Now let her go, and I'll give it to you."

I couldn't believe my eyes. Liam couldn't be serious. He wasn't. Everything we'd worked for, everything that had happened on the stupid trip here, and he would just hand it over? For me? No. He couldn't.

"Liam. Don't…" I wheezed, my words turning to a moan as Tobias gripped my heart tighter.

"Now, be a good God King and toss it over," Tobias urged.

"Not until you let her go," Liam said, motioning with his hand.

I saw Liam take a step forward. It was just an inch, but I knew he would do the unthinkable. He would try to save me, because he was good. He was everything that Tobias and I could never be.

No. Kaden couldn't get the book. My life wasn't a good trade-off for the world. I wasn't worth it. I mustered as much strength as I could and grabbed hold of Tobias's arm. Even that slight movement made me spit more blood, but I held Liam's gaze.

"You promised," I choked, nodding toward him. He knew what I meant: take care of Gabby. Deal or not, it was the one thing he'd promised me.

A look I had never witnessed on him crossed his features. It was the same emotion that Kaden had worn the day Zekiel died.

Fear.

I saw his eyes widen, the color fading to bright silver as he reached forward, a single word forming upon his lips.

I never heard it. Before he could give it voice, I yanked Tobias's hand out of my chest—along with my heart.

FORTY-FIVE

DIANNA

Darkness. That's all there was—yet my body felt warm and whole. I was held in a tight embrace as if I were wrapped in a lover's arms. I couldn't move, but I also didn't want to. Was this Asteraoth? Had I finally found peace?

The middle of my chest throbbed, erupting in a fierce and piercing pain, spreading through every part of my being. It was liquid heat, drenching me from the inside out. I tried to move, fight, kick, anything to get away from that horrible blinding agony. It felt as if someone had poured lava into the space where my heart was supposed to be. Had I not ripped my heart out? Was Tobias finishing the job? No, that was wrong, too; I'd felt Tobias rip into my chest and shred it. So then, where was I? What was happening to me?

"Come on. Come on..."

I heard someone pleading, a mix of sobbing and begging. My thoughts stopped as a warm liquid filled my throat. Ambrosia. That's the only way I could describe it. My whole being suddenly felt alive. It had to be the greatest thing I had ever tasted. My nerve endings tingled, sparking and firing with life. With every gulp, I gained more control of my limbs.

I wasn't dead. I wasn't even close to death. Not when I felt like this. The world came rushing back to me as I took another long pull. The sound of the wind, the birds, and a groan filled my ears. I gripped whatever the source was of this amazing elixir, holding it to my mouth greedily.

My eyes shot open, and my vision cleared. The stars slowly came into focus, along with the silhouette of a large figure crouched over me. All I could see was the pure silver of his eyes, and I realized the amazing thing I tasted was indeed blood—Liam's blood.

He knelt on one knee, the other foot flat on the ground, cradling me against him. My head was on his powerful thigh, and he had his wrist shoved in my mouth. My eyes were adjusting to the dark, and I could see the lines of pain on his face. The groan I had heard earlier was from him. In my need, I wasn't feeding gently. I took my teeth from his flesh and moved my head to the side.

"No." I reached up, trying to push him away.

"Dianna, I physically put your heart back into your chest with my bare hands," Liam snapped. "Now, drink!" He shoved his wrist back into my mouth, not giving me time to respond.

I bit again, gently this time, holding his wrist with both hands as the sweet flavor filled my mouth. I moaned as my body healed in places I hadn't realized I was hurt. Liam swallowed hard as I drew another mouthful out of him.

I knew what it felt like to be on the receiving end of a bite. There was venom in our fangs. Most mortals described the sensation as a warmth that sent shock waves to their core, akin to desire. It made it easier to feed if the person allowing it felt pleasure instead of just pain, and it could be intimate. It was a characteristic that we had passed down to the vampires and every blood-drinking creature. Evolution was a tricky bitch. We had to feed just like the lesser creatures we spawned, and blood carried life. It held the purest and most potent magic in the world. It was the only thing that determined the living from the truly dead.

"Easy," Liam murmured.

I looked up at him, my lips gentling as I swirled my tongue over the wounds I had made before moving his wrist away from my mouth. "That's enough. I'm fine now. Promise."

"Dianna—" He started to say something else, but I was already trying to stand up.

Liam grabbed my upper arm, helping me to my feet. I glanced at his wrist and saw he was healing, but slower than normal.

"Thank you." I paused, gesturing toward his wrist. "For that, and putting my heart back in my chest."

Liam looked at me, a shadow of a scowl tightening his features beneath the layer of dirt and grime. He gave me a curt nod, but I could see what looked like anger tightening his expression. I raked my eyes down his body, checking for wounds. Liam's clothes looked like they had gone through a shredder. He was covered in ashes, dried blood, and gore, his hair plastered to his skull with gods knew what. I didn't see any critical wounds on him, but the silver sheen I had grown accustomed to seeing on his skin was gone.

I looked down at my torn and tattered clothes. There was a hole in the front of the tank I was wearing, and it was covered in blood. I pulled the ruined material away from my body and could see the shiny raised flesh between my breasts where my heart had been ripped out. I lightly touched the spot, still tender from healing. Had he really put my heart back? I had to have been dead for a moment before he tried to feed me. He'd saved me. He always saved me.

The stars were bright in the open night sky above. We were in a grassy expanse, but I could hear the whisper of the breeze in the trees lining the edge of the field. A few feet away, there was a giant hole in the ground.

"What happened?" I asked.

"Which part, Dianna?"

Yeah, he was mad.

His hands flew to his hips. "The part where you did not hesitate to take your own life, or the part where Tobias secured the last existing relic of Azrael?"

I looked down for a second, pursing my lips. "I guess both?"

"It is not funny." He ran a hand over his face in weary frustration.

"I wasn't making a joke. I did what needed to be done. You were going to risk the book for me. I saw it, saw your hesitation. I know the face you make when you're calculating."

He took a step forward, and I noticed he swayed, even if he did not. "You had no idea what I was going to do and should not have attempted to discern my intentions. You've known me for mere minutes in the grand scheme of things and should not assume you know what I will or will not do."

"So, you weren't going to save me?" My brow ticked up as I folded my arms.

"Yes, I would have saved you and the book, but you gave me no choice. You chose *for* me."

I scoffed. "You wouldn't have, and Tobias would have gotten the book. I—"

"You do not know what I am capable of!"

It was the first time Liam had ever raised his voice at me, and I flinched. Not because he scared me, but because of what I heard in those words. Liam didn't yell at me as Kaden had, or degrade me as others did. He shouted, and his voice trembled with fear.

"Liam..."

"You gave me no choice! No choice. You let Tobias rip your heart out. He grabbed the book, and I flew through the collapsing temple with the remains of you. There's your recap."

"I did what I thought was right."

"For who?"

My head reeled back. "For you, for the world, for my sister. You and everyone have done nothing but preach about how important this damned book is."

"'Preach'? As if you have done a single thing during this entire fiasco but preach about our partnership! Yet you did not trust me enough to know I could have saved you *and* gotten hold of the book."

"I'm sorry, okay? Is that what you want to hear? I'm sorry, but I gave you the perfect opportunity for this to be done. Don't spin this around and make me the bad guy here. You're pissed, but I didn't ask you to save me. I gave my life so that you and everyone else would have theirs."

"And what of yours, Dianna? You always do this! You willingly try to throw yours away as if it means nothing. As if *you* mean nothing."

He stopped and turned away, as if he couldn't look at me. Pain stabbed me, but it was just for a moment, because he spun back and pointed at me. "You should have trusted me more, Dianna. After everything we have been through, why would you think I would ever let anything happen to you?"

I didn't say anything, because I honestly couldn't find words. It had never occurred to me Liam would try to bring me back, yet here I stood.

He looked around the destroyed terrain. "We have to leave now. I don't know how long it will take for Tobias to reach Kaden." He met my gaze, his eyes tired.

"It's dark enough that I can fly us out of here without us being seen."

He shook his head as he raised his hand, rubbing his temple. "Too risky, and you were just … dead." His voice cracked on the word.

I started to argue, but stopped when I saw him sway on his feet. "Liam. Are you okay?"

"Fine. I'm fine," Liam said, right before his eyes rolled up into his head, and he fell forward. I caught him, stumbling beneath his dead weight as I tried to keep him from hitting the ground face-first.

FORTY-SIX

DIANNA

"Where are you now?"

I turned away from the window, cradling the phone between my ear and shoulder. "Outside of Charoum. I tried to fly back, but the sun came up, and I doubt a winged beast carrying a man would go over great in the news. Plus, I'm tired."

I could hear the people in the room with her, the machines, and her shoes on the floor as she walked. "Is this because of what happened in El Donuma? The recent quakes have been all over the news. Logan and Neverra seem on edge, acting like the end of the world is near. They dropped me off at work and left. So, now I'm stuck with the regular celestial bodyguards, and everyone is being weird."

My hand went to my chest. I could feel the rhythmic beat beneath my skin. A single scar lay between my breasts now. I would notice, but it wasn't anything that others would pay attention to. It was just a small mark, but for me, it would always be a reminder of how far Liam was willing to go for me.

"Yeah, about that… Tobias showed up."

"What?" Gabby practically screamed before catching herself. I heard her apologize to someone next to her before she whispered,

"What? Are you okay? Well, I mean, I guess you are okay, since I'm talking to you. So, that's good. Is he dead?"

I turned toward the bed where Liam slept. His chest rose and fell, but it was slower than usual.

"No, but I was. I think. For a second, at least. I don't know—"

"What?! Wait—what does that mean, Dianna?" Gabby was screaming for real and didn't seem to care who heard.

I shook my head, rubbing my hand over my forehead. "It's a long story, but we were tricked into getting the book. Tobias showed up and raised every dead person he could in probably a three-mile radius. We fought, we lost, and Liam brought me back."

"'Back' as in resurrection? As in—"

I cut her off. "Shh, don't say it too loud. I don't think it's a good thing. Liam said necromancy is forbidden. That's what Tobias does, and it's all reanimated flesh, like in the zombie movies, you know? What Liam did was different. I mean, does it even count if I never turned to ash? Does that mean I didn't really die?" I sat by the window, watching the neighborhood children play.

Gabby was quiet for a while.

"Say something."

"I'm sorry. I'm just taken aback. That's a big deal, regardless of if you truly passed or not. You're saying Liam restored your heart, Dianna. The one thing you can't grow back." She paused again, which only drove my already erratic nerves insane. "How close have you two gotten on this trip, D?"

I turned back, glancing at my sleeping savior. "It's complicated."

"Dianna! You didn't," she all but gasped.

"Listen, it's different. Liam is different. Look, just let me explain when I get back, okay? Promise to not hate me until then."

"Fine, fine." She cleared her throat, then she lowered her voice. "So, that means Tobias has the book, then?"

"Yeah. Don't tell the others. Not yet. I feel like it's something that Liam needs to address."

"Of course." She grew quiet once more.

"Listen, I'll be fine. So don't worry. I'm probably going to try to sleep for a while and then head out once it's dark again. Hopefully,

Liam wakes up soon." I heard the noises on her end pick up. "I'll call you back later, okay?"

"Okay. Remember that I love you."

"Love you, too." I smiled into the phone before hanging up.

A soft knock tapped on the bedroom door, and the homeowner peered in. He was a nice-looking gentleman with a large family. I had compelled him to let us stay. Liam's blood let that small part of me work in overdrive. We were currently in one of their teenage sons' rooms.

"Everything all right, Miss Dianna?"

"Yes." I nodded and smiled. "You and your family should head out. Go to a nice dinner or a movie. Just get out of the house and live a little."

His eyes held a far-off glazed look for a moment. "You're right. A movie sounds great."

He left, closing the door behind him. I heard the commotion downstairs as the kids yelled in excitement. Footsteps ran up the stairs and then down as keys were grabbed. The front door opened and closed, leaving us in silence.

I crawled onto the bed with Liam, the two of us barely fitting. I draped myself over him, curling up against his side, making the small space work. Once we had gotten settled, I had showered and gotten Liam cleaned up as best I could. I had borrowed clothes for both of us, and they fit well enough. I slid my fingers through his hair, brushing back the dark waves threatening to curl toward his brow. He didn't move, his breathing slow and deep.

"Why did you do that?" I whispered—the same words I had whispered the first time he fed me his blood when he thought I had died.

I snuggled into him, wrapping my arm around his and placing my head on his chest. I closed my eyes, listening to the slow beat of his heart, the rhythm now matching my own.

MY BODY ACHED AS I STRETCHED ACROSS THE BED, MY ARM SHUFFLING through the covers, reaching for Liam—and coming up empty.

I was alone.

I sat upright and stopped. What the fuck? I looked around the room that did not belong to a teenage boy who loved sports and was living in the suburbs with his family. Drapes danced in the wind, swirling around the large bed frame. Furniture not of this world took up much of this chamber, birds chirping from the large open window. Oh no—was this another blooddream? My hand reached for the small scar on my chest, my fingers rubbing it through the fabric of my shirt.

Something crashed outside the room, and I jumped. I could hear the muffled sound of raised voices and pushed the drapes aside to pad across the cool floor. I didn't even bother with the large doors, just walking through the wall. It sounded like a lot of people were gathered, but for what? I walked down the massive corridor, taking in the art carved into the walls. It was as beautiful as the first time I'd seen it.

"The boy never listens!" I heard someone shout, shaking me from my admiration of my surroundings.

"The *boy* is standing in front of you." It sounded like Liam, and he was pissed.

I broke into a run, following the sound of continued shouting. I entered what reminded me of a cathedral and skidded to a halt. The ceiling was so high, I wondered how they had even hung the massive chandelier. It moved and danced, glowing with shades of blue, purple, and silver, reminding me of a small galaxy.

The guards flanking the doors held their weapons tight, and several hundred more stood against the walls inside. This place was huge. It was no wonder Liam had told Drake he had seen bigger when we had toured their mansion. Several guards turned in my direction, and I froze, thinking I could be seen. I relaxed when a few celestials passed through me, and I realized they were looking at them, not me.

Duh, Dianna, it's a memory.

I took a deep breath and stepped forward. Celestials gathered around a dais. A row of large chairs sat atop it, allowing whoever was sitting in them to see the entire room and everyone in it. The thrones were made of pure gold, and the legs were carved to depict different alien creatures.

There had to be at least twenty deities in attendance. Many of the gods and goddesses bore marks like Liam, with long, vein-like lines of light that seemed to coalesce in their eyes. The light on the others seemed to waft off of them in waves, not tied into their skin. They were beautiful, but in an alien way, too perfect, too defined. The celestials were watching intently, their blue-lined skin a contrast to that of the gods.

Instinctively, I moved closer to the far wall as I watched. I knew this was a dream, but every fiber in my being told me to run. I stayed by one of the empty chairs, grabbing the edge as I peered over. From this angle, I could see Liam. His hair was like it had been the last time I was here. The long, wild curls lay across his armor, held back by the twin braids on either side of his face and contained by small, bejeweled metal bands.

Whatever was happening, it must be after he had formed The Hand, because those I recognized were all wearing matching armor. Had they just come back from battle?

Logan moved past a few celestials to stand close to Liam. He held his head high and gripped the hilt of one of those ablaze weapons, ready to strike if needed.

I scanned the crowd and saw Vincent. He was at the back of the group, sitting to the side of the dais. He looked even more pissed than he usually did. Several claw marks marred his chest and arm, but he wasn't actively bleeding.

"You did not listen, Samkiel, and it nearly cost you several celestials. They are not made to be your toys, you insolent fool!" a woman snapped, and my head turned toward her. The goddess had long white hair, and silver rings completely covered her fingers. She wore a shimmering dress beneath her armor, light dancing off of her pauldrons every time she moved. The silver lines on her body pulsated with her anger as she pointed at Liam.

"It is done, is it not, Nismera?" Liam responded, wiping the blood off of his sword.

So, that was Nismera—the one who had made Vincent and hurt him, too, from what Liam had said.

"Yes, I am quite well," Vincent groaned.

Liam turned toward Vincent, waving his hand in his general direction. "See, he is fine."

The room erupted, everyone talking over each other. The door behind me opened, and several more guards entered, a handful of celestials following. Okay, full house it was, then. They were dressed in shiny armor, thicker than what Liam and his warriors wore. A bird with multiple wings was engraved on their breastplates.

The noise in the room died as they made their way to the dais and removed their helmets. One of the taller warriors tossed a large bleeding head at the feet of the gods, blood gathering around the neck like a reflective pool. It had two thick horns that curved back in a spiral. Emerald-green flecks of light gleamed beneath its scales, even in death. Its mouth gaped in four directions, exposing hooked teeth that glistened with venom.

"I bring the head of an Ig'Morruthen," a feminine voice said. "One of many Samkiel and his warriors bested in battle."

I knew they hunted Ig'Morruthens and everything in between, but seeing how easy it was for them to take the head off something that would give me nightmares shook me.

To my surprise, I recognized the warrior that had tossed the head: Imogen. She was strikingly beautiful, even covered in the blood of one of my own. She came to stand by Liam, greeting him with a kiss. I felt the pit of my stomach roll, and my eyes darted away. So, she was a leader, as well. *Great. That's perfect. Not jealous at all.*

"Lady Imogen, can you attest to the actions of Samkiel?"

I remembered that voice, and I recognized Liam's father in all his glowing glory, although an air of frustration surrounded him in this moment. He sat upon the center throne, one hand on his head as he rubbed his temple. I smirked. My Liam was more like his father than the younger version of himself had been.

"With all due respect, your grace, the task was completed," Imogen said with a slight bow.

Liam wore a smug look on his face and extended his arms out as if to say, "*See, I told you.*"

I rolled my eyes as the gods all burst into angry bickering, talking over each other and yelling. I sighed. It was pointless.

"So, you would rather the Hynrakk realm stay open while they ravaged and slaughtered countless?" Liam practically yelled to be heard.

Several of the gods turned toward him, the light around them pulsating. Even I knew nothing good happened when they strobed like that.

The god in the chair on the far right had been eyeing Liam with malice. He jumped from his throne and strode toward Liam, menace radiating off of him. He was tall and lean with angular features, his muscles rippling as he clenched his hands into fists. The circular gold blades strapped to his back glowed in response to his aggression.

"You are an arrogant and foolish boy!" he snapped, the floor rumbling as his power flexed.

I would give Liam credit: he didn't back down or look remotely shaken. He folded his arms and stood his ground, licking the inside of his lip. "A boy who did what you could not, Yzotl."

Yzotl raised his hand toward Liam, and a loud booming siren filled the hall. I covered my ears and crouched, the noise making my teeth clench. As soon as it started, it was over. When I looked back toward the thrones, Liam's father was on his feet. His staff was stuck in the floor between them, silver light dancing from the cracks it had created in the stone.

"Silence!" he said, his voice resonating with power. Every being in the room obeyed. "There shall be no more arguments from either party. What my son has done was arrogant, impulsive, and above all, selfish." He stopped, his gaze focused on Liam.

Liam shook his head in disgust, clearly not surprised that his father did not have his back. But I could also see his hurt. I wanted to reach out to him, but knew I couldn't.

The other gods nodded and murmured their agreement, but their expressions fell when he continued. "But nevertheless, the threat is eliminated. People are safe because of his actions. Where would we be if we chastised the means by which we keep others safe?"

"Typical," Nismera scoffed, standing from her throne. "It matters not what the boy does; you will always choose his side, consequences of his disobedience be damned. Seems repetitive, Unir."

Unir glared at Nismera, the glow in his eyes intensifying, but he made no move. Others seemed to agree with her, slowly nodding. She didn't say any more before she shot out of the room in a streak of light. Many others looked at Liam and Unir with disgust before leaving the room. I hadn't realized how bright they had made the area until just Unir remained. The room held a dim glow as he lifted the spear from the cracked floor, his eyes never leaving Liam.

"Your pride, egotism, and insolence will be the reason they will turn on you," Unir said with a shake of his head. "You cannot lead them, or anyone, if they don't respect you. Have I taught you nothing? Years of training, educating you, yet you resort to barbaric tactics. How can you ever hope to lead?"

"Father, I—" Liam started, but his father only held up his hand.

"I am ashamed of you. I had such high hopes, and now I am left to clean up your mess. Again."

He stared at Liam, but when Liam didn't say anything, he shook his head one more time and disappeared.

I started toward Liam, no longer caring that I was in a dream. My steps faltered when the ground began to shake.

I looked at my feet, the marble floor melting away to reveal a rocky, blood-stained expanse. Shouts from behind me had me ducking just in time as a golden beam of light sailed over my head. Screams and the sound of metal on metal filled my ears. It was the gods—and they were fighting each other.

The beasts the gods rode were massive. They had wicked talons on their feet, and their eyes glowed. At first, I thought their bodies were covered with fine hair, but looking closer, I saw tiny finger-feathers billowing on them in waves. They were beautiful, but also terrifying. One was coming right for me, and forgetting this was a dream, I ducked behind a large rock formation.

I watched as a god was run through with one of those engraved weapons. He collapsed, holding his midsection. He groaned once before the light dancing off of him exploded, a wave of energy rushing away from where he had been.

A terrifying roar shook the air as thick black clouds roiled over-head. Wings bigger than any I could ever conjure beat at the sky, fire pouring from the gaping maw. Ig'Morruthen. A chill ran up my spine, fear gripping me at what I could become. I didn't want to be a monster.

The ground rocked once more, and I saw another golden light shoot into the sky, followed by several blue ones. Kaden was right. The books were right. They *could* die.

Okay, I needed to wake up now. I turned around—and gasped. Liam stood right in front of me, blood dripping from his hair and armor as a long green-and-gold-lined cape billowed behind him. His gaze was focused on something behind me.

"Are you happy, Samkiel? This is what you wanted, yes?" Nismera said, her voice sultry even in this setting.

Liam spun his sword twice as he walked to my left, staring at the goddess. "I never wanted this." The weapon he held wasn't the dark one I had seen before, but an ablaze one.

"You're a fool if you think we would ever let you lead us." I turned as she came into view. Her armor was stained with blood, and she gripped a red blade, the gold hilt gleaming with jewels. "Look around you, Samkiel. You shall get the fame you so desperately crave. They will know you now for what you truly are: World Ender."

Liam rushed forward, slamming the blade down where Nismera had stood.

"Come on, World Ender. Summon your death blade. Show them who you are." Her smile dripped venom as she charged.

His strike went right through my incorporeal form and almost clipped her. "No."

"Coward." Nismera dodged just in time, bringing her blade up. Their weapons clashed, again and again, both skilled fighters. Every move the goddess made, Liam parried, and vice versa. More screams rang out as the ground shook again.

The sky flashed, and I knew another god had died. It must have distracted Liam long enough for Nismera to get the upper hand. She swiped her blade at Liam's legs. He tried to dodge, but it was too late. A long gash appeared on Liam's left calf, blood pouring from the deep wound. He yelled in pain and dropped to his knees. Nismera advanced, and Liam raised his sword to block her swing. Her blade cut through his sword at the hilt, slicing the palm of his hand.

"Did you really think you could best me, you cocky, ignorant fool? I am stronger than you."

Nismera kicked Liam square in the chest, and he tumbled backward. I tried to move forward to help, to do something, but it was like I no longer had control of my body.

She placed her thick, armored boot on his chest, her sharp heel sinking into his breastplate. She leaned forward and placed her sword at Liam's throat, blood pooling around the tip.

"You see, World Ender, this is your legacy. I hope that as the light bursts from your chest as you die, you know that all of this destruction is because of you."

Nismera raised the sword, and I could see she meant to drive it into Liam's throat. Then a bright light hit her chest, sending her flying back.

Unir lowered his spear, power sparking at the tip. He was wounded, blood covering his armor.

Liam struggled to his feet, his leg and neck bleeding. He half walked, half crawled to his father.

Finally able to move, I ran to them. I wanted to help, but my hands went through them both. Fuck.

Liam reached his father right as Unir half collapsed into his arms. Liam struggled to prop him up, pushing him back against the wall. Unir held his side, seeming surprised when he felt the blood.

"Father?" Liam said, his voice breaking as he looked at Unir.

Another bright light exploded nearby, and the ground shook again, causing them both to nearly fall. Unir made a disgruntled noise as he struggled to correct himself. I knew from the amount of blood he was losing that he didn't have much longer.

"You..." His voice was filled with pain. "I am truly sorry. I only wished to save you. All of you."

"Father." Liam shook his head, tears streaming down his face. I recognized that desperation. He knew his father's final moments were a breath away, and he was trying to keep from breaking.

The ground shook, and another burst of blue light erupted. I heard footsteps approaching and turned to look. Several celestials stood around us, wearing armor similar to Nismera's. They were not here to help.

"Father," Liam whispered, "do not leave me. Please, I am so sorry. I will listen better. I swear it. Please, Father, I cannot do this without you. I do not know what I am doing." His voice shook, uncaring of their increasing audience.

"Yes, you do. You always have." Unir struggled to force the words out.

Liam watched with dawning horror as his father's face started to glow.

"How precious. A dying father who cares for something other than his own sickening greed to rule."

The voice came from behind the other celestials. It was the God Yzotl. His armor was draped in blood from the top of his helmet to the tip of his blade. It shone silver and cobalt. It was the blood of their own.

Unir grabbed the spear, pushing Liam back as he shot to his feet with the last bit of strength he had. He spun it once over his head, sending a beam of golden light at the god. Yzotl bounced the beam from his sword, redirecting the power and sending the blast right back at Unir. It hit Unir dead center, creating a massive hole through his breastplate.

The world stopped for a split second as Liam's father looked at him and smiled, a single tear streaking his cheek. "I love you, Samkiel. Be better than us." Then cracks formed across his body, and he took one more breath before bursting into a thousand purple and yellow lights.

Liam's scream echoed over the battlefield. His howl of pain and rage vibrated through every inch of the falling Rashearim. My heart broke at the sound of his sorrow. I watched as Liam dropped his head into his hands, sobbing violently. More gods slammed to the ground, surrounding him. Liam didn't seem to notice, and if he did, he didn't care.

Yzotl stepped forward with a smile of pure hate on his face, stopping in front of Liam's kneeling form.

"So, this is our king? A sobbing child!" Yzotl shouted as the other gods laughed. "How pathetic." He reached down and gripped Liam by his hair. He yanked him up, forcing him to his feet. Hate and grief were etched into Liam's features.

Yzotl's smile turned to a shocked gasp just before his entire being turned into a thin sheet of ash.

Everyone stopped, unsure of what had just happened. Liam didn't move. He did not advance. He just stayed there with his head hung.

It didn't take long before another worked up the courage. He charged, and Liam spun on his good leg, stabbing the black-and-purple blade through his skull. Energy did not burst from him like it had with the others. His skin turned a deep black before disintegrating. More gods grew the courage to rush Liam, and each one met the same fate. He was so quick that I couldn't even tell he moved, until all that was left was ash and sand.

Liam didn't so much as hesitate as he grabbed the blade with both hands, flipping it once and driving it into the ground. Energy like I'd felt when I first met him shook the planet, spreading out in every direction. The power of the blade surged with a dull thud, the air forced out as if a bomb had gone off. Everything that wave touched burned to ash, leaving only Liam on a dusty, deserted battlefield. That was the last thing I saw before Rashearim exploded.

FORTY-SEVEN

LIAM

My eyes blinked open, and I nearly slammed them closed again. I raised my hand, shielding them from the sunlight streaming through the window. I looked around the unfamiliar room, trying to get my bearings. It was a small space, and I was confused by the shirts hanging on the white walls, each of them with a number printed on the fabric. I turned as Dianna moaned where she slept next to me.

Dianna.

She shifted restlessly in her sleep, and her eyebrows drew together. I reached over, holding my hand above her chest. The rhythmic beat of her heart was strong, and I almost wept in relief.

I peeked under the blanket covering me and saw that the clothes I wore were new and clean. She had moved us and taken care of me, too? I shook my head in disbelief. She claimed to be this dreadful beast, yet all she did was look out for others.

I was happy knowing she was alive, but upset that it had happened at all. My dream had come true, just as I had seen it. My eyes closed, the memory of watching her die replaying in my mind. I heard the words leave my lips as my vision blurred. It had been my night terror made real. I saw her eyes, saw the light leave as she yanked his hand out of her. His smile had been cruel and satisfied as I'd rushed to her, falling to my knees to catch her body before it hit the floor. I'd barely registered the whomping sound of his wings as he'd grabbed the book and took to the air. He'd left the crypt, and there had been a clash and a clatter as hundreds of dead fell. Then there was nothing. The world went completely silent without her.

My tears had refused to stop falling, and I hadn't understood that pain. I had not felt like that in centuries—not since my father died. I had cradled the empty shell that was Dianna, searching for the light in her gorgeous face. No longer would she laugh at the most inappropriate times. She wouldn't correct me over the most idiotic things.

She was gone, and I'd felt like a part of me was, too. I had known her for mere months, but in that short time, I had grown deeply attached to her. She'd helped me in my darkest moments, steadily pulling me from that deep-seated hatred I felt for myself. She'd helped me even when I'd been less than kind to her—and now she was gone.

I remembered grabbing her heart and placing it back in her chest. I remembered flying through that empty tomb with her and exploding into the night with her cradled in my arms. All I'd known was that I couldn't lose her—not without fighting for her. I had promised, and so I'd drawn a blade and sliced my palm to pour myself into her. She couldn't leave me like this. I'd concentrated on picturing her whole once more, laughing, happy, and sassy. I'd seen her smiling again. Didn't she understand how important she was? I knew I couldn't raise the dead or restore lost life, but I had to try.

I had promised her.

The flesh beneath my hand had started to mend from the inside out. Her body jolted as I'd forced more power into her. Veins, muscles, and tissue knitted as her heart regrew, restoring itself. It had jumped once, twice, and a third time before picking up a rhythmic beat. The tissue above that was next, her ribs and sternum mending. The muscles had filled back in, and her skin smoothed over, silky and unblemished. My body had ached as I'd poured more of my power into her. The light beneath my hand flickered, and I hadn't cared.

I pulled my hand back, making sure I did not touch her.

It had worked, but I worried what the cost would be.

I was careful not to wake her as I shifted out of bed and took a few steps to the door. I slipped out of the room and found myself in a hall-way. The walls were crowded with pictures of smiling mortals. Dianna must have taken over a home. I couldn't hear anyone else in the house and needed to hurry before the family returned.

I jogged down the stairs to the open living room. It was filled with the clutter of an active family and a large gray couch. I stood in the middle of the room and took a deep breath, closing my eyes. I concentrated on Logan, trying to summon a connection with him. The familiar tug was there, but then it stopped. Strange—that had never happened before. I tried again, but ran up against a wall that my power could not penetrate.

"Resurrection has a cost."

My father's voice echoed through my mind. Fuck. I clenched and unclenched my fingers. If I could not summon Logan the normal way, I would need to do it the mortal way.

I walked toward the well-lit kitchen, searching for a phone. I picked up the small black device and dialed the number Logan had forced me to memorize.

It rang once and was answered with a sharp, "Hello?"

"Logan. It's Liam. I need you to meet me somewhere. Only you."

I TOLD LOGAN EVERYTHING, THE SAME WAY I HAD DONE YEARS BEFORE on Rashearim. I told him about El Donuma in gritty detail. I told him of the fight, Dianna's death, her resurrection, and the new threat we faced.

"It has been eons since we have faced an actual threat. These weren't the usual soulless beasts I have encountered previously. No, this was much worse," I said as we sat in the large living room.

Logan's gaze searched mine before he pointed toward the ceiling and the room where Dianna still slept. "You did the unthinkable, Liam."

"I know."

"Even if she didn't truly die, resurrection is taboo. Forbidden. The horror stories we heard about the damage it could cause... It could have backfired, and you could have ended up an empty husk."

"I know." My voice came out a little harsher than I intended.

"Do you love her?"

I sighed and leaned my head back, resting it on the sofa. "Why does everyone keep asking me that?"

"Well, she is a very attractive female with a very persuasive vocabulary that some..." He paused as he raised a single brow. "... men who haven't had female attention in a while may find alluring." He made a noise in his throat, clearly uncomfortable.

"Does your wife care if you speak so fondly of other women?" I arched my eyebrow at his response.

"I... No... I'm talking about for you," Logan retorted, frustrated.

I said nothing, and he sighed, realizing my agitation.

"All I'm saying, Liam, is this isn't you. You wouldn't risk this for just any woman. I know you. That kind of power... You don't know the damage it could cause, and not just for you or her, but for the universe. They always spoke about a catalyst that unbalanced everything. You know that."

He was so wrong. If he knew what I had done to Rashearim, the gods there, he would think differently. He would know that I was completely aware of my destructive nature and how dangerous I was to everyone around me. I ran my hands roughly through my hair as I sat there. "I know."

I felt the weight of the couch shift next to me as Logan sat. "Thank you for telling me. I do miss the days when you would actually talk to me." He laughed, but I knew it was forced. "So, what's next?"

"Have you heard from the vampires I sent?"

Logan nodded his head. "Yes, they made their presence very known. Gabby likes the loud one a lot, and they seemed to bond over some stories I didn't care about."

I snorted, folding my arms, knowing Logan had the same disposition toward him as I. "That's Drake."

Logan shrugged. "Neverra is with them both. I think she spoke of coffee or something. I made a few other celestials go with them. Regardless of if Gabby likes them, I don't. I don't know what it is, but

I don't want to leave the girls alone with them for too long. And if what you said about the Four Kings still being alive is true, well then, they can't be trusted."

I turned my head, and a small smile formed. Logan's protectiveness toward Gabby would make Dianna happy. "Drake may be boisterous, but he is harmless. He is more of an annoying flirt."

A low growl ripped through Logan's chest. "If he flirts with Neverra, I'll rip him to pieces."

A small laugh coursed through me before I sighed, leaning forward and rubbing my head. "Yes. That is fair. I don't know. Something just feels off."

"A possible side effect, maybe?"

"Maybe … or maybe something else is stirring. It feels like I can't keep my head above water." I let out a long breath. "I need to get to the council. If Victoria brought any more of Azrael's scrolls or texts from Rashearim, I am hoping they will know of them."

"If you go to the council, Imogen, Cameron, and Xavier will bombard you the moment you set foot in the city."

"I know. That's why you are coming." I paused, rubbing my hand under my chin before looking toward the stairs. "… and Dianna."

His eyes widened. "How are you going to sneak an Ig'Morruthen past the council?"

"It's not an Ig'Morruthen; it's Dianna. She was mortal at one time. Have some respect."

Logan nodded, but I saw a glint in his eye. Was he testing me?

"My apologies," he said sincerely, a corner of his mouth lifting. A test, indeed.

I nodded, moving on. "With that being said, I do have a plan for that, too. To start, I need you to find us some clothing, so that we will fit in. I am too drained to summon any garbs at the moment."

"Done," Logan said without asking any further questions.

I stared at the ceiling, feeling as if I had missed something. "Something is wrong, Logan."

"We'll figure it out. If worse comes to worst, you have a queen on your side."

I snorted at his statement before dropping it. He was right. Dianna gave us a better chance, but just a slight one. She was powerful, but she refused her nature, which kept her at a disadvantage. Although, I might have had a solution for that, but it was not one I wished to share with him.

"You're right," I replied, Logan's look of shock nearly making me smile. "Their power far outmeasures any Otherworld creature. Even my father feared the Kings of Yejedin."

Logan sucked in a breath at my revelation. "What I don't get is how they got here? The realms and gates have been locked for so long that nothing with that much power should exist."

"I'm starting to think they have been here a lot longer than we thought. Moving behind the scenes, planning and waiting for ... something," I said.

"Waiting for what, though?" Logan asked.

"That is a very good question."

Logan stood and wiped his hands on his pants. "I will go get us something to wear and be right back."

"One more favor," I asked without getting up.

He stopped, turning slightly. "Yes?"

"I need you to distract Imogen."

"Oh, may the old gods protect me." He sighed before disappearing from the room in a flash of cobalt light.

The living room fell silent once more as I rubbed my hand over my face. I should have been faster and killed Tobias when I had the chance. I should have made my move and gotten to him before he got his hands on her. She had sacrificed herself for me, for the world, and I'd resurrected her without a second thought. My own father would not bring back my mother, the one person he had loved with every atom of his being. Yet I'd brought back a smart-mouthed, ill-tempered, caring woman. I was as selfish and weak as they claimed, because I hadn't brought her back for the world, or even for her. I brought her back because I didn't think I could exist without her.

"A god does not think of his own wants or needs, but of the needs of others, the ones he protects."

My father's words rang in my head. He was right then, and he was even more right now. Even Tobias had seen it, and he was correct when he'd said that Dianna had gotten under my skin. My minor curiosity with her had morphed into a deep caring and protectiveness that I could not control. It had cost me the Book of Azrael. But the most terrifying part was that a part of me didn't care. Dianna was worth it.

A scream echoed through the house, and I was on my feet and up the stairs before the echo of it had even faded. I burst through the door to find Dianna sitting up in bed, clutching her chest. She turned to me, her eyes wide and unmoving.

"You really are a World Ender."

FORTY-EIGHT

DIANNA

L iam's eyes narrowed, his brows furrowing as he stepped into
the room. I was on my feet and backing away before I registered what I was doing.

"Don't come any closer." I raised my hand, and he stopped.

"Dianna. It's me," he said, raising his hands as if I were the one to
fear. "Put the fire away, please."

I looked down to see I was holding twin flames. I hadn't felt it or
even known I'd summoned it.

"You destroyed Rashearim. That's why they call you World Ender.
It's not just some weird egotistical name. You obliterated an entire
planet with your sword. I saw it."

Liam's face dropped. He tensed, realizing there were no more
secrets between us, no more lies. I knew everything now. "Yes."

"You slaughtered hordes of Ig'Morruthens."

"Yes."

"Is that what you would have done to me in the beginning?"

His eyes searched mine, and I knew he would never lie to me. "If it
was necessary."

My heart hammered, instinct overriding logical thinking. The
beast inside me stirred for the first time, cautious of him. "Is it necessary now?"

"No." He shook his head, a look of pain etching into his features. "How could you ask me that?"

I clenched my hands, extinguishing the flames. "I saw your father die."

For the first time since he'd entered the room, he looked away from me. I saw the flash of torment before he composed his features and could look at me again.

"I saw the agony in your eyes and heard the scream that shook the world. That blade I saw—the same one you wielded the night you saved me." His hand fisted as my gaze focused on the silver-and-black ring. "I want to see it."

His eyes met mine, and he didn't say a word as he flicked his wrist, summoning the Oblivion blade. Black-and-purple smoke danced within the blade, and I could feel its power from across the room.

"It is Oblivion. The purest form of the ever after. I created it out of agony, grief, and regret after my mother died. Her death was close to my ascension. They say you must go in with a clear mind when you forge your weapon. I did not. Sorrow is a powerful emotion, and one gods cannot afford to feel, much less express. It is the same with love. It makes even the most powerful of us rash, erratic, and unpredictable." He spun the blade before it disappeared back into his dark ring. "My father's death broke me. It is why I left. Why I hid away, and why I was the man I was when you first met me. What you witnessed was the end of Rashearim. It was the end of my home. No one else living knows what occurred that day, and I would like to keep it that way."

I nodded, finally understanding. The tension in my shoulders eased. "That's what you see when you dream."

"Yes." He looked as if he wanted to say something else, but stopped himself.

"That's why you hate that name so much. It's a constant reminder of what you've lost."

He nodded slowly. "My father's staff, the one you saw. It helped shape planets and healed others. Unir was known throughout the cosmos as the World Bringer, and I, Samkiel, will forever be known as the World Ender."

My eyes softened as the fear that had gripped me when I woke released its hold. I had seen the fight and knew how they had treated him. A part of me felt compassion for him. I should have been scared, or at the very least cautious and suspicious. He and his had killed thousands of creatures just like me. Yet all I felt was sorrow.

I moved closer. His eyes raked over me hungrily, but I could see him bracing himself for my repudiation.

"Is that why you were so upset that I died? Because your father had given his life for you?"

Another curt nod. "Among a list of many, but yes, I do not want anyone else to die for me. I have grown tired of it, and I am not worth it, Dianna."

His eyes slid away from mine, disgust crossing his features. I knew it wasn't aimed at me, but at the painful memories I had dragged into the light.

"Liam. What are the consequences?" He sighed and rubbed his eyes with his thumb and forefinger. "I saw it in your memories. 'Resurrection has a cost.' What will ours be?"

"I do not know."

His eyes met mine again as a bright blue light lit up the room. I blinked as Logan appeared between us. Logan took a moment to take in his surroundings before looking at me, his eyes lingering on my chest. Sorrow darkened his eyes, and I realized he knew what had happened. He placed a pile of cream-colored fabrics on the bed and said to Liam, "I brought what you requested."

"Thank you, Logan."

"No problem." Logan smiled at me. "Well, are you ready to sneak into the council and pray to the gods we don't get caught?"

My eyes widened as I looked between the two of them. "Wait —what?"

"This is a terrible idea. Why do we have to sneak in again? You're in charge of everything. Just ask for the information," I whispered as Logan, Liam, and I hid behind a massive column.

"I cannot. If one or more knew Azrael had made a book that contained the information that could lead to my demise, and did not share that information, then there are people here who cannot be trusted," Liam whispered back, his breath tickling the hairs atop my head.

Fair point.

Logan turned toward me, wearing the tight black pantsuit that fit him like a glove. Rustic gold belts across his chest and shoulders formed a vest. A thin black shawl hung off his shoulders and moved with the wind. He had told me it was what The Hand wore when inside the council halls. "You guys got this. I'll distract Imogen and the other council members. Just play the part, and remember: the less talking, the better."

My eyes narrowed as I whispered back, "It's not my fault you guys gave me less than an hour to learn your language."

Several footsteps approached, echoing through the great hall. It was an opulent wide-open space sitting in the shadows of mountains that nearly pierced the sky. They were much larger and more majestic than anything I had ever seen. The trees in the surrounding forests were tall, the foliage lush, and the colors breathtaking. The ceiling was open and framed all the galaxy had to offer. Everything here was brighter, clearer, sharper. I wanted to admire it more, but we had a job to do.

"She's coming," Logan said to Liam, looking over my head. "I'll distract her as long as I can, but hurry."

Liam pressed his hand to the small of my back, and I leaned into the pressure. He had touched me at every opportunity since I'd awakened in that tiny room. It was not in the same fun way as before, but more as if he were afraid I would disappear if he wasn't touching me.

I watched Logan approach a small group of celestials. They parted as he joined them, and then I saw her. Her blonde hair was braided on the sides, and she wore a beautiful white dress. It was sheer, but not see-through. When she saw Logan, her eyes lit up, her smile adding a flush to her high cheekbones. She was even more gorgeous in person than in Liam's dreams. *Dammit.*

I memorized her form and called forth the power needed to change. A moment of concentration, and I looked just like her, clothes and all. I looked at Liam, who nodded his approval and ushered me around several more columns. Our soft-soled shoes whispered over the glossy floor.

Once we were out of sight, we picked up the pace, jogging through the maze of corridors and staircases. Despite our exertions, Liam's voice was steady as he said, "The third floor holds the council chambers. We just need to get past the few guards there, and we should be good. Logan double-checked that there are no meetings today."

As we hit the second floor, we stopped running; we strolled calmly so as not to draw attention. I waved at a few celestials as we passed, and Liam nodded in their direction. Their eyes almost bugged out of their heads as they saw us, which I assumed was because of Liam's new look. I don't think anyone here had seen him with short hair. Plus, the cream-colored shirt and pants ensemble made his skin seem to glow, the silver lines that traced the shape of his body shining through the thin fabric.

We passed through several rooms, weaving between thick columns as if we were in no hurry to reach our destination. Liam suddenly changed direction and pulled me into a passageway hidden behind a red-and-gold-trimmed curtain. I slammed against him, my nose bouncing painfully against his hard chest.

"Fuck," he said, holding the curtain back so he could peer out. He scanned the far side of the room as if he'd spotted someone.

"Liam, you cursed! Where does the 'follow all the rules' guy learn to talk like that?" I teased, poking my index finger against his chest.

"Probably from the dark-haired, foul-mouthed woman whose vocabulary screams indecency." He glanced down at me for a split second, a grin tugging at his lips before he went back to peering beyond the curtain. I turned, our bodies pressed so closely that I nearly groaned. I took a deep breath to gain some control and peered beneath his arm.

A tall, muscular, brown-skinned celestial in the same uniform that

Logan had worn smiled down at a woman in an off-white jumper. Okay, so he was a member of The Hand I hadn't met yet. Gods, why were they all so beautiful? His hair was dreaded and pulled back in a thick double ponytail that spilled down his powerful back. Blue lights ran along his arms and neck, arrowing toward his piercing eyes. His teeth flashed white as he laughed at something the woman said, and they turned to leave.

"He's a member of The Hand. Why are we hiding? Are you worried about him seeing us?"

Liam shook his head. "No, I'm not concerned about Xavier. I'm concerned about the one who rarely leaves his side."

We came out from behind the thick curtain as Liam nodded toward the large staircase.

"Why?"

Liam started to say something, but was tackled from the side. I heard the air leave his lungs, followed by a deep, resonant laugh. I spun, flames dancing on my palms. My eyes widened as I watched a blonde man lift Liam off the floor, his feet dangling. He picked him up effortlessly, as if they weren't the same size.

"Cameron. You will put me down if you value your job and your life."

Cameron. Zekiel had mentioned him in Ophanium. I remembered Liam saying something about him as well. I closed my hands into fists, snuffing out the flames and putting them behind my back.

Cameron dropped him, and Liam glared, adjusting the front of his shirt.

"Did you think you could sneak into the great halls, and I would not scent you?"

Scent? My lips turned up. Could he smell Liam through the entire building? Could he smell *me*? Uneasiness hit my gut. On the plus side, Liam and I had not had sex or anything even remotely close before we came here. On the downside, would my ruse even work on Cameron? I thought I might like this one, if it weren't for the fact that he might ruin what we were here to do.

He laughed once more, drawing my attention back to him. He wore the same clothes as Logan, but I already knew he was a part of

The Hand. His fair skin was flushed a shade of pink at his excitement in seeing Liam. His blonde hair was braided into a thick mohawk, the end reaching the middle of his back.

He turned toward me, taking his time as he looked me over. I froze, nervous that he had seen the fireballs I had threatened to throw at him, or smelled that I wasn't Imogen. His head tilted to the side as he glanced behind me. A slow, mischievous smile curved his lips. "Oh, I see. You all were playing another exciting round of 'hide the battle sword'?"

A thick, rich laugh came from behind me, and I looked over my shoulder to see that Xavier had returned.

"Cam, you speak too freely. One day, Samkiel will remove your head."

"No." Cameron smirked. "He likes me too much."

"Debatable," Liam said as he moved back to my side. "Where did you learn to speak like that? Onunian is not our predominant language."

Cameron shrugged. "Logan visits often. He fills us in on what the mortals have been up to and brings us the best cuisine. Chocolate is damn near orgasmic!"

"Ah," Liam said, grabbing my hand and turning toward the stairs. "Very well, then. Imogen and I have other business to attend to, and I am sure the two of you have something you need to be doing."

Cameron stepped in front of Liam and me, keeping us from moving. "Hmm, business. What business? I just saw her leaving with some members of the council, and Logan, who didn't even say hi. What's gotten into you guys? Imogen says that matters on Onuna are escalating. Logan has been visiting less. There have been secret council meetings, and your sudden return from your cave after centuries of being gone. The most surprising bit is this new look of yours. Is there something we should know?"

Liam and I froze, my mind spinning as I tried to formulate an excuse, but Liam beat me to it. "If there was, you would be alerted. Now, move."

"Touchy, touchy," Cameron said, and Xavier snickered quietly.

"Imogen, you usually make him a little bit nicer after your rendezvous. What happened? Losing your touch?"

Cameron strolled close to me, his hands clasped behind his back. He stopped, grinning from ear to ear. I felt my temperature rise as I clenched my fists, willing my fire to stay put. I had no claim on Liam, but their words rubbed me the wrong way. Would it be that simple, that normal, for him to fall back into his ex-lover's arms? Was that why he wished to go home so badly? My chest ached with thinking such thoughts.

"Losing my touch? Ridiculous. Why else do you think he came back?" I gave them my best Imogen grin. I tried to remember how she moved from my short glimpse of her and prayed that my attempt worked.

Xavier busted out laughing, and Cameron grinned at me. However, Liam was not amused.

"Enough." Liam tugged me toward the stairs. "We have more important things to attend to than your failed attempts at humor. Xavier, do not encourage him."

Xavier held up his hands. "Hey, I can only do so much."

Cameron winked at Xavier, which seemed to only make the fearsome warrior smile more. There was a history between the two. I could feel it. "Be nice, Samkiel. I was only joking. It's not like we see you—"

His words stopped, his smile fading as we walked past them. I didn't catch it at first, but then he was in front of me, and I knew he knew. He had seen or felt something that told him I wasn't who I said I was.

His blue eyes flared a shade brighter as he studied me. Liam went stiff at my side as Cameron took not one, but two sniffs at me. He scowled, all humor gone, and for the first time, I saw how perfectly dangerous he was. Xavier appeared at his side, staring at me like I'd grown horns.

"What is it?" Xavier asked, touching Cameron's arm.

It seemed to pull him from his death-stare trance. Could I really fight two members of The Hand if I had to escape? Sure, Liam was more open to the possibility of an Ig'Morruthen helping, but they were not.

Liam carefully stepped in front of me, his broad back blocking the others from sight. "Cameron." It was a demand, not a question.

"Your scent, Imogen. It's different." Cameron craned his neck to stare at me around Liam. "You smell like spices."

Xavier looked at me, narrowing his gaze. I had no idea what this obsession with scent was, but it apparently meant a lot to them both.

"I brought her some perfume," Liam said, causing Cameron to finally take his eyes off me.

Just like that, a switch flipped. That fun-loving grin came back, and I could breathe again.

"Oh, well, that makes sense." Cameron shrugged, and Xavier relaxed. "At least he finally listened to your messages. All that pining and unrequited love was getting on my nerves."

Liam was done as he pulled me past them, heading towards the stairs. "Your job will be terminated by the end of the day," he called over his shoulder as we took the steps two at a time.

I heard Cameron whisper to Xavier, "Wait—he is kidding, right?"

"Yes, yes, although you seem to love to antagonize him."

"It is a gift and a curse."

I saw Liam roll his eyes, and I smiled, knowing he had picked up the gesture from me. "Both of you go do something productive for once. Now," I called out.

Liam turned to me, his face a mix of shock and amusement.

"Hey, Logan told me to play my part," I whispered.

Xavier and Cameron snickered, and I turned to grin at them. They were staring after us, Cameron leaning against Xavier. Regardless of their seemingly sweet natures, I could feel the power that radiated from them. They were focused on me, and I swore they saw straight through my illusion. I gulped, the hairs on my arms standing.

It terrified me.

FORTY-NINE

DIANNA

"What's with Cameron and that weird smelling thing?" Liam came around the corner carrying a few books before placing them on the table. "Cameron's senses are heightened, even for us. It is a small gift from the god that molded him, and another reason he was let go from that rank and fell under my leadership."

"So, he's pretty much an excellent tracker. Good to know," I said, turning away from the balcony and the view of the mountains. "So, what do you have here on the Kings of Yejedin?"

"Everything," Liam said, shuffling through the pile of scrolls and papers he had pulled from the massive stacks that surrounded us. I had seen libraries before, but this—this was something else. The shelves reached to the ceiling and wrapped around the room. Stairs made of the same red and gold I had seen in his dreams led to the upper levels, and walkways crisscrossed overhead.

He was studying a book, pacing as he read. He waved his free hand, calling forth more scrolls and papers. They added themselves to the stacks on the large stone table in the center of the room. I smiled at his careless use of his power. I loved looking at Liam, so I was surprised when my gaze kept being pulled to the view outside the balcony. It was as if I were being drawn to it.

"Your mountains and trees glow with a color I'm not sure I have ever seen before. They seem almost iridescent. It really is gorgeous here. I wish I could see more, especially at night."

"I'll escort you back another time," he said absently.

I was a bit annoyed that he said it so casually. This place was special, sacred. I could feel it in the pulse of the planet and smell it in the air. But he just so casually offered to bring me back here for a visit, as if he brought monsters and the mortal enemy of these people here all the time.

"Oh, yeah? How are you going to do that when I'm locked up? Are you planning on kidnapping me once this is done?" I never forgot about what could happen at the end of our arrangement.

He placed the book down on the table, running his finger along a section while reaching for another scroll. "Well, Kaden has the book now, so we will probably be at this longer than expected. I suspect we will be back here more often than not."

I walked over to the table, worrying my lip and suddenly unsure of myself. Shock and hope warred within me. I didn't belong here, but the wild beauty of this place called to me, and I ached to explore it with him. My voice was low and hesitant, but I forced the words out. "I would love to see the stars from here. I want to know if it's just as pretty as in your dreams."

Liam lifted his gaze from the book and regarded me. "It will be done."

Liam didn't seem to be in a joking mood, and I didn't blame him. He returned his attention to his research as I sat in one of the large hand-carved chairs. I pulled one of the books closer and opened it. The pages felt rough against my fingertips, and the brown-tinted paper seemed sturdy and impervious to the effects of aging. The book was pristine, but I could feel the weight of its age. I couldn't read the text; I was only able to make out one or two words. Instead, I flipped through, looking at the pictures. Not seeing anything of interest, I set that one down before grabbing another.

"So, do I get my own estate or something if I'm queen?" I asked into the quiet, not realizing I had intended to ask the question.

He glanced up, furrows of concentration between his eyebrows. "I am not sure. I would assume you would be half ruler of the Yejedin realm," he said, sinking into a chair.

"Cool. I get my own realm." My nerves were shot, and unease hit my gut once more. "Does this make us actual enemies now?"

Liam's eyes softened, as if he knew why I was asking. "No. You'd still have to best me."

I gave him a small smile before picking up a large beige book. The wear and tear on the pages made it seem ancient. I flipped it open, and a picture of a large beast greeted me. It was drawn in gray ink, the image somehow raised off the page. I ran my fingers over it, tracing the lines. The creature's body was covered in armored scales, and it had no limbs. A flowing fanned tail looked almost delicate against its otherwise bulky shape. Its mouth was agape, displaying hooked, razor-sharp teeth. The words written below the drawing were foreign to me, but one stood out: *Ig'Morruthen.*

"Is this what I am?" The words left my lips on a whisper.

I heard Liam approach, the heat of him warming my suddenly cold body as he stopped behind me. I flipped through several more pages of different beasts drawn in painstaking detail. My heart sank with each new image. Some had more teeth or claws, and others had long tentacles, while others had no facial features at all.

Liam reached from behind me, grabbing the book. I looked at him over my shoulder. He closed it with one hand, his features turning soft. "In a way, yes. That is what you came from. But you are not the same, Dianna."

"Do you think I will grow horns like that? That crown thing? What if it makes my forehead permanently big?"

His smile was gentle as he ran a hand across my forehead, his fingers gently combing my hair from my face. "It is already large. I doubt anyone would notice."

I grabbed another book and swatted at him. He chuckled low in his throat and backed away. I held the ancient tome like a weapon as I glared at him. "I'm being serious."

He gripped the book but didn't pull it away as he stepped in close again. "I am unsure of what you could be, if I am being a hundred percent honest. You surprise me and are unlike anything I have ever experienced. So, to answer your question, I do not know."

"That was nice." A small smile formed on my lips. "Sort of."

"I'm a nice guy." He smiled back.

"In the bedroom maybe, but outside of it, not so much," I teased, playfully swatting at him again.

He dodged my attempt before releasing the book, his hand brushing over my hair once more before he stepped away. I noticed he kept the one with all the drawings. "Focus, Dianna."

I looked through the new book I held to find it was about weapons. My mind still gnawed at the images of the fabled beasts, but I pushed them aside. I propped my chin on my fist as I turned through the pages.

Liam returned to pacing as he closed and picked up yet another book. "Most of these records have dates listing artifacts made, items long lost, or those locked away by my father. I am having a hard time pinpointing the last known files of Azrael, which is peculiar."

"They probably destroyed them," I said nonchalantly, resting my cheek on my hand. I flipped another page, this one showing me a cool sword-chain weapon. "The ones who knew about it. I mean, why make a god-killing weapon and then keep records of it on a planet where a god lives?" I said, looking at him over the book.

Liam had stopped and was staring at me. My eyes widened as he went rigid, and a smile formed on his face. "Dianna. Your intelligence is terrifying at times."

"Thanks, I guess."

He looked toward the open sky behind me and then to the door. "How do you feel about vortexes?"

"Come again?" I asked, closing the book and pursing my lips.

MY SCREAMS EVENTUALLY DIED IN MY THROAT AS WE LANDED SOFTLY ON a thick, rippling black mass. I pushed off Liam as I turned away from him. Unable to stand upright, I bent over, placing my hands on my knees.

"Never..." I paused as I felt my stomach lurch. "...do that again."

"I apologize, but I did warn you it would be quite a trip."

I spun on him and quickly covered my mouth with my hand, trying to keep my last meal where it belonged. It took a moment, but when I was sure I wasn't going to pass out, I said, "Yeah, a trip, like a short one. I felt like we'd been shot from the world's largest catapult and then slammed to a full stop."

He studied me, the silver lines on his skin pulsating. "Are you all right?"

I nodded once as I placed my hands on my hips. "Yes. No. Maybe. Just give me a minute, so I don't vomit."

His face held concern, but when the thick black mass above us rippled, it had his full attention. It looked like we stood on the edge of the universe. Purple, gold, and silver stars flashed across the velvety expanse.

"What is this place?"

"The creature we meet today is the last of its kind. Its species played a huge role in the mythologies of thousands of civilizations. They were known as fates, hunted and slaughtered because beings across all realms feared their powers. My father made a home for the last one here. I am the only one who has access to this place because I had no use for him and no reason to harm him. As you recall from my memories, my attention lay elsewhere."

I spun in a slow circle as I tried to process the alien landscape.

"Roccurrem, I seek your counsel." Liam's voice echoed off the empty space before dying. I reached out, grabbing Liam's arm as several small star-like masses passed overhead. He looked down at my hand and then back at me. "You are safe."

"Yeah, sure. Whatever you say."

The expanse of black seemed to grow at one edge as all light rushed toward it. A silent pop echoed, and a creature stepped out. It had form, but not. Three black orbs spun where its head should be, and it had no legs nor any definition to his lower body. Its shape was nebulous, swirling and bending. Lights danced and floated around it as if it were made from the fabric of the universe. As it glided toward us, my instincts blared a warning. There was something off about this being.

"Samkiel, God King, World Ender, you seek guidance on information you have already obtained." When it spoke, its voice whispered from every direction. The sound floated around the room and through me, going in one ear and out the other. I shuddered. Creepy was an understatement. "And you bring a creature whose livelihood is death."

"She is not a creature, and she is friendly." He stopped and glanced at me over his shoulder. "Sometimes."

My grip tightened on his arm, and Liam pressed on. "I need to know what was in the Book of Azrael."

"You know already."

"If there is a weapon made to kill me, why do we have no archives of it? Why is there no mention?"

"One whose blood runs silver took what you seek long ago."

"A god?"

"Yes."

Liam's brows furrowed. The floating, weird genie thing seemed to be speaking in riddles, confusing me more.

"There are no gods left," Liam said. "Even if one had erased the archives, there would be a trace. Azrael died on Rashearim long before I destroyed it. How did Victoria even get her hands on it without dying, too?"

"Secrets are long buried in your family, World Ender. Long before your creation. The celestial of death had a master—a master who foretold of the great demise. The texts you seek were written and hidden to maintain balance, for if the realms bleed, chaos will return."

"Because of her resurrection?" I watched his throat bob as he spoke.

Those floating heads danced to the right and then back, spinning toward the left. "No."

"Does her resurrection..." Liam stopped, pain spreading across his face. "Is she okay?"

I hadn't realized he was that worried about my return. It surprised me that he would ask this creature about me instead of focusing on the book. I squeezed his arm lightly as the creature in front of us spoke.

"You worry about an abomination soaked in death. How interesting."

"She is not an abomination," Liam seethed.

"She is, and cannot die by normal means. You resurrected nothing."

It was my turn to speak up. "So, I'm not going to be a weird, decaying zombie or anything?"

The heads swiveled to the right and then left, as if confused by my question. The floating mass around it expanded slightly before returning to normal. "You are Ig'Morruthen, a creature made for destruction. You are an agent of death, despair, fire, and chaos. The ancient ones before you made worlds shudder, made gods tremble, and Primordials ashamed of their creation. You are a beast of legend, yet you wear a suit of flesh and tissue."

That seemed to enrage Liam. He stepped forward, and I tightened my grip, stopping him from moving further from me. "She is not a *creature*, and if you speak to her like that again, there will be no more fates left in this universe or the next."

Roccurrem's head swiveled and stopped, as if he were as shocked as I was. "Very interesting, indeed."

I shrugged, squeezing Liam's arm once more.

"Ignore him. He gets cranky when he doesn't eat." Liam smiled and looked at me with frustrated amusement.

I patted his arm and said, "How do we find out what's in the book?"

"You will know soon enough."

"How are the Kings of Yejedin still alive? How did they make it past the seals on the realms after the Gods War?" I could feel Liam's frustration and hear it in his voice. Roccurrem spoke in riddles, and Liam was in no mood to be denied the answers he sought.

"Your family is full of secrets, Samkiel. Secrets that far outstretch this world."

"What?"

The swirling mass around it seemed to shine brighter before dimming. "You are the key that connects the ones seeking revenge. There must always be a Guardian. Unir perceived the end, knew the consequences, and took action. Realms were locked—and your death will open them all. It is foretold. Chaos will return, and chaos will reign. You have seen a fraction of it."

Liam went rigid, a shuddering breath escaping him.

"Seen it? How has he seen it?" My eyes darted between them. "Are you talking about the nightmares?"

"He sees as his father and his father before him did. Distorted as it may be, it still rings true. The realms will open again."

"But if they open, that means Liam will die."

"So it is written; so it shall be."

"No." I looked up at Liam, his gaze focused and far away. Whatever floating-head-guy meant, it had struck a chord deep within him. My hands tightened enough to make him look at me. Pain flashed there. "As long as I am here, nothing will happen to you. I *promise*—and I don't need a pinkie for it."

The smile he forced was barely recognizable. I turned back to Roccurrem. "Can you give us some good news or something?"

One head seemed to look at me as the others continued to spin. I immediately regretted opening my mouth.

"The prophecy remains. One falls, one rises, and the end begins. It was foretold and will remain. One carved from darkness, one carved from light. The world will shudder."

I felt the room quake as Liam's power seeped from him. "Was this all part of another godsdamned test?"

"A test indeed, but to solidify the realms. That is how it is, and how it shall be. The universe needed to see, needed to know."

"Needed to know what?"

The room shook once more, and the floating heads spun counterclockwise and then back. "You are running out of time, Samkiel."

I let go of Liam's arm as I stepped forward, no longer concerned about this swirling creature that spoke in tongues. "Is that what you do in this mythical land? Speak in riddles the entire time? How are you any help?"

"Dianna." Liam's voice was but a whisper. The anguish that shone behind his silver eyes made me want to tear the world apart.

"You don't know everything," I said, my anger rising.

"It seems the King of Gods has found a new home." The creature's form shifted. One head swiveled, speaking to me as the other two agreed in unison.

"That doesn't make sense either. You know his world is destroyed, you floating ass!" I snapped. I took Liam's hand. "Let's go. There is no help to be found here." I was over this place and over that creature.

Roccurrem's voice echoed once more off the empty space, everywhere and nowhere at once. "There will be a shuddering crack, an echo of what is lost and what cannot be healed. Then, Samkiel, you will know this is how the world ends."

I stopped and slowly turned around. I knew my eyes glowed red, and I was ready to throw as many fireballs as it took to make it shut up. But it was too late. The creature said no more as it melted into shadows, its body returning to the backdrop of the galaxy, the weight of its presence fading away.

THE LIBRARY RUSHED AT US AS WE PORTALED IN. PAGES FROM THE OPEN books we'd left behind fluttered from the force of our entry. The trip back was less nauseating, and after a few deep breaths, I regained my equilibrium. The suns were still high in the sky. We must have only been gone for a few minutes.

"Why didn't we go to the floating man in the first place, instead of wandering all over the world?" I asked.

Liam paced back and forth, his hands raking through his hair. "One, he speaks in past, present, and future, so half of his information has either already happened or will happen. Two, I did not think the book even existed, much less that it was important."

I nodded and worried my lower lip. "Okay, fair. So, what's our next plan?"

Liam shrugged as he continued to pace. "I do not know."

"What do you mean, you don't know?"

He stopped abruptly, placing his hands on his hips as he tilted his head back. He stared at the ceiling as he spoke. "I saw it. This is how the world ends. That's what the dream said. The same dream where I saw you..." He stopped, lowering his head to look at me. I saw the sheen of tears in his eyes.

"Liam?" My voice was soft, questioning.

"I saw it. The sky ruptured, just like on Rashearim. War was what Logan said when I first returned, and I thought we would never see it again. I thought the worst was behind us, and I could rest, but I was so wrong." He started to pace once more. "I am always wrong, or off by a few seconds. I was not fast enough to save my father. Instead, he died saving *me*." His voice cracked, and I flinched at the sound. For the first time since I'd met him, he seemed unsure and raw. He waved a hand toward me. "I was not fast enough to save you. So, what am I doing, Dianna, besides fucking everything up?"

"Liam." I stepped toward him, but he recoiled from me.

"That is all I am good for. They call me World Ender for a reason. I guess that is truly all I am. Now Onuna will fall. What's two, right?" A harsh, self-deprecating laugh escaped him, and I knew I was losing him. Every emotion he'd kept buried was threatening to break free and tear him apart. All that grief and depression was rearing its ugly head.

The room shook, and I stumbled back, but caught myself. The rows of shelves lining the walls vibrated as every object not attached to something levitated.

I looked around as the tremors slowly built. "Liam. I need you to calm down, okay? We will figure it out together, like we always do."

"There is nothing to figure out, Dianna. It cannot lie. Everything it predicted will come to pass. Do you not understand that?"

I threw my arms up. "Fine! Then we face the end of the world together."

I hoped I could break through the echoing void trying to claim him. The birds in the nearby trees jolted from their perches and took flight as the ground shook again. I was terrified that if he didn't breathe or calm himself down, the whole building would fall.

"I failed." I heard him whisper. "Again."

"No, you didn't."

"Yes, I did! You heard it. I had one chance to have that damned book." His voice rose an octave higher. "I failed because I chose you over the book—over the world! I was selfish because of you. You crawled beneath my skin like some parasite. You have infected me, and it has cost me the world. So now, I have to prepare armies once more for war. *War*, Dianna."

I felt my cheeks blister as my heart jumped in my chest. I was angry and pissed and sad for him, all at the same time. "You're right. I wasn't worth it."

"That is just it, Dianna. To me, you *are* worth it—and that makes me the most selfish bastard and the most dangerous god to ever exist. I did it in a second, without thinking or worrying about the conse-quences, and I would do it again and again. What I feel for you is overwhelming, and I cannot stop it. I do not know what I am doing. Do you understand that? I have the weight of the entire universe on my shoulders. I had a plan, and then you crashed into my life, making me ignore all reason. You make me trek through Onuna, taking me to places with loud music and overly sugary treats. You make me stay at castles with pretentious vampires. You make me laugh, make me smile, make me feel. You make me feel normal and allow me to forget that I am the sole ruler, because you see *me* when you look at me. I hate it, Dianna! I hate that I have known you for what others would consider mere minutes. In the grand scheme of things, our time together means nothing. I have known and bedded others longer than you have been in my life, yet I felt nothing but fondness for them. I hate that you affect me so much, that you care so much when I do not deserve it."

His sudden admission made me pause. My world shifted, because what he felt for me, I felt too. I had grown so attached to him. I cared for him more than anyone before him. It terrified me. I felt the tears roll down my cheeks as I stepped in close, resting my hands against his chest. "Well, I hate it, too." My voice cracked. "I didn't ask for this—to feel for you as much as I do. I honestly hated you at first."

A small snort escaped him as he nodded, and tears spilled down his cheeks. "Same."

"Ass." I popped him gently, which only made my vision blurrier. "Look, I get it. I get that you would have had the book, and the world would be fine. But how is that a choice? How? How is that you being selfish? What's the point in all of this if these are the kinds of choices you have to make?"

The room shook again, and I reached up and cupped his face, forcing him to look at me. Tears and fear shone in those piercing silver eyes. "Hey, stop, look at me. I don't care what that floating tool says. Liam, your father saw something in you that needed to be saved. Unir saw a future, and whatever it was, he believed with his entire being that you would make it a reality. Your friends see the worth in you. It's why they are so loyal, why they love you, even now. You saved them without knowing it. You gave them a purpose beyond just following. They would follow you into Iassulyn, because you gave them a choice. You gave them free will and a reason to be. I've seen the memories, Liam. I get that you think you've failed, but you haven't. You won't."

His voice was cracked and broken. A god, defeated and tired. "How can you be so sure? I've done it before."

"Because you're strong and resilient. At times, you're a complete dick, sometimes annoying and bossy, but underneath all of that, you care. You love, whether you admit it to yourself or not. Liam, you are not some mindless creature. You never were. You don't listen to what anyone says, and you shouldn't. If those all-powerful beings that were above you really knew everything, Rashearim wouldn't have fallen. I don't care what anyone says. Follow your heart. You have to. The world doesn't need more of them. It needs more of you. I heard what your father said, what he told you. He wanted you to be better—better than them. That means giving a damn, Liam."

He shook his head slightly as I wiped his tears away with my thumbs. "I do not know what I am doing. I don't think I can survive going through it again."

My fingers made light passes across his cheeks. "That's fine. We'll figure this out together, okay? We will do our usual, where I come up with an idea, and you disagree, and then we argue about it until you eventually come around to my amazing foolproof plans." He huffed, as if laughter alone failed him, but the tremors making the room shudder slowly eased. "Besides, you're one of the strongest people I know. You put everyone before yourself—even cold-blooded Ig'Morruthens who get on your nerves and drive you crazy." I smiled softly, rubbing my finger across his cheek one last time.

"You do not get on my nerves all the time. Sometimes you are mildly amusing."

I smiled, dropping my hands from his face. "'Mildly amusing,' huh? I'll take that. We will get the book back. I promise. Just don't destroy this world, too."

He took a few shuddering breaths, in and out. "I am truly sorry. I do not know why I cannot control it."

"Panic attack."

"What?"

"It sounds crazy, but that's what it reminds me of. When I first saved Gabby, I would wake up sweating, my heart feeling like it wanted to burst out of my chest. I kept thinking I hadn't managed to save her, but it wasn't real. It was miserable, but I got through it because I had her. She helped me—and I'll help you."

He lifted his hand and ran his fingers through my hair. It was the same thing I had done for him on the nights when his nightmares overcame him. It was soft, soothing, and caring. "I do not deserve you."

"Definitely not. I know I don't truly get it, but you have a million-and-something eyes full of admiration looking to you for guidance. That's a lot of responsibility, to be honest. Even the strongest would falter under that pressure, Liam."

"You have no idea." He was quiet for a moment as his expression softened, his eyes roaming over my face. "I can't do this without you."

I sniffled and blinked back more tears, my cheeks still stained from before. "Obviously."

I studied his features in the light of the setting suns. He looked tired even as his body glowed. It was as if his body were absorbing energy from these stars. I didn't know how long he had been keeping the world in balance, but wouldn't even a god grow weary?

Liam carried the weight of worlds on his shoulders and was essential in maintaining the order of the universe. Without him, chaos would reign. That was what Kaden wanted, and Liam was the only thing standing in his way. Liam carried that burden with no promise of it ever being lifted. It was a wonder he hadn't cracked sooner and said fuck it all. But I knew he couldn't. He wouldn't. He would fight until the last breath left his body.

"The weight of the world," I whispered before I realized what had left my mouth.

He looked down at me, his face somber. He released me with a sigh and a brief half smile. "That's what it feels like."

"I'm sorry."

He regarded me for a second, as if the words surprised him. Shit, they surprised me, too.

"Don't be. It's my birthright."

I snorted. "Which only means you had no choice in the matter." I forced a smile as he nodded.

"In reality, yes."

The images from the blooddream played back to me. The Liam from those dreams had been so carefree, but I realized it was because he was lost. He had been fighting against a destiny that was coming for him, whether he wished it or not. I wished I could protect him, keep him safe, and help him.

"Regardless of what happens or what you decide, I will stand by your side. I will fight this fight with you. You will not be alone, and I will do all I can to keep you safe."

He closed his eyes briefly before looking at me once more. "You've already done too much. You risked your life for me to get that book. Dianna, you saved Logan when you didn't even know him! You helped me without a promise of anything in return. You fought one of your own to help save the world, and gave your life in the process," he said, his eyes dropping from my face to my chest. The dress I wore for my Imogen disguise was a little loose in the chest area, given our different sizes. It didn't expose me too much, but you could see my sternum. I knew he wasn't looking at my breasts, but at the almost invisible scar.

A pained expression passed across his features as he swallowed. He lightly traced the mark directly over my heart, and my body responded. It felt like a shot of electricity went through every fiber of my being. I shivered, goose bumps dancing across my arms and legs. It didn't hurt, but his touch excited me more than any man who had ever laid hands upon me. I didn't flinch from the sensation, but leaned into it, my breath catching. Liam had literally held my heart in his hands, and I would let him touch me in any way he wanted.

I sucked in a breath, my voice shaky as I said, "But you saved me."

"Barely." He slowly pulled his hand away, clenching his fist as he realized what he was doing. He lifted his gaze, his eyes roaming over me as if he were trying to memorize everything about me. It made me feel vulnerable, which was childish. I had been with men and women, but whenever Liam looked at me or touched me, it was as if I had never been with anyone. The mere sight of him set my blood aflame as if he stoked a fire deep in my soul—and I wanted it to burn. I wanted more. I wanted him.

"I thought I'd lost you." It was a whisper, and his gaze flicked to mine as if he were shocked he had said the words out loud.

"You know better than that. I'm impossible to get rid of." I shook my head with a smile playing on my lips as I threw his words back at him. "Like an infection."

He didn't laugh or smile, and he didn't attempt a joke as his eyes bored into mine. "If that is true…" The fear in his gaze shifted, becoming another primal emotion. "… then I wish for you to infect me."

He slid his hand across my collarbone, the roughness of his callused palm sending a bolt of electricity through my very being. I was caught in his gaze and could feel my pulse pound as his large hand wrapped gently around my neck. He tipped my chin up with his thumb, and my lips parted in anticipation. Hot, molten silver filled his eyes as his gaze dropped to my mouth, and my core went liquid. I pushed to my tiptoes as he leaned forward, neither of us caring about the line we were about to cross.

We both knew we shouldn't. There was no future for us, and there never would be. Liam was a Guardian, a savior, a protector of this realm and every realm in between. I was an Ig'Morruthen, the beast of legend he and his friends hunted. I was the monster under the bed. Stories were told of me to keep all divine beings in line. We were destined to fight until the sky bled and the worlds shook. But when he touched me, cradled my face as if I were the most fragile, beautiful being in the world, I melted. I didn't feel like a monster with him, and I realized I never had. I felt his breath touch my lips, and my body sang in response—right as the door slammed open.

Liam and I broke apart, both turning to face the unknown threat.

Logan stood there, his eyes wild and rage snapping around him. "We have a problem."

"I assure you, I am fine now."

Logan waved his hand towards the mess of the room. "No, not that. Neverra was taken, and…" Logan turned his gaze on me. "Gabby is missing."

FIFTY

DIANNA

The obsidian door tore off its hinges and flew across the room as I kicked it open. I stormed inside, both hands burning wildly. No one was here, but I had assumed that since I'd set the entire island of Novas on fire the moment Liam and I had arrived.

"It's empty." Liam strode past me, an ablaze weapon at his side.

"I told you to call Oblivion."

He looked at his hand, then back at me. "No."

"They don't deserve an afterlife, Liam."

Where I had expected anger, a look of worry crossed Liam's face. "Dianna, you know what it can do. You are here, and your sister may be as well. I am not risking either of you."

I shook my head, passing him as I headed toward the hallway.

We took the stairs up, and I slammed both hands against the double doors, sending rocks and rubble flying into the open expanse of the throne room.

"If anyone is here, the noise alone will alert them, Dianna. Try to be quieter."

I said nothing, not wanting to admit what I already knew. The island was abandoned, which meant she was gone. My chest hurt, my breath coming out in ragged gasps as I squared my shoulders.

"Search here. I'll be back."

I strode past the chairs and empty lanterns that decorated the sides of the room. The walls didn't move how they did when Kaden was in the castle. They were cold and empty. Exactly how I felt, knowing she was out there somewhere with *him*. I forced myself not to think about what he could be doing to her, but I quickened my pace. I reached the rooms upstairs and shredded Alistair's and Tobias's areas, but found nothing.

I stepped over the shards of wood, torn sheets, and broken furniture. I held myself up with one arm against the doorframe as I turned toward the end of the hall. It had been a waste of time to search those rooms. I had known I wouldn't find anything. But I was a coward and was trying to avoid that door.

It was the same door I'd beaten on when Kaden had locked me out because I'd failed him. I'd begged for forgiveness because I knew the cost of my failure. My chest heaved as I stared at it. It was my past. I didn't have to be that creature anymore. I didn't feel my feet move until I was in front of the door, my hand resting on the knob. With a turn and a push, it swung slowly out of my way.

My steps echoed in the quiet, the silence oppressive. The room still looked immaculate, as if it were waiting to be occupied. I stopped in front of the dresser and ran my hands over the top. The framed picture of Gabby and me that Kaden had grudgingly allowed me to keep was still there. We had gone to the beach because it was her favorite place. In the photo, I was hugging her, both of us smiling at the camera. She grasped the hat she wore as the thin cover-ups we wore over our bikinis blew in the wind. It was the only picture I'd had in this damned place, because I'd begged to keep it. Kaden hated it, and I couldn't even think about what he had demanded of me to allow me to keep it.

My hands shook as I gripped the frame. The glass broke, distorting the image beneath into a mosaic. I turned and threw it against the wall. I screamed and tore into that damned dresser, ripping the drawers from the base and throwing them in every direction. Clothes, a mix of mine and his, littered the floor. I spun and grabbed the mirror next, tossing it toward the door. Glass exploded, dust shimmering in the air, the noise a harsh crescendo through the house. *House.* That was a fucking joke; it was a prison.

My breath was coming in painful pants as I looked at the bed. The same bed he had fucked me on. The same bed where I had cried myself to sleep when I was left alone, unable to see the one person who gave a damn about me. I ripped the bedposts from the frame, breaking them over my knee and tossing the remains to the side. I threw one of them so hard that it stuck in the wall. My groans and screams echoed as I raged.

A vice-like grip clamped down on my arms, and I spun, ready to attack. I stopped when Liam's face came into focus. "Dianna! Dianna. Stop. This isn't helping us."

"She's not here," I snapped, pushing at him hard enough that he let go of my arms.

He stood there, stunned. "What?"

"She's not here. Kaden has her, and she's dead. I know it." I couldn't breathe, couldn't think.

"She isn't dead, Dianna."

"She is. I know it. They aren't here. Look around! They haven't been here for a while now. Can't you tell? The whole fucking cave is dormant. The rooms have not been touched since I left."

"Hey, look at me. She isn't dead." He held my hand palm up next to his, the thin scar of our deal still present. "If she were, we would know. Besides, he will not kill her. She is the last tether he has on you, the last string he can pull. He knows she is the only thing he has to keep you in line. If she is gone, he has no control, no power over you. Do you understand? He took her to draw you out, make you erratic, and it's working. I need you to focus, okay?"

"How can I focus?" The words fell out on a whimper as I pressed my hand to my forehead, turning away from him.

Liam reached for me again, but I stepped back. He watched me carefully as I pulled away from him, his brows drawing together. He was not used to this side of me. I didn't want to be comforted. I wanted to find my sister.

"You don't know that," I said. "You don't know him."

"I know men in power. You are every bit an intrinsic part of this as

Kaden and me. He wants power over you, gods know why, but I know he will not sever that tie. Trust me. Please."

My chest heaved as the words rang through me. Trust him. He had asked for it when we lost the book after him bringing me back, and I should have then. His expression softened as I sighed and nodded slowly.

"Now, help me search the rest of the island," he said, backing toward the door.

I took a deep breath and followed him, glass shards crunching beneath my foot. I stopped and looked down to see the picture of Gabby and me. My hand shook as I picked it up, tracing the lines of her happy smile. That beach trip she had obsessed over…

"What is it?" Liam asked, appearing again at my side.

"It's a trip we took. We dove off the cliffs that day, but she made me go first because she was scared. I always went first. I had to make sure it was safe. She depends on me to protect her, and I…" My words trailed off as I held the picture too tight.

"We will find her."

"Liam." I turned toward him, my vision once again a shimmering mess. "I'm scared."

I SAT WITH ONE LEG UNDERNEATH ME ON THE OVERSIZED BED IN HER room in Silver City. The comforter was a sideways mess beneath me. She must have been late waking up for work. That was the only time Gabby didn't make her bed. She was way too tidy to leave anything in disarray. I held one of the green pullover sweaters she loved, rubbing the material between my fingers.

Liam and I had made it back about an hour ago. Novas had been a dead end. Kaden had abandoned the island and had apparently been away from it for a while. The map from Ethan was also a dead end. I checked the places myself and found nothing other than empty caverns and mines. I didn't know where else to go, where else to search. It was as if they had vanished.

I brought the sweater to my face and inhaled deeply of her scent as tears filled my eyes. If she did what he asked, she would live. Then I could save her. I would never stop looking, and I would find her and save her, just like she had saved me all those times. All the times Kaden was too rough, too mean, too hateful, I'd always had a place to go.

A home. She was my home.

Just let me save you this time, Gabriella. Let me save you.

A light tap had me dropping the sweater to my lap and looking toward the open bedroom door. Liam stood there, and I turned away. I didn't want to see him, and a part of me thought he knew it. I didn't want to be comforted or touched.

"Did you find Drake or Ethan?" I asked. "Logan said they were with them."

"No."

I nodded, sighing as I looked down at the sweater in my lap. Maybe Kaden had taken them, too.

"It appears a lot of your old contacts are missing as well, not just them."

I set the sweater aside and stood up. "Okay, so we search elsewhere."

He reached out, grabbing me as I tried to walk past him. "Search where? We have checked the places you knew. Your informants are gone. Where else do we go?"

"I don't know!" I yanked my arm out of his grip. "You're a god; do something godly! Could you feel if she were near or something?"

He shook his head, his mouth forming into a solid line. "It doesn't work like that."

"Then we keep searching."

I exited the room and heard his footsteps close behind.

"Search where, Dianna? Where else?"

"I don't know."

"He has to have another hideout, a place he may have taken you besides the island. There is no way he can hide in this realm that well."

I shook my head, continuing toward the door.

"Let me help you, Dianna. Stop and think. Where else could he have taken her?"

I spun, my temper and pain at the boiling point. He kept asking me questions as if I had all the answers. "I don't know!" I snapped, fisting my hands in my hair. My world shook—and I realized it wasn't just my world, but the room, too. "I don't know, okay?"

Liam looked at me, his eyes widening for a second before scanning the room. I didn't know why he regarded me as if I had made it shake. He had done it. It was always him.

I took a deep breath and let it out on a slow, steady sigh. "I just need to think."

But thinking was the last thing that happened as static lit up the room, the TV behind us turning on.

"Dianna."

FIFTY-ONE

LIAM

Dianna's eyes bled crimson as she yelled at me. I was used to her fury; I had seen it before. But the power that blasted off of her and shook the room was new. She was slipping, and I felt it. She was filled with fear, and something darker I could feel lurking, waiting for its chance. I was losing her.

Static hit the air, and the large TV in the center of the room blinked on. We turned toward it and took a step closer. Words scrolled along a small red banner at the bottom, telling us that this was a live feed. A man and a woman sat reclined in anchor chairs, their suits ripped and smeared with blood. They were dead—which meant Tobias was there.

"Good evening, and welcome to KMN news at night. Tonight's top story is 'A king with a broken crown that wasn't even his to begin with.'" The woman shuffled the pages in front of her as she spoke, and her words made my jaw clench.

The man turned toward her. I could see the bruises on his neck, and as he tried to smile, it looked like his jaw was barely hanging on. "Now, Jill, this has been a story circulating for ages. A man gifted with a title and a throne, but childlike in his ideals, and no follow-through."

Jill nodded in agreement. "If you think about it, Anthony, it's pretty sad. A whole planet was destroyed because he just couldn't cut it."

I knew every jab was directed at me, but I didn't care. I had heard it all before. My concern wasn't for me, but for Dianna. Every instinct I had was telling me we were on the cusp of something catastrophic.

"Well, Jill, that's what happens when you send a boy to do a man's job. Speaking of jobs, let's check in with Casey for the weather."

The camera swung to the other side of the room, focusing on a woman standing with a small device in her hand. Her suit was also in tatters, and I could tell that Tobias's magic was the only thing keeping her upright. The screen behind her turned into a large map with what looked like clouds dancing across certain areas.

"Thanks, Anthony and Jill. The forecast calls for clear skies and sunny weather for the next few days, but the incoming apocalypse may put a stop to that. If that happens, we may be looking at thunderous clouds as the realms rip open. Precipitation will be heavy with a copper smell as his blood rains from the sky. We're predicting a few quakes, but those should subside before the planet tears itself apart. Back to you, Jill."

"Thanks, Casey. When can we expect this drastic change?"

"Oh, very soon," her voice said from off-screen.

Jill's smile was a little too wide. "Can't wait."

Anthony chuckled lightly, his jaw bobbing obscenely as he folded his hands together and regarded the camera. "I guess it would be a good idea for everyone to get inside, huh?"

"Oh, Anthony, there's no hiding from this. Now, we do have a special guest with us tonight. Quite a few, actually."

Anthony pointed to her. "You know what, Jill? You're right. Now let's welcome our co-host tonight, Kaden."

The camera swung again, and a jolt went through me. His suit was dark, and he had his feet propped up on a desk. I had seen him before, sitting atop a throne made of bones, wearing horned armor. He smirked out at me from the screen, his face wholly visible, and I got my first good look at my enemy. He was relaxed, as if his hands and the white shirt he wore beneath his suit were not stained with blood. His collar was unbuttoned, and I could see the glint of a silver chain around his neck. Kaden licked his fingers clean and smiled at the camera.

The air in the room shifted as Logan and Vincent popped in. They spoke over each other as Dianna stared at the screen, her body unmoving.

"Liam. It's on every channel, every station."

Kaden just sat there, staring back as if he could see her.

"What?" I asked, not taking my eyes from her.

"Globally. We checked."

"Where is it coming from? Can you pinpoint a location?"

Vincent shook his head. "That's the thing. It's as if the frequency is coming from everywhere and nowhere at once. There is no way to turn it off."

My next questions died as Anthony started talking once more.

"Now, Kaden, please tell us, what exactly is the Otherworld?"

My adrenaline spiked, knowing this wasn't something mortals needed to learn. Not like this. Logan said they'd tried to stop the feed, but couldn't.

"Sounds like something out of a movie, am I right?" Jill laughed.

Kaden sat up, leaning over the side of the table and clasping his hands together. "I can agree, but it is so much more. See, you all think monsters do not exist, that they are created from the imaginations of mortals. But you are oh so wrong. Every monster has an origin based in reality."

Jill nodded along, as if she could even comprehend what was happening. She was Tobias's puppet, just like the ones in El Donuma. They all were. "So, you're saying every supernatural creature is real?"

"Everything and so much more. The only problem is that the population is practically nonexistent in this realm."

It was Anthony's turn to speak, and he placed his hand under his wobbly chin to listen. "How so?"

Kaden smiled, still staring intently into the camera. "I'll tell you a story. Once upon a time, in a world far, far away from here, lived a vile and vicious king, ruler to all and adored by many, but he bore secrets—dark, ghastly secrets he kept buried even from the ones he claimed to love the most. He believed peace was achieved through force. He used and abused those under his command until they meant nothing to him any longer. Once his goal was achieved, they were discarded like trash. Then one day, he bore a son, a being like him, pure of light and everything he wished for in his new world. His son was next in line to rule, but there was concern."

"Concern?" Jill's disjointed voice asked.

"Oh, yes. Concern he would be just like the ones before him, just like his father. The truth slowly came to fruition, and friends turned to foes. There was an uprising. Blood of the gods spilled across stars you can't even see now. It was the Gods War, but it was so much more than that." Kaden's eyes gleamed as if he had been there and reveled in the chaos.

"What happened next?"

Kaden sighed and leaned back, folding his hands in front of himself. "Well, what your legends say about the great and powerful Samkiel... He saved the world, did he not? Everyone that stood against them was locked away by his blood. Every realm, every world sealed." He paused as he reached under the table. There was a loud thud as he slammed the Book of Azrael onto the desk. His smile was venom and rage as he glanced at the camera. "Well, for now, at least."

Static sizzled in the air, oppressive, thick, and heavy. I was losing my patience. He spoke of my father and my world as if he knew them personally, yet I had no recollection of him or his name. I turned to Logan and Vincent.

"Go, see if you can find where he is. I need every celestial form here to Ruuman searching. He cannot hide from us, not when this is on every station around the world. Once you find him, summon me immediately."

They both nodded before shooting from the room in a flash of blue light. Words from the screen filtered in as I glanced back at the TV. Kaden's hands were covered in thick black gloves. He flipped through the Book of Azrael as if it weren't a powerful, ancient, decaying artifact containing the means of my death.

Jill clutched her chest as if she could feel. "That is such a sad story."

"Is it? I like to think of it as a rebirth. A new beginning, some would say. See right here." He pointed one finger at a page as Jill and

Anthony leaned toward him. "This is the key to opening the realms now."

"Such a pretty weapon."

"I agree, and once I make it, this world will bleed. I am betting that there are thousands, if not millions, of pissed-off beings looking for a little bit of payback."

Anthony's head tilted. "Well, what happens to us mortals if this comes to pass?"

Kaden laughed and slammed the book closed, the sound making me grimace. "Well, you die." He stopped and shrugged as if he hadn't just condemned the world. "Or you are all enslaved. It's really up in the air right now."

Jill and Anthony laughed as if that were the funniest joke they'd ever heard. Once Jill had control over herself, she said, "Well, that sounds lovely. Can't wait!"

Anthony cleared his mangled throat. "Now, usually we have a hot topic round sponsored by Jeff, but since you dismembered him, I guess you'll have to do the hot topic round. So, tell us, Kaden, what's the hot topic tonight?"

"Well, love, of course."

"Love?" All eyes turned toward the camera, and I knew this next part was for Dianna. I shifted closer to her.

"Why, yes."

Jill waved her hand and said, "The stage is all yours." Anthony and Jill froze in place, and I knew Tobias was slowly releasing his hold on them. They stared straight ahead as their eyes turned the glassy white of the dead.

"Now, I know you're all thinking that I am evil incarnate, but you would be wrong. I love love—and no one loves harder than Dianna."

A picture of Dianna and me popped up on the screen, and I realized he had been a lot closer to us than I'd assumed. How had I not felt it? My gaze swung to Dianna. She was fixated, her arms folded as she glared, radiating pure rage. As I studied her, I knew she had felt him—those times she had those chills. She had sensed him, but hadn't known what it meant.

Kaden's eyes flashed red in the studio lights as he stood and moved closer to the camera. He removed the gloves, one finger at a time. "I gave her everything I could. A trade, some would say, for what she asked." He rubbed at his jaw with one blood-stained hand.

A picture of Dianna popped up on the screen and stayed there, taking up one of the corners. "All that she is, all of her power, is because of me, yet I've met dogs that are more loyal. She can't keep her legs closed—not that I can complain. It only took me saving her sister before she let me bend her over. Which I'm sure she let you do too, Samkiel." The picture switched to one of Dianna smiling up at me at the carnival. "I hope you enjoy her while you can, because make no mistake, she will turn on you, too."

I watched as he flicked his eyes toward someone off-screen. The pictures faded, and his demeanor changed. Dianna's stance did not waver; it was as if her body had turned to stone. I stood next to her, my gaze flicking between her and the screen as my gut churned. I had no idea what his plan was, but I couldn't leave to search for him—not when she needed me.

"Dianna, tsk, tsk, tsk, you know better. You know I have eyes everywhere. This world belongs to me, my love, and I was never far away. Didn't you feel me?"

My heart sank further, the pit of my stomach rolling. I was right; she had sensed him. It was inconceivable that I had not. How had I not known that he was so close? And not just once.

"I'm just curious, though. What were your intentions with this failed relationship? Just for fun? Stopping me? Saving the world? And then what? You think he loves you? Cares for you? Ask him how many men and women he has whispered those words to. How many have fallen at his feet, hoping to stand by his side? You are nothing to him, and you never will be. You are a monster, no matter what he tells you, no matter what you pretend. Do you think you could rule at his side, Dianna? Even after I'm gone, do you think *they* would accept you— after everything you've done? He's truly immortal, Dianna. Have you thought about that? We aren't. Do you really hate yourself so much that you would be comfortable being his consort for the rest of your life while he marries an actual queen? He will need an equal, someone to rule by his side, to bear his children into this perfect world of theirs."

Kaden's nostrils flared and his fists clenched. Anger bubbled below the surface of his calm facade. His eyes burned with red embers, but then he glanced beyond the camera and seemed to remember that he was not alone. He shrugged and braced his hands on the table.

"Let's play a game. Say you two succeed. The realms are saved, and people sing and cheer in the streets. Deep down, Dianna, do you really think he would choose you after all of this is over? Be realistic." He clicked his teeth, shaking his head slowly. "I don't. I think even if I don't win, you will still lose."

Kaden paused for a moment, maybe realizing he had revealed too much. I glanced at Dianna, and her body had gone so rigid that she looked like she would break with one touch. She was so closed off that I couldn't feel anything from her, which was terrifying. Dianna was never contained.

"Now." Kaden clapped his hands together before rubbing them twice. "Back to business. See, here's the thing, Dianna. I wanted you by my side, you know? My perfect, beautiful weapon for what's coming." He sighed in disappointment and rubbed his chin before pointing at the camera. "But alas, you have chosen the wrong side. It's okay, though. I think I can forgive you and let you come home. I just need to teach you a lesson first."

He stopped speaking and waved someone forward. The camera panned back and turned slightly. The new angle allowed us to see Kaden, a closed-off corridor with a curtain above it, and the audience. I looked closer and saw that the crowd was full of Otherworld creatures. Eyes fluoresced in various colors, and I saw more than a dozen pairs of gleaming red eyes. The Irvikuva stood in the back corridor with their wings spread, making sure no one tried to leave.

There was a ripple as Drake stood and started toward Kaden. My lips curled in a silent snarl at his betrayal of her friendship and love. How could he have done this to her? I had trusted him against my better judgment because she believed him to be her friend. The coward refused to look at the camera as he stopped beside Kaden.

"Come on, Drake. Center stage is yours, buddy," Kaden mocked, slapping a hand on Drake's back as if they were old friends. "Drake told me all about you and your new boyfriend's little trip to El Donuma. He told me when you would arrive, how long you stayed, and your next move. Camilla filled me in from there."

He waved toward the audience, and Camilla nodded, her head held high. I recognized several others. Santiago was there, his and Camilla's covens intermingled. Elijah sat next to a few mortals from the Kashvenia embassy. I guess she was not the only one betrayed; it seemed some of the mortals under my jurisdiction had switched sides, too.

Pure, unadulterated rage made my rings vibrate, and I could feel the heat behind my eyes. I reached out, placing my hand on Dianna's arm. Her skin beneath the shirt felt heated. I rubbed my thumb in small, slow circles, trying to ground her and let her know I was here for her, even if those she had trusted most were not.

"True loyalty from the beginning, Dianna," Kaden said, patting Drake on the back. "Why don't you head back to your family, old friend."

Drake strode away from Kaden without looking at the camera once. I watched as he joined Ethan and a dark-haired woman I assumed was Ethan's wife—the wife who had been too busy to greet us while we were staying in Zarall. The pieces started to click together, and I didn't like the picture they made. Had they sold Dianna out for the wife?

"You see, Dianna…" his voice droned on.

I needed to get Dianna away from the pull he had on her. He sliced her open with every word, and I could feel the grip he had on her tightening. It was like talons dipped in acid digging into her, even from a distance.

"Dianna." My voice was soft, and I felt her shift. The air grew heavy, as if a storm were brewing in the room. "Remember what I taught you. Do not let him bait you."

I couldn't tell if she heard me or not. Her breathing was coming in small pants, her eyes glazed and unfocused as she stared straight ahead.

Kaden's voice cut in, followed by a whistle as he looked directly into the camera and said, "Tobias, if you would be so kind? There is one last thing I would like to show my sweet, precious girl."

The camera shook as Tobias stepped out from behind it, turning to flash an ice-cold grin I knew was meant for Dianna. He disappeared behind the large dark curtain and returned, dragging a hooded figure with him. The woman struggled against him, kicking her legs but failing to gain traction against the slick floor. Tobias threw her at Kaden's feet. Kaden leaned down and grabbed her under her arm with one hand before pulling the hood off with the other.

Gabriella.

I heard it then, in sync with my own: the pounding of her heart and mine. They beat rapidly, mine bashing itself so hard against my ribs that I wondered if it would burst. I tried taking deep breaths, hoping to slow mine, and in turn, hers. We watched as Gabby kicked out and Kaden dropped her. She tried to scoot away, but several of Kaden's Irvikuva snarled and snapped behind her, forcing her to stop.

Dianna jerked away from my touch to drop to the floor in front of the TV. I didn't think she was even aware of how close she got as her hands gripped the sides of the screen.

Kaden whistled, signaling one of the Irvikuva. Gabby grunted in pain as the beast grabbed her by the arm. The creature looked at Kaden, and when he nodded, tossed Gabby toward him. Kaden caught her, grabbing her hard enough that she winced. He dragged her closer to the camera.

"Do you like the present Drake brought me, Dianna? He even snagged me a member of The Hand," he said as a deadly smile curved his features. He squeezed Gabby's face as he stared at the camera. "Say hello to big sister, now."

"I hope you rot in whatever dimension you're from. Permanently!" Gabby spat, defiance apparent in every line of her body.

Kaden laughed and looked out at the creatures in the audience. "Feisty, isn't she? Just like her sister."

The crowd laughed, and I wanted to rip every single one of them to pieces. White-hot rage skittered through my body at the blatant disrespect. They would pay. I would make sure of it.

Kaden's eyes were bright red as he held her close. She glared at the camera with all the fury she could muster, even as her eyes filled with tears.

"Now, is there something you want to say to big sis? You know she's watching." His smile was downright venomous as he squeezed Gabby's face a fraction tighter, his thumb caressing her jawline.

Gabby's eyes bored into the screen in silent desperation. It wasn't for herself, but for the one she knew stared back at her—the one person who had given up her life for hers. Her eyes clouded with unshed tears as the world held its breath. Even the creatures behind Kaden were silent. It was a defining moment in what was to come. Kaden held the world in his grasp, and he reveled in it.

"Remember…" Gabby swallowed, a single tear sliding down her cheek. "Remember that I love you."

Kaden jerked upright, taking Gabby with him as he stood. He laughed as Gabby seemed to release a breath, her chest heaving from the fear we all felt.

"See?" Kaden turned toward the room, waving his free hand, his other wrapped around Gabby's neck, holding her in place. "That wasn't so hard, was it? And they say I'm cruel." He smiled at the camera, this time his eyes boring into mine as he cupped Gabriella's chin. "Would you like to see the true beast that rests under Dianna's pretty skin, Samkiel? Do you think you will care for her still? Let's find out."

He did it so quickly that it even startled me. But we all heard it—the crack. I felt it resonate through the ties that made me a protector of this realm. No one moved. No one breathed. It was as if time had slowed down. I watched the light leave her eyes. Kaden dropped her and turned away with a satisfied smirk. Gabby's body thudded to the ground, her neck contorted. Her small, lifeless hand was outstretched, attempting to reach through the screen, desperate for the one she loved the most.

I hissed, flexing my hand as a blinding white heat danced across my palm. I glanced down, and my heart stuttered as a glowing yellow line seared across my palm, bright and iridescent, before disappearing.

The blood deal had reached its completion in the most horrid way.

"Blood of my blood, my life is sealed with yours until the deal is made complete. I grant you my maker's life in exchange for my sister's life. She shall remain free, unharmed, and alive, or the deal is broken."

I smelled it before I saw it. A single tilt of her head, and a world-shattering boom filled the room. Not a boom; a scream. It was so loud and painful that it shook the building, and I knew it could be heard throughout the realms. Wings and scales replaced skin and limbs as the beast ripped its way into the world. The flames that erupted from her were so hot and bright that they blinded me. The force of her massive tail slammed me through walls, concrete, and glass. My vision was consumed with the inferno as the building was engulfed.

My head throbbed and my ears rang as I sat up, cupping them. Moisture coated my palms even as my eardrums healed. My clothes were burned and torn, clinging to me where they had melted into my skin. I patted out some embers along my sleeve as another soul-shattering scream split the air. The sound tore a fissure in the world. It was pure pain and rage, an echo of ruin. My dreams came flooding back, and I realized I had gotten it wrong. My translation was mistaken. There were too many words and languages in my brain.

"This is how the world ends." That's what Roccurrem had said. *"There will be a shuddering crack, an echo of what is lost and what cannot be healed. Then, Samkiel, you will know this is how the world ends."*

But it was not this world.

No, it was mine.

It was Dianna.

Acknowledgments

First and foremost, I want to say thank you to all the readers. The fact that you even wanted to pick up this book means the world to me! Thank you endlessly. Also, thank you to every single person I have met and become friends with on this journey, and I hope you enjoyed the first installment of Liam and Dianna's adventures.

Next, I want to say thank you to Rose & Star Publishing for believing in me! Jeanette and Ally, you own my very heart. Thanks for letting me blow your phones up with a thousand messages for the last few months. Liam may have lost his home, but I found mine with you! This has been quite a ride, and I am so lucky to have a home for my crazy, loveable, chaotic characters.

Aisling, my amazing editor, thank you so much for seeing my world and loving every single part. Thank you for believing in me as well and not being afraid of Dianna and her chaotic ways. I also apologize in advance for the five books.

Siobhan, Alex, and Kaven, where do I begin? First you have to unblock me now, since the entire world is probably on your side for Gabby. I'm sorry—just know I love you! Thank you guys for being the best beta readers a girl could ever ask for. Your feedback and reactions made my life, and I treasure you guys.

Kaven, thanks for letting me talk your ears off with this, and thank you for the tremendous and endless support.

Alex, thanks for letting me scream and cry to you even though it was 2:00 a.m. in Scotland at the time.

Siobhan, thanks for loving the playlist and continuously listening even after you finished. Thank you for the amazing aesthetics and never getting tired of me talking about them. I can't wait to visit you in New York this Christmas!

Thank you to my mom and sister, whom I love dearly. The family bond in this entire series is a reflection of them for me—the undying love and the ability to do anything for the ones you love. We have been through hell and back, and I hope you both know how much I love you.

Lastly, once again, I just want to thank everyone who read this. You are everything, and you all deserve the world, and I hope you find someone (if you don't have someone already) who would throw away an ancient book for their love for you, too. Thank you, Thank you, and Thank you!

KEEP READING FOR AN EXCLUSIVE BONUS
CHAPTER FROM AMBER NICOLE . . .

CINNAMON BLUES

CAMERON

"Let it go."

My head whipped toward Xavier as he leaned against the council chamber doors. We listened, standing guard as we had done for eons now. Most of the time, the noise inside was the same old, same old, but it seemed Onuna had a power grid blow that caused some structural damage. My biggest concern was Samkiel's random stop-by and his sudden departure. I didn't even get to see Logan, just the treat he brought by.

"Nah." I sighed, folding my arms a fraction tighter. "I mean, you don't think it's a little weird that Samkiel returns from nowhere with Imogen? The last I heard, she couldn't even get him to talk to her, and he was still refusing to leave that secluded, run-down place. Now they are working together, but he didn't tell us?" I blew a breath out. "I don't believe it at all."

His chuckle bounced off the marble halls before he covered it with a cough. He pushed off the wall, the golden tassels of his council garbs dancing as he moved. "So what, do you think he's lying, or she is?"

I shrugged. "Or another working theory."

His brows rose. "Oh?"

"I smelled cinnamon, but something else. It was there one second and gone the next."

His head reared back slightly. "What else did you smell?"

"Smoke."

The council doors opened, and Xavier and I straightened at our posts, both of us clasping our hands behind our backs as if we weren't dozing off a few seconds ago. The council members exited one by one, a few placing papers beneath their arms, still lost in conversation.

Elianna's eyes caught mine as she tucked her journal away. It was a look I knew well. She was hoping I'd make an excuse to annoy her later. If she was seeking my comfort in broad daylight, it meant whatever they were talking about for the last few days was something stressful enough that she needed the release, but I didn't have time for it.

Xavier faked a smile toward Levithan as he stalked past. I forced my eyes from his grin just in case Elianna caught on to why I frequented her bed chamber so often.

Xavier and I waited until everyone left, their footsteps receding down the hall before we shoved each other, fighting over who would enter the room first. I tripped him, and Xavier laughed as he stumbled over his feet. Gods, I loved the sound of his laugh. Who could blame me?

Xavier shoved me into the room, and I faked a fall to the left. The sound of someone clearing their throat had us both looking toward Imogen. She had a disgruntled look on her face and both hands on her hips. Papers were still scattered over the surface of the massive council table, and my eye caught on one labeled *Vortexes*. I ran my fingers across it before Imogen slapped my hand away.

Xavier sighed and took a seat, placing his hands on the table.

"Why do you both look like you're up to no good?" Imogen asked, sliding her hands across the long ends of her council garbs and taking a seat.

Xavier cut his eyes to me, widening them for a second. I rolled mine and sat down, placing my feet atop the council table. I said nothing but folded my hands over my stomach and just waited. He said he wanted to ask because he had tact. I disagreed. I thought I had so much tact it was falling out of my ass.

"What took so long this evening, Immy?" Xavier asked.

Imogen sighed as she shook her head. "Levithan called an emergency meeting because one of the vortexes was opened here on Rashearim, and there was a report of a Shift on Onuna." She shook her head. "I'm unsure what it all means, but everyone is scurrying."

I sat up a tad straighter, and Xavier leaned forward, both of us focused on Imogen now. "A Shift? On Onuna?"

A Shift happened so infrequently that they were hard to pinpoint. The birth of powerful rulers could cause one. When they ascended and reached their full potential, whether good or evil, a Shift often occurred. We had heard of those who could bend magic to their will, and the backlash could cause them. They were a raw power imbalance that the elders claimed could shift the very universe on its axis.

Imogen nodded. "A city block lost power and sustained some damage, but it was felt nonetheless."

Xavier cut his eyes towards me. So that was why we both had jolted awake the other night.

Imogen went on. "The council spoke to Vincent, and Samkiel is there working on it, so we just wait until we're needed, I suppose."

"Samkiel hasn't called?" I asked as Xavier looked at me.

"No." She sighed. "Surprisingly not. I know he went back and has been there for a minute. Logan claims everything is fine, and Vincent backs him up, but I don't know. Something feels off."

"Yeah, probably because you're here and not with him."

Imogen's brows furrowed. "Why would I be with him?"

Xavier cleared his throat. "I mean, we saw you two the day of the vortex incident."

"Yeah," I added as Imogen's eyes darkened in confusion. "I mean, Logan even dropped off another one of those cool chocolate cake things."

Xavier's eyes cut to mine.

"Which is so not the point," I said.

Imogen's lip lifted. "I haven't been with Samkiel."

Xavier glanced at me, and I folded my arms. "You know what, Imogen? I'm hurt."

"What?" she asked.

"I consider us best friends, but here you are, sneaking around with each other again, and you didn't even tell us."

"Cameron—" Xavier started.

I lifted my hand, cutting him off. "No, I'm serious. Wasn't I the one who helped cover for all the little training sessions you were always late to? What about when Athos lost her mind over a dress I helped you steal? The worst part is that you are sneaking around. Since when? You've always been terrified you'd lose your chair on the council board. Now you two are back to making doe eyes at each other and sneaking around Rashearim like old times."

"What are you talking about?" Imogen glared at me. "I haven't been sneaking around with anyone, least of all Samkiel. No one but Logan, Neverra, and Vincent have seen him in ages."

Xavier's face grew slack, but I knew the game Imogen was playing. I let a breath loose as I leaned over, taking her hand in mine and patting it slightly.

"Look, I get it. I'm not one to judge. You've caught me in some crazy positions before and never even batted an eye. So Samkiel gets out of his depressive funk and gets a haircut. He's hot, we get it. We've all known. It's no surprise. No one is going to judge you if old feelings have come back. But lying to your best friend? Ouch."

She scowled, and her hand whipped out, popping me upside the head. "I am not sleeping with him, nor have we even remotely come close to that in well over a thousand years. You both know I am with Jiraiya."

"Terrible decision, honestly," I said. Imogen glared at me, and I held up a hand. "Just saying the guy sucks and, to be honest, seems a little sketchy."

"Anyway," Imogen enunciates, stretching the word. "You'd better tell me right now if Samkiel has been here. Has he?"

Xavier and I looked at each other, and I rubbed the side of my head.

"Yes," Xavier said, "and with you. Two days ago."

"Yeah, and then you all have been locked in here since," I said. "We thought it was something major."

"That's impossible," Imogen practically squealed. "I was with Logan in the atheneum two days ago . . ."

Her words drifted off, and my heart pounded in my chest. Imogen, above all, was truthful, and I was stupid to continue to brush it off. I knew that, but there was just no other explanation for what we both saw and felt. My hand dropped as I looked at Xavier. I knew he could read every expression that crossed my face. I just prayed he never gained the ability to read my thoughts.

"Well, if you weren't with him," Xavier cast her a glance, "then who was?"

Imogen's face melts into a cool calm, but I see her adrenaline spike. Samkiel had lied to us, but more importantly, he snuck someone onto Rashearim who could bend their shape here, too. Not only that, but Logan knew.

Imogen's throat bobbed. "I'm not sure, but I have a feeling that with everything that's been happening, we are about to find out."

Then, Samkiel, you will know this is how the world ends.

**But it was not this world.
No, it was mine.
It was Dianna.**

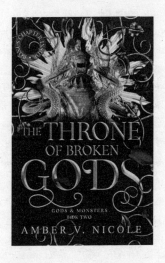

**Keep reading for sneak peek at the next
stage of Dianna and Samkiel's story . . .**

OUT NOW

The world once made sense. My sister got sick and Kaden saved her, giving her breath again when the world threatened to take it. He changed me, making me one of his own, gifting me with extraordinary powers that made even creatures of the night flinch. In return, I did what he said and cared for him in my own way. Sure, my work schedule wasn't the best, and things sometimes got messy. "Kill this person, Dianna. Maim him, Dianna. Bring me that, Dianna." He had a lot of demands, but it was easy. It made sense. Everything made sense until him.

A god king, they called him the World Ender. I didn't mean to bring him back, but when I slayed one of his celestials in battle, he returned with a vengeance, and the world stopped. The last living god walked this plane once more, and the Otherworld shuddered.

Kaden sought an ancient relic and set us to finding it. I snuck into the mortal council to see if the World Ender had brought it with him. My need to keep Gabby safe had been the driving force in my life for centuries, but there was something about the World Ender. Like a moth drawn to a flame, I couldn't stay away from him. That was my first mistake. My second was being captured. He and his minions imprisoned me, trying and failing to extract my secrets. During a failed rescue attempt, I made a choice based in fear, love, and a deep desire to keep Gabby safe that changed everything.

So came the hard part. Another trade for Gabby's life, and a deal made with my enemy, the World Ender. His people would protect her while I helped him hunt for the artifact. For her, I would do it. I had no choice. They say that the enemy of my enemy is my friend, but the consequences of my betrayal would cut me deeply.

I stayed with Liam, worked with him. Days turned to months as we searched for the relic. Angry glares transformed into heated stares, arguments transformed into laughs, and that spark between us turned into searing flames. Our hate for each other faded, replaced by something far deadlier and far sweeter.

After staying weeks with allies and navigating the growing tension between us, we finally had a solid lead and set out to finish our mission. We found the Book of Azrael in a long forgotten tomb and fell into a trap. In a desperate act to save Samkiel and the world, I risked my life. Samkiel saved me instead of claiming the book.

With the book in enemy hands, we went to Plan B and traveled to the remains of his world. We visited a fate that revealed a prophecy of what was to come and how the end of the world was in sight.

Unbeknownst to us, traitors lived in our midst. Individuals I had trusted with both my life and Gabby's belonged to Kaden. They took advantage of our absence, and for my betrayal, they took the one person I loved most and delivered her to Kaden.

We returned to Onuna immediately, searching for her to no avail, until a broadcast that reached around the world and through the realms. Kaden had a message for us, for me, and he wanted the world to hear it, too.

It was only a snap, a single crack, and the world that once made sense, made sense no more.

"This is how the world ends," the fate had whispered, and I was going to show them just how right fate was.

Dianna

ONE

SAMKIEL

It had been twenty thousand, one hundred and sixty minutes since she left, and I had counted every single one. My eyes skittered toward the large clock on the other side of the room. Sixty-one now.

"So, a giant, scaled-winged beast destroys half of Silver City and just disappears?" The anchorwoman shifted in her seat as she stared at me. Jill was her name, right? Or was it Jasmine?

Scorching-hot metal bit at my skin as I pushed a large sheet off of me. The ground rumbled as I dug myself out of the hole my body had made when I crashed to the street. My ears rang, and when I touched them, my fingers came away wet. The silver shine on them told me everything I needed to know. Blood. She had screamed so loud that it had burst my eardrums.

I threw my head back as another heart-shattering roar lit up the sky. It was pain and anger and utter heartbreak. It shook the nearby windows, and I wondered if it could be heard throughout the realms. One mighty clap of wings, then another, and she was airborne. Thunder cracked the sky in her wake, the speed of her ascent displacing the air. Lights and sirens bellowed on the street as flames tickled the buildings all around me.

I couldn't stop thinking about our time together, every second, from the first to the last. Dianna's words echoed as if we were back at that cursed mansion.

Her smile had awoken something in me, and for the first time in a millennium, I felt the ice I'd encased my heart in crack. She gazed at me through those thick lashes, her hazel eyes filled with warmth, as if I was worth something. She held a single small finger out, and I held my breath. What was wrong with me?

"Pinkie promise, I will never abandon you, Your Highness."

More of those odd words of hers, but they meant something to me. Everyone I held dear had left me. I'd lost them and secluded myself, yet this creature... No, this woman promised me something I had begged for. Such simple words, such a simple act, had fractured something in me and shifted my world.

I stared at the empty night sky, watching her dark wings beat across the sky, her sleek form disappearing into the roiling clouds, away from me.

"You promised," I whispered as the sirens continued to wail.

Noise flooded the newsroom, pulling me from the memory and slamming me back into the present. Hot lights blazed down on us. I did not remember the name of the woman sitting across from me, even though several people had reminded me.

Disappeared? That's what they were saying. She had ripped a hole through that building and my chest as she fled.

I plastered a smile onto my face, one made of falsehoods and despair. I leaned forward. "*Disappeared* is a misnomer, to say the least. As you know, it is very easy for powerful creatures to hide."

A slight blush grazed her cheeks, and my stomach rolled. How easy mortals were to manipulate with a smile and kind words. They had no clue what was coming, the casualties I feared would happen soon.

"Yes, and speaking of which, what would you like the people to call you?" She shifted closer, tucking a strand of hair behind her ear. "Since you have officially returned?"

I did not think or pause. I knew the answer and had denied it for far too long.

"Samkiel." I forced another broken smile. Could they not see?

"Samkiel is fine." Liam was a shield I hid behind, as if I could pretend to be anything other than the World Ender. Liam was my attempt at a new start, even if it was a broken one. And Liam had cost me everything. If I had been the king every text was written for, been the protector the old gods built monuments for, maybe I could have saved her, helped her more. So, no; Samkiel was who I was, who I would forever be, and Liam died with whatever part of Dianna's heart fractured that night.

BACK AT THE GUILD IN BOEL, I SPLAYED MY HANDS ON THE TABLE.

Vincent sighed beside me and folded his arms. "They had questions they were supposed to stick to. I apologize."

Vincent gave the thin man behind me a hard stare. He adjusted his glasses and flipped through the tablet he carried everywhere. "I swear they picked their own questions, my liege. I would never..." He paused. "I'll fix it."

I sighed and walked to the window before turning to face them. Gregory. That was his name. He was a member of the council, sent as an advisor to help ease the growing animosity among the mortals. Vincent approved of him. It seemed everyone approved of Gregory. They all saw I needed extra assistance, but Gregory could not help me with my problem.

"What is your job title once more?" I asked Gregory, cutting a glare at Vincent again, knowing he had more of a hand in this than the shivering celestial.

Greg's throat bobbed. "Article 623 in the House of Dreadwell states that all ruling monarchs must have an advisor. With all due respect, my liege, your parents had one, and you need one, too. I should have been appointed to you the second you returned, but that did not happen. Since you have fully come back, the council feels it is past time that I assume my station. I am more than adept at dealing with the media. I have experience in political, legislative, and judicial matters as well. I am the qualified party."

"Ah." I nodded, the air in the room growing heavy. Vincent shifted and shuffled some papers on his desk. "As the qualified party, I can assume accidents like today will not happen again. Correct?"

Gregory looked at Vincent and then down, avoiding eye contact with me. "I will go handle this current situation."

"Fantastic," I said and turned to the window, looking out at the clear sky and the mortals below.

His footsteps receded, and I heard the door close a second later.

The power flickered, and I took a deep breath, steadying my nerves. Lights buzzed, and I took another breath, inhaling through my nose and slowly exhaling through my mouth.

"You have to expel some of that." Vincent neared, slipping his hands into his pockets. "Another thunderstorm wouldn't hurt," he said, nodding toward the window.

I shook my head. "It's been raining for days."

"And it's dried. Do it. You need it."

My head lifted, and I felt the familiar tingle beneath my skin as I summoned the energy. I felt every atom. They bounced off each other, building the storm. A tendril of power whipped out of me, and I took another breath. The sun disappeared, thick clouds rolling across the sky. Thunder rocked the world, the clouds broke open, and rain poured down like someone had turned on a great faucet. I heard the curses of mortals down on the street as the wind howled.

"Feel better?"

"No."

My reflection glared back at me from the rain-spattered window. The suits they draped me in were supposed to make the mortals see me as more approachable, but I knew it was actually to show them I was not falling apart. My face was clean-shaven and my hair trimmed short. They wanted me seen as whole and not the broken king they knew so little about.

Fake a smile. Look presentable, as if your entire world is not in shambles. Pretend. Pretend. Pretend.

That's what Vincent said, what he preached. He wanted the mortals to feel secure and not as if the world was on the verge of yet another catastrophe.

Lightning streaked across the sky, and the door opened. My eyes searched the reflection in the window. I longed to see her burst through the door, carrying a plate of food for me, a smile blooming across her cheeks, as she had done at the Vanderkais' mansion.

"See, it's grumpy, just like you."

I spun as the image of her faded, and Logan rushed in, carrying a smaller tablet than Greg's.

"We found something."

I pushed away from the window and was at Logan's side in an instant.

Logan handed me the tablet, with a graph displayed on the screen. Blue, yellow, and red lines all showed an upward trend. I scanned the screen, noticing the small numbers along the bottom. Time was labeled over thirty minutes, yet it still made no sense.

"What am I looking at?" I sighed, rubbing my brow.

Vincent retreated behind his desk, watching Logan and me.

"The waves you see show electromagnetic interference, pretty much what TV or radio give off during a broadcast. They spiked right here when Kaden started talking, and stayed that way until he..." He stopped, and I knew a part of him hurt for Gabby's death, even if he never spoke of it. "Anyway, it stopped shortly after."

"And?"

Vincent cleared his throat. "Logan thinks it was broadcasting not just to us, but beyond Onuna."

Logan sneered at Vincent. "I'm not wrong. It spiked, and to a degree that made it accessible to not only every TV and radio in this realm, but further."

Vincent rolled his eyes. "Whatever you say. I think there is no possible way it could reach past this realm. They are closed, and even if it could be done, who would Kaden be reaching out to? Everyone is dead. You really think some cosmic entity survived this long and wants a special broadcast on Dianna?"

"Why am I just now hearing of this?" I asked with a frown, looking between the two.

Logan cleared his throat. "Vincent thought it was a pointless lead on yet another dead end, but once I saw the graph, I knew I was on the right track."

Vincent cleared his throat. "We need to focus on making sure the mortals are comfortable, not chase our tails on hints and guesses. The spikes could be from the energy both of them expelled when she—"

"You do not answer to Vincent," I snapped. I did not mean to talk to him like that, but I knew I had done so often over the last two weeks.

Logan scowled at Vincent as I leaned forward and took the device. Ignoring their stare-down, I studied the screen. "If, by chance, Logan is not wrong, who would he speak to? More importantly, why would they be interested in Dianna and her sister?"

Logan shrugged. "I don't know, but I do know there was an energy spike high enough that it not only affected every bit of technology, but hit satellites as well. We may not be able to reach realms, but—"

"But nothing. It's impossible," Vincent said, cutting Logan off.

Their bickering faded into the background as I stared at the chart. Logan was not wrong about the spike, but it was the line that followed that made the noises, lights, and world fade away. It dropped immediately after Gabby died, a flat, steady line that dragged across the screen. Her echoing scream roared back into my head.

"Thank you, Logan," I finally said, stopping them mid-argument. Still looking at the tablet, I turned and left.

"We still have one interview left!" Vincent called, but he did not follow.

"Cancel it."

"I can't," I heard Vincent whisper.

"Well, you do it, then," Logan replied to him.

Their voices faded away as I headed toward the main conference room. I took the elevator up several floors, my eyes scanning, memorizing that graph as a million and one possibilities ran through my head. If Logan was correct, who cared enough to want to witness such a thing?

I pushed open the mahogany double doors, the lights in the conference room already on. The dark leather chair spun toward me and stopped, facing me. Manicured nails tapped on the desktop, and she smiled at me.

"Is this new?"

Dianna.

And don't forget to keep an eye out for

GODS & MONSTERS BOOK 3

Coming soon!

HEADLINE
ETERNAL

HEADLINE
ETERNAL

FIND YOUR HEART'S DESIRE...

VISIT OUR WEBSITE: www.headlineeternal.com

FIND US ON FACEBOOK: facebook.com/eternalromance

CONNECT WITH US ON X: @eternal_books

FOLLOW US ON INSTAGRAM: @headlineeternal

EMAIL US: eternalromance@headline.co.uk